By the same author

TIM POWERS

The Stress of Her Regard

Grafton
An Imprint of HarperCollins*Publishers*

047986181
CLITHEROE
6/00 donation

Grafton
An Imprint of HarperCollins*Publishers*
77–85 Fulham Palace Road,
Hammersmith, London W6 8JB

Published by Grafton 1993
9 8 7 6 5 4 3 2 1

First published in Great Britain by
HarperCollins*Publishers* 1991

ISBN 0 586 07283 7

Set in Meridien

Printed in Great Britain by
HarperCollinsManufacturing Glasgow

For Dean and Gerda Koontz,
for ten years of
cheerful, hospitable and tolerant friendship

And with thanks to
Gregory Santo Arena and Gloria Batsford and
Gregory Benford and Will Griffin and
Dana Holm Howard and Meri Howard and
K. W. Jeter and Jeff Levin and Monique Logan and
Kate Powers and Serena Powers and
Joe Stefko and Brian M. Thomsen and Tom Whitmore

– and to Paul Mohney,
for that conversation, many years ago
over beers at the Tinder Box, about Percy Shelley.

. . . yet thought must see
That eve of time when man no longer yearns,
Grown deaf before Life's Sphinx, whose lips are barred;
When from the spaces of Eternity,
Silence, a rigorous Medusa, turns
On the lost world the stress of her regard.

— Clark Ashton Smith, *Sphinx and Medusa*

PROLOGUE
1816

— Bring with you also . . . a new Sword cane . . .
(my last tumbled into this lake —)

        — Lord Byron, to John Cam Hobhouse,
                        13 June 1816

Until the squall struck, Lake Leman was so still that the two men talking in the bow of the open sailboat could safely set their wine glasses on the thwarts.

The boat's wake stood like a ripple in glass on either side; it stretched to port far out across the lake, and on the starboard side slowly swept along the shore, and seemed in the late afternoon glare to extend right up the green foothills to move like a mirage across the craggy, snow-fretted face of the Dent d'Oche.

A servant was slumped on one of the seats reading a book, and the sailors had not had to correct their course for several minutes and appeared to be dozing, and when the two travellers' conversation flagged, the breeze from shore brought the faint wind-chime melody of distant cowbells.

The man in the crook of the bow was staring ahead toward the east shore of the lake. Though he was only twenty-eight, his curly dark red hair was already shot with grey, and the pale skin around his eyes and mouth was scored with creases of ironic humour.

'That castle over there is Chillon,' he remarked to his younger companion, 'where the Dukes of Savoy kept political prisoners in dungeons below the water level. Imagine climbing up to peer out of some barred window at all *this*.' He waved around at the remote- white vastnesses of the Alps.

His friend pushed the fingers of one skinny hand through his thatch of fine blond hair and peered ahead. 'It's on a sort of peninsula, isn't it? Mostly out in the lake? I imagine they'd be glad of all the surrounding water.'

Lord Byron stared at Percy Shelley, once again not sure what the young man meant. He had met him here in Switzerland less than a month ago and, though they had much in common, he didn't feel that he knew him.

Both of them were voluntarily in exile from England. Byron had recently fled bankruptcy and a failed marriage and, though it was less well known, the scandal of having fathered a child by his half sister; four years earlier, with the publication of the long, largely autobiographical poem *Childe Harold's Pilgrimage*, he had become the nation's most celebrated poet — but the society that had lionized him then reviled him now, and English tourists took delight in pointing him out when they caught glimpses of him on the streets, and the women frequently threw theatrical faints.

Shelley was far less famous, though his offences against propriety sometimes appalled even Byron. Only twenty-four, he had already been expelled from Oxford for having written a pamphlet advocating atheism, had been disowned by his wealthy father, and had deserted his wife and two children in order to run away with the daughter of the radical London philosopher William Godwin. Godwin had not been pleased to see his daughter putting into all-too-real action his abstract arguments in favour of free love.

Byron was doubting that Shelley would really be 'glad of the surrounding water.' The stone walls *had* to be leaky, and God knew what kinds of damp rot a man would be subject to in such a place. Was it naïveté that

10

made Shelley say such things, or was it some spiritual, unworldly quality, such as made saints devote their lives to sitting on pillars in deserts?

And were his condemnations of religion and marriage sincere, or were they a coward's devices to have his own way and not acknowledge blame? He certainly didn't give much of an impression of courage.

Four nights ago Shelley and the two girls he was travelling with had visited Byron, and rainy weather had kept the party indoors. Byron was renting the Villa Diodati, a columned, vineyard-surrounded house in which Milton had been a guest two centuries earlier; and though the place seemed spacious when warm weather let guests explore the terraced gardens or lean on the railing of the wide veranda overlooking the lake, on that night an Alpine thunderstorm and a flooded ground floor had made it seem no roomier than a fisherman's cottage.

Byron had been especially uncomfortable because Shelley had brought along not only Mary Godwin, but also her stepsister Claire Clairmont, who by a malign coincidence had been Byron's last mistress before he fled London, and now seemed to be pregnant by him.

What with the storm clamouring beyond the window glass and the candles fluttering in the erratic draughts, the conversation had turned to ghosts and the supernatural – luckily, for it developed that Claire was easily frightened by such topics, and Byron was able to keep her wide-eyed with alarm, and silent except for an occasional horrified gasp.

Shelley was at least as credulous as Claire, but he was delighted with the stories of vampires and phantoms; and after Byron's personal physician, a vain young man named Polidori, had told a story about a woman who'd been seen walking around with a plain skull for a head, Shelley had leaned forward and in a low voice told the company the reasons he and his now abandoned wife had fled Scotland four years earlier.

The narration consisted more of hints and atmospheric details than of any actual story, but Shelley's obvious conviction — his long-fingered hands trembling in the candlelight and his big eyes glittering through the disordered halo of his curly hair — made even the sensible Mary Godwin cast an occasional uneasy glance at the rain-streaked windows.

It seemed that at about the same time that the Shelleys had arrived in Scotland, a young farm maid named Mary Jones had been found hacked to death with what the authorities guessed must have been sheep shears. 'The culprit,' Shelley whispered, 'was supposed to have been a giant, and the locals called it "the King of the Mountains."'

'"It"?' wailed Claire.

Byron shot Shelley a look of gratitude, for he assumed that Shelley too was frightening Claire in order to keep her off the subject of her pregnancy; but the young man was at the moment entirely unaware of him. Byron realized that Shelley simply *enjoyed* scaring people.

Byron was still grateful.

'They captured a man,' Shelley went on, 'one Thomas Edwards — and blamed the crime on him, and eventually hanged him . . . but I knew he was only a scapegoat. We — '

Polidori sat back in his chair and, in his usual nervously pugnacious way, quavered, 'How did you know?'

Shelley frowned and began talking more rapidly, as if the conversation had suddenly become too personal: 'Why, I — I knew through my researches — I'd been very ill the year before, in London, with hallucinations, and terrible pains in my side . . . uh, so I had lots of time for study. I was investigating electricity, the precession of the equinoxes . . . and the Old Testament, Genesis . . .'

He shook his head impatiently, and Byron got the impression that, despite the apparent irrationality of the answer, the question had surprised some truth out of him. 'At any rate,' Shelley continued, 'on the twenty-sixth of February – that was a Friday – I knew to take a pair of loaded pistols to bed with me.'

Polidori opened his mouth to speak again, but Byron stopped him with a curt 'Shut up.'

'Yes, Pollydolly,' said Mary, 'do wait until the story's over.'

Polidori sat back, pursing his lips.

'And,' said Shelley, 'we weren't in bed half an hour before I heard something downstairs. I went down to investigate, and saw a figure quitting the house through a window. It attacked me, and I managed to shoot it . . . in the shoulder.'

Byron frowned at Shelley's poor marksmanship.

'And the thing reeled back and stood over me and said, "You would shoot *me*? By God I will be revenged! I will murder your wife, I will rape your sister." And then it fled.'

A pen and inkwell and paper lay on a table near his chair, and Shelley snatched up the pen, dipped it, and quickly sketched a figure. 'This is what my assailant looked like,' he said, holding the paper near the candle.

Byron's first thought was that the man couldn't draw any better than a child. The figure he'd drawn was a monstrosity, a barrel-chested, keg-legged thing with hands like tree branches and a head like an African mask.

Claire couldn't look at it, and even Polidori was clearly upset. 'It – it's not any kind of human figure at all!' he said.

'Oh, I don't know, Polidori,' said Byron, squinting at the thing. 'I think it's a prototypical man. God originally

13

made Adam out of clay, didn't He? This fellow looks as if he were made out of a Sussex hillside.'

'You presume!' said Shelley, a little wildly. 'How can you be certain this isn't made of Adam's rib?'

Byron grinned. 'What, Eve is it? If Milton ever glimpsed *that* with his sightless eyes, I hope it wasn't during his visit here – or if it was, that she isn't around tonight.'

For the first time during the evening Shelley himself looked nervous. 'No,' he said quickly, glancing out the window. 'No, I doubt . . .' He let the sentence hang and sat back in his chair.

Belatedly afraid that all this Adam and Eve talk might lead the conversation into more domestic channels, Byron hastily stood up and crossed to a bookshelf and pulled down a small book. 'Coleridge's latest,' he said, returning to his chair. 'There are three poems here, but I think "Christabel" suits us best tonight.'

He began to read the poem aloud, and by the time he had read to the point when the girl Christabel brings the strange woman Geraldine home from the woods, he had everyone's attention. Then in the poem Geraldine sinks down, 'belike through pain,' when they reach the door into the castle of Christabel's widowed father, and Christabel has to lift her up and carry her over the threshold.

Shelley nodded. 'There always has to be some token of invitation. They can't enter without having been asked.'

'Did you ask the clay-woman into your house in Scotland?' asked Polidori.

'I didn't have to,' replied Shelley with surprising bitterness. He turned away, toward the window. 'My – someone else had invited it into my presence two decades previous.'

After a pause Byron resumed his reading, and recited Coleridge's description of Geraldine exposing her withered breast as she disrobes for bed —

> Behold! her bosom and half her side —
> A sight to dream of, not to tell!
> O shield her! shield sweet Christabel!

— And Shelley screamed and jackknifed up out of his chair and in three frantic strides was out of the room, knocking over a chair but managing to grab a lit candle as he blundered past the table.

Claire screamed too, and Polidori yelped and raised his hands like a cornered boxer, and Byron put down the book and glanced sharply at the window Shelley had been looking out of. Nothing was visible on the rain-lashed veranda.

'Go see if he's well, Polidori,' Byron said.

The young doctor went into the next room for his bag, then followed Shelley. Byron refilled his wine glass and sat down, then looked at Mary with raised eyebrows.

She laughed nervously and then quoted Lady Macbeth: ' "My lord is often thus, and hath been from his youth." '

Byron grinned, a little haggardly. 'No doubt "the fit is momentary; upon a thought he will again be well." '

Mary finished the quote. ' "If you much note him, you shall offend him and extend his passion." '

Byron looked around the long room. 'So where did he see "Banquo's ghost"? I'm a fair noticer of spirits, but I didn't see anything.'

'He — ' Mary began, then halted. 'But look, here he is.'

Shelley had walked back into the room, looking both scared and sheepish. His face and hair were wet, indicating that Polidori had splashed water on him, and he reeked of ether. 'It was . . . just a fancy that took momentary hold of me,' he said. 'Like a waking nightmare. I'm sorry.'

'Something about . . .' began Polidori; Shelley shot him a warning look, but perhaps the young doctor didn't notice, for he went on. '. . . about a woman with – you said – eyes in her breasts.'

Shelley's squint of astonishment lasted only a moment, but Byron had noticed it; then Shelley had concealed it, and was nodding. 'Right, that was it,' he agreed. 'A hallucination, as I said.'

Byron was intrigued, but regard for his obviously ill-at-ease friend made him decide not to pursue whatever it was that Shelley had really said and Polidori had misunderstood.

He winked at Shelley and then changed the subject. 'I really think we should each write a ghost story!' he said cheerfully. 'Let's see if we can't do something with this mud-person who's been following poor Shelley around.'

Everyone eventually managed to laugh.

A shadow passed over Chillon's blunt towers and across the miles of lake between the grim edifice and the boat, and Byron shifted around in his seat by the bow to look north; a cloud had blotted half the sky since he had last scanned that side.

'It looks as if we'd better put in at St Gingoux,' he said, pointing. His servant closed his book and tucked it away in a pocket.

Shelley stood up and leaned on the rail. 'A storm, is it?'

'Best to assume so. I'll wake the damned sailors – *what's wrong*?' he demanded, for Shelley had leapt back from the rail and was scrabbling through the pile of their baggage.

'I need an *eisener breche*!' yelled Shelley – and a

16

moment later he leapt to his feet with Byron's sword cane in his fist. 'Over your head, look out!'

Half thinking that Shelley had gone absolutely mad at last, Byron sprang up on to the yard-wide section of rail around the bowsprit and calculated how long a jump it would take to land him near the mast-hung haversack, which in addition to wine bottles contained two loaded pistols; but the urgency in Shelley's voice made him nevertheless risk a quick look overhead.

The advancing cloud was knotted and lumpy, and one section of it looked very much like a naked woman rushing straight down out of the sky at the boat. Byron was about to laugh in relief and say something sarcastic to Shelley, but then he saw that the woman-form was not part of the distant cloud, or at least wasn't anymore, but was a patch of vapour much smaller than he had at first thought – and much closer.

Then he met her furious gaze, and he sprang for the pistols.

The boat rocked as the cloud figure collided with it, and Shelley and the boatmen yelled; when Byron rolled up into a crouch with a pistol in his hand he saw Shelley swing the bared sword at the woman-shaped cloud, which hung now just above the rail, and though the blade stopped so abruptly that the top half of it snapped right off, the cloud seemed to recoil and lose some of its shape. There was blood on Shelley's cheek and in his hair, and Byron aimed the pistol into the centre of the cloud and pulled the trigger.

The sharp explosion of the charge set his ears ringing, but he could hear Shelley shout, 'Good – lead conducts electricity pretty well – silver or gold's better!'

Shelley braced his tall, narrow frame against the rail, and with the broken sword aimed a real tree-felling stroke at the thing. The now turbulent cloud recoiled again, no longer resembling a woman at all. Shelley

17

swung again, and the blade struck the wooden rail a glancing blow; Byron thought his friend had missed his target, but when a moment later Shelley hit the rail again, straight down this time, he realized that he had intended to chop free a wooden splinter.

Shelley let go of the broken sword – it tumbled over the side – and with his thin hands pried up the splinter. 'Give me your other pistol!'

Byron dug it out of the fallen sack and tossed it to him. Shelley jammed the wooden splinter into the barrel and as Byron shouted at him to stop, aimed the weirdly bayonetted gun into the cloud and fired.

The cloud burst apart, with an acid smell like fresh-broken stone. Shelley slumped back on to the seat. After a moment he took a handkerchief out of his pocket and began blotting his bleeding forehead.

'You're damned lucky,' was all Byron could think of to say. His heart was pounding, and he shoved his hands into his pockets so Shelley wouldn't see them trembling. 'Jam a gun barrel like that again and it'll blow your hand off.'

'Necessary risk – wood's about the worst conductor.' Shelley pushed himself back up and stared anxiously at the sky. 'Have the boatmen get us in, fast.'

'What, you think we're likely to see another?' Byron turned back to the ashen boatmen. 'Get us in to shore – *bougez nous dans le rivage plus près! Vite*, very goddamn *vite*!'

Facing Shelley again, he forced himself to speak levelly. 'What was that thing? And what . . . did . . . it . . . goddamn . . . *want*?'

Shelley had wiped the blood off, and now folded his handkerchief carefully and put it back in his pocket. He apparently had no scruples about being seen to tremble, but his eyes were steady as he met Byron's glare. 'It wanted the same thing the tourists in Geneva want, when they point me out to each other. A look at something perverse.' He waved to keep Byron silent. 'As to what it was – you could call it a lamia. Where better to meet one than on Lake Leman?'

Byron stepped back, dispelling the mood of challenge. 'I never thought about the name of this lake. A leman, a mistress.' He laughed unsteadily. 'You've got her in a temper.'

Shelley relaxed too, and leaned on the rail. 'It's not the lake – the lake's just named after her kind. Hell, the *lake's* more an *ally*.'

The man at the tiller had tacked them more squarely into the offshore breeze, and the castle of Chillon swung around to the port side. The wine glasses had fallen and shattered when the cloud-thing impacted with the boat, so Byron picked up the bottle, pulled the cork with his teeth, and took a deep gulp. He passed it to Shelley and then asked, 'So if wood's the *worst* conductor, why did it work? You said – '

Shelley took a drink and wiped his mouth on his sleeve. 'I think it has to be . . . an extreme, electrically. I think they're like pond fish – equally vulnerable to either rapids or stagnation.' He grinned crookedly and had another pull at the wine. 'Silver bullets and wooden stakes, right?'

'Good Christ, what are we talking about here? It sounds like vampires and werewolves.'

Shelley shrugged. 'Not a . . . coincidence. Anyway, silver's the best electrical conductor, and wood's about the worst. Silver's generally been too expensive for the kind of people who are credulous of the old stories, so they've traditionally had to make do with iron stakes. *Eisener brechen*, the stakes are called – it's a very old term that means "iron gap," sort of, or "iron breach" or "iron violation," though *brechen* can also refer to the refraction of light, or even to adultery. Evidently in some archaic context those things were all somewhat synonymous – odd thought, hm? In fact, it was an *eisener breche* that I was calling for at your house four nights ago. Polidori, the idiot, thought I had said "eyes in her breasts."' Shelley laughed. 'When I came to myself again, I had no choice but to go along with his foolish misunderstanding. Mary thought I had gone mad, but it was better than letting her know what I'd really said.'

'Why were you calling for one that night? Was this creature we saw today outside my window that night?'

'It, or one very like it.'

Byron started to say something, but paused, staring back north across the water. A sheenless wave of agitation was sweeping toward them. 'The sail, *desserrez la voile*!' he yelled at the sailors; then, 'Hang on to something,' he added tensely to Shelley.

The wind struck the boat like an avalanche, tearing the sail and heeling the boat over to starboard until the mast was almost horizontal, and water poured solidly in over the gunwales, splashing up explosively at the thwarts and the tiller. For several seconds it seemed that the boat would roll right over – while the shrill wind tore at their rail-clutching hands and lashed spray across their faces – but then, as reluctantly as a tree root tears up out of the soil when the tree is forced over, the mast came back up, and the half-foundered boat swung ponderously around on the choppy water. One of the boatmen yanked the tiller back and forth, but it just knocked loosely in its bracket; the rudder was broken. The winds were still chorusing through the rent sail and the shrouds, and had raised a surf that was crashing on the rocks of the shore a hundred yards away.

Byron took off his coat and began pulling at his boots. 'Looks like we swim for it,' he yelled over the noise.

Shelley, gripping the port rail, shook his head. 'I've

never learned how.' His face was pale, but he looked determined and oddly happy.

'Christ! And you say the lake's your *ally*? Never mind, get out of your coat – I'll get us an oar to cling to, and if you don't struggle, I think I can manoeuvre us around those rocks. Get – '

Shelley had to speak loudly to be heard, but his voice was calm – 'I have no intention of being saved. You'll have enough to do to save yourself.' He looked over the far rail at the humped rocks withstanding the battering of the surf, then looked back at Byron and smiled nervously through his tangled blond hair. 'I don't fear drowning – and if you give me an oar to cling to I promise you I'll let go of it.'

Byron stared at him for a couple of seconds, then shrugged and waded aft, bracing himself on the rail, to where his servant and one of the sailors were frantically filling buckets from the pool sloshing around their thighs, and heaving the water over the side; the other boatman was pulling at the shrouds in an effort to get what was left of the sail usefully opposed to the wind. Byron grabbed two more of the emergency buckets and tossed one toward Shelley. 'In that case bail as fast as you can, if you ever want to see Mary again.'

For a moment Shelley just held on to the rail; then his shoulders slumped, and he nodded; and though he snatched the floating bucket and scrambled to help, Byron thought he looked rueful and a little ashamed, like a man who finds his own willpower to be frailer than he had supposed.

For the next several minutes the four men worked furiously, sweating and gasping as they hauled up bucketful after bucketful of water and flung it back into the lake, and the man working the sail had, by swinging the boom way out to starboard, managed to get at least a faint surge of headway in spite of the loss of the rudder. And the wind was losing its fury.

Byron risked pausing for a moment. 'I – was wrong in my – estimation of your courage,' he panted. 'I apologize.'

'Quite all right,' Shelley gasped, stooping to refill his bucket. He dumped it over the gunwale and then collapsed on one of the benches. 'I *over*estimated my grasp of science.' He coughed, rackingly enough to make Byron wonder if he was consumptive. 'I recently eluded one of those creatures and left it behind in England – it's practically impossible for them to cross water, and the English Channel is a nice quantity of that – but somehow it didn't occur to me that I might run across more of them here . . . much less that they'd . . . *know* me.'

He hefted his bucket. 'Switzerland especially,' he went on, 'I had thought, would be free of them – the higher altitude – but I think now that what drew me here to the Alps is the same . . . is the *recognition* . . . that this is . . . I don't know. Now I don't think I could have fled to a more perilous place.' He dragged his bucket through the water, now shin deep, and then got to his feet and hoisted the bucket up on to the rail. Before dumping it he nodded around at the Alpine peaks ringing the lake. 'They do call, though, don't they?'

The labouring boat had rounded the point, and ahead they could see the beach of St Gingoux, and people on the shore waving to them.

Byron poured out one more bucketful of water and then tossed the bucket aside. The cloud had passed, and looking south to the Rhône Valley he could see sunlight glittering on the distant peaks of the Dents du Midi. 'Yes,' he said softly. 'They do call. In a certain voice, which a certain sort of person can hear . . . not to his benefit, I believe.' He shook his head wearily. 'I wonder who else is answering that particular siren song.'

Shelley smiled and, perhaps thinking of their recent emergency, quoted from the same play his wife and Byron had been quoting four days ago. 'I suppose it's many another who is "like two spent swimmers that do cling together and choke their art."'

Byron blinked at him, once again not sure what to make of what he said. '"Many *another*"?' he said irritably. 'You mean many *others*, don't you?'

'I'm not sure,' said Shelley, still smiling faintly as he watched the shoreline grow steadily closer. 'But no, I think I mean *each* like two spent swimmers.'

A rescue boat was being rowed out toward them across the sunny water, and already some of the sailors on it were whirling weighted rope-ends overhead in wide, whistling circles. The sailors on Byron's boat scrambled to the bow and began clapping their hands to show their readiness to catch and moor the lines.

BOOK ONE

A Token of Invitation

Of the sweets of Faeries, Peris, Goddesses,
There is not such a treat among them all,
Haunters of cavern, lake, and waterfall,
As a real woman, lineal indeed
From Pyrrha's pebbles . . .

> — John Keats, *Lamia*

And Venus blessed the marriage she had made.

> — Ovid, *Metamorphoses*
> Book X, lines 94 and 95

Chapter 1

> . . . and the midnight sky
> Flares, a light more dread than obscurity.
>
> – Percy Bysshe Shelley

'*Lucy*,' the barmaid was saying in an emphatic whisper as she led the two men around the foot of the oak stairway, 'which I'd think you could remember by now – and keep your damned voice down until we get outside.'

The flickering lantern in her hand struck an upwardly diminishing stack of horizontal gleams from the stair edges rising away to their right, and Jack Boyd, who had just asked the barmaid her name for the fourth time that evening, apparently decided that taking her upstairs would be a good idea, now that he had at least momentarily got straight what to call her.

'God, there's no mistaking you're one of the Navy men,' she hissed exasperatedly as she spun out of the big man's drunken embrace and strode on across the hall to the dark doorway of the reserve dining room.

The off-balance Boyd sat down heavily on the lowest stair while Michael Crawford, who'd been hanging back in order to be able to walk without any undignified reeling, frowned and sadly shook his head. The girl was a bigot, ascribing to all Navy men the faults of an admittedly conspicuous few.

Appleton and the other barmaid were ahead of them, already in the dark dining room, and now Crawford heard a door being unbolted and pulled open, and the sudden cold draught in his face smelled of rain on trees and clay.

Lucy looked back over her shoulder at the drunken pair, and she hefted the bottle she had in her left hand. 'An extra hour or two of *bar service* is what you paid for,' she whispered, 'and Louise's got the glasses, so unless you two want to toddle off to bed, trot yourselves along here — and don't make no *noise*, the landlord's asleep only two doors down this hall.' She disappeared through the dining room doorway.

Crawford leaned down unsteadily and shook Boyd's shoulder. 'Come on,' he said, 'you're disgracing me as well as yourself.'

' "Disgracing"?' mumbled the big man as he wobbled to his feet. 'On the — contrary — I intend to marry . . .' He paused and frowned ponderously. 'To marry that young lady. Her name was what?'

Crawford propelled him into the dining room, toward the open door in the far wall and the night beyond it. Lucy was waiting for them impatiently in the far doorway, and by the wavering glow of her lamp Crawford noticed the lath and plaster panelling on the walls, and he remembered the ornate double chimney-stacks he'd glimpsed over the roof when the stagecoach had turned off the Horsham road this afternoon; evidently the inn's Georgian front had been added on to an old Tudor structure. He wouldn't be surprised if the kitchen had a stone floor.

'We'll make it a *double* wedding tomorrow,' Boyd went on over his shoulder as he bumped against chairs in the dark. 'You wouldn't object to sharing the glory, would you? Of course this means I won't be able to be your groomsman — but hell, I'm sure Appleton would be groomsman for both of us.'

The pattering hiss of the rain was much louder when

they were out on the roofed porch, and the chilly air sluiced some of the wine fumes from Crawford's head. The porch, he saw, began at the door they'd come out of and extended south, away from the landlord's room, almost all the way to the stables. Appleton and Louise had already sat down in two of the weatherbeaten chairs that stood randomly along the deck, and Lucy was pouring wine into their glasses.

Crawford stepped to the edge of the porch so that the curtain of rain tumbled past only inches in front of his nose. Out in the dark yard he could dimly make out patches of grass and the shaggy, waving blackness of trees beyond.

He was about to turn back to the porch when the sky was split with a dazzling glare of white, and an instant later he was rocked back on his heels by a thunderclap that he was momentarily certain must have stripped half the shingles from the inn's roof. Thinly over the crash he could hear a woman scream.

'Damn me!' he gasped, taking an involuntary step backwards as the tremendous echoes rolled away east across the Weald to frighten children in distant Kent. 'Did you see that?' His ears were ringing and he was speaking too loudly.

After a few seconds he exhaled sharply, and grinned. 'I guess that's a stupid question, isn't it? But no kidding, Boyd, if that had struck any closer, it's a different sort of church ceremony you'd be bringing me to tomorrow.'

It was an effort to speak jocularly – his face was beaded with sudden sweat as if he'd stepped out into the rain, and the air was sharp with a smell like the essence of fright, and for a moment it had seemed to him that he was participating in the earth's own shudder of shock. He turned and blinked behind him – his eyes had readjusted to the darkness enough for him to see that his companions hadn't moved, though the two women looked scared.

'No chance,' Boyd called, sitting down and filling his glass. 'I remember seeing Corbie's Aunt clinging round your head in a storm off Vigo. The stuff *likes* you.'

'And who,' spoke up Appleton, his voice expressing only amusement, 'is Corbie's Aunt?'

Crawford sat down himself and took a glass with fingers he willed not to tremble. 'Not who,' he said. 'What. It's Italian, really, supposed to be *Corposanto* or *Capra Saltante* or something like that. Saint Elmo's Fire, the English call it – ghostly lights that cling to the masts and yardarms of ships. Some people,' he added, pouring wine into his glass and waving it toward Boyd before taking a deep gulp, 'believe the phenomenon's related to lightning.'

Boyd was on his feet again, pointing toward the south end of the yard. 'And what are those buildings down there?'

Lucy wearily assured him that there weren't any buildings at that end of the yard and told him to keep his voice down.

'I saw 'em,' Boyd insisted. 'In that flash of lightning. Little low places with windows.'

'He means them old coaches,' said Louise. She shook her head at Boyd. 'It's just a couple of old berlines that belonged to Blunden's father that haven't been moved in thirty or forty years – the upholstery's probably shot, not to mention the axles.'

'Axles – who needs 'em? Mike, whistle up Corbie's Aunt again, will you? She'll motivate the hulks.' Already Boyd was off the porch and striding jerkily across the muddy yard toward the old coaches.

'Oh hell,' sighed Appleton, pushing back his chair. 'I suppose we have to catch him and put him to bed. You didn't think to bring any laudanum, of course?'

'No – I'm supposed to be on holiday, remember? I didn't even bring a lancet or forceps.' Crawford stood up, and was a little surprised to discover that he wasn't annoyed at the prospect of having to go out into the rain. Even the idea of going for an imaginary ride in a ruined coach seemed to have a certain charm.

He had left his hat in the taproom, but the rain was pleasantly cool on his face and the back of his neck, and he strode cheerfully across the dark yard, trusting to luck to keep his boots out of any deep puddles. Behind him he could hear Appleton and the women following.

He saw Boyd stumble and flailingly recover his balance a few yards short of the vague rectangular blackness that was the coaches, and when Crawford got to that spot he saw why – the coaches sat on an irregular patch of ancient pavement that stood a few inches higher than the mud.

A yellow light waxed behind him, bright enough to reflect gold glints from the wet greenery and to let him see Boyd clambering up the side of one of the coaches – Appleton and the women were following, and Lucy still had the lantern. Crawford stopped to let them catch up.

'*Gallop, my cloudy steeds!*' yelled Boyd from inside one of the coaches. '*And why don't you sit a little closer, Auntie?*'

'I guess if he's got to go crazy, this is the best place for it,' remarked Lucy nervously, holding up the steaming lantern and peering ahead through the downpour. 'These old carriages are just junk, and Blunden's not likely to hear his ravings out this far from the buildings.' She trembled and the light wavered. 'I'm going back inside, though.'

Crawford didn't want the party to end – it was the last one he'd ever have as a bachelor. 'Wait just a minute,' he said, 'I can get him out of there.' He started forward, then paused, squinting down at the pavement. It was hard to be sure, with the rain agitating the muddy water

31

pooled on it, but it seemed to him that there were bas-relief carvings in the paving stones.

'What was this, originally?' he asked. 'Did there used to be a building here?'

Appleton cursed impatiently.

'Back in the olden days there was,' said Louise, who was clinging to Appleton's arm and absently spilling wine down the front of his shirt. 'Romans or somebody built it. We're always finding bits of statues and things when the rains fatten the creeks in the spring.'

Crawford remembered his speculations on the age of this establishment, and he realized that he'd misguessed by a thousand years or so.

Boyd yelled something indistinct and thrashed around noisily in the old coach.

Lucy shivered again. 'It's awful cold out here.'

'Oh, don't go in just yet,' Crawford protested. He handed his wine glass to Appleton and then awkwardly struggled out of his coat. 'Here,' he said, crossing to Lucy and draping it over her shoulders. 'That'll keep you warm. We'll only be a minute or two out here, and I *did* pay you to keep serving us for a couple of hours past closing time.'

'Not for out in the damned rain you didn't. But all right, a couple of minutes.'

Appleton glanced around suddenly, as if he'd heard something over the gravelly hiss of the rain. 'I – I'm going in myself,' he said, and for the first time that evening his voice lacked its usual sarcastically confident edge.

'*Who are you*?' Boyd yelled, all at once sounding frightened. A furious banging began inside the coach, and in the lamplight it could be seen to rock jerkily on its ancient springs; but the racket seemed dwarfed by the night, and disappeared without any echo among the dark ranks of trees.

'Good night,' said Appleton. He turned and began leading Louise hurriedly back toward the inn buildings.

'*Get away from me*!' screamed Boyd.

'My God, wait up,' muttered Lucy, starting after Appleton and Louise. The rain was suddenly coming down more heavily than ever, rattling on the inn roof and the road out front and on lonely hilltops miles away in the night, and over the noise of it Crawford thought for a moment he heard a chorus of high, harsh voices singing in the sky.

Instantly he was sprinting back after the other three, and only after he caught up with Lucy did he realize that he'd been about to abandon Boyd. As always happened in moments of crisis, a couple of unwelcome pictures sprang into his mind – an overturned boat in choppy surf, and a pub across the street from a burning house – and he didn't want to take the chance of adding the back yard of this inn to that torturing catalogue; and so when Lucy turned to him he quickly thought of some other reason than fright for having run after her.

'My ring,' he gasped. 'The wedding ring I've – got to give to my bride tomorrow – it's in the pocket of the coat. Excuse me.' He reached into the pocket, groped around for a moment, and then came up with it between his thumb and forefinger. 'That's all.'

By the light of the lamp she was carrying he could see her face tighten with offence at the implied insult, but he turned away and started resolutely back through the rain to where Boyd was screaming in the darkness.

'I'm coming, you great idiot,' he called, trying to influence the night with his confident tone.

He noticed that he was carrying the wedding ring in his hand, holding it as tightly as a sailor undergoing surgery bites a bullet. That wasn't smart – if he dropped it out here in all this mud it wouldn't be found for years.

Over the noise of the rain he could hear Boyd roaring.

Crawford's tight breeches didn't have any pockets, and he was afraid the undersized ring would fall off his own finger if he wound up having to struggle with Boyd; in desperation he looked around for a narrow upright tree branch or something to hang the ring on, and then he noticed the white statue standing by the back wall of the stable.

It was a life-sized sculpture of a nude woman with the left hand raised in a beckoning gesture, and as Boyd roared again Crawford splashed across the mud to the statue, slipped the ring on to the ring finger of the upraised stone hand, and then ran on to the derelict coaches.

It was easy to see which one the crazed Navy lieutenant was in – the carriage was shaking to pieces as if it had a magically sympathetic twin that was rolling down a mountain ravine somewhere. Hurrying around to the side of it, Crawford managed to get hold of the door handle and wrench the door open.

Two hands shot out of the darkness and grabbed the collar of his shirt, and he yelled in alarm as Boyd pulled him inside; the big man threw him on to one of the mildew-reeking seats and lunged past him toward the doorway, and though a web of rotted upholstery had got tangled around Boyd's feet and now sent him sprawling, the big man had managed to get at least the top half of his body outside.

For a moment Crawford seemed to hear the distant singing again, and when something brushed gently against his cheek he let out a roar as wild as any of Boyd's and jackknifed up on to his feet; but before he could vault over the other man, he braced himself against the wall – and then he relaxed a little, for he could feel that all the loose threads of the upholstery were bristlingly erect like the fur on the back of an angry dog, and he realized that the same phenomenon must have been what made the shreds of the seat upholstery stand up and brush his face a moment ago.

Very well, he told himself firmly, I admit it's strange, but it's nothing to lose your wits over. Just some electrical effect caused by the storm and the odd physical properties of decaying leather and horsehair. Right now your job is to get poor Boyd back to the inn.

Boyd had by this time freed himself and crawled out on to the puddled pavement, and as Crawford climbed down from the coach he was getting shakily to his feet. He squinted around suspiciously at the trees and the ruined carriages.

Crawford took his arm, but the bigger man shook it off and plodded away through the rain toward the inn.

Crawford caught up with him and then matched his plodding stride. 'Big beetles under your shirt, were there?' he asked casually after a few paces. 'Would have sworn rats were scrambling up your pant legs? I'll bet you *wet* your pants, in fact, though as rain-soaked as you are nobody'll notice. *Delirium tremens*, we doctors call this show. It's how you know when to back off on the drink.'

Ordinarily he wouldn't have been as blunt as this, even with someone he knew as well as he knew Jack Boyd, but tonight it almost seemed to be the most tactful approach – after all, no one could be blamed for suffering a case of the galloping horrors if the cause was simply a profound excess of alcohol.

Actually he was afraid Boyd had not been quite that drunk.

The party was clearly over. Lucy and Louise were complaining about having to go to bed with wet hair, and Appleton was evasively irritable and, as if to confirm the soured mood, the landlord muttered angrily in his room and caused either his knees or the floorboards to

35

creak threateningly. The women abandoned the lantern and fled to their rooms, and Appleton shook his head disgustedly and stalked upstairs to go to bed himself. Crawford and Boyd appropriated the lantern and tiptoed to the closed door of the taproom and tried the lock.

It wouldn't yield.

'Probably just as well,' sighed Crawford.

Boyd shook his head heavily, then turned and started toward the stairs; halfway there he paused and without looking back said, 'Uh . . . thanks for getting me . . . out of that, Mike.'

Crawford waved, and then realized that Boyd couldn't see the gesture. 'No trouble,' he called softly instead. 'I'll probably need something similar myself sooner or later.'

Boyd stumped away, and Crawford heard his ponderous footsteps recede up the stairs and down some hall overhead. Crawford tried the taproom door again, with no more luck than before, briefly considered finding out where the barmaids' rooms were, and then shrugged, picked up the lamp and went upstairs himself. His room wasn't large, but the sheets were clean and dry and there were enough blankets on the bed.

As he got undressed, he thought again of the overturned boat and the house across the street from the pub. Twenty years had passed since that rowboat foundered in the Plymouth Sound surf, and the house had burned down nearly six years ago, but it seemed to him that they were still the definition of him, the axioms from which he was derived.

Long ago he had started carrying a flask so that he could banish these memories long enough to get to sleep, and he uncorked it now.

Thunder woke him up hours later, and he lifted his head from the pillow and reflected sleepily on how nice it was to be drunk in bed when the lanes and trees and hills outside were so cold and wet . . . and then he remembered the wedding ring he had left in the yard.

His belly went cold and he half sat up, but after a moment he relaxed. You can get it in the morning, he told himself – wake up early and retrieve it before anyone else is up and about. And who's likely to be rooting around out behind the stables, anyway? Sleep's what you need right now. You're getting *married* later today – you've got to get your rest.

He lay back down and pulled the blankets up under his chin, but he had no sooner closed his eyes than he thought, *stableboys*. Stableboys will probably be working out there, and I'll bet they're on the job early. But maybe they won't notice the ring on the statue's finger . . . a gold ring, that is, with a good-sized diamond set in it. Very well, then surely they'll report the find, knowing that they'll be rewarded . . . after all, if they tried to sell it they'd get only a fraction of its real value . . . which was two months' worth of my income.

Damn it.

Crawford crawled out of bed and found the lamp and his tinder box, and after several minutes of furious striking he managed to get the lamp lit. He looked unhappily at his sodden clothes, still lying in the corner where he'd thrown them several hours ago. Aside from one change of clothes, the only other things he had brought along to wear were the formal green frock coat and embroidered waistcoat and white breeches in which he was to get married.

He pulled the wet shirt and breeches on, cringing and gasping at the cold unwieldiness of them. He decided to forego the shoes, and just tottered barefoot to the door, trying to walk so steadily that his shirt would not touch him any more than it had to.

* * *

37

He almost abandoned the whole undertaking when he unbolted the outer door of the spare dining room and a rainy gust plastered his shirt against his chest, but he knew that worry wouldn't let him get any rest if he went back to bed without fetching the ring, so he whispered a curse and stepped out.

It was a lot colder now, and darker. The chairs were still on the porch, but he had to grope to know where they were. The south end of the yard, where the stables and the old carriages were, was darker than the sky.

The mud was grittily slimy between his toes as he stepped off the porch and plodded out across the yard, and he hoped nobody had dropped a wine glass out here. His heart was thumping hard in his chest, for in addition to worrying about cutting his feet he was remembering Boyd's eerie ravings of a few hours ago, and he was acutely aware of being the only wakeful human being within a dozen miles.

The statue was hard to find. He found the stable, and plodded the length of it, dragging his hand along the planks of the wall, with no luck; he was about to panic, thinking that the statue had been carried away, when he rounded the corner and dimly saw the inn buildings away off to his left, which meant that he had somehow been checking the south wall instead of the west one; he reversed course and carefully followed two more walls, conscientiously making the right-angle turn between them, but this time he found himself dragging his numbing fingers along the wall of the inn itself, which wasn't even connected to the stable; he shook his head, amazed that he could still be this drunk. Finally he just began stomping out a zigzag pattern across the nighted yard with his arms spread wide.

And he found it that way.

His fingers brushed the cold, rain-slick stone as he was groping back toward the stable wall, and he almost sobbed with relief. He slid his hand up the extended stone wrist to the stone hand – the ring was still there. He tried to push it up off the statue's finger, but it was stuck somehow.

An instant later he saw why, for a flash of lightning abruptly lit the yard: and the stone hand was now closed in a fist, imprisoning the ring like the end link of a chain. There were no cracks, no signs of any fracture – the statue's hand seemed not ever to have been in any other position. Rain was streaming down the white stone face, and its blank white eyes seemed to be staring at Crawford.

The nearly instantaneous crash of thunder seemed to punch the ground spinning out from under him, and when his feet hit the mud again he was running, racing the tumbling echoes back toward the inn, and it seemed to him that he got inside and slammed the door against the night just as the thunder crashed over the inn like a wave over a rock.

When Crawford awoke, several hours later, it was with the certainty that horrible things had happened and that strenuous activity would soon be required of him to prevent things from getting even worse; his head was throbbing too solidly for him to remember what the catastrophe was, or even *where* he was, but perhaps, as he told himself blurrily, that was something to be grateful for. More sleep was what he wanted most in the world, but when he opened his eyes he saw a smear of nearly dried mud on the sheet . . . and when he threw back the covers he saw that his feet and ankles were caked with it.

With a gasp of real alarm he bounded out of bed. What on earth had he been doing last night? Sleepwalking? And where was Caroline? Had she thrown him out? Perhaps this place was some kind of madhouse.

Then he saw the portmanteau under the window, and he remembered that he was in a village called Warnham, in Sussex, on his way to Bexhill-on-Sea to get married again. Caroline had died in that fire nearly six years ago. Oddly, this was the first time since her death that he had even momentarily forgotten that she was gone.

So how had his feet got so dirty? Had he walked to this inn? Surely not barefoot. No, he thought, I remember now, I took the stagecoach here to meet Appleton and Boyd – Boyd is to be my groomsman, and Appleton is letting me pretend to Julia's father that his elegant landau carriage is mine.

Crawford let himself relax a little, and he tried to conjure some cheer in himself, to see his recent fright and present sickness as just the consequences of old friends out carousing.

If I was in the company of those two last night, he thought with a nervous and self-consciously rueful smile, God knows there are any number of ways I might have got so dirty; I suppose mayhem is assured – I only hope we didn't commit any *murders* or *rapes*. As a matter of fact I do seem to recall seeing a nude woman . . . no, that was only a statue . . .

And then he remembered it all, and his fragile cheer was gone.

His face went cold and he sat down. Surely that must have been a dream, that closed stone fist; or maybe the statue's hand never had been open, maybe *that* was what he had imagined, and he had really just drunkenly pushed the ring at the hand and then not noticed it fall when he had let go of it. And then there must have been something else, a bit of wire or something, around the stone finger when he saw it later.

With the blue sky glowing now in the swirls of the window's bull's-eye panes, it was not too difficult to believe that it had all been a dream or a drunken mistake. It *had* to be, after all.

In the meantime he had lost the ring.

Feeling very old and frail, he unstrapped the portmanteau and pulled on his spare set of travelling clothes. Now he wanted hot coffee – brandy and water would be more restoring, but he had to go find the ring with as clear a head as possible.

Appleton and Boyd weren't up yet, which Crawford was glad of, and after choking down a cup of hot tea – the only drink available in the kitchen – he spent an hour walking around the inn's muddy back yard; he was tense but hopeful when he started, but by the time the sun had climbed high enough to silhouette the branches of the oaks across the road he was in a fury of despair. The landlord came out after a while, and though he expressed sympathy, and even offered to sell Crawford a ring to replace the one he'd lost, he was unable to remember ever having seen any statue of a nude woman in the area.

Finally at about ten Crawford's two companions came tottering down for breakfast. Crawford sat with them, but nobody had much to say, and he ordered only brandy.

Chapter 2

I set her on my pacing steed,
  And nothing else saw all day long;
For sideways would she lean, and sing
  A faery's song.

— John Keats, 'La Belle Dame Sans Merci'

The storm clouds had scattered away northward, and
Appleton folded down the accordionlike calash roof of
his carriage so that as they drove they could bake the
'drink-poisons' out of their systems in the summer sun;
but most of the roads between Warnham and the sea
proved to be very narrow, walled on either side with
stones heaped up centuries ago by farmers clearing the
moors, and to Crawford it several times felt as if they
were driving through some sunken antediluvian
corridor.

Ancient oaks spread branches across the sky overhead,
seeming to strive to provide the corridor's missing roof,
and though Appleton's hired driver cursed when the
carriage was slowed for a while by a tightly packed flock
of two dozen sheep being languidly goaded along by a
collie and a white-bearded old man, Crawford was glad
of their company — the landscape had been getting too
close-pressing and inanimate.

At about noon they stopped at a tavern in Worthing,
and on a chestnut-shaded terrace overlooking the glittering expanse of the English Channel they restored
themselves with several pitchers of bitter ale, and a
dozen pickles, and three vast beef-and-gravy pastries

with each man's initials stamped into the crust so that they could keep straight which was whose when they unwrapped the uneaten ends later in the day.

Eventually Crawford pushed his plate away, refilled his glass, and then squinted belligerently at his companions. 'I lost the ring,' he said. The sea breeze blew his brown hair back from his forehead, letting the sun catch the grey hairs at his temples in the moments when he wasn't shaded by the waving branches or the seagulls sailing noisily back and forth over the shore slope.

Appleton blinked at him. 'The ring,' he echoed blankly.

'The goddamn *wedding* ring, the one Jack's supposed to hand to me tonight – I lost it last night, when we were larking about in the back yard of that inn.'

Jack Boyd shook his head. 'Christ, I'm sorry, Mike, that was my fault, going crazy the way I did – I got no business drinking so much. I'll buy you a new one somehow – '

'No, I'm to blame,' interrupted Appleton with a smile which, though rueful, was his first genuine one of the day. 'I was soberer than you two, but I got scared of the dark and ran out on you – hell, Michael, I even saw you take the ring out of the pocket of your coat, after you'd draped the coat over the barmaid who was getting chilled, and I knew it was risky, but I was in such a sweat to get back inside that I didn't want to bring it up. I insist you let me pay for it.'

Crawford stood up and drank off the last of his ale. Even now his face had not lost quite all of the deep-bitten tan acquired in shipboard life, and when he smiled he looked vaguely foreign, like some kind of American or Australian. 'No no, I'm the one that lost it – and anyway I've already bought a replacement from the landlord back there. It cost me half my travelling money,

43

but I think it'll do.' He held out a ring on the palm of his hand for them to look at.

Appleton had at last regained his usual manner. 'Well, yes,' he said judiciously, 'these southern rustics will probably never have seen *real* gold . . . or any kind of metal, conceivably. Yes, you ought to be all right with that. What's the name of the place again? Undercut-by-the-Sea?'

Crawford opened his mouth to remind him that it was called Bexhill-on-Sea, but, now that at least a tenuous sort of cheer had been restored, he didn't want to seem stuffy. 'Something like that,' he said drily as they wrapped up the leftovers and started back toward where the hired driver waited by the carriage.

The roads were open now, with the sea generally visible to their left as the carriage rocked along past the stone jetties of Brighton and Hove – Boyd made deprecatory remarks about the little boats whose ivory sails stippled the blue water – and even when they turned to follow the Lewes road inland across the South Downs, the green fields stretched broadly away to the hills on either side, and the walls between the fields were low.

The only jarring moment came when they were passing the north face of Windover Hill, and Crawford awoke from an uneasy doze and saw the giant figure of a man carved crudely into the chalk of the distant hillside; Crawford instantly scrambled up into a crouch on the seat and grabbed the door as if he intended to vault out of the carriage and simply run back toward the sea, but Boyd caught him and pushed him back down into the seat.

He stared fearfully at the figure, and his companions shifted around to see what had so upset him.

'For Christ's sake, Mike,' said Boyd nervously, 'it's only an old Saxon hill figure, like there's dozens of throughout these parts. The Wilmington Long Man, that lad's called. It's just a – '

Crawford, still not completely awake, interrupted him – *'Why is it watching us?'* he whispered, staring across the miles of farmland at the pale outline on the hill.

'You were having a dream,' said Appleton a little shrilly. 'What do you drink for if it gives you dreams like this?' He dug a flask out of his coat pocket, took a deep swallow, and then leaned forward and ordered the driver to go faster.

Late in the afternoon they passed the first outlying stone-and-thatch cottages of Bexhill-on-Sea; a few miles farther and they were among the shaded lanes of the town, driving past rows of neat seventeenth-century houses, all built of the local honey-coloured limestone. Flowers brightened the boundaries of the yards and lanes, and the house at whose gate they stopped was hardly visible from the road because of the hundreds of red and yellow roses that bobbed on vines woven around the posts of the front fence.

As Crawford climbed down from the carriage to the grass, a boy who had been crouched beside the gate leapt to his feet and sprinted across the lawn and into the house. A few moments later the abrupt, mournful wail of a bagpipe startled birds out of the trees overhead, and Appleton, who had followed Crawford out of the carriage and was now trying to pull the wrinkles out of his coat, winced when he heard it.

'Blood sacrifice?' he asked politely. 'Planning some sort of druid rite, are you?'

'No,' said Crawford defensively, 'uh, it's going to be a traditional Scottish ceremony, I understand. Wrong end of the island, of course, but . . .'

'Christ,' put in Boyd anxiously, 'they're not going to

make us eat those stuffed sheep stomachs, are they? What do they call it? Havoc?'

'Haggis. No, the food'll be conventional, but . . . oh, they'll have whitened Julia's eyebrows with antimony, and I sent ahead a jar of henna so the bridesmaids could stain her feet with it after they wash them – '

He was reaching toward the back of the carriage for his portmanteau when he froze.

'Hey, Mike,' said Boyd, leaning down from the carriage to grab Crawford's shoulder, 'are you getting sick? You're suddenly pale as a low sky.'

Crawford shivered, but then continued his interrupted reach to the boot; with trembling fingers he began unbuckling the leather straps. 'N-no, I'm fine,' he said. 'I just . . . remembered something.'

Mention of the washing of feet had brought back a hitherto-lost memory of last night – he *had* washed his feet, and taken off his muddy trousers too, after fleeing back to his room from the statue; and he hadn't cleaned up because of any particular fastidiousness, it seemed to him now, but out of an irrational fear of Sussex dirt. So he must have gone outside one more time . . . at least. He searched his memory now for any recollection of it, but could come up with nothing.

Could he have been searching for the ring again? The question frightened him as soon as he posed it to himself, for it implied the conceivability of some *other* reason. He forced himself to concentrate on unstrapping his luggage.

People were coming out of the house now. Crawford recognized the minister who had had him and Julia to tea at the local rectory a fortnight ago; and the man behind him was Julia's father; and the lady in the blue velvet stole – whose shuffling, undersea-creature gait was the result, he decided, of a reluctance to look down at the stepping stones for fear of disarranging her tall

46

rose-studded coiffure – must have been Julia's aunt, though previously Crawford had only seen her in a housedress, with her hair pulled up in a tight bun.

And the scowling girl hanging behind, he thought warily, must be Julia's twin sister Josephine. She's got Julia's colouring, I suppose, but she's far too thin – and why does she hunch her shoulders so? Maybe this is the defensive 'mechanical' pose Julia told me she assumes in stressful situations – if so it's even less attractive, and far less funny, than Julia described it.

Away from the leather-and-meat-pie smell of the carriage, he noticed for the first time the smells of rural East Sussex – clay and flowers and a whiff of a distant dairy. It was all a long way from the musks of sick people and the sharp reek of vinegar-washed hospital walls.

He had got his bags free, and he set them down on the road's gravel verge just in time for the boy, rushing back again, to pick them up and wrestle them in a sort of running waddle back toward the house. Remembering that Josephine disapproved of her sister's marrying a physician – particularly one who currently specialized in an area of medicine that was by tradition the domain of unprofessional old women – Crawford pretended not to see her, and instead made a show of greeting her father and aunt.

'Julia's upstairs,' her father said as he led the new arrivals toward the house, 'worrying about her hair and her clothes. *You* know how brides are.' Crawford thought he heard Josephine mutter something behind him, and then the old man seemed to realize that he had said something awkward. 'By which – uh – I mean merely – '

Crawford forced a smile. 'I'm sure she needn't worry about such things,' he said. 'I've never seen her looking less than splendid.'

47

Visibly relieved to have got past his apparent reference to Crawford's first wife, old Mr Carmody nodded rapidly, blinking and smiling. 'Oh, to be sure, to be sure. The very image of her departed mother, she is.'

Crawford was glancing back toward the road and the carriage as Mr Carmody said this, and so he saw the expression on Josephine's narrow face change instantly from spite to vacuity; she kept walking, but her arms and legs were stiff now, and her head, when she looked away, moved in one abrupt jerk, like the instantaneous movement of a spider. Her nostrils were wide and white. Clearly *this* was her mechanical pose.

He looked ahead at her father, expecting more apologetic mumbling for having brought up what was clearly another touchy subject, but the old man stumped on unaware, grinning and shaking his head at some comment Appleton had made.

Crawford raised an eyebrow. The old man didn't seem unobservant or thoughtless — but surely, if the subject of his deceased wife was so evidently traumatic to one of his daughters, he ought sometime to have noticed? He'd have had twenty years to stumble across the fact, for the twins' mother had bled to death minutes after having given birth to Josephine, the second of them.

Once inside the house, the travellers were given mugs of cider and plates of bread and cheese, and, as they worked their way through the snacks, they pretended to enjoy the efforts of the young man wringing doomful melodies out of the bagpipe. At last Mr Carmody halted the recital and offered to show his guests to their rooms.

Crawford obediently went to his room and washed his face in the basin on the dresser, but then he went back out into the hall and stole down to Julia's room. She answered his knock and proved to be alone in spite of the wedding preparations, and she was still dressed casually in a green cotton dress. With her shoes off she seemed even shorter than usual, making her abundant figure and narrow waist even more startling. Her long brown hair was still slightly damp from a recent washing.

'You're nearly a full day late,' she said after she'd kissed him. 'Break a wheel?'

'Delayed by a rough delivery,' he told her. 'A charity ward case – her family only got her to the hospital after some midwife had made an almost fatal hash of the job.' He sat down on the window seat. 'I finally got to see your sister, out front just now. She really doesn't look well.'

Julia sat beside him and took his hand. 'Oh, poor Josephine is just upset that you're taking me away. I'll miss her, too, but I've got a life of my own. She's got to . . . become Josephine.' Julia shrugged. 'Whoever that may turn out to be.'

'Somebody in some trouble, I think. How long has she been doing that mechanical trick?'

'Oh, ever since she was a baby, practically – she asked me once when we were children what I did to keep the night-scaries from getting me when I was in bed at night. I asked her what *she* did, and she said she would rock back and forth like a pump-arm or a clockwork or something, so that the scaries would say to themselves,' Julia assumed a deep voice, 'oh, *this* isn't human, *this* isn't prey – this is some kind of a *construction*.' Julia smiled sadly.

'She did it out in the yard a little while ago, though, when your father mentioned your mother. She could hardly have thought the night-boogers were after her then.'

'No, she isn't afraid of ghosty things anymore, poor thing. Now she just does her clockwork trick when things happen that she can't bear – I guess she reckons that if Josephine can't stand whatever's going on right now, it's best if Josephine stops existing for a while, until it's over.'

'Jesus.' Crawford looked out the window at the sunlit leaves in the high branches. 'Is that . . . I mean, did you and your father . . . you *have* tried to help her over this, this thing about her, your mother, have you? Because – '

'Of course we have,' Julia spread her hands. 'But it's never done any good. We've *always* told her that my mother's death wasn't her fault. She just won't listen – ever since she was a little girl she's had the idea that she killed her.'

Crawford looked out the window at the path on which he'd first seen Josephine, and he shook his head.

'We really have tried to help her, Michael. You know me, you know I would. But it's useless – and really, *try* to imagine what we've gone through living with her! Good lord, until only a few years ago she'd every now and then believe she was me – it was humiliating, she'd wear my clothes, visit my friends – I can't . . . *tell* you how I felt. You must have known some young girls when you were growing up, you must have seen how easily their feelings get hurt! Honestly, I really thought sometimes that I'd have to run away, make new friends somewhere else. And of course my friends had a fine time then pretending to mistake *me* for *her*.'

Crawford nodded sympathetically. 'Say, she's not going to do it now, is she?' He winced at the thought of Josephine making some scene by pretending that *she* was his bride.

Julia laughed. 'That would be dramatic, wouldn't it? No, I finally stopped it by following her one day and confronting her as she was harassing some of my friends. And even then she tried to continue the . . . *pretence* for a minute or so. My friends nearly choked, they were laughing so hard. It was hard for me to do, to humiliate both of us that way, but it worked.'

Julia stood up and smiled. 'Now you're not supposed to be in here — scat and get dressed, we'll be seeing each other soon enough.'

The wedding was performed at nine o'clock that evening in the wide Carmody drawing room, with the bride and groom kneeling on cushions on the floor. During almost the entire ceremony the late summer sun slanted in through the west windows and glowed gold and rose in the crystal glasses ranged on a shelf, and as the light faded and servants brought in lamps, the minister declared Michael and Julia man and wife by the authority vested in him.

Josephine had been the strikingly unemotional maid of honour, and at this point she and Boyd were supposed to go out to the kitchen and come back, Josephine with an oatcake and Boyd with a wooden stoup of strong ale; the stoup was to be passed around the company after Crawford took the first gulp, and Josephine was to break the oatcake ceremoniously over Julia's head, symbolically assuring Julia's fertility and bestowing good luck on the guests who picked up the crumbs from the floor.

But when Josephine held the little cake over Julia's head, she stared at it for a moment and then lowered it and crouched to set it carefully on the floor. 'I can't break her in half,' she said quietly, as if to herself, and then she walked slowly back to the kitchen.

'Well, so much for children,' said Crawford into the resulting silence. He drank some of the ale, and covered his embarrassment with a savouring grin. 'Good brewers they have hereabouts,' he said quietly to Boyd as he passed the stoup to him. 'Thank God it was the biscuit that they made her carry, and not this.'

Actually, Crawford wanted to have children — his first

51

marriage had produced none, and he hoped the defect had been poor Caroline's and not his . . . and he didn't want to believe the rumour that Caroline had been pregnant when the house she'd been living in burned down, for at that point he had not even spoken to her for a year.

He was, after all, an obstetrician – an *accoucheur* – and in spite of the two years he had spent stitching up the wounds and sawing off the shattered limbs of His Majesty's sailors in the wars with Spain and the United States, delivering babies was what he did best. He wished Julia's mother could have been attended by someone with his own degree of skill.

The difficult delivery at St George's Hospital had made him and Boyd miss the stagecoach they were originally to have taken south from London early yesterday and while they had waited in the taproom of the coaching inn for the next one, Boyd had irritably asked him why, after all his complicated surgical training, he should choose to devote his career to an area of medicine which not only made him late for his own wedding, but which 'old wives have been handling just fine for thousands of years anyway.'

Crawford had called for another pitcher, refilled his glass and then tried to explain.

'First off, Jack, they *haven't* been handling it "just fine." Most expectant mothers would be better off with no attendance at all than with a midwife. I'm generally called in only after the midwife has made some awful mistake, and some of the scenes I've walked in on would make you turn pale – yes, even you with your scars from Abukir and Trafalgar. And there's a difference when it's an infant, a person who . . . who you can't think up any *well-at-any-rates* for – you know, "Well at any rate he knew what he was getting into when he signed on," or "Well at any rate if the man ever lived who deserved it, it was him," or "Well at any rate he had his faith to sustain him through this." An infant is . . . what, innocent, but more than that, not only innocent but *aware* too. It's a person who hasn't seen or understood or agreed to anything, but will, if given time – and therefore you can't be satisfied with a merely good rate of survival for them, the way you can with . . . oh, tomato seedlings or pedigreed dog litters.'

'Still,' Boyd had said, 'it'll no doubt be squared away and systematized before long. Is there really enough there to occupy your whole *life*?'

Crawford had paused to drain his glass and call for another pitcher. 'Uh . . . yes. Yes. Plain old prudery is what has kept it so primitive – it's made a, a fenced-off *jungle* of this area of medicine. Even now a male doctor can usually only assist at a delivery if they've got a sheet draped over the mother – he has to do his best with groping about blindly underneath, and so a lot of times he cuts the umbilical cord in the wrong place, and the mother or the child bleeds to death. And no one has *begun* to figure out what sorts of foods an expectant mother should eat or not eat in order to have a healthy child. And the goddamned "literature" on the whole subject is just an accumulation of bad guesses and superstitions and misfiled veterinary notes.'

The fresh pitcher arrived, and Boyd paid for it. Crawford, still absorbed in his subject, laughed then, though his frown didn't unkink.

'Hell, man,' he went on, automatically refilling his glass, 'only a few years ago I looked up in the Corporation of Surgeons' library a Swiss manuscript catalogued as being on the subject of caesarian birth, in a big portfolio known as *The Menotti Miscellany* . . . and I discovered that it wasn't about birth at all – the person who catalogued the manuscript had simply looked at the drawings in the wrong order.'

Boyd frowned at that, then raised his eyebrows. 'What, you mean it was a manuscript on how to insert a *baby* into a woman?'

'Nearly. It was a procedure to surgically implant a little statue into a human body.' Crawford had had to raise his hand at that point to silence Boyd. 'Let me finish. The manuscript was in a sort of abbreviated Latin, as if the surgeon who wrote it had just been making notes to himself and never expected them to be read by anyone else, and the drawings were crude, but I soon realized that it wasn't even a woman's body but a *man's* body the thing was being put into. And yet for hundreds of years this manuscript has been catalogued as a work on caesarian delivery!'

Through the inn's window he had seen the coach entering the yard then, and he drained his mug in several long swallows. 'There's our transport to Warnham, where we meet Appleton. Anyway,' he said as they got up and hefted their baggage, 'you can see why I don't agree that childbirthing is likely to become an orderly art any time soon.'

Crawford and Boyd had dragged their baggage out of the building and across the pavement to the coach. The horses were being changed and the driver was gone, presumably into the taproom they had just left.

'*Well?*' said Boyd finally. When Crawford gave him a blank look, he went on almost angrily, 'So why did this Macaroni person want to put a statue inside of somebody?'

'Oh! Oh, right, of course.' Crawford had thought about it for a moment, then shrugged. 'I don't know, Jack. It was seven or eight hundred years ago – probably nobody'll ever find out. But my *point* was – '

'I got your point,' Boyd had assured him tiredly. 'You like birthing children.'

* * *

54

And here his new sister-in-law was messing up the traditional fertility rituals of his wedding. Crawford smiled as Julia broke away from her father and the minister, who were talking by the drawing room window, and crossed to where he and Boyd were standing.

'Well, it was *mostly* traditional Scottish, dear,' she said, bending down to pick up the biscuit Josephine had left on the floor. 'And it wasn't actually an oatcake anyway – it was a Biddenden cake from just across the Weald in Kent.' She handed it to Crawford.

'I remember those, Miss – uh, Mrs Crawford,' said Boyd, who had grown up in Sussex. 'They used to be given out at Easter, didn't they?'

'That's right,' Julia said. 'Michael, oughtn't we to be getting aboard Mr – aboard your carriage and leaving? It's getting dark, and Hastings *is* a few miles off.'

'You're right.' He dropped the biscuit into his coat pocket. 'And we're supposed to be on the Calais boat by noon. I'll begin making our goodbyes.'

Appleton and Boyd were staying on and taking separate coaches back to London tomorrow. He found them and shook their hands, smiling to conceal a sudden, momentary urge to go back with them, and to leave to braver souls the whole undertaking of marriage.

Julia had come up beside him and touched his shoulder. He nodded to his friends, then turned and took her arm and began leading her toward the front door.

The moon ducked in and out of muscular-looking clouds overhead as the landau rattled along the shore road, and a wind had sprung up that nearly drowned out the distant respiration of the waves. Crawford pulled the fur robe more tightly around Julia and himself, thankful that the carriage roof had been put up; and he was charitably hoping, as he watched the steam of his breath plume away, that the driver had had a lot of old Mr Carmody's brandy before they'd left.

The wildness of the night seemed to have got into the horses, for they were nearly galloping in the harnesses, their ears laid back and sparks flying from their hooves even though the road wasn't particularly flinty – the carriage arrowed through the luckily empty streets of St Leonards only about ten minutes after leaving Bexhill-on-Sea, and shortly after that Crawford could see the lights and buildings of Hastings ahead, and he heard the driver swearing at the horses as he worked at reining them in.

The carriage finally slowed to a stop in front of the Keller Inn, and Crawford helped Julia step down on to pavement that seemed, after the wild ride, to be rocking like the deck of a ship.

They were expected, and several young men in the inn's livery sprinted out of the building to haul the luggage down from the boot. Crawford tried to pay for the ride, but was told that Appleton had covered it, and so he made do with tipping the driver lavishly before the man got back up on to the seat to take the carriage back to Appleton's house in London.

Then, suddenly both impatient and self-conscious, Crawford took Julia's elbow and followed the baggage-laden servants into the building. Several minutes later an amber glow of lamplight flared to define an upstairs window, and presently it went out.

Morning sunlight, fragmented by the warped glass of the windowpane, was spattered and streaked like a frozen fountain across the wall when Crawford was awakened by the maid's knock. He was stiff and feverish, though he hadn't had an appreciable amount to drink the night before, and for the first few minutes, while he was facing the sunny wall, he thought he was still in Warnham, and that it was tonight that he was supposed to get married.

Brown stains on the quilt in front of his eyes seemed to confirm it. That's right, he thought blurrily, I went out barefoot into the muddy yard last night . . . and had some kind of drink-spawned hallucination, and failed to find the wedding ring. I'd better go look for it again this morning. Vaguely he wondered what the mud had consisted of – there was certainly a strange smell in the room, like the heavy odours of an operating theatre.

And why were these bluish quartz crystals lying on the sheet? There must have been half a dozen of them, each as big as a sparrow's egg. He could understand having picked them up – they were eye-catching little pebbles, knobby but bright with an amethystine glitter – but why scatter them across the bed?

The maid knocked again. With a groan he rolled over –

– And then he screamed and convulsed right out of the bed and on to the floor, and he crawled backwards across the polished wood, piling up carpets at his back, until the wall stopped him, and he was still screaming with every quick breath.

The brown stains had not been mud.

His lungs were heaving inside his ribs with the stress of his inhuman shrieking, but his mind was stopped, as static as a smashed clock; and though his eyes were clenched tightly shut now, all he could see were bones jutting terribly white from torn and crushed flesh, and blood everywhere. He wasn't Michael Crawford now, nor even a human – for an endless minute he was nothing but a crystallized knot of horror and profound denial.

He consisted of an impulse to stop existing – but the very fact of breathing linked him to the world, and the world now began to intrude. Hugely against his will he became aware of sounds again.

The maid had fled, but now there were masculine voices outside the door, which shook with knockings loud enough to be heard over Crawford's continuing screams. Finally there was a heavy impact against the panels, and then another, and the third one splintered the door broadly enough so that an eye could peer in, and then a gnarled hand snaked through and pulled back the bolt. At last the door was swung open.

The first two men into the room rushed to the bed, but after a glance at the crushed, redly glistening ruin that had last night been Julia Crawford, they turned their stiff, pale faces toward Crawford, who had by now managed to stifle his screams by biting his fist very hard and staring at the floor.

Crawford was aware that the men had stumbled out of the room, and over the noise he himself was making he could hear shouting and a racket that might have been someone being devastatingly sick. After a while men – perhaps some of the same ones – came back in.

They hastily bundled up his clothes and shoes and helped him get dressed in the hall, and then they took him – carried him, practically – downstairs to the kitchen; and when exhaustion had stopped his ever hoarser screaming they gave him a cup of brandy.

'We've sent someone to fetch the sheriff,' said one man shakily. 'What in the name of Jesus *happened*?'

Crawford took a long sip of the liquor, and he found that he was able to think and speak. 'I *don't know*!' he whispered. 'How could that – have happened! – while I was *asleep*?'

The two men looked at each other, then left him alone there.

* * *

He had known at a glance that she was dead — he had seen too many violent fatalities in the Navy to entertain any doubt — but if a body in that condition had been brought to him after a sea battle, he would have assumed that a mast section had fallen across it, or that an unmoored cannon had recoiled and crushed it against a bulkhead. What had *happened* to her?

Crawford recalled that one of the men who broke into the room had glanced at the ceiling, apparently half expecting to see a great gap from which some titanic piece of masonry would have fallen, but the plaster was sound, with only a few spots of blood. And how had Crawford not only come through unscratched, but *slept right through it*? Could he have been drugged, or knocked unconscious? As a doctor, he was unable to discover in himself the after-effects of either one.

What kind of husband sleeps through the brutal murder — and rape, possibly, though there would be no way to derive a guess about that from the devastated body upstairs — of his own wife? Hadn't there been something about 'protecting' in the vows he'd taken last night?

But how could a killer have got into the room? The door was bolted from the inside, and the window was at least a dozen feet above the pavement, and was in any case too small for even a child to crawl through . . . and this murder wasn't the work of any child   Crawford estimated that it would take a strong man, even with a sledgehammer, to crush a ribcage so totally.

And how in the name of God had he slept through it?

He was unable to stop seeing that smashed horror in the bed, and he knew that it completed a triumvirate, along with the burning house in which Caroline had died and the overturned boat in the surf that had drowned his younger brother. And he knew that these things would forever be obstacles to any other subject for his attention, like rough boulders blocking the doorways and corridors of an otherwise comfortable house.

He wondered, almost objectively, whether he would find a way to avoid dying by his own hand.

He had refilled his brandy cup at least once, but now he was nauseated by the sharp fumes of it, and out of consideration for their kitchen floor – *That's good*, interrupted his mind hysterically, *their kitchen floor! How about the floor upstairs, and the bed and the mattress!* – he decided to go outside into the garden.

The fresh sea breeze dispelled his nausea, and he walked aimlessly down the narrow, shaded lanes, trying to lose his abhorrent individuality in the vivid smells and colours of the flowers.

He put his hands into the pockets of his coat, and he felt something which, after a moment's puzzlement, he was able to identify as the Biddenden cake Josephine had failed to break at the wedding the night before. He took it out of the pocket. There was a raised pattern on the crumbly surface and, looking closely, he saw that it was a representation of two women physically joined at the hip. Crawford had read of twins who'd been born so, though he didn't know why the town of Biddenden should celebrate one such pair on their biscuits. He crumbled the thing up in his hands and scattered it over the path for the birds.

After a while he began to walk back toward where the rear wall of the inn rose above the greenery, but he halted when he heard voices behind a hedge ahead of him, for he didn't want to have to talk to anyone.

'What do you mean, "should have restrained him"?' came a man's voice angrily. 'I'm not a member of the Watch – and anyway, nobody would have guessed that he could walk away. We *carried* him down the stairs to the kitchen.'

'Murderers are generally good actors,' said another voice.

Crawford was suddenly dizzy with rage, and actually reeled back a step; he took a deep breath, but before he could shout he heard another voice say, 'Did you hear how his first wife died?' — and he sagged and let the breath out.

Chapter 3

I will drain him dry as hay:
Sleep shall neither night nor day
Hang upon his pent-house lid;
He shall live a man forbid:
Weary se'nnights nine times nine
Shall he dwindle, peak and pine:
Though his bark cannot be lost,
Yet it shall be tempest-tost.

— Shakespeare, *Macbeth*

'*First* wife? No. How did you?'

'The father and sister of the dead lady upstairs got here a few minutes ago – they're in the dining room. They say his first wife ran off with a Navy man who got her with child, and Crawford found out about it and burned down the house she was living in. Her Navy man tried to get into the burning house to save her, but Crawford fought him, on the street out front, long enough to make it impossible for anyone to get inside.'

Crawford's eyes and jaws and fists were all clenched tight, and he had to crouch to keep from falling over. He could hear the blood pressure singing in his head.

'Jesus,' said the first man. 'And did you see what he did to the Carmody girl upstairs? Like a mill wheel rolled over her. And then he went back to sleep! The doctor says, judging from her temperature and the way the blood's dried, that she was killed around midnight. So old Crawford was sleeping there next to that thing for something like seven hours!'

'I'll tell you one thing, I'm not searching this damn garden without a pistol in my hand.'

'That's a point. Yeah, let's . . .'

The voices drifted away then. Crawford sat down in the grass and held his head in his hands. These people were so wrong, about so many things, that he despaired of ever getting it all straightened out . . . but the worst of it was that Mr Carmody apparently *believed* that old story about Caroline's death.

It had been about six years ago – Caroline had left him, but though he had known which house she was living in in London, he hadn't been able to work up the nerve to go and confront her; it was too much like making a perilous leap from one high rooftop to another – an error would be fatal. He might simply fall, simply ruin any possibility that she would come back to him . . . for there would be only one chance, she wouldn't feel that she owed him more than one conversation.

And so for ten days he had ignored his medical practice to sit all day in a pub across the street from the house she was in, trying to judge the perfect moment to see her and ask her to return.

And before he did, the place had caught fire. Crawford thought now that the Navy man might have set it intentionally when he'd learned – when he had got the impression – that she was pregnant.

When smoke had begun gouting out of the upstairs windows, Crawford had dropped his beer and sprinted out of the pub and across the street, and he'd been slamming his shoulder against the front door when the sailor had opened it from inside, to come lurching and coughing out in a cloud of acrid smoke. Crawford had bulled past him, shouting 'Caroline!' – but the sailor had caught him by the collar and whirled him back outside.

'Hopeless,' the man had wheezed at him. 'Only be killin' yourself.'

But Crawford had heard a scream from inside. 'That's my wife,' he gasped, tearing away from the sailor.

He had taken only one running step back toward the house when a hard punch to the kidney brought him to his knees; but when the Navy man grabbed him under the arms to haul him out on to the street, Crawford drove an elbow, with as much force as he could muster, back into the man's crotch.

The sailor collapsed forward, and Crawford caught his arm and spun him out into the street, where he fell and rolled moaning in the dust. Crawford turned back toward the open door, but at that moment the upper floor gave way and crashed down into the ground floor, exploding out through the doorway such a burst of sparks and heat that Crawford was lifted off his feet and tossed right over the hunched sailor.

His eyebrows and a lot of his hair were gone, and his clothing would have been aflame in moments if some-one had not flung on him the contents of a pail of water that had been brought to douse the wall of one of the surrounding houses.

The fire was officially declared an accident, but rumours – and even a couple of street ballads – hinted that Crawford had set it in revenge, and then prevented the Navy man from getting inside to rescue Caroline. Crawford thought the sailor himself might have started the rumours, for a couple of the onlookers at the fire had remarked acidly on his hasty solo escape.

And this thing now was far, far worse. Of *course* people will take it for granted that I killed Julia, he thought. They won't listen to me. And already errors have begun to creep into the story – such as the doctor's statement that she died at around midnight. I *know* she was still alive at dawn. I remember drowsily making love to her while the curtains were just beginning to lighten; she was straddling me, sitting on top of me, and while I don't know if I ever did wake up fully, I know I didn't dream it.

I can either stay, and be arrested, and almost certainly hang . . . or I can run, leave the country. Of course, if I run, everybody will conclude that I did kill her, but I don't think my voluntary submission to arrest and trial would make them think any differently.

All I can do, he thought, is run.

He felt better after deciding; at least now he had a clear goal, and something to think about besides Julia's intolerably sundered body.

He stood up cautiously — and instantly there was a shout and the stunning *bam* of a gunshot, and a tree branch beside his head exploded in stinging splinters.

And then Crawford was running, back through the lanes of the garden, toward the back wall. Another shot boomed behind him and his left hand was whiplashed upward, spraying blood across his eyes, but he leapt, caught the wall with his right hand, and contorted his body up and outward through empty air; a moment later he hit rocky dirt hard on his side, but as soon as he had stopped sliding he made himself roll back up on to his feet and hobble down a slope to a rutted, building-shaded alley.

Only when he saw the man on the horse at the street end of the alley did he realize that he had picked up a fist-sized stone, and almost without volition his arm drew back to fling it with all his remaining strength.

But, 'Michael!' the man called softly in a familiar voice, and Crawford dropped the stone.

'My God,' he gasped haltingly, limping forward with wincing haste, 'you've got to . . . get me out of here! They think . . .'

'I know what they think,' said Appleton, swinging down out of the saddle. 'Can you — ,' he began, but then he looked at Crawford more closely. 'Good heavens, are you shot?'

'Just my hand.' Crawford now looked at it for the first time, and his pupils contracted with shock. The index and little fingers looked flayed, but his ring finger was gone, along with his wedding ring, leaving only a ragged, glistening stump from which blood was falling rapidly to make bright red spots on the dirt and the toes of his boots.

'Jesus Christ,' he whispered, suddenly wobbly on his legs. 'Jesus, man, look what . . .'

His eyes unfocused, but before he could fall, Appleton stepped forward and slapped him across the face twice, forehand and backhand. 'Faint later,' he said harshly. 'Right now you've got to ride or die. Tourniquet that as soon as you're beyond pursuit — there's fifty pounds and a note in the saddlebag, but it seems that what you'll need soonest is the string I tied around them. Foresightful of me to have used it, eh?'

Voices could be heard shouting on the far side of the wall, and somewhere hooves were knocking on cobblestones. Appleton gave the ashen Crawford a leg up into the saddle, clearly half expecting him to tumble right back to the ground on the other side of the horse.

But Crawford took the reins in his right hand, kicked his boots into the stirrups, pushed his heels down to be able to grip the horse, and, when Appleton gave the horse a loud slap across the thigh, he hunched forward as his mount sprang away west down the broad Hastings street in the morning sunlight. He clamped his teeth on the stump of his missing finger and worked very hard at not being violently sick.

Only the highest chimney-pots still glowed in the reddening sunlight as the stagecoach lurched and lunged its slow way up the crowded length of Borough High Street in London, and when it stopped in front of an inn near the new Marshalsea Prison, Crawford was the first passenger to alight from the carriage.

In a back corner of a Brighton tavern at midmorning he had tied a clean cloth around his finger-stump and then drenched it in brandy before gingerly pulling on a pair of gloves. Now, after more riding and no rest and finally, after abandoning the exhausted horse, six straight hours jammed between two fat women in the London coach, he was obviously fevered – his hand was throbbing like a blacksmith's bellows, and his breathing was hotly metallic and echoing in his head.

He had used some of Appleton's money to buy clothes and a new leather portmanteau to carry them in, and though it was light luggage compared to what he had left behind in the Hastings hotel room, he had to repress a groan when he picked it up from where the coachman had casually set it down.

As he walked away up High Street he stayed in the shadows under the overhanging second storeys of the old half-timbered houses, for he was nervous about all the prisons around him. Ahead of him to the left, on the Thames bank, stood the burned-out ruin of the famous Clink, and behind him, just south of the new prison where the stage had stopped, was the King's Bench Prison. Why the hell, he thought peevishly, didn't Appleton *think* of the alarming nature of this area, and send me somewhere else?

The Borough's many sewage ditches always smelled horrible, but after this hot summer day the fumes seemed to hint at some sort of cloacal fermentation, and he worried about compounding his fever in the bad air. At least it was medical students he was going to stay with.

The street was clogged with homeward-bound coster-monger carts, every one of which seemed to have a dog riding on top, but soon he could see, over them, the arch of London Bridge – and remembering the instructions in Appleton's note, he turned right down the last street before the bridge. He turned right again at the next corner, and found himself, as the note had said, on Dean Street. He walked down to the narrow house that was number eight – it was right across the street from a Baptist chapel, another dubious omen – and obediently rattled the doorknocker. A headache had begun behind his eyes, and he was sweating heavily under his coat.

As he waited on the cobblestones, he mentally reviewed Appleton's note. 'Pretend to be a Medical Student,' Appleton had written. 'You're a bit old, but there are older. Be frankish about your Navy experience, for you could have been a Dresser to a Naval Surgeon without getting any Credentials, but be vague about questions touching on whose Lectures you are attending. It's unlikely that you will be recognized, but of course don't talk about Obstetrics. Henry Stephens will not press you for Answers once he knows that you are a Friend of mine, Nor will he let others do so.'

The door was pulled open by a sturdy young man who was shorter than Crawford. Crawford thought he looked more like a labourer than a medical student. His reddish-brown hair had obviously been pushed back from his forehead only a moment before.

'Yes?' the young man said.

'Is,' said Crawford hoarsely, 'uh, Henry Stephens at home?'

'Not at the moment. Can I be of any help?'

'Well . . . a friend of his told me I might be able to get a room here.' Crawford leaned against the doorframe and tried not to pant. 'Help pay for the joint sitting room, I think it was.' His voice was hollow and rasping from his screaming this morning.

'Oh.' The young man stared at him for a moment,

then swung the door open. 'Uh, do come in. Tyrrell moved out a week ago, I guess you heard, and we could use the help. You're,' he said dubiously, 'another medical student?'

'That's right.' Crawford stepped forward into the warmth and lamplight, and sank into a chair. 'My name is – ' Belatedly he wondered what name to give. His mind was a blank – all he could remember was that in the note Appleton had said *Be frankish.* ' – Michael Frankish.'

The young man seemed to find the name plausible. He held out his hand. 'I'm John Keats – currently a student at Guy's Hospital, right around the corner. Are you at Guy's?'

'Uh, no, I'm at . . . St Thomas's.' He was pleased with himself for having remembered the name of the hospital across the street from Guy's.

Keats noticed the dark bandage on the stump of Crawford's finger then, and it seemed to upset him. 'What – your finger! What happened?'

A little flustered, Crawford said, 'Oh, it – had to be amputated. Gangrene.'

Keats stared at him anxiously for a moment. 'I gather you had a rough trip,' he ventured finally as he closed the door. 'Would a glass of wine sit well?'

'Sit like corn upon the head of Solomon,' said Crawford, too tired to bother with making sense. 'Yes,' he added, seeing Keats's bewildered look. 'What area of medicine are you studying?' he went on hastily, speaking more loudly as Keats went into the next room.

'Surgical and apothecary,' came the answer. A moment later Keats reappeared with a half-full bottle and two glasses. 'I'm going to the Apothecaries' Hall this Thursday to take the examinations, though I won't be able to practise until the thirty-first of October.'

Crawford took a filled glass and drank deeply. 'What,

Hallowe'en? I thought you said *surgical*, not witchcraftical.'

Keats laughed uncertainly, the look of anxiety returning to his face. 'I become of age then; the thirty-first is my birthday. My – ' He paused, for Crawford was staring at several knobby little bluish crystals on a bookshelf.

'What,' asked Crawford carefully, 'are those?'

A key rattled in the front door lock then, and a tall man opened the door and entered. He didn't look as young as Keats, and his face was leanly humorous.

'Henry!' exclaimed the younger man with obvious relief, 'this is Michael . . . Myrrh? . . .'

'Michael, uh, Frankish,' Crawford corrected, standing up but not really looking away from the little crystals. Their facets made bright needles of the lamplight, and seemed to increase the fever pressure behind his forehead. 'Arthur Appleton . . . told me to look here for a place to stay. I'm a student at St Elmo's.' He shook his head sharply. 'Thomas's, that is.' He coughed.

Henry Stephens gave him a good-naturedly sceptical smile, but just nodded. 'If Arthur vouches for you, that's good enough for me. You can – what, are you off, John?'

'I'm afraid so,' said Keats, taking a coat from a rack by the door. 'Got to see to Dr Lucas's poor charges. Good to have met you, Michael,' he added on the way out the door.

When the door had closed, Stephens sank into a chair and picked up the wine glass Keats had left. 'St Elmo's, eh?'

Though exhausted, Crawford smiled and changed the subject. 'Dr Lucas's charges?'

Stephens bowed a fraction of an inch. 'Young John is a dresser for the most incompetent surgeon at Guy's – Lucas's dressers always have plenty of festering bandages to change.'

Crawford waved at the odd crystals. 'What are those?'

Stephens may have realized that Crawford's casual manner was a pose, for he looked sharply at him before answering. 'Those are bladder stones,' he said carefully. 'Dr Lucas is given many such cases.'

'I've seen bladder stones,' said Crawford. 'That's not how they look. They look like . . . spiky limestone. These things look like quartz.'

Stephens shrugged. 'These are what get cut out of Lucas's patients. No doubt they're tired of it – any day now I expect the administrators to summon Lucas and tell him, "Doctor, you're beginning to exhaust our patients!"' Stephens leaned back in his chair and chuckled quietly for several moments. Then he had a sip of wine and went on. 'Keats isn't a brilliant student, you know. The boys assigned to Lucas never are. But nevertheless Keats is . . . perhaps more *observant* than the administrators guess.'

Crawford knew he was missing something. 'Well . . . ' he said, trying to keep his eyes focusing, 'why has he *saved* the things?'

Stephens shook his head in humorous but apparently genuine disappointment. 'Damn, for a moment I thought you might know, you were looking at them so intently! *I* don't know . . . but I remember one time he was playing with them, holding them up to the light and all, and he said, mostly to himself, "I should throw these away – I know I can have my real career even without using them."'

Crawford had another sip of wine and yawned. 'So what's his *real* career? Jewellery?'

'Nasty sort of jewellery that'd be, wouldn't it? No.' He looked at Crawford with raised eyebrows. 'No, he wants to be a poet.'

Crawford was nearly asleep, and he knew that when he slept it would be for a good twelve hours, so he asked

71

Stephens which room would be his, and when he was shown it he threw his portmanteau on to the floor. He fetched his drink, and stood for a moment in the hall and swirled the inch of wine in the bottom of the glass.

'So,' he asked Stephens, who had helped him carry blankets from the linen closet, 'what's poetry got to do with bladder stones?'

'Don't ask *me*,' Stephens told him. '*I'm* not on intimate terms with the Muses.'

At first he thought the woman in his dream was Julia, for even in the dimness — were the two of them in a cave? — he could see the silver of antimony around her eyes, and Julia had whitened her eyebrows with antimony for the wedding. But when she stood up, naked, and walked across the floor tiles toward him, he saw that this was someone else.

Moonlight climbed a white thigh as she padded past a window or cleft in the cave wall, and he smelled night-blooming jasmine and the sea; then she was in his arms and he was kissing her passionately, not caring that her smooth skin was as cool as the stone tiles under his bare feet, nor that there was suddenly in his nostrils an alien muskiness.

Then they were rolling on the tiles, and it was not skin under his sliding fingertips but scales, and he didn't care about that either . . . but a moment later the dream shifted, and they were in a forest clearing where the moon made spots of pale light that winked like spinning silver coins as the branches overhead waved in a Mediterranean wind . . . she slithered out of his embrace and disappeared in the underbrush, and though he crawled after her, calling, unmindful of the thorny branches, the rustling of her passage grew steadily more distant and was soon gone.

But something seemed to be answering his call — or

was he answering a call of its? As in many dreams, identities blurred into one another . . . and then he was looking at a mountain, and though he'd never been there, he knew it was one of the Alps. It seemed miles high, blocking out a whole corner of the sky even though the thin clouds streaking its breast with sunset shadow let him know that it was many miles distant — and, in spite of its broad-shouldered, strong-jawed look, he knew it was female.

Pain in the stump of his missing finger woke him before dawn.

Two mornings later he was scuffing his way up the broad front steps of Guy's Hospital, blinking at the Greek-looking pillars that stretched away overhead from the top of the front door arch to the roof two storeys above; but the sunlight seemed too harsh up there among all that smooth stone, and he let his gaze drop back down to the heels of Keats's boots, which were tapping up the steps just ahead of him.

For the last couple of days he had been attending lectures at both Guy's and St Thomas's, confident that he would be able to get Appleton to acknowledge the signature he had forged on his application papers — if Crawford should decide to make it official and actually become a surgeon again under the name of Michael Frankish.

And he was fairly sure he wouldn't be recognized. For one thing, Dr Crawford had always worked in hospitals north of the river and, for another, he no longer looked very much like Dr Crawford — he had recently worked very hard to lose weight so as to look his best at the wedding, and he now found himself losing more, involuntarily; and nobody who had known him a week ago would have described him as hollow-cheeked and sunken-eyed, as he certainly was now.

At the top of the steps Keats paused and frowned back at Crawford. 'Are you sure you're not too sick?'

'I'm fine.' Crawford fished a handkerchief from his pocket and wiped his forehead. He was dizzy, and it occurred to him that Newton must have been right when he'd said that light consisted of particles, for today he could feel them hitting him. He wondered if he was going to faint. 'What have you got today – Theory and Practice of Medicine?'

'No,' Keats said, 'this morning I'm helping out in the cutting wards – people recovering from lithotomies.'

'Mind if I . . . follow along?' asked Crawford, attempting a carefree smile. 'I'm supposed to hear about Anatomy from old Ashley, but he'll just put me to sleep. And I'm sure I'd pick up more real acquaintance with the subject by touring the wards than by sitting through a damn lecture anyway.'

Keats looked uncertain, then grinned. 'You were a surgeon's dresser on shipboard, didn't you say? Sure, you'll be used to dealing with much worse than this. Come along.' He held the door open for Crawford. 'Matter of fact, I'm taking the exam tomorrow, and then leaving for two months at Margate – you might very well be my successor with Dr Lucas, so it's only right that I show you around.'

They reported to the senior surgeon, who didn't even look up when told that Michael Frankish was to be Lucas's new dresser; he just gave Crawford an entry certificate and told him to use the boot-scraper before going upstairs to the wards.

It took a little over an hour to tend to all of Dr Lucas's patients.

As a student Crawford had not minded tending to the people recovering from surgeries in the cutting wards; the operating theatre itself was far worse, a horrifying pandemonium in which burly interns struggled to hold some screaming patient down on the table as the surgeon sweated and cursed and dug with the knife, his shoes scuffing streaks in the bloody sand on the floor as he braced himself for each resisted thrust . . . and just as nightmarish, if quieter, were the 'salivating' wards, where syphilitics drooled helplessly as a result of the mercurial ointment rubbed into their open lesions . . . but the cutting wards were where a student could see healing actually occurring, quietly, day by day.

Dr Lucas's cutting wards were different. After changing the first heavily slick, malodorous bandages, Crawford could see that Stephens had not understated the old surgeon's skill — Crawford had never seen clumsier incisions, and it was clear that at least as many would die of the bladderstone operation as benefit from it.

A grey-haired clergyman was on his knees beside one of the last beds they came to, and he looked up when Keats bent over the patient. The old cleric seemed to have been deep in prayer, for it took several seconds for his eyes to focus on the newcomers, and even then all he managed to do was nod and turn away.

'Excuse me, Reverend,' said Keats, 'got to change the bandages.'

The clergyman bobbed his head and backed away from the bed, and he thrust his hands inside his cassock — but not before Crawford noticed blood on his fingers. Puzzled, Crawford looked up at his face, and saw the man quickly lick his upper lip — had there been blood there too?

The minister met his gaze for a moment, and the old face tightened with some emotion like hate or envy; one of the bloody hands emerged from the robe for a moment with the ring finger folded inside the fist, and then a spotted finger pointed at Crawford's own left hand. The old man mimed spitting at Crawford, then turned and scuttled out of the room.

Keats was leaning closer to the figure in the bed, and now he reached over and opened one of the eyes. 'This one's dead,' he said, softly so as not to alarm the patients in beds nearby. 'Could you find a nurse? Tell her to fetch a doctor and the porter so we can get this into the charnel house.'

Crawford's heart was beating fast. 'My God, John, that minister had blood on his hands! And he gave me the most horrible look before he ran out of here.' He waved at the corpse in the bed. 'Do you think . . . ?'

Keats stared at him, and stared off the way the old man had gone, and then grabbed the blankets and pulled them down to peer at the diaper-like bandage; in that instant Crawford thought Keats looked older than the clergyman had. After a few moments Keats spoke. 'He didn't kill him, no,' he said quietly. 'But he was . . . looting the body. The blood of . . . certain patients has a . . . certain value. I'm fairly sure he wasn't a real minister, and I'll see to it that he's kept out in the future – let him go haunt the wards at St George's.' He waved at Crawford. 'So get the nurse.'

Though both disgusted and intrigued by Keats's words, Crawford's mood as he walked down the hall was one of dour amusement at being ordered around a hospital by a twenty-year-old . . . but his amusement turned to incredulous horror when he started down the stairs.

A nurse was walking stiffly up the stairs, and he had raised his hand to get her attention, but when she looked up he recognized her. It was Josephine Carmody, apparently deep in her mechanical persona.

His hand paused only a moment, then went on up to scratch his scalp as if he had never intended the gesture to be a wave, and he lowered his eyes and moved to pass her. His heart was thudding hollowly, and he felt drunk with panic.

She was too close to him when she drew the pistol from under her blouse, and instead of shoving the muzzle into his ear, she only managed to slam the flesh-warmed barrel against the back of his neck. She took a step back to get a clear shot.

Crawford yelled in alarm and swung his right fist hard up against her gun hand.

Breath whistled through her teeth and the pistol flew out of her grasp, but it clanked against the wall and then tumbled down three steps and Josephine dived after it.

Crawford didn't think he could get to her before she could come up with it, so he went clattering back up the stairs in a half crawl. She didn't shoot, but he could hear her clump-clumping up after him, and somehow her imperturbable clockwork stride was more terrifying than the pistol. He was whimpering as he ran back down the hall to the room in which Keats waited for him.

Keats looked up in surprise when Crawford came lurching back into the windowless ward. 'Did you find a – ,' he began.

'Quick, John,' Crawford interrupted, 'how can I get out of here besides by the stairs?' – but the metronomic clumping had reached the floor they were on. 'Jesus!' he said shrilly, and ran back out into the hall.

Josephine was standing ten yards away, pointing the pistol straight at him. He sat down and threw an arm across his face, hoping she'd fire quickly and not take time to aim – and then something burst out of the ward doorway to his right.

The gun boomed and flashed, and he wasn't hit. He lowered his hands –

– and saw a glittering thing like a rainbow-coloured serpent curling its heavy, scaled body in the air between him and Josephine; he was dazedly trying to make out whether it had wings that were beating too fast to see, like a hummingbird, or was hanging from some kind of spiderweb, when it simply disappeared.

The hallway's stale air shook, and Crawford shivered in a sudden impossibly icy draught.

Josephine was staring wide-eyed at the space where the thing had been, and when she turned and ran back to the stairs it was with an animal grace that was the very opposite of her mechanical pose.

Keats was beside Crawford. 'Get in here,' he was saying harshly, 'and deny having seen anything.' He dragged Crawford back into the ward, where the patients were querulously demanding to know what was going on and who would carry them to safety if the building was under attack by Frenchmen. Keats told them that a nurse had gone mad and fired a pistol, and to Crawford's surprise that explanation seemed to calm them.

'Act stupid,' Keats whispered. 'They'll assume you are anyway, to be assigned to Lucas. Tell them this fellow' — he waved at the corpse in the bed — 'was this way when we got here.'

Crawford was about to protest that the patient really *had* been dead when they'd arrived, but before he could speak he looked down at the figure in the bed.

The body was collapsed, like a trolling net with the stiffening hoops taken out of it, and the mouth was now gaping and charred and toothless. When Crawford looked up, Keats was staring at him coldly.

'Your . . . *rescuer* . . . came out of that,' Keats said. 'If the old scavenger in the clergyman suit hadn't drained off some of the potency first, the thing probably would have killed that woman, in addition to stopping her shot.'

Chapter 4

The stones . . .

. . .

Began to lose their hardness, to soften, slowly,
To take on form, to grow in size, a little,
Become less rough, to look like human beings,
Or anyway as much like human beings
As statues do, when the sculptor is only starting,
Images half blocked out. . . .

— Ovid, *Metamorphoses*

Taking Keats's advice, Crawford thickened his voice a little and let his mouth tend to hang open when they were questioned by the senior surgeon; total bewilderment he didn't have to feign, nor a tendency to jump at any sudden motions around him. The senior surgeon told them that the nurse who had fired the gun had fled the hospital, so Crawford was able to say that he'd never seen her before and had no idea what she had hoped to accomplish. The condition of the corpse in the hospital bed was blamed on the ricocheted pistol ball, and it required an acting ability Crawford hadn't known he possessed to nod and agree that that sounded likely.

Keats was through for the day, and Crawford knew that his own days as a medical student were over now that Josephine had somehow found him, and so the two of them walked homeward together up Dean Street. Men were unloading bales of old clothes from several wagons by the south corner of St Thomas's Hospital, and the yells from the vehicles of the merchants and cabbies

79

blocked behind them were almost drowned out by the clamour of the dozen boys and dogs playing around the halted wheels, and for several minutes as Keats and Crawford shouldered their way through the crowd neither of them spoke.

Finally they were past the worst of the noise, and Crawford said, 'John, what *was* that thing? That flying snake?'

Keats seemed bitterly amused. 'Are you really trying to tell me you don't know?'

Crawford thought about it. 'Yes,' he said.

Keats stopped and stared at him, obviously angry. 'How is that possible? How the hell much do you expect me to *believe*? Am I supposed to think, for instance, that your finger was really amputated because of gangrene?'

In spite of the fact that Keats was shorter than he and fourteen years his junior, Crawford stepped back and raised his hands placatingly. 'That was a lie, I admit it.' He wasn't sure he wanted to share any of his recent personal history with Keats, so he tried to change the subject. 'You know, that fake priest was staring at my . . . at where my finger used to be.' He shook his head in puzzlement. 'It seemed to make him . . . *angry*.'

'I daresay. Can you really not know about all this? He thought you were there for the same reason he was, and he was angry because you pretty clearly didn't need to be anymore.'

'He was – what the devil are you saying, that he was there to get a *finger* amputated? And jealous because I'm missing one? John, I'm sorry, but this doesn't even – '

'Let's not talk about it in the street.' Keats thought for a moment, then looked hard at Crawford. 'Have you ever been to the Galatea, under the bridge?'

'Galatea? No. Is that a tavern? It sounds as if . . .' He let the sentence go, for he'd been about to say *as if the*

80

barmaids are living statues. Instead he said, 'Why is it under the bridge?'

Keats had already started walking forward. 'For the same reason that trolls hang about under bridges,' he called back over his shoulder.

The Galatea was indeed a tavern under London Bridge. After shuffling down a set of stone steps to the narrow river shore — into the shadows of the beached coal barges, where the two of them picked their way over unconscious drunkards and piles of rotting river weed — they stepped into the dank darkness under the bridge, and at one point even had to shuffle single file along a foot-wide ledge over the water, and Crawford wondered if there was another entrance for deliveries or if all the food and drink was delivered to the front door by boat.

They passed the place's warped windows before they got to the door; lamplight made luminous amber blobs in the crude glass, and it occurred to Crawford that sunlight must never get this far in under the wide stone belly of the bridge overhead. Nine tiny lamps burned over the door, and Crawford wondered if they might be just the remainders of a pattern of now mostly missing lights, for their positions — four in a cluster, then two, then three — seemed intentional.

Keats was in front, and pushed open the door and disappeared inside. When Crawford followed him in, he saw that there was no consistent floor to the place — every table was on its own shoulder or slab or projection of primordial masonry, connected by stairs and ladders to its neighbours, and each of the half-dozen oil lamps hung from the ceiling on a chain of unique length. Considering the place's location, Crawford wasn't surprised that it smelled of wet clay.

There were only a few customers huddled down there on this summer morning, and Keats led Crawford past them, in a winding, climbing course, to a table on an ancient pedestal in what Crawford assumed must have been the back of the place. One of the lamps swung in a subterranean breeze a couple of yards above the scarred black tabletop, but the shadows were impenetrable around them as they sat down.

'Wine?' suggested Keats with incongruous cheer. 'Here you can get it served in an amethyst goblet – the ancient Greeks believed that wine lost its power to intoxicate if it were served that way. Lord Byron used to drink wine out of an amethyst skull.'

'I read about that – but it was just a skull, I think, a plain old bone one,' said Crawford, refusing to be intimidated by Keats's manner. 'A monk's, I believe. He dug it up in his garden. And yes, wine would be just the thing on a day like this – sherry, if they've got a thick, strengthening one here.'

A big, moustachioed man in an apron climbed up beside Keats and smiled at the two of them; Crawford guessed that he had grown the moustache to partially conceal the no doubt cancerous bump that disfigured his jaw. 'Well now, look who we have here!' the man exclaimed. 'After some company, are you, my men? Neffy on this fine day? I'm not sure who's around right now, but there'll certainly be several who'll pay for – '

'Have you met my friend?' interrupted Keats. 'Mike Frankish, Pete Barker.'

Barker bowed slightly. 'Anyone who can persuade Mr Keats to grace my estab – '

'Just drinks,' interrupted Keats. 'An oloroso sherry for my friend, and I'll have a glass of the house claret.'

The man's smile remained mockingly knowing, but he repeated their orders and went away.

'He didn't know you.' Keats sounded thoughtful. 'And Barker knows all the neff-hosts in London.'

'What is that, and why did you think I was one?'

The drinks arrived then, and Keats waited until Barker had climbed away into the darkness again. 'Oh, you *are* one, Mike, or you'd be gripping the sides of the operating table right now while some doctor probed your abdomen for that pistol ball. But I knew it when I first saw you. There's no mistaking the mark – kind of an ill look about you that's all in the eyes. At first. Clearly you only became one recently – you couldn't live with the mark on you in any city for very long without noticing the kind of attention you'd be drawing – and anyway your finger still hasn't healed, and their bites heal quickly.'

'It wasn't bitten off, damn it,' Crawford said. 'It was *shot* off.'

Keats smiled. 'I'm sure it seemed that way. Try telling that to the neffers, though – the people you'll be meeting who live the neffer life.'

More mystified than ever, Crawford drank some of the syrupy sherry and then set the glass down hard. 'What,' he said levelly, ignoring a faintly echoing groan from the darkness behind him, 'is that?'

Keats spread his hands and opened his mouth to speak, then after a moment exhaled and grinned. 'A sexual perversion, actually. More often than not, anyway. According to the police, it's a taste for congress with certain sorts of deformed people, like Barker there with his big jaw. According to its devotees, though, it's the pursuit of . . . *succubae, Lamiae.*'

Crawford was both unhappy and amused. 'So I'm the sort who'd mistake Barker for a beautiful female vampire, am I? Goddammit, John – '

'No, you're not one of the *pursuers*.' He sighed. 'The problem is that there *aren't* any pure-bred lamiae, pure-bred vampires, anymore.' He squinted at Crawford. 'Hardly any, that is. And so people nearly always make do with remote descendants of that race. And it's generally some sort of . . . tumour . . . that distinguishes

83

such. The tumour is the evidence – the substance, in fact – of the kinship.'

'And just knowing that some person, like your man Barker there, is descended from Lilith or somebody is enough to make him irresistible to these deviates? I swear to you, John – '

Keats overrode him. 'The thing that blocked that pistol shot this morning was no half-breed. That was the most . . . poisonously *beautiful* example I've ever seen, and there are wealthy neffers that would get you a baronetcy and a manor and lands in exchange for just half an hour with it, even if they knew it would kill them.' He shook his head almost enviously. 'How on earth did you meet it?'

'Hell, man, you were there; it jumped out of that dead lad's throat, you said.'

'No, it was able to use him as a . . . a channel, because he was one of the people with a trace of their stony blood – or, conceivably, a victim of one such – but it *came* because it knew *you*.' He stopped, staring up into the darkness, then went on in a whisper. 'Knew you and *felt some obligation* to you, as if you were . . . an actual member of the family, not just prey, like what the patrons of the Galatea would love to be. How did it happen? When did she bite off – ' He smiled. '*Shoot* off your finger?'

'I never saw the thing before, honestly. And the finger was shot off by some man in Sussex. He didn't *look* like a vampire.'

Keats looked sceptical.

'Damn it, I'm telling the truth! And how do you happen to know all this stuff, anyway? Are *you* a snarfie?'

The young man's smile was like smiles Crawford had seen by firelight aboard battle-locked ships at night, on the faces of young sailors who had survived much already and hoped to survive until dawn. 'I guess maybe I am. I'm told I have the look, and the old *habitués* here think I'm very priggish to avoid this place, not give them the benefit of my situation. But if I am one, it was a consequence of my birth, and no choice of mine; I'm a . . . what, a *pursuee* rather than a pursuer. I'm pretty certain you are too.'

Keats stood up. 'Ready to go? Come on, then. This is a good place to be out of.' He threw down some coins and started toward the ladder closest to the distant grey glow that was the front windows.

A groan echoed hollowly from the other direction, from the dark depths of the place; glancing that way, Crawford thought he saw a cluster of figures around the foot of a cross, and he hesitantly took a step toward them.

Keats caught him by the arm. 'No, St Michael,' he said softly. 'Anyone who's here is here voluntarily.'

After a few seconds Crawford shrugged and followed him.

Lamplight fell across Crawford's eyes as he blundered past one table, and the elderly man sitting at it stared at Crawford for a moment – and then bit one of his fingers, struggled out of his seat and followed Crawford all the way to the door, whining like a begging dog and waving his bleeding hand enticingly.

Back up at street level, Crawford's nervousness only increased. He was fairly sure Josephine hadn't followed them from the hospital, but she might well have given up on the idea of personal revenge and gone to the authorities, who could easily find out where he lived from the hospital records. Sheriffs might be waiting for him at the Dean Street house right now.

He was wondering how fully he could trust Keats

when Keats spoke. 'Since you haven't even referred to it, I guess you knew the nurse.'

Deciding to trust the boy brought no feeling of relief. 'Yes. She's my sister-in-law. She thinks I murdered my wife Saturday night.' He peered ahead nervously. 'Could we walk along the bankside to the west?'

Keats had his hands in his pockets and was staring at the pavement, and for several seconds he didn't answer. Then he squinted up at Crawford; it wasn't quite a smile. 'Very well,' he said quietly. 'We could have a beer at Kusiak's — it's your round, and I have the feeling I'd better get it while I can.'

They dodged across High Street between the jostling wagons, slowing again when they were under the over-hang of the houses on the west side of the street. 'She seems fairly sure of it,' Keats remarked when they were walking down one of the narrow streets that paralleled the river. 'Your sister-in-law, that is.' The old house-fronts to their right were bright with sunlight, and Crawford led Keats along on the left side of the street.

'Everybody is. That's how I lost my finger, actually — somebody shot at me while I was running.' Crawford shook his head. 'We, she and I, were in a locked room with a tiny window, and when I woke up in the morning, Julia — that's my wife, or was — was — '

Abruptly he was crying quietly as he walked along, not even sure why, for he knew now that he hadn't really loved Julia; he quickly turned his face toward the doors and brick walls and windows that were passing at his left, hoping that somehow Keats wouldn't notice. Behind one of the windows a fat merchant met his tear-blurred gaze and wheeled around in alarm to look at the far doorway of his office, evidently supposing that Craw-ford had seen something lamentable behind him.

'Not tuberculosis, I gather,' said Keats in a casual tone, looking ahead attentively for Kusiak's. 'More often than not it's tuberculosis, or something so close to it that the doctors don't bother to look further. That's how my mother went.' He was walking faster, and Crawford had to blink his eyes and hurry to keep up. 'It had been coming on for years. I . . . knew it was my fault even when I was a child – when I was five I stood outside her bedroom door with an old sword, trying to keep out a thing I'd dreamt about. It wasn't the fact of its being a *sword* so much, I remember, as the fact that it was *iron*. Didn't do any good, though.' He stopped, and when he wheeled around there were tears in his eyes too. 'So don't assume that I agree with your sister-in-law,' he said angrily.

Crawford nodded and sniffed. 'Right.'

'What are your plans?'

Crawford shrugged. 'I thought I could become a surgeon again under the name Frankish – my real name is Crawford, and I'm – '

'Crawford the *accoucheur*? I've heard of you.'

'But that plan went to hell when Josephine recognized me. The sister-in-law. I suppose she's been doing nurse work at several London hospitals in case I might try getting back into medicine. So I guess I'll leave England. No court would judge me innocent if it came to a murder trial.'

Keats nodded. 'Damn few neffers in the judiciary . . . that would admit to their knowledge, anyway. Here's Kusiak's.'

The inn they had arrived at was a broad, two-storey place with a stable at the side and a dock out back so that patrons could arrive by boat; Keats led the way into the taproom, which, with its oak panelling and leather-upholstered chairs, was a reassuring contrast to Galatea's. Crawford hoped he didn't still smell of the place.

'You . . . said you thought you were to blame for your mother's death,' he said when they had found a table by

87

a window that overlooked the river. 'How is that? And does that mean I'm responsible for Julia's?'

'Jesus, man, *I* don't know. If so, it was obviously unintentional on your part. I think there's a number of ways these things can attach themselves to people, but *most* of them involve the people's actual consent. In my case I'm pretty sure it was because of the night on which I was born. I think the things can *get at* infants born on the night of the thirty-first of October — some normal protection is missing on that night, and if you're born then you're . . . honorary family to these things. You're adopted. They can . . . *focus their attention* on such a newborn, and then, once they've focused on anyone, they seem to keep track of him throughout his life. And keep track, keep disastrous track, of his family, too. A glass of claret, please,' he added to the aproned girl who had walked up to the table.

'And a pint of bitter,' added Crawford.

'Do you have a family?' Keats asked when the girl had walked away toward the bar. A river beer-seller's bell could be heard ringing far out across the water.

Crawford thought of the foundered boat, the burning house, and the imploded corpse in the bed. 'No.'

'Lucky man. Think hard before ever changing that status.' He shook his head. 'I have two brothers and a sister. George and Tom and Fanny. We're orphans, and we've always been very close to each other. Had to be, you know?' He held his hand up and stared at it. 'The — *thought* — of anything like this happening to them, of their becoming a part of this . . . especially Fanny, she's only thirteen and I've always been her favourite . . .'

Crawford had to keep reminding himself that Julia really had died inexplicably and that he really had seen that levitating serpent this morning; what Keats was telling him might not be the true explanation, but there would never be a *natural* explanation for it.

88

The drinks arrived, and Crawford remembered to pay for them. He took a sip of the beer, then opened his mouth to speak.

Keats spoke first. 'You want me to fetch your things from the house and bring them to you somewhere and be careful not to be followed.'

Disconcerted, Crawford shut his mouth and then opened it again. 'Uh, right, as a matter of fact. I'd be very damned grateful . . . and though I can't reward you now, as soon as I get settled abroad, I'll – '

'Forget it. I may need a favour myself someday from a reluctant neff-host.' He raised his eyebrows. 'Switzerland?'

Crawford could feel his face getting red as he stared at the younger man, for he knew that he hadn't told anyone about his travel plans, and he himself didn't know why he had decided to go to the Swiss Alps – Keats seemed to know more about Crawford than Crawford himself did.

'Look,' he said levelly, 'I'm willing to admit that I've stumbled into something . . . *supernatural* here, and you obviously know more about the whole sordid business than I do. But I'd appreciate it if you'd just tell me what you know about my situation straight away, and save your sense of dramatic timing for your goddamn poetry.'

Keats's confident smile was gone, and he suddenly looked young and embarrassed. '. . . Stephens?' he said. 'Told you?'

'He did indeed. And how can you go on about how contemptible all these people are, these neffers, when you've saved those disgusting bladder stones to help you write your stuff? Do they work like good luck pieces? I suppose someday you'll have old Barker's deformed jawbone on your mantel – and then Byron and Wordsworth and Ashbless had better just fold up their tents and go home, right?'

Keats grinned, but his complexion was looking spotty. 'Not your fault,' he said tightly, almost to himself. 'You don't know enough about it all for me to take offence . . . *much* offence, anyway.' He sighed and ran his fingers through his reddish hair. 'Listen to me. I *am* one of the people who've attracted the attention of a member of this other race; as I said, it happened on the night I was born. If I wanted to use that connection to help my writing – and I think I could, these things may very well be the creatures remembered in myth as the Muses – I could summon my . . . my what, my fairy godmother, call it. I certainly wouldn't have to hang around the neffy wards looking to snatch a bladder stone or a cup of blood, in the hope of getting the kind of dim contact that only really shows up in the warping of certain dreams.'

Crawford started to speak, but Keats waved him to silence and went on.

'Did you know – but no, you wouldn't – that it's fashionable among neffers to carry a blood-spotted handkerchief, so as to seem consumptive? It implies that you really got the attention of one of the vampires, that one of them can spare the time to devour you. Quite an honour . . . but *I'm* a member of the goddamned *family*. So are you, clearly. They pay so much attention to us that they won't *let* us die – though they've got no such scruples about members of our real, earthly families.' Keats shook his head. 'But my poetry is my own, damn you. I – I can't help a lot of my situation – the protection, the extended life – but I will *not* let them have anything to do with my writing.'

Crawford spread the fingers of his maimed hand. 'Sorry. So why *do* you save those things?'

Keats was staring out the window at the river. 'I don't know, Mike. I suppose it's for the same reason I didn't quit when the hospital administrators decided I was ignorant and unobservant enough to be assigned to Lucas. The more I know about these creatures, these vampires, the more likely it is that I'll be able to get free of the one that oversaw my birth . . . and killed my mother.'

Crawford nodded, but he thought that Keats was lying, and mostly to himself. 'The hospital administrators know about this stuff?'

'Sure . . . though it's hard to say to what extent. A lot of patients vary from the human norm, of course, especially once you get a look inside them, but there's a consistency to the neffy variations. And they're generally less dramatic, too – the kidney and bladder stones just look a little *quartzy*, or the skin turns hard and brittle when they stay out too long in the sun, or they see fine at night but are blinded by daylight. I guess the hospital has decided to try to ignore it – not turn patients away for no reason, which would cause talk, but give the neffy cases to the most inept staff members. I wonder if something like today's adventure has ever happened before – the senior surgeon sure closed the book on it in a hurry.'

'So why am I going to Switzerland?'

Keats smiled – a little sadly. 'The Alps are the biggest part of the neffer dream.' He stared out at the river as if for help in explaining. 'There's supposed to be a plant in South America that gives people hallucinations if they drink a tea brewed from its leaves – like opium, but in this case everybody sees the same vision. A vast stony city, I understand. Even if a person hasn't been told what to expect, he'll still see the city, same as every other person who's taken the drug.'

He paused to finish his wine, and Crawford waved for a refill. 'Thanks. Anyway, being a neffer is similar. You dream about the Alps. A couple of months ago they brought a child from one of the worst Surreyside rookeries to the hospital because he was dying of consumption, and he didn't last long here; but *before* he died, he found a piece of charcoal and drew a beautiful picture of a mountain on the wall by his bed. One of the doctors saw it and wanted to know what book the boy had copied the perfectly detailed picture of Mont Blanc from. Everybody just said they didn't know — it would have been too much trouble to explain to him that the boy had done it out of his head, and that he had never seen a book nor ever been east of the Tower, and that his mother said he'd never drawn anything in his life, not even in mud with a stick.'

'Well, maybe I won't go there. Maybe I'll — I don't know — ' He looked up and saw Keats's smile. 'Very well, damn it, I have to go there. Maybe the way out of this whole entanglement is there.'

'Sure. Like the exit from the very bottom of Dante's hell — and that just led to Purgatory.' Keats got to his feet and put his hand for a moment on Crawford's shoulder. 'You may as well wait for me here. I'll make sure I'm not followed, and I'll tell you if I see any official-looking types hanging about. If I haven't come back in an hour, you'd better assume I've been arrested, and just go with what you've got on your back and in your pockets.'

Chapter 5

Desire with loathing strangely mixed
On wild or hateful objects fixed.

— Samuel Taylor Coleridge

After Keats had left, Crawford estimated the amount of money in the inner pocket of his coat — he hadn't spent much of Appleton's fifty pounds, and he figured he still had a fairly good stake — probably eighty pounds, certainly seventy. A little reassured, he waved to the girl and pointed at his empty glass.

He would travel and live cheaply now, and make his money last. In London a person could live, albeit without many new clothes or much meat in the diet, on fifty pounds a year, and things were sure to be less expensive on the continent. And with even a year's leeway he certainly ought to be able to find himself a niche somewhere in the world.

All he had to do was get across the English Channel, and he was drunkenly confident that he'd be able to do that; hadn't he been a shipboard surgeon for nearly three years? He assured himself that he still knew his way around a dock, and that even without a passport he would be able to get aboard a ship somehow.

The new beer arrived, and he sipped it thoughtfully. I suppose Julia's been buried by now, he thought. I think I know now why I wanted to marry her — because a doctor, especially an obstetrician, ought to be married, and because I wanted to prove to myself that I could have children, and because all my friends told me what a stunning catch she was ... and partially, I admit, because I wanted to obscure my memories of my first wife – but why did she want to marry *me*? Because I am, or was, a successful London doctor who seemed sure to come into real wealth before too long? Because she loved me? I guess I'll never know.

Who were you, Julia? he thought. It reminded him of what she had said about her sister: 'She's got to become Josephine – whoever that may turn out to be.'

It seemed to him that what he would remember about England would be its graves: the grave of his older brother, who from out in the surf had shouted to young Michael for help, twenty years ago – shouted uselessly, for the sea had been a savage, elemental monster that day, crashing on the rocks like grey wolves tearing at a body, and Michael had sat on the high ground and watched through his tears until his brother's arm had stopped waving and he could no longer identify the lump in the fragmented waves that was his body; and Caroline's meagre memorial, which was just the initials and dates that, one drunken night, he had furtively carved into the wall of the pub that had been built on the site of the house that had burned down with her in it; and now Julia's grave, which he would never see. And each one was a monument to his failure to be what a man was supposed to be.

And how much, he wondered, of *me* will I be leaving here, buried in the foam at the bottom of this glass when I leave this inn and walk to London Dock? A lot, I hope. All the Michael Crawfords I tried to be: the ship's surgeon, because Caroline had preferred a sailor to me; the man-midwife, because there seemed to be value in the innocence of infants. He held his glass up and winked at the warped *in vitro* reflection of his own face

94

in the side of it. From now on it's just you and me, he thought at the image. We're free.

Suddenly Keats was at the window, looking tense. Alarmed, Crawford stood up and unlatched the window and pulled it open.

Instantly Keats pushed his portmanteau in over the sill. 'She's right behind me. Dump this out and give it back to me – she'll be suspicious if she sees me without it now.'

'Christ.' Crawford took the bag and hastily carried it over to a table that had a tablecloth on it, unbuckled the straps and upended the bag; trousers and shirts tumbled out on to the table, and several rolled pairs of stockings fell off and wobbled across the floor. The barmaid called to him sharply, but he ignored her and ran back to the window. 'Here,' he said, shoving the portmanteau back out into Keats's hands. 'Thanks.'

Keats nodded impatiently and made a *get down* gesture.

Crawford nodded and stepped away from the window, but peered out from around the edge with one eye. The barmaid was saying something behind him, and he dug into his pocket and threw a one-pound note over his shoulder. 'I want to buy that tablecloth,' he rasped without looking around.

Keats was walking away from him, out on to the pier, swinging the leather portmanteau ostentatiously. Don't overplay it, Crawford thought.

A moment later another person walked in front of the window, following Keats, and Crawford instinctively cringed back, for it was indeed Josephine, moving with all the indomitable purpose of one of the gear-driven figurines that emerge from German clock-towers to ring the bells. Crawford hoped for Keats's sake that she hadn't managed to get her pistol reloaded.

Still peering out the window, Crawford backed across

the hardwood floor to the table that had all his clothes on it; he flipped up the ends of the tablecloth and balled them up in his good fist.

At the end of the pier Keats glanced back and saw Josephine advancing at him; he swung the portmanteau around like a discus thrower and then let it sail off the end of the pier; Crawford's whispered curse coincided with the distant splash.

'A pound's enough for the goddamn tablecloth, I trust,' he said bitterly, thinking of how much he'd paid for the portmanteau.

'Yes sir,' said the barmaid, who edged away from him as he strode across to the street door, swinging his impromptu luggage with a sort of furious nonchalance.

He crossed London Bridge and, after walking east through the Billingsgate fish market, he sauntered as carelessly as he could past the Customs House and the Tower of London, envying the surrounding fish-sellers and housemaids and labourers their indifference to these imposing stone edifices that seemed to personify law and punishment. He kept glancing behind him, but he didn't see any following figure that walked as though it had been wound up with a key.

He could tell by the shops he passed that he was approaching the docks. All the grocers had posted signs assuring the public that the barrels of beef and pork and biscuit they sold would keep forever in any climate, and every other shop window seemed to be crowded with brass sextants and telescopes and compasses – and the stiff paper compass-cards printed with the crystallized-looking rose indicating the directions. These shook with the rattling passage of every carriage as if fluttering in some otherwise-undetectable magnetic wind.

His tablecloth bundle was attracting the rude attention of a crowd of street boys, so he stepped into a shop that displayed luggage in the window – but the proprietor, after greeting him civilly enough at first, took a second look at Crawford's face and then asked him how he dared to bring 'filthy bones and teeth and marbles' into a store run by a Christian; the man actually drew a pistol from under the counter when Crawford tried to explain that his bundle just contained clothes and that he wanted luggage, so he fled back out to the street and the clamouring children.

One of the boys ran up behind him with a knife, slashed the bottom of his bundle and then yanked on the bulge of garment exposed; the sleeve of his green velvet jacket wound up hanging out, with a pair of undershorts from his more heavy-set days somehow caught in the lacy cuff.

Crawford whirled around so fast that the sleeve-and-shorts stood out behind him like a tail, but he wasn't quick enough to see which boy had done it – though he did see the luggage shop proprietor standing in the shop doorway looking after him, and Crawford thought he saw the man make a hand-signal to someone across the street.

Just what I wanted, Crawford thought hysterically – an inconspicuous exit.

A pub door banged open farther down the street and two skinny, sick-looking men came hobbling out toward him, each of them waving a bloody handkerchief; they were both jabbering at once, but Crawford caught the word 'stone' and another word that seemed to be 'neffy-limb.'

He turned around to run back the way he'd come, but he thought he glimpsed stiff limbs swinging in the crowd, and a rigid, expressionless face . . . and so he swung his bundle around in a fast circle, much as Keats had done with his portmanteau, and let go of it. The tablecloth blew open and clothing billowed out in all directions and shoes flew into the crowd, and Crawford ran down an alley.

Enough people ran squabbling into the street after the explosion of valuable clothing to cause a raging traffic jam, but several members of the crowd came pelting along the alley after Crawford; he rounded a corner into a narrow old brick court and then, before his pursuers could appear behind him, he found a door, yanked it open and stepped inside, and then drew it closed behind him. There was a bolt on the inside, and he slid it across the gap into its bracket.

He was at the back of a crowd of men, evidently some class of labourers, in a low-ceilinged room that smelled of beer and sweat and candle wax, and though he wasn't very successful in his efforts to breathe slowly, the men near him just glanced his way, nodded civilly and returned their attention to whatever was going on in front.

'Pile of old sail pieces here by the door,' came an authoritative voice from the far end of the room.

Crawford heard steps on the cobbles outside, and someone rattled the door at his back; but none of his companions made a move to let the person in, and a moment later the footsteps clumped away.

'Pick 'em up as you go out,' the voice at the front of the room added, and the whole crowd began shuffling forward across the floor of what Crawford now recognized as a pub. Old sail pieces? he thought. What are we expected to do, wash windows?

No one gave him a second look as he filed out the pub door into the sunlight again, following the example of his companions and picking up several sheets of coarse cloth from a pile by the doorway. Once out in the yard the men around him began tying the rags around their shoes and ankles, and Crawford imitated them as best he could.

'More like this 'ere, mate,' said one old fellow, tightening Crawford's wrappings and pulling the overlap wider. 'Loose like that and you're sure to get gravel in there, and then it's harder to get it out of your shoes than if you wasn't wrapped at all.'

'Aha!' said Crawford. 'Thanks a lot.' His gratitude was doubly sincere, for now he knew what sort of employment he had inadvertently volunteered for; these men were ballast-heavers, whose job it was to shovel gravel into the holds of ships that had discharged their cargoes and now needed extra weight in the holds to keep them from heeling too far to the wind. He had seen such work done often enough, he thought, to be able to do it himself. And it ought to get him aboard a ship.

The docks were vast, a series of interconnected canals and basins and pools; masts and spars and the diagonal slashes or droops of rigging fenced out the misty sky except for directly overhead, and the slow progress of a ship in the middle distance being towed in or out could be read by the way its profile blended and separated in the stationary pattern. Sitting in the stern of the ballast-heaver boat, Crawford eyed the hulls they poled and rowed their way between — towering away above if the ship had been unloaded and was riding high in the water or, if it was still laden with cargo, low enough so that he could have jumped and touched the railings — and he wondered which one might be his transport out of England.

The load of gravel in the boat smelled of the weedy river bottom it had lately been dredged from, but whenever there was a cold gust of breeze he could catch on it the smells of foreign lands — a heartening mix of tobacco and coffee aromas from one direction, a curry of conflicting spices from another, and the decayed smell of hides from a third; and the songs of the sailors on various

99

ships made a cacophonous, multilingual opera to fill in the moments when the released chains of the cranes weren't springing noisily upward and the coopers weren't hammering barrels. He was glad conversation in the boat was practically impossible.

When the boat was finally turned toward the bow of the ship they were to ballast, another boat was already working on the port side. Crawford hiked himself up on his thwart and looked to refresh his memory of how the job was done.

A platform had been set up on poles that fitted into the boat's gunwales, and men were shovelling gravel from the boat's waist up on to the platform, where other men scooped it up and poked spadeful after spadeful into a yard-wide porthole in the side of the ship. Soon the view was cut off, as Crawford's boat rounded the bow to load the starboard side, but he had seen enough to dampen his hope of getting aboard a ship this way. The Navy ships he'd sailed on had used stone blocks for ballast, and the heavers had had to be aboard the ships to stow it, but these men never even *touched* the ship except with the blades of their shovels.

Damn, he thought, it looks as if all I've done is committed myself to a day's hard work — and without pay, since I'm not on the work list. Should I just dive overboard and swim away? I've got no luggage to worry about anymore.

The men on his own boat had already stood up and erected the scaffolding. 'Up on the stage with ye,' growled an old fellow near him, pushing him forward, and a moment later Crawford found himself trying to climb up on to the platform while gripping the shovel someone had thrust into his hand. By the time he had clambered up on to the platform and was able to get to his feet, another man was already standing there and digging his shovel into the gravel that the men below were flinging up on to the sagging beams.

Crawford got to his feet and scooped up a couple of pounds of the stuff and swung the load toward the ship, but he nearly overbalanced and had to lean back quickly, and his shovelful of gravel slid off the blade and down into the dirty water between the boat and the ship's hull. He felt he had done well to hang on to the shovel.

'Drunk, are you?' asked the man beside him. 'Work below if you haven't got sea legs.'

Stung that a landsman should say this to him, Crawford shook his head and dug the blade in again; he hefted a load of the gravel and then watched the way the man flung the stuff in through the porthole. A moment later it was his turn again, and he did it just the way the other man had, using the shovel blade against the rim of the porthole to catch himself before dumping the gravel inside, and then bracing it there again to push himself back upright afterwards.

'That's better,' the man allowed, and Crawford was embarrassed to realize that he was blushing at the praise.

After an hour his arms were aching with the effort, but it was only when his finger stump began to bleed that he thought he would have to stop. He was about to feign some kind of illness when a banging started up nearby and the men below stopped tossing the gravel up on to the stage.

The other ballast-heaver boat appeared from around the ship's bow, and he could see that the noise was being made by two of the men in it clanging their shovels together overhead like actors portraying a fight with broadswords; and when he saw the men below him drop their own shovels and begin pulling baskets from under the gunwales he understood that this was the ballast-heavers' customary supper ritual. He put

101

down his shovel and let his arms hang limp at his sides, ignoring the blood that pattered regularly on to the wet boards of the stage.

His companion had jumped down into the boat and was scrambling to get at the baskets, but for a moment Crawford just watched, catching his breath and wondering if each workman had brought his own food or if this was some kind of common supper, provided by the contractor, that he might hope to get a bite or two of.

Just when he had decided to climb down and try for a bit of food, there was a yell of alarm from another ship, and when he looked up he saw a broad wooden pallet falling from a crane; it was tipping as it fell, and among the several tumbling crates that had been on it Crawford could see a man, his arms and legs waving uselessly as he dropped down through the misty air. From this vantage point it was difficult to guess whether he would hit the deck of the ship he had been helping to unload or splash safely into the water.

And, without thinking, Crawford turned and leaped across the gulf between the boat and the ship and caught the edge of the porthole; one kick and a convulsive jackknifing slither got him through it, and then he crossed his arms over his face an instant before he ploughed headfirst into the heaped wet gravel and did an avalanching somersault down to the pebbled deck.

He sat up, cradling his bad hand and whimpering softly. The hold was dark, the only illumination being the beams of grey light slanting in through the dusty air from the portholes, but he could see that the deck was crisscrossed with knee-high partitions to divide it into low, square bins. He got up and walked to the farthest, darkest corner of the deck, being careful to step over the partitions and not kick them, and in the last bin he lay down, confident that he couldn't be seen.

He hoped that the dock worker had hit the water.

For what seemed like an hour he waited, wondering if the ballast men would deduce where he had disappeared to, but eventually another shovelful of gravel came cascading in, and then another, and he knew that he was safe for now.

After a while he heard men come into the hold and begin shifting the piles, shovelling the gravel from one bin into another and arguing about whether one side had more weight fore or aft than it should, but they finished up and left without getting to the one he was hiding in. After that there was nothing to hear but the occasional faint thud of booted feet on some upper deck, and distant cries from out in the dock, and nothing to watch except the ponderously slow dimming of the light from the portholes.

He slept, and didn't wake up until the ship was rocking in ocean swells, and moonlight rimmed the porthole edges and raised faint points of glitter on the higher gravel piles. The hold was chilly, and he wished he hadn't lost the rest of his clothes. Despite the sea air, his head was filled with the smell of river-bottom rock.

Then he heard gravel shift, once, somewhere out across the deck, and he realized suddenly that it was the same noise that had awakened him.

A rat, he told himself nervously. Fattened on whatever cargo this ship carried to London, and now left with nothing to nibble on except gravel and my face. Better not sleep anymore. Too cold anyway – and getting colder by the moment.

The rattle came again, prolonged this time as though someone were letting the gravel run out from between cupped hands; then there was a noise like something heavy being dragged along. In the darkness the hold seemed vast, and the noise sounded far away, but he got an impression of terrible weight moving out there.

Crawford was suddenly much colder. Whatever that is, he thought, it isn't a rat.

Dimly he could see that something had stood up in some farther region of the deck, something tall and broad. It wasn't human.

Crawford stopped breathing, and even closed his eyes in case the thing could sense his gaze, and though he knew that even the most laboured heartbeat can't be heard at any distance, he was afraid that the shaking his own heart was giving him would knock him audibly against the partition of the bin.

But a moment later he was horrified to realize that a perverse impulse to *make* some noise was building in him; he managed, with some difficulty, to suppress it.

The thing was moving – walking, to judge by the regular, ponderous jars Crawford felt through the deck – and he opened his eyes in fear or even eagerness in case it might be coming toward him; but it was crossing to one of the portholes, and as it got closer to the moonlit circle he could see it more and more clearly.

Its torso seemed to be a huge bag at one moment and a boulder in the next, and the surface of it was all bumpy like chain mail; and when it had plodded its way on elephantine legs to the porthole, he could see that its head was just an angular lump with shadows that implied cheekbones and eye sockets and a slab of jaw.

Oddly, it seemed female to him.

It didn't have arms to rest on the porthole rim, but Crawford sensed something weary about it – he got the impression that it had had no particular purpose in getting up . . . that it was just looking thoughtfully out at the sea as any sleepless voyager might.

For many long moments neither of them moved; Crawford lay stiff with something like terror, trying not even to tremble in the intense cold, and the thing by the porthole just stared out, though it didn't seem to have eyes. Then finally it stepped back, grinding gravel to powder under its inconceivable feet, and it turned and faced Crawford across hundreds of feet of deck.

He was in total darkness, but he knew intuitively that the figure saw him, saw him by his body heat rather than by any light, and recognized him, knew him. Crawford wondered desperately how long he would be able to continue to keep from screaming – and again he almost *wanted* to scream, wanted it to come toward him.

But the thing didn't approach him. It turned away and shambled back out across the deck into the darkness from which it had emerged, and after a few minutes he heard a long, rattling whisper of sifting gravel, and he knew that the thing had relaxed its sketchily anthropoid form back into the tiny stones that had comprised it.

It took Crawford a long time to get back to sleep.

Chapter 6

Ye that see in darkness,
Say, what have ye found?

— Clark Ashton Smith, *Nyctalops*

Something bumped against the hull, and Crawford awakened instantly, thinking that the gravel creature was up and moving around again — but the whole ship was creaking and rocking, and he could hear voices and the clumping of boots from overhead, and he guessed that they were arriving at their destination. After a few minutes his guess was confirmed by the splash of the anchor hitting the water. It was still night, unless somebody had fastened covers over the portholes.

He stood up quietly and groped his way to the porthole he'd come in through, being careful not to blunder out across the deck, and even when he was still yards short of the porthole the incoming land-scented breeze let him know that there was no cover in place, and that dawn had not yet come.

He poked his head out, and by starlight he could see a long stretch of land across a wide expanse of calm water, and he knew the ship was in some harbour. The air was hardly chilly at all now, leading him to believe that the ship must have sailed south — so this was France, or just possibly if they had made very good speed and exhaustion had made him sleep much longer than he thought, Spain.

He took off his boots and tied them together with his

belt so that he could carry them while swimming, then set them down and peered out to fore and aft, trying to decide when he'd best be able to jump into the water unobserved . . . but when gravel shifted somewhere on the deck behind him he just sprang through the porthole in a somersault, touching the rim with nothing but his fingertips.

He hit water feet first, and plunged far down into the shockingly cold depths.

And he woke up completely; the seawater cleared his head of the feverish confusion that had plagued him throughout the last week, and as he began frog-kicking back up toward the water's invisible surface he was already making plans.

He would return to England somehow and vindicate himself – after all, he was a respected doctor, and no jury could judge him even *physically* capable of doing what had been done to Julia – and he would shake this weird obsession with Switzerland. Keats's tales were self-evidently the fantasies of an imaginative would-be poet. Crawford didn't understand how he could even have listened to such nonsense.

Then he broke the surface and gulped air, and the doubts fell in on him again. He began paddling toward the stern of the ship, for the sound of voices seemed to be louder up by the bow, and he had already dismissed his momentary hope of returning to England and vindicating himself. You've already crossed the Channel, he told himself; the Alps – the majestic, towering, dream-known Alps – are ahead of you. You can't possibly turn back now.

Hell, he thought, even if you *could* go back safely . . .

When he rounded the high, square stern he saw that the ship's anchorage was a good distance out from shore. The sky had only begun to glow a deep predawn purple over some hills far away across the black water on his

107

right, but he was able to see a shoreline ahead of him, and patches of trees that seemed to shine faintly on the rising land beyond.

He looked back up at the ship, and was blinded by the relatively glaring light that shone from the cabin windows; he glanced away for several seconds as he quietly trod water, and then squinted back, avoiding looking directly at the lights. There was one man visible on deck, his face and hands strangely luminous against the dark sky, but he was looking at the mainland, not down at Crawford, who turned away and began paddling silently toward shore.

After ten minutes of swimming he stopped berating himself for having jumped without grabbing his boots, for he knew now that he'd never have been able to drag them along with him all this way . . . but he was sorry that he'd used his belt to tie them together.

It made him nervous to be swimming in deep water without anything to lean on if he should get tired – he was reminded of dreams in which he could fly, but was always hundreds of feet in the air when his arms began to cramp from the furious flapping necessary to keep him aloft. Could he still get back to the ship? He turned and looked back, but the ship was now as distant behind him as the shore was ahead. Fighting down panic, he resumed his course. He had never felt as alone and unprotected . . . and when his knees and feet eventually bumped against sand, and he realized that he had reached shallow water, he wanted to nuzzle the gritty stuff like a strayed sheep finally found by the sleepless shepherd.

The sky was grey in the east now, and the trees on the distant hills had lost their luminosity. When he stood up and began wading to shore he saw low buildings – houses and a church tower – a few hundred yards ahead, and he paused, wondering what to do now. The surf swirled around his bare ankles, feeling warmer than the air now.

His French was no better than utilitarian – assuming this *was* France, which he hoped, for he knew *no* Spanish – and this didn't look like a gathering spot for cosmopolitans. France and England had been at war too recently for the general populace to be eager to help a lost Britisher. The only marketable skill he had was doctoring, and he couldn't imagine a crowd of peasants being eager to let him set their broken bones . . . much less let him attend to their pregnant wives.

Would the shopkeepers accept British money? *Wet* British money? If not, how was he even to get beer and bread and dry clothes?

The bell in the church tower began ringing, rolling its harsh notes away across the echoless grey salt flats, and he wished he were Catholic so that he could ask for sanctuary; or a mason or a rosicrucian or something, able to turn to his secret brethren for help.

As he walked up the sand slope it occurred to him that he *was* a member of a secret brotherhood . . . though he didn't know if they were at all concerned with helping one another.

Let's see, he thought, do I know any passwords? Neffy? God knows what that might mean in French. Should I wave a bloody handkerchief? Stick a pebble in my cheek like a squirrel and wink at people?

Then he remembered what Keats had said about the unmistakable 'look' a neffer had – he'd said that Crawford must newly have become one, or he'd be used to getting attention from strangers who could recognize that look.

So he just walked around the little town, shivering in the onshore breeze and smiling at the fishermen who trudged past him down the broad lanes toward the beached dories, and then at the people who began ambling up to open the shops. Many of them looked twice at the haggard, soaked figure, but none of their gazes seemed to hold the kind of interest he was looking for.

Eventually he found a warm chimney and leaned against it, and it was there that the very old man in the dun-coloured cassock found him. Crawford noticed him when he was still a dozen yards up the street – and the old man was hunching along so slowly, seeming to put the whole weight of his frail body on his gnarled walking stick with each step, that Crawford had plenty of time to study him.

Strong-looking yellow teeth were exposed when the leathery cheeks pulled back in a grin, and from deep in wrinkle-bordered sockets glittered an alert and humorous gaze; but Crawford wanted to look away, for it was somehow clear to him that longevity had been more costly to this man than it was to most. The figure stopped in front of him.

Then the old man spoke, and Crawford swore softly to himself, for the language had the rhythmic precision of southern Europe and the Mediterranean, and none of the skating, back-of-the-nose elision of Picardy or Normandy.

For several seconds he tried to recall any Spanish phrases . . . and couldn't. But perhaps the man also spoke French.

'Uh,' Crawford began, desperately mustering his words, *'Parlez-vous français? Je parle français – un peu.'*

The old man laughed and spoke again, and this time Crawford understood a few words; apparently the old man was insisting that he was speaking French.

'Oh, really? Well, *bonjour, Monsieur.* Listen, *non j'ai un passeport, mais –'*

The old man interrupted with a question that sounded like *Essay kuh votray fahmay ay la?*

Crawford blinked, then shook his head and shrugged. *'Repetez, s'il vous plaît – et parlez lentement.'* It was the French sentence he always used most – a plea to repeat and speak more slowly.

The old man complied, and Crawford realized that he was indeed speaking French, but was pronouncing all the usually unaccented final *e*'s. The question had been, *Is your wife here?*

'Non, non . . .' Good God, he thought, has he got me confused with someone else? Or did he see my wedding ring? No, that's right, it went with the finger. *'Non, je suis seul,* alone, you understand. Now *envers mon passeport . . .'*

The old man put a finger to his lips, then winked and began limping away, waving his stick in front of him between each step as if to hold Crawford's attention.

But something else had already caught his attention – the old man, too, was missing his wedding-ring finger.

The old man led him out of the village east along the shore, skirting hills that were purple with a richness of heather Crawford hadn't seen since leaving Scotland, finally to a tiny house made from the bow half of an overturned fishing boat. The sawn sides had been boarded across and fitted with a low door and a head-sized window, and a few yards away crude wooden steps led down among piled rocks to a tide pool that was overhung with tangles of nets and lines and scaffolds.

Crawford's guide dragged open the little door for him, and Crawford sidled inside in something like a fencer's crouch. Archaic-looking books and liquor bottles filled the dim triangular room, but there was a square indentation in the dirt floor, and Crawford sat down there.

The bow corner of the room was a little fireplace, and Crawford moved some pans aside so as not to have to sit on his feet . . . He paused before setting the pans down, for though they were of an ordinary silvery colour, they were much lighter than any metal he'd ever handled.

The old man was grinning again when he followed Crawford in and perched on a stack of books, and in his outlandish French he remarked that Crawford was sitting where the old man's wife had always sat; but before Crawford could apologize or ask if the wife was likely to appear soon and demand her seat, the old man was talking again.

He introduced himself as François des Loges, a poet, and assured Crawford that this was indeed France – a village called Carnac, on the south Brittany coast near Vannes. There was a government office in Auray, eight miles distant, and Crawford's passport problem, whatever it was, could be rectified there.

Crawford was beginning to get used to the old man's accent, and he could see why he had mistaken it for Spanish at first; not only did the man pronounce all the terminal *e*s, he also gave words like 'mille' an almost Spanish or Italian lilt, and he rolled his *r*s. It was recognizably French, but seemed to be French as it had been spoken when the Romance languages were still more parallel than divergent.

Des Loges had pulled a straw plug out of a bottle as he was speaking, and now poured brandy into two blue crystal cups. Crawford sipped the liquor gratefully, and then, setting aside his doubts of the old man's ability to give arbitrary and illegal orders to Customs officials, asked what he would be expected to do in return.

The brandy in des Loges's cup caught a gleam of morning sunlight through the warped glass of the little window, and threw a spectrum of purple and gold across the weathered planks that were the wall. '*Qui meurt, a ses loix de tout dire,*' he began.

Crawford mentally translated this as *A dying man is free to tell all.* As des Loges went on, Crawford had to keep interrupting with requests that he talk more slowly, and even so he wasn't sure he was understanding the old man's speech.

Des Loges seemed to be saying that he had imprisoned his wife – though he waved toward the sea when he said it – and was now free, with help from the right sort of person, to get away forever. The in-laws might not be pleased – here, for some reason, he nodded toward the pans Crawford had moved – but they couldn't touch him. He picked up one of the lightweight pans, made a face, and tossed it out the door on to the dirt outside. 'Disrespectful, I know,' he added in his strange French, 'but they're not even good for cooking – they're always getting pitted, and they discolour sauces and eggs terribly.'

He had had many women during his life, he told Crawford, but he wouldn't tell anyone where these 'yquelles' resided currently. None of them could get at him now, that was the important thing. He pointed at Crawford's maimed hand and, with a grin, said he was sure Crawford understood.

Crawford was pretty sure he *didn't* understand, though, especially when the old man concluded his speech by saying, '*Les miches de Saint Estienne amons, et elles nous assuit,*' which seemed to mean, 'We love the loaves of St Stephen, and they pursue us.'

But when des Loges stood up and asked Crawford if they were in agreement, Crawford nodded and assured him that they were. If he can get my passport stamped, he thought, then I *will* help him do whatever this procedure is that'll protect him from his in-laws, or from loaves of bread, or whatever it is. And even if he can't, even if he's crazy, at least he's a contact in a foreign land – and I'm ahead already by a roof and a glass of brandy.

* * *

The old man threw Crawford a pair of ancient shoes to put on, and from behind the door he lifted a cloth sack and indicated that Crawford could carry it – remarking, as they left the little house, that he had bought extra food and drink when he had heard that Crawford was coming.

Startled, Crawford asked him how he had heard that – but des Loges just winked, pointed at Crawford's hand again and then pointed to the tide pool below them. Crawford stepped to the edge of the rocks and looked down, but the only thing he could see in the pool was a knee-high pyramidal stone with a square base.

Walking back away from the water, Crawford looked around for some sign of a paddock where horses or donkeys might be kept, but the little boat-house was the only structure on the heathery hillside. Was old des Loges planning to *walk* eight miles at his crippled-bug pace?

He was glad that the shoes were a good fit – and a moment later he wondered if des Loges had bought them when he had bought the food, having been told Crawford's shoe size in advance too.

Then he saw that the old man had dragged out from behind the house a child's wagon with a rope attached to its front, and that some kind of shoulder-harness was tied to the far end of the rope. As Crawford watched incredulously, des Loges climbed into the wagon, with his knees tucked up under his chin, and tossed the harness-end of the rope into the dust at Crawford's feet.

The old man helpfully pantomimed putting the harness on.

'In case I didn't get the idea, eh?' said Crawford in English as he picked the thing up. He slowly put it on, feeling the stiffness in his joints and wishing he hadn't spent the night curled up in a cold wooden bin. 'Well,

I'll tell you this – you'd better be able to get me a passport.'

Very clearly, des Loges asked him if, for the walk, he would prefer stone-soled shoes.

Crawford declined the offer.

'Ah, *le fils prodigue!*' remarked des Loges in his barbarous French, shaking his head.

Crawford leaned forward against the rope and the wagon creaked forward, but then he realized that he was still carrying the bag. He stopped and walked back and, over protests, made des Loges hold it. Then, with that small victory won, he walked back until the rope was tight again and began pulling. Within the first few minutes he had figured out the most comfortable way to wear the harness, and the easiest-to-maintain pace.

As he plodded away from the sea, leaving the village behind as the ground slowly rose, the only smells were of sun-heated stone and the spice of heather, and the only violations of the sky's quiet were Crawford's heavy breathing and the creaking of the wheels and the monotonous skirling of the bees.

After what might have been an hour he crested a hill, and found himself facing a broad, shallow inland valley . . . and he stopped abruptly, letting the wagon roll forward and bump him in the calves, for an army of giants stood in ranks across the distant grey-green slopes.

Then he heard the old man laughing at him and he realized that the figures in the valley weren't men but were upright stones – the landscape reminded him vaguely of Stonehenge.

A little embarrassed at having been startled by the sight, he began walking down the north slope of the hill; but after the wagon had twice more bumped him from behind, he decided that it would be easier to let the wagon roll down the hill ahead of him backwards while he trudged along after it, hauling back on the rope and acting as a brake.

In this ludicrous posture they were passed by a party of six unamused monks on donkeys, and des Loges added to Crawford's humiliation by choosing that time to recite, in a loud and sarcastic voice, a local legend that held the stones to be a pagan army that had been chasing one St Cornely toward the sea until the saint turned, and, by the exertion of his virtue, petrified them all in place.

A slender arm of the sea extended far inland, narrowing to a river eventually, and the buildings of the little town of Auray clustered around the mouth of the river and mounted in steep lanes and terraces up the flanks of the hills on either side.

From the old man Crawford had learned that the history of the whole area was peppered with miracles and apparitions – only a mile away to the east was the Chapelle Ste Anne, where the Virgin had appeared to a peasant named Yves Nicolazic and told him to build a church there, and down the road a little way stood a cross marking a fourteenth-century battlefield, the unshriven casualties of which were condemned, according to popular belief, to wander the hills until the Last Day – but the citizens weren't prepared for the procession that came plodding and creaking and barking into town at a ceremonious pace just at sunset on that Friday.

All day Crawford had alternately sweated in the sun and shivered in the sea breezes as he dragged the wagon along the rutted road, and at lunch he and his passenger had each drunk an entire bottle of claret with the bread and cheese and cabbage des Loges had packed; just before they resumed their journey the old man had bitten eye-holes into the cloth bag and pulled it over his head like the hood of a bucolic executioner, and Crawford had followed his example by donning as a hat the hollowed-out shell of the cabbage head.

Having finally reached Auráy, these many hours later, the cabbage was wilted but still clinging to his head, and he was noctambulistically intoning the refrain to a song des Loges had begun singing hours ago; and the melody, or perhaps the wing-flapping motions with which the wagon-bound old man had chosen to accompany it, had attracted a following procession of barking dogs. Children ran into houses and several old women blessed themselves fearfully.

Des Loges broke off his singing long enough to tell Crawford where to turn and which one of the fifteenth-century buildings to stop in front of; and when the wagon rolled to a halt and he was finally able to take off the harness, Crawford blinked around at the steep streets and old houses and wondered what he was doing here, weary, fevered and cabbage-decked.

They'd stopped at a two-storey stone building with half a dozen windows upstairs but only a single narrow one at street level. The eaves projected a good yard out beyond the wall, and the building was just perceptibly wider at the bottom than at the top, and Crawford thought the place had a forbiddingly oriental look. A thin, middle-aged man in an outmoded powdered wig was staring down at them in consternation from one of the upstairs windows.

'This had better be *it*, François,' the man called.

'I'll see that the widow is delivered to you in a lace dress and a veil,' answered des Loges in his archaic French, 'and that Mont St Michel stands in for her father! But Brizeux! — until my cousin here resumes his travels I can't spare the hospitality.'

The man in the window nodded tiredly. 'Everybody needs help in passing on. One moment.' He disappeared,

117

and a few moments later the street door was pulled open. 'Come in, come in,' Brizeux said, 'God knows you've drawn enough attention already.'

The morning sunlight overwhelmed the lamplight inside, and it wasn't until the door was closed again that the ranked shelves of ledgers and journals regained their air of significance.

Brizeux led them into a private office and waved toward a couple of velvet-upholstered chairs; dimly on the faded cloth backs Crawford could see the outline of the embroidered Napoleonic *B* that had been cut off recently and, more faintly, the shadow of the fleur-de-lys that had preceded it. Brizeux was as erratic in his politics as the chair, addressing his guests as 'citoyens' one moment and as 'monsieurs' the next. His French, at least, was pure Parisian.

Crawford looked at the man curiously. He was nearly a caricature of a law clerk, fussy and shabby and ink-stained and smelling of book-bindings and sealing wax, but he seemed to hold a position of authority here — and, to Crawford's surprise, he seemed to be willing to give Crawford a passport.

He opened a drawer in his desk and dug out a double handful of passports and then shuffled through them, squinting up at Crawford from time to time as if to judge the fit. Finally, 'Would you be more at ease as a veterinarian or as an upholsterer?' he asked.

Crawford smiled. 'A veterinarian.'

'Very well. Henceforth you are Michael Aickman, forty-two years old, late of Ipswich, who arrived in France on the twelfth of May. Your family is doubtless worried about you.' He handed Crawford the passport.

'What happened to the original Michael Aickman?' he asked.

Brizeux shrugged. 'Waylaid by criminals, I imagine.

118

Perhaps he was carrying a lot of money . . . or perhaps his assailants simply killed him for his passport, which could be sold to,' he permitted himself a sour smile, 'certain unscrupulous public officials.'

'And how much would a public official charge for one of these?'

'Quite a bit,' said Brizeux cheerfully, 'but in your case des Loges here has elected to . . . pay your bill for you.'

Crawford glanced at des Loges and began to wonder what, exactly, the ancient man expected in return; but Brizeux had now initialled the passport and was flipping through the pages to show him what his new signature looked like, and Crawford pushed the worry away.

'You'll want to practise it until you can do it instinctively,' said Brizeux, grinning up at him as he handed the document across.

It occurred to Crawford that Brizeux resembled young Keats – not in much, for Keats was young and burly and Brizeux was grey and frail, but very strongly in the eyes. The eyes of both of them, he realized, had the same unhealthy brightness, as if they were infected with the same rare kind of fever.

When they were outside again des Loges began hobbling back toward the wagon.

'No! We'll take a regular coach back,' said Crawford in slow, carefully pronounced French. 'I'll pay for it.' His feet had been throbbing painfully ever since he had stopped pulling the wagon, and he could feel them swelling in the borrowed shoes.

'No doubt you could satisfy the coachman, but what *I'd* need to be paid isn't yours to offer,' laughed des Loges, not looking back or pausing.

'Wait, I mean it. I would think you'd prefer it yourself, that can't be the most comfortable position to be in all day – or all night, in this case. Why don't we just – '

The old man had stopped, and was looking back at him. 'Didn't you look at the wheels?' he demanded in his barbaric French. 'Why do you think I asked you if you wanted stone shoes?'

Crawford walked bewilderedly to the wagon, crouched beside it and spat on one of the wheels and rubbed off the caked mud. The rim of the wheel was studded with flat stone ovals – no wonder the grotesque vehicle had begun to seem ponderous during the day! He looked up at the old man blankly.

'Your wife never told you?' asked des Loges in a quieter voice. 'Travel over stone doesn't age us, you and me. A family courtesy, you might say. I wore stone-soled shoes for more years than I can count, but age crept up anyway, when I'd change them or take a stroll barefoot for a treat, and now I just don't have the strength for it anymore. I've got a stone base to my walking stick, though, and I make sure to lean on it. Every little bit, right?'

'Uh . . . right.'

'I'll give you a pair of stone soles before you go. And wear them, you hear me? You'll be good for centuries more, easily, just so *you* don't insulate yourself from *your* wife.'

'But I'm *not* married, certainly not to one of these . . . things.' His fever suddenly seemed much worse, and his breath was as hot as a desert wind in his head. 'Am I? Could my wife have been one of them?'

'Sure – a fellow-husband can tell it just to glance at you, even without the evidence of your finger.'

Crawford shook his head uncomprehendingly. 'But she's dead . . . so I can hardly keep from *insulating* myself from her.'

'I really doubt that she's dead.'

Crawford chuckled dizzily. 'You should have been

120

there. Crushed like a press-full of grapes for wine, she was, and on our wedding night.'

Des Loges's walnut-wrinkled face softened in what might have been pity. 'Boy, *that* wasn't your wife.' He shook his head, then climbed into the wagon. 'I got your passport – now pull me home so that you can do your part of the bargain.'

Crawford considered just walking away, hiring a carriage to take him at top speed to the Swiss border, and leaving this old man to walk, or hire some child to pull his wagon – but, almost in spite of himself, he remembered Appleton with the horse and money, and Keats with his luggage.

He bent over stiffly and picked up the harness.

The sun set before they were five miles south of Auray, but des Loges refused to consider spending the night in an inn, even when Crawford pointed out that there was no moon tonight to see by; and so Crawford plodded on, wondering feverishly if there would ever again be a time when he wasn't dragging this wagon around the Brittany hills.

The moon was indeed in its dark phase, but as his eyes grew accustomed to the dark he discovered that he could nevertheless see it as a faint ring in the sky. The ground seemed to have a dim glow too, and several times when he heard noises in the surrounding fields he glimpsed patches of phosphorescence moving behind the wild shrubbery; and when an owl sailed past he was able to follow its silent flight for several long seconds before it swooped toward some small animal.

As the miles unrolled away behind, Crawford settled into a comfortable, metronomic pace, and when a pebble worked its way into his shoe through a gap at the side of the sole, he was reluctant to break his stride and take the shoe off – but after a few seconds he realized that the pebble wasn't at all uncomfortable. It might have been a fever-born delusion, but that foot, the whole leg, in fact, felt much less tired, springier; and so when he did pause it was to find another pebble and poke it into his other shoe. Behind him, des Loges laughed softly.

This time he wasn't startled by the valley of the standing stones, even though at night the figures looked much more like motionless men lined up across the miles of nighted plain for some unimaginable purpose. Luminous mists played over the stones in the starlight, and Crawford, dizzy and sick, thought the mists greeted him; he nodded back and waved his maimed hand.

It was past midnight when he pulled the wagon up beside the inverted half-boat that was des Loges's house. When they had got inside, the old man gave him a cup of brandy and showed him a corner he could sleep in.

At noon the next day Crawford was awakened by the old man calling to him from outside. He came stumbling out of the tiny house, blinking in the glaring sunlight, but it wasn't until he walked out to the rocks and looked down into the tide pool, and saw old des Loges sitting in the water next to the angular rock, that he remembered escaping from the ship and acquiring a passport.

And now you've got to do him this favour, he thought as he squinted around and scratched under his unfresh shirt. I hope it's something you can do quickly, so as to be on the road again before the sun moves too much farther west. Nothing like the sleep-late life of a fugitive! He shook the pebbles out of the battered shoes, pulled them on and then climbed down the sandstone boulders to where des Loges sat.

The old man was dressed in the same dun cassock he'd been wearing the day before, and the clear sea water was rocking and swirling around his upper chest. The roughly hewn pyramidic stone was submerged, but

Crawford could see that a segmented necklace of silver and wooden beads and some kind of onionlike bulbs was draped around the base of it — the buoyant wood and vegetable sections arched upward and waved in the currents, but the silver sections held the strange jewellery down on the sand.

Crawford glanced around again, uneasily, for all at once he knew that something bad was supposed to happen here, and he didn't know what direction it was likely to come from.

The old man was grinning up at him. 'Married in the mountains, divorced by the sea!' he piped. 'It's high tide now, but after you've liberated me, do please break that garlic necklace, will you? I'm not selfish, and I do like to pay my debts.'

Though mystified, Crawford nodded. 'Got you. Break the necklace.' He dipped a toe into the water and winced at the chill. 'You're . . . getting divorced?'

'That's the ceremony I want you to perform,' des Loges told him. 'It shouldn't be any problem. I'm a frail old man, and anyway I promise not to struggle.'

'Do I have to get in the water?'

Des Loges rolled his eyes. 'Of *course* you've got to get in the water! How are you going to drown me if you don't get in the water?'

Crawford grinned. 'Drown you. Right. Listen, I — ' Glancing at the necklace-bordered stone, he realized that it had a square base — and there had been a square dent in the ground where des Loges had said his wife always sat. 'How does this divorce work?' he asked unsteadily.

Des Loges was watching the tide anxiously. 'You drown me. It's just a token killing, really — suicide won't work, you see. Accident or murder only, and with the wife,' he waved toward the stone, 'incapacitated. And it has to be you — I knew it had to be you when I first heard you were on your way – because you're *married into the family*. They won't interfere with *you*; anybody else they could stop, or at least visit vengeance upon.'

Crawford was reeling, and had to kneel down. 'That rock, there, in the water by you. Are you trying to – is that your – '

'Brizeux has no family, no children!' des Loges shouted. 'There's no one at stake but he and I, and we know what we're doing. For God's sake, the tide's going out – hurry! You promised!'

As if to give Crawford a head start, the old man bent over and shoved his face into the water; and with his four-fingered hand he beckoned furiously.

Crawford looked again at the sunken pyramid . . . and a voice in his head said, *No. Get away.*

Crawford turned and ran, as fast as his stiff legs could propel him, east – toward Anjou, and Bourbonnais and, somewhere beyond, Switzerland.

Chapter 7

I said 'she must be swift and white
And subtly warm and half perverse
And sweet like sharp soft fruit to bite,
And like a snake's love lithe and fierce.'
Men have guessed worse.

— A. C. Swinburne, *Felise*

And always, night and day, he was in the mountains,
and in the tombs, crying, and cutting himself with stones.

— Mark 5:5

Like the fingers of a vast, invisible harpist, high-altitude winds were drawing plumes of snow from the top of distant Mont Blanc and casting them out across the whole southwest quarter of the sky; and in spite of the sunlight that raised steam from the slate roofs of the *riegelhausen* around him and made him carry his coat instead of wear it, Crawford shivered with something like sympathy as he watched the faraway mountain, and for a moment he could vividly imagine how these Geneva streets would look from the viewpoint of a person with a telescope on the summit.

Blue sky glittered in the puddles of rainwater between the cobblestones underfoot, and in the west a rainbow spanned the whole valley between Geneva and the Monts du Jura. Looking down from the too bright sky, Crawford saw a young woman approaching him hesitantly from across the street.

Though her fair hair and lace-trimmed red bonnet

implied that she was a native, her pallid beauty seemed suited to some less sunny land, and her sick smile was jarring among these gaily painted housefronts — it seemed to Crawford to be somehow fearfully eager, like the smile of an unworldly person loitering around a foreign waterfront in the hope of selling stolen property or hiring a murderer.

'*L'arc-en-ciel*,' she said hoarsely, nodding over her shoulder at the rainbow but not looking at it. 'The token of God's covenant to Noah, hmm? You look, pardon me, like a man who knows the way around it.'

Crawford assumed she was a prostitute — the Hôtel Angleterre was just ahead, after all, and no doubt many of the English tourists who could afford to stay there would appreciate a girl who didn't require the services of an interpreter — and he was chagrined, but not very surprised, to realize that he was not tempted to take her upstairs somewhere. He had just spent a full month in traversing France, and never during that time, even when he was working alongside very healthy young girls in the vineyards, had he felt any stirring of erotic interest. Perhaps the death of his wife was still too recent . . . or perhaps his intensely sexual dreams, the near nightmares that plagued him and left him drained and fevered in the mornings, were leaving him no energy for the pursuit of real women.

But before he could reply to her ambiguous remark, there was a scuffling on the side of the street she'd come from.

'It's that damned atheist, let him lie,' a gruff man's voice called, and then a girl cried, 'A doctor, someone go for a doctor!'

Crawford automatically pushed the young woman aside and loped past her across the street.

'I'm a doctor, let me through,' he said loudly, shoving his weathered but newly bought portmanteau between the people who were clustered in a rough semicircle against the wall of a tavern. They backed away to let him in, and at the focus of the crowd he found a frail-looking youth lying unconscious on the stones, his wispy blond hair clinging damply to his forehead.

'He started talking crazily, wildly,' said a girl who was crouched beside him, 'and then he simply fell over.' Crawford realized that she was the one who had called for a doctor. She was English, and idly he noted that he would once have found her, too, attractive, though in contrast to the Swiss girl she was dark-haired and plump.

He got down on one knee and felt the young man's pulse. It was rapid and weak. 'It looks like sunstroke,' he snapped. 'Got to get the temperature back down. Get me wet cloths – anything, a sail . . . curtains, a cloak – and something to fan him with.'

A couple of people ran away, presumably to get the wet cloths, and Crawford pulled off the unconscious man's jacket and began unbuttoning his shirt. A moment later he had peeled it off too, and he tossed both garments over his shoulder. 'Soak up some rain water with these,' he yelled, 'and give them back to me.'

Crawford stood up then and began flapping his own coat back and forth over the thin torso. It occurred to him that this young man resembled someone he'd met recently.

'Wasting your time, my good man,' said one foppishly dressed Englishman cheerfully. 'That's Shelley the athe-ist. Let him die and the world's a better place.'

Crawford was about to say something about the Hippocratic Oath, but another man had just limped up from the direction of the hotel, and this new arrival swung around to give the tourist a frigid smile. 'Shelley is a friend of mine,' he said tightly. 'If *you* have friends, perhaps you would be so kind as to have one of them arrange a time when you and I can meet somewhere at your convenience and . . . *reason* with each other?'

'Good God,' muttered someone in the crowd, 'it's *Byron.*'

Crawford, still flapping his coat, glanced over at the newcomer. He did seem to resemble the author of *Childe Harold's Pilgrimage* as the drawings in the London papers had portrayed him – with a moody but classically handsome face under a wind-tossed mane of dark curls. Crawford had vaguely heard that the man had left England, but he hadn't known he had come to Switzerland. And who was this 'atheist' Shelley?

The English tourist's face was dark and he was looking away, back toward the hotel. 'I . . . apologize,' he muttered, then turned and stalked off.

The blonde young woman who'd talked to Crawford about the rainbow came hobbling over with a blanket and a bucket of water – and before she let Crawford dunk the blanket she shook into the water a handful of what seemed to be white sand. 'Salt,' she said impatiently, as if Crawford should have thought of it himself. 'It makes the water a better conductor of electricity.'

Byron seemed startled by the remark, and looked more closely at her.

'Great, thank you,' Crawford said, too busy to bother with her odd remark. He balled up the blanket and plunged it into the water, and then draped the sodden fabric over Shelley's thin frame – noting, as he tucked it around him, a wide, corrugated scar on the young man's side, below the prominent ribs. One of the ribs, in fact, seemed to be missing.

The English girl who had called for a doctor smiled up at Crawford. 'You must have been a ship's surgeon,' she said, 'to have instinctively called for a *sail*.'

Both Byron and Crawford looked at her uncomfortably.

'Oh, hello, Claire,' said Byron. 'I didn't see you there.'

'Yes,' Crawford put in shortly. 'I was in the Navy in my youth.'

Just then another man came bustling up. 'What's going on here?' he demanded. 'I'm a physician, let me pass.'

'The situation's well in hand, Pollydolly,' said Byron. 'It seems Shelley has had a sunstroke.'

'According to whose diagnosis?' The man with the implausible name glared around at the crowd and then focused on Crawford. Crawford noticed that he was young – in his twenties, probably, and trying to hide the fact behind his ostentatious moustache and blustery manner. 'Yours, sir?'

'Right,' said Crawford, 'I'm a surgeon – '

'A barber, that is to say.' The newcomer smirked. 'Well! While I won't argue that Shelley could benefit from the services of – of one of your trade, I can't applaud your – your methods of – '

'Oh, save it, Polly,' interrupted Byron. 'This man seems to be doing fine – look, Shelley's coming round now.'

The young man on the pavement had half sat up, and was hugging Claire; he hadn't yet opened his eyes. 'Her conscious tail her joy declared,' he said in a thin, high voice, obviously reciting something; 'the fair round face, the snowy beard, the velvet of her paws, her coat that with the tortoise vies . . .'

Obviously embarrassed for his friend, Byron laughed. 'That's from Thomas Gray's poem about the favourite cat that drowned in a tub of goldfish. Here, let's see if we can't get him up – '

'*Mommee!*' Shelley yelled suddenly. 'It *wasn't* Daddy, it was the tortoise-thing from the pond! You *must* have known, even if it did make itself look like him! It lives in the pond, in Warnham Pond . . .' His eyes flew open then, and he blinked around without evident recognition at the faces over him. Crawford and the thin, sick-looking young woman were standing next to each other, and Shelley's gaze stayed on them for a moment, then darted away.

Warnham, Crawford was thinking. That's where I lost my wedding ring.

Byron grabbed Shelley under the arm and hauled him to his feet. 'Can you walk, Shelley? Here's your coat, though some helpful soul has mopped the street with it. Sir,' he added, turning to Crawford, 'we're in your debt. I'm staying at the Villa Diodati, just north along this shore of the lake, and the Shelleys are my neighbours – do visit us, especially if . . . if we can be of any aid to a fellow traveller.'

Byron and Claire each took one of Shelley's arms and led him away, and the physician with the ludicrous name followed, after shooting Crawford a baleful squint. Crawford again noticed that Byron was limping, and now he remembered reading that the young lord was lame – clubfooted.

The crowd was dispersing, and Crawford found himself walking beside the thin girl who had asked him if he knew a way around rainbows. 'Sometimes they *appear* to be reptiles,' she remarked, as casually as if she were resuming a conversation.

Crawford was worrying about having admitted to being a surgeon and one-time Navy man. 'I daresay,' he answered absently.

'I mean, I'm certain it wasn't *really* a tortoise.'

'I suppose that is unlikely,' he agreed.

'My name is Lisa,' she said.

'Michael.'

She rocked her head dreamily, and Crawford noticed

her high cheekbones and large, dark eyes, and he was again sourly aware of how attractive he would once have found her.

'Have *you* ever seen one that regal?' she asked him softly. 'His mother was damned fortunate. The closest to real love *I* ever had was the hand of a statue . . . I lived with it for years, but then I became anaemic, and people noticed that I couldn't be out in the sun anymore, and so the priests came with the salted holy water and killed it. I suppose I'm grateful – I'd certainly be dead today if they hadn't – but I still look for rocks on the slopes of the mountains.'

'The hand of a statue,' echoed Crawford, thinking again about Warnham.

'I was luckier than most,' she said, nodding as if in agreement. She glanced at him shyly and licked her lips. 'Have you brought with you any . . .' She blushed, then went on in a lower voice, '. . . any loaves of St Stephen? We could, you and I could, be together through them – ' She took his hand, and drew it across her cheek, then kissed the palm; the gesture seemed forced, but for a moment he had felt the hot, wet tip of her tongue. ' – we could share in their interest in us, Michael, and at least be interested in each other that way . . .'

Crawford realized that this was what Keats had told him about, and had something to do with what des Loges had wanted him to do; and he admitted to himself that he recognized the same ill glitter in Lisa's eyes that he had seen in the eyes of Keats and that government clerk, Brizeux – he would have to study his own face in a mirror sometime.

'I'm sorry,' he told her gently. 'I don't have anything.'

'Oh.' She dropped his hand, though she kept walking beside him. 'You have had recently, though – you shine with it like *ignis fatui*, will-o'-the-wisps, over a stagnant pond.'

He glanced sharply at her, but she was looking list-lessly ahead and seemed to have meant no offence.

'Maybe you could come to the mountains with me sometime and look for rocks,' she said, beginning to draw away from him. 'I know a couple of high places where landslides have exposed the metal, that silvery metal that's as light as wood, and we could check all the rocks nearby, for live pieces.'

He nodded and waved as she receded into the crowd. 'Sounds like fun,' he said helplessly.

Visits to a few of the nearby hotels and inns convinced him that he couldn't afford to lodge within Geneva's walls, so he took a coach through the villages northward along Lake Leman's east shore; and in one of them he found a room for rent in a sixteenth-century log house, the windows of which looked down over narrow lanes to a beach grooved by the keels of the fishing boats that had been dragged from there down to the lake that morning.

He slept until dark, and then spent most of the night staring out across the lake at the remote, sky-banishing blackness that was the Jura; sometimes he turned to face the northeast corner of his room and, beyond the panelling, beyond the house and the hills of the Chablais and the Rhône River, he could sense the separate majesties of the Bernese Alps far away in the night – Monch, the Eiger, and the Jungfrau.

Some time after midnight the sky began slowly to ripple and gleam in vast curtains like the Aurora Borealis, and the stars went out; the massed trees around the lake began to shine faintly, and for just a few moments, like someone who hears a distant music when the wind is right, he thought he could feel through his heels the reverberations of a long-ongoing litany from the very heart of the stony earth. He slept, and dreamed of the cold woman again.

She was in the room with him in this dream, and that was a first — when he had dreamed of her in England and France he had always seemed to meet her on an island where ruins shouldered up between ancient olive trees, and the two of them had made love on a floor of marble tiles that was streaked by alternate bands of moonlight and the shadows of broken pillars. Always her skin was cold, and after she had drained him she slithered away so rapidly into the viny shrubbery that he knew her shape could no longer be human . . . and it had maddened him, every time, to be unable to follow her, for in the dream he was somehow convinced that her reptilian shape would prove to be as erotically beautiful as her human one.

Tonight she seemed to come in as a mist between the casements, but she was in her human form by the time he looked fully at her. She was naked, as always before, and he was so dazzled by the sight of her that he hardly noticed her arm snake out and turn his shaving mirror to face the wall. Then her white fingers reached out and unbuttoned his shirt, and his lungs seemed to clog full with ice when her cold nipples pressed against his chest.

He fell backwards on to the bed and she followed and straddled him, and he realized, with no feeling except gratitude, that it was *she* he had made love to in the hours before the dawn when he found Julia's body. Now she bent down to give him a passionate kiss — her hair fell in coils around his ears, and he abandoned himself to her.

Her flesh warmed around him as the hours were achingly chiselled away, and when at last she rose from the bed she was actually glowing faintly, like the bricks lining a smithy's stove. She leaned down and took his limp hand as if to kiss it, but when she lifted it to her

133

lips it was only to bite the stump of his missing finger. The blood spurted rackingly into her mouth, and the strained bedjoints squealed as he convulsed into unconsciousness.

He cringed when the morning sunlight touched his face, and though the effort made his legs shake and sent him gasping and sweating back to bed, he managed to drag the curtain across the torturing bright gap. The bedsheet was blotted brown with blood from his freshly torn finger stump.

Only after sunset was he able to venture outside, and at twilight he found himself on a ledgelike walkway notched across the lake-facing side of an ancient stone house, and after leaning on the iron railing for half an hour, watching silent lightning play over the mountains beyond the far shore, he noticed a boat out on the face of the water.

It was a small sailboat, its mainsail blue under the salmon sky, skating toward him on the breeze that twitched at his coat collar and made the water's sky-reflecting skin flutter like a sheet of gold-leaf held up to a whisper. There was one solitary figure aboard.

A set of stone steps slanted down to the water at Crawford's left, and when it became clear that the boat was headed directly toward him he found himself slowly walking to the steps and then descending them. By the time the boatman was close enough to swing broadside to the wind and loose the sail, Crawford was waiting for him on the stone dock at the water's edge, and he caught the painter-rope the boatman tossed to him.

Crawford tugged the boat in to the dock, and as he crouched to loop the rope around a weathered wooden post, Percy Shelley stepped agilely from the rocking boat on to the unmoving stone.

The line secured, Crawford straightened up. It was the first time he'd seen Shelley's face under normal conditions, and he flinched.

'The resemblance is not coincidental,' Shelley said with a kind of grim amusement. 'She's my half sister.'

Crawford didn't have to ask who he meant . . . and he remembered some of the things Shelley had said during his heat-stroke delirium. 'Half sister? Who – who was her father?'

Shelley's face was haggard but merry. 'Can I trust you?'

'I – don't know. Yes.'

Shelley leaned against the wooden post. 'I'm pretty sure I can trust you in exactly the same way I can trust a flower to turn toward the sun.' He made a slight bow. 'That will suffice.'

Crawford frowned at that, and wondered why he should believe anything that Shelley might tell him. Well, he thought, he *is* her brother – *visibly* he's her brother.

'You asked about her *father*,' Shelley was saying. 'Well, to start with, father isn't really the right word. These things are . . . can assume either sex. It was . . . Christ, there's no point in trying to define it. It looked like a giant tortoise, as often as not, and if it had any more motivations than do the animalcules that you can see through a microscope in a drop of vinegar, it's news to me. I've studied . . . his . . . species for years, but I still can't see *motivations* behind the *consistencies*.'

Crawford thought of the cold woman, of her ageless beauty. 'Which of you is the elder?'

Shelley's grin widened, but looked even less cheerful. 'That's hard to say. Our mother gave birth to both of us on the same day, so you could say we're twins. But *her* seed was implanted in my mother's womb long before mine was – these things must have a longer gestation

135

period – so it would be just as valid to say she's older. But then again she lived as a sort of encysted stone in my abdomen for nineteen years, until 1811, when I managed to cut her out of myself – you must have noticed, the other day, the scar from my "caesarian" – so you could say she's younger than I am. The only thing I can say with any assurance is that we did have the same mother.' He laughed and shook his head ruefully. 'At least for *you* it wasn't *incest*.'

Crawford was suddenly light-headed with jealousy. 'You – ' he choked, 'when did you – '

'The stones have ears. Let's talk out on the lake.' Shelley waved toward the boat.

Crawford turned to the knobby post around which the painter was tied, and for the first time noticed that the top of it had been crudely carved into the form of a grimacing human head, and that several long iron nails had been pounded into the face . . . long ago, to judge by the black rust-lines that streaked the splintered visage like tears.

'That's a *mazze*,' called Shelley, from behind him. 'The word's Italian for "club." You see a lot of them in the Valais, southeast of here.'

Crawford was gingerly untying the rope from around the thing. 'What's it *for*?'

'Back in the fifteenth century, when the Swiss were breaking free of the Hapsburgs, those things were a sort of roster for the rebels; if you wanted to go fight the oppressors, you indicated it by pounding a nail – an *eisener breche*, they called them – into one of these heads.'

Crawford touched one of the nails. It rocked in its hole, and impulsively he pulled it out of the face and put it into his pocket.

Shelley was taking in the freed rope, and Crawford stepped aboard before the vessel could drift out of reach. The wooden hoops around the mast clattered as the sail was raised, and then, even as Crawford settled himself comfortably on the thwart, Shelley was deftly working the sheet to put the bow around into the wind and begin tacking out away from shore. The sky had already darkened to the colour of wet ash.

'When did,' Crawford began, but his voice came out too shrill; he swallowed, and then in a more normal tone he said, 'when did you . . . sleep with her?'

'Long before you married her,' Shelley assured him. 'Actually it was shortly after her birth – her birth from me, that is. I met her on the street, and I made myself believe that it . . . that what I had cut out of myself had been nothing more than a stone – I do suffer from bladder stones.'

Shelley twitched at the mainsail sheet, and the boat leaned as it skated out across the face of the lake. 'I made myself believe,' he went on, 'that this woman who had sought me out couldn't have anything to do with that bloody lump, that diseased rib, that I had flung into the street a couple of months before. But of course they were one and the same . . . though it was very difficult for her to maintain a human form back then. Even now she has to relapse into something else . . . rocky or reptilian . . . after any length of time.' The wind shifted, and he smoothly let the shift become a change to a fresh tack. 'It was my first sexual experience.'

'And have you . . . had her, since?' It made Crawford's teeth hurt to ask.

'No. It was – no offence, but it was too horrible to want to repeat. She was too nearly *me*, after all those years of living inside me, and it was like masturbation – having sex with the dark side of myself.'

'Too *horrible?*' Crawford's hands had clenched. 'Can you swim?'

'No, I can't – and you'd harm her, very likely kill her, if you drowned me. We're twins, remember, and very

137

closely linked. But I didn't seek you out this evening in order to insult her. Do you – '

'You're the second – no, third! – person who has thought I'm married to her,' Crawford interrupted. 'Why do you think that?'

Shelley glanced over at him quizzically. 'Well, because she's let me know, for one thing. And you're missing your wedding-ring finger, which is generally a sign of being married to one of these – as a matter of fact, wedding bands were originally a symbolic protection against *succubae*, the idea being that that finger was thus banded with metal to the body. And you've got a different look from all the people who are just *prey* for these things – a practised observer can always recognize a *member of the family*.'

The shore had so receded behind them that Crawford, looking back, couldn't make out the dock anymore, and Shelley let the sail spill the wind; within moments the boat had rocked to a stop and was drifting. Crawford thought he caught a hint of light and movement in the sky, but when he looked up there was nothing to see except the dark clouds.

Shelley looked up too, a little nervously. 'Wild lamiae? We ought to be protected from *them*, at least, now that *she's* here – though one almost drowned me on this lake a couple of months ago.' A minute went by in silence, and he relaxed.

'So,' Shelley went on, 'you *did* marry her. They can't initiate it, there has to have been a token of invitation on your part. I wonder why you can't remember it. Did you . . . I don't know, speak marriage vows to a rock, put a wedding ring on a winged lizard . . .' He grinned. '. . . have sex with a statue in a church?'

Crawford's stomach had gone cold. 'Christ!' he whispered. 'Yes, I did!'

Shelley's eyebrows were halfway to his hairline.

'Really? A statue in a church? I don't mean to seem vulgarly curious, but – '

'No, no, I put a wedding ring on the finger of a statue. In Warnham, a month ago. And when I went back, late at night, to get it, the – later I decided it was a dream – the statue's hand was closed, so I couldn't get the ring off.'

'That was it,' said Shelley flatly. 'That was her. And it wasn't as . . . *random* an action, I'll wager, as you imagine; just like the loss of your finger, hmm? She was there, she was directing things. She needed a vehicle aboard which to follow me to Europe, so she manoeuvred you into volunteering to be one.'

'Did she kill my wife? The woman I married the next day, who . . . who was killed on our wedding night, while I slept?'

Shelley bared his teeth in a snarl of sympathy. 'Christ, did that happen? Yes, it has to have been her. She's . . . a jealous god.' He tugged at his hair. 'There was a girl I was interested in in Scotland, in 1811, shortly after I cut my sister out of myself; Mary Jones the girl's name was. My sister killed her – tore her to pieces. The authorities said it must have been done with big sheep shears, and they picked the biggest, stupidest citizen as the culprit, but anyone could see that no human being with anything less than a, a *cannon* could have so destroyed the girl's body.'

'Right, exactly,' Crawford said in a clipped whisper, 'that's what happened to Julia. But you know something? I'm . . . not sorry. Damn me for saying it, but I'm *not sorry*. I mean, I wish Julia were still alive, that is, I wish I'd never met her – I wish I had known I was marrying her, the . . . the cold woman, your sister, so that I could simply have *avoided* Julia. Is that horrible of me?'

'Profoundly, yes.' Shelley shifted around, draping an

arm over the tiller bar. 'But I'm glad to hear that you feel that way – it means you'll probably cooperate with the plan I have in mind. You see, I have a wife and children – and, on top of that, I'm about to get a divorce and re-marry; and my half sister, *your* wife, will kill all of these people if she can, just as she killed your Julia. But she can't cross water, especially salt water, by herself – she's got to ride across with a human to whom she's closely related: by blood, as in my case, or by marriage, as in yours. Now, she married you in order to chase me across the Channel – '

'That's a lie,' Crawford said.

Shelley gave him a pitying look. 'Very well, it's a lie. In any case, wouldn't you like to make sure that when I return to England she stays here with you, and doesn't ride back across the Channel with me?'

'She wouldn't,' said Crawford, his voice louder and belligerent. 'You're just flattering yourself. Go ahead, go back to England – she won't follow you.'

'You're probably right,' said Shelley soothingly. 'I'm sure you are. But why don't you help me make it *certain*, by just cooperating with me on a couple of . . . procedures. Nothing complicated, I got my wife to do them just before I left England in May. I just want you to – '

'I don't have to physically *bind* her to me – and I won't insult her, and shame myself, by trying.'

Shelley stared at him, and though it was too dark to see clearly, his expression seemed to be one of bewilderment. 'Very well. Right. Then let's put it this way – how would you like to learn, learn from her *brother*, remember, what sorts of behaviour you should avoid, if you want to keep her? What she likes, what she hates?'

'I don't need this.' Crawford stood up, rocking the boat. 'And *I* know how to swim.'

He dived over the side.

The lake water was cold, and seemed to clear his head

140

of the feverish complacency that had been surrounding him like a warm fog; now there was just panic. I should climb right back aboard, he thought, and find out how to keep her from following him ... and then do the opposite. How can I want to keep her? My God, *she killed Julia*! And now somehow you –

His head broke the surface of the water and he was breathing the evening air, and he forgot all about going back to the boat. The prospect of swimming several hundred yards while wearing boots and a coat didn't seem daunting, and he turned toward the shore they'd embarked from and began crawling through the water with a steady, ponderous stroke. Behind him Shelley was calling to him, but he didn't bother to listen.

As he swam, the water seemed gradually to become a denser fluid, like mercury – so that he floated higher and could propel himself along with less effort, almost as if the water were repelling him; and a warm wind had sprung up at his back, thrusting at his clothes and hair and lending him impetus. Thank you, he thought to the mountains and the sky. Thank you, my new family.

Shelley tried to follow him, but the wind over the lake was impossibly erratic, and finally he had to let the sail flap loose. His night vision had been diminishing ever since he had taken the knife to his own lower ribs in 1811, but he could still see well enough to make out the wide whirlwind that drew spray up in a dim funnel and centred on the receding lump of agitation that was his brother-in-law.

Simultaneous lightning crazed the night sky over the Jura on one horizon and Mont Blanc on the other, and a few moments later the thunder rolled back and forth across the lake, sounding to Shelley like the majestic laughter of the mountains.

* * *

For the next week Crawford never went out by day. Often when the sun had set behind the black slopes of the Jura he would climb up the rocky foothills by starlight, or slouch down the steep cobblestoned lanes to the shore of the lake, and then just wander aimlessly. He was acutely aware of smells now, relishing the wild spice scents of the upland flowers, and repulsed by the smoke that whirled away along the shore at dusk when the returned fishermen were cooking their garlicky sausages. There were no tourists out here, and the locals seemed to hurry away when he approached them, and so whole days went by without his speaking a word.

The memories of his past life had lost their driving power – his only concern these days was to be back in his room every evening by midnight for the arrival of *her*.

And he had only one worry, but it was a consuming one – she was becoming less substantial. The dreams were losing their vividness, and he could find only the faintest red spots now when he looked for her bites in the mornings; he treasured the memory of the first bite, and sentimentally kept picking at it so that it wouldn't heal.

He had never turned the mirror back to face the room, but he knew what he would see if he did – the bright, ill-looking eyes and hectically spotted cheeks that distinguished the faces of so many of the people he'd been meeting lately.

When he came back up the hill on the tenth night, he found half a dozen people awaiting him outside the rooming house. One of them was the old woman who owned the place. His bag had been packed, and it sat on the grass behind them.

'You cannot stay here any longer,' said the landlady clearly in French. 'You did not tell me that you are consumptive. The quarantine laws are very strict – you must go to the hospital.'

Crawford shook his head, impatient to get upstairs. 'It is not genuine consumption,' he managed to reply in the same language. 'Honestly, I am a doctor, and I can assure you that I suffer from an entirely different malady, one that – '

'One that can perhaps bring worse things yet down upon us,' said the burly man nearest Crawford's bag. 'The teeth of the middle.'

For a moment Crawford thought the man was making a reference to his bitten finger stump, but then he remembered that that was the name of a cluster of nearby mountains: the *Dents du Midi*.

Crawford was afraid it might be midnight now, and that she might be waiting for him . . . or not waiting. 'Look,' he said unsteadily in English, 'I've paid for the goddamn room, and I'm gonna – '

He tried to push past them, but an outflung palm thrust him back with such force that he wound up sitting on the grass well behind where he'd been standing. His portmanteau thudded on to the ground next to him.

'Within my grandfather's lifetime people like you were burned alive,' the landlady called. 'Be grateful that you are simply required to leave.'

'But it's the middle of the night!' Crawford gasped, still nearly breathless from the push. 'Uh, *mais, c'est en pleine nuit!* They close the Geneva gates at ten! What do you expect me to – '

The burly man pulled something silvery out from under his coat, but Crawford didn't wait to see whether it was a crucifix or a knife; rolling painfully to his feet, he seized his bag and, wheezing curses, limped away down the hill.

He hoped to walk to Geneva and talk or bribe his way

into the city, and then get a room somewhere, but she came to him while he was still on the road.

He had his portmanteau slung over his back as he strode along, and all at once it seemed to grow shockingly heavy; he fell under its sudden weight and rolled several yards down the lakeward slope . . . and then, with an overwhelming burst of gladness, he realized that the glowing-eyed creature that was crouched on his back and lowering its open mouth toward his neck was *her*. And he was awake – this was no dream.

When her teeth punctured the skin of his throat he was abruptly somewhere else . . . even some*one* else. He was lying on a bed, and he knew he was on the west coast of France, booked to sail for Portsmouth tomorrow. Mary Godwin, his wife-to-be, slept beside him, but his thoughts tonight were of his present wife, Harriet, and their two children, all three of whom he had left behind in England. Then he became aware that his thoughts were being monitored, and he hastily closed his mind . . . and Crawford was himself again, sprawled across the dewy grass slope under the stars while the cold woman drew hot blood from his throat.

He realized dimly that the flow of his blood into her had briefly linked his mind to Shelley's.

But now she was speaking to him in his mind, and he forgot everything else. She didn't use words, but he learned that she had to go away somewhere to fulfil a five-year-old promise, and that there were only two vessels available to her for such a voyage – and one of them was leaving now. She would give his . . . name, face, identity . . . to certain sorts of . . . people, who would try to protect him if he got into danger.

And he had better be . . . *faithful* to her.

He tried to remonstrate, to tell her how much he needed her, but even though he shouted at her, staring

144

into her weirdly luminous eyes as her ivory face hovered over him, he wasn't sure she heard him.

Eventually she left him, but it was too cold on the grassy hillside for him to go to sleep. He got to his feet, refastened his clothes and, with infinite weariness, resumed his interrupted walk to Geneva.

In Le Havre, in northern France, Percy Shelley stepped aboard the ship that was to take him to England . . .

. . . And Crawford was alone. She was gone, not only somewhere else but not watching over him anymore. The night was instantly darker; his night-vision had suddenly diminished, and he began dragging his feet as he walked so that he could feel the texture of the road and notice if he strayed off it.

Shelley had been right after all — and had failed to leave her on this side of the Channel.

Chapter 8

I saw pale kings, and princes too,
Pale warriors, death-pale were they all;
Who cry'd — 'La belle Dame sans merci
Hath thee in thrall!'

I saw their starv'd lips in the gloam
With horrid warning gaped wide,
And I awoke, and found me here
On the cold hill side.

— John Keats, 'La Belle Dame Sans Merci'

... seals — necklaces — balls &c. — & I
know not what — formed of Chrystals
— Agates — and other stones — *all of &
from Mont Blanc* bought & brought by
me on & from the spot — expressly for
you to divide among yourself and the
children ...

— Lord Byron, to Augusta Leigh,
8 September 1816

Lord Byron didn't appreciate having to be up early and
having to be in a carriage with Dr Polidori; either burden
alone, he felt, he could have taken, indeed often *had*
taken, in stride — but both at once today was asking too
much. He really couldn't be held to blame if he lost his
temper.

Byron's gigantic travelling carriage was making poor
headway through the traffic around Geneva's north
gate; the carriage had been built in England, copied from
the celebrated one of Napoleon's that had been captured

at Genappe, and it contained a bed and a table and silverware ... but it was an unwieldy vehicle for manoeuvring through crowds.

The young physician didn't seem to mind the delay, though. Polidori had done a lot of strenuous exercises before they had set out, making a show of his disciplined gasping, and now he was squinting at the distant mountains visible against the blue sky behind the gables and spires of the town, and he was whispering under his breath.

Byron couldn't stand it. He knew that it was some wretched bit of the physician's own verse that he was reciting. Why did the man have to have literary ambitions?

Mostly because the physician disapproved, Byron poured himself another glass of Fendant wine.

Sure enough, Polidori glanced over at him and frowned. 'That's your fifth glass of wine today, my lord, and you've only been up for a couple of hours!' He cleared his throat. 'It has been ... medically and mathematically proven, that wine, in excessive amounts, has ... catastrophic effects in the ... digestive sphere – '

'When I meet a man with a *digestive sphere*, Pollydolly, I'll send him straight to you. What *I've* got is a stomach, and it's partial to drink.' He held the wine up to the sunlight and admired the way the sun made an amber smouldering in the glass. 'Liquor's an old friend of mine, and it's never betrayed my trust.'

Polidori shrugged sulkily and resumed staring out the window; his lower lip was sticking out more than usual, but at least he had stopped his *sotto voce* recitations.

Byron grinned sourly, remembering an exchange he'd had with the envious young physician four months ago, when the two of them had been travelling up the Rhine. 'After all,' Polidori had said, 'what is there that you can do that I cannot?' Byron had grinned and stretched languorously. 'Why, since you force me to say,' he had answered, 'I think there are three things.' Of course Polidori had hotly demanded to know what they could be. 'Well,' Byron had replied, 'I can swim across this river . . . and I can snuff out a candle with a pistol ball at a distance of twenty paces . . . and I can write a poem of which fourteen thousand copies sell in one day.'

That had been fun; especially since Polidori had been unable to argue. Byron demonstrably *had* done all those things – except swim the Rhine, but he was known to be a powerful swimmer, who had once swum across the mile of treacherous sea between Sestos and Abydos in Turkey – and Polidori couldn't even claim to be able to do one of them. That dialogue, like this morning's, had sent the young physician into a sulk.

The crowd had finally opened up in front of them, and Byron's driver was able to whip up the horses and get the carriage out through the gate.

'*Finally*,' snapped Polidori, shifting awkwardly on his seat as if to imply that the carriage's construction ought to have provided passengers with more room.

Just to annoy the young man further, Byron leaned forward and opened the communication panel. 'Stop a moment, would you please, Maurice,' he called to the driver. He was about to say that he wanted to let the horses rest for a while; but then, glancing out the window, he saw an arm and the back of a head showing like nearly submerged reefs above the sea of daisies along the side of the road.

'What *now*, my lord?' sighed Polidori.

'It's some physician you are,' Byron told him sternly. 'People are dying by the side of the road, and all you can be bothered to do is recite poetry and tell me about digestive trapezohedrons.'

Polidori was aware that he was missing something. He blinked out of one of the windows in what would have been, if aimed in the right direction, a brave show of alertness. '. . . People dying?' he mumbled.

Byron was already out of the carriage and limping across the grassy shoulder. 'Over here, you moron. Exercise your arts on this poor – ' He paused, for he had rolled the limp body over, and he recognized the face.

So did Polidori, who came stumping up then. 'Why, it's just that false doctor who nearly gave Shelley pneumonia! Did I tell you I made some inquiries, and found out that he's actually a *veterinarian*? I expect he's just drunk. There's no – '

Byron had looked closely at the wasted face, though, and was remembering how close he had come to a similar disaster in his youth – and he remembered too the protective carnelian-quartz heart a friend had subsequently given him, and the strangely crystalline skull he himself had later dug up at his family estate and had made into a goblet.

'Lift him inside,' Byron said softly.

'What, a drunk?' protested Polidori. 'On your famous upholstery? Let's just leave word – '

'*I said get him inside!*' Byron roared. 'And pour some wine into that amethyst cup that's packed in the same case with my pistols! And then,' he went on gently, putting his hand on the startled young physician's shoulder, 'calculate how much I owe you. Your services are no longer required.'

For a moment Polidori was speechless. Then, '*What?*' he sputtered. 'Are you mad, m'lord? A *veterinarian*? Not even a surgeon, as he claimed that day, but an *animal doctor? To replace me*, a graduate of *Edinburgh University*? Five glasses of wine in a morning, no *wonder* you're talking this way! As your physician, I'm afraid I must – '

Byron had certainly not intended to hire this unconscious person as Polidori's replacement, but the young man's denunciation of such a course made him perversely seize upon it. 'I have,' he said in his coldest tone, easily overriding Polidori's shrill protests, 'no further right as an *employer* to ask you to do anything; but as a fellow *human being* I'm asking you to help me carry my new personal doctor into my carriage.'

Though choking with rage and perhaps weeping, Polidori complied, and in a few moments Michael Crawford was sleepily spilling wine down his throat and his muddy shirt-front while sitting on the leather upholstery of Byron's carriage. Soon the vehicle was under way again, and Polidori was walking shakily back toward the gates of the city of Geneva.

Crawford expected the wine to hit him hard, what with his empty stomach and weakened constitution – but instead it seemed to clear his head and restore some of his strength. He emptied the cup, and Byron refilled it.

'I told you to come to me for help, if you needed it,' Byron said.

'Thank you – but I didn't need any until last night.'

Byron stared at him, and Crawford knew he was considering his thin face and fever-bright eyes. 'Really.' Byron sighed and leaned back, replacing the bottle in the sloshing ice bucket on the floor. 'What happened last night?'

Crawford looked speculatively at Byron, noting for the first time Byron's own symptoms – the pale skin, the intense eyes. 'I lost my – ' What, he couldn't precisely say *wife*; protector? Lover?

But Byron was nodding knowingly. 'Not for long, you haven't,' he said, 'unless you climbed one of these mountains between then and now. How long has it been since . . . "melancholy marked you for her own"?'

'Since . . . ? Oh. A month or so.'

'Huh.' Byron refilled his own more mundane glass with a not-quite-steady hand. 'You must have been bitten hard, to get here so quickly. I've been their prey since I was fifteen.'

Crawford raised his eyebrows, reflecting that these poets tended to have drawn the deadly attentions of their vampires very young – Keats had fallen into the power of his at birth, and Shelley had been consecrated to them before he had even emerged from his mother's womb!

Byron was staring at him. 'Yes, that is young. It took me a long time to get here.' He drank some more of his wine and squinted out his window at the lake.

'I do owe you help,' he said quietly, perhaps to himself; then he sighed and turned to Crawford. 'My family estate was some kind of focus for the things – there are such places even in England, ask Shelley sometime – and one of them made his tenancy legal by actually renting the place. Hah! Lord Grey de Ruthyn, he called himself. He liked me, and wanted me to live there with him – my mother thought that was *prestigious*, and made me go, and he knocked on the door of my room the first night I spent there. Like a lunatic I invited him in . . . but it was my mother's fault too.'

He frowned and lifted the bottle out of the bucket again, then stared at the dripping label. 'Of course she paid for it later,' he remarked, 'as the families of people like us generally do. Did you know that? And Lord Grey has been . . . attending to me ever since, in one form or other, one sex or the other.'

He shuddered and poured some of the wine into his glass. 'But now my sister, half sister, actually, has begun to show the symptoms of his attentions, and I won't have that. And Claire's foetus is mine, and even my bastards won't suffer it if I can prevent it.'

'*Can* you prevent it?' asked Crawford. 'Without dying yourself?'

'I hope to. Switzerland is dangerous – they seem to

have a stronger foothold in this country than anywhere else – but I believe that at the same time, ironically, it's *possible* here to climb up out of their field of power, and throw off their yoke.' He pointed at Crawford's cup. 'Drinking wine from an amethyst cup is a good way to start.'

Crawford remembered something Keats had told him in the Galatea. 'I thought neffers liked to do that – and *they* certainly don't want to . . . throw off any yoke. They seem to be *seeking* that yoke.'

'Neffers?' Byron seemed amused by the word. 'I know the sort of people you mean – God knows I've been hounded by them. One of them, Lady Caroline Lamb, cut her hand at a ball I was at four years ago, and waved her bloody fingers at me, to entice me. Christ. Anyway, they misunderstand the real nature of the quartzes. Some tantalizing dreams can be induced by the use of them, but such dreams are just . . . echoes still ringing in the remoter halls of a castle after the inhabitants are long gone. Some crystals can give more vivid echoes than others, but none of them can recall the departed tenants; in fact, such crystals tend to *repel* a living member of the nephelim. Not that there are many such left anymore.'

Crawford took a deep sip of the wine, and he could feel alertness and energy trickling back into him. 'Nephelim?'

'You're not a biblical scholar,' Byron observed. 'The nephelim were the "giants in the earth" they had in those days, the descendants of Lilith, who sometimes laid with the sons and daughters of men – it's one of the ways they can reproduce, through human wombs. Ask Shelley about *that*, sometime, too, but catch him when he's tranquil. They're the creatures God promised to protect us from when He hung the rainbow in the sky as a sign of his covenant.'

'I thought that was a promise of no more floods.'

'No – did you ever read the Greek version of the flood? Deucalion and Pyrrha?' The carriage shook as it crossed an unevenness in the road, and some of the wine splashed out of Byron's glass on to his shirt front, but he didn't appear to notice.

'Sure. They were the only survivors of the flood, and the oracle told them to repopulate the earth by throwing behind them the bones of their mother; and they figured out that the mother being referred to was the earth, so they threw stones behind them as they walked across the mud,' Crawford's voice was becoming more thoughtful, 'and the stones they threw became humans.'

The image of throwing stones had reminded him of St Stephen, who had been stoned to death, and suddenly he was sure that the phrase *loaves of St Stephen* referred to stones – dangerous stones.

'Almost right,' Byron said. 'That's actually a much older story, which those primeval historians confused with their own stories about a relatively recent flood. The things that the stones turned into *looked* like people – it's mimicry – but they were this other species, the nephelim. The rainbow, I'm told, is a reference to the fact that the nature of sunlight changed sometime, God knows when, and now it's bad for them – in heavy doses it can even crystallize them, freeze them where they stand. They turn into a sort of dirty quartz. Lot's wife was one of these creatures, and that's what happened to her – it wasn't actually salt that she became a pillar of.'

'So quartz crystals repel them because they're . . . bits of dead friends?'

'More than that.' Visibly drunk by now, Byron waved his hand in the air as he groped for an analogy. 'If you were a glass of water in which three dozen spoonfuls of

153

sugar had been dissolved, would you – I don't know – collect rock candy?'

'Uh . . . *oh!* I get it! It might provoke the whole glassful into crystallizing.'

'Exactly. I don't think it's a rig bisque . . . uh, a big risk for them, and I've heard that unless they're diminished they can change to crystal or stone and back again without any . . . with relative impunity, but it does repel them.' He nodded heavily and pointed at Crawford's cup. 'And wine drunk from an amethyst cup, amethyst being a quartz, is a tiny but real first step in freeing yourself. It will help clear you of the fevers those creatures induce – so drink up.' Byron blinked at him owlishly. 'Assuming, that is, that you *want* to be rid of the creature that did this to you.'

Crawford raised the cup, then hesitated; he licked his lips nervously, and his forehead was suddenly chilly with sweat – but a moment later he tilted the cup up and drained it in three big swallows, and held it out for a refill.

'That's a start. You have a family? Brothers, sisters?'

Crawford shook his head.

'No? There's no twin-half, no mirror image, that you're trying to save? Then you must be split yourself – one of the ones who is "like two spent swimmers that do cling together and choke their art."'

Oddly, Crawford found himself remembering the raised figures on the oatcake Josephine had refused to break. He shrugged, then asked, 'Are you a twin of this sister of yours?'

Byron seemed suddenly ill at ease; he answered with an air of duty, as if he owed some degree of honesty to Crawford. 'Well, almost closer than that – it's all my own fault, but it's why Lord Grey is so jealous. These things *are* jealous, you know – they don't want you to love any being but themselves, not even yourself. That must be why they attack families – our families are extensions of us.' He shook his head sombrely. 'Poor Augusta. I've *got* to get free of this creature.'

Though it was just the sort of thing they had come to the Continent to see, few of the English tourists who were clustered on the couches in the lobby of the Hôtel d'Angleterre had succeeded in getting a glimpse of the infamous Lord Byron or his friend Shelley, who habitually listed his occupation as 'atheist' in hotel registers. Rumour had it that the two men were living carnally with two sisters in a house across the lake, but hired boat excursions and rented telescopes had all failed to make the private lives of the pair accessible to the public.

So Polidori found an audience when, over a restorative bottle of mineral water, he began describing how badly his former employer had treated him. Most of his listeners wanted stories to bring home about the daughters of William Godwin, but one young woman pushed through the crowd that jostled around the young physician to ask for more details about the drunk who had caused Polidori to lose his job this morning.

'That was the craziest thing I ever saw Lord Byron do,' declared Polidori, shaking his head. 'This man claimed to be a doctor when we first saw him three weeks ago, a Navy doctor, but *I* got a look at his *passport*. His real name is Michael Aickman, and he's – ' Polidori paused for effect ' – a *veterinarian*.'

Laughter and bemused head-shakings followed this, and then one old fellow revived the laughter by opining that an animal doctor was perhaps the most *appropriate* attendant for such as Byron and Shelley; but the girl who had asked the question turned away, abrupt as a weathervane in a sudden gale, and walked stiffly to the opposite side of the lobby – she sat down on a bench and, in a quick series of tiny releases and catches, lowered her head into her hands.

After several minutes of deep breathing, Josephine Carmody was able to raise her head.

It had been a shock to learn that Michael Crawford was so close – this had to be him, she had tracked him as far as this city – and the shock had now knocked her back, for the first time in nearly two months, into her Josephine personality.

For most of the fifty-seven days since Julia's murder, she had been the woman-shaped machine, thoughtlessly and automatically following Crawford's trail east across France to Switzerland. The machine could sleep in ditches, and eat disgusting food, and earn money by opening its hydraulically powered legs to the occasional well-to-do man who found it attractive, without worrying about what it was doing, or why.

A few times she had been Julia, and that had not been too bad. When she'd been Julia she had had to use her money, any money there might have been, to check into hotels and get cleaned up and buy clothes. Always she had inquired at the desk if there were any messages from her husband, Michael Crawford – and always she was told that there were not any, and she decided to press on and meet him 'at a later point in our itinerary.'

Sometimes when she was Julia she would write cheery notes home to her mother, who had always been a prey to melancholy, and was particularly sad now that her only daughter was married and moving away from home. Julia's father had told her that her mother blamed herself for the death of Julia's twin sister, who had died at birth. Julia thought this was awfully sensitive and motherly of the old darling, but at the same time unrealistic. Why, the whole thing might have turned out so much worse! The second twin could very easily

156

have been born *alive*, but at the expense of Julia's mother's life!

It was the Julia personality that she hoped eventually to occupy for the rest of her life, as soon as Josephine or the machine had succeeded in killing Michael Crawford.

His death had to come first, of course, for she could hardly inhabit a world that also contained the man who had . . . who had done something that it was impossible for her to think about, something to negate Julia's very existence. *A bed soaked in blood, piled with terrible fleshy ruin . . .*

She flailed her mind away from the inadmissible image.

When Crawford was killed and erased from the world, she would be able to relax and be Julia. She knew she could do it – hadn't she had lots of practice?

She touched the lump under her dress that was the pistol, and smiled jerkily. She stood up all in one movement and marched out of the lobby with a precision a soldier might have envied . . . though several men looked after her uneasily, and one small boy burst into tears as she went scissoring past him.

It wasn't until night fell that Crawford began to miss the cold woman.

At first he wasn't sure what was bothering him – he thought it might be the measured thudding of Byron's foil tip against the wooden silhouette on the wall of the dining room, but when Crawford took his wine out on to the balcony and stared down the slope at the darkening lake, it seemed to be the birds and the wind in the orchard that had him on edge. He drained his glass and went back inside for the bottle, but when he had refilled the glass and emptied it twice he knew that it wasn't drunkenness he wanted. And he wasn't hungry, and he wasn't any more worried than usual about his situation.

He was leaning against the railing with increasing pressure, and he wondered if his problem could be simple sexual deprivation . . . and then he knew what it was that was missing. He missed *her*, and the orgasmic amnesia that had for three weeks freed him from his intolerable memories of a boat in heavy surf, and of a burning house, and of an unthinkably mutilated body in a bed.

But she was gone, and had forbidden him to follow her . . . and he didn't want to follow her, anyway. He swore to himself that he didn't.

For the first time in quite a while he thought of Julia, and of how totally he had failed to avenge her – he had, for God's sake, gone to bed with her murderer, and then told Shelley that he wasn't particularly sorry about the way things had worked out.

Rain began spotting the rail and coldly tapping the backs of his hands; he shoved them into his coat pockets, and the fingers of his right hand curled around some small, gritty object. A sudden wind blew the wet hair back from his forehead as he pulled the thing out and turned it over in his palm, but it wasn't until lightning flared distantly out over the lake that he recognized the ancient, rusted nail he had pulled out of the wooden face nine days ago. The nail's head proved to be broad and flat enough for it to stand on the rail with its point toward the sky.

He held his right hand out flat, as though about to lay it on a Bible for the taking of an oath, and then he lowered it until the cold point dented his palm.

He pressed down very slowly, and felt his skin painfully stretch and then abruptly part; and by the time another person's hand slapped his forearm from below, knocking Crawford's hand up and sending the nail spinning away into the darkness, he had been able to feel the iron probing between the metacarpal bones.

He turned and saw Byron behind him, silhouetted against the yellow glow of the windows. Byron had tucked the fencing foil under his arm, and the bell-guard and grip bobbed in front of him now as though he'd been run through.

'No, my friend, believe me, patience is all that's required,' Byron said softly, taking Crawford's left elbow and leading him toward the doors. 'I can assure you that if you'll only wait, the world will flay you much more thoroughly than you ever could yourself.'

Back inside, Byron tossed the foil on to a couch and poured wine into two fresh glasses. A couple of dogs wandered into the high-ceilinged room, followed after a moment by one of Byron's tame monkeys; neither man paid them any attention, and the animals began tossing couch pillows around.

'What were you punishing yourself for?' Byron asked Crawford in a conversational tone as he handed him a glass.

Crawford took it in his right hand, and blood quickly slicked the base and ran unnoticed down his sleeve. He considered the question as he drank. 'Deaths I did nothing to prevent,' he said finally.

Byron grinned, but in such a fellow-soldierly way that Crawford couldn't take offence. 'People close to you?'

'Brother . . . wife . . . and wife.' Crawford took a deep, ragged breath. 'I tell you, seeing that thing, that vampire, recede . . . is like watching a tide recede from some evil waterfront. All the horrible old skeletons and wrecks and deformed creatures are exposed to the sun and the air, and you would rather have drowned in the high tide – than lived to see these terrible things again.'

'You're a fugitive?'

Crawford considered lying, but then decided that sometimes one fugitive could trust another. He nodded.

'And a genuine doctor?'

Crawford nodded again. 'The veterinary story, the whole Michael Aickman identity, is . . . a pose. My real name is – '

Byron shook his head. 'I don't want to know.'

The monkey had snatched both of the cushions and climbed up on to the back of the couch, to the noisy outrage of the dogs. A tall, burly man strode into the room, saw the disturbance and crossed to the couch.

'Damn it, Byron, you're running a bestial pandemonium here!' he called, having to speak loudly because the monkey was protesting his attempts to take the cushions away.

'That's old news, Hobby,' replied Byron. 'Ask any of the tourists at the d'Angleterre.' He limped back to the table and poured a third glass and held it out to the newcomer. 'This is my new medical man, by the way – Michael, this is John Cam Hobhouse – John, Michael Aickman.'

'Got rid of that idiot Polidori, did you? Good work.' Hobhouse pried both cushions out of the monkey's grip and pitched them through the open doorway. The animals all scrambled after them in a rush, and the room was suddenly quieter. He took the glass and sat down on the couch and stared at Crawford. 'Do you write poetry? Dramas?'

The question surprised Crawford, for during the past couple of months he *had* found himself composing verses in his head – it always happened at night, while he was waiting for sleep to take him, and it was always as involuntary as the jerking of a limb during a dream of falling; but he hadn't written any of the verses down, so he shook his head. 'Not me.'

'Thank God.'

'Hobhouse has always been a steadying influence on me,' said Byron. 'He kept me out of scandals when we were adolescents at Cambridge, and two weeks ago he

160

came here all the way from England just to chase Claire Clairmont away.'

Hobhouse laughed. 'I'm honoured if my arrival had that effect.'

'Hobby was even groomsman at my wedding, and it certainly wasn't *his* fault that I turned out to be marrying a modern Clytemnestra.'

Crawford recalled that, in Aeschylus's *Orestia*, Clytemnestra had been the wife and murderess of Agamemnon. 'Some of us just shouldn't attempt marriage,' he said with a smile.

Byron looked at him sharply. After a moment he said, 'I'm about ready to leave Switzerland . . . move on south to Italy. How does that sound to you?'

The idea made Crawford obscurely uncomfortable, as Byron seemed to have known it would. 'I . . . don't know,' Crawford said. He glanced through the window into the night. *I can't*, had been his first thought; *this is where she'll come looking for me, when she comes back.*

His face reddened as he realized it, and he reminded himself that he wanted to be *rid* of her – wanted, as a matter of fact, to stay here for a while to test Byron's idea that the nephelim shackles could be shaken off in the high Alps.

'But before we go,' Byron went on, 'I want to take a tour of the Bernese Alps. I spent a day on Mont Blanc recently with Hobhouse and another friend, but I don't yet feel that I've really made the . . . beneficial acquaintance of these mountains.' He winked at Crawford, as though to imply that there was a meaning in his words that was for Crawford alone. 'Hobhouse tells me he's free to come along for the trip – are you?'

Crawford exhaled with relief. 'Yes,' he said, trying to sound casual.

Byron nodded. 'You're wiser than Shelley. I think the only way to be quit of the sirens is to answer the call, go

161

right up into their pre-Adamite castles, and then by the grace of God come back down alive and sane. To go back without having done that is to . . . come to terms with an illness, rather than get a cure.'

Hobhouse snorted impatiently at what he clearly considered to be a snatch of poetic nonsense – but Crawford, who knew something about illness and cures, shivered and gulped his wine.

Chapter 9

The stones are sealed across their places;
One shadow is shed on all their faces,
One blindness cast on all their eyes.

— A. C. Swinburne

The rain continued throughout the next day, and it seemed to Crawford that Byron spent most of the day limping up and down the damp stone stairs and shouting at people; the irascible lord found fault with the way the servants were packing his clothes, and he kept changing his mind about what dainties he wanted the cook to stock the travelling-basket with and, having splashed through the courtyard to the stables, he swore aloud at the grooms' perverse inability to grasp his instructions about how the horses should be harnessed.

Crawford, who had encountered such masters on shipboard, expected to see in the servants' faces the resentful stubbornness that promised slow and minimal work, but Byron's servants just rolled their eyes and grinned and tried to follow their employer's most recent instructions; clearly Byron inspired at least as much loyalty as irritation among them.

The following morning dawned sunny, and the touring party managed to set out at seven o'clock. Crawford sat with Byron and Hobhouse and Byron's valet in a big, open charabanc carriage, rocking sleepily on the cold leather upholstery and blinking back through the dappled sunlight at the grooms and servants who were bringing along the saddle horses. Crawford was glad the monkey had been left behind.

All day they travelled eastward along the road that skirted the north shore of the lake, and when dusk had claimed all of the landscape except the distant rose-lit peaks of Mont Blanc and the Aiguille d'Argentières, they stopped for the night at an inn in the port village of Ouchy, just below the blocked-out piece of sky where the lights and spires of Lausanne fretted the slope of Mont Jurat. Byron retired early, but the sheets on his bed proved to be damp, and he spent ten minutes swearing and stripping them off and flinging them around before he finally wrapped himself up in a blanket and returned to bed.

The company was up, if grumbling, at five the next morning, and they were all dressed and fed and mounted and clattering away eastward while the workmen around the quay were still shovelling up frozen horse-droppings in the shadows of dawn; and only the highest pastures had begun to glow emerald in the peak-descending sunlight when the travellers, who had been aware of the dark face of the lake edging higher and higher up the embankment at their right, found the road ahead of them sheened with water, so that the trees bordering the right side of it seemed to have grown up out of the lake in single file, a sunrise phenomenon as wondrous as the rings of mushrooms Crawford remembered finding on dewy lawns when he was a boy in Scotland. To make the carriage lighter in case a wheel should find a submerged pothole, Crawford and Byron and Hobhouse got out and rode horses, and the horses' hooves, splashing in the fetlock-deep water, made a wake that stretched far out across the brightening lake.

They spent that night at Clarens, on the east shore of the lake, and on the next day they hired pack mules and started into the mountains.

* * *

Breakfast was a stop under the pine trees on the slopes of Mont Davant. One of the servants started a fire and made a pot of coffee, and paper-wrapped pieces of last night's chicken were passed around by Byron's valet, and Byron himself circulated among the crouching company with a magnum bottle of cold white wine, filling up any cups that had been emptied of coffee.

Byron eventually sat down on a sunlit heap of brown pine needles near where Crawford was trying, for the first time in at least a week, to shave.

Even though he had nothing but cold water, Crawford had managed to work up some lather from the cake of soap he'd borrowed from Hobhouse, and now he was carefully drawing a straight razor down his lean cheek. He had propped a small mirror on a fallen black branch that lay against a trunk, and after every slow razor-stroke he peered curiously at his reflection. Because of the altitude, or perhaps the early morning wine, his own face looked less familiar, and more like the face of some imbecile, every time he glanced at it.

When he was done he wiped his face on his coat-tail and took one last look in the mirror. By now he couldn't recognize himself at all, and the visage in the mirror seemed to be nothing more than a bumpy blob of flesh with eyes and holes and dots of blood arranged randomly on it. He pondered it thoughtfully for several minutes.

'Did you ever notice,' he asked Byron finally, 'how foolish your face looks?'

Byron glanced sharply up from his wine, obviously startled and angry. 'No, Mister Aickman,' he said, 'how foolish *does* my face look?'

'No no, I mean if you stare at your own face for long enough it stops looking familiar – or even like any face at all. It's the same effect you get if you repeat your name over and over again; pretty soon the name sounds like nothing but frog croaks.' Crawford waved, a bit drunkenly, at the mirror. 'I've been shaving, here, and now I can't recognize myself at all.'

He was glad he had had several glasses of wine, for he found the bestial face in the mirror obscurely frightening.

Still frowning, Byron took the mirror and stared into it for nearly a full minute; finally he shook his head and handed it back. 'It doesn't work for me – though sometimes I wish I *could* fail to recognize myself.' He sipped his wine. 'And it would certainly be a relief to be able to hear the syllables "By-ron" without . . .' He made a fist.

'Without having to take it personally,' Crawford suggested. 'Without it being a . . . call to the battlements.'

Byron grinned, and it occurred to Crawford for the first time that the poet was younger than himself. Crawford dropped the mirror into his jacket pocket and got up to return Hobhouse's soap and razor.

They were attacked an hour later, when the road had become so steep that everybody had had to get out of the carriage and ride or walk, and even the baggage had been taken out of the boot and strapped on to the backs of the mules. Crawford was riding one of the saddle horses, alternately warmed and chilled as the horse climbed through slanting bars of sunlight and tree-shadow; ahead of him swayed one of the baggage-laden mules, and beyond it rode Byron, leading the plodding procession.

The horses moved slowly, audibly sniffing the cold air from time to time, though Crawford could smell only morning-damp earth and pine needles.

Crawford, still a little drunk, was singing a song that old des Loges had sung interminably on that day, nearly two months ago now, when Crawford had pulled him in a wagon from Carnac to Auray and back. The song, which of course Crawford knew only in des Loges's debased dialect, recounted how badly the songwriter had been treated by the woman he loved.

After the first stanza had gone ringing away through the pine trees that towered up from the slopes above and below them, Byron reined in his horse to listen; and when Crawford came to a stanza in which the singer compared himself to laundry beaten on rocks in a stream, Byron let the mule pass him and then edged his own horse between Crawford's and the road's edge, so that he could comfortably talk to Crawford as they rode.

'Who set Villon to music?' Byron asked.

Crawford had heard of the fifteenth-century poet François Villon, but he'd never read him. 'I didn't even know that's who wrote it,' he said. 'I learned the song from an old madman in France.'

'It's the "Double Ballade" from *The Testament*,' said Byron thoughtfully. 'I'm not sure I ever really paid attention to it before. Do you remember the rest?'

'I think so.'

Crawford began the next verse – which lamented the fact that even the penalties for practising witchcraft wouldn't deter young men from pursuing women like the one that ruined the singer – but suddenly and for no apparent reason his heart was pounding, and a dew of sweat had sprung out on his temples.

The wine, he thought – or the disquieting lyrics of the song.

Then the path shook to a heavy, splintering crash on the uphill slope at their right, and Crawford heard branches snapping and drifts of pine needles hissing like fire as something big came sliding down toward him.

Byron had just grabbed the reins of Crawford's horse and tried to pull both of them back, out of the path of whatever was tumbling down the slope, when the thing roared like an earthquake and sprang at them.

Dazzled by the blue sky, Crawford wasn't able to see the thing until, in midair, it erupted from the shadows – then he got an instant's glimpse of a mad-faced, eyeless giant before the thing collided with him and punched him right out of the saddle.

The downhill slope was steep, and Crawford fell through four yards of chilly air before he hit the muddy slope; but he landed feet first and slid, and so it was his feet and legs and rump that took the worst of the beating against the low branches and upward-projecting rocks; and when he finally jolted to a stop against a tree trunk dozens of yards down the slope, flayed and wrenched and whooping with the effort of getting air into his abused lungs, he was at least still conscious and not badly broken physically.

They were in the mountain's shadow, and even after he had brushed the leaves and dirt and blood out of his face, it took several seconds for Crawford's eyes to adjust to the cathedral dimness; he *heard*, more than watched, as the roped-together bundle of luggage rolled noisily down the slope, finally stopping with an expensive-sounding internal crash against a tree trunk. After that, all he could hear was the diminishing rattle of dislodged dirt-clods tumbling away far below.

His breathing was a confusion of hiccups and frightened sobs. He was trying hard to believe that the rushing bulk had been a boulder, and wishing passionately that he had stayed back down in the lowlands.

He was cramped in tension, his nerves uselessly braced for some crushing, malevolent impact; it didn't come, and after several seconds he cautiously let himself relax a little.

He hitched himself up to a less painful position and looked around for Byron. After a few moments he saw him, perched on a rock above Crawford and to his left, chewing his knuckle and staring down at him.

'Aickman,' Byron said, just loudly enough for his voice to carry across the abraded slope, 'it's important that you do exactly as I say – do you understand that?'

Crawford's stomach was suddenly icy, and his muscles had tightened up again. He managed to squeeze the word '*Yes*,' out of his rigid lungs.

'Don't move – if you move, it'll get you. You can't slide away faster than it can jump on to you.' Byron stretched and reached under his jacket.

'Where,' said Crawford stiffly, 'is . . . it?'

Byron had drawn his pistol, and was looking closely at the leaves and dirt around him, as if he'd dropped something. 'It's – do keep calm now – it's right over your head. I suppose you could look, if you can do it slowly.'

Crawford felt drops of sweat run down his ribs under his shirt as he slowly forced the muscles of his neck to tilt his head up; he saw the upper slope, bristling with trees that obstructed a view of the road, and then he saw the outer branches of the tree he was braced against, and finally he gathered his tattered courage and looked straight up.

And it took all of his self-control not to recoil or scream, and he was distantly resentful that he couldn't just die in this instant.

The thing was clinging upside down to the trunk, its projecting snout only a few feet above his face. It had no eyes, nor even eye sockets, and its corrugated grey hide and anvil-shaped face were anything but mobile, but he could tell that he had excited its profoundest attention. A mouth opened under the snout, exposing teeth like petrified plates of tree fungus, and the creature began to stretch its neck downward.

'Lower your head,' called Byron tensely.

Crawford did, trying hard not to be sudden about it, and he let the motion sweep his gaze across Byron's perch. Byron was kneeling up on the rock and aiming his pistol in Crawford's direction, and Crawford saw that a stumpy section of tree branch was now projecting from the muzzle.

'God help us both,' Byron whispered, and then he screwed his eyes tightly shut and pulled the trigger.

The deafening bang and the spray of splinters struck Crawford simultaneously, and he convulsed and lost his balance and slid away from the tree; and though he was able to dig his fingers and toes into the dirt and drag to a stop five yards farther down the slope, he couldn't make himself lift his head until he heard the creature fall heavily out of the tree and then begin to crawl uphill, away from him.

The thing, he saw then, was moving slowly on all fours toward Byron, lifting its long legs high over its body with each step, as if it were crawling through deep mud, and audibly snuffing the air with its upraised, elongated face. The young lord had stood up on his rock and was waiting for it, his spent pistol gripped clubwise in a white fist, his face even paler than normal but resolute. Crawford wondered why he wasn't scrambling back uphill, and then remembered his lameness.

People were calling now from up on the road, but Crawford was busy digging a fist-sized rock out of the slope, and he had no breath to answer them. The effort of flinging it upward made him slide another yard downhill, but he had thrown accurately — the stone thudded against the nightmarishly broad back of the creature.

He coughed out a hoarse cry of triumph — which became a grating curse when he saw that he had not even slowed the monster down.

'Save yourself, Aickman,' said Byron in a voice that was flat with control.

With despair Crawford realized that he was not going to obey. His heart was still pounding alarmingly in his ribcage, and he knew he could accomplish nothing, but he began climbing uphill after the slow, snuffling, misshapen thing.

Peripherally he noticed a silent flare of green above him and to his right, and he paused to look.

It was morning sunlight in the top branches of a pine tree; dawn was finally, belatedly, coming to this west-facing mountainside. Beyond the tree was a slanting ridge that stood higher than the rest of the slope, and on the humped spine of it dew glinted dazzlingly in the brown carpet of pine needles.

He shifted to look back at Byron and the monster, and something jabbed him painfully in the side; he reached into his coat pocket and pulled out an uneven fragment of his broken shaving mirror.

And an idea came to him. *The nature of sunlight changed sometime*, Byron had told him four days ago when they'd been discussing the nephelim, *and now it's bad for them*; and Crawford remembered, too, stories he'd heard in childhood about trolls who turned to stone at the first glint of dawn, and vampires that had to retreat into the earth to hide from the sun . . . and he remembered that Perseus had found a mirror useful in defeating Medusa.

He tucked the mirror fragment back into his pocket and resumed his scrambling crawl – but he was moving toward the sunlit ridge now, away from Byron and the monster.

Behind him he could hear Byron calling taunts at the indomitable thing, but Crawford didn't look back until he had reached the ridge and climbed up the projecting tree roots on to the rounded hump of it.

He was in sunlight now, and he fumbled the broken

pieces of mirror out of his pocket and held up the biggest piece – but he could no longer make out Byron or the creature in the dimness below him. In panicky haste he caught the sun in the glass and began sweeping the bright spot of reflected glare back and forth across the shadowed hillside.

He heard the earthquake-roar again at one point, and with desperate hope he jerked the spot of light back to where it had just been – and though it was what he had hoped for, he shuddered to see that terrible head turn slowly toward him, and he nearly flung the piece of mirror away. The thing in the light shook its head and resumed climbing, flexing and stretching its long legs in the air – Crawford could now see Byron, only a few yards above the advancing form – but Crawford forced his hand not to shake, and to hold the spot of light in the centre of the broad back.

The thing stopped again, and again the trees shook to a roar that was like a mountain shifting on its hell-foundationed base. Now the figure turned around and began ponderously levering its bulk across the slope toward Crawford.

He almost dropped the mirror and ran. Smoke-coloured slabs of tooth were bared in what was unmistakably outraged fury, and its pincers were tearing up head-sized chunks of dirt, and even splitting stones, as it advanced toward him; and he knew that physical damage was not by any means the worst thing to be feared when facing such an entity as this. But he held his ground and forced his bladder to stay tight and kept the light centred on the thing's neck . . . where he could now see a torn spot, probably where Byron's branch-missile had struck it.

The thing was getting closer, and the shifting roar of its breathing now sounded like a distant, valley-filling orchestra; was the thing *singing*? Crawford found himself following the theme, and the tragic grandeur of it caught at the breath in his throat; lyrics sprang spontaneously into his mind, coruscating tapestries of language as intricate as the depths of an opal, and it seemed to him that this must be some antediluvian march composed by sentient planets to celebrate a wedding of suns.

But the music was fading, as if a wind had sprung up between himself and the vast but far-distant orchestra. The long-legged thing was only a few yards away now, but it was moving much more slowly, and it seemed to Crawford that a gold and purple aura was flickering around its head; and at last with an audible crack it froze.

For several taut seconds it continued to stare eyelessly at him while he held the light on its neck.

And at last it tipped, slowly at first and then with a massive rush, and its shoulders jarred the earth several yards downslope and then it was just a tumbling statue breaking up as it receded away, more audibly than visibly, below them.

When the crashing racket had diminished to silence, Crawford could hear someone clambering down the slope above them, and soon he heard Hobhouse shouting angrily.

'Here we are, Hobby,' called Byron, his voice quavering only slightly. 'And the luggage is wedged against a tree down here. Did the horses fall too?'

'Damn you for not answering before,' yelled Hobhouse, grudging relief evident in his tone. 'Yes, one horse fell, but not far and he's not hurt. What was that roaring? And what did you shoot at?'

Crawford had climbed, much more slowly and carefully now, halfway to Byron's perch, and when he looked up he saw the young lord wink at him. 'Some species of mountain lion, I believe!' A frown crossed his haggard face for a moment, and he called, 'Don't tell

173

them about it back in England, there's a good lad! Hey?
No sense worrying poor Augusta.'

Soon Crawford had joined Byron on his rock, and
from there he could see men hopping down the mountainside on a rope.

Byron held out his hand, which Crawford now
noticed was torn and bloody. 'Earn your keep, doctor.'

Crawford took his hand and looked at the ragged
wound. 'What did you catch it on?' he asked, proud that
he could speak levelly.

'Our . . . assailant,' Byron said. 'Before you managed
to get your reflector working, that thing got up here. I
pushed him back, and he slid down a little, but . . . he
got his teeth into me.' His smile was brightly bitter.
'Redundant, in my case, of course . . . but this confirms
my resolve to divest myself entirely of the connection,
in the' – he swept his bloody hand in a gesture that
encompassed the entirety of the Alps – 'in the high
places.'

Crawford looked down at the stump of his own
wedding ring finger, on which the bite scar was still
visible, and he tried, with at least some success, to be
glad that he was going along.

Byron developed a fever as they continued up the
mountain and the sun burned its slow arc across the
empty vault of the sky, and when they reached snow he
took delight in showing Crawford how the sweat from
his forehead, falling on a snowbank, made 'the same
dints as in a sieve.' Several times he slipped and fell on
the ice, and Hobhouse, clearly alarmed, kept throwing
glances of suspicion at Crawford – who, doubtless
because of the thinner air, was beginning to feel a little
dizzy and disoriented himself.

Byron, though, was full of hectic cheer; at one point
he gaily called Hobhouse's attention to a shepherd

playing upon a pipe in a sky-bordering meadow across the valley – 'just like the ones we saw in Arcadia fifteen years ago . . . though, now I recollect it, they all carried muskets instead of crooks, and had their belts full of pistols' – and later, when their guide asked them to cross one mountain ledge in a hurry because of the danger of falling rocks, Byron just laughed and asked Hobhouse if he remembered the crowd of Greek workmen he had seen in 1810, who wouldn't carry an ancient statue to Lord Elgin's ship because they swore they'd heard the statue sobbing at the prospect of being sent across the water.

He seemed to recover himself for a little while at the peak of Mont Davant, from which vantage point they could see most of Lake Leman far below them to the west, Lake Neufchatel to the north and, ahead of them in the east, the remote, towering, patriarchal peaks of the canton of Bern.

He and Crawford had wandered away from the rest of the group, and were standing on a wind-scoured rock outcrop above the plateau of powder snow. Both men were sweating and shivering.

'You lied, I think,' remarked Byron in the echoless silence of the sky, 'when you told Hobhouse that you don't write poetry – hmm?'

Crawford, nervous about the abyss overhead, sat down and gripped the rock with damp hands. 'Not precisely,' he managed to answer. 'I haven't *written* any – but I do find myself building . . . verses, images, metaphors, in my head, when I'm half asleep.'

Byron nodded. 'These creatures aren't especially good visually, but they are purely matches in a powder keg when it comes to language. I wonder how many of the world's great writers have owed their gift to the . . . ultimately disastrous attentions of the nephelim.' His laughter was light and sarcastic. 'And I wonder how many of them *would* have freed themselves, if they could have.'

Crawford was sick, and he wasn't letting himself think about all the narrow ledges and steep climbs that lay between him and normal ground — and he was still trembling from their encounter with one of Byron's precious nephelim that morning, and didn't relish hearing anything even remotely good about the creatures. 'I wonder if that was mistletoe,' he snapped.

Byron blinked at him. 'If what was?'

'The twig you shot at that beast this morning. Isn't that what Balder the Beautiful was killed with, in the Norse myths? A dart made of mistletoe? I guess that makes you Loki, Odin's evil brother.'

Byron frowned, and Crawford wondered if he could actually be feeling bad about having shot at that monstrosity this morning.

'Balder,' Byron said softly. 'You're right, a wooden stake killed him. Christ! Do all of our most affecting legends, as well as our literature, derive from these devils?' He shook his head and looked down the west side of the mountain, and Crawford knew he was thinking of the hideous statue that lay shattered in the bottom of a ravine far below them.

Finally Byron looked up and met Crawford's gaze. 'Loki came to a bad end, didn't he?' Byron said. 'But I'm afraid his is the only example we can follow with any self-respect.' He shivered and started back toward the others.

When the innkeeper handed her back her passport, Julia Carmody hoped that she could now let her phantom sister lie dormant in her head until . . . until the day when the sister would emerge, do what she had to do, and then disappear forever.

Julia had had to be Josephine two days ago in order

to pick up the bank draft from her father at the Poste Restante in Geneva, and tonight, here in Clarens, getting a room had required that she show her passport; but she didn't want to touch the passport again until she was crossing international boundaries on the way home to Bexhill-on-Sea. And she didn't *ever* want to think about the anguished note that had accompanied the bank draft.

With luck she'd be home comfortably before Christmas, and her father would accept the way things were, or had turned out to be, and then she would be Julia for the rest of her life, and she could expunge the name and identity of Josephine from her memory.

A boy carried her bags upstairs, and when he had opened the door to her room she took only the hastiest glance inside, for she knew in advance what she would see – the same disgraceful thing she had seen in every rented room she'd been in since the twenty-first of July, her wedding day – and she had her sentence of French prepared.

'Oh!' she exclaimed after her first glimpse of the bed. '*Mon Dieu! Voulez-vous changer les draps!*' The sheets, as she had known they would be, were grossly blotted with dried blood.

The boy, of course, pretended to see nothing wrong with the sheets, but she gave him a handful of francs to have them changed anyway. A harassed-looking chambermaid was summoned, and when she had changed the offending bedclothes and departed, Julia opened the lake-facing window and lay down on the bed.

At dusk a wind from the mountains brought rain, and the rattle of it in the drainpipes woke her up. The room was dark and the curtains were flapping against the dark sky –

– And she couldn't remember who she was.

She was empty, a staring-eyed vacuum, and it was horrible. Dimly her body knew that there were several personalities who inhabited its head from time to time, and now it wanted one of them, any one of them, to appear; the throat buzzed with a sort of beseeching whimper . . . and suddenly, as if it was a gift from outside itself, the body had grateful access to language.

'*Come,*' it croaked. '*Come in. I'm open to you. I need you.*'

Personality animated the body then – she was Julia again, but she was worried about this new development. Would this recur, this blankness? And could she count on it always being the Julia personality who would step in to fill the vacancy? Would it –

'Good evening, Julia,' came a soft voice from the window side of the room.

She whirled in that direction with a gasp, and saw a bulky silhouette against the emerging stars; and she knew instantly that the Julia personality had not been the only entity that had responded to her body's desperate invitation.

Oddly, she wasn't frightened. 'Good evening,' she said hesitantly. 'Can I . . . light the lamp?'

The figure chuckled – from its voice she knew it was masculine. 'Of course.'

She opened her tinderbox and struck the flint and steel over the lamp's wick, and yellow light grew and filled the room. She turned around to face her visitor.

He was a big, burly man with a prominent nose, and he was dressed, astonishingly, in the most formal court habit – a purple frockcoat with gold embroidery, a jabot and cravat, white silk stockings and black pumps. Awed, she curtsied.

He bowed and crossed to her, and though he limped, and winced when he reached out for her hand, his eyes were kind when he lifted her hand to his full lips.

'I can help you,' he said, still holding her hand, 'with

178

. . . what you're here for. I can lead you to the man you want to find. He was protected against you before, but his protector is in another country now.' He shook his head; the motion seemed to hurt him, and Josephine saw red lines like veins or cracks on the skin of his neck. 'I wasn't going to disobey her, and hurt him – I just wanted to *look* at him – but he and his friend hurt me, terribly. So I'll help you.'

He released her hand and limped across to the bed and lay down on it. Julia looked at the hand he'd kissed, and realized that the new sheets were fated to go the way of the first set, for blood was dripping energetically from a bite on the knuckles.

Her heart was hammering in her breast, and before she went to join him she turned away to catch her breath. The lamplight had grown brighter, and had made a dark mirror of the window panes, but she had been avoiding looking at her own reflection ever since her identity had started to become fragile two months ago, so she pulled the curtains across the glass. She didn't notice that, in the reflection, she was alone in the room except for a fragment of broken statuary on the bed.

Chapter 10

We talk of Ghosts; neither Lord Byron or M. G. L[ewis] seem to believe in them; and they both agree, in the very face of reason, that none could believe in ghosts without also believing in God. I do not think that all the persons who profess to discredit these visitations really discredit them, or, if they do in the daylight, are not admonished by the approach of loneliness and midnight to think more respectably of the world of shadows.

— Percy Bysshe Shelley, 17 July 1816

For the next two days Byron's touring party moved uneventfully east through the Enhault and Simmenthal valleys, and on Sunday the twenty-second of September they crossed the Lake of Thoun to Neuhause and then resumed the horses and carriage for the fourteen-mile trip east through Interlaken and south to the village of Wengen, which lay at the foot of the range that included the Kleine Scheidegg, the Wengern, and beyond them, the more than cloud-tall Jungfrau.

The sky was darkening and overcast by the time they found rooms at the house of the local curate, but Byron insisted on saddling a horse and going for a closer look at the mountains while there was still any light at all, and so Hobhouse, Crawford and a guide mounted up to accompany him.

From the cobblestoned road outside the vicarage they could see a waterfall bisecting the dark wall of the mountains, seeming to be more cloud than water in the distance; the slowly swaying column stood nearly a thousand feet from its mist-hidden base to its skyey source, and Byron shuddered and said it looked like the tail of the pale horse on which death is mounted in the Apocalypse. With that observation he galloped away up the road, leaving the other three to follow.

Rain swept over them after they'd gone only a few miles, but it wasn't until the thunder began frightening the horses that Byron would listen to Hobhouse's demands that they turn around.

Byron was in a wild mood, and because the man was his patient Crawford rode beside him. Byron was waving his cane over his head — which alarmed Crawford, for it was a new sword cane, and Byron had refused to let the guide carry it for fear that it might draw lightning — and he was shouting verses into the rain.

Twice Crawford recognized phrases he had heard in his dreams.

Hobhouse's cloak turned out to be anything but waterproof, and so they left him in a cottage and rode on toward the curate's house to get a man to bring him back an umbrella and a stauncher cloak.

A flare of lightning lit the valley at the same instant that thunder cannoned against the mountains, and Byron stood up in the stirrups to brandish his cane at the sky. He looked across at Crawford and laughed to see him cringing in his saddle.

'Tomorrow we'll climb to the peaks, never mind what the weather is,' Byron yelled over the rain. After a moment he added, 'Do you believe in God, Aickman?'

Crawford shrugged miserably; his own cloak was not much better than Hobhouse's. 'I don't know,' he called back. 'Do you?'

Byron settled back on to the saddle. 'I'm an agnostic with option to buy,' he said. 'But I can't see how . . . I mean, can there be supernatural phenomena without there being, too, a God? — In the *absence* of any God?'

Crawford bleakly reviewed the course of his own life, especially the last two months of it. 'I'm afraid,' he called finally, not at all happy with the answer he had come to, 'that the more absences there are, the more things are possible. And so if there's an absence the size of *God*, then there probably isn't *anything* so appalling that we can count on not meeting it.'

His statement seemed to sober Byron. 'It's just as well you chose to disguise yourself as a veterinarian, Aickman,' he called through the rain. 'You'd have made an alarming philosopher.' He spurred his horse and rode on, leading the way back to the curate's house.

The figure silhouetted against the yellow light from the open door proved to be the curate himself, and when the travellers had dismounted he curtly asked to see Byron and Crawford alone in his room.

'Some problem about the fee, I expect,' muttered Byron as the two of them hung up their wet cloaks and followed the old man up the stairs; but Crawford had seen the look of distaste and sorrow on the lean, wrinkled face, and he wondered if they were all simply going to be thrown out, as he had been from the rooming house near Geneva eight days ago.

The old clergyman's room was right up under the steeply slanted roof, with a very low wall on one side and a high one on the other, and the windows that ran at ankle height along the low side were so small that Crawford guessed a lamp was necessary here even on the sunniest day. Rows of old leather book spines along shelves on the high wall seemed to blot up the light from the old man's lamp as he set it down on a low table and then lowered himself on to the narrow bed and waved toward two chairs at the other end of the room.

'I . . . did not know who you were,' said the old clergyman, speaking English with a heavy German accent, 'when you came here. I would not have let you stay.' Byron had just sat down, and now pushed his chair back to stand up again, but the old man raised his hand. 'You may stay now, I will not turn you out. But I have heard from the people about you – you, *besonders*,' he added, looking at Crawford.

'Means "especially,"' put in Byron helpfully. 'What did they tell you about us? That old incest story again? Those girls *weren't* sisters, you know – Mary Godwin had entirely different parents than the Clairmont girl, even if they do both have the same stepfather. And in any case, is it really worth the effort of your disapproval? These are things that every day occur.'

'This is nothing to do with . . . plain carnal congresses,' the old curate said. 'Worse stories are about. The people tell me that you have dealings with . . . unheavenly spirits, the things which walk the valley of the shade of death.'

'A nice phrase,' said Byron, grinning. 'I like it. So we've sinned against your . . . *ordinances*? Prove it and punish us, if you can.'

The old man shook his head wearily. 'The mountains, the high places, are not the path to redemption now, not anymore. That was long ago – and dangerous even then. Salvation, redemption, are now to be found through the sacraments.' He turned to Crawford, and his lined old face was rigid, as if with the effort of concealing his loathing. 'Even such as *you* might be able, through them, to escape damnation.'

Byron laughed uneasily. 'Don't be so hard on the lad, Father, he's not nearly as bad as all that. My God, you're eyeing him as if you think he'll steal the gold chalices off your altar.'

'Or turn the wine in them to vinegar,' said Crawford, his voice quiet with anger, 'just with a look. Is this Christian charity as it's practised in Bern?' He stood up, rapping his head against the low ceiling. 'The Church has become a more . . . *exclusive club* since the founder's day, it's clear. No doubt the Devil is more hospitable.'

'Wait,' said the curate, 'sit. I want to see you in Paradise, but I also want to see all my parishioners there. If you go to the mountains now, in the state you're in, things will be roused that will do none of my people any good.' He nodded to Crawford. 'Another like you is already in the Alps, but I can do nothing about him, and in any case he's keeping to the low passes and travelling only at night . . .'

He had slowly lifted the stopper from a decanter of brandy on a shelf by the bed, and he turned toward a row of glasses beside it. 'Will you stay down here, away from the mountains? I can promise you redemption, if you truly want it – and I can promise you death, if you persist in your course. You have not ever had better counsel than what I am saying.'

Crawford sat down, a little mollified, but he shook his head. 'No. I'm going up there.'

Byron nodded agreement. 'I don't get dissuaded from my courses by this kind of counsel.'

The curate closed his eyes for a moment, then shrugged and poured the brandy into three of the glasses. He stood up to hand one to each of his guests, and then hobbled back to the bed and sat down.

Behind him a human shadow appeared on the wooden panelling of the wall, though there was no form casting it. The dim silhouette shook its head slowly, and then faded.

Crawford's heart was thumping, and he looked at Byron; Byron's eyes were wide – clearly he'd seen it too. Both of them put their glasses down on the floor.

'None for me, thanks,' said Crawford, standing up.

'Me neither,' said Byron, who had already got to the door and opened it.

The old man was quietly sobbing on his bed as they drew the door closed behind them, and Crawford wondered if he was repenting having tried to poison his guests, or sorry that the attempt had failed.

On the way back to where Hobhouse waited they passed a big, six-wheeled wagon that had got bogged down in the sudden mud. Byron, still in his wild, contentious mood, insisted that they get out and push, even though the wagon seemed to have at least a dozen torch-carrying attendants who were already labouring at it, and so he and Crawford and the servant got off their horses and dug their heels into the mud and helped shove at the thing.

The attendants didn't seem grateful for the help, especially when Byron got up into the bed of the wagon to direct the work, but they put up with it until the wagon was rolling again, then made Byron get down and whipped up the horses and resumed their southward progress.

'Coals to Newcastle,' laughed Byron as he got back on to his horse.

'How's that?' asked Crawford wearily, wishing his boots weren't now full of cold mud.

'The big box they've got in the back of that is full of ice – it leaked on my hands when I leaned against it – and they're heading into the Alps.'

At seven o'clock the next morning they set out toward the mountains again, fortified with coffee and brandy – their own – against the eternal chill that made fragile cloud-plumes of human speech and then snatched them away into the cobalt sky. Crawford and the guide were on mules, while Byron and Hobhouse rode horses.

The waterfall was now glowing in sunlight; Byron called attention to the rainbow that hovered around it like a halo, but Hobhouse sniffed and said he wasn't impressed with a rainbow that had only two distinct colours in it.

'At least they're regal colours, Hobby,' said Byron, and only Crawford heard the tremor in his voice. 'Purple and gold, after all.'

The mountains themselves were too big — too high and distant and vastly jagged — for Crawford to comprehend; looking at them was like looking through a telescope at the alien features of the moon. It was only the unnaturally clear air of this high country that let these sights be visible in such awful totality — back down there behind the travellers, in the zones where mankind flourished, hazes and mists and smokes mercifully limited the extents of human sight. As the hooves clopped along the uphill stone path toward the feet of the sky-spanning peaks, Crawford kept catching himself thinking of the mountains as ancient, living entities, and he was nervously reminded of the story of Semele, the human mother of Dionysus, who was struck dead by the sight of Zeus in his undisguised, inhuman glory.

The sun blazed on the expanses of snow and ice, and by midmorning they had all donned blue-tinted goggles to protect themselves from snow-blindness.

The oily scent of the pines was diminishing as the travellers got higher, like the taste of juniper in a glass of gin that's being refilled with icy vodka, and Crawford thought that all smells, and even the ability of the air to carry them, would soon be among the things he and the others had left behind. The pines they were passing now were all withered and stripped of bark, and Byron stared at them sombrely and said that they reminded him of himself and his family.

Crawford thought the remark was a little too affected and theatrical, a little too *Byronic*, to be genuine, and he wondered if Byron himself could always distinguish between his own emotions and his poses.

The road grew steeper, and at one point they had to angle across the path of a recent avalanche; no trees still stood in the wide, swept-looking track of it and, blinking up the slope at the inaccessible steepnesses from which it had come, Crawford was surprised to see a broad silvery vein glittering in a freshly exposed stone face. He asked the guide about it, and the man answered, uncomfortably, that it was the *argent de l'argile*, or silver from clay, and that in a day or two it would have withdrawn back into the body of the mountain.

After a thoughtful pause, Crawford asked if it was a particularly lightweight metal, but the guide just turned away and began pointing out peaks ahead of them.

Soon they were moving in single file along narrow switchback ledges up the face of the Wengern, and Crawford discovered that his mule behaved as though it were carrying its usual width-tripling bales of cargo – the beast plodded along the very precipice edges of the paths to avoid snagging its nonexistent baggage against the mountain wall. No amount of yanking or swearing could make the beast move in closer to the wall and, after an hour or so of the almost tightrope-walking pace, Crawford had got used to it, and only turned pale when his mount would knock loose a section of the edge with its hoof and have to scramble to right itself.

Josephine was on foot, but her new friend had given her a splinter of stone to press deeply into the flesh of her palm, and for hours she had been able to jog along after Byron's party without fatigue; and on the ledgy paths up the mountain she was able to keep pace with her quarry effortlessly. Her transfixed palm had stopped bleeding hours ago, and her hand only hurt when she accidentally touched the rock wall with it.

'I can't accompany you,' her friend had told her at dawn when he had had to leave. 'But take this piece of me' – he had handed her the little stone claw then – 'and keep it, me, enclosed in your flesh, and I will be with you in spirit, and guide you.'

And he certainly had. Several times she had encountered a choice of ways, but each time the stone spike pulled her decisively, if painfully, one way or the other – it had always kept her on Crawford's trail, even when her eyes were watering so badly in the glare of the sunlit snow, in spite of her goggles, that she couldn't see where she was going; and her only concern now was not to follow so closely that someone in Byron's party might look back along some straight traverse and see this solitary female figure following after them.

She had seen only one party of tourists – a dozen men standing around a tent that seemed to conceal a big wagon – and they seemed to have pitched camp for the day. Clearly they wouldn't be interfering with her plans.

Her pistol was loaded and tucked into the waistband of her skirt; her friend had told her of another way to get Crawford, but the mere description of the procedure had made her sick – with a weak, horrified attempt at humour she had told him that she didn't have eyes for it – and she was resolved to make the gun serve.

Scuff marks in the snow told her that her quarry was still ahead of her, but all at once the stone imbedded in her hand began pulling upward. Startled, she glanced up.

The face of the mountain directly above her *was* somewhat sloping and bumpy, but surely not enough so that she could climb it, she thought – especially with a gored hand! Her arm was stretched out above her head now, and she tried to pull it down. The stone only grated between the bones of her palm, making her nearly faint with the pain, and then it pulled upward harder.

The only way she could lessen the agony was to fit her free hand and the toes of her boots into irregularities in the rock wall and pull herself up; she did, and was permitted several seconds of relief, but the stone soon resumed its tugging, and she had to do it again.

The stone seemed to want her to get above Crawford quickly. And though she was in such pain that the world had gone dim, and terrified that she might slip and find all her weight hanging on her maimed hand, it never occurred to her to pull the guiding, torturing stone out of her palm.

By noon Byron's party had reached a valley only a few hundred feet short of the Wengern's summit, and they dismounted to tie up the horses and mules and proceed on foot to the top.

Crawford's legs were uncomfortably quivery after the hours in the saddle, and he kept shaking them and stamping around to get rid of the feeling ... and he noticed that the odd tingling went away when he was walking downhill. Just for the relief of it he took several long strides back down the road, and then it occurred to him that Byron had done the same thing only moments before.

He looked across at Byron, and found himself intercepting his stare. Byron walked across the slanting, snow-dusted rock surface to him, and when he was standing beside Crawford he spread his hand in a gesture that took in Hobhouse and the guides and the servants, none of whom seemed a bit impelled to walk downhill.

'They're not sweating the way you and I are, either,' he told Crawford quietly, his breath wisping away as visibly as smoke. 'It's not an effect of riding, or scanty air. I believe that, like hydrophobia, it's a consequence of having been *bitten*.' He smiled tightly and waved up at the snowy summit. 'There's a cure up there, but the venom in us doesn't want us to get it.'

They heard the rolling thunder of an avalanche, but there wasn't even a mist of powder snow to be seen over the mountain when they looked up – it must have been on the south side.

Crawford wanted nothing so much as to be off this mountain – to be at sea level or, better, below sea level, living in the Dutch low countries, no, living in a deep, sunless cave . . . that would be best of all. Even with the blue-tinted goggles on, the sun glare on the steep snow slopes was blinding, and he kept having to push them up to wipe the stinging sweat from his eyes. 'The venom,' he told Byron hoarsely, 'is persuasive.'

Byron took off his coat as they walked back toward Hobhouse and the assembled servants and beasts. 'Only a few hundred feet left to go,' he said. 'We can be back here within the hour, and back at the curate's house before dark.'

Josephine had heard the avalanche too, and her flinty guide seemed to take it as an excuse to let her rest for a little while on the foot-wide diagonal ledge she'd been hobbling along for the last quarter of an hour. She was a hundred yards west of Byron's party and a bit above it, and she had missed the sunlit valley and was shivering in a wind that spun across the shadowed face of the mountain like the bow-wave cast up by a ship; but the momentary cessation of the agony in her hand made her mid-cliff crouching place seem luxurious.

For several minutes she basked in the rest, and then the bone-grating tug started up again, and with a whispered sob she straightened her knees and looked up at the nearly vertical slope that still loomed above her – and then she realized that the stone was pulling downward.

What is it, she thought wildly, suddenly terrified at the notion of climbing backwards – has Crawford started down again already?

No, came a voice in her head, *but we can't go any farther up. Wait for him below – get him when he descends.*

With a wave of despair colder than the wind, Josephine realized that she might not be able to survive the descent even with the spiritual strengthening she'd get from having killed Crawford . . . but that she *certainly* wouldn't survive without it.

I can't, she thought; I can't make it down without having spilled his blood on the rocks and snow.

The stone spur in her hand pulled at her insistently.

It's *you*, she thought at it; *you* can't go any higher. Well, I can.

The effort leached the colour from her face and outlined her teeth starkly against her bloodless lips, but she managed to brace herself, flex her arm until she thought her sleeve would burst, and then actually pull her hand up off the stone claw.

Blood sprayed brightly in all directions as if she'd been shot, and for a moment the redly glistening stone hung suspended in the air – and then, with a scream that she heard only in her mind, it sprang away downward in the shadow of the mountain.

Her strength was going with the blood that was now jetting out of her and steaming in spatters on the ledge. Josephine clutched her ruined hand to herself and pressed her face against the rock wall, and her sobs were as grating and patient as the natural noises of the mountain.

Then she pulled the ribbons from her hair and knotted them tightly around her wrist – and, much more slowly now that she was unassisted, she resumed creeping up the side of the mountain.

* * *

Byron had glanced sharply across the sunlit rock face at Crawford, who now nodded to let him know that he had heard the psychic scream too – though Hobhouse and the guide, on a ledge below them, didn't seem to have sensed anything.

'A lot of people hereabouts seem to find high altitudes uncongenial,' Byron remarked tightly, shaking sweaty hair out of his face.

Crawford was aware, with a sense that was neither quite hearing nor touch, of the minds of Hobhouse and the others below; and he would have given in to the increasing reluctance and depression if he had not constantly been reminded of his dead wife Julia; it almost seemed that he sensed her mind, too, on the mountain.

At last he pulled himself up over the last rock outcrop on to the rounded summit, even though every atom of his body seemed to be screaming at him to go back down – and then suddenly he was standing up on the wind-scoured irregular plateau, and the discomfort was gone, and the breeze was invigoratingly cold in his open, sweat-drenched shirt. He was tempted to scratch a line into the rock to mark the level at which the venom could finally be left behind.

The air seemed to be vibrating, at a frequency so high that it was scarcely discernible. He felt safe for now in ignoring it.

The summit was about a quarter the size of a cricket field, looking particularly tiny under the dominating, empty sky; he took several wobbly strides across it to look at the valleys and peaks spread out vastly distant below him – and at the Jungfrau that, miles away, still towered above. It seemed to him that he felt lighter for all the immense volume of air that he was now on top of, and he thought he must be able to jump much higher here than he could on the ground.

'I don't think *people* have any problem at all,' he called back to Byron.

Then Byron, who had been looking more sick with every upward yard, dragged himself up over the last lip of stone on to the roughly level expanse, and suddenly his dark eyes glittered with renewed vitality.

'You're right,' he said, some cheer back in his voice. He stood up, shaky as a newborn colt, and took a few steps toward Crawford. 'If only we could *live* up here, and so be sure that the people we met were in fact people!'

Crawford sniffed the cold air uncertainly. He could no longer sense the vibration in the air, but he was sure it was still there, undetectable now because of being horribly higher in pitch. 'I'm not sure . . .' he began.

Then abruptly his initial exhilaration was gone. There was something ominous about the atmosphere on the summit, a frigid vastness that both diminished him and made him seem perishable, in fact actively decaying, in his own eyes; glancing at Byron, he guessed the young lord was feeling it too, for his momentary cheer was gone – now his mouth was pinched and his eyes were bleak.

The sky was darkening and taking on an orange tint, and though it made him dizzy to do it Crawford glanced up at the sun, wondering if the climb could have taken a lot more time than he had thought; the sun, though, was still high in the firmament, indicating that the afternoon was still fresh – but now Crawford was distracted by something else.

There were lines in the sky, faint luminous streaks spanning the heavens from the northern horizon to the Italian peaks in the south; and though it was such a weird phenomenon that he could feel the hairs at the back of his neck stirring, it was at the same time distantly familiar. He had the feeling that he had seen this effect

193

before, unthinkably long ago . . . and that the effect had been more pronounced then, the lines brighter . . . and despite the depression that had been increasing in the last several seconds and now sat on his shoulders almost like a physical weight, he was obscurely glad, for the sake of the rest of humanity, at least − for the sake of the infants being born now − to see that the lines had faded since.

Irrationally, he was reminded of the compass-cards shaking in the shop windows by the London Docks, and his whimsical idea that they were fluttering in some magnetic wind.

He tried to trace the memory of the sight of these sky-bands − something about particles from the sun − the particles could come down to the earth's surface when the bands were weak, and they were poisonous to the . . . the other sentient race on earth, the . . .

He let the thought go; suddenly it seemed presumptuous for a creature as insignificant and despicable as himself to attempt cogitation.

Byron was talking, in an oddly muffled voice. Crawford's face was buffeted by a momentary puff of wind when he looked across at him, but he noticed that Byron's voice was not quite in synchronization with the movement of his lips.

And even through the muffling effect of the air Crawford could hear the leaden fear in Byron's voice. 'Behind you,' Byron was saying. 'Do you see a person there?'

Crawford turned, ignoring another abrupt punch of wind, and his shoulders slumped in despair when he recognized the figure that stood a few yards farther up the slope.

It was Julia, his wife − but she was as translucent as tinted glass. He couldn't tell whether the trouble he was having in getting a breath into his lungs was a consequence of the altered air or his own shock.

'It's a ghost,' said Byron hoarsely. 'It's the ghost of my sister Augusta. God, when can she have died? I've got letters from her within the month!'

Josephine peered over a shoulder of rock at Michael Crawford and pulled the pistol out of her skirt. She had pushed her goggles up on to her forehead when the light began to dim and redden, and now she could see perfectly – though breathing was getting difficult.

She had lived in the shadow of self-loathing all her life, and so the summit's psychic field made no changes in her.

And the climb had actually become easier shortly after she had got rid of her flinty guide – toward the end she had seemed almost able to *swim* up the side of the mountain – and she now had the strength, even with her ruined left hand, to cock the gun. She raised it and aimed it at the centre of Crawford's torso.

He and Byron were standing slightly below her and no more than eight yards away – it was an easy shot, but she braced the gun barrel on a rock to make it certain. Finally she sighed and pulled the trigger.

Through the blinding flare of the detonation she saw her target spin away – but then she noticed the figure standing farther up the slope, and she recognized *it* as Crawford. Had she shot the wrong person?

But the person up the slope, she now saw, wasn't solid – the light was glowing right through its substance. Why, she thought with relief, *that* isn't Crawford; that's just his ghost.

Crawford heard the bang, and turned – and then he sprang away to the side, for he had seen a shiny ball rushing through the air toward him as fast as an angry bee.

And all at once he felt as if he had jumped into an invisible haystack. He heard the pistol ball buzz past him, and felt the shock wave of its passage ripple across his body like a caress, but he was too stunned to do anything more than stare down at his feet, which were suspended a yard above the rock surface. He was floating, supported only by the gelatinous air.

It took several long seconds for him to settle to the ground; and only when he had landed did it occur to him to look back in the direction the bullet had come from.

By the reddening light he saw a figure standing behind a bulge of rock eight yards away. Crawford couldn't guess who it might be, but he assumed the person would have as much trouble moving as he was having, and that he would be safe in ignoring him or her for a little while.

And if the person had another pistol, and shot at him more successfully in the meantime, wouldn't that actually be a good thing?

He turned back to Julia. She was walking down the slope toward him and Byron, and somehow *she* was able to walk in this thickened air . . . though it seemed to Crawford that she was getting more transparent. He wondered if his nausea and light-headedness were indications of near panic.

Byron might not have heard the shot. 'I don't need to know how she died,' he said now in a choking voice. '*I* killed her. I seduced her, God damn me! That's what I tried to tell you, that day I picked you up in my carriage. Incest – it wasn't *her* fault, she was never strong-willed, and she did resist me at first. And then I left her alone in England with our child . . . and my horrible ex-wife.'

Byron frowned and clenched his jaw, and Crawford

knew he was resisting the despair the mountain's psychic field was inducing. 'My ex-wife drove Augusta to this, I'm certain – I *won't* take *every* bit of blame here, God damn it! – Augusta was so like me, and that harridan I married didn't have *me* around to torment any longer.'

The phantom was only a few yards away now, and it was definitely Julia. She was looking directly at Crawford, and her face suddenly curdled into an expression of almost imbecilic hatred. He flinched back and raised his hand, his sleeve rippling so rapidly that it was momentarily a smoky blur; he would have dived back the way they'd come and scrambled or tumbled back down to the valley where Hobhouse and the servants waited, but Byron caught his arm.

The phantom was fading away to complete transparency even as he watched . . . even as the light got redder and the air got thicker. It now required real muscular effort to breathe. And then she was gone.

But she had only made way for something else – the thick air was humming with the *imminence* of something else. Crawford tried to scramble back to the place where they'd come up to the summit, but the air was too thick now to push through – it seemed to squeeze his ribs, compressed by the bulk of some approaching thing.

Something was forming, but not on this mountaintop – something immensely bigger and farther away, looming down and across the miles – from the peak of the Jungfrau.

It was made of arcs of darkness that gathered out of the dimming sky, and though it never did attain anything much like *form*, something in his blood or his spine or the oldest lobe of his brain recognized it as feminine and leonine, and as it leaned down over the three people on the Wengern summit, eclipsing the whole sky, its malevolence was as palpable as the cold.

Tears sprang from Crawford's eyes and hung in the air like gelatinous gnats.

The thing in the sky spoke, shivering the crystal air with a voice like rock strata shifting. *'Answer my riddle or die,'* it said. After a long pause it spoke again. *'What is it that walked with four limbs when the sunlight had not yet changed, and now is supported by two, but will, when the sunlight is changed again and the light is gone, be supported by three?'*

Crawford exhaled, and the spent breath was a bulk in front of him, pushing his head back against the resisting air.

'Four, two and three,' Byron managed to say. 'It's . . . the riddle . . . of the . . . sphinx.' Even in this dimming red light Crawford could see that Byron's face was hollowed and pale. 'We're facing . . . the sphinx.'

Crawford forced himself to look up at the thing. She seemed to be a lens, warping the magnetic lines into her shape; she was less substantial now than she had been in the days when she had caused the seven great gates of Thebes to be closed in fear of her, and been portrayed in towering stone on the plain of Gizeh, but she had clearly lost none of her power, at least in these high regions.

Crawford fought the induced self-loathing and made himself remember the legend; Oedipus had been confronted by the sphinx, and she had asked him what creature walked on four legs in the morning, two legs at noon, and three legs in the evening. According to the story, the answer had been 'man,' who crawls in infancy, walks on two legs in maturity, and walks with a stick in old age. He opened his mouth to force the word into the air, but then he hesitated.

Why was the thing asking? And had Greek mythology preserved the answer correctly? Why would the sphinx want him to say *man*? And, as a matter of fact, *man* didn't seem to *be* the correct answer to this version of the riddle – there was nothing about infancy that he could think of that corresponded to 'when the sunlight had not yet changed.' Whenever that might have been, he didn't think humans would even have been around.

Who had been? The nephelim? And was the sphinx one of that species? Was he supposed to say *you*, instead of, in effect, *me*?

He remembered the flash of primordial memory he'd had when he first saw the streaks in the sky – something about the *other* sentient race on earth. Could this riddle be the equivalent of a diplomatic demand of recognition, in which case the answer would be, 'Both of us'?

Byron opened his mouth to answer it himself, but Crawford waved at him urgently, forcing his hand through the thick air, and Byron noticed and remained silent.

'Remember the ... consequences ... of a wrong guess,' Crawford told him. 'And I don't think ... mythology recorded . . . the right answer.'

The thing was leaning down closer to them, and Crawford was looking up into the darkness of her gigantic eyes. They were as inorganic as frost crystals, and it was wildly disorienting to recognize intelligence – albeit a profoundly alien intelligence – behind them.

He saw that her mouth was opening, and then the whole summit of the mountain seemed to tilt toward that vast, black maw.

He went with his last guess. 'Sentient life on earth,' he called, forcing the words out.

Something changed then.

The menacing shape still loomed above them, but after a moment Crawford realized that the sphinx was gone – what had been the arch of her wings was now a pattern of cloud on one side and the shadowed flank of the Jungfrau on the other, and the face, which had given such a strong impression of femininity, was just a pattern of stars in the dark sky. The sphinx had receded back to the remoteness of the Jungfrau's peak.

And the air was finally beginning to loosen — apparently he had given the right answer.

Josephine saw that her shot had somehow missed Crawford — had he actually leapt out of the way? — and she slumped limply, releasing the pistol. Several seconds later her knees and the pistol bumped against the snow-dusted stone.

She remembered the procedure her night-visiting friend had told her about, the alternative to shooting Crawford; she had been confident that the pistol would make it unnecessary, and in any case she wasn't sure how well it would work in this strange, red-lit, slowed-down world — clearly her guide had never intended for her to be here — but she now had nothing else.

At least she had no self-regard to impede her.

Though her voice clogged with tears, she managed to begin pronouncing the syllables he had taught her, and the air boiled away from in front of her as if the words were a violation of the very space here — again it occurred to her that she was not using this procedure as her friend had intended.

And, as she was speaking, she pulled the goggles off her head and swung them as hard as she could against the stone. One lens broke, and she caught one of the slow-flying fragments of tinted glass, wrestled it to a stop, and then hesitantly forced it up through the air to her face.

It took every bit of her courage and resolve to do it, but her recitation of the litany didn't even falter when she punctured her own left eye with the piece of glass.

* * *

Crawford turned now toward the person who had shot at him – and his heart sank, for he recognized her, and he wondered if he might one day have to kill her. Then he noticed the dark streak down one side of her face, and he realized that she was bleeding.

Good, he thought exhaustedly. I hope the gun blew up in her hand, I hope she's dying.

She seemed to be pulling something out of her eye. Whatever it was, she now pressed it against the stone, and he heard her sob: *'There, damn you – render yourselves visible to such as this.'*

Big drops were forming on the stone now, and bulging up, as if the summit were a wet ceiling viewed upside down. Angularities began to form inside the bulges, and then Crawford was able to make out orbs with hollows like eye sockets in them.

Byron tried to walk through the slowed air, then cursed and simply began swimming; it was an awkward way to travel, and at first he propelled himself backwards as often as forwards, but after a few moments he had frog-kicked over to where Crawford stood.

'Who is that?' Byron demanded, treading air beside Crawford's shoulder. 'And what the hell are those things growing up around her?'

The bulges were breaking open, releasing waving stick-arms and grimacing heads that glistened nastily in the red light . . . but they were all grown together, so that they formed a hideous centipedelike monstrosity instead of separate figures, and half of them seemed to be partially imbedded in the rock.

'Who cares?' said Crawford, lifting his legs and spreading his arms so that he could swim too. 'Let's get back down.' He began struggling through the air toward the route they had climbed up.

After a few hard-won yards he looked back at Byron.

201

'This slowed-time effect probably ends at the brink – don't go sailing over the edge.'

'*Him*,' yelled Josephine, beyond Byron. 'You're supposed to go after *him*!'

Crawford focused on her. She was trying to run through the resistant air, but she wound up simply flailing in place, several inches off the ground, and then the melted-together things had seized her and seemed to be clumsily trying to force her down against the stone – to make her into one of themselves? Were they the decrepit ghosts of people who had died up here?

May they enjoy her company, he thought grimly, turning away.

Then, horribly, the things began to speak, and he had to turn back again. '*Thought you could abandon your mother, did you, slut?*' chittered one of the peeled-looking heads, its voice disorientingly out of synchronization with the motions of its mouth, as several birdy hands fumbled at Josephine's face. '*After killing me! What mother wouldn't hate a daughter who killed her even as she was trying to give the daughter life?*'

'*I had to marry that horrible little nonentity,*' squealed another head, '*it was the only way I could get away from you! And then he killed me in that inn! Thus your fault – you killed your own sister!*'

Several hinged limbs had wetly wrapped around her ankles, and a nearby head added its yapping voice to the babble. '*I was always hidden away in your head so that you could be* Julia, *or a* machine, *and I've rotted in there! You starved me, your own self, and I hate you for it!*'

Josephine fell to her knees under the ungainly assault, and she rocked her head back and wailed hopelessly into the barred red sky . . . and just for a moment she reminded Crawford of – of whom, not Julia – of his brother, who had been pulled under the waves in the savage surf off Rame Head.

With a convulsive jackknife motion that tore his shirt against the unyielding air and punched the breath out of him, Crawford turned around and began dragging himself back through the air toward her.

Chapter 11

In the wind there is a voice
Shall forbid thee to rejoice;
And to thee shall Night deny
All the quiet of her sky;
And the day shall have a sun,
Which shall make thee wish it done.

— Lord Byron, Manfred

The headwind deafened him and peeled his lips back from his teeth at every forward thrust — he was glad of the goggles over his eyes — but between strokes the air was as still as stagnant water, and over his own tortured breathing he could hear a couple of the heads begin to pay attention to him. *'Drinking in a pub while I was screwing another man, and drinking there still while I burned to death!'* one head called to him.

Another opened its mouth just as he clawed his way forward into the wind again, and he wondered who it would claim to be. His brother? Julia again, but tailored for his despair this time?

When the wind of his forward motion abruptly stopped, he stretched his arm out ahead and managed to grab Josephine's wrist; then he spread his legs wide to help moor himself to the air, and pulled until his lungs felt as if wires were being twisted in them, but nothing happened.

Various ghostly limbs had grown together into a sort of ectoplasmic rope below him, and a head sprouting from a thigh was winking furiously at him. *'You still owe me my death,*' the thing hissed. '*I got your passport, and you promised!*'

Crawford pulled again, and though the effort wrenched a sob out of him he heard several ghost-limbs snap. 'Kick!' he gasped to Josephine.

Josephine looked up at him, and he saw a glint of recognition in her one good eye; and then she began kicking wildly at the jabbering heads, sending jawbones and fingers slowly arching away through the red light. She kept kicking the things even after she was free, and Crawford had to yank at her arm again several times to get her attention.

'Come on, goddamn you,' he told her. 'Swim!'

But her goggles were gone, leaving her completely blind except when holding still, so he had to drag her through the air. They were losing their buoyancy, and several times Crawford had to kick off from the ground as they floundered over to where Byron stood. Her empty eye socket left a trail of little globes of blood in their wake, all of them settling toward the ground as quickly as drops of vinegar through oil.

The air was loosening, and the sky was brightening back through orange toward the remembered blue, and when Crawford saw the translucent figure of Julia forming again, ahead of them, it occurred to him that he should have expected this. This phantom and the sphinx evidently each existed at specific intensities of the time-slowing they'd been experiencing – each of the apparitions only became visible or invisible as a viewer approached or receded from its characteristic point on the time spectrum.

It's like looking through a telescope, he thought – nearby things blur out to invisibility as you focus farther away, then reappear when the scale gets back closer to normal. And *this* phantom lives only a few degrees outside of normal focus ... unlike the sphinx, which

205

was only barely visible even when time had slowed so extremely that the light was deep red and I could hardly drag air into my lungs.

The phantom's eyes were bitter with hatred. It stood between them and the way down from the summit – they would have to step through it to climb down.

The self-loathing that he had been trying to hold at arm's length increased in weight, but he knew it was being induced in him, and he tried to fight it.

'Augusta's ghost,' said Byron, faltering and settling to the stone surface.

'No it's not,' said Crawford wearily. His lungs were exhausted with the work of breathing, and felt ready to stop altogether. 'I'm seeing it as . . . my dead wife, and God knows who our . . . lunatic friend here is seeing. Those weren't real ghosts back *there*, either – the one pretending to be my wife said that I'd killed her, which' – he turned to speak directly into Josephine's blood-streaked face – 'my wife's genuine ghost would know was *not true.*'

Byron looked back at him, desperately hopeful. 'Really? Then might Augusta still be alive? If this isn't – '

Crawford nodded, and reluctantly inhaled. 'This thing, and those wormy phantoms that almost got this damned girl, are simply reflecting us, our . . . guilts and fears. And magnifying them, horribly. The sphinx's castle is . . .' He paused, groping for a phrase. '. . . is guarded by distorting mirrors.'

Byron seemed to be almost convinced – and then the phantom woman spoke.

'I'm glad to be dead and rid of you at last,' said the thing that seemed to Crawford to be Julia. 'You only diminished me, just cut me down like a tapestry you could trim into a momentarily pleasing garment, and then discard. You never *knew* me. You've never known anyone. You've always been alone.' And then her face

206

changed, and Crawford saw his own features smiling coldly out of the insubstantial face. 'This is the only one you were ever concerned about.'

Then abruptly it was Julia again, but Julia as he had seen her last, bloody and shapeless and jagged with broken bones, somehow still standing upright and staring at him with her ruptured and protruding eyes.

'Was this enough?' asked the horribly extended mouth. 'Or do you require even more, from the people you tell yourself you love?' Behind the figure Crawford sensed waves crashing on rocks, and flames roaring out from under eaves.

Byron was apparently being shown something similar, for his face had gone ashen. 'If this is even *possible*,' he whispered, perhaps to Crawford, 'there can be no God – and no punishments but those we choose to take.' He waded through the thinning air away from the figure, away from the safe way down, to a lip of stone over a sheer drop.

He turned an unreadable look on Crawford. 'It's not so difficult to die,' he said, and then leapt out into space.

The next thing Crawford realized was that he was swimming after Byron, and he knew vaguely that he was giving in to the mountain's psychically goading field, but also that he was fleeing from overwhelming exhaustion and horror and failure. He had reached the close limits of his self-regard, and now unquestioningly accepted what the phantom had said.

If I'm the only one I love, he thought dimly, then I'll require it of myself, too – and when my body is a smashed, sun-dried framework of leather and bones wedged in the bottom of some Alpine ravine, I'll be free of Michael Crawford, and everyone . . . and maybe, too, I'll have paid off at least the bulk of my debts to my brother and wives.

He gave a wordless shout of renunciation and then leapt right after Byron.

The suicide impulse disappeared the moment he was in the air.

Through fear-squinted eyes he saw the whole Lutschin Valley spread out below him in the orange light, the rugged peak of Kleine Scheidegg to his right, and the Schilthorn far away ahead across the valley, and Byron's back mercifully blocking the view of the sea of cloud directly below; he was falling perceptibly . . . but then someone had grabbed him from behind and was swimming back up against the weakening air.

Instinctively he reached out below him and grabbed Byron's collar with one hand and began flailing at the air with the other; then Byron was swimming back upward himself, and Crawford was more being pulled than pulling.

Looking up, he saw a figure in a dress silhouetted against the sky, and he realized that it was Josephine who had grabbed him and hauled him back. She was swimming strongly upward with her legs and her free hand, but the air was thinning fast; all their struggling was only holding them in place, and the light was brightening to yellow.

'Never make it back up,' Crawford panted to his companions above him. 'Slant in toward the slope – at least be against stone when gravity comes back full on.'

The other two nodded, and then they had all let go of each other and were swimming furiously toward a snow-piled stone shoulder slightly below them and to their left.

'Aim high!' Byron yelled.

They were still a good four yards out away from the ledge when the sky turned blue and they were suddenly flying through unresisting air . . . but the force of their

208

previous swimming had left them with some forward momentum, and so instead of plummeting straight down, they tumbled forward in a parabola that slammed them on to the ledge they'd been aiming at.

Crawford's head collided sickeningly hard with the rock wall, but through the shimmer of near unconsciousness he saw Josephine sliding toward the edge, and he managed to grab her wet hair – he couldn't nearly have held on to her full weight, but he did halt her slide for a moment, and she got her legs under herself and was able to scramble back up on to the rough surface.

Byron was sitting up at Crawford's left, massaging his knee and grimacing. 'You can see I was ready to meet my maker,' he said. 'I landed on my knees.' But in spite of his jocular tone, his face was as pale as dirty snow, and he didn't look squarely at either of the others.

Crawford peered nervously over the edge, wincing to see the vast volumes of empty air and cloud that the three of them had nearly fallen through, and then he looked at Josephine.

She looked horrible in the bright, restored sunlight – her left eye was just a gory hole, and blood was streaked all over her face and matted in her hair, and her hand seemed to have been shot through. He wondered if she could survive.

'Thank you,' he told her hoarsely. 'You saved . . . him and me both.'

Her right eye was wide and staring at him, and she looked like a wild animal broken but alive in a trap – he leaned away from her and gripped the rock more tightly, wondering if he would be able to kick her off into the abyss if she were to attack him – but then something seemed to click inside her head, and she bared her blood-flecked teeth in what might, under dramatically different circumstances, have been a warm smile.

'Michael!' she said. 'You rogue, I've been looking for you all over Europe! And here I find you on top of an *Alp*, for Heaven's sake!' The eye swivelled past him toward Byron. '*Hel*lo, I'm Mr Crawford's wife, Julia.'

Byron shook his head weakly. 'Pleased to meet you,' he said in a barely audible whisper. 'Who's Mr Crawford?'

'That's me, my real name,' said Crawford. He got his feet under him, though it chilled his belly to do it and, crouching and gripping the wall, he looked left and right along their ledge. 'We've got to get down off this mountain – her eye needs medical attention right away . . . and you and I aren't at our best, either.'

At the right limit of their ledge the rock wall wasn't impossibly steep, and seemed bumpy enough to provide hand and foot holds, but he had no idea where climbing it would lead them, and in any case he was pretty sure none of them had enough strength left for a real climb. To the left the ledge became narrower and more out-wardly slanted, though it did seem to continue around the mountain for some distance. Neither way looked attractive.

'Let's try yelling,' he said. 'Maybe Hobhouse can get a rope down to us.'

Crawford and Byron took turns shouting, and after only a few minutes their shouts were answered from above; soon a rope came hitching and snaking down the slope from above, finally coming to a stop when its end had passed them, and though it hung a few yards to the right of the ledge, climbing across to it looked like it wouldn't be difficult. And then hanging on, Crawford thought, won't be any problem at all – they'll have to *break* my fingers off it.

He turned to Byron, who had been watching over his shoulder. 'The girl first, I think. We can tie it around her. I don't know how she's stayed conscious this long, and there's certainly – ' He stopped, for he had looked past Byron, and Josephine was gone. 'My God, did she fall?'

Byron's head whipped around to the left. 'No,' he said, after a moment. 'Look, there's blood and scuff marks way out along that end. She's gone that way.'

'*Josephine!*' Crawford yelled. Then, after a fearful glance toward the summit, '*Julia!*' There was no answer.

Byron joined in, and they called several more times, with no results except to alarm Hobhouse, who kept shouting down advice about breathing deeply and avoiding looking down.

Finally they abandoned the effort and let themselves be roped up to where the others waited. Hobhouse was pompous with worry, and insisted on knowing what the hell had happened, and Byron rolled together a snowball and threw it at him as a prelude to explaining.

Byron told them only that Aickman's wife had fallen from the summit with them and was injured and alone on a ledge somewhere below, but the guide didn't even believe that. He insisted that on the high mountains it was a common thing for tourists – or even seasoned mountaineers – to imagine that they saw people who weren't really there, frequently people from their pasts; and that often the sufferers of this delusion sat down and waited interminably for the imaginary others to catch up.

In support of his opinion he pointed out how visibly distraught Byron and Crawford both were, and noted the bad knock Crawford's head had taken and, most telling of all, he observed that only a few minutes had passed between the time Byron and Crawford had disappeared on to the summit and when the party had heard the two of them calling from the ledge below. This one-eyed wife would have had to appear the moment

Byron and Crawford had climbed out of sight of the others – just in time to slide with them down to the ledge they'd been roped up from – and then disappear instantly afterwards.

And by the time the touring party had descended the mountain without having seen any sign of Josephine or her passage, even Crawford was willing to admit that the guide might be correct. After all, he told himself at one point as he looked back at the peak, you *have* been feverish lately, and lots of people have been to the top of the Wengern without having encountered thickened air and slowed time, or suicide promptings, or phantoms, or the sphinx.

Byron had retracted the story entirely, and asked Hobhouse and his servants to forget about it – and when his horse and Crawford's mule both sank up to their shins in the clayey mud of a morass which everyone else had passed over safely, he only laughed. '*Don't* try,' he called across to Crawford as they both were floundering in the mud, and the servants were tugging on the reins, 'to tell me that the mountain doesn't want us to leave.'

Crawford kicked his legs to keep from sinking farther into the chilly, clinging mud, and he tremblingly shrugged. 'When I'm sure of anything,' he answered, 'I'll let you know.'

The sun was low when Josephine clambered up on to the path and started back toward the village of Wengern.

She was hardly anyone now.

When she had walked all the way back down to where the road widened out and the trees were crowded and aromatic in the darkness on either side, she began to hear faint songs on the branch-combed air, and she knew that things were awakening with the passing of the day.

She was dimly aware that her night-visiting friend

had lost his power over her and would need a new invitation to have access to her again.

She wondered if he would get one and, if he did, who would extend it.

She had tied a cloth around her empty eye socket, and her hand was only seeping blood now – they might very well become mortified, but her injuries didn't seem likely to kill her tonight.

For the moment free of all the hatreds and fears and constrictions that had defined her personalities, she actually sniffed the pine- and snow-scented air with enjoyment, and her bloodstained cheeks kinked into a battered version of the small smile of a contented, sleeping child.

Byron's party continued eastward the next day, crossing the Kleine Scheidegg Mountain and moving on through the green valley between the Schwarzhorn and the Wetterhorn to the Reichenbach Fall, where they halted to rest the horses and mules, and then looping back west to the town of Brienz on the north shore of Lake Brienz.

They stayed at an inn, and though there was fiddling and singing and waltzing downstairs, Byron and Crawford retired early to their rooms. Crawford recognized in them both the signs of recovery from long fever. Crawford didn't dream at all.

Everybody slept later than usual, but by nine the next morning Hobhouse and Byron and Crawford and a couple of servants were aboard a boat crossing the lake of Brienz, while the horses were being brought around along the north shore. The boat Byron had hired was rowed entirely by women, which struck Byron as so novel that he insisted on taking an oar himself next to the prettiest of the rowers, up in the front.

Crawford was perched in the bow of the long, narrow boat, watching the patterns of early autumn leaves on the flat water sweep past on either side; from time to time he looked up, but always to starboard, where the slate roofs of the village of Oberried serrated the north shore and, far more distantly, the white peaks of the Hohgant and the Gemmenalp dented the blue sky. He avoided looking out over the port side, for the view in that direction was dominated by the towering, broad-shouldered bulk of the Jungfrau, and the glitter of the sun on its snows was uncomfortably like the glitter of watchful eyes.

The summer was gone, along with a lot else — but since climbing the Wengern it all seemed to have taken place in someone else's life, someone Crawford had known and felt sorry for a long time ago. He was reminded of Shelley's story about having cut his encysted sister out of his side, and he felt as though he had now done something similar.

Maybe, he thought with a smile, Josephine only pulled part of me back up from that abyss I jumped into — maybe some part of Michael Crawford did go plummeting away into those cloudy canyons.

The lake current was taking the boat in close to the north shore, almost into the shade of the overhanging pine branches, and when the little vessel rounded the point of a low, wooded promontory, Crawford saw several men on the shore running away from a large boulder that sat in the shallows. Smoke seemed to hover behind it.

One of the men glanced at the boat, and then flailed to a stop. '*Frauen!*' he yelled to his companions, '*im boot!*'

'Women in the boat, they say,' remarked Hobhouse, who was lounging on a thwart at the stern end.

Byron lifted his oar out of the water and squinted at them. 'Of course there are women in the boat,' he said. 'Did he think we'd be rowing it ourselves?'

Crawford pointed at Byron's oar. 'Well, you are, after

all.' He looked ahead again. The boat was bearing down on the boulder, and smoke was definitely curling up from behind it.

The men on the shore were yelling urgently to the people in the boat.

Crawford didn't understand what they'd said, but Byron and the boatwomen evidently had – they all began working the oars furiously to put distance between the boat and the shore; and they had managed to slant sharply out away from it when the boulder abruptly became a cloud of flying stone fragments, and a resounding *crack* punched a wall of air and hard spray against the boat and its passengers; splinters flew as rock bits clipped the rails, and when Crawford had cuffed the spray out of his eyes he saw a cloud of smoke unfolding above a patch of choppy, foamy water where the boulder had sat. He turned to the port side and saw rings appearing farther and farther out on the lake as rock pieces went skipping away across the flat water. In the distance the Jungfrau looked on impassively.

Byron and Hobhouse were on their feet, and they both shouted furious curses until the men on the shore had run away into the woods.

'Damn me!' Byron said, sitting down and pulling a handkerchief out of his pocket. 'No one's hurt? Pure luck – those idiots could have killed us.'

The women were talking excitedly among themselves, but they seemed to have recovered from the shock, and soon resumed their rowing.

'I think it was bad luck that they saw you rowing,' said Crawford. 'It made them think we were by ourselves, unaccompanied by any innocent locals.'

Hobhouse groaned. 'You really should be writing novels, Aickman! Why do all of Byron's physicians feel called on to indulge so in – in *morbid fancies?* Those men were just careless louts trying to get an obstruction off their beach without going to the trouble of hauling it away! Look, if they had wanted to *murder* us, why didn't they simply *shoot* us? Or, if they had their hearts set on actually blowing us up, why not simply pitch a bomb at us? Why go to the trouble of dragging a big damned rock down to the water and blowing *it* up when we're nearby?'

'Maybe because it *was* a rock,' said Crawford. 'That is to say, because it was a *rock*. Things that can protect you, that can . . . oh, say, raise a shadow to prevent you from drinking poisoned brandy,' he went on, glancing at Byron, 'might not have the power to block or deflect pieces of one of the sentient stones, one of the *living* ones. Maybe they can't interfere with *family*. Is this making sense?'

'Oh, yes, excellent sense,' said Hobhouse nervously. 'Do take my hat, old fellow. And maybe a nap would be a good idea – after all, yesterday was a strenuous – '

'Hush a moment, Hobby.' Byron leaned forward. 'Go on, Aickman. Let's say that is the only way they could have killed someone with such protections. Why would they *want* to do it? If someone wanted to stop us from going to the mountain, that's one thing; but why try to kill any of us *now?* We would pose no further threat to them. We have no more connection with these things.'

Crawford reluctantly let his gaze go back to the Jungfrau. 'Maybe that's not altogether true,' he said softly.

Byron shook his head and picked up his oar. 'I don't believe it – and I *won't* believe it, watch me. I don't mean to seem to speak *ex cathedra*, but I think you have to concede that, in these matters, I have a good deal more – '

Crawford was scared, and it made him irritable. 'More like *ex catheter*, actually.'

Byron barked one hard syllable of laughter, but his

eyes were bright with resentment. 'Hobhouse is right,' he said. 'I have unfortunate taste in doctors.' He resumed his seat beside the prettiest rower, and began animatedly talking to her in German.

Hobhouse gave Crawford an amused look that was not without sympathy. 'I think you've lost a job,' he said.

Crawford sat down and reached over the gunwale to trail the fingers of his four-fingered hand in the cold water. 'I hope I've lost a lot more than that,' he said.

The sunlight had begun to slant in through the window from the west, and Mary Godwin put down her pen, stretched back in her chair and looked out the window at the housefronts and gardens and fence-walking cats along Abbey Churchyard Lane.

Their unconventional household – herself, Shelley, their nearly eleven-month-old son William, and the ever more obviously pregnant Claire – had been back in England for just a little more than three months; and often, especially at times like this when she had spent a few hours rewriting her novel, she was startled to look up and see the low Welsh mountains on the horizon beyond the Bristol Channel instead of the snowy majesties of the Alps.

Shelley had seemed nervous during the crossing from Le Havre to London, though it had been an uneventful trip – the only annoyance had been when the London customs officer had leafed through every page of the manuscript of Lord Byron's third canto of *Childe Harold's Pilgrimage*, evidently supposing that Shelley was trying to smuggle lace into the country between the sheets of paper. Shelley had been entrusted with delivering the manuscript to Byron's publisher, and he didn't want anything to happen to it.

She waved a page of her own manuscript in the air

now to dry the ink. She was apparently the only one to have taken up the challenge Byron had tossed out on that rainy evening almost exactly six months ago, when she and Claire and Polidori and Shelley and Byron had been sitting in the big upstairs room at the Villa Diodati on the shore of Lake Leman, after Shelley had had that nervous seizure and run out of the room.

'I really think we should each write a ghost story,' Byron had said when Shelley had returned and the awkward moment had passed. 'Let's see if we can't do something with this mud-person who's been following poor Shelley around.'

She'd had a nightmare shortly afterwards – a figure had seemed to be standing over her bed, and at first she had thought it was Shelley, for it had resembled him closely; but it had not been him, and when she had reared up in horror it had disappeared.

She had used the vision as the basis of a novel; it was the story of a student of natural science who assembled a man out of lifeless parts, and who then managed by scientific means to endow the thing with unnatural life.

Shelley had been very interested in the tale; he encouraged her to write it out, and to freely use incidents from his own life to amplify it. She'd taken him at his word, and the story had become almost a biography of Shelley, and a chronicling of his fear of being pursued by some kind of double of himself, a sort of dreaded twin that was destined to kill everyone he loved.

Shelley had even suggested the name of the protagonist, a German word meaning something like *the stone whose travel-toll is paid in advance*. She had wanted to use a more English-sounding name, but it had seemed important to Shelley, and so she had obediently called the protagonist Frankenstein.

The story took place in the Swiss locales Mary and he had lived in, and the name of the protagonist's infant brother, slain by the monster, was William, the same as the son Mary had had by Shelley; the areas of science involved in the monster's vivification were ones Shelley was familiar with, and the books the monster read were those Shelley had been reading at the time.

And, based on Shelley's description of the intruder he'd wounded in his house in Scotland in 1813, she wrote a scene in which the monster's face is seen leering through the window of an inn at its creator, who later tries unsuccessfully to shoot it; though here Shelley had showed some hesitation, and made her omit certain details. The physical description of the monster couldn't actually be that of the thing Shelley had shot in his parlour on that occasion – Mary remembered the drawing of it that he'd done from memory, that night in Switzerland, and how much it had upset Claire and Polidori – and for some reason she couldn't mention the fact that Shelley had pulled a muscle in his side, at the scar under his ribs, during the encounter.

She hoped the book would be published, but it seemed already to have fulfilled its main purpose, which was to draw out and dispel Shelley's outlandish fears. He was much calmer now that he was back in England and she'd written the story out – it almost seemed that she had taken the fears one by one from Shelley's head and transferred them to the novel.

And Shelley seemed comfortable without them – 'Maybe she *did* stay over there with Aickman,' he had said recently while half asleep, and Mary got the clear impression that the 'she' he'd referred to was the thing that he feared.

Mary hoped that the worst of their problems were now behind them, and that they'd soon be buying a house to raise children in.

She heard Shelley put a book down in the next room,

and then she heard him yawn. 'Mary,' he called, 'where's that letter from Hookham?'

Mary frowned slightly as she put the sheet of paper down and stood up, for while Hookham was Shelley's publisher, this letter was probably in answer to the inquiry Shelley had made a month ago about the situation of Harriet, Shelley's wife. Mary was determined to get Shelley to divorce Harriet and marry *her*, and she hoped the woman wouldn't have got herself or the two children into some situation Shelley would feel called on to help out with.

'It's on the mantel, Percy,' she said cautiously. Soon she heard paper tear, and wondered if she should go into the sitting room and wait expectantly while he read it, but then she decided that she shouldn't seem to care.

She hoped that the news, whatever it might be, wouldn't drag Shelley back to London – the city never seemed to have a good influence on him. Only yesterday he had returned from a visit to the London suburb cottage of one Leigh Hunt, a mildly revolutionary poet and editor, and the visit had apparently almost caused Shelley to suffer a relapse back into his fear of supernatural enemies – for he had met there, he said, a young poet who was 'clearly marked by the attentions of the same breed of antediluvian devils' who had supposedly harried Shelley back and forth across the map.

'You can see it in his face,' Shelley had told her, 'and even more clearly in his verse. And it's too bad, for he's as modest and affable a fellow as I've ever met, and he celebrated his twenty-first birthday only a month and a half ago. He has none of the pose and morbidness that neff – that this crowd usually affects. I advised him to postpone publishing his verse; I think the advice offended him, but every year that he can avoid drawing the attention of . . . certain segments of society . . . will be a blessing.'

Mary tried now to remember what the name of the young poet had been. She remembered that Hunt had nicknamed him, to Shelley's considerable disgust, 'Junkets.'

John Keats, that's what the name was.

She heard Shelley shout in the next room, and ran in to see him sprawled across the couch, the letter clutched in his hand.

'What is it, Percy?' she asked quickly.

'Harriet's dead,' he whispered.

'Dead?' Out of love for him, Mary made a determined effort to share his grief. 'Was she sick? How are the children?'

'She wasn't *sick*,' said Shelley, his lips pulled back from his teeth. He stood up and crossed to the mantel and picked up a piece of smoked glass that had been sitting there since they'd gone out to view a recent solar eclipse. 'She was *killed* – as her murderess promised me she would be . . . that was four years ago, almost, in Scotland. God damn it, I didn't do enough – not nearly enough – to protect her.'

'Murder*ess*?' said Mary. She'd been wondering how to tactfully take the piece of glass away from him, but this last statement had jolted her.

'Or murder*er*, if you'd rather,' said Shelley impatiently. 'I – ' He wasn't able to finish, and for a moment Mary thought it was rage, rather than grief, that choked him. '*And she was pregnant when they found her body!*'

Mary couldn't help being glad to hear it, for Shelley had been separated from Harriet for more than a year. 'Well,' she ventured, 'you *have* always said she was of weak character . . .'

Shelley stared at her. 'What? Oh, you mean she'd been unfaithful. You don't understand any of this, do you? Mary, *she undoubtedly thought it was I. You* should

221

be able to grasp that, *you* thought it was I who was standing over – ' He shook his head and clasped the piece of glass in his fist.

Suddenly Mary was afraid that she did understand, and she was frightened. She remembered his strange fears, and all at once they didn't seem so ludicrous. 'Percy, are you saying that – this thing you're afraid of – '

Shelley wasn't listening. 'And her body was found floating in the Serpentine Lake in Hyde Park. The *Serpentine!* Was *that* damned . . . *joke* . . . necessary? She – he, it – can't really have thought that I'd have failed to recognize its handiwork without this . . . this *hint*.'

Blood was dripping now from his fist, but Mary had forgotten about trying to get the piece of glass away from him. 'Perhaps,' she said unsteadily as she sank into a chair, 'you'd better tell me more about this . . . this . . . this *doppelgänger* of yours.'

Shelley left for London later that day, and in a letter that Mary received two days later Shelley proposed marriage to her; they were wed two weeks later, on the thirtieth of December, but Mary's joy was marred a little by her suspicion that he had married her mainly to get legal custody of his two children by Harriet.

Two weeks after that, Claire's child by Byron was born, a daughter that Claire christened Allegra, and by the end of February all of them had moved to a house in the little town of Marlow, thirty miles west of London.

Here Mary's fears began to dissipate. Shelley failed to get custody of Harriet's children, but Mary's son and Claire's daughter appeared to be healthy, and she soon discovered that she was pregnant again herself; the baby, a girl, was born in September, and they named her Clara.

Even Shelley was, tentatively, beginning to relax

again. He kept a skiff moored on the bank of the Thames, only a three-minute walk from the house, and frequently went rowing up and down the waterway, though he still refused to learn to swim.

It was only in his writings that he seemed to express some of his old fears. He wrote a number of poems, but devoted most of the year to writing a long political poem that he at first called *Laon and Cyntha* but later retitled *The Revolt of Islam*. Mary carefully read all his verse – she was a little alarmed by a poem called 'Marianne's Dream,' in which a city consisting of mountains is destroyed by fire, and marble statues come briefly to life – but there was only one stanza, in *The Revolt of Islam*, that really disquieted her:

> Many saw
> Their own lean image everywhere, it went
> A ghastlier self beside them, till the awe
> Of that dread sight to self-destruction sent
> Those shrieking victims . . .

Summer, 1818

I wish you a good night, with a Venetian benediction, 'Benedetto te, e la terra che ti fara!' – 'May you be blessed, and the *earth* which you will *make*' is it not pretty? You would think it still prettier if you had heard it, as I did two hours ago, from the lips of a Venetian girl, with large black eyes, a face like Faustina's, and the figure of a Juno – tall and energetic as a Pythoness, with eyes flashing, and her dark hair streaming in the moon-light – one of those women who may be made any thing.

– Lord Byron, 19 September 1818

When he couldn't take any more of the ceremony, Percy Shelley left the circle of people and walked away; in a few long strides he had followed his shadow to the top of a low hill, where a wind-twisted old olive tree seemed to point back south across the calm water of the lagoon toward Venice. Shelley turned his gaze in that direction, and the irregular glittering line that was the city seemed to him to be dominated by churches, from the Roman-esque campanile of San Pietro di Castello in the east to, at the western end, the low walls of the Madonna dell' Orto.

Our Lady of the Kitchen Garden, he translated that last phrase mentally. A month ago Byron had told him that the church had been dedicated to San Cristoforo until 1377, when a crude statue, supposedly of the Blessed Virgin, had been found in a neighbouring garden. Neither Byron nor Shelley had been in a mood to visit the place.

For a few minutes Shelley picked at the splinters and blisters he had inflicted on his left palm before dawn this morning; then he looked back down the hill toward the knot of people.

Mary and Claire were standing off to one side, near the flowers the English Consul had brought, and even from this distance Shelley could see that Claire was uneasily watching Mary, who simply stared at the ground.

He knew they'd have to be leaving Venice soon, now. Byron would be wise to leave too ... but of course he wouldn't – not with that Margarita Cogni woman living with him, and with the best poetical work of his life only begun.

This was a Friday, and it occurred to Shelley that he and Claire had arrived in Venice five weeks ago tomorrow night, looking for Claire's baby – Allegra was nineteen months old now, and for the last four months the child had been staying in Venice with Byron, her father. Claire was desperate to see the child, and Shelley had agreed to help her. He had been looking for an excuse to visit Byron, an excuse that would look plausible to any minions of the Austrian government of Italy who might be keeping track of the extravagant English lord.

Their gondola had come in to the city from the mainland – they must have passed close by this island, though in the dark and the storm they could never have seen it – and though the string of lights that was Venice had been nearly invisible through the thrashing downpour beyond the gondola's rain-streaked window, the water had been no choppier than it was today, for the long islands of the Lido to the east protected the lagoon from the wild Adriatic.

Pulling a long splinter from his palm now, he grinned bleakly. The lagoon's always calm, he thought. Even

225

though the city's not ritually married to the sea anymore, the sea evidently still has a . . . soft spot for the
place.

They had arrived at an inn at midnight, and even before
they could go to their rooms the fat landlady, learning
that they were English, felt called on to tell them about
the wild countryman of theirs, an actual lord, who was
living in a palace on the Canal Grande amid a menagerie
of dogs and monkeys and horses and all the whores that
the gondoliers could ferry to him.

Claire had turned pale, imagining her infant daughter
living in the midst of this pandemonium, and for a while
Shelley had thought he would have to send for some
laudanum to get her to bed. At last she had gone to
sleep – but before going to bed himself Shelley stood for
a long time at the window, watching the dark twisting
clouds.

He had known Claire as long as he had known Mary,
which was to say two years before Claire had gone to
London at the age of eighteen to seduce the notorious
Lord Byron; that had been a project he'd helped her
with, for he was instinctively unpossessive of his women
. . . though Claire couldn't really be said to be *his*. Shelley
had always found her attractive, and often in their
travels he had shared a bed with her and Mary, but he
had so far not ever made love to her.

He certainly had no reason *not* to – she and Mary and
he were in agreement about the unnatural laws, forced
on people by the twin oppressors Church and State,
concerning marriage and monogamy. And now at the
age of twenty she seemed more beautiful to him than
she ever had – just thinking about the way she had
fallen asleep against him in the gondola, the black
ringlets of her hair spilled across his shoulder and one
warmly soft breast pressed against his arm, made his

heart pound again and almost set him tiptoeing to her room.

Idealist though he was, he was a shrewd enough judge of women to know that she wouldn't be alarmed or particularly reluctant.

But it would certainly complicate his situation. Experience had made her realistic, but she couldn't help taking any such – liaison? – as at least partially a promise of getting her daughter Allegra back, and he was not by any means sure he'd be able to talk Byron into that.

It was getting late. A stagnant smell had begun drifting into the hallway on the draught from the window, and he guessed that the canals, when all the gondolas and grocer's boats were retired for the night and no longer agitated the water into the bright choppiness so dear to painters and tourists, gave off this nocturnal evidence of their great age.

It humbled him, and he went quietly to his own room.

The next afternoon Shelley had gone alone in a low, open gondola to the palace Byron had leased. Shelley had been uneasy, for he hadn't told Byron he was coming, and he knew Byron detested Claire and had said that if she were ever to arrive in Venice he would pack up and leave.

The previous evening's storm had blown away, leaving the sky starkly blue behind the pillared and balconied palaces of green and pink stone that walled the broad waterway, and Shelley had blinked at the needles of sunlight reflected from the gold trim and gleaming black hulls of the gondolas that were ranked like slim cabriolets in front of the Byzantine structures.

Dozens of the narrow craft were moored to striped poles that stood up in the water a few yards out from the palace walls, and several times Shelley noticed wooden heads – *mazzes* – at the tops of the poles; once he was even close enough to see the gleam of a nail-head in one of the crudely carved faces. Shelley had heard that the *mazzes* now represented opposition to the Austrian rulers of Italy. It's still resistance to the Hapsburgs, he thought.

The gondola passed under the ornate, roofed bridge that was the Rialto, and soon afterwards the gondolier began trying to point out the palace Byron was renting, on the left ahead.

The Palazzo Mocenigo was actually several big houses which had at one time been united by one long, neoclassical façade of grey stone. No one was visible on the balconies or at the huge triple windows of the palace as the gondola glided across the water toward it, and when the gondolier had poled them in under the shadow of the huge palace, and brought the craft to a rocking stop at the puddled stone steps, Shelley couldn't see anyone in the dimness beyond the open arches of the ground floor.

He stepped out, paid the gondolier, and was looking back out across the wide face of the canal when, simultaneously, the gondola he'd just quitted emerged into the sunlight with a flash of gold, and the door on the landing behind him was echoingly unbolted.

The person who pulled the door open was Byron's English valet, Fletcher, and he remembered Shelley as a frequent visitor at the Villa Diodati in Switzerland; his master, he told Shelley now, had only awakened a little while ago and was in his bath, but would certainly be glad to see him when he emerged. He held the door open so that Shelley could enter.

The ground floor of the palace was damp and unfurnished, and it smelled of the sea and of the many sizeable cages that were stacked against the back wall; stepping around a couple of locally useless carriages in the dimness, Fletcher led him to an ascending marble stairway, and by the sunlight slanting down from above,

Shelley was able to see the animals in the cages . . . monkeys, birds and foxes. He knew that if he had brought Claire, she would have theatrically insisted on searching the cages for Allegra.

Upstairs, Fletcher left him in a wide, high-ceilinged billiard room on the second floor, and went to tell Byron he was here; and as soon as Shelley had leaned back against the billiard table, a little girl wandered into the room from the direction Fletcher had taken.

Shelley recognized Allegra instantly, though she had grown taller even in just these last four months, and was beginning to show the Byronic dark hair and piercing eyes – and when he took some billiard balls from the table and, smiling, crouched down to roll them one by one across the threadbare rug to her, she smiled back, clearly recognizing her old playmate; and for several minutes they amused themselves by rolling the balls back and forth.

Claire had given birth to her while they were all living back in England, at a time when that country had begun to weigh on Shelley: only a month before her birth he had learned of the suicide of Harriet, his first wife; and two years before that, his first child by Mary had died of some sort of convulsion near London. The infant Allegra had for a while been more company to him than Mary or Claire, and he had missed her during these last four months.

'Shelley!' came a delighted call from another room, and when he looked up he saw Byron striding toward him from an inner archway. The man wore a colourful silk robe, and jewels glinted in the brooch at his throat and the rings on his fingers.

Shelley got to his feet, being careful not to let surprise show in his smile – for Byron had put on weight in the two years since Shelley had seen him in Switzerland, and his hair was longer and greyer; he looked, Shelley thought, like an ageing dandy, making up in finery for what he had lost in youth.

Byron seemed to know his thoughts. 'You should have seen me last year,' he said cheerfully, 'before I'd met this Cogni girl; she's my — what, housekeeper now, and she's thinning me down fast.' He peered past Shelley. 'Claire's not with you, I hope to God?'

'No, no!' Shelley assured him. 'I'm just — '

A tall woman appeared in the archway then, and Shelley paused. She stared suspiciously at him, and he blinked and stepped back, but after a moment she appeared to make up her mind favourably about him, and smiled.

'Here's Margarita now,' said Byron, a little nervously. He turned to her and, in fluent Venetian Italian, explained that Shelley was a friend of his, and that she was not to turn the dogs on him or throw him into the canal.

She bowed, and said to Shelley, *'Benedetto te, e la terra che ti fara.'*

'Uh,' said Shelley, *'grazie.'* He squinted at her, and wished the curtains were not drawn across the tall windows at the far side of the room.

Little Allegra was standing behind Shelley's leg now, gripping it tight enough to hurt, and after a moment he looked down at her and noticed how wide her eyes were, and how pale she was.

Her grip loosened when Margarita turned around and disappeared back into the depths of the house.

'Where's Mary?' Byron asked. 'Have you all moved out to this coast? You were staying at that spa, last I heard, near Livorno.'

'Mary's still there. No, I came here to talk to you about . . .' He touched Allegra's dark curls. '. . . about our children. There was something you said in a letter — '

Byron held up a pudgy hand. 'Uh,' he said, 'wait.' He

turned away and walked to the curtained window, and when he turned back Shelley could see that he was frowning and chewing his knuckles. 'I think I remember the letter. I don't think I still believe – still find mildly interesting, that is, I never *believed* – the things I wrote about. I told you to destroy it – did you?'

'Yes, of course. In fact I'm here in person only because you told me I wasn't to write to you here about it. But whether you still credit the story or not, my daughter Clara is sick, and if those Armenian – '

'Hush!' Byron interrupted, glancing quickly toward the archway. Shelley thought there was exasperation, but a little fear, too, in the look. The smile he turned on Shelley a moment later seemed forced. 'I've got horses stabled on the Lido, and I often go riding in the afternoons. Want to come along?'

'Sure,' answered Shelley after a pause. Then, 'Are we bringing Allegra?'

'No,' said Byron irritably. 'She's – there's nothing to be afraid of here.'

Shelley glanced down at Allegra; she looked unhappy, but not extremely so. 'If you say so,' he said.

The warm morning breeze was from the mainland, and from Shelley's sunny hilltop vantage point the priest's Latin was just a low, intermittent murmur, like the droning of bees in a far field.

Mary was looking up the slope at him now, and even from this distance he thought he could read anger in her expression.

Don't blame me, he thought unhappily. I did everything I could to avoid this, everything short of sacrificing my own life.

I suppose I should have done that. I suppose I should have. But I did a lot nonetheless – far more than even you, the authoress of *Frankenstein*, could ever know, or believe.

The Grand Canal broadened out as it merged with the wider Canal della Guidecca and, when the domes of the Church of Santa Maria della Salute were shifting massively past across the oceanic horizon on their right, Byron had the gondolier pull in at the left shore, among the ranks of gondolas moored in front of the Piazzetta. The gondola's blade-shaped prow bumped the step, sending a cloud of startled pigeons swirling noisily up into the sunlight.

The Ducal Palace loomed at Shelley's right, and its bottom two storeys of Gothic pillars made it look to Shelley like a Venetian block deprived of the sea, the once secret opulence of its supporting pilings exposed now to the air.

Byron told the gondolier to wait, and when they had got out and walked up the half dozen steps to the pavement, he led the way out across the warped mosaic pavement of the square. Shelley slowed to stare up at the white statues atop the pair of hundred-foot-tall columns fronting the water, but Byron only snarled and limped on ahead.

'I . . . thought we were going to the Lido,' Shelley ventured when they were halfway to the square tower that stood across the Piazza from the Basilica of St Mark. 'Isn't that farther – '

'This whole enterprise is *certainly* foolish,' Byron snapped, 'but I need to make sure it's not *absolutely impossible* too. I lived near here when I first came to Venice – there's a man we have to see.'

Despite Byron's lameness, Shelley had to hurry to keep up with him. 'Why should it be impossible? I mean, why lately? Surely the Austrians won't – '

'*Shut up!*' Byron glared back the way they'd come;

then he went on in a clipped whisper, 'They *will*, and soon, according to what I've heard.'

Shelley knew his friend's moods well enough to wait for him to speak at times like this. For most of a minute they walked together in silence past the pillars of the palace's west face.

'For a couple of years now,' Byron said, more calmly, 'a man has been . . . is . . . being moved south from Switzerland, laboriously and at huge expense . . . he's Austrian, some kind of ancient patriarch who can pretty much command anything he likes. He's incalculably old, and determined to become a good deal older.' He squinted sideways at Shelley. 'I think I actually saw the wagon he was being carried in, during my tour of the Alps two years ago. There was a box in it like a coffin, leaking ice water.'

'Ice water,' Shelley repeated cautiously. 'Why would – '

Byron made a quick motion with a jewelled hand. 'That part's not important. He needs to get here. The necessity of getting him here may be the main reason the Austrians took Italy, and why they put a stop to the annual ritual marriage of this city to the sea . . . anyway, we can't discuss it now. Wait till we're on the Lido, with the lagoon between us and this place.'

Several identical long banners had been hung vertically from the roof of the Libraria Vecchia on their left, and were curling and snapping in the breeze and throwing coiling shadows on to the sunlit pavement below; Shelley could make no sense of the trio of symbols painted on each of them – at the top was what seemed to be a downward-pointing crow's-foot, then a vertical line, and then at the bottom an upward-pointing crow's-foot with the middle toe missing, like a capital Y. Holes had been punched right through the thick paper at the ends of the lines, as if the marks were the footprints of something with claws.

'What does that symbol mean?' he asked Byron, pointing at the banners.

Byron glanced toward the library, then away. 'I don't know. I'm told it started showing up here and there during the last four years.'

'Since the Austrians took possession,' said Shelley, nodding. 'Four points, then two, then three . . . and they look like footprints. What walks on four points, then two, then three?'

Byron stopped and looked at the banners, and his eyes were a little wild. He started to speak, then just shook his head and hurried on.

Shelley followed, wishing he could pause to look around at the structures ringing the broad square – he gaped up beyond the towering pillars at the vast gold-backed paintings in the highest arches of the basilica as the two of them hurried past, but Byron wouldn't halt, or even slow down. Shelley got a quick look at the brightly blue-and-gold-faced clock-tower, and a glimpse of bronze statues on the top platform of it, before Byron had dragged him around the corner of the basilica.

A smaller square lay beyond the church, and Byron led them across it and into one of the narrow alleys between the buildings that were its north boundary.

Suddenly they had left all grandeur behind. The alley was scarcely six feet wide, and the overhead tangle of chimney flues and balconies and opened shutters kept it in deep shadow except where occasional lamps burned far back in the shops that occupied the ground-floor gothic arches. It seemed to Shelley that anyone could find any shop here just by following his nose, so clear were the smells of fruit stalls, metal workers and wine shops, but the vendors nevertheless shouted the virtues of their wares up and down the alley, and Shelley could feel a headache coming on.

After a few moments he became aware of a regular metallic pinging amid the cacophony, and glancing to the side he saw that Byron was rhythmically bouncing a coin off the pillars he passed. Shelley was about to ask him to stop it when a ragged boy ran up and said something in hopelessly staccato Italian.

Byron gave him the coin and rattled out a reply, then turned around, retraced a few steps and limped through an arch into a tiny courtyard. Iron stairs curled away upward, and potted plants on the steps raised a jungle of leaves to block any stray rays of sunlight, but Shelley could see a crowd of ragged men standing by the far wall.

There was a metallic clinking here too – the men were lagging coins at the wall, each trying to land his coin closest to the wall, the winner taking all the coins.

After a moment one of them, a fat old man who was visibly drunk, scrambled over to the wall and began scraping up the accumulated money while the others swore and dug in their pockets for more.

Several of them noticed Shelley and Byron then, and began edging away, but the fat one looked up and then reminded his fellows sharply that gambling was legal 'in questo fuoco' – Shelley was puzzled by the phrase, which seemed to mean 'in this focus.'

Byron asked the man something that sounded like *Is the eye restored yet?*

The fat man waved broadly and shook his head. '*No, no.*'

Byron insisted that he needed to be sure, and that the man check right now.

The drunken man raised his arms and began protesting to various saints, but Byron crossed the tiny courtyard and handed him some money. The man relented, though with almost theatrical reluctance.

He waved at the other gamblers and they repocketed their coins and hurried away toward the arch. When they were gone he bit his finger – hard, to judge by his expression – shook a drop of blood on to the paving stones, and then walked to the far wall, tossing one of his coins and catching it.

'Stand back,' whispered Byron.

The man was facing the wall now, but squinting over his shoulder at the spot of blood and humming atonally as he repeatedly tossed and caught the coin; then he was looking straight at the wall in front of him and tossing several coins – juggling them, in fact – and the humming was echoing weirdly between the close walls. Shelley could feel the hair standing up on his arms, and the scar in his side began to throb.

Suddenly one of the coins was flung very hard straight up – Shelley watched it, and saw it glint for an instant in the sunlight high above, and then it fell back into the shadow and he could only hear it pinging as it tumbled down through the iron stairway; finally it spun off a flowerpot and clinked to the ground and rolled across the pavement, wobbled for a moment and fell over flat. It was several yards away from the spot of blood.

Shelley restrained a shrug. The juggling had been good, but if the idea had been to land the coin on the blood, the trick had been an absolute failure; of course, after all the bouncing around it had done, it *would* have been incredible if it had landed on it.

He turned to Byron with raised eyebrows.

Byron was staring at the coin sourly. 'Well,' he said, 'it *is* still possible – though I still think it's damned foolish.' He nodded to the fat man and then turned and stalked out of the court. Shelley also nodded, though bewilderedly, and followed him.

They were out of the alley and halfway across the Piazzetta when Shelley noticed Byron cock his head as if listening; Shelley listened too, and heard a cracked old voice singing something in what sounded like Spanish – or was it archaic French?

He looked around and saw that the singer was a startlingly aged man a dozen yards away, hobbling north across the square, away from the Ducal Palace and the two tall columns by the canal; the man leaned heavily on a cane that clicked when it touched the warped pavement.

Shelley remembered Byron's report of an unbelievably old Austrian being carried toward Venice in order to have his life prolonged even further, and he wondered if this aged fellow was here for the same reason; somehow he thought not.

Just then the old man looked up and met his gaze, and waved – Shelley noticed that his left hand was missing a finger – and called something that sounded like *Percy*.

Startled, Shelley waved. 'Do we know him?' he asked Byron.

'No,' Byron replied, grabbing his arm and pulling him away, toward where their gondola waited. 'But I've heard the song before.'

Claire looked up the hill toward where he was standing and, though she didn't move her head, she rolled her eyes in a way that clearly summoned him. He sighed and stood away from the olive tree's twisted branch and started back down.

The little box was being carried over from the boat, and Hoppner, the English Consul, had removed his hat. The hot morning sun gleamed on his bald head and on the varnished box.

Several emotions tightened Shelley's chest as he

stared at the box; but when he noticed that the lid had been nailed shut his only feeling was one of relief.

The Lido was a long, narrow spit of sandy, weedy hillocks, streaked with shadows in the late afternoon, and aside from a few fishermen's net-draped huts, the wooden building that was Byron's stable was the only structure visible along the desolate island.

Byron's grooms had left for the Lido at the same time that Byron and Shelley left the Palazzo Mocenigo, and had been waiting on the shore for a while when the two of them stepped out of the gondola on to the low dock.

The day had turned chilly, and Byron quickly had the grooms saddle up two horses; minutes later the two men had ridden across the spine of the Lido and were galloping away down the eastern shore, the Adriatic on one hand and the low, thistle-furred hills on the other.

For a while neither of them spoke; the wind was snatching the tops from the waves and flinging occasional gusts of spray across their faces, and Shelley tasted salt when he licked his lips.

'When you wrote to me,' he called finally, 'you said that in Venice a means could be found to free ourselves and our children from the attentions of the nephelim.'

'Yes, I did,' replied Byron tiredly. He reined in, and Shelley did the same, and they walked their horses down the slope toward the water.

'It's . . . *just possible*,' Byron said, 'that one can, here, just as in the Alps, break their hold and break their attention – lose them, the way you can lose tracking dogs by walking up a stream. You've got to invoke a blindness – for one thing, it can only be done at night.' He spat into the water. 'Evidently you can even restore life to a freshly perished corpse, if the sun hasn't yet shone on it; vampires' victims never truly *die*, of course, but if you do this right you get the resurrection without

238

the vampirehood – the person is still a normal, mortal human, revived from death just this once.'

Byron laughed. 'And of course then you'd be best advised to take ship immediately to the other side of the globe, so that your devil won't be likely to stumble across you again – put a *lot* of salt water between yourself and her. I was thinking very seriously about South America.' He gave Shelley a defiant stare. 'I no longer think I need to.'

Byron was clearly not comfortable with the subject, so Shelley tried to approach it obliquely. 'It sounded as though you asked that man about an eye,' he said. 'Whether or not it had been restored.'

'The eye of the Graiae,' Byron said. His horse had come to a halt and begun chewing up clumps of the coarse grass. 'You remember the Graiae.'

'The . . . what was it, three sisters that Perseus consulted before going off to kill the Medusa?' Abruptly, and irrationally, he was sure it had been *Perseus*, not *Percy*, that the very old man had shouted to him in the Piazzetta earlier.

'Right,' said Byron. 'And they only had one eye among them, and had to hand it back and forth to take turns seeing, and Perseus snatched it from the hand of one of them, and wouldn't give it back until they answered his questions. When I first came here after leaving Switzerland, I spent a lot of time at a monastery full of Armenian priests and monks on one of the islands in the lagoon; I was . . . nervous about some metaphysical nonsense that doctor told me.'

'Who, Polidori? Oh! No, you must mean the very neffy one – Aickman.'

Byron looked annoyed that Shelley remembered the name. 'That's the one. He and I climbed the Wengern after you went back to England, and it really did exorcize us, as I told you it would – I *felt* the psychic infection sweated out of me, and I'm still not sure what we saw and what we only imagined we saw up on the summit.'

He squinted out across the Adriatic. 'Odd to be speaking of restoring the eye – I *think* I saw a woman cut out her own eye up there. In any case, this Aickman fellow, afterwards, tried to convince me that the . . . shall we call them *lamiae?* . . . would still, even after the exorcism, keep track of us, still be able to recognize us as good prospects, as people with a weakness for their particular . . . *infection.*'

Shelley thought of the woman he'd seen at Byron's palace. 'What are you writing these days?' he asked.

Byron laughed again and shook his head, but Shelley thought the laugh was forced. 'No, no, I haven't relapsed. I *am* writing my best thing to date, a . . . sort of epic, called *Don Juan*, but the fact that it's good is to my credit, not some . . . some *vampire's.*' He was looking Shelley in the eye as he spoke, as if to prove his sincerity.

'Oh, I don't doubt you,' Shelley began, 'it's just – '

'In any case,' Byron interrupted, '*you* are hardly the one to be lecturing *me* about all this.' He was still smiling, but his eyes were chilly.

'You're right, you're right,' Shelley said hastily. 'Uh, back to what I was saying. Was it word of this . . . exorcism possibility . . . that brought you to Venice in the first place?'

'I . . . can't recall.'

Shelley nodded. 'Very well. So what's all this about the Graiae and their eye?'

Byron nudged his horse into a slow walk. He sighed, apparently tired of this subject. 'The Armenian fathers claim that the three sisters were examples of the real, Old Testament nephelim giants, and were captured in Egypt way the hell of a long time ago. They were staked out in the sun until they turned to stone, and then they were carved up for use in architecture, and shackled by having certain restricting designs cut into their bodies. They became drained of energy – unconscious, asleep. But they still had their eye – except that it wasn't really an eye, and what they did with it wasn't precisely *see*.'

Shelley rolled one hand in an *And?* gesture.

'I wish I could have Father Pasquale explain it to you. With the eye they didn't so much see as know. They knew, down to decimal points even finer than God Himself ever bothered to figure to, every detail of their surroundings; and therefore they could predict any future event with absolute certainty – as easily as you were able to predict which corner of the room would receive one of those billiard balls you and Allegra were rolling around this afternoon.'

He stared out at the sea for a moment before going on. 'Now the world isn't usually as *knowable* as this – it *isn't* by nature hard and fast in its tiniest details, and that's why we have the luxury of despising or admiring people, for if our courses really were as predestined as, say, the parabola of a dropped stone, we could hardly . . . make moral *judgements* . . . about the bodies that found themselves conforming to those courses, any more than we can blame a rock that falls on us. Fortune-tellers – and Calvinists – would like living around these things when they're awake and have their eye, because the Graiae's sight forbids all randomness, all free will. When they have their sight, the Graiae not only check on things, but also *check* them.'

'But according to that fat man they don't have it, their eye hasn't been restored,' said Shelley. A wave surged in and swirled foam around his horse's ankles. 'How did that juggling establish that?'

'Well, Carlo's an expert coin-tosser, so good at it that he works right up against the bounds of what's possible; and if you take that as a given, then by having him juggle and try precision-tossing, you can monitor the bounds of the possible. If the eye had been restored, his coin would have landed a good deal closer to the spot of blood; and if they were *awake* and had the eye, it would have landed squarely on it.'

'And what if they'd been awake this afternoon when he did it? Awake but still blind?'

'That's what you've come to Venice to do – wake them up while they're still blind – that's what I was hinting about in my letter. As to what would happen to Carlo's coin if he was to toss it in that circumstance – I don't know. I've asked him, and he's tried to explain, but all I can gather is that the coin wouldn't even exist between the moment of being tossed and the moment of coming to rest; and where it came to rest would have nothing to do with how he threw it; and the penny that landed wouldn't in any valid sense be the same one that was thrown.'

Shelley was frowning, but after a few moments he nodded slowly. 'There's a sort of insane consistency to it,' he said. 'We're trying to undo determinacy, predestination; these things, these three primordial sisters, cast a . . . a field, say. If they've got their eye, it's a field of inviolable determinacy – but if they're blind, it's a field of expanded possibilities, freedom from coldly mechanical restrictions.' He grinned at Byron, his eyes bright. 'You'll remember that Perseus was careful to ask them his questions while they were casting their blind field – so that what he asked wouldn't be impossible.'

'I hadn't thought of that,' said Byron. 'And you're right, if they're awake but still blind, then many things ordinarily impossible are possible within their focus.'

'And they're in Venice, the Graiae? And your priests told you *how* to wake them up?'

'I'm not too confident about waking them, certain very rare fuels have to be acquired . . . but yes, they're here – you saw two of them an hour ago standing at the

242

southern end of the piazza. The third fell into the canal when they were trying to set them up, way back in the twelfth century.'

Shelley blinked. 'Those columns?'

'Right. The doge at the time, Sebastiano Ziani, promised any favour, any *onesta grazia*, to whomever could stand the pillars up in safe captivity there on the pavement in front of the Ducal Palace. Some fellow named Nicolo il Barattiere did it – though he did drop one of them in the canal – but then he demanded the eye as payment. In other words he demanded that uncertainty – gambling – be legalized in the vicinity of the square, in the focus of the sisters' attention. The doge had to stand by his promise, but to counteract it he built the prison right there, and had executions held between the pillars. Blood, fresh-spilt blood, is evidently a fair replacement for the missing eye. Of course, they haven't had executions there for quite a while now.'

Shelley was trying to hold on to his impression that all this made some kind of sense. 'Why should blood be an effective replacement?'

Byron turned his horse back the way they'd come, and set off at a walk. 'I'm just quoting the priests now, and I know what you think of priests – but they said that blood contains the . . . what, the complete, unarguable *plan*, the *design*, of the person it comes from. There's no – '

'That has to be why they need to drink *human* blood,' interrupted Shelley excitedly. 'In order to take human *form*. They couldn't do it without the plan, the design, that's in the blood. If they just drank animal blood, the only forms they could assume would be animals.'

Byron shrugged a little testily. 'That could be. Anyway, in blood there's no room for change – no uncertainty, in other words. It's a pretty powerful embodiment of predestination. Semen would be the opposite, the embodiment of undefined potentiality. In fact, if you could have sex with a woman, there in the square, that would be a perfect blinder for them.' He laughed and put the spurs to his horse. 'I'll volunteer to try, if you like.'

Shelley was shaking his head. 'How can the Austrians *want* to restore the eye, and make everyone in the area brute slaves to mechanical causality?'

'Well of course they've supposedly got this ancient member of the ruling Hapsburg family – some old fellow named Werner who's apparently been hibernating in the Hapsburg castle in northern Switzerland for the last eight centuries. They want to keep him alive for another few centuries, and medicines and life-prolonging magics work much better near the Graiae – assuming they're awake and can pay their razory sort of attention to things. The Austrians have apparently been busy shipping him south through the Alps ever since 1814, when they acquired Venice. I – ' He laughed uncertainly. 'I believe they've got him packed in ice.'

Shelley shrugged. 'Very well. But back when Venice was a *republic* – why did the *doges* want the pillars to have the eye? The doges were always enemies of the Hapsburgs.'

'The Graiae, with the eye, promote *stasis*, Shelley,' said Byron impatiently. '*Every* ruler wants to maintain the status quo. And I don't see that that's so pernicious, either. Your *fields of expanded probability* sound to me like the . . . unformed darkness that was on the deep before God said "Let there be light."'

'Maybe it is like that – maybe it's God who imposes restrictions on us to keep us from becoming all that we're capable of becoming, all we dream of. Certainly religion does that. Without the shackles of religion, mankind would be free to – '

Byron laughed. 'You haven't changed, Shelley. I'll

admit that it was cruel of nature to allow mankind self-awareness; death is going to sever every one of us from his memories and everything that he — uselessly — sought, and we all know it, and that's unbearable. But it's also the way the world works — you needn't blame it on priests and religion. Hell, religion can at least make us believe, for a while, sometimes, that our souls *are* grand and immortal and perfectible.'

'You're talking the worst kind of fatalism,' said Shelley sadly.

'And you're talking Utopia,' answered Byron.

Shelley managed to get Byron to agree on a plan of action, and Shelley and Claire Clairmont left Venice three days later; Shelley was to return as soon as possible with his whole family: Mary, and their two-and-a-half-year-old son, William, and their one-year-old daughter Clara.

He wrote to Mary even before leaving Venice, telling her to bring the children with all possible haste to Byron's hilltop villa in the mainland town of Este, where Shelley would be awaiting them. He had had to be a bit evasive in the letter, for he couldn't tell her, especially through the Austrian-controlled mail, that he intended to take the whole family northwest to Venice in the middle of some night, awaken the blind Graiae and slip free of the attention-net of the vampiric nephelim, and then flee the Western Hemisphere forever.

Mary and both of the children arrived at Byron's villa twelve days later, on the fifth of September, and Mary insisted on simply resting there for a week or so, relaxing in the gardens of the villa, which had been built on the site of a Capuchin monastery that had been destroyed by the French. Byron had told Shelley that consecrated ground might have certain protective properties.

The children seemed happy to get a respite from travel, and even Shelley decided that a few days of rest could do them no harm.

He was finding that he was able to write very well here, in fact; he began by doing translations of the Greek classics, and had now moved smoothly from translating the *Prometheus Bound* of Aeschylus to actually trying to write the last play of that ancient, uncompleted trilogy.

He wrote during the long, hot days in the breezy summer house, which was reached by leaving the back of the main house and walking through a shady tunnel of vine-tangled trellises, and at night he often went out there to watch the bats fly out of the battlements of the ruined medieval fortress of Este; sometimes too, at night, he would stare out across the hundred and twenty miles at the spine of the Apennine Mountains to the south.

Those mountains had dominated the southeast corner of the sky when he and Mary and the children had recently been living near Livorno on the opposite coast, and the peaks had fascinated him then too. He had written a fragment of a poem while living there, and on many nights now he recalled it while staring south at the mountains over the monastery's fallen walls:

> The Apennine in the light of day
> Is a mighty mountain dim and grey,
> Which between the earth and sky doth lay;
> But when night comes, a chaos dread
> On the dim starlight then is spread,
> And the Apennine walks abroad with the storm,
> Shrouding . . .

He had taken the poem no further; he wasn't sure what the mountain might be shrouding.

As it happened, they wound up spending eighteen days at the villa; then, one Monday afternoon late in the month, two things happened to convince Shelley that he'd better get the family on to Venice as fast as possible.

Clouds had sailed darkly up the Po Valley, and the light was leaden and dim by four o'clock; storm clouds bunched and flexed vastly in the south, like gods miraculously rendered in tortured, animate marble, and Shelley, sitting over his manuscript in the summer house, glanced up at the sky from time to time. He was hoping it wouldn't rain for a while, for he was writing a more purely powerful sort of verse than anything he'd ever written before, and he was unwilling to stop the flow of words for any reason – not for rain, nor even to reread the verses to see if they made consistent sense.

'*Ere Babylon was dust*,' he found himself writing, '*The Magus Zoroaster, my dead child, / Met his own image walking in the garden . . .*' And Shelley looked up and saw a figure walking in his own garden, behind a vine-choked lattice, a silhouette against the distant grey bulks of the clouds and the Apennines.

It seemed for a moment to be himself, but when it emerged from behind the arbour he saw that it was a much shorter figure – was, in fact, his infant daughter Clara.

The seeming connection between what was going on inside his head and what was going on outside had momentarily scared him, and so it was with considerable relief that he called out to Clara and pushed his chair back and got to his feet, holding out his arms to pick her up.

But she didn't advance. In the metallic light she gave him a smile that scoured his own smile from his face, and then she walked back behind the arbour.

His heart was thumping alarmingly in his chest, but he was reaching for the door to the garden – when he heard familiar footsteps echoing in the trellised passage behind him, approaching from the direction of the house.

Suddenly glad of an excuse to put off going into the garden, he turned around and pulled open the house-side door, and saw Mary walking toward him with Clara in her arms.

'Dinner's ready, Percy,' Mary said, 'and you've got a letter from Byron.'

He slowly turned to look back out at the garden. There might have been a flicker of motion behind the lattice, but he turned his back on it, put his arm around Mary and escorted her back to the house, hurriedly enough to startle her.

'Where are you?' asked Byron in the letter. 'The *man* is nearly here, I'm told, and the – *Apparatus* – is in Mestre, just across the lagoon. "If 'twere done, 'twere well done quickly." Go at once, if all this still seems sound to you, to Padua – think of some excuse – and I will write to you there and tell you if it be not too late. Destroy this letter *now*.'

Shelley put the letter down and looked across the dinner table at Mary. She was the only one looking at him, for Claire was busy feeding the two children; and Mary's gaze was fearful, so he made himself speak lightly. 'I've got to go to Padua tomorrow,' he said. 'Byron has news of a doctor for Claire.' It seemed a fair excuse – Claire *had* been ill, and he had taken her to a Paduan doctor only a week earlier. 'And it seems that this *medico* might be able to cure little Clara's malaise, too – be ready to follow with her when I send for you.' He glanced toward the back of the house, and then added, 'And of course bring young William, too.'

Mary brought him a plate of steaming pasta and vegetables, but he seemed unaware of it, staring at little Clara as she licked some of her own puréed serving off

248

the spoon Claire held to her mouth, and he was thinking about the image of her that he'd seen walking in the garden. What did that mean? Had he waited too long?

The trusting innocence of the child was a shocking reproach to him, was like a hook turning in his side; she deserved a normal life, normal parents. There can't be a God, he thought, if a child like this can be fathered by a man like me.

Byron's letter was all Shelley ate that night.

Byron's follow-up letter was waiting for Shelley in Padua, and after reading it he immediately bundled Claire into a carriage back to Este, for Byron said the gambit *was* still possible. Bewildered, Claire asked about the doctor they had supposedly come to see, and Shelley hastily told her that they had missed him, but would undoubtedly catch him when she returned with Mary and the children.

When Claire had gone, he went to the Palazzo della Ragione and walked alone through its great hall, appreciating the way its vast dimensions dwarfed him; for he couldn't, now, justify the eighteen days he had wasted at the villa in Este, and he wanted Percy Shelley to seem insignificant, a background character, a figure in a crowd, whose errors couldn't possibly have serious consequences.

Two days later Mary and Claire and the children arrived in Padua, at eight-thirty in the morning.

Little Clara was sicker, her mouth and eyes twitching in a way Shelley recognized – his first child by Mary, a girl who had not even lived long enough to be named, had shown similar symptoms just before dying, four years earlier.

Over the exhausted Mary's objections he insisted that the Paduan doctor had turned out to be no good, and that they must press on immediately to Venice. The weather had not cleared up — they were standing in the square in front of the church of Saint Anthony, and rain had darkened and shined Donatello's equestrian statue of Gatamelata — and the children were crying.

For an hour they waited under a narrow awning for the coach that would take them to the coastal town of Fusina, where they could get a boat to Venice; at last they saw the coach come shaking across the flagstones of the square toward them and when it had squealed to a stop and Mary had climbed aboard, Shelley picked up Clara to hand her in.

As he hefted the infant in front of himself he looked closely at her, and noticed two inflamed puncture marks on her throat.

So much, he thought bitterly, for Byron's idea that sanctified ground might be a protection against the nephelim — or perhaps the French had somehow neutralized the ground of the Capuchin monastery when they had knocked down the walls. The French, too, he recalled, had badly wanted to take Venice.

At the malodorous Fusina docks he found that their travel permits were not among the luggage, though Mary swore she had packed them. The customs guards told Shelley that he and his family wouldn't be able to cross to Venice without the papers, but Shelley selected one of the guards and took him some distance away across the puddled pavement and talked to him for a few minutes in the shadow of an old stone warehouse; and when they returned, the suddenly paler guard said, gruffly, that they could cross after all.

The handkerchief with which the officer wiped his forehead as they strode past him was artistically spotted with old, dried blood.

* * *

250

During the long gondola ride Clara's convulsions grew worse, and Shelley's thin face was stiff as he stared alternately down at the child and up at the setting sun visible through the breaking rain clouds, for Byron had told him that the procedure had to be done at night.

When their gondolier poled them to a stop at the wave-lapped steps of a Venice inn, Shelley climbed right into another gondola and went to find Byron; the sun was low and glinting redly off the nail heads in the faces of the wooden *mazzes* atop the blue-and-white striped mooring poles in front of the Palazzo Mocenigo when he disembarked, and Fletcher took him quickly upstairs to where Byron waited in the billiard room. Allegra was with him, but Shelley didn't see Margarita Cogni.

'I may have waited too long,' Shelley said, his voice tight with controlled emotion. 'Clara's nearly dead.'

'It's still not too late,' Byron told him. 'They haven't . . . *bestowed the eye* on the Graiae yet.' He waved tensely toward the window. 'Meet me at sunset on the piazza – I'll have Allegra with me, and you have Clara, at least; that will do, I think, if she's the only one getting the special attention. And then be ready to hide in some church somewhere until we can find a ship to take us all to America.'

'A *church?*' said Shelley incredulously. 'No, I won't – *you* may see nothing wrong with expressing . . . *implicit allegiance* to the Church, but I'm not going to let Clara and William grow up with blinders on. Even just as a gesture – '

'Listen to me,' said Byron, loudly enough to override him. 'It won't be a *gesture*, and you may well not be able to raise your children at all if you don't do it. There's evidently some truth to the idea that churches are sanctuary – it seems to have something to do with the salt in the holy water, and the stained glass, and the gold

251

patens they hold under the chins of the people who line up to receive Communion.'

Shelley looked unconvinced. 'The *patens?* Those are the little discs with handles, aren't they? What good are they supposed to do?'

Byron shrugged. 'Well,' he said, 'the story *today* is that those metal discs are to catch any crumbs, but they're very highly polished, and Father Pasquale hinted to me one time that they were originally used to make sure that each communicant could cast a reflection.'.

When Shelley got back to the inn, Mary was sitting on a gaudy couch in the entry hall, and Clara was thrashing in her lap; and even as he crossed the stone floor toward them he saw the baby subside and go limp. He ran the last few steps, and lifted the body from Mary's arms.

Claire and some man Shelley didn't know were standing nearby, and the man now stepped forward and explained in Italian that he was a doctor. Shelley let him examine Clara while he held her, and after a moment the doctor said quietly that the child had expired.

The silence that followed seemed to shake the air in the hall all the way up to the arched and painted ceiling; Shelley asked the man to repeat what he had said, more slowly. The man did, and Shelley shook his head and demanded to hear it again; the dialogue was repeated several times, while the doctor grew visibly less patient, until finally Shelley couldn't pretend any longer that the man might have said something else. Still holding the dead child, he sat down heavily beside Mary.

The Magus Zoroaster, my dead child, he thought crazily, *met his own image walking in the garden.*

Chilly air swept through the hall a few minutes later when the canal-side door was opened, but Shelley didn't look up; Richard Hoppner, the English Consul, had to cross the room, glance at the doctor for a confirming nod, and then crouch by Shelley and call his name a couple of times before Shelley even realized that he was there.

'I can handle all the details, Mr Shelley,' Hoppner said gently. 'Why don't you leave your daughter with us, and you and Mrs Shelley can go to your room; I'm sure the doctor here can give you something for your nerves.'

Shelley's mind was an aching vacuum − until he remembered something Byron had said during their ride on the Lido, a month and a day ago: *Evidently you can even restore life to a freshly perished corpse, if the sun hasn't yet shone on it . . . ;* and then his thin lips curled into a desperate smile.

Shelley stood up, still holding the little body, and walked slowly to the window. Only the top spires of the churches still glowed gold.

He turned back to Mary, and even through her tears she saw his expression clearly enough to visibly flinch at it.

'It's still not too late,' he said, echoing what Byron had said to him less than half an hour ago. 'But I have to take her . . . out, for a while.'

Hoppner protested, waving at the doctor to enlist his aid, and he looked relieved when Mary stood up to speak.

But she didn't say what he'd apparently expected. 'Maybe,' she said to Hoppner in a voice harsh with grief and fear, 'you'd better let him take her.'

Hoppner began remonstrating with her now, in a louder voice, but she didn't take her eyes off Shelley's face. 'No,' she said, interrupting Hoppner, 'he just . . . wants to take her to church, to pray over her. He'll bring her back by . . .'

'By dawn,' said Shelley, striding toward the door.

* * *

253

When his gondola emerged into the Grand Canal from the narrow Rio di Ca' Foscari, he recognized the man poling a nearby craft as Tita, Byron's gondolier, and he waved; in a moment Byron's gondola had pulled in alongside, and Byron was gripping the two gunwales to hold the boats together.

He saw Clara's corpse, and swore. 'Pass her across,' he said, 'and get in yourself; I've just heard that there are Austrian soldiers in the piazza – they're apparently getting ready to restore the eye – and they'd catch on to what we're attempting *instantly* if we let them see you bringing a *corpse* up to the pillars.'

Shelley had started to hand the body across, but halted. 'But we've got to bring her, the whole point of this – '

Byron gently took the body from him and laid it down on one of the leather seats in his own gondola. Shelley noticed that Allegra, Byron's daughter by Claire, was crouching wide-eyed in a seat up by the bow.

'We're going to bring her,' Byron assured him. 'We simply can't let them see that she's dead.'

Shelley climbed across into Byron's gondola and then tried to pay the gondolier who had picked him up from in front of the inn, but the man clearly hadn't known until now that he'd been ferrying a corpse, and he poled his craft away without accepting any money.

'A good sign,' said Shelley a little hysterically as he sat down beside his dead daughter. 'She can't be dead if the ferryman won't take two coins.'

Byron laughed grimly and then ordered the imperturbable Tita to go on – and to watch for any canal-side *spectaculos di marionettes*. He gingerly lifted a cloth bundle from his pocket and unwrapped it; it contained a tiny iron fire-pot, and he blew on the air-slits. Shelley saw a glint of red light from within.

Shelley was willing now to let Byron handle things,

and he didn't even ask for a reason when Tita manoeuvred the gondola to a stop beside a pavement near the Academia di Belle Arti where a puppet show was going on by early lamplight.

Byron wrapped the fire-pot in the cloth and replaced it in his pocket; then he climbed out and limped over to the stage and managed to interrupt the show long enough to talk to one of the puppeteers behind the stage. The audience didn't seem to mind, and several people cried, delightedly, *'Il matto signore inglese!'* — the mad English lord! Shelley saw money change hands, and then Byron was limping back with one of the big Sicilian marionettes in his arms. It was of a knight in golden armour, and strings and iron rods dangled from it.

When Byron had got back into the gondola and ordered Tita to resume their journey, he began untying the sections of armour from the marionette and tossing them to Shelley. 'Dress Clara in these,' he said curtly. Shelley did as he was told, and when Byron handed him the visored golden helmet he tried to fit it over Clara's head.

After several minutes of wrenching, 'It doesn't fit,' he said desperately.

The canal was in shadow now, and darkening by the moment — the water was already streaked and stippled with the reflections of coloured lights from the many-windowed palaces they were passing.

'It's got to,' Byron told him harshly. He was staring ahead at the night-silhouetted domes of Santa Maria della Salute. 'And quick — we've only got another minute or so.'

Shelley forced the helmet on, hoping Allegra wasn't watching.

The gondola pulled in to the *fondamenta* in front of the torchlit piazza, and as Shelley stood up and stepped across from the rocking boat on to the stairs he saw that there were indeed Austrian soldiers on the pavement – ranks of them – and he saw too that charcoal and straw and bundles of wood and canvas bags had been piled around the bases of the two columns. A man was splashing some liquid on to the piles. Shelley smelled fine brandy on the breeze.

He turned to Byron, who now stood beside him with Allegra. 'Intense heat wakes them up?'

'Right,' Byron answered, starting forward, 'with the proper fuel, and just so it isn't done in sunlight. The Austrians are ready; the eye must be in Venice now. I wish I'd thought to bring Carlo.'

Tita stayed by the gondola, and the odd foursome – Byron, Allegra and Shelley carrying the ghastly marionette – strode out across the square.

Several of the Austrian soldiers stepped forward as if to stop them, but began laughing when they saw what Shelley carried, and they called to him in German.

'They want to see the puppet dance,' whispered Byron tensely. 'I think you'd better do it. It'll be a distraction – I'll try to ignite the fires – now, while the eye isn't here yet – while they're watching you.'

Shelley stared at him in horror – and noticed a very old man standing behind Byron, leaning on a cane. There was a moment's glint of light beneath the old man's plain brown robe, and Shelley realized that he was carrying a concealed lamp. Did he, too, intend to light the fires prematurely, while the Graiae were still blind?

The old man met his gaze, and nodded, as if answering his thought – and suddenly Shelley remembered having seen him here a month ago; he had called something that had seemed then to be *Percy*, but Shelley was now surer than ever that the name called had actually been *Perseus*.

'*Do it*,' snarled Byron. 'Remember, if this works, it won't have been disrespect to a corpse.' He shoved Allegra toward him, which added to Shelley's distress — what would *she* make of this?

With tears in his eyes, Shelley took hold of the two iron rods in one hand and the strings in the other, then let the body slide out of his arms so that it dangled above the warped pavement — and, as Byron sidled away in the shadows, Shelley began yanking at the strings and rods, making the body dance grotesquely. Torchlight glinted red on the helmet, which was lolling loosely at the level of his belt.

His teeth were clenched and he wasn't permitting himself to think, except to hope that the impossibly hard thudding of his heart might kill him instantly; and though over the rushing of blood in his ears he was vaguely aware that the soldiers had begun muttering, it wasn't until he sneaked an upward glance through his eyebrows that he realized that they were dissatisfied with the show — that they'd seen better, that they had higher standards when it came to this sort of thing.

Somehow that made the whole situation even a little bit worse. It occurred to him that he now knew something that perhaps no one else in the world did — that there was no curse more horrible than, *May your daughter die and be made into a puppet which finds disfavour before an audience of Austrian soldiers.*

Then an urgent shout rang among the pillars of the Ducal Palace, and Shelley had completely lost his audience. He stopped jiggling the body and looked up.

Two of the soldiers had grabbed Byron, but the lord managed to tear one arm free and throw his fire-pot into the heaped straw at the base of the western column — the column, Shelley remembered, that was surmounted by a statue of Saint Theodore standing on a crocodile.

One of Byron's captors let go of him to rush to where the fire-pot now lay flaming.

We're committed now, thought Shelley – or at least Byron is.

At the same moment the old man in the brown robe shambled awkwardly to the other column, opened his robe and, with a full-arm swing, lashed a lamp on to the pavement at the base of it. Burning oil splashed across the straw.

The soldier who had started toward the first pillar evidently saw this as the greater threat, for he veered toward the burning straw at the base of the second one and began trying to kick the stuff away; his trousers began flaming, but he didn't stop.

'*Feuer!*' the soldiers were yelling now, and they were rushing away from Shelley and his marionette; the old man swung his heavy walking stick at the Austrian who was trying to kick the fire away from the second column, and the apparently weighted end of the stick caught the man solidly in the belly; he folded up in midair and hit the pavement and lay there, writhing and still burning.

A man who was clearly an Austrian officer sprinted up, his fire-thrown shadow dancing across the pillared wall of the Ducal Palace, and he was waving to someone back by the dark bulk of the basilica. '*Das Auge!*' he was yelling. '*Komm hier! Schnell!*'

One soldier levelled a rifle at the very old man and squinted down the barrel. Shelley grabbed Allegra's hand. Things were getting out of control – people might very well die here tonight.

Byron had torn free of his remaining captor and flung him to the ground. Two of the soldiers had dragged their burning fellow away toward the canal, apparently hoping to throw him into the water, but his rifle still lay on the pavement. Byron limped over to it, picked it up and hurried back to where Shelley stood with the children.

In the instant before the soldier fired his rifle at the old man, Shelley saw a thing burst vividly but silently into existence in the air between the soldier and his target; it was a winged serpent as big as a large dog, and firelight glittered on scales and blurs of wings as the snaky thing curled in the air.

After the bang Shelley heard the rifle-ball ricochet off the thing and go rebounding away among the pillars as the echoes of the shot batted between the palace and the library.

Byron grabbed Shelley's arm. 'Get back – all we can do now is hope the fires get hot enough before they can restore the eye.'

The winged serpent disappeared, and the sudden chill in the air made Shelley wish irrationally that he had brought a coat for Clara.

In the red light he could see several of the Austrians hurriedly carrying a wooden box from the direction of the basilica.

'It's the eye,' said Byron. 'Hold Allegra.'

The Austrian officer was gesturing urgently to the men with the box, and yelling something to them about the fires being nearly hot enough.

And Byron swore, made the sign of the cross and then raised the captured rifle to his shoulder. It took him only a moment to aim at the advancing men, and then he fired.

The box fell to the stones as its lead carrier buckled, and Byron barked a quick, harsh laugh, which was echoed by the old man. Shelley was holding Allegra's hand so tightly that she had started to cry.

The officer cast a desperate glance toward Byron and Shelley, and then snatched at his belt – Shelley turned his back and crouched in front of Allegra, but when he glanced fearfully over his shoulder he saw that it hadn't been a pistol the man had been reaching for.

The man had drawn a knife and, even as Shelley watched, he slammed the edge of it against the throat of one of the soldiers Byron had struggled with. Blood sprayed across the stones as the man folded backwards and down, his hands clutching uselessly at his split neck.

'*Blood!*' yelled Byron, throwing the rifle down, 'He's spilling blood! That will provide an eye!'

Shelley unceremoniously dropped Clara and rushed forward, intending to drag the bleeding body away, out of the focus of the Graiae, but the officer had spun around and cut the throat of another soldier – and as Shelley ran toward him, shouting in horror and still twenty feet away, the officer looked him square in the eye and lifted the blade under his own chin and dragged it deeply across his throat. He knelt down almost gently, leaning forward.

Blood was puddled across the uneven pavement now, and Shelley floundered dizzily to a halt, wondering if it was delirium that made the paving stones underfoot seem to ripple, as if thirsty for the fare they hadn't got since executions had stopped being done here.

But the air was rippling too, like a bird in a trap, and Shelley thought the very fabric of the world here was quivering in protest – then abruptly it stopped, and though the fires were still raging and lashing bits of burning straw up to the weirdly underlit statues on top of the columns, and the soldiers were shouting and running back and forth as chaotically as ever, Shelley felt a heavy stillness settle over the square; and he knew it was too late.

The Graiae were awake, and they could see.

He backed hesitantly across the solid pavement to where Byron stood. Byron tossed Clara's ludicrously costumed body to him and began leading Allegra back toward the gondola.

Shelley followed numbly, and their shadows were wiggling across Tita and the gondola long before they reached the steps. As Byron lifted Allegra into the gondola Shelley noticed how pale he was, and he remembered the soldier Byron had shot.

Shelley looked back – and the hair stood up on the back of his neck for, impossibly, the blood was now sliding rapidly across the square from the base of one column to the base of the other, horizontally, as though the whole pavement had been tilted up; and then as he took a sideways step to see better, it rushed back the other way, toward the column at whose base it had been spilled.

The stars seemed to be crawling in the sky, and when Shelley turned back to get into the gondola he noticed that the shadows cast by the fires were particularly hard-edged, with no blurriness.

Shelley could feel vast attention being paid to him; he had to glance up to make sure nothing had leaned down out of the sky to focus vast eyes on him. There was nothing to see but the hard-gleaming stars.

'It's the columns,' said Byron hoarsely, pushing him into the gondola. 'They're – apparently fascinated by you.'

As Shelley climbed in and sat down, Allegra edged away from him, up toward the bow, and for an anguished moment he thought she hated him for the way he had treated Clara's body; but then she pulled one of the seat cushions over her face and, in a muffled voice, called, 'Why is the eye staring so hard at *you*, Uncle Percy?' – and he realized that she had only wanted to get away from the object of the Graiae's overpowering scrutiny.

And they *were* staring hard at him, he could feel the

intense interest. His heart laboured in his thin chest, as if extra work was required to push his blood along against the resistance of their attention.

Byron untied the mooring ropes and climbed in last.

The water was uncharacteristically choppy as Tita poled them away from the *fondamenta*, though the sky had cleared of storm clouds hours ago and the stars shone like needles. Again the stars seemed to be moving in the sky, rocking just perceptibly like toy boats on an agitated pond. Shelley leaned out of the gondola and clawed sweaty hair back from his forehead to see what was happening in the canal.

Something was splashing heavily in the water fifty yards away, out in front of the church of Santa Maria della Salute, and spray glittered dimly in the starlight – Tita was audibly and uncharacteristically praying as he wrenched at the oar – and then for a moment something vast had risen partway out of the water, something made of stone but alive, and its blunt head, bearded with seaweed and crusted with barnacles, seemed to be turned toward the glaringly lit piazza with terrible attention in the moment before it crashed back into the water and disappeared.

The oppressive sense of being cosmically stared at lifted from Shelley's chest.

'The third pillar,' Byron said hoarsely. 'The one they dropped into the canal in the twelfth century. We've awakened it too.' He looked almost fearfully at Shelley. 'I think even it wants a look at you.'

Shelley was glad he had blocked Allegra's view of it – she had already seen far too much tonight – and he tried to broaden his narrow shoulders to keep her from seeing anything more; but the water seemed to be settling down, and the thing didn't rise again.

Soon the church of San Vitale blocked the rearward view, and he let himself lean back. He looked anxiously at Allegra. She was apparently calm, but he wasn't reassured.

He didn't stay long at the Palazzo Mocenigo.

He did remember to take the armour off Clara's abused body – and to borrow a couple of tools from the shaken Byron, who didn't ask why or even look at him as he handed them over – before flagging a gondola in which to return to the inn where Mary and Claire waited.

Shelley walked back down the hill in the morning sunlight to where Mary and Claire stood. The tiny coffin had already been lowered into the grave, and the priest was shaking holy water down into the hole. Too little too late, Shelley thought.

Goodbye, Clara. I hope you don't resent the last thing I did for you – the unspeakable going-away present I gave you just before dawn, after we'd got back to the inn and everyone but you and me had gone to sleep.

Did I really delay so long in Este, he asked himself, and let this happen to my child, just because my *writing* was going so well? Am I guilty of the same self-imposed blindness as Byron, who is clearly ignoring the connection between his concubine Margarita Cogni and his recent poetry?

Maybe, he thought now, maybe if I had jumped out of the gondola on the trip from Fusina to Venice, when Clara was at least still alive – drowned myself then, even as late as that – my dreadful sister would have died too, and Clara wouldn't have had to die. But no, by then she'd already been bitten.

He looked again at his abraded left hand.

The coffin had been shut last night, when he had stolen down to the spare room where the landlord had told them to put it, but Shelley had lifted the lid and taken Clara's cooled little wrist in his hand. There had been no pulse, but he had felt a patient vitality there, and he knew what sort of 'resurrection of the dead' would await her if he didn't take the ancient precaution.

It hadn't taken him long, even trembling as he was and blinded with tears.

When he had finished, he had closed the coffin again, and despite being an atheist he prayed, to whatever benevolent power there might be, that no one would open it – or at least no one unburdened by an awareness of the truths behind superstitions.

He threw Byron's iron-headed hammer into the canal; the wooden stake, which had so ravaged his hands and had so much more horribly ravaged little Clara's body, he left imbedded in her chest.

INTERLUDE

February 1821

. . . This consumption is a disease particularly fond of people who write such good verses as you have done . . . I do not think that young and amiable poets are at all bound to gratify its taste; they have entered into no bond with the Muses to that effect . . .

— Percy Bysshe Shelley, to John Keats, 27 July 1820

I fear much there is something operating on his mind — at least so it appears to me — he either feels that he is now living at the expence of some one else or something of that kind.

— Dr James Clark, Keats's physician in Rome

Write to George as soon as you receive this, and tell him how I am, as far as you can guess; and also a note to my sister — who walks about my imagination like a ghost — she is so like Tom. I can scarcely bid you good-bye, even in a letter. I always made an awkward bow.

— John Keats, to Charles Brown, 30 November 1820

Here lies one whose name was writ in water.

— John Keats, epitaph for himself

Even on this chilly day there were a dozen artists, mostly English tourists, who had set up easels in the Piazza di Spagna, at the foot of the wide marble stairs that terraced the Pincian Hill below the twin bell towers of the Trinita dei Monte church. As Michael Crawford strode across the piazza toward the tile-roofed rooming house that was Number 26, his boots scattered piles of the little yellow husks that littered the pavements wherever the lower classes of Rome gathered, and he looked with sour amusement at the loungers eating plates of the boiled beans that had shed the husks.

These weren't precisely beggars – they stood here in hopes of being asked to model for paintings. In order to solicit such employment they liked to assume, as if by accident, poses they thought they were particularly suited for: here, leaning against the stairway coping, a hollow-cheeked, bearded young man rolled his eyes heavenward and mumbled under his breath, clearly hoping to be asked to pose as some suffering saint or perhaps even Christ; while over by the Bernini fountain a woman in a blue shawl clutched an infant to her breast and made beatifically magnanimous gestures with her free arm; the weather was evidently too chilly for any appearance by the sun-basking representatives of the *dolce far niente*, the 'sweet to do nothing' life, but saints and madonnas and even entire Holy Families stood in shivering clusters along the shallow grey slopes of the steps.

For a moment Crawford was whimsically tempted to drop his bag and stand idly here himself, just to be able to see, when an artist finally did ask him to pose, what sort of character the artist might think he represented. A Hippocrates? A Medici poisoner?

But he quickened his pace, for even in Rome winter could be deadly to victims of consumption, and the man he was going to see was supposedly very far gone with that disease; and the man's nurse, for whom Crawford had been given some medicine that was now in a vial in his coat pocket, was apparently suffering from a nervous disorder that made her a danger to both herself and her patient.

Though Crawford's step was still light and he was only forty years old, his hair was almost completely grey. He

266

had been working as a doctor again for two years now, largely on retainer for a man named Werner von Aargau, and the retainer work had, during the last twenty-six months, taken him all over Europe. He was glad to be back in Rome again.

He had met von Aargau in Venice, in the winter of 1818. Crawford, nearly destitute in those days, had been doing some late night drinking by lamplight in a canal-side café when he'd been startled to his feet by the nearby screech and clang of swordplay, and when he had flung down his drink and rushed along the canal bank a dozen yards, he had come upon a young man sprawled on the ancient pavement beside a dropped sword, his shirt soaked with blood.

Over the diminishing drumbeat of fleeing footsteps Crawford had been able to hear the young man's rasping breath, and so he had crouched down and used the sword to cut a bandage from the victim's silk jacket and tie it tightly over the cut in his belly; Crawford had then run back to the café and enlisted help to drag the semiconscious body back there, and when they had got the young man stretched out on the floor beside one of the tables, he had stitched up the wound with a skewer and kitchen twine.

The young man had regained consciousness as Crawford and a couple of volunteers were boating him to the nearest hospital, and when he learned who had stitched him up he had weakly dug a purse from his pocket and insisted that Crawford accept it; and when Crawford looked into it, later in the evening, it had proven to contain a dozen gold *louis d'or*.

Thinking to use up the money sparingly, Crawford had spent a little of it to hire a cheap room and buy a plate of hot pasta in unfresh oil, but the next morning a footman had knocked at his door and summoned him to the hospital. Crawford never did find out how the footman had known where to find him.

To Crawford's astonishment the young man whom he had stitched up only the night before had been cheerfully sitting up in the hospital bed, apparently lucid and unfevered; and when Crawford had haltingly begun to express his gratitude for the money, the young man had interrupted to say that no amount of money could repay the debt he owed Crawford for having saved his life – and that he had a proposal of employment, if Crawford happened to need such.

Crawford had looked down at his own shabby clothes, then looked up with a wry smile and asked what sort of work it might be.

The young man had proved to be one Werner von Aargau, a wealthy humanitarian and patron of the arts. He explained to Crawford that he not only *funded* artists and politicians and religious leaders, but got the finest medical care for them too when they needed it, and he asked Crawford if he'd like to work for him as a surgeon, since his skills in that area were clearly so great.

Crawford had told him that he was only legally qualified to practise veterinary medicine, and hadn't made a success of that – he'd come to Venice, in fact, only to try to borrow money from an acquaintance he hadn't seen in a couple of years, and he'd been wasting the evening in that café only because he'd parted from the acquaintance on bad terms, and wanted to blunt his pride with drink before approaching the man.

Von Aargau had assured him that his skills were first-rate, and that he could be provided with impeccably forged medical credentials, and – since von Aargau would call on him only infrequently – that he could build and maintain a medical practice all of his own, in whatever speciality he would like to pursue.

That had made up Crawford's mind for him.

Crawford hadn't felt that he had the right to ask about the nature of the quarrel that had led to their meeting; but, before accepting von Aargau's offer, he *had* worked up the nerve to ask him how often swordsmen tried to kill him in the middle of the night.

Von Aargau had laughed and assured him that it was infrequent – but when Crawford had stitched him up on the blood-puddled café floor, he had noticed a broad scar below the young man's ribs, and he knew that the canal-side assassin's blade had not been the first to violate the integrity of von Aargau's hide.

Later he learned that von Aargau was obscurely but powerfully connected with the new Austrian government of Venice, and that he was particularly hated and feared by the Carbonari, an ancient, secret society that was currently striving to drive out Italy's foreign masters. Von Aargau warned Crawford that he'd be regarded by these people as an agent of the Austrians himself, even though he'd only be doing medical work; he would be wise, von Aargau had said, to avoid neighbourhoods where the post-mounted wooden heads called *mazzes* were to be found, for the *mazze* was virtually the Carbonari flag.

This didn't deter Crawford, and within a month he had a post at the Hospital of Santo Spirito in Rome, on the bank of the Tiber between the imposing dome of St Peter's on one side and the fortifications of the Castel Sant'Angelo on the other.

He took an apartment on the far side of the river, a couple of rooms overlooking the fountain of Neptune in Navona Square, and every morning that he wasn't on an assignment for von Aargau he would walk through narrow streets to the Ponte Sant'Angelo and cross that bridge, always a little happier if there were other pedestrians on the bridge too, for then he didn't feel so outnumbered by the tall stone angels that topped

269

pedestals every few yards along the stone balustrade on either side.

The Hospital was actually a collection of hospitals, each devoted to a different sort of sufferer; Crawford worked in the foundling hospital, caring for the infants that were delivered anonymously through a little wall grate that was opened when a bell was rung outside on the street. The infants always arrived at night, and Crawford never saw any of the reluctant parents who rang the bell, and sometimes when he was giddy with exhaustion it seemed to him that no one was ever out there when the bell rang and the babies appeared in the basket, that the infants were put in the basket by the city itself, perhaps in the person of one of the stone angels from the bridge.

He didn't see von Aargau after leaving Venice, but every month or two someone representing the wealthy young man would call on him at his apartment. Crawford frequently worked more than ten hours at a time, but these messengers would never visit him at the hospital, preferring to wait in the street outside his apartment even if it was cold or raining; once he had asked one of them about it, and the man had explained that they weren't comfortable on the Vatican side of the river.

The assignments they brought him were always for the same ailment – a pseudo-tuberculosis that von Aargau insisted be treated with garlic and holy water and closed windows . . . and often laudanum, to make sure the patient would sleep through the night.

Of course Crawford was aware of the implications of the treatment – and he hadn't failed to note the paired puncture marks on the bodies of many of these special patients. But he had long ago come to accept the fact that his life would never again remotely resemble what it had been before that night, four and a half years ago,

270

when he had put his wedding ring on to the finger of a statue in the back yard of a Sussex inn; and at least this arrangement permitted him to do the only thing in life that still seemed to have any value: caring for the newly born, the little helpless people who had not yet had the chance to act, to fall from grace.

Number 26 was at the south end of the Piazza di Spagna, and Crawford stepped through the archway of the old house and climbed the stairs to the second-floor landing, where he stepped out into the hall and began counting the room doors as he walked along the worn wooden floor; he'd been told that his new patient had the two corner rooms, overlooking the piazza. Piano music – something by Haydn – rippled softly on the still air.

He found the right door and knocked on it, and as he waited for a response he reviewed what he'd been told of this case.

The patient was a young Englishman, a poet, and he suffered from consumption – but it was a sort of consumption that called for a course of treatment exactly the opposite of what von Aargau usually recommended. In this case *no* garlic was to be administered, or even permitted into the room, and any religious paraphernalia was to be *thrown out*, and the windows were to be left *open* at night.

Crawford knew very well that in any civilized medical college von Aargau's methods would be cause for derision and expulsion – conceivably even imprisonment – but he had seen dying patients recover because of them.

The piano music had stopped the instant he had knocked, and now furniture creaked and thumped on the other side of the door for several seconds. Finally the door was unbolted and, when it was pulled open by a harassed-looking young man, Crawford guessed from the present haphazard placement of several of the chairs that they had been braced against the door moments earlier.

Crawford was puzzled until he noticed the piano – certainly rented – that stood in the far corner of the room. Italian law required that every piece of furniture in a room occupied by a consumptive be burned after the invalid had died, and so these people couldn't risk having the landlady burst in unannounced and catch the sick man in this expensively furnished room.

'*Si?*' the young man quavered, speaking with a thick English accent. '*Cosa vuole?*'

'English is fine with me,' said Crawford, stepping around him into the room. 'I'm Michael Aickman, a doctor. I've been sent to look at a young man named John Keats – I gather he's to be found through here,' he said, crossing to the inner door.

The young man had looked relieved at not having to speak Italian, but now he looked worried again. 'Can't Dr Clark come? Did he send you? The nurse has just gone for the mail, and she's got to go home shortly after she gets back, but – '

'No, I'm not from Dr Clark. I work at Santo Spirito, across the river, but I'm on an independent assignment now. Excuse me, but I was told that Mr Keats is very ill, and I'd like to begin immediately – could you tell him I'm here?'

'But we . . . we can't *afford* another doctor! Even now Clark is giving us a break on his fee, and the nurse is working for nothing. You – '

'My bill is prepaid – by an anonymous good Samaritan who watches over people like destitute poets who get ill. So if you would announce me?'

'Well . . .' The young man stepped in front of Aickman and rapped on the door. 'John? There's a doctor here, he says somebody's paid him to take care of you . . . maybe it was Shelley, or Brown back in England.'

272

Aickman frowned slightly at the first name, and suddenly needed a drink. 'I'll wait out in the hall while you talk,' he said quickly, turning away and fumbling under his coat.

In the hall he twisted the cap off his flask and then tilted it up to his mouth; after several deep swallows of the brandy, he replaced the cap and tucked the flask back into his pocket. Usually he covered the smell on his breath by chewing cloves of garlic, but he'd been told that this Keats person wasn't to be exposed to the stuff, so he'd left it behind. Oh well, he thought – maybe this young man won't sniff a gift physician in the mouth.

The thought struck him as funny, and he was still chuckling to himself when he re-entered the apartment.

The young man at the door sniffed the air and stared at him. He turned quickly to the closed door, and Aickman heard him whisper, 'My God, John, your instincts are good – he's *drunk!*'

Crawford was about to get stern with this ungrateful pauper when there was a laugh from beyond the closed door, and then a frail voice called, 'Drunk? Oh, very well then, Severn, let him in.'

Severn rolled his eyes but pulled the door open, and Crawford strode past him into the next room as imperiously as he could. Severn followed him.

It was a narrow room, with a bed against one wall and a window in the other. The young man in the bed was emaciated and hollow-eyed, but looked as if he had once been sturdily built – and when he looked up, Crawford recognized him.

This was the same youth who had helped him evade Josephine in London four years earlier, and who had been the first to tell him about the nephelim. What had been the name of that evil pub Keats had taken him to, under London Bridge? The Galatea, that was it.

Keats seemed to recognize him, too, and for a moment

he looked frightened; and the smile he put on now seemed forced. 'Doctor . . . ?'

'Aickman,' said Crawford.

'Not . . . let me see . . . Frankish?'

What a memory the boy had! 'No.'

The air in the room was thick with the yeasty, bakery smell of a starving human body – conventional medical wisdom held that consumptives should eat virtually nothing. Crawford crossed to the window, unlatched it and pushed the frames open.

'Fresh air's important in the treatment of the sort of Pthisis you suffer from,' Crawford said. 'It's fortunate that your bed's close to a window.'

Below him he could see the tourist painters, and the broad steps sloping up the hill, and the clusters of shivering saints huddled against the balustrades. The spire in front of the church of Trinita dei Monte cast a long winter shadow, as if it were the gnomon of a sundial meant to indicate seasons rather than hours. Beyond the church were simply wooded green hills, for this was the northern edge of the city.

'Another thing that is – ,' he began, then paused. He had been leaning on the window sill, and now there was grease on his hand. Even without bringing his hand to his nose he could smell garlic. 'What's this?' he asked quietly.

Keats looked wary, but Severn laughed. 'We have our dinners sent up here from the trattoria downstairs,' Severn explained, 'and it costs us a pound a day, but the food was just *terrible* at first! So finally one evening John here just took the plates from the porter and, smiling the whole time, dumped them all out the window, and handed the empty plates back! Since then they've brought us excellent food – and the landlady didn't even charge us for the dinners that wound up in the square.'

He peered at Crawford's hand. 'Uh, I guess he accidentally got a little on the window sill while he was at it.'

'Accidentally,' Crawford repeated thoughtfully, smiling at Keats. 'Well, we can't expect you to get well with putrefying food lying about — I'll have this nurse of yours wash that off as soon as she gets back. Now it's important that you — '

'I don't want you,' Keats said steadily. 'I'm fine with Clark, I don't need — '

Crawford promised himself another drink very soon. 'I've dealt with a dozen cases like yours, Mr Keats, and every one of my patients has recovered. Can Clark claim a similar record? Is Clark even confident that this is consumption? Aren't there some symptoms that . . . puzzle him?'

'That is true, John,' put in Severn, 'Clark did speculate that it might be something to do with your stomach, or your heart . . .'

'My brother is dead, Frankish,' said Keats loudly, his wasted face made even gaunter now with anxiety and helplessness. 'Tom died in England two years ago, of *consumption* — ' Keats paused to cough harshly, but after a few seconds forced himself to stop. 'And,' he went on, his voice hoarse, 'he wasn't even eighteen yet . . . and two years before that — just after I met you, in fact — he started getting *letters in verse* from something signing itself "Amena Bellafina", and I'm sure your Italian is good enough for you to translate that into something like "pleasant succession of sweethearts" — though *bella* can also mean "final game" — '

Keats's voice had been getting more and more strained, and now he gave way to the cough that had been building up inside him; he fell back on to the bed and rocked there as the terrible coughing tore through his chest and brought bright blood to his lips.

Crawford knelt beside him and took his thin wrist.

Any conventional doctor would be sharpening his lancet now, and calling for a cloth and bowl and bolsters and a sponge soaked in vinegar, but at some point since leaving England Crawford had lost his faith in phlebotomy – somehow bleeding a patient seemed too much like rape now, and he doubted that he'd ever do another bleeding in his life.

Keats's pulse was strong, which was uncharacteristic of consumption – but Crawford had known all along that this wasn't consumption. Camphor, nitre, white henbane – he wouldn't be prescribing any of those for this ailment.

Keats was subsiding, breathing deeply, but he seemed to be unconscious.

'Delirium, doctor?' asked Severn, and when Crawford glanced up at him he noticed for the first time how exhausted Keats's friend was.

'Just about any doctor would tell you so.' Crawford stood up. 'How long have you been looking after him?'

'Since September – five months. We sailed from England together.'

Crawford led the way back into the other room. 'How long have the two of you been here in Rome?'

'Since November. We landed in Naples on Keats's birthday, Hallowe'en.'

'The trip from England took more than a month?'

'Yes.' Severn collapsed into a chair and rubbed his eyes. 'The weather was bad when we left, and for two whole weeks we just sailed back and forth along the south coast of England, waiting for it to clear up; finally we were able to start out across the Channel, but the trip was horrible, and then when we got to Naples we were quarantined aboard the boat for ten days.'

'Why?'

'We were told that there had been a typhus epidemic in London.'

276

'Huh.' Crawford, who worked in Rome's biggest hospital and was often called in on cases that required a speaker of English, had not heard of any such epidemic. 'Hallowe'en's his birthday,' he said thoughtfully, remembering now that Keats had told him that four years ago.

That would be why the medical treatment von Aargau had prescribed was the opposite of what he usually had Crawford do in these pseudo-consumption cases – usually the patients had to be insulated with garlic and holy water and closed windows, so that the source of their diminishment couldn't get at them; but because of his birth date Keats was an adopted member of the nephelim family. *He* was different – re-exposure to the poison was the only thing that would keep *him* alive.

And, he thought, Keats must know this – so why is he intentionally keeping . . . her . . . out?

Just as he thought the word *her*, he noticed the title of a book lying on the table – *Lamia, Isabella, The Eve of St Agnes, and Other Poems* . . . by John Keats. He picked it up.

'John's second book of poems,' Severn said.

The weight of the vial in his pocket reminded Crawford that he had to wait for the nurse, and no serious remedial measures could be taken for Keats until dark anyway, so he looked over at Severn. 'I'd like to wait and talk to this nurse you mentioned. All right if I read some of this?'

Severn waved. 'Surely. Can I make you some tea?'

Crawford took out his flask and unscrewed the cap, ignoring Severn's scandalized stare. 'Just a glass, thanks.'

Lamia was a narrative poem about a Corinthian youth who married a creature that was sometimes a woman and sometimes a sort of winged, jewelled serpent, and how he died after a friend banished her. *Isabella* told the story of a well-born girl whose brothers killed her plebeian lover, whose head she later dug up and planted in a pot of basil which she subsequently watered with her tears. Crawford wondered if the two poems weren't really the same story – a female mating beneath her station, to the unintended ruin of the genuinely loved male.

At last footsteps approached up the hall, and Severn put down the magazine he'd been reading and got to his feet. 'That will be Julia, the nurse,' he said.

Crawford stood up too, still holding Keats's book – but he dropped it when Severn opened the door and the nurse walked in.

For a moment he was sure it was Julia, *his* Julia, his second wife, who had died so horribly in a Hastings inn; then he noticed that the shape of the jaw was subtly wrong, and the forehead was too high, and he coughed to stifle an embarrassed laugh.

But when she glanced at him he saw that one of her eyes didn't track properly, and wasn't quite the same colour as the other one, and the hairs actually stood up on the back of his neck when he realized who this was.

'Julia,' Severn was saying, 'this is Dr Aickman. The hospital across the river sent him – gratis! – to look in on John.'

Josephine nodded at Crawford with no evident recognition, and he was reminded of how much he had aged since she had last seen him. 'Dr Clark agreed to taking you on as a consultant?'

Crawford was trying to figure out if anything besides sheer, appalling coincidence could have led her here, and he missed her question and had to ask her to repeat it. When she did, he shook his head wearily and reached down to the table for his flask.

'No,' he said, lifting it to his mouth. 'Excuse me,' he said a moment later as he lowered it and wiped his mouth with his free hand. 'No, but I can show you credentials and testimonials that I guarantee outrank anything Clark can produce – *and* I can guarantee Mr Keats's recovery.'

Josephine didn't look reassured. 'And has Mr Keats had anything to say about this?'

'John doesn't want him,' put in Severn, apparently offended afresh by Crawford's drinking. 'Aickman wants John to sleep with the window open . . . oh, and he wants you to wash off the *window sill*.'

It was clear from the way Severn said this that he expected the nurse to be offended at being asked to perform a menial chore, but Crawford saw the flash of real alarm in her eyes.

'*Who* sent you?' she asked quietly. 'Not the Santo Spirito, *they* don't object to garlic and holy water and closed windows!'

Severn stared at her blankly, but Crawford stepped closer to her and spoke directly into her face. 'I never said the Santo Spirito sent me. All I say is that my methods will heal him.' He remembered that she suffered from some sort of nervous malady herself, and wished he could pry her jaws open and dump the contents of the vial down her throat right now.

At the same time he was blurrily aware that he wasn't handling this as tactfully as he could; the reference to Shelley, and then the sudden intrusion of Josephine and a hundred memories from his supposedly dead past, had jolted him. He only carried the flask in order to be able to render himself unconscious during those times, generally late at night, when he was tempted to invite his nonhuman spouse back – and here he'd been sucking at it liberally in the middle of the day.

Von Aargau had made him memorize a procedure to use if some assignment should prove to be beyond him, and he was afraid he might very well have to use it, for the first time, today. Von Aargau had frowned when he'd described it, though, and very clearly hoped that Crawford would never have to do it.

'Look,' Crawford said now, desperately, 'give me one night. If he hasn't shown an astonishing improvement by tomorrow morning, I'll pay the entirety of Dr Clark's bill – and a salary for you, too,' he added, turning to Josephine, 'covering the entire time you've been working here.'

Josephine's expression didn't change, but Severn smiled incredulously. 'Really? Will you put that in writing? Great God, that would – '

'No,' interrupted Josephine sharply, 'he can't stay. John doesn't want him. And I don't need pay for this job – I've saved some money, and on my days off from here I have paying patients, and I'm not being charged rent at the St Paul's Home . . .'

'Excuse me, Julia,' said Severn a little stiffly, 'but it's hardly your place to make decisions of this sort. If this man is willing to pay Clark's bill – '

The door behind them was pulled open then, and when he turned around Crawford was astonished to see that Keats had got out of his bed and was standing in the doorway.

'My brother,' Keats whispered, then fell.

Crawford and Severn leapt forward and caught him, and then carried him back to his bed.

'You told us,' Crawford told him softly, 'how Tom died of consumption.'

Keats shook his head impatiently. 'My other brother, George – he's well enough, I trust – I talked him into going to America – I even had to lend him the money to do it – and he's over there now, with the whole Atlantic lying between him and my . . . Godmother, devilmother . . . and my brother Edward died when I was only six . . . but *my sister*, Fanny, she's only seventeen! And she's in England! Christ, can't you understand? I – ' He broke into a booming cough, and seemed to lose consciousness again; but a moment later he opened his eyes and stared at Severn and, through bloody lips, said, 'I'm sorry, Joseph. I know it would be nice to get out of Clark's debt. But this . . . Aickman fellow has got to leave. Don't ever let him come back.'

Crawford leaned over the bed. 'You want to die, is that what you're saying?'

Keats rolled his head to the wall. 'No, you idiot, I don't *want* to die. Christ . . .'

Severn took Crawford roughly by the arm and forcibly marched him out of the room, through the front room and into the hall. Crawford was too surprised to resist, for Severn hadn't seemed to be at all forceful.

'He's engaged to a girl in England,' Severn said harshly, 'and he knows he'll never see her again. She writes letters, but he can't bear to read them anymore. He won't even let me open them.' There were tears in his eyes, and he cuffed them away impatiently. 'And his new book is finally getting the kind of attention he's hoped for all his life. And he's not some . . . some *ascetic recluse*, he's – he was – a vigorous, healthy young man, and he's in *Rome*, but he can't even go out and *look* at it. And *you* think he *wants* to die.'

Crawford started to speak, but Severn pushed him hard, and he took several drunken steps backwards down the hall.

'If I see you here again, I'll – ' Severn began, then just shook his head helplessly and re-entered the apartment and shut the door behind him.

Crawford swore, not least because he'd left his flask inside, then turned and walked back toward the stairs.

Blood made terrible ink; Crawford's fingertip was a slashed ruin by the time he had stabbed the pen nib into it often enough to scrawl the note to his Austrian bosses. Finally he put the pen down and sucked on his finger as he read the note.

He won't cooperate; nor will the nurse. Sorry.

By the time he had found and pocketed the special whistle von Aargau had given him, the blood had dried on the paper. He was supposed to leave the note in the hand of any piece of statuary – not difficult anywhere in Italy, and very easy in Rome. He walked down the stairs from his rooms over Navona Square – just a dozen blocks from Keats's place – and, still sucking his finger, stared around at the three wide fountains in the long square.

The fountain of Neptune was closest, so he walked over to it and looked speculatively at the stone figures arranged across its wide pool. Neptune himself was too busy shoving a spear down into some sort of octopus – his hands were just fists around the shaft of the spear – but there was a pair of marble cherubs who seemed to be tormenting a wild-eyed marble horse nearby, and there was room under the hand of one of them for the note, if he folded it tightly.

He folded it up, then stepped over the coping, splashed his way to the horse, and stuck the bit of paper under the stone fingers.

It chilled him a little to be putting something into a statue's hand, but he thrust out of his mind the long-ago memory of another statue in the back yard of a Sussex inn.

He looked up as he waded back to the fountain's coping, wondering if anyone might wonder what he'd been up to and try to pry the note out, but only one old woman seemed to have noticed his action, and she was crossing herself and hurrying away.

Very well, he told himself as he clambered out, his trouser legs flopping wetly around his ankles, the note's in place, now all you've got to do is let von Aargau's people know there's a note to be picked up. God knows how they'll receive my signal, or be able to tell which stone hand in the city is holding the note, but that's their job.

He unpocketed the whistle and started to raise it to his lips, but then it occurred to him that he was already a bit conspicuous in his wet trousers, and that standing in the middle of the square puffing on a little whistle *too* would make him seem to be some sort of third-rate street performer.

He hurried into the shade of a narrow alley, and then puffed at the whistle in the *four-two-three* pattern von Aargau had described to him. As von Aargau had told him to expect, it produced no audible sound. He blew the signal pattern again.

Sand and tiny pieces of gravel were sprinkling down into the alley and, looking up even as he blew the pattern one more time, he saw that a flock of pigeons that had been nesting under the ancient tile eaves were scrambling out and scattering noisily away into the sky; and church bells had begun ringing in random cacophony all over the city — but a moment later all sounds were masked in the hiss of a sudden downpour of rain, and in moments the pavements and stone building fronts were all dark. He put the whistle away and hurried out from under the overhanging eaves into the abruptly rain-swept square.

Before he could cross the twenty yards back to his building he heard a clatter of hooves on pavement and, squinting to his left, northward, he saw a dozen men on horseback ride into the square and jerk their mounts to a halt.

Though they were nearly a hundred yards away,

Crawford could see that they were staring intently at everyone and asking quick questions of the people nearby – but the old woman who had seen Crawford wade into the fountain was gone, and in the rain Crawford's wet trousers apparently raised no suspicions, for he got to his front door without being stopped.

He had glanced at the stone cherub as he passed it, and he'd thought he'd seen a faint wash of blood streaking the neck of the stone horse. More than ever the cherubs seemed to be torturing it.

Back up in his room he threw off his wet coat – and noticed that it *clunked* when it hit the back of a chair. He picked it up again and felt in the pockets, and a moment later he had dug out from among the folds of his handkerchief the vial of medicine he had been supposed to give to Josephine.

He sat down in the chair with the vial in his hand and stared out of the rain-streaked window at the lead-coloured afternoon sky.

How in hell had *Josephine* wound up there – and calling herself *Julia*? Obviously she hadn't followed him, for she'd been attending Keats for at least several days before Crawford had even got the order to go over there. And, even more obviously, it was clear that she and Crawford had not been there for the same reason.

And why, he wondered, does she want Keats to die?

More to the point, why does *Keats* want to die? He was worried about his little sister – does he think his survival would mean his sister's death?

Would it mean that? He recalled that Byron and Shelley – and Keats, too, back in London – had had some such idea about the families of the nephelim's prey.

Crawford shifted uncomfortably in the chair and wished he hadn't left his flask at Keats's place, for he didn't want to think clearly, or remember clearly, right now. None of these questions was his problem anyway – he was only trying to save someone who would otherwise die. Where was the ethical problem in that? Perhaps he should go downstairs and get a bottle to bring back up here.

The thought reminded him of the vial he still had in his hand, and he held it up to the lamplight, which glowed red through the milky fluid within. He remembered that von Aargau's representative had told him to give it to the nurse in some strong-tasting medium like stew or hot spiced punch and, because her nervous ailment made her needlessly suspicious, not to let her know he was giving it to her.

He pulled out the cork and sniffed the stuff. The harsh, acidic smell was distantly familiar, and reminded him of the first hospital he had ever worked at – something to do with the syphilitic ward. Did Josephine have syphilis? That disease could certainly affect her mind adversely. Perhaps this was the explanation of all her weird behaviour.

He smelled it again. The memory was circling in his head like a fly, always seeming on the point of alighting. Something to do with his having got in trouble, having mixed something wrong . . .

And then he had it, and his belly went cold and, just for one moment of weakness, he wished he had got that bottle of liquor and had drunk himself insensible and not ever opened this vial.

The vial contained quicksilver dissolved in acid mineral spirits, a virulent poison which was sometimes accidentally produced by careless medical students when mercury was being prepared for use on syphilitics in hospitals.

Von Aargau had sent him there to kill Josephine.

But he's my employer, one part of his mind instantly pointed out, it's through him that I'm able to care for all the foundling infants in Rome — if I break with him I'll lose the position and have to go back to being a mediocre veterinarian, once more trying to work up the nerve to borrow money from Byron; and, realistically, quite a number of those infants will die without my care, and *Josephine* is hardly a creature with potential, hardly anybody's idea of a *tabula rasa*, a blank slate — hell, she's a slate that's had bad maths scrawled on it and then been waxed so that nothing can ever be written on it again. I've treated *sheep* that had more of a right to live.

He started to recork the vial, intending to put it back in his pocket to await a future decision, but found he couldn't do it. Was he really even willing to *consider* giving her the poison?

This would be his first murder by *action* rather than by inaction, wouldn't it?

But, he asked himself plaintively, is saving *Josephine* worth losing the position at Santo Spirito? Somebody else, sure, Keats, his damned sister, the next person to walk across the square, in fact, but *Josephine*? All those infants who'll need my help, who'll die without me, just so that this . . . wretched construct named Josephine can lurch a few more unhappy miles and years before giving in wearily to death?

Of course, by the time I lie down to die, at the age of seventy or so, all the children I'll have delivered and cared for will have grown up to become coarse, brutish adults; and hell, Josephine herself was a baby once — her mother died giving birth to her.

This . . . protectiveness you feel toward newborns, this value you see in them — at what point, exactly, does it all wear off? When is it that a person stops qualifying for life, according to your definition?

Josephine certainly didn't acknowledge it when she saved your life on the Wengern Alp.

His heart pounding at the prospect of all the questions

he'd now no longer be able to evade, Crawford crossed slowly to the window, opened it, stared down at the grey street for a moment and then carefully poured the liquid in a long, separating stream into a puddle under a rain gutter. He considered throwing the vial itself across the pavement into the fountain of Neptune, but decided that it would probably fall short — and if it didn't, that it might hit that poor stone horse.

The thought of the horse reminded him of the note he'd left under the cherub's hand. Had von Aargau's people had time to find it yet? If so, they might very well be on their way to do what Crawford had failed to do.

He threw on his wet coat, ran out of the room and down the stairs, leaving the window and the door open, and sprinted across the rain-slick stones and then cleared the three-foot-tall coping of the fountain in a flying leap. His legs twisted out from under him when he hit the water, and he wound up more swimming than wading as he floundered to the horse.

The note was gone.

Von Aargau's people wouldn't be able to deal with Keats until dark, but killing Josephine could be done at any time.

For one falsely hopeful moment he hoped that the rain would have washed the blood-letters away . . . but then he remembered how efficient von Aargau's organization was when it came to dealing with blood.

Where had Josephine said she lived? St Paul's Home — that was in the Via Palestro. Crawford knew the place, for it was where the hospital hired most of its nurses. It was at the east end of the city, more than twice as far away from here as Keats's place.

The jets of water from the fountain's mechanism were being torn to bits by the hammering rain as he climbed out on to the pavement again, and he had to squint to see as he began running, miserably, east.

As he jolted along through the rain he thought about this last case von Aargau had assigned him. Every previous pseudo-consumption patient had been a powerful pro-Austrian politician or writer; why should von Aargau want to save Keats, an obscure poet whose political sympathies, assuming he had any at all, were probably more in line with the Carbonari's? In fact, how had von Aargau even come to *hear* of Keats? Lots of tubercular patients came to Rome hoping to stave off death.

It made no sense . . . unless von Aargau – through his employee, Crawford – was representing the only figure in the conflict who was being thwarted: the lamia herself. And of course the lamia would just as soon see Josephine dead, since Josephine was abetting Keats in his resistance to the lamia's will.

The thought brought Crawford to a wheezing stop in a narrow street, and he leaned against a lamp-post to catch his breath and order his thoughts.

Had he been working for the nephelim cause, these two years? It seemed unlikely, since in every one of von Aargau's cases, except that of Keats, he'd been *insulating* the patient from a vampire; but of course von Aargau had never prescribed any measures that would *free* a victim from a vampire – just . . . hold it at arm's length for a while.

And Keats, Crawford reminded himself, is a member of the nephelim family. For that matter, so was I. I wonder if, considering the nature of the work von Aargau has been giving me, that fact could have been a factor in von Aargau's hiring me. Am I still, in some sense, a member of the family?

It would explain why von Aargau needed *me*, specifically; the nephelim would have no scruples about stopping a *non*member who dared to obstruct them.

Abruptly Crawford wondered if von Aargau's canalside duel had been staged for his benefit, so that apparent gratitude would conceal the *real* reason von Aargau had been so insistent about hiring him.

That cut in his belly was real, though, Crawford thought. What kind of man could inflict that kind of wound on himself intentionally . . . and then heal so rapidly and totally?

Well, it doesn't matter whether von Aargau is on the side of the nephelim or not, he told himself firmly – just the fact that he sent me there as an unwitting poisoner has made it impossible for me to continue working for him.

He toppled forward into his plodding, splashing run again, resolutely not letting himself think about how cold and wet he was, nor about how cold and wet he was likely to be in the future, now that he would have to give up his employment and return to the life of a penniless fugitive . . . though he did damn Josephine, in jerky whispers through rain-numbed lips, for not having died in the Alps.

The ground floor of the building next to St Paul's Home was a trattoria, and yellow lamplight from inside gleamed on the abandoned cups and dishes that stood half-filled with rainwater on the tables out on the pavement; only one hooded man still sat in a chair by one of the tables, and he got to his feet as Crawford came limping around the corner from the Via Montebello. The grey sky had begun to darken toward black, and the amber glow of lamplit windows gilded the dark puddles.

'It's all right, doctor,' the man said in a low voice. 'Go home. Others are taking care of it even now.'

Crawford paused, panting too hard to speak, then nodded and leaned on one of the tables as if to let his heartbeat slow down; one hand gripped the edge of the table and the other closed on the neck of a half-empty bottle of wine.

His eyes rolled up and he took a raspingly deep breath and his feet shuffled for balance, and then he lashed the bottle up across the shadowed face; the glass shattered against the cheekbone and the man cartwheeled away to slam into the side of the building.

Crawford was on the limp body even before it had finished collapsing to the pavement, and bits of glass were still rattling and spinning among the legs of the tables as he yanked a flintlock pistol from under the unconscious man's coat and then turned toward the nurses' home next door.

The building was fronted by an arch that opened on to a small courtyard, and he ran inside and, blinking in the darkness, groped his way past half a dozen wooden statues of saints to a set of wrought-iron steps. Orange light now glinted overhead, and he heard boots scuff echoingly.

Men were coming down the stairs above Crawford, cursing and grunting — apparently carrying something heavy. Pausing only to cross himself, he tucked the pistol into his belt and started quickly up the iron stairs.

A bobbing lantern somewhere farther up silhouetted the bottom-most man, who was peering down over his shoulder to see where he was stepping, and he was the first to see Crawford.

'Out of the way, Aickman,' he gasped, 'we've got her.'

Crawford could now see that the burden the men were carrying was a rolled carpet that sagged in the middle, and he knew it must contain Josephine; the man who had spoken was holding up one end, and Crawford hoped it was where her feet were.

290

Crawford smiled and nodded agreeably – and then leapt up four more steps, grabbed the back of the man's collar and pulled, hiking his feet up so that his entire weight was behind the pull.

The man toppled over backwards with a panicked yell, and though Crawford tried to twist him around in midair, Crawford was still between the stairs and the heavy body above him when they slammed into the iron stair-treads several yards down; all the breath was punched out of him in one harsh, agonized bark, so that when, a moment later, the dropped roll of carpet thudded solidly into them before going end over end down the stairs, he could only scream in his mind as he felt broken rib-ends grind together in his chest.

The man on top of him had his legs in the air and, screaming and flailing uselessly at the brick wall, he slowly overbalanced and then went tumbling away himself in a backward somersault, off Crawford. The stairs were ringing dully.

Someone leapt over Crawford and ran on down the stairs, and then someone else hoisted him roughly to his feet, and he was dimly aware of angry faces in lantern light, and loud questions being shouted at him.

He was only able to shake his head. His battered lungs were heaving in his chest, trying to draw in air, and he was distantly aware of hot blood running down his chin from his nose.

Finally one of his questioners spat an impatient curse and looked past Crawford down the stairs. 'I can't get any sense out of him, Emile, but there's been too much noise,' he called, loudly enough for Crawford to hear him over the ringing in his ears. 'Never mind taking her to the river – kill her here, and leave Marco where he is and let's be on our way.'

Crawford turned and began frantically shambling down the stairs, his feet flopping and slipping under him, his hands clutching the rail, and sweat springing out coldly on his ashen face. He was able to breathe now, but only in great rasping whoops.

When he got down to the narrow courtyard he was sure he would have to pause to vomit; but by the light from the quickly descending lantern behind him he saw the man who'd hurried past him on the stairs – Emile, apparently – bend over the carpet and drive a knife twice, hard, into the streetward end of the carpet roll.

The light was good enough now for Crawford to see blood on the blade as Emile drew back his arm for a third stab. The roll was heaving now, and Emile seemed to be trying to judge where Josephine's neck was.

Crawford drew the pistol from his belt – tearing some skin, for the jagged lock mechanism had apparently been driven into his stomach – and, whimpering in horror, pointed it at the man and fired it.

Recoil punched the pistol out of his hand, but Emile spun away from the carpet and sat down hard against the wall, and Crawford hunched across the pavement to him, stumbling over the limp body of the man he'd pulled down the stairs, and hurriedly searched Emile's blood-wet pockets.

He found another pistol and, turning on his heel so fast that he thought he might pass out, aimed it back up at the men who by now were nearly at the bottom of the stairs. Lights had been lit behind several of the courtyard-facing windows, and women were screaming and calling for the *guardia*.

'Run,' Crawford choked, 'or I'll . . . kill you too.'

They backed up cautiously until they were out of his line of sight, and then he heard them scramble away – farther up the stairs or down some hall.

Crawford gingerly pushed the pistol down inside his belt, then crouched by the still-heaving roll of carpet.

He noticed that there were two nuns peering at him

from a doorway. '*C'è una donna ferìta qui dentro – forse marta – aiutatemi srotolare!*'

The nuns exclaimed in alarm but hurried over to him, and in less than a minute had unrolled Josephine.

She sat up, and Crawford was relieved to see by the blood on one of her ankles that Emile had been stabbing the wrong end of the carpet. He looked around until he saw Emile's dropped knife, and he automatically bent and picked it up.

The men on the stairs had carried their lantern away with them, but enough lamps had been lit behind the nearby windows now for Crawford to see that Josephine was deep in her mechanical defence – her eyes were wide and her head was snapping back and forth, and she got to her feet like a rusty iron puppet, apparently unaware of the blood coursing down over her right foot.

Crawford glanced nervously back up the stairs, then limped over to her. 'We've got to get out of here, Josephine,' he said. 'Those men won't leave the area until they've killed you.'

She stared at him blankly and recoiled from the arm he'd put around her; he was ready to simply drag her away, but then he remembered the nonsense she'd spoken to Byron and him on the Wengern, and remembered the name under which she'd been working for Keats.

'Julia,' he said, 'this is Michael, your husband. We've got to get out of here.'

The rigid blankness left her face, and she gave him a grotesquely delighted smile. She seemed about to speak, but he just grinned as cheerfully as he could and led her toward the arch and the street beyond, waving Emile's knife reassuringly back at the bewildered nuns.

He bumped into one of the life-size wooden statues, and in a moment of panic stabbed at it with the knife, striking it in the face.

The knife-grip was suddenly red-hot, and he snatched his scorched hand away. His palm was red, with a black spot in the centre.

He thought he heard a shout far away in the night, and on a sudden impulse that he didn't bother to analyse, he left the knife sticking in the wooden saint's cheek.

He pulled Josephine out into the street.

The rain was coming down even more heavily than before, raising waves of splash-spray that swept like nets across the pavement. There were no carriages on the street, and he hadn't brought any money anyway. He had one arm draped around Josephine; with the other he drew Emile's blood-slick pistol, and he kept glancing back at the nurses' home as the two of them reeled across the street.

They had nearly got to an alley on the far side when something punched his thigh like a hammer blow, and he folded, at the same moment feeling Josephine jerk and pitch forward away from him; and as he landed on his hands and knees on the cobblestones he realized that the two heavy *bams* that had for a moment battered the building fronts had been gunshots.

He knew he was being killed, but he was too exhausted and hurt to derive any alarm from the thought, only depression and a leaden impatience that it was taking so long, and hurting so much.

He wondered if Josephine was dead and, if not, if he could somehow get her free of this before the men behind them came over to finish off the job. He swung his head dizzily back and forth, squinting in the cold rain, and finally saw her sprawled only a few yards from him. Her skirt, already dark from the rain, was pulled up, and he could see the quickly diluted blood running from two gashes in her right calf.

He crawled over to her, dragging his shot left leg, and

lifted her face. Her hair was full of fresh, hot blood — evidently she'd been shot in the head — but he put his ear to her mouth.

She was breathing, in fast gasps.

Over the ringing in his ears he could hear footsteps thudding and splashing, louder by the second, behind him. He had dropped the pistol when he fell, but it was next to Josephine's head, and he picked it up; he rolled over, careful not to jar his mercifully numb left leg, and sat up, facing back the way he'd come. It was hard to see through the rain, and he pushed wet hair away from his eyes with his free hand.

He raised the pistol in shaking hands. He could dimly see two figures approaching through the veil of rain, and he waited for them to come closer.

They did, in great bounding leaps, and at nearly the last moment he remembered to click the hammer back, wondering if he could pull the trigger on a human being again.

Then there was the sound of hoofbeats from the direction of the Via Montebello, and the two men in the street halted and turned toward the noise, raising pistols of their own.

Not caring who the newcomers might be, but grateful for the diversion, Crawford aimed at one of the men in the street and, unconsciously whispering curses and fragments of half-remembered prayers, carefully squeezed the trigger of Emile's pistol.

The *bang* hammered his already abused eardrums and the gun's barrel clouted his face as the recoil kicked it up and back — and the man he'd been aiming at did a backflip and disappeared in the spray of the rain above the pavement. Crawford reversed the spent pistol and held it by the hot barrel and waited for the last man to come for him — but the horsemen were galloping forward now, and then he was dazzled into momentary blindness by a muzzle-flash as the last of Crawford's attackers fired his gun at the riders in the moment before being ridden down.

Crawford couldn't see if the man's shot had hit anyone. One of the riders reined in his horse long enough to fire a shot down into the body under the horses' hooves, and then to call, perhaps to Crawford, *'Questo e' fatto dai Carbonari, chiamato dalla mazze'* – and then all of them rode away south. Crawford tried to watch them, but the rain, and the red dazzle-spots floating in his vision, made them invisible within a few yards.

This was done by the Carbonari, summoned by the mazze, Crawford translated mentally – and he was profoundly grateful for the impulse that had made him stick the iron blade into the wooden head – and grateful too that the men on horseback hadn't recognized him from having glimpsed him earlier this evening in Navona Square.

But of course he had changed his allegiance since then.

Still sitting on the street, he laid the gun down and put his hand under his thigh, scraping the backs of his knuckles against the wet cobblestones.

He found the tear in his trousers and, though it nearly made him faint with sheer horror, he gingerly probed the hole in his leg with a fingertip. It was bleeding, but not so copiously as to indicate a torn artery. There was no exit wound, so the ball must still be inside – that was good news in some ways, bad in some others. The wound was still numb, but a hot ache was building up in there, and he knew he needed medical attention soon.

Still sitting up, he now hiked himself back so that he could assess the damage to Josephine's head. In the rainy darkness he felt the shape of her skull, but it didn't seem to have been shattered; and her face was fine, except for some rough-feeling scratches on her cheek and jaw from having collided with the street. Then he noticed a hard lump at her right temple, and he traced its outlines gently with his fingers.

It was the pistol ball. It had evidently struck the back of her head at an angle and, instead of punching straight through the skull into the brain, had skidded along the outside of the bone like the tip of a filleting knife.

She's been lucky – but she could still easily die of this. And even if she lived, her brain might sustain damage from the concussion. Of course with *her*, he thought, it would have to be a *lot* of damage, for anyone to be able to tell.

She shifted and groaned, then all at once sat up. One arm came up like a hinged rake and clawed sopping hair back from her forehead. 'Is,' she said in a voice like a shovel going into gravel, 'the sun . . . down yet?'

When he'd recovered from his surprise at her abrupt return to consciousness, Crawford laboriously raised his eyes to the dark sky. 'Uh,' he said, 'I think so.'

'We have to go to . . . Keats. To his apartment.'

Her voice was entirely without inflection, and Crawford found it hard to believe that there was anyone at all behind it. He wondered if her personality – or personalities – were still unconscious from the pistol shot, leaving this . . . this machine to work the vacated body.

'Keats's place,' he echoed. 'Why?'

'This is . . . not the one that knows. But we have to . . . go there.'

Crawford thought about that. They'd be likely to meet more of von Aargau's men there . . . but none of them could know of his defection yet. All the witnesses to it were dead – or at least, as in the case of the man whom he had pulled down the stairs, injured and unconscious.

He could claim . . . what, that he had gone to *help* the assassins, and had been shot at by Carbonari.

Von Aargau's men would help him – he was a fellow-employee. They would certainly get him medical help, and they might even loan him some money.

Of course they'd *kill* Josephine . . . damn her.

'That's the one place we *can't* go,' he told her, trying to speak clearly in spite of the powerful dizziness that made the whole street seem to spin. 'The people who shot us just now – more of them will be there. They'd kill . . . us.'

She stood up. 'Stay or come along,' she said. 'This is going there.'

Crawford's hands were shaking as if he'd been drinking coffee all day. He was only breathing every five seconds or so, in great, shuddering sighs, and a cold, sweaty nausea was beginning to crawl up his throat from his stomach. He'd seen these symptoms in wounded sailors aboard ships, and he knew he was in danger of 'freezing up' – going into a state in which all the body's functions just slowed down and stopped.

He tried to think clearly. He could knock on a door in this street, and take his chances with whatever sort of doctor was summoned, or he could walk the near mile to Keats's place with some assurance of getting the best possible care.

The rain had stopped, and the night didn't seem to be as cold as it had been.

'Let me put a tourniquet on this first,' he said.

Though Crawford sweated and swore and sobbed, and leaned ever more heavily on the fortunately mechanical Josephine, and had to sit down many times to loosen and retie the tourniquet, and toward the end started begging forgiveness from the ghosts that seemed to be walking with him, the devastated pair of them eventually came dragging and lurching into the Piazza di Spagna.

Wild piano music was playing somewhere nearby, and Crawford blinked around, trying to figure out where it was coming from and what the tormentingly familiar melody was. After a moment he realized that he had heard it only in certain unrestful adolescent dreams.

There didn't seem to be anyone in the square – the saints on the steps had of course all left many hours ago, at dusk, and if any of von Aargau's men were here, they were apparently inside the building that was Number 26 – but the square flickered with a diffuse white light, and when Crawford forced his eyes to focus he saw that the second floor of the building was alive with the brushlike illumination of St Elmo's fire.

Corbie's Aunt is paying Keats a visit, he thought blurrily – and then he noticed the two figures that stood outside the door. Somehow in the weird light he couldn't tell if they were robed or naked.

One was male and the other, which he recognized instantly even after four years, was female. He sighed profoundly, and knew that even if he had had his flask with him, he wouldn't have had the strength to resist, not now, not injured and exhausted like this.

He hoisted himself away from Josephine's shoulder and began limping forward. The music strengthened and jumped up into the higher octave.

Josephine started forward too, and though she was weaving drunkenly he fleetingly got the impression that she was *somebody* again. The music was in cut-time now, and wilder, like a horse galloping down a steep road at night.

'Run,' he whispered harshly to Josephine, even though he had little breath to spare. 'You'll die here. This has . . . nothing . . . to do with you.'

He looked over at her, and saw on her face the same

hungrily despairing expression he knew was on his own. '*He* has to do with me,' she said. Her voice was a defeated monotone, but he still thought she had recovered from her mechanical mode.

The woman at the doorway kept her brightly reptilian eyes on Crawford as he approached, and when at last he paused, a few yards in front of her, she smiled, baring inhuman teeth.

'*You lost me in the Alps,*' she hissed. '*Invite me back now and I'll heal you entirely, and you can forget everything.*'

She held out to him a hand – it was slightly more like a jewelled bird-claw than like a woman's hand, but he remembered it sliding languorously over his naked body four years ago, and his heart was pounding with the desire to take it. The music was doing arabesques around his rapid heartbeat now, and he thought he could almost remember the steps of a dance so ancient and wild that trees and rivers and storms took part in it.

A moment later Josephine rocked to a halt beside him, and the male figure said to her, '*You lost me in the Alps. Invite me back now and I'll fulfil you, and you can forget everything.*'

The parallel statements had fitted into the music like sections of gold thread in a vivid tapestry, and almost seemed to be lyrics, implying more to come.

Tears were running down Crawford's face – he didn't see how he could be expected to resist her any longer. For four years now he had ignored his nocturnal urges when he could, and had drunk himself insensible when he could not, and had lived with the memories that she could rid him of, and had not once given in to the temptation to call her – but now, surely, he could do it, could surrender his despised identity and just become an extension of her.

Faintly over the music he thought he caught an echo

of harsh coughing; and then, 'Not yet,' grated Josephine beside him. 'Upstairs – free Keats to die.'

Crawford had vaguely assumed that she was talking to herself, but when he raised his arms toward the faintly luminous female figure in front of him, Josephine struck them down.

The music, which had been rising, fell off a little.

He blinked at her impatiently. '*We* do? Why?'

She waved her hands helplessly. 'Because . . . because of the *sister*,' she said. She seemed to have trouble talking, but then words came in a rush. 'We can't let the sister die, not again. We've got to buy ourselves out of debt. *Then* we can go to hell.'

I never *had* a sister, he thought – and then, for the first time in quite a while, he remembered the boat foundering in the Plymouth Sound, and remembered his brother's arm waving, for a while, in the savage water.

He stepped back, and though he was talking to Josephine his eyes were on the lips and the flickeringly lit eyes of the woman in front of him. 'But they're dead!' he said loudly. 'What can we do about it now, except forget it?'

'*Nothing*,' the woman in front of him said. '*Come to me.*' Her bare breasts were nacreous white, and seemed to be very finely scaled, and he knew how they would feel under his hands, or against his bare chest. The music surged, booming through the square and away up the steps to ring in the dark forest beyond the church.

'Save this one,' interrupted Josephine, and again he wondered if she was talking to herself, for she was talking almost too softly to be heard. 'Do what's left.'

'I . . . can't.' Crawford took a step forward, reaching for the inhuman woman and opening his mouth to pronounce, gratefully, the long-resisted invitation – he could feel the appropriate point in the music approaching.

'*Wait!*' screamed Josephine, so harshly that he actually slowed for a moment to glance back at her.

She darted a hand to her face and seemed to dig and pull, and a moment later he was startled to see that she had gouged out her false eye. She popped it into her mouth and bit down hard, and even through the muffling of her cheeks he heard glass crunch.

Then Josephine had pulled him back and locked her arms around him and was kissing him furiously, her dry lips opening and leading his tongue into a mouth that was full of blood and glass splinters and — startlingly — crushed garlic.

The piano screamed.

And all of Crawford's years-pent-up eroticism battered at him now in a sudden, hot flood — he responded passionately, grabbing the blood-thick hair at the back of her head with one hand so that he could crush her face into his, and pulling her pelvis hard against him with the other. The pistol ball under her scalp was hot against his fingers, and he could feel the one in his thigh radiating heat.

For ten intolerably drawn-out seconds they reeled there on the pavement, grinding against each other as the echoes of the music's shrill last chord resounded away among the domes and streets of Rome and into the sky.

And then the night broke, and the rain came down again in a cold torrent, and when Crawford lifted his ravaged mouth from Josephine's he saw two heavy but hummingbirdlike flying serpents hanging unsupported in midair, curling and snapping their long tails, at eye level in front of the door to Keats's building; the music had either stopped or gone very quiet, and the chitinous buzz of their blurred wings underscored the hiss and rattle of the rain, and Crawford could smell the musk of them over the dry-wine scent of the wet street.

The smell only repelled him, and he knew he was immune to the lamia's attractions for at least a while now.

In the relative silence the buzzing of the reptilian wings wavered up and down the scale, and became words.

Silver in your blood, and garlic.

It was impossible to tell which of the hovering things produced the words – perhaps they both did, in unison, still singing the night's song though the music had retreated.

Though more exhausted than ever, Crawford was now coldly clearheaded, and he realized that von Aargau's assassins must have used silver bullets. 'Yes,' he said, and the cloud that was his breath reeked so of garlic that the serpents swung ponderously away through the chilly air. 'Get out of our way.'

The serpents slowly moved farther back, one on each side of the door, though their eyes glowed with a terrible promise.

Crawford kept one arm around Josephine as the two of them lurched between the buzzing things, through the doorway. They stumbled up the dark stairs, spitting blood and glass and holding on to each other for support.

The music had resumed, and was whirling up around them like bubbles in a glass of champagne. Crawford knew now that they would find none of von Aargau's men here – clearly the job had been left to other sorts of agents.

When they got to the second-floor landing they could see Keats's door, for it was open, and the inside of the apartment glowed as bright as noon. Josephine pulled a scarf out of her pocket and tied it around her head slantwise, so that her empty eye socket was covered.

Crawford forced himself to walk forward through the hailstorm of crystalline music, trying to remember what

Josephine had said out front, and why it had seemed compelling — and, forlornly, reminding himself that his flask, at least, was inside.

Little long-legged things with big eyes pirouetted out of his way as he shuffled up the hall, and he heard whispering and chittering from a dozen swinging sacks that were attached by some sticky stuff to the ceiling, and creatures like starfish clinging to the walls waved tentacles at him, but none of the lamiae's unnatural retinue obstructed the two humans, who advanced hand in hand toward the open door.

Crawford was the first to peer around the doorframe, and he was surprised to see that it was the meek Severn who was wringing the demonic music from the piano — it was a radical change from the polite Haydn he'd been playing earlier — but then he noticed that the young man's eyes were closed, and that a thing like a cat with a woman's face was crouched on his shoulder and whispering into his ear.

Josephine bumped Crawford from behind, and he stumbled into the room.

The street-side wall was gone, and beyond where it had stood rose a grassy hill, with the dawning sun glittering on dewy flowers; for one stunned moment Crawford wondered if he had somehow lost an hour or two while climbing the stairs — but then he looked at the windows facing the steps, and he saw blackness beyond them, and even, in spite of the sunny glare, the orange spots of a few streetlamps; and, looking back toward the open side of the room, he saw that the foot of the hill met the floor and was flush with it, even though this was an upstairs room, and he noticed too that the sun was rising in the south.

The music was brighter and more adventurous, though still carrying an undertone of dark glamour, and now Crawford saw two young people, a man and a

304

woman, running hand in hand up the sunny hill . . . and then he recognized the young man as John Keats, looking healthy and tanned.

'I think we're too late,' he said to Josephine, whose hand he still held.

'No,' she said. He looked at her, and then followed her stare toward the door to the other room.

Keats stood there, the real Keats, leaning against the frame, his eyes blazing from his wasted face as he watched the illusion on the far wall, and Crawford suddenly knew that the woman on the hill with the phantom healthy Keats was an illusory image of the woman he was engaged to marry.

Then the illusion faded, and the copy of Keats's poems on the table flew up into the air. The book swelled and grew in size as it moved toward the wall where the illusion had been projected, and when it was nearly as tall as Crawford the covers swung open like a pair of doors, presenting the text on two of the pages. The spine of the giant book bumped against the wall, and clung.

The verses printed on the pages seemed to glow darkly against the white paper . . . and then suddenly it was a different book hanging there, clearly a book of poems Keats had not yet written, and the verses fairly sprang off the rapidly turning pages into Crawford's mind – and, he could see, into the minds too of Josephine and Keats himself.

The music was unbearably sad now, conjuring images of future sunsets none of them would live to see, evening breezes none of them would live to feel; and it had a Latin tone to it, reminding the hearers that they were in Italy, in *Rome*, where the grandest accomplishments of mankind were as commonplace as the onion-sellers on the streets . . . and that the invalid Keats, who would so desperately appreciate it all, would die before seeing any of it.

The Temptation of St Keats, Crawford thought. He looked around for his flask, and saw it on the table where the book had been, and he wished passionately that he dared to cross the room to it.

The woman Crawford had seen on the illusory hill was in the room now, watching the succession of brilliant poems, and after a moment she turned and held out a hand toward the dying young man standing in the bedroom doorway. Her eyes glittered like crazed glass in the lamplight, and Crawford wondered if she still much resembled Keats's fiancée . . . and if it still mattered.

Crawford noticed that when she turned away the magnified pages faded – and when he looked again at his flask it rose up in the air and flew across the room to him; without bothering about how it had happened, he took it out of the air and unscrewed the cap and took a deep gulp of the brandy.

The real book was in one of the woman's hands, and Keats's bony hand reached out toward the other, and Crawford drank some more, hoping to drown all concern for the doomed sister of the young poet, all concern for all betrayed sisters, and brothers . . .

He looked away, toward the wall where the book had been hanging – the book was gone, and he was jolted to see instead the image of Julia, his dead wife, smiling and walking down a country lane, between tall chestnut trees; as she walked, pieces of her were falling off into the dirt – first a hand, then an entire arm, then a foot – though she moved along as smoothly as ever, and her smile didn't falter. Behind her came a little dark thing that clicked and whirred as it moved, and it was picking up the fallen pieces and fitting them on over its own rusty limbs.

Josephine's hand tightened convulsively in his, and he looked at her – her single eye was fixed intensely on the illusion.

306

He looked back at it — and then stared in horror, for what he saw now was storm-surf and cliffs under a steel-coloured sky, and the keel of an overturned boat sliding across the foam-streaked faces of the waves. He knew he would see his brother's raised arm any moment now, if he didn't look away . . .

And there it was! No, the scene had changed — the shifting blue surface was now a field of flowers, and the person waving was a young girl; a moment later he heard her yell, *Johnny* . . .

Crawford looked back toward Keats, and saw that he had lowered his hand and was staring at the illusion. The woman followed his gaze and then, with an impatient hiss, clicked her fingernails together, and the street-side wall was restored, all visions banished. The room seemed suddenly very dark.

Crawford guessed that Josephine, and then himself, and then Keats, had been involuntarily projecting the scenes, had for a few moments made helpless use of the lamia's magical tools while her attention had been distracted by Keats's near surrender. His summoning of the flask must also have been done by magic borrowed from her.

And the final vision, the vision of Keats's sister, had undone all her work. Keats was shaking his head and turning back toward the bedroom. The woman followed him, and Josephine dragged Crawford after them. In the corner Severn was torturing a high-pitched, urgent tune out of the piano, but no one seemed to be listening.

The bedroom window was open to the rain, according to the directions Crawford had tried to give this afternoon, and he wondered if poor Severn had been duped into washing the window sill and asking the vampire in.

Keats had fallen across his unmade bed, and it really looked as though the exertion of standing up had been too great a strain on his ruined lungs – there was a bubbling undertone to his desperate wheezing now.

The woman hurried to him, holding the book of poetry. '*Quickly,*' she said, '*sign the book, save yourself.*' She took a pen from the top of the dresser and, when he raised a weak hand to fend her off, she jabbed the pen point into his palm. '*Sign,*' she repeated, holding the pen toward him.

Keats took the book from her, but there was bitter disappointment on his face, and he shook his head again. He looked past her to Josephine, who had been his nurse. 'Water,' he whispered.

The inhuman woman moved toward Josephine, but Crawford stepped in front of her and coughed garlic fumes in her narrow face; she recoiled, her hair shuddering and contracting away.

Josephine turned to the open window, scraped the palm of her hand along the rain-wet sill and then took a step toward the bed with her hand cupped in front of her.

Keats reached for her.

Suddenly the room was tilting – or seemed to be: when Crawford grabbed at the window sill to keep his balance he saw that the streets outside were still parallel to the sill and the floor, and for an irrational moment he thought the whole world must be falling over sideways.

Josephine took another step, a very uphill one, but then started to topple backwards toward the sitting room door, which was beginning to seem like part of the floor. Keats, apparently insulated from the gravitational tricks, lunged desperately for her, but was too far away, and too weak to get up and step toward her.

Crawford hiked his good foot up into the window frame and then sprang out across the room in the direction that felt like *up*; his open hands slammed into the small of Josephine's back, shoving her into balance,

308

and he fell away backwards and hit the wall hard enough to blind him for a moment with the pain in his broken ribs.

Josephine had grabbed one of the posts of Keats's bed and, holding herself up by it, she extended the hand in which she still cupped some of the water she'd scraped from the window sill.

'God help me,' Keats whispered, then dipped his finger into the dirty water in Josephine's palm and scrawled with it on the open page. Crawford saw that the poem the book was opened to was *Lamia*.

The woman retreated still farther when his finger touched the paper, and the room was suddenly level again – and then Josephine was toppling forward and, in catching herself, she pushed her wet fingertips across Keats's waxy forehead. At that instant the inhuman woman disappeared, with a thin wail that made Crawford's teeth ache.

The music had stopped, though the air still seemed to ring with it, and they could hear Severn blundering about in confusion in the next room. 'John?' Severn called. 'Are you all right? I seem to have fallen asleep . . .' Clearly the cat-woman thing had disappeared from his shoulder.

Keats's eyes were closed, but his lips were moving; Crawford leaned closer. 'Thank you, both of you,' Keats said softly. His eyes opened for a moment and he looked at Crawford. The water that ran down from his forehead found and filled the pain-wrinkles around his eyes and, after a moment, coursed down his cheeks like tears. 'I told you once that I might . . . someday need a favour from a reluctant neff-host.' He sighed, and turned to the wall. 'Now please go. And send Severn in – I want to tell him what my . . . epitaph is to be.'

* * *

Severn nodded when Crawford delivered Keats's message and, though there were tears in his eyes and he started forward at once, he waved toward the couch. 'Sit down,' he called softly over his shoulder. 'I'll have Dr Clark right over to look at you two.'

But when Severn had gone into Keats's room and closed the door, Crawford took Josephine's elbow and started toward the door. 'We can't stay,' he whispered clearly to her, hoping she was capable of understanding him. 'Anywhere else would be safer – men will be coming here who'll kill both of us.'

To his relief, she nodded.

He led her down the hall toward the stairs – several people were staring fearfully out past doors open only a crack, and crossed themselves as the two wet, battered figures limped past – and then down the stairwell to the street and the still saintless steps that fretted the Pincian Hill.

He didn't pause when they left the building, but propelled Josephine quickly out across the square, past the boat-shaped Bernini fountain, to an alley on the far side. He relaxed a little then, but nevertheless made Josephine hurry south along the alley; for when the Austrian forces found that Crawford and she had already got out of the building, they'd certainly search the nearby area.

Luminous grey had begun to infuse the sky to the east, and the long clouds were like wet bandages slowly absorbing blood as the first rays of dawn touched the steeples and towers overhead. Crawford had found a rolling, half-up-on-the-toes gait that eased some of the pain in his left thigh, though he still found himself putting a lot of his weight on the uncomplaining Josephine. Both of them suffered occasional violent fits of shivering, sometimes so bad that they had to stop.

At the Church of San Silvestro he paused to rest and,

as he leaned against the stone wall and let his hot lungs slow down, he read a plaque on the wall claiming that the head of John the Baptist was kept somewhere on the premises. It reminded him of Keats's poem *Isabella*, and he wondered feverishly what the priests watered the head with, and what they hoped would grow.

'The convent here,' began Josephine suddenly, startling him, 'is the post office now. I went there for Keats and Severn yesterday, to see if any of Keats's friends in England had sent him money. Nobody had.'

'It would have been too late anyway,' Crawford observed. He stared at her. She seemed to be lucid, and he wondered who she thought she was. 'How did you wind up *here*? It wasn't because of me, was it?'

'No,' she said. 'Originally it was for haruspication.' She leaned against the wall next to him and stared into the brightening sky. The white of her eye was blotted with bright red. 'A doctor told me that word, when he figured out why I was a nurse. He made me leave. That was in . . . I don't know, Fabriano, Firenze . . . I'm a nurse everywhere I go now. I need to be.'

Even in his pain and exhaustion Crawford vividly remembered her brief stint as a nurse in St Thomas's Hospital four years ago, and he wondered if she had discovered this necessity then. 'So what's . . . haruspication?'

'Divination by the examination of entrails,' she said, clearly reciting a phrase she'd been told. 'I get a lot of jobs because most nurses don't like to work surgery; I need to, though, I – need to look in there.'

Crawford knew he'd be having trouble following this even if he'd been alert and uninjured. 'To . . . what, see the future?'

Her torn lips actually curved into a smile. 'Maybe to see my own future, in a way. I hope. No, to . . . see what's inside people. Inside *people*. It gives us . . . it gives *me* . . . dreams, and the dreams are pulling me out of . . .' She paused, then shook her head in despair of expressing whatever her thought was.

'What kind of dreams?'

'Of performing surgery on myself – always in the dreams I'm on the table, sitting up a little, and I've knifed open my whole torso, and I'm digging around in my own entrails and pulling things out to throw away. If I can just get rid of all of them . . .'

Crawford stared at her, the expression on his haggard face a mix of concern and horror. 'Things? What things?'

She shuddered, and swayed against him as if she were about to faint. 'Gear-wheels,' she said; 'springs, bolts, chains, wires . . .' She let the sentence drift off.

Crawford put his arm around her and wordlessly held her.

Crawford led her southwest to Navona Square, and then, peering from around the corner of a shop, he watched the square and the window of his apartment for several long minutes. When at last he was fairly sure that no Austrians had traced him here yet, he told Josephine to wait, and hobbled across the square and into his building, re-emerging a few minutes later with a valise and a walking stick. It had been a risky action, but he had felt that he and Josephine would have no chance at all without some money and his medical kit, and if they were to make any progress at all he needed to be able to take some of the weight off his shot leg.

A greengrocer had stopped his cart near the alley where Josephine was waiting, and the man was now setting out baskets of leeks and potatoes on the cobblestones, and from the open door of a bakery across the street Crawford could smell hot rolls and coffee; he was considering going over there and spending some of his money, but then he heard the greengrocer call across to the baker, asking if he knew why there were so many soldiers riding up and down every street and alley a few blocks north.

Crawford gave Josephine the valise, then took her elbow again and began hitching himself along southward. The stick didn't seem to help much, but despite his throbbing, stiffening leg he was unwilling to hire a carriage, both because the drivers had probably been told to watch for them and because he didn't want to use the little money he had on anything less than food and shelter.

Eventually he realized that the stick was supposed to be held in the hand away from the bad leg, and after that discovery the walking became a good deal less painful. The sweat began to cool on his face, and he was able to relax a little.

It occurred to him that Josephine had not answered his question. 'So how *did* you wind up with Keats?' he asked.

She shrugged. 'Dr Clark gets a lot of his nurses from the St Paul's Home, and when it's for an English tourist he prefers an English-speaking nurse.'

'Then why did you stay on with him? *He* didn't need surgery.'

'No,' she said, seeming to recover energy as they walked, 'and when I was assigned to him I almost *didn't* stay, I almost quit. But he . . . had a look that I used to have; and he was trying to get away from it too . . . and he was trying to save his sister . . . I don't know, I guess I decided I could learn more about what's inside people by working for him.'

She looked squarely at Crawford for the first time in quite a while, her one eye red but alert below the slanted scarf, and when he saw the cuts on her lips he found himself remembering the glass-splintery kiss they'd shared in the street, and he touched his own lacerated mouth.

'It can't have been easy,' he said, his voice quiet, 'to get a glassblower to make a glass eye filled with chopped garlic.'

'Actually he did it for nothing. He said he understood why I wanted it, why I wanted to have an emergency source of garlic ready to hand at all times; he said he admired me for it.'

Crawford thought about the flask he had been keeping for roughly the same purpose, and he wondered if the man he'd bought it from had admired him for it; he certainly hadn't seemed to.

The thought of the flask made him take it out and uncap it, though, and he tilted it up to his mouth; the alcohol stung in the cuts on his lips and tongue, but the rich pungency did so much to restore his energy and alertness that he made Josephine take a mouthful too.

Three times they saw parties of soldiers on horseback in the streets north of them, and twice they heard children demanding to be allowed to go see the dozens of boats that were landing and disgorging soldiers along the Tiber's banks, so Crawford and Josephine walked southeast, making their way through twisting alleys and lanes and avoiding the wider streets, and finally, when they followed the narrow Via di Marforio to its end and then descended a set of steps, they found that they were at the eastern end of the shallow valley that was the Roman Forum, and had left the noise and activity of modern Rome behind.

It was a long, uneven field, cross-hatched with ancient pavements that still mostly held back the rank grass; weathered pillars stood up here and there across the field in just discernible patterns, hinting at the grand temples and basilicas that were long gone. Ahead of the two fugitives and a little to their right loomed a massive square edifice of stone encompassing three arches, and Crawford took Josephine's hand and started toward the high, broad central arch.

The rising sun beyond it made a dark silhouette of the huge structure, and Crawford was unable to make out any of the bas-reliefs or Latin inscriptions cut into the stone.

'The Arch of Septimius Severus,' said Josephine abruptly. 'He was one of the cruellest emperors of Rome, but at least there was nearly no literature produced during his reign.'

Crawford blinked at her. 'Is that right? Well, that's – '

'Somewhere in the vicinity of this arch would be a good place to deal with our injuries.'

'I'm not sure I follow – ' he began; but then he thought of the producers of literature he'd met since leaving England four years ago, and he nodded slowly. 'You think the old boy might still cast a . . . sphere of influence, eh? Well, what the hell – we certainly can't afford to scorn any good luck charms.'

Ahead on the left, three low walls of pink brick made a shadowed little enclosure, and Crawford led her to it. When they were crouched down, out of the sight of any early morning strollers, he opened his medical kit, unfolded a clean white cloth and spread it across the ancient pavement, and then, hoping that she hadn't exaggerated her nursing experience, he began laying out instruments.

Cutting the pistol ball out of Josephine's scalp was easy and only superficially bloody, and within a few minutes Crawford had sutured up the incision and applied brandy-soaked bandages to it and to the entrance wound. And it was little trouble for her to sew his shirt tight to bind his cracked ribs.

Getting the ball out of his thigh would be more difficult, as he had to pull down his trousers and then lie on his stomach and give Josephine directions on what to do with the forceps.

The wound had started to close, and he almost lost consciousness when she began probing with the cold instrument.

'Sorry,' she said, after he had smothered a scream with his fist.

''S all right,' he whispered quickly, wishing he didn't have to save the last dribble of brandy for dressing the wound. He was suddenly bathed in cold sweat, and he wondered if he was about to be sick. 'Talk to me as you do it, will you? Anything.'

She pushed the closed jaws of the forceps in a little deeper, and it was all he could do to keep from leaping up and yanking it out. The cold steel in his leg contrasted with the fresh, hot blood running down the sides of his thigh and puddling on the gritty pavement under him.

'Well, I told you why *I* was there, at Keats's,' she said calmly. 'Why were you there, and working for his vampire?'

'I wasn't,' he gasped, 'working for the goddamn vampire. Well, I guess I was, but I didn't – *Jesus, slow, do it slower!* – I didn't know it. I was working for the Austrians. Hell, most of the work I did for him, this fellow von Aargau, and the Austrians – *goddamn!* – was *protecting* people from vampires.'

He felt the tip of the forceps touch the silver ball. 'Stop,' he said hastily, 'you're there. Now God help me – back out a little, open the forceps *very slowly*, and then try to grab the ball. I mean *take hold* of the ball. Firmly, squeeze it, you understand, but – don't – do anything *jolting*.'

He saw her shadow nod. 'The Austrians and the . . . stone people are allies, I think,' she said thoughtfully as

316

she worked the metal in his leg and the blood puddle reached his knee, 'but they're different kinds of life, and can't – I've got hold of the ball. What now?'

Crawford gripped the edges of the broken marble paving blocks under him. 'Slowly,' he whispered. 'Pull.'

She began pulling, so gently that at first he wasn't aware of it. 'They couldn't possibly really understand each other's goals,' she went on. 'At best it can only be an alliance of convenience. I'll bet the only people you protected from vampires were people important to the Austrians.'

'That's true,' he said tightly. He could feel the tugging now. 'Except for Keats – and that was apparently just an attempt to keep Keats's vampire happy.' The tugging got stronger.

'A failed attempt,' said Josephine calmly as she slowly increased the pull, pressing down with her free hand on his bare, blood-sticky thigh. 'She's without a host now. He knew he had to die, and he did. He was even talking about suicide at one time.'

'Without a host,' Crawford echoed. 'After twenty-five years.' Suddenly he remembered Severn's story about Keats having been kept quarantined in Naples Harbour until his birthday, the 31st of October – and he was certain that the quarantine had been an Austrian courtesy to Keats's vampire: to delay Keats's arrival, and disillusionment, and possible deathwish, until the night when the vampire could scout Rome for a newborn infant to adopt, as she had adopted Keats himself a quarter of a century earlier. The Austrians had in effect donated an Italian child so that the vampire would not, no matter what Keats did, be left without a host.

She was provided with a field of hosts to choose from, Josephine, he thought bitterly. And he wondered if the infant the vampire had chosen was one of the ones that had been anonymously handed to him through the grating in the wall of the foundlings' hospital at Santo Spirito.

'Here it comes,' said Josephine, 'don't tense up.'

The forceps, gripping the pistol ball, was much wider now than when it had gone in, and Crawford could feel it tearing muscle as Josephine kept inexorably tugging upward. His eyes and jaws were clenched shut and he was breathing in great, whispered sobs, and the sweat was puddling under him and diluting the blood around his leg.

At last he felt it pop out and, though the blood began to well more quickly from the wound, he went limp in relief. Even when she doused the wound with the last of the brandy he didn't twitch at the pain, and after she had tied a bandage around the thigh he was even able to pull his trousers up by himself.

He rolled over carefully, then sat up, feeling chilly and weak. 'Thank you,' he told her hoarsely. 'I've never worked with a steadier nurse.'

She turned away, toward the sun, and then awkwardly bent down to pick up the ball Crawford had cut out of her scalp. She rolled the two silver lumps in her palm, then drew her hand back as if to throw them out across the ruinscape.

'Don't!' he said.

She lowered her arm and looked at him questioningly.

'They're silver,' he said, 'and we don't have much travelling money.' He began struggling up on to his feet, using his walking stick like a barge-pole.

'Are we travelling together?' she asked, with no expression discernible on her face.

He paused, realized that his words had implied that . . . and that in fact it was what he would prefer. He straightened up, and then nodded cautiously. 'If you'd like to. We can travel as brother and sister, and get work at some hospital somewhere. Uh . . . I do have to ask this; if the question makes no sense to you . . . just tell me so.' He took a deep breath. 'Do you still think I killed Julia?'

She walked away from him, picking her way over fragments of fallen pillars, and she stopped beside a eucalyptus bush and picked one of its poisonous leaves and, as she absently tore it to pieces, stared out across the ruins to the ivy-masked arches that fretted the steep face of the Palatine Hill.

Crawford followed more slowly, bracing his stick in the cracks in the old pavement.

When he stood beside her he opened his mouth to speak, but she held up her hand. 'You think I don't know that I'm Josephine,' she said quickly, as though it was something that had to be said but that no one wanted to hear, 'and that it's Julia that's – that's d-dead.' She shook her head, a grin of unhappiness cramping her face, and tears spilled from her eye and made highlights on her lean cheek. 'I *do* know it, I do; I just . . . can't *stand* it. Julia was such a . . . so much better a person than I ever was. She was always terribly kind to me, in spite of all the trouble I was to her. I *should* be dead, and she should be the one that's still alive.'

She looked away from him but held out her scarred, deformed left hand, and he took it. 'I know you didn't kill her. And I know what did.'

Hand in hand, but with not the slightest erotic interest, they made their halting way forward across the shattered floor of the Forum, toward the southeast, where the high, crumbled red shoulder of the Colosseum rose above the skyline of more modern churches.

'Have you ever had that done,' she asked him after a while, 'what I did for Keats right there at the end? If not, I could do it for you any time you liked. Anyone can, you know. What do the Catholics call it?'

Crawford tried to remember the details of the previous

319

night. The midmorning sun was drying his clothes, and he felt a lot better than he had a couple of hours ago, but exhaustion still clung to him like children on his back. 'What,' he said finally, 'letting him sign his book, with the water from the window sill? I don't think the Catholics – '

'No,' she said, 'when I smeared my wet hand across his forehead, so as to – '

'I thought that was accidental,' Crawford said, 'just you catching your balance.'

She looked at him in exasperation. 'No. It was what made his vampire leave. Damn it, what do they call it, not Confirmation – '

'Oh.' Crawford stopped walking for a moment. 'Yes. Yes, I might want you to do that for me sometime – let me think about it.' He started walking again, and added, as an afterthought, 'Baptism, they call it.'

BOOK TWO

1822: Summer Flies

And a fair Shape out of her hands did flow –
A living Image, which did far surpass
In beauty that bright shape of vital stone
Which drew the heart out of Pygmalion.

A sexless thing it was, and in its growth
It seemed to have developed no defect
Of either sex, yet all the grace of both . . .

And o'er its gentle countenance did play
The busy dreams, as thick as summer flies . . .

Percy Bysshe Shelley, *The Witch of Atlas*

. . . thou shalt be in league with the stones of
the field . . .

Job 5:23, quoted without comment
in Shelley's 1822 notebook

Chapter 12

Fruits fail and love dies and time ranges;
Thou art fed with perpetual breath,
And alive after infinite changes,
And fresh from the kisses of death;
Of languors rekindled and rallied,
Of barren delights and unclean,
Things monstrous and fruitless, a pallid
And poisonous queen.

— A. C. Swinburne, *Dolores*

Pisa, on the northwest coast of Italy near Livorno, was clearly a relic of what it had once been. The houses were classical Roman, but the paint was blistering off the shutters on the windows, and the clean architectural lines were blurred now with water stains and cracks, and some of the streets were simply abandoned, with vines and weeds claiming the fallen buildings.

The yellow Arno still flowed powerfully under the ancient bridges, but the buildup of the river-mouth delta had tripled the city's distance from the sea in the centuries since Strabo had called Pisa one of the most valorous of the Etruscan cities. Charcoal-burners and cork-peelers laboured in the *maremma*, the salt marsh that now surrounded the city, but the local commerce subsisted mainly on European tourists.

Most of the tourists came to see the cathedral and the famous Leaning Tower, but a few came with medical problems to the university – where an English-speaking doctor was a Godsend – or to try to catch glimpses of the two infamous poets, exiles from England, who had lately taken up residence in the city and were supposed to be intending to start some sort of magazine; such literary-minded tourists were advised to hurry, though, for the poets had evidently got themselves into some sort of trouble with the local government, and were expected to be moving on soon.

As Michael Crawford made his way eastward along the Lung'Arno, the crowded street that overhung the north side of the Arno, he was not paying any particular attention to the people around him. Two men were beating out mattresses over the bridge ahead, and a woman was singing as she leaned from a third-floor window and hung laundry on an alley-spanning clothes-line, but Crawford, glancing at the ground from time to time to judge where to seat the tip of his walking stick, didn't see the old man who was hobbling toward him.

The river was deep and fast-moving on this overcast April Thursday, and all the boats were moored along the river wall below the sun-bleached stone houses — even the adventurous Shelley's skiff was tied up, though it was on this side of the river, across the rushing water from the Tre Palazzi where he lived. Clearly he was visiting Byron at the Palazzo Lanfranchi, probably for the last time before moving north to the Bay of Spezia.

And Byron had decided to spend the summer in Montenero, ten miles to the south. It looked to Crawford as though the English colony in Pisa was breaking up; Byron and Shelley had formed the hub around which the rest of them had revolved like spokes.

Crawford and Josephine would stay on, of course. They worked as a brother-and-sister doctor-and-nurse team with the medical faculty at the university, and he was confident that their value there would keep the official anti-English sentiment from affecting them.

Byron was the cause of it all, anyway, and he was

leaving. His current paramour was a young lady named Teresa Guiccioli, whose brother and estranged husband were known to be active in the anti-Austrian Carbonari, and Byron had apparently been initiated into the secret society himself, and frequently bragged about having stored guns and ammunition for the informal army when he had been a guest in the Palazzo Guiccioli in Ravenna.

The Pisan government had not been pleased when Teresa and her brother, and then Byron himself, had moved to their city; and the hostilities had reached a near crisis a month ago, when Byron and Shelley and four other members of the local English circle had got into a scuffle with a rude Italian dragoon at the south gate. The dragoon had punched Shelley in the face with the guard of a sabre, and in the ensuing *mêlée* one of Byron's servants had stabbed the dragoon with a pitch-fork; the man had eventually recovered from the wound, and the servant had been imprisoned, but now government spies routinely followed Byron and Teresa and her brothers.

Crawford certainly *hoped* that he and Josephine were under no suspicion.

He had continued to practise medicine as Michael Aickman after he and Josephine fled Rome. He'd been afraid von Aargau might have removed his faked cre-dentials from the official records in Rome, but the university here had been impressed enough by his documentable experience and obvious competence to dispense with checking his papers too thoroughly, and he and Josephine had come here with the hope that at last they could settle down. Crawford thought they could live together as brother and sister for the rest of their lives — neither one of them was likely to marry.

He was forty-two now, and nearly always walked with a cane because of the stiffness that he'd never been able to work out of his left leg, and he spent a lot of his free time reading and gardening; and Josephine had been getting steadily saner during this unstressful last year. The wines and cooking of Tuscany had filled her figure out too, so that she looked a good deal like her dead sister now, and the Italian sun had tanned her skin and brought out a whole spectrum of copper and gold and bronze in her long hair. She and Crawford had become friendly with the Pisan English, and were frequently guests at Byron's Wednesday-night dinners, but the two of them were really more Italian than English now.

Crawford had been looking down to his right at the surging water and, when he looked up to make sure not to pass the white marble façade of Byron's house, he did see the old man, who was also walking with a cane – but Crawford was too busy with his own thoughts to give the man more than a passing glance.

Byron stepped out on to the second-floor balcony now, his greying hair blowing in the breeze, and Crawford started to wave up at him, but halted the motion when he saw the grim expression on the lord's thinned face. A moment later Percy Shelley strode out of the Palazzo's front door. He too looked upset.

'Percy!' Crawford called, lengthening his stride. 'What's up?'

Shelley blinked at him for a moment as if without recognition, then shook his head. 'Can you and your sister come with us to Spezia?' he asked harshly. 'I have reason to believe that wc'll be needing . . . *your sort* of medical expertise.'

Crawford had never really managed to like Shelley. 'I don't see how we could, Percy, not right now. Mary or Claire is pregnant?'

'As a matter of fact we think Mary might be again – but that wasn't exactly . . .' He gestured impatiently. 'I

326

can pay you both more than you're making at the university hospital.'

Crawford knew this wasn't true – Shelley was in debt to any number of people, even his English publisher. 'I'm sorry. We really couldn't leave Pisa. You know Josephine isn't well. Her nervous condition . . .'

For a moment Shelley looked ready to argue – then he just shook his head and stalked past him; a moment later he was hurrying angrily down Byron's private landing steps to his moored skiff, his boots tapping on the wet stone.

Crawford looked up at the balcony, but Byron had gone back inside. He let his gaze fall back to the street, and at last he noticed the old man and a moment later he had quickly stepped forward into the recessed door-way of Byron's house, and was rapping the knocker hard against the wood of the door, for he thought he had recognized him.

He thought it was . . . what had the name been? . . . des Loges, the crazy-talking old man who had got the Aickman passport for him in France – and then asked him to drown him in exchange for the favour – six long years ago and more than five hundred miles from here.

'Come on, Fletcher,' he whispered to the locked door. He told himself that des Loges couldn't have recognized *him* – he no longer looked anything like the young, dark-haired Michael Crawford who had crawled up on to the beach at Carnac in late July of 1816.

And perhaps it hadn't been des Loges at all. What would the man be doing *here*?

Could he be looking for Crawford?

The thought scared him, and he hammered the knocker again, harder.

At last Byron's servant dragged the door open, an expression of grieved surprise on his seamed face.

'Sorry to have been so insistent, Fletcher,' Crawford

said breathlessly, and a moment later the servant's eyebrows climbed even higher, for Crawford had hurried inside and pulled the door closed himself. 'There's a . . . an old creditor of mine out there, and I don't want him to see me.'

Fletcher shrugged and nodded, and it occurred to Crawford that, over the years, Byron had probably burst into a number of the houses he'd lived in with the same excuse for haste.

'Shall I announce you,' Fletcher inquired, 'or were you just . . .?'

'No, he actually is expecting me. We were supposed to ride out to shoot in the *maremma*.'

'I'll tell my lord you're here,' said Fletcher, starting up the stairs, 'though he might not be in the mood.'

Crawford lowered himself on to one of the sofas, and then stared unseeingly at the painted flowers on the high ceiling and wondered what had so upset Shelley and Byron. Had they had a fight?

It wasn't impossible. Shelley was often visibly annoyed by Byron's bawdy talk, and by the slight but ever-present condescension which the fact of being an English peer gave him, and, above all, by his refusal to speak to Claire or let her visit their daughter Allegra, whom he had left behind in a convent in Bagnacavallo, on the opposite coast of Italy.

Shelley would be reluctant to break with Byron, for the lord was the most important contributor and subsidizer of the *Liberal*, the proposed magazine that was to publish Byron's and Shelley's newest poetical works and save Shelley's friends the Hunt brothers from bankruptcy — Leigh Hunt and his wife and children were already supposed to be in transit to Pisa from England — but the right provocation at the right moment could have set off Shelley's temper.

* * *

328

Even before he and Josephine had arrived in Pisa, over a year ago now, Crawford had known that Shelley was living in the city, and that Byron was expected – but he'd confidently dismissed a momentary suspicion that it was Shelley's inhuman twin, rather than the university, that had made the place look good to him.

In fact he had at first planned to have nothing to do with the English poets . . . but then he had met Byron one evening a couple of months ago on the Lung'Arno.

Crawford had instantly recognized Byron, and after a moment of hesitation he walked up to him and introduced himself. Byron had been chilly at first, but after they had shaken hands he was suddenly full of cheer, recounting nostalgically exaggerated stories about Polidori and Hobhouse and some of the inns they'd stayed in during that tour of the Alps six years earlier. Before the two of them had parted that evening, Crawford had found himself accepting an invitation to dinner at the Palazzo Lanfranchi that Wednesday night.

Josephine hadn't accompanied him that first time, and Shelley had been a little more surprised than pleased to see Crawford again, but gradually Crawford and Josephine had become a part of the group of English who were drawn to Shelley's house on the south side of the river and Byron's on the north.

Josephine seldom spoke, and sometimes upset the Shelleys by staring intently into vacant corners of a room like a spooked cat, but Byron claimed to like her occasional abrupt, random statements, and Jane Williams, who with her husband was staying with the Shelleys, was trying to teach her to play the guitar.

Byron never referred to having met Josephine on the Wengern, and Crawford believed he had managed to make himself forget most of that day.

Crawford had wondered what it had been about that handshake that had so warmed Byron to him, until one

329

day a couple of weeks ago when he'd been drinking with Byron, and the lord had held up his own right hand, on the palm of which Crawford saw a black mark similar to the one that had been burned into Crawford's hand when he had stuck the knife into the face of the wooden statue in Rome, accidentally summoning the Carbonari. 'Yours is darker,' Byron had observed. 'They must have used a fresher knife in your initiation, when they had you stab the *mazze*. Did you know that any one knife is only good for so many stabs? After enough use in initiations all the carbon has been thrown off into flesh, and the knife isn't steel anymore, just iron.'

Crawford had just nodded wisely, and he was careful never to contradict Byron's impression that he had been initiated into the Carbonari . . . partly because he suspected that he *had* been, that night.

Byron was limping down the stairs now, and Crawford looked away from the ceiling.

'Good afternoon, Aickman,' Byron said. He was slim and tanned after having lost a lot of weight he'd apparently put on in Venice, but today he looked harassed and unsure of himself. 'What did Shelley say to you out there?'

Crawford stood up. 'Just that he wanted Josephine and me to go with them to Spezia.'

Byron nodded ruefully, as though this confirmed something. 'He won't be coming along today – and I'm damned if I'll go over there to fetch Ed Williams – so I guess it's just you and me.' He gave Crawford a look that was almost a glare, then grinned. 'You won't be putting any silver bullets into me, will you?'

'Uh,' said Crawford, mystified, 'no.'

The two of them rode out through the Porta della Piazza, the same southern gate where Shelley had been

330

punched and the Italian dragoon stabbed a month ago, but though pistols bristled from the tooled leather holsters that fringed Byron's Hussar saddle, the soldiers of the Pisan guard looked down from the walls with nearly none of the alarmed suspicion that they had shown in previous weeks. They all knew that Byron was leaving the city soon. Also, there were only two armed riders today. Previous shooting parties had consisted of half a dozen or more.

'The Shelleys and their damned children,' snapped Byron when the walls were well behind them, and wild olive trees and thickets of saw-grass lined the road. 'Have they *reared* one? Percy Florence is still alive and in his second year, but how much longer do you imagine he'll survive? Their son William died three years ago, you know – a year after little Clara died in Venice – and way back in 1814 or so they had a child that died after two weeks. They hadn't even named it yet! And I seem to recall that he had at least one child by his first wife – no doubt any such are long dead. I don't think Shelley is *interested* in the welfare of children – *particularly* if they're his own.'

'That's obviously nonsense,' Crawford said, driven by his knowledge of Shelley to risk contradicting Byron. 'You know how he feels about his children . . . when he's had them.'

Far from getting angry, though, Byron actually looked abashed. 'Oh, you're right, I know. But they do always die. And now they think Mary's pregnant again! You'd think he'd give up sex – abandon the whole notion as a bad job.'

As I've done, thought Crawford.

They rode on without speaking, and the only sounds were the sea wind in the trees, and the sandy thudding of the horses' hooves. Crawford pondered Byron's remark about a silver bullet. Did Shelley imagine that

331

Byron was the prey of a vampire? He *had* been, of course, before getting to the top of the Wengern.

Crawford looked across at his companion, noting the hollowed cheeks under the greying hair, and the brightness of Byron's eyes. And the poetry he was writing these days was the best he'd ever done – Shelley had said recently that he could no longer compete with Byron, and that Byron was the only one *worth* competing with, now that Keats was dead.

Suddenly Crawford was sure that Byron *had* given in again – probably while he'd been staying in Venice, to judge by Shelley's description of the woman he'd been living with there. Would it have been the same vampire that had been preying on him before? Probably. As he'd guessed in Switzerland six years ago – to Byron's displeasure – they seemed to keep track of their previous lovers even when they'd been barred from them.

But Teresa Guiccioli was obviously not any sort of vampire – she frequently accompanied Byron and his friends on the afternoon rides, and even went to Mass at the cathedral. How was Byron keeping her safe from the jealous attentions of his supernatural lover?

He found himself thinking of the feel of his own vampire's cold skin, and he hastily fumbled under his coat for his flask. He hadn't had sex with anyone – anyone *human* – since his disastrous wedding night six years ago, and he had come to the bleak conclusion that making love to the thing that was Shelley's twin had spoiled him for sex with his own species.

He still sometimes thought about the painful but releasing kiss Josephine had given him in front of Keats's house a year ago in Rome, but the memory never quickened his pulse, and he and Josephine had never referred to it.

He and Byron had reached the field at the outskirts of the Castinelli farm where they always did their shooting, and Byron swung down off his horse and grinned up at Crawford. 'Join you in that?'

'Certainly.' Crawford handed the flask down and then dismounted, and walked with Byron to the ravaged tree around which they habitually set up their targets. Byron took a second deep sip of the brandy, then handed the flask back, and as Crawford tethered the horses he crouched over some stakes they'd pounded into the ground last time. He was wedging halfcrown pieces into the splintered heads of a couple of the stakes.

'Allegra's dead,' he said over his shoulder.

'Oh.'

Crawford had never met the five-year-old daughter of Byron and Claire Clairmont, and though he knew that Claire cared passionately for the child, he had no real idea of how Byron had felt about her – clearly he blamed himself at least to some extent, since he had made such a point earlier of impugning Shelley's ability to take care of children.

'I'm sorry,' Crawford said, blushing at how inane it sounded.

'I had her in a convent, you know,' Byron went on, still facing away from him and adjusting the stakes. His tone was light and conversational. 'I've got certain protections for myself and Teresa, but they're not foolproof, and I thought . . . that in a consecrated place, far away from me and everyone else who's known to these creatures . . . but it doesn't seem to . . .' His shoulders were rigid, and Crawford wondered if he was weeping, but his voice when he spoke again was just as steady. 'Our poor children.'

Crawford thought of his own agonized resisting of the urge to invite his lamia back – which in his case was, among other things, resistance to the offer of enormous longevity – and he thought too of the cost at which Keats had managed to save his own younger sister.

'Your . . .' Crawford began, wondering if Byron would challenge him to a duel for what he was about to say, 'your poetry means that much to you?'

Byron stood up lithely and limped back toward the horses, still without having faced Crawford. In one flash of motion he drew two of the pistols and spun toward Crawford and the tree; and, in the next stretched instant of panic, Crawford had time to wonder if this was where he would die, and to notice that Byron's hands were shaking wildly and that his eyes were shining with tears.

The two detonations were one ear-hammering blast, but Crawford caught the brief, shrill *twang* of at least one of the coins as it was punched away across the field.

One muscle at a time, Crawford relaxed, dimly aware through the ringing in his ears that Byron had reholstered the pistols and was walking back toward the tree; and beyond the glittering dots swimming in front of his eyes he watched him limp on past the tree, out into the grass; Byron's head was down, and he was apparently looking for the coins, both of which were gone.

'It has,' Byron called back after Crawford had crossed to the tree and was leaning against it. 'Meant so much to me,' he added. He was kicking at the grass ten yards away and peering intently at the ground. 'I . . . I suppose I really *did* know what Lord Grey was, what sort of thing he was, at least, when I opened my bedroom door to him in 1803. By the time I found out that I had doomed my mother and imperilled my sister, of course, it was too late. Still, I didn't want to believe that he was responsible for my . . . life's work, my writing, the thing that I . . . that made me *me*, do you know what I'm saying?'

'Yes,' Crawford managed to reply.

'I did *suspect* it – and so I've always taken inordinate

delight in physical accomplishments – swimming and shooting and fencing and carnality. But none of those things are enough – not to justify all the deaths and hatreds and . . . betrayals, that have been my life.' He stooped and picked up a wad of silver, then held it up with a frail smile. 'Not bad, eh? The coin's wrapped right around the ball.' He began limping back toward the tree.

Still remembering the way Keats had chosen to die, Crawford said, 'But why did you *ask him in again*? After you had managed to cut free of him in the Alps?'

'I had stopped *writing!*' Byron shook his head and pitched the coin away. 'It . . . it turned out that I couldn't stand that. I wrote *Manfred*, yes, but that was mostly from memory, stuff I'd composed mentally before we climbed the Wengern; and then in Venice I started the fourth Canto of *Childe Harold*, but it was just plodding . . . until I met Margarita Cogni – and then I made myself believe that she *wasn't* Lord Grey again in a differently sexed body, and that the sudden improvement in my writing would have happened anyway.' He started back toward the horses. 'I find I'm not really in the mood for shooting – how about you?'

'To hell with shooting,' Crawford agreed bewilderedly.

'And now Allegra's dead,' Byron said as he untethered his horse and swung up into the saddle. His eyes narrowed. 'But before the . . . thing can get my sister and my other daughter, I'm going to ditch it again, and then go someplace where I can *accomplish* something, make my name mean something – in some more valuable arena than poetry.'

Crawford climbed back up on to his horse. 'Like?'

'Like . . . what, freedom – fighting for it – for people that haven't got it.' Byron frowned self-consciously. 'It seems like the best way to atone.'

Crawford thought of the bas-relief coat-of-arms on the door of Byron's carriage, and of the many-roomed

335

palace he shared with his monkeys and dogs and birds. 'Sounds awfully democratic,' he said mildly.

Byron gave him a sharp look. 'That's sarcasm, isn't it? Apparently you don't know that my first speech in the House of Lords was in support of the frame-breakers, the English labourers who were being jailed, and even killed, for breaking the machines that were taking away their employment. And you know how involved I've been with the Carbonari, trying to help them throw off the Austrian yoke. It's been . . .' He shrugged and shook his head. 'It hasn't been enough. Lately I've been thinking about Greece.'

Greece, Crawford recalled, was struggling to free itself from Turkey; but it was such a distant conflict, and so overshadowed with echoes of Homer and classical mythology, that he dismissed the notion as mere Byronic romanticism.

'So you're planning to return to the Alps?' Crawford asked.

'Perhaps that. Or Venice. There's no *terrible* hurry . . . in the meantime I can continue to *resist* the thing's attentions, as I've been doing. The Carbonari have been resisting them for centuries, and Teresa's family is deeply schooled in Carbonari lore. You noticed, I trust, that Teresa is . . . that she remains untouched by this particular *ailment*.'

Byron seemed angry, so Crawford didn't question him further – though he was now very curious to know whether Byron's affection for Teresa had sprung up before or after his discovery of her family's vampire-repelling skills.

They had ridden for several minutes back toward the centuries-forsaken walls of the city when Byron noticed a figure ahead of them, silhouetted against the grey sky on a rise in the track through the marsh. Crawford squinted in the direction Byron indicated, and saw that the figure was running wildly – toward them – and then he went cold with recognition.

'It's Josephine,' he said tightly, spurring his horse forward.

She began waving when she saw the horses, and her arm didn't stop metronoming back and forth until Crawford had ridden up to her, reined in and dismounted, and grabbed her arm and forced it back down to her side. She was panting so desperately that he made her sit down, and her eyes were wide open, the glass one staring crazily up into the grey sky.

Byron dismounted too, and held the reins of both horses, staring at Josephine with lively interest. Crawford hoped she would turn out to have had some purpose in running out here; he never permitted anyone to make fun of her odd behaviour, but it was discouraging how many times she gave people the opportunity.

After a minute Josephine had regained her breath. 'Soldiers from the garrison,' she said, 'at our house. I hid when they broke in, and then I climbed out the kitchen window when they were all in the main room.'

Byron swore. 'You two weren't even anywhere *near* the damned gate when Tita stabbed that dragoon! And they just broke in? I'm going to deal with this, they can't start harassing all my acquaintances – '

'I . . . I don't think it was about the dragoon,' she said, staring hard at Crawford with her one eye.

'Well?' Crawford demanded impatiently after a pause. 'What *do* you think it was about? You can talk in front of Byron,' he added, seeing her hesitate.

'They were talking about three men who were killed in Rome last year.'

Crawford's belly suddenly felt very empty, and he instinctively looked past her at the city walls. '. . . Oh.'

Byron's eyebrows were raised. 'You killed three men in Rome?'

Crawford exhaled. 'Apparently.' He looked back, along the road that led to the Castinelli family's farm-house, and he wondered how much the old farmer might charge to let him and Josephine sleep on his kitchen floor tonight.

'Byron, could you please have a message delivered to Shelley when you get back? Tell him that the Aickmans will take him up on his offer of employment after all – but that he'll have to bring clothes and supplies for us, and pick us up on the road outside the city.'

Chapter 13

The realm I look upon and die
Another man will own;
He shall attain the heaven that I
Perish and have not known.

— A. E. Housman

The entire Shelley household — which, after a hasty stop at the Castinelli farmhouse, included Crawford and Josephine — left Pisa the next day; and four days later Crawford and Shelley and Edward Williams spent an hour carrying boxes through the shallow surf of the Gulf of Spezia's eastern shore, setting the boxes down on the sand-swept portico of the old stone boat-house that Shelley had rented, and then wading back to the anchored boat for more.

Away from each side of the house stretched a seawall that divided the narrow strip of beach from the trees masking the steep slope behind the house, and the nearest neighbours were a dozen fishermen and their families in the little cluster of huts called San Terenzo, two hundred yards to the north. There was a road somewhere up the hill, but the only practical access to the shoreside dwellings was by sea, and Shelley was anxious for the delivery of the twenty-four-foot boat that he'd had built at Livorno, and aboard which he hoped to spend most of the hot summer days.

The house was called the Casa Magni, which Crawford thought was an awfully splendid name for so desolate and inhospitable a place. Five tall arches opened on the ground floor, but except for a narrow pavement the house fronted right on the water and, behind the arches, the flagstones of the vast, house-spanning chamber were always rippled and gritty with sand from the high tides.

The ground-floor chamber was used only for storage of boating equipment, and everyone had to sleep and dine in the rooms upstairs – Crawford remembered hearing descriptions of Byron's palace in Venice, and he wondered why both poets seemed to like dwellings that were just about literally *on* the water.

On the evening after their arrival Claire returned unexpectedly soon from a walk along the narrow beach and, climbing the stairs to where everyone else was sitting around the table in the long central dining room, she heard Shelley saying something about Byron and the convent at Bagnacavallo; when she got to the top of the stairs she crossed the room and asked Shelley if her daughter was dead, and Shelley stood up and answered, quietly, 'Yes.'

She stared at him with such white-faced fury that he actually stepped back, but then she turned and ran into the room she was sharing with Mary, and closed the door; Mary slept in Shelley's room that night, contrary to their habit.

Even in his bunk in the men's servants' room in the back of the house, Crawford could hear Claire sobbing wildly until dawn.

During the next several days Shelley went on a number of solitary hikes up and down the beach, climbing the weirdly bubbled and wavy volcanic rocks and frequently cutting himself on them, but at sunset he could generally be found leaning on the rail of the terrace that fronted the Casa Magni's second storey, staring out across the four miles of darkening water at the tall, craggy silhouette of the peninsula of Portovenere across the Gulf.

One evening Crawford followed him and Ed Williams out on to the terrace after dinner; Shelley and Williams were talking between themselves, and Crawford, shaded from the moonlight by the ragged canvas awning, leaned against the house wall and, as he sipped a glass of *sciacchetra*, a locally made sweet amber wine, he stared speculatively at his new employer.

Crawford had wondered why Shelley had been so determined to bring his whole entourage to this particular section of bleak coast; at times like this, when Shelley would desultorily maintain a conversation as he scanned the empty waters and the structureless shores, he seemed to be waiting for something – and at such times too he often rattled certain quartzy beach pebbles in his fist, like a man working up the nerve to roll dice on a horrifyingly large wager.

The only sounds on the warm breeze tonight were the measured crash of the surf on the rocks below the terrace, and the hoarse whisper of the wind in the trees behind and above the house, and the clicking of the rocks in Shelley's fist – and so Crawford spilled most of his wine on to his hand and wrist when Shelley suddenly gave a choked yell and grabbed Williams' arm.

'*There!*' Shelley said in a whispered scream, pointing out over the rail at the white foam streaking the dark waves below. '*Do you see her?*'

Williams, his voice shrill with fright, denied seeing anything; but when Crawford hurried to the rail and looked down he thought he saw a small human form hovering over the waves, beckoning with one white arm.

Shelley tore his gaze away from the sea and looked at Crawford; even in the evening dimness Crawford could see the whites of his eyes all around the irises.

'Don't interfere, Aickman,' Shelley said. 'She's not for you this – ' He paused then, for he had looked back out

341

at the sea, and the look of alarmed anticipation was struck from his face, leaving only a look of sick, tired horror. 'Oh, God,' he wailed softly. 'It's not her.'

Crawford looked out again at the dark, surging ocean. The pale figure was farther out, and now he thought he saw several – no, dozens – of impossibly hovering human forms far out over the face of the night's sea, and he flinched back, coldly aware of how alone he and his companions were on this desolate northern coast, and of how very many miles outward the featureless water extended.

In the moment before it disappeared, seeming to rise into the ash sky and disappear against the stony shoulder of Portovenere, Crawford got a glimpse of the face of the child-figure Shelley had pointed out; the face was porcelain white, and seemed to be showing all its teeth in a broad smile.

Shelley collapsed on the rail, and if Williams hadn't grabbed his shoulder he might have fallen over the rail on to the narrow pavement below; but after a moment Shelley straightened up and pushed his disordered blond hair back from his face.

'It was Allegra,' he said quietly. 'Don't, for God's sake, tell Claire.'

Crawford stepped back into the shadows and chewed sweet wine from his trembling knuckles.

During the long summer days the heat seemed to flow through all of them like a drug. Even the children were stunned by it – the Shelleys' two-year-old son, Percy Florence, spent most of his time drawing random squiggles in any shaded patches of sand he could find, and the Williamses' two children, one of whom was barely a year old, spent much of each day crying – it seemed to Crawford that they cried with a sort of slow patience, as

342

if a lot of it would have to be done and they didn't want to wear themselves out early.

Claire just stumbled around in a daze, and Crawford didn't think it was caused by her admittedly heavy drinking. All she could talk about was how Byron had used Allegra as a way to make her unhappy; in fact, so frequently did she say 'He never did *anything* for Allegra!' that Crawford and Josephine would often whisper the sentence to each other when Claire opened her mouth to speak, and more often than not had correctly anticipated what she'd been about to say.

Mary was unspecifically ill much of the time, and had taken on the status of an invalid, and when she did leave her room it was generally to talk to Edward Williams and his wife Jane, who of all the group were bearing up best.

Ed Williams was a year younger than Percy Shelley, and though he had literary ambitions, and had even written a tragedy, he was a bluff outdoorsman, always tanned and cheerful and ready to help with the various maintenance jobs the boats and house required. His wife Jane, too, seemed unaffected by the domineering sun, and was always ready to cheer up the rest of the party with her guitar playing in the evenings, when at last a cooling breeze would sweep in off the water to break the sweaty choke-hold of the day.

Crawford liked both the Williamses, and was profoundly glad that they were here to share the impromptu exile.

At noon of the fourth day after the apparition of Allegra had beckoned to Shelley from the twilight surf, they saw a sail appear around the headland of Portovenere.

For once the day was grey and storm-threatening, and when the watchers on the terrace realized that the sail was that of Shelley's new boat, the *Don Juan*, being

343

delivered at last, Shelley smiled nervously and remarked to Crawford how appropriate it was that his craft should first be seen emerging from the port of Venus.

That's right, thought Crawford, with a sudden chill that wasn't the cold wind's doing, *Portovenere – that's what it means*.

The boat was an imposingly big craft when seen up close – two masts stood up from the polished deck, each sporting a gaff-rigged mainsail and topsails, and three jibsails extended like an upswept mane from the tapering neck of the long bowsprit – and, after she was moored and the delivery crew had come ashore, Shelley hired one of them, an eighteen-year-old English boy called Charles Vivian, to stay on as a part of her permanent crew.

On a sunny afternoon three days later they took the *Don Juan* out for her first real sail with Shelley as captain, and tacked their way effortlessly across the sparkling blue water of the Gulf to within a hundred yards of the cliffs of Portovenere. Jane Williams and Mary were aboard, seated in the stern near where Shelley worked the tiller, and Shelley had insisted that Crawford come along too, in case the outing should make the pregnant Mary ill.

At one point Shelley gave the tiller to Edward Williams and walked up to where Crawford sat leaning against the forward mast. 'Six months more, then?' Shelley asked him.

Crawford realized that he was talking about Mary's pregnancy. 'Roughly,' he answered, shading his eyes with his hand as he squinted upward. 'Be born in the late autumn or early winter.'

Shelley stood easily on the deck, keeping his arms folded and only leaning to compensate for the rolling. 'Mary doesn't like it here,' he said suddenly. 'She hates the loneliness, and the heat.' He had to speak loudly for

Crawford to hear him, but the wind was on the starboard quarter and was flinging their voices away over the bow. 'I think she knows I have to be here, though. To . . .' He shivered and looked past Crawford at the cliffs, shaking his head.

Crawford wished Byron had followed them all here, instead of moving farther south for the summer; despite the differences between the two poets, he was the best person to get Shelley to express himself clearly.

'To . . . ?' echoed Crawford helpfully.

Shelley dropped his gaze to him again. 'I may . . . it's possible I may . . . suffer, here, this summer.'

Shelley had often complained to Crawford about bladder stones and hardening of the skin and fingernails; the symptoms seemed to be aggravated by exposure to sunlight, and Crawford started to advise him for the dozenth time to be careful always to wear a hat, but Shelley waved him to silence.

'No, not all that.' Shelley rubbed his eyes.

'I may not be quite the same man, come autumn, as I am now and have been,' Shelley said. 'You're a doctor — if the sort of thing I'm describing does happen, I'd be grateful if you'd authoritatively tell Mary that it was — oh, you know, a brain fever induced by a mortified cut or something, that left me not as . . . as *intelligent*, not as *insightful*, as the man she married.' His tanned face was hollowed and pinched, making him look much older than his thirty years. 'Don't ever let her — suspect that I did it intentionally — for her, and for our surviving son, and for the child she carries.'

Without waiting for a reply he turned away and strode aft, and a few moments later Crawford got to his feet and leaned on the starboard rail, staring out to the open sea and away from Portovenere. Summer lightning made it seem that flickering white-hot wires were turning in the terribly blue sky just above the horizon, and the recent storms had driven in toward shore hundreds of gigantic Portuguese men-o'-war that now hung below the surface of the water like big malignant pearls.

Shelley continued to take his long walks, mostly after dark now; and after Williams built a little rowboat out of wood and tarred canvas, Shelley began rowing it out to where the *Don Juan* was moored offshore, and spending his days aboard the big boat, feverishly writing page after page of poetry. *The Triumph of Life* was what he was calling his new, long work.

The summer seemed to Crawford to be flying past. Josephine bunked with the rest of the women servants, and had been recruited as a sort of assistant to Antonia, the Italian nanny who took care of the Williamses' two children and young Percy Florence Shelley, and so he hardly saw her except at dinner; and she was subdued then, firing off none of the weird, conversation-stopping remarks that had so upset Mary and Claire when they all used to gather around Byron's table in Pisa.

Mary tended to hide out in her room, and the Williamses stayed together, often out on the boat with Shelley, and so it was almost with a sense of relief that Crawford recognized the man he met on the beach on a twilight evening a month after that first outing aboard the *Don Juan*.

Crawford and Josephine had been busy all day attending to Mary, who had begun bleeding from the womb and for a swelteringly strenuous couple of hours had seemed on the verge of having a miscarriage; the fit had eventually passed, to Shelley's intense relief, and Mary had fallen into a restless, sweaty doze. Josephine had returned to the children and Shelley had stalked back to his own room to resume the writing that so absorbed him, and Crawford had gone for a long walk south along

346

the beach, only turning back when the sun had dipped behind the island off the tip of Portovenere.

As soon as he turned his steps back toward the north, Crawford had noticed the man standing on the sand a hundred yards ahead of him, and when Crawford had taken a couple of dozen steps in that direction he had recognized him.

It was Polidori, the arrogant young man who had been Byron's poetry-writing personal physician before Byron had dismissed him, and given the job to Crawford, in 1816. The carefully tended little moustache and the curled hair and the self-consciously dignified stance were unmistakable.

Crawford waved and called out to him, and Polidori turned to stare in response.

Crawford started toward him along the sand – but at one point the shoreline led Crawford inland around a boulder, and when his course took him again out to where he could see some distance of beach, Polidori was gone, presumably up the wooded slope.

Still holds a grudge, thought Crawford. I wonder why he's visiting Shelley.

As he trudged up to the Casa Magni, Crawford saw Shelley at his usual station for this time of night, leaning from the rail on the second floor and staring out over the sea. Shelley started violently when Crawford hailed him, but relaxed when he saw who it was. 'Good evening, Aickman,' he called down quietly.

'Evening, Percy,' returned Crawford, pausing below the terrace. 'Didn't mean to startle you. What did Polidori want?'

Shelley's momentarily regained composure was suddenly gone. His narrow fingers gripped the rail like the claws of a bird, and his whisper was shrill as he told Crawford, 'Get up here – and say nothing to anyone.'

Crawford rolled his eyes impatiently, but obediently

blundered through the empty ground floor to the stairs, climbed them to the dining room level and passed by Jane Williams and Mary and Josephine without speaking, though he picked up a glass and filled it from a decanter on the table, and then walked out to join Shelley on the terrace. The wind was from the sea, and he looked nervously out across the face of the water before looking at Shelley.

'So why are you afraid of Polidori?' he asked quietly, taking a sip of the wine.

Shelley stared at him. 'Because he's dead. He killed himself last year, in England.'

'Well, your information's faulty. I saw him down the beach not half an hour ago.'

'I don't doubt you did,' said Shelley unhappily. 'This is an easy place for them to come to, the Port of Venus.' He waved out at the ocean. 'Remember Allegra?'

Crawford was suddenly very tired. 'What,' he asked listlessly, 'are you saying?'

'You know what I'm saying, damn you. If someone dies after being bitten by a vampire, and nobody . . . kills the body in the right way, he comes back, he digs his way out of his grave and *comes back*. Though it's hardly *him* anymore. I stopped Clara . . . but the nuns at Bagnacavallo didn't stop Allegra, and clearly nobody pounded a stake into Polidori's corpse either.'

He shook his head, looking even wearier than Crawford felt. 'Eggshells are all humans are to these things – the bite carrics their . . . what, eggs, spores . . . and in the ground the spores replace the organic stuff of their dead host with their stonier substance, like the primeval fish and plants you can find petrified in rocks.' Crawford tried to interrupt, but Shelley went on. 'I wish it were possible to be certain, absolutely *certain*, that no bit of the soul of the original host was still present in the remade body – but the revivified ones do seem to seek out people they knew when they were alive.'

He turned to Crawford, and there were tears in his eyes. 'What if Allegra, the real child, is still . . . *in* that head, somewhere, like a child lost in the catacombs of an overthrown castle? Christ, I remember playing with her, rolling billiard balls back and forth across the floor of Byron's palace in Venice with her . . . years ago.'

'Why did you come here?' Crawford asked, thinking of the fragility of Josephine.

'Because I want to make a deal with her.' Shelley smiled shakily at him. '*Her* – not Allegra. You know who I mean. And, like the rest of her tribe, she'll be more accessible in this place. I want to . . . buy her off.'

'With what?'

Shelley took the glass from Crawford's hand and drained it. 'With myself – or what makes me *me*, anyway; with the . . . greater part of my humanity.'

Crawford stared at him. 'Will she take it?'

'Oh, she'll *take* it, sure enough; I just hope she'll remember to adhere to the bargain.'

Crawford shuddered, but didn't try to talk him out of it.

That night Crawford was shaken awake by another of the servants, who told him he'd been shouting in his sleep; Crawford blurrily thanked the man, but was almost sorry he'd been awakened – for, though he couldn't remember any of the dream, it was evident to him that it had been intensely erotic, and it was the first time in two years that he'd had any such feelings. At the same time he knew that even in the dream it had only been a tantalizing glimpse of something passing by, not anything for him.

He didn't sleep for the rest of the night, and when at dawn he took a cup of coffee out on to the terrace he saw Shelley, pale and haggard, rowing the little boat out to the *Don Juan*; Shelley was facing him, and when he saw Crawford he nodded grimly.

The next day a three-masted frigate sailed into the Gulf and fired a four-gun salute to the moored *Don Juan* — it proved to be Byron's new ship, the *Bolivar*, en route from Genoa to where her future owner awaited her in Livorno; aboard her were a Captain Daniel Roberts and a friend of Shelley's and Byron's from the days in Pisa, Edward John Trelawny.

Shelley was delighted to see Trelawny again, and even Mary revived somewhat from her semi-invalidhood, and for two days the Casa Magni was a cheerful place, with boat trips to Lerici for roses and carnations and spicy Ligurean food and strong coffee, and long, animated conversations around the dining table, and the sound of Jane Williams's guitar echoing over the water.

Trelawny was a tall, bearded soldier-of-fortune who had known Edward Williams in Geneva; he had asked for an introduction to the Pisan circle mainly in order to meet Byron, whose adventurous poetry he admired, but as it happened he had become friends primarily with the Shelleys. He and Shelley were the same age, and though the one was big and dark and the other frail and fair, they were equally skilled at shooting and sailing, and now spent many hours together in pistol practice and in discussion of improvements Shelley wanted to make on the *Don Juan*.

The holiday atmosphere brought the children out, and Crawford saw Josephine frequently during the two festive days; and on Saturday night when a group took the *Don Juan* a mile north along the coast to Lerici for dinner, and there proved to be too many people for the longest table the restaurant had, he found himself sitting at a small separate table with her.

The waiter brought a steaming platter of trenette

noodles covered with green pesto sauce redolent of basil and Ligurean olive oil and garlic, and Josephine said, 'I hate this.'

She was forking a lot of the noodles on to her plate, so Crawford knew she didn't mean the food. 'We could leave,' he said quietly.

She looked up at him. 'You know why we can't.'

The smile he gave her was as affectionate as it was wry, for he knew she wasn't referring to the danger of arrest. He nodded. 'The children.'

'He's got something in mind, in coming here,' she said. 'Hasn't he? Something he thinks will save them.'

Crawford took some of the pasta himself, and while he nibbled at it he quietly told her about the vague deal Shelley had hoped to make with his unhuman sister, and that he had apparently already made it.

'The one you're married to,' said Josephine. 'Are you . . . comfortable with the fact that she might be around?'

'*Used* to be married to,' he said. 'I got a divorce in the Alps.' He went on hurriedly, 'No, I'm not comfortable with the fact. She . . . killed Julia, after all. As a matter of fact I think she *was* around, night before last – I sort of . . . felt her, in my sleep, I think.'

Josephine reddened and looked away. 'I know what you mean. Do you think Percy . . . ?'

It was a new thought to Crawford, and he fought down the instant jealousy it roused in him. 'I don't know. That might have been part of the bargain, I suppose – he did . . . have her, once before, in 1811.' He despised himself for remembering the year; 'Yes, I imagine that probably was part of it.'

She drank some wine and smiled unhappily at him, and he knew she had been aware of his momentary envy. 'It's all just so damned horrible, isn't it?'

Crawford reflected her smile.

* * *

351

Edward Williams piloted them all back home, skating the *Don Juan* across the calm water under a full moon, but when they got back to the Casa Magni Crawford couldn't sleep, and eventually got out of bed and went out to the dining room to read.

The wind was strengthening, and the windows rattled with each gust in eerie counterpoint to the boom of the surf on the rocks, and Crawford kept being distracted by a remark Williams had made about the tides being capricious along this shore. Williams had seemed to find it amusing, but now, as the moon hovered over the massy shoulder of Portovenere, the thought made Crawford uneasy.

After a while Claire came silently out of Mary's room and closed the door behind her. She smiled and nodded to him, but her face was drawn, and he wondered what dream had driven her out of bed. She seemed sober.

'I've got to get out of here, Michael,' she whispered, sitting down in a chair across the table from him. 'Back to Florence. This is a bad place.'

He glanced out at the moon, and nodded. 'Shelley should have done this alone,' he whispered back.

She stared at him. 'Done what?'

He realized that she wasn't aware of Shelley's vague purpose in coming here, and he began to frame some answer having to do with the man's poetry, but suddenly she was looking past him, toward the window, and her mouth was pinched shut and her eyes had gone as wide open as they could. Then she was up out of her chair and running toward the closed door to the terrace.

The violence of the movement startled Crawford half out of his own chair, and when he glanced at the French door he lunged out of the chair entirely and got to the door an instant before she did, and held her back.

There was a little girl out on the terrace, holding up white hands toward the light inside, and though she was silhouetted by the moon, Crawford could see her darkly shining eyes and white teeth as she mouthed inaudible words through the glass.

'What are you doing,' Claire panted, struggling to get out of Crawford's arms, 'that's my daughter! That's Allegra!'

'It's *not*, Claire, I swear to you,' Crawford snarled, spinning her back across the floor to crack her hip against the table. 'It's a vampire. Your daughter *died*, remember?'

One of the candlesticks wobbled and then clanked over, and then Shelley's door opened, and Crawford could hear people stirring in the rear rooms.

Claire ran back toward the glassed door, and Crawford caught her, holding her too tightly in his fear.

Josephine, wrapped in a robe, padded up, stared expressionlessly for a moment at the swaying thing on the terrace, and then stood between it and Claire.

Claire's eyes blazed at Shelley, who was blinking around sleepily. 'Allegra's on the terrace,' she told him clearly. 'Tell these two to let me go to her.'

Shelley was suddenly wide awake. 'It wasn't her, Claire,' he said quietly, keeping his eyes away from the windows. 'Ed,' he added to Williams, who had appeared from his own room, 'pull the curtains across, will you? And Josephine, get Claire a glass of something to let her sleep.'

Williams walked slowly across the room to the windows, and Crawford, still holding the struggling Claire, glanced at him impatiently.

Williams was staring at the child outside as he dragged the drapes across, and though there was no change in Williams' expression, Crawford thought there had been some kind of communication through the glass in the instant before the curtains cut out the last of the moonlight. He tried to catch Williams' eye as the man walked back across the room, but Williams was staring at the floor.

Claire sagged in Crawford's arms, and he led her to a chair and lowered her into it as Josephine hurried back to the women's servants' room.

Shelley's alertness had faded, and he was blinking around as if he couldn't remember what had just happened – more than ever Crawford was sure he must have consummated his bargain with the lamia, and he gripped the back of Claire's chair very hard. He didn't want to go back to the lamia himself – he swore to himself that he didn't – but he remembered with torturing vividness how hungrily she used to come into his arms, and he remembered his hands on her, and hers on him.

Josephine had returned with a bottle of laudanum, and Claire dazedly drank the dose Josephine measured out, and then let herself be led back to her bed.

Without a word Williams returned to his own room and closed the door.

'You didn't expect this?' Crawford asked.

'Not Allegra, no,' Shelley said softly, shaking his head. 'I couldn't believe it when we saw her the other night – I was told that the body was shipped back to England. God knows what child's body *was* sent there. I – '

'What do you recommend we do about it?'

'. . . All go back to bed?' Shelley ventured.

Not trusting himself to speak, Crawford nodded stiffly and returned to his room.

He still couldn't sleep. He lay staring up at the ceiling, wondering if he should go take some laudanum himself to drive away the memories of cold breasts and a hot tongue, and glaringly alive but inorganic eyes, and the total loss of self to which he had so gratefully surrendered during that most peaceful week of his life in Switzerland six years ago.

Shelley was having her — perhaps even now, at this moment — and her thoughts were all of Shelley and not of him.

He sipped brandy from his ever-present flask instead, and at dawn managed to fall into an uneasy doze.

At eight he was again shaken awake, this time by Shelley, who was pale beneath his tan and clearly on the verge of weeping. 'Mary's had a miscarriage,' he said tightly, 'and is haemorrhaging badly. Hurry — I think she may bleed to death.'

Crawford rolled out of bed and pushed back his hair. 'Right,' he said, trying to gather his wits. 'Get me brandy and clean linen, and send someone to Lerici for ice. And get Josephine — I'll need her.'

Chapter 14

. . . The Magus Zoroaster, my dead child,
Met his own image walking in the garden.

— Percy Bysshe Shelley

. . . He had seen the figure of himself which met him as
he walked on the terrace & said to him — 'How long do
you mean to be content?'

— Mary Shelley

The sheets had been peeled back from Mary's bed, and blood seemed to be everywhere; it not only soaked the bedclothes and the mattress, but was spattered on the walls and smeared across her face — evidently she had reacted violently when she'd become aware of what was happening to her. By the grey, fog-filtered light from the windows, the blood seemed to be the only colour in the room, and it was only after the first stunned moment that he even noticed Mary's naked form lying among it.

The low ceiling of the long-ago hotel room in Hastings seemed to press down on the top of his head, and for several seconds he just stared in mindless horror at what seemed to be Julia's exploded corpse.

'Aickman!' Shelley said loudly.

Crawford dragged himself out of the memory. 'Right,' he said tightly.

He crossed to the bed and knelt, quickly pressing the heel of his hand against Mary's lower belly.

'Someone's going for ice?' he asked sharply.

'Ed Williams and Trelawny are, in the *Don Juan*,' Shelley told him.

'Good. Get me a bowl of brandy.'

Josephine hurried in a moment later, and when Crawford glanced back at her he could see that the spectacle had a traumatic effect on her, too – but she took several deep breaths, and then in a flat voice asked him what needed to be done.

'Come over here.' When she had crossed to the bed and leaned over, he spoke to her quietly. 'It's too late for the foetus. Now we've got to stop the bleeding. Get me a pot of very damned strong tea, and then roll a cylindrical bandage for packing her, and soak it in the tea – the tannin should help. And be ready to bandage her tightly around the hips, with a pad over the uterus here, where my hand is.'

He felt that someone else had entered the room and was standing behind him, but he was talking calmly to Mary now, reminding her that he was a doctor, and telling her to relax.

He saw some of the tension go out of the tendons in her neck and legs, and when Shelley returned with the bowl of brandy Crawford rinsed his free hand in it and then gently put a finger into Mary's vagina to try to ascertain the source of the bleeding. As he'd feared, it was inaccessibly far up.

He felt strong disapproval radiate from the person behind him, but ignored it.

He heard Josephine return, and smelled the tea she had brought.

And suddenly it was Julia's destroyed body that he was probing with such grotesque intimacy, and the room was again the one in which he'd spent his wedding night in Hastings. He drew back with a smothered yell and looked around wildly; Josephine and Shelley were the only other people in the room – God knew whom

357

he had imagined to be standing behind him – and Josephine was trembling so hard that tea was shaking out of the pot she held as she stared in horror at the fearful bed.

It's a hallucination, Crawford told himself desperately. This is like what happened in Keats's apartment in Rome.

He took a deep breath and closed his eyes, and when he opened them again it was Mary in the bed, and Shelley was looking at him anxiously. Crawford turned to Josephine – her face had relaxed again, but she was just staring blankly out the window, into the fog. Clearly she had shared the hallucination.

'Josephine,' he said, to no response. 'Goddammit, *Josephine!*'

She stirred, and blinked at him.

'What's the year, and where are we?' he demanded.

She closed her eyes, then after a moment whispered, 'Twenty-two, Gulf of Spezia.'

'Good. Remember it. Now get the bandage out of the teapot and wring it out and hand it to me – it doesn't matter if it's a bit hot, I want to try diaphoretics anyway, until the ice gets here.' Easily said, he thought, but how are we to induce real sweating without burnt hawthorn or calx of antimony or elder flowers or camphor? More than ever he regretted the loss of his medical kit in Pisa.

He saw Josephine's questioning look when he turned to her to take the bandage. 'Well, wrap her up in blankets, at least, when I'm done here,' he said, 'and then have her drink as much of that tea as she can.' He turned back toward the bed.

The whole front of Julia's head was crushed, but there was a shifting of the bloody flesh where the eye sockets might have been, and he guessed she was trying to open her eyes. A hole opened beneath them, and managed to pronounce the words, '*Why, Michael . . . ?*'

He closed his own eyes again. 'Percy,' he said unsteadily, 'go to the kitchen and get me garlic, anything with garlic in it. We're getting that kind of resistance here.'

'Why, Michael . . . ?' said Josephine behind him in an eerily accurate echo.

When he opened his eyes he saw Mary again — he gave her what he tried to make a reassuring smile, then glanced past her, out the window. The sky was still lost behind the fog, and he prayed that the sun would disperse the stuff soon.

The visual hallucinations stopped when Shelley followed his instructions about rubbing the window frame with the garlic bread he'd found, though Crawford — and, visibly, Josephine — continued to hear Julia's voice outside, repeatedly asking him, '*Why?*'

Crawford's measures slowed the bleeding, and when the ice was brought upstairs at nine-thirty he had Trelawny fill a metal hip-bath with salted water and chunks of the ice; then he had Shelley help him lift Mary out of the bed and lower her into the tub.

She shuddered violently at the chill, but it very shortly stopped the bleeding.

The fog was breaking up, and distantly across the Gulf the ridge of Portovenere glowed green and gold in the morning sun. Crawford stripped the bed, wrapped the tiny foetus of Shelley's dead child in the ruined sheets, and walked out into the dining room. Shelley followed him.

'There's a shovel downstairs,' Shelley said bleakly, 'in the corner by the spare oars.'

Shelley dug the grave, in the slope behind the house; it didn't have to be very deep, but tears were running down his cheeks and it took him nearly half an hour. At last Crawford laid the bloody bundle in the hole.

He straightened, and Shelley began shovelling dirt into the hole, and Crawford mentally said goodbye to the child that had been in his care. He had lost babies before, but – perhaps not rationally – this loss filled him with more guilt than had any of the others.

'She didn't honour your deal, did she?' he asked Shelley in a brittle tone.

Shelley threw the last shovelful of dirt on to the low mound. 'No,' he said hollowly. 'She did take what I offered – I won't ever write any more poetry, she gnawed out that part of my mind – but I guess she . . . didn't remember, not for very long, anyway, what her part of the bargain was supposed to be.'

'This is what – the third child you've lost to her? The fourth, that's right. And this time Mary nearly went too. You've got one child left, Percy Florence, upstairs. How long do you think it'll be before she kills *him*?' Crawford had sometimes taken the two-year-old boy out rowing in the little boat when his father was off in the *Don Juan*, and he didn't like to think of coming out here again some morning to bury Percy Florence.

Shelley blinked around at the walnut trees standing up from the slope, then out at the sea. 'I don't know. Not long, I suppose. I wish she could be stopped, but this was my best – '

'It was not,' interrupted Crawford harshly. 'In Switzerland, when you talked to me in that boat on the lake, you told me that it'd be a bad idea for me to pitch you into the water, remember? You said that if you were to drown it would probably kill her, because of how closely you're linked, being twins and all. Well, if you want to save Mary and your remaining son, why don't you do that? Drown yourself? Why didn't you do it *years* ago, before she killed your children?'

He had expected Shelley to get angry, but instead he seemed to consider seriously what Crawford had said. 'I don't know,' he mumbled again, then plodded slowly away toward the house, leaving Crawford to carry the shovel.

After stowing the shovel, Crawford took off his bloody shirt – he hadn't had time yet this morning to put on shoes – and walked out across the pavement onto the sunlit sand and waded into the clear blue water. When the waves were lapping around his waist he kicked himself forward and began swimming, and he rolled in the waves and scrubbed at himself until he was sure all the blood was off him. It didn't make him feel much cleaner.

He lay flat in the water and floated, listening to the pulse of his own blood. His bloodstream was currently a closed loop, not open to anyone, and for a while he thought about Shelley's submission to his lamia, and then he made himself stop thinking about it.

He was pretty far out by now – fifty yards, he guessed. Treading water awkwardly in his long trousers, he turned and looked back at the old stone edifice all of them were living in. The awning over the terrace was ragged and faded, and the walls and arches were streaked with rust stains, and at this moment he couldn't see why anyone would come here except to die and leave their bones to bleach on the white sand.

A robed figure stepped out from the darkness between the arches and began picking its way over the sun-bright rocks, and he recognized it as Josephine. Apparently she wanted a thorough bath too.

At the surf line she threw off her robe, and he was surprised and alarmed to be able to see, even at this distance, that she was naked. Shelley and Claire, and even the Williamses sometimes, liked to go swimming nude, but Josephine had certainly never done it before. Crawford hadn't even known she could swim.

She swam out at a southward slant, and he decided she hadn't noticed him bobbing far out on the glittering face of the water; he paddled along after her, more slowly because of the drag of his trousers.

They were a good hundred yards south of the Casa Magni when her head disappeared beneath the surface, and suddenly Crawford guessed what her purpose was. In an instant he had shucked off his trousers and was swimming as powerfully as he could toward where she had disappeared.

A cluster of popping bubbles told him he had found her – apparently she was emptying her lungs as she sank – and he jackknifed in a surface dive and struggled down against the buoyancy of the salt water. He could see her white body below him, and he kicked himself farther down. The sudden rush of water hurt his eyes, and he was weirdly reminded of swimming through the thickened air on top of the Wengern.

He grabbed a handful of her hair, and then began thrashing back up toward the rippling silver sheet overhead that was the surface; she clawed at his hand and forearm, and he could feel his lungs heaving with the effort to breathe in water, but he knew that if he let her succeed in drowning he would almost certainly decide to follow her, so he kept tugging and kicking.

At last his head broke the water, and he was whoopingly gasping air, and then, in a move that pushed him back under, he hoisted her up so that her head was out of the water. Her naked back was pressed against his chest, and he could feel her lungs working.

Not too late, he thought desperately.

He grabbed her under the arms when he came up again, and with his free arm and his legs he began dragging them back toward shore. She was moving weakly, but he couldn't tell if she was trying to help or to get free of him. He managed to keep her face above the water most of the time.

His vision was darkening and his bad leg was beginning to cramp when at last he felt sand under one bare foot, and he managed to conjure up one last explosion of effort that left them both sprawled naked on the hot sand.

Though bleakly sure that any more work would burst his heart, he rolled her over onto her stomach, spread his hands on her ribs just under the shoulder blades, and bore down, feeling the sand abrading her skin under his palms. Water gushed from her mouth and nose.

He did it again, forcing more water out, and then again; at last, with the coloured sparkling of unconsciousness filling his sight, he rolled her onto her back and pressed his mouth onto hers and blew his own breath into her lungs – waited a moment while it rushed back out – and then put his mouth to hers once more.

The exhalation he gave her took his consciousness with it.

He couldn't have been insensible for more than a few seconds, for the water she'd spewed out was still a patch of bubbles on the sand when he raised his head from her breast and stared anxiously into her face.

Her eyes were open, and for one long moment met and held his. Then she rolled out from under him and spent a good minute coughing up more water. She was facing away from him, and seemed to be almost clothed in clinging sand.

At last she got unsteadily to her feet. Crawford watched her, then hastily got up himself when he saw that she was walking back toward the water.

'I'm only rinsing off the sand,' she snapped when she heard his footsteps splashing behind her in the shallows.

He stayed close to her; and, when he saw that she

really didn't intend to swim out again, he decided that getting rid of the caking sand was a good idea, and he got down and let the waves wash over him, too.

Then they were walking back up the sand slope, and she took his hand. They kept walking, through the dry, floury sand, to the sudden coolness of the leaf-carpeted shadows under the trees, and when he released her hand it was just so that he could put his arms around her. She lifted her face to his and held him tightly.

He kissed her, deeply and with all the passion he had thought lost forever; and she was responding feverishly. In a moment they were lying in the leaves, and with each thrust into her it seemed to Crawford that he was pushing further away all the awarenesses of failure and death and guilt.

Later Crawford walked naked back up the beach to the Casa Magni, almost grateful now for the solitude of the area, and he managed to get upstairs to his bunk without being seen by anyone but Claire Clairmont, who had clearly started drinking early today, and simply blinked at him as he strode past her. Once dressed, he went into the women's servants' room and bundled up some clothes for Josephine.

When he returned to the clearing in which they had made love, he found her sitting up and staring out at the sea. She took the clothes with a grateful smile, and when she had dressed she hugged him for several seconds without speaking.

He was relieved, for during the walk back from the Casa Magni he had tried to imagine what he would find when he got to where he had left her – he had pictured finding her gone, and her body washing up some days later; or catching a glimpse of her, mad-eyed and with her fingers chewed bloody, scampering away through the trees like a wild beast; or hunched up as he'd seen a few over-stressed sailors get, with her knees to her face and her arms around her legs and nobody at all at home behind her eyes. He had hardly dared to hope that she'd be not only alive and sane but *cheerful* too.

Then she leaned back and looked up at him happily. 'Found you at last, darling!' she said. 'What on *earth* have you been doing in this desolate place, with all these horrible people?'

'Well,' he said, suddenly cautious, 'we're working for Shelley, you and I are.'

'Nonsense. You've got your practice in London, and *I* certainly don't work! Do finish up whatever dreary little affairs you have here, and quickly – my mother must be wild with worry by this time, even though I've been sending her letters.'

He was far too tired to argue now. 'I guess you're right,' he sighed, holding her close again so that she wouldn't see the weariness and disappointment in his face, 'Julia.'

Trelawny left aboard the *Bolivar* two days later, though Captain Roberts stayed on at the Casa Magni so as to be able to help Shelley sail the *Don Juan* down to Livorno for Leigh Hunt and his family were finally due to arrive there in two weeks; at last Hunt and Shelley and Byron would be able to start their magazine, though Shelley seemed to have lost some of his enthusiasm for the project.

Shelley was, in fact, devoting all his attention to refitting the *Don Juan*, presumably to make it a more imposing vessel, better able to stand comparison with Byron's ostentatious *Bolivar*. He and Roberts and Williams were adding a false stern and bow to make the vessel look longer, and had dramatically increased the amount of canvas she could spread.

They also re-ballasted her; Crawford pointed out that

the vessel rode a little higher now than it had before the refitting, but Shelley assured him that they knew what they were doing.

On the evening of Trelawny's departure, Crawford was standing with Shelley and Claire on the terrace and watching the *Bolivar*'s sails recede to the south against a cloudless bronze sunset, when Josephine stepped out onto the terrace from the dining room and gave Crawford an unfriendly look.

'Can I speak to you in our room, Michael?'

Crawford turned to bare his teeth out at the sea and squint his eyes shut, then let his face relax as he turned around. 'Of course, Julia,' he said, following her back inside.

Shelley had given up his room when Josephine told him that she and Crawford were married, and Crawford now missed his old bunk in the servants' quarters.

She shut the door when he had followed her into the room. 'I told you this morning,' she said, 'that I wanted a definite answer from you about when we're leaving this ghastly place.'

'Right.' He sighed, and sat down in a chair by the window. 'Shelley's sailing south to Livorno a week from yesterday, to meet Byron and this Leigh Hunt fellow. Shelley said you and I can ride along.'

'Why how frightfully generous of him! – considering that you've been working here for nearly two months without a penny of pay. You still haven't explained to me why you failed to demand passage on the *Bollix* or whatever its foolish name was.'

'Yes, I did. Mary Shelley – and Claire, lately – are patients of mine, and I don't want to leave them while their conditions are in doubt.' He tried to look sincere as he said this – the truth was that he had been delaying leaving the Casa Magni because he thought she was more likely to recover her real, Josephine personality

366

here, where she'd lost it, than in the cosmopolitan atmosphere of Livorno, or back at home in the now alien nation of England.

'Very well.' Her tone was brittle with resentment. 'But we stay not one day longer than next Monday, do you understand me? This place is horrible and these people are horrible. Have you made that Shelley person understand *yet* that you and I are *not* brother and sister?'

'Oh yes,' he said hastily. Actually he had only got Shelley to stop referring to them as such.

'How does he think we *could* be, and be married?'

'I don't know.' Incest is nothing unusual to this crowd, Julia, he thought – Shelley and his 'sister,' Byron and his half sister – but it wouldn't help to tell you that.

'And when will you abandon this ridiculous "Aickman" name?'

'As soon as we leave,' he told her, not for the first time.

She turned her head parrotlike to peer out the window. 'I would think you'd be more concerned about getting proper medical help for your own wife,' she said, 'than applying your evidently inadequate skills to *strangers*. This eye that you've proven unable to do anything about is getting *worse*.'

I doubt that, he thought, unless you've managed to crack it.

Yesterday he might have taken this complaint as a good way to try to remind her of the Wengern and all the rest of the events of her life as Josephine, but after last night's dinner he had finally given up trying to provoke that.

In the afternoon yesterday he had forcibly held her down on their bed and told her about Keats, and fleeing Rome, and living in Pisa and working at the university there, and he'd been optimistic when her sobs and protests had ceased and she had relaxed under him; but when he had got off her – and, in a tone made hoarse by hope, said, 'Welcome back, Josephine' – she had sat up so jerkily that he had almost thought he heard the clatter of gears and ratchets in her torso.

She had stayed in her mechanical mode all evening, snapping her neck from one position to another and moving awkwardly as if on hinged limbs, and Claire had fled the dining room and young Percy Florence had burst into tears and demanded that his mother take him away from the 'wind-up lady.' When she recovered, some hours later, she was Julia again.

And so he had abandoned, at least for the moment, the idea of calling Josephine back – he had decided that he was at least minimally better off with Julia than with the wind-up lady.

He was eerily sure that Josephine's body was doing a perfect imitation of his dead wife, based on its two decades of close acquaintance with the subject; in effect he was only getting to know his wife now, six years after her death, and he was dismayed to find that he didn't like her at all.

She had made it clear two days ago that she would not welcome any sexual advances as long as the two of them were still in this house, and he was sure that part of her chronic resentment arose from the fact that this declaration had not sent him packing.

The truth was that he no longer wanted sex with her. He knew now that he loved poor Josephine – who, for all he knew, might be dead herself, no longer even a dormant spark in her own abdicated brain.

The thought reminded him of Shelley's agonized speculation that Allegra might still be alive and aware somewhere in her own nightmarishly revivified skull. We're all prisoners in our own heads, he thought now as he considered the memories that bound himself, but at least most of us can speak to other people through the bars, and sometimes reach between them to clasp someone else's hand.

'I did meet one gentleman here,' Julia went on, 'an Englishman, last night on the beach. One of Shelley's friends who came on that ship, I suppose. I hope he didn't leave on it today. He's a *physician*,' she added, emphasizing the word. Crawford was only a surgeon. 'He said *he* could restore sight to my eye. He *promised* it.'

Crawford blinked in puzzlement for a moment – then he was on his feet, and leaning down to speak directly into her face. 'Don't go *near* that man,' he said harshly. 'Don't ever invite him in, do you understand me? This is important. He's a . . . a murderer, I promise you. If you ever again speak to him I swear I will never leave here, and my London practice can go to hell.'

She smiled, visibly reassured. 'Why, I believe you're *jealous!* Do you really imagine that I'd flirt – or do anything *more* than flirt, at least – with another man, when I'm married to a successful doctor?'

He forced an answering smile.

Shelley launched the refitted *Don Juan* on Saturday – he and Williams and Roberts kept her out all day and well into the evening, slanting and tacking across the calm water of the Gulf, and returning her to her mooring only when the moon began to be veiled with clouds; Shelley's spirits remained substantially restored until, during the late dinner, Claire tremulously told him that twice during the evening she had seen him pacing the terrace . . . before the *Don Juan* had returned.

Josephine only rolled her eyes impatiently and muttered something about alcoholism, but Shelley threw down his fork, got up, and pulled the curtains across the windows. 'From now on we'll keep these closed after dark,' he said.

Remembering Josephine's meeting with what must

have been the resurrected Polidori, Crawford nodded. 'A good idea.'

Claire, halfway through her third tumbler of brandy, frowned, as if she could nearly remember some reason why Shelley should be opposed in this; she hastily drank some more of the brandy, and the momentary kinks of alertness relaxed out of her face.

There was something ill about Edward Williams' smile that made Crawford stare at him even before he spoke. 'But we can – we can open them later, can't we, Percy?' Williams asked nervously. 'I only mean that – that it's sort of pleasant to be able to look out over the Gulf at night.'

Crawford glanced at Shelley, and saw that he had noticed it too.

'No, Ed,' Shelley said tiredly. 'Look at the goddamned Gulf all you want during the day. The curtains stay closed from sundown to sunup.' He looked at Crawford and Josephine. 'I think the Aickmans will be willing to . . . *wash the windows* with a solution that will help to enforce this.'

'*Windows!*' protested Josephine. 'Impossible! My husband is a *doctor*, and *I'm* certainly no one's *maid*! How do you dare to imagine that – '

'I'll do it, Percy,' said Crawford quietly. 'After everyone's gone to bed.'

Josephine got up from the table and stormed into their room.

A couple of hours later, when the lights had been snuffed, Crawford smashed several dozen garlic cloves into a bucket of salt water, then dragged it into the dining room and pulled the drapes back and, with an old shirt, slopped the mixture across the window panes and the flat stones of the floor.

He was glad that there were no lights in the room, for he didn't want to be able to recognize the several human forms that were bending and gesticulating silently in the darkness on the terrace outside.

Shelley and Roberts and the English boy Charles Vivian took the *Don Juan* out by themselves the next day, for Williams had a fever and only wanted to lie in bed all day. Crawford offered to examine him and do what he could in the way of prescribing something, but Williams hastily assured him that it wasn't necessary. Crawford was nearly moved to tears to see the sick brightness in the man's hitherto clear and humorous eyes.

At about noon Crawford put on a pair of cut-off trousers Shelley had given him and went downstairs. The wind was shaking the trees on the slope behind the house, and the *Don Juan*, running with the wind, was a speck of white on the southern horizon. Crawford walked into the water and began swimming. Since the death of Mary's foetus a week ago he had been taking a long swim every day.

The water was bracingly chilly, and revulsion at his situation made him swim out quite a distance before he relaxed and floated on his back, at last letting himself enjoy the sun on his face and chest.

Today was Sunday. They were to sail for Livorno tomorrow, and then he would have to decide what to do about Josephine. He couldn't possibly go back to England with her — could he, in good conscience, book passage for both of them and then jump ship, leaving her to travel alone? No — whether she was his wife or the woman he loved, he was bound to take better care of her than that. And Josephine might one day come back. He couldn't assume that she was gone forever.

Twice more he had felt the lamia's nearness in the night — both times 'Julia' had recoiled from him, thinking he was about to violate their agreement about not having sex until they left Spezia — and he knew Shelley was still helplessly paying his part of the bargain. The expense of spirit in a waste of shame, he thought, mentally repeating a line from one of Shakespeare's sonnets that Shelley had haltingly recited recently.

Crawford wondered if the lamia did the same things with Shelley that she had done with him – and if Shelley was satisfying her as he had. He couldn't believe Shelley was. And he wondered if Williams was actually having sex with the resurrected Allegra, or just being chastely bitten by her.

He didn't know what to do about Williams – drag him into the Alps and up the Wengern? With *Julia* along? – and, though he had garlicked the windows and threshold of the children's room, and given Jane Williams ludicrous-sounding instructions not to let the children talk to strangers when they were outside, he bleakly wondered how long it would be until one of them, probably Percy Florence, began wasting away.

At last he let his legs sink and looked back toward the house, and a slight chill passed across his belly; he had drifted out while he'd been carelessly floating, and was now about twice as far from shore as he had thought. His heart was thumping hard in his chest as he began swimming back toward shore.

He couldn't see that he was making any progress at all, and he cursed his four-fingered left hand and his stiff left leg.

After several minutes he was breathless from swimming against the tide, and he thought that in spite of his struggles he had drifted out farther. The sun was hot on his balding scalp, and glittered blindingly on the glassy waves.

He forced himself to breathe slowly and tread water. You swim in at a *slant*, he told himself, that's what everybody says. This is *not* where you die, understand me?

372

He tried to see which way the tide had taken him, so as to be able to swim inward in the same direction, but now he couldn't make out where the house was. The stretch of green-speckled brown that was the mainland seemed featureless, and farther away than ever. The harsh purple sky and the sun seemed to be squeezing it away.

He took several deep breaths and then kicked himself up as high out of the water as he could, and yelled, '*Help!*' – but the effort left him breathless, and the sound had not seemed to carry.

Tread water, he told himself; you can do that all day, can't you? Hell, I remember a time in the Bay of Biscay when Boyd and I trod water for two hours straight, as an endurance contest, with friends swimming out to us to deliver fresh bottles of ale, and we only quit because it was clear that waiting for one of us to give up would require that the contest continue until well past dark. This current is much likelier to sweep you ashore somewhere than to take you right out of the Gulf into the open sea.

But even though he traded off between using his arms and using his legs, he could feel his muscles tightening like wires under his skin. Nearly a decade had passed since that contest, and he had clearly lost his youthful fitness somewhere along the line during the intervening years.

He forced himself to breathe evenly and slowly.

The loneliness was appalling. He was a tiny pocket of frightened agitation on the vast, indifferent face of the sea, as frail as a candle in a lost toy boat, and he thought that he wouldn't even mind drowning if he could hear another person's voice just once before going under forever.

He could call her.

The thought sent a shiver through his body. Could

she get to him quickly enough? On such a sunny day? Somehow he was sure she could – she loved him, and she must have understood that he hadn't *really* wanted to divorce her in the Alps. It might not even necessarily mean abandoning Josephine – once he was safely back ashore he could figure out some way to deal with that poor lunatic; certainly he'd be able to do more for her that way than by drowning out here.

He had been trying to favour his stiff left leg, but suddenly it knotted up tight with a muscle cramp that wrung a scream out of him. He flailed his arms to keep from sinking, but he knew that he had only perhaps a minute left.

And then to his own horror he realized that he wouldn't do it, wouldn't call her. It meant that he was going to die out here, right now, but something – his love for Josephine, the love she had clearly felt for him on that too brief afternoon a week ago – made dying preferable to being possessed again by the lamia.

He tried to pray, but could only curse in angry panic.

The water closed over his head, and he looked up at the image of the sun wiggling on the surface. One more clear glimpse of it, he told himself desperately, just one more gasp of the sea air.

He made his hands claw out and down through the water, and his head poked out into the air – and he heard oar-locks knocking.

A moment later he heard Josephine's voice screaming, '*Michael!*'

He discovered that he did still have a little strength left. He was sobbing with the pain of it, but he made his arms keep pushing the water out and down, and when an oar had spun through the air to splash near him, he managed to pull himself over to it and wrap his aching hands around the wide part of it.

A rope had been tied to the other end, and he nearly

374

lost his grip when the line began to be pulled in; but at last his head collided with the planks of the boat, and he was being dragged in over the gunwale. He even managed to help a little.

His left leg was folded up tight, and hurt so badly that he really thought the bones might snap. He touched his thigh, and the knotted muscles were as hard as stone.

'Cramp,' he gasped, and a moment later she was massaging it with hands that had been made bloody by strenuous inexpert rowing. Her left hand, the one she had ruined on the Wengern, was itself visibly becoming clawed with cramp, but she worked strongly, with a nurse's expertise, and after a minute the knot in his leg had been ground out.

For a long time he lay sprawled against one of the thwarts, just filling and emptying his lungs, his eyes shut. At last he sat up a little and looked around. The boat was one that Shelley had found too big to be convenient for rowing, and had stowed downstairs. There was no one in it but himself and Josephine.

He stared at her until he had regained his breath enough to be able to speak; then, 'Who are you?' he asked bluntly.

At first he thought she wouldn't answer; then she whispered, 'Josephine.'

He lay back again. 'Thank God.' He reached out and gently held her flayed, twisted hand. 'How in hell did you even get this boat out of the house?'

'I don't know. I had to.'

'I'm glad you noticed me out here. I'm glad *you* noticed me out here.' Julia, he thought, would never have done this.

Josephine sat back and pushed sweaty hair off her forehead. Her glass eye was staring crazily into the sky, but her good one was focused intently on him. 'I . . . woke up from fright, I came back into my body, staring out the window at you and knowing you were in trouble. I had heard her noticing it – you understand? – and that was what gave me the strength to . . . push her aside, push J-Julia out. And then I was running down the stairs and wrestling this thing out through the arches and over the pavement and into the water.'

He saw that she was barefoot, and that there was blood on the floorboards too.

'Josephine,' he said unsteadily, 'I love you. Don't let Julia, your ghost of Julia, take your body, not ever again.'

'I – ' For several seconds she tried to speak, then just shifted around toward the bow and shook her head. 'I'll try not to.'

That night was Midsummer's Eve, and the two of them stayed up later than everyone else, though they could hear Ed Williams talking quietly, presumably to his wife, in his room.

Only one lamp burned, the lamp Shelley insisted burn all night, and Crawford and Josephine had finished the bottle of wine left over from dinner and were slowly working on another one that he had opened after that. They had talked for more than an hour, rarely even brushing any important topics, when, simultaneously, the latest pause in the conversation became the end of it and Crawford noticed that they had finished the wine.

He stood up and held his hand out to her. 'Let's go to bed.'

They went into their room and closed the door and undressed, and then in the darkness – for he had pulled the curtains across their window – they made long, slow love, stopping short of climax again and again until finally it was unstoppably upon them.

After a while Crawford rolled off her and lay beside

her, feeling her hot, dewy flank against his side; he opened his mouth to tell her softly that he loved her –

– And a shriek from another room interrupted him and sent him bounding out of bed.

For lack of anything else he pulled on Shelley's cut-off trousers, then opened the door and stepped into the dining room; he could hear Josephine behind him struggling into clothes.

The door to the Shelleys' room was open, and the tall, thin figure of Shelley came out quickly but without any sound. His eyes were glowing like a cat's in the lamplight and, before pulling the curtains aside and disappearing onto the terrace outside, he crossed to Crawford and kissed him lightly on the lips. Crawford saw teeth glint in the open mouth, but they didn't touch him.

Then Shelley came out of his room again, and Crawford realized that this was the real one – and when he realized who the first figure must have been, his chest went hollow and cold and he had half turned toward the terrace door before he remembered Josephine.

He made himself turn his back on the terrace and face Shelley.

Chapter 15

But the worm shall revive thee with kisses,
Thou shalt change and transmute as a god
As the rod to a serpent that hisses,
As the serpent again to a rod.
Thy life shall not cease though thou doff it;
Thou shalt live until evil be slain,
And good shall die first, said thy prophet,
Our Lady of Pain.

– A. C. Swinburne, Dolores

'Where did it go?' Shelley demanded.

Not trusting himself to speak yet, Crawford simply pointed to the curtains.

Shelley collapsed against the wall and rubbed his eyes. 'It was trying to strangle her – strangle Mary.' He held up his hands, which were scratched and bloody, 'I had to tear its hands away from Mary's neck.'

The Williamses and Josephine were in the dining room now, and Shelley had pulled the curtains aside and, crouching, was licking his finger, rubbing it along the floor by the windows, then moving and licking it again. When he had hunched and licked his way down the whole length of the windows he looked up.

'There's no salt nor garlic here,' he said, staring straight at Edward Williams.

Williams flinched, then mumbled, 'Is that what that was? The smell – I just thought I'd wash them better – ' He had buttoned up the collar of his nightshirt, but Crawford could see a spot of blood staining the fabric at his neck.

Shelley's lips were a straight white line. 'All of you go back to bed,' he said, 'except you, Aickman – we've got to talk.'

'Josephine can hear it,' Crawford said.

Shelley blinked. 'I thought her name was . . . ? But very well, let her stay. Bed for the rest of you.'

Shelley was twisting a corkscrew into a fresh wine bottle when the Williamses closed their door, and he poured wine into the only lately abandoned glasses that Crawford and Josephine held out.

'We can't leave tomorrow,' Shelley said quietly.

Crawford was glad that the person at his side was no longer Julia. 'What are you talking about?' he whispered. 'This makes it more urgent than ever that we leave! Did you see Ed's neck? Will you wait until your last child is dead? I don't – '

'Let him speak, Michael,' interrupted Josephine.

'She's particularly accessible here,' Shelley went on, 'and what I have in mind – the only thing left for me to try – requires that she be accessible.'

'What is it?' asked Crawford.

'You should know,' Shelley told him with hollow gaiety. 'It was your idea.' When Crawford still stared blankly at him, Shelley added, with some impatience, 'That I drown myself.'

Crawford flinched. 'I – I wasn't serious. I was just – '

'I know. Angry at the death of that unborn child. But you were right, it is the only way to save Percy Florence and Mary.' He smiled now – maliciously, Crawford thought. 'But you'll have to do something too. And I wonder if you won't find it harder than my own task.'

The next day the sun burned more hotly than ever in the empty cobalt sky, and when Captain Roberts returned from a run up the coast for supplies – largely more wine – he reported that the narrow streets of

Lerici were crowded with religious processions imploring rain.

That night was the Feast of St John, and after sunset the people of San Terenzo came dancing down the coastline through the surf, singing holy songs and waving torches; Shelley stood at the rail of the terrace, even after night had fallen and the songs had degenerated into drunken, savage chanting and the figures in the surf had begun to throw rocks at the Casa Magni.

Finally a torch was flung at Shelley, and missed only because Crawford pulled him out of the way, and Shelley dazedly allowed himself to be led back inside. The noise continued until only shortly before dawn, when the fishermen went reeling and singing back to their boats and nets.

The shouting and the oppressive heat had kept anyone from getting any real rest, and when Crawford went downstairs to watch the fisher-folk go lurching and splashing home he saw the dim silhouette of Mary Shelley standing by the seawall and talking to someone up on the wooded slope beyond it.

He hurried toward her, thinking that one of the drunken fishermen might be bothering her, but he paused when he heard her laugh softly.

'John, you know I'm married,' she said. 'I couldn't possibly go with you. But thank you for the . . . attention.'

She turned back toward the beach and Crawford saw that she was holding a dark rose up to her chin, so that its petals seemed to be a part of the bruising that mottled her throat. He looked past her at the shadowy slope, but could see nothing there – though he could hear a slithering rustle receding up through the trees.

Crawford walked forward, sliding his feet in the sand so that she'd hear him approaching and not be startled when he spoke. 'That was Polidori?' he asked.

'Yes.' She sniffed the rose and stared out at the dark sea.

'You shouldn't be speaking to him,' Crawford began wearily. He hoped the coming day wouldn't be so hot as to make sleeping impossible. 'He . . . he's not . . .'

'He told me about it, yes,' she said calmly. 'His suicide, back in England. He thinks they're the Muses, thinks these vampire things are. Maybe he's right – though they weren't that for him. Even after he summoned one and let himself be bitten, he still couldn't write anything publishable . . . and so he killed himself.' She shook her head. 'The poor boy – he was always so *envious* of Percy and Byron.'

'If you know that much about him,' Crawford said, forcing himself to be patient, 'then you must know how dangerous such people are once they've been resurrected. That is *not* Polidori, not anymore – that's a vampire inhabiting his *body*, like a hermit crab using some sea-snail's shell. Are you *listening* to me, damn it? Hell, ask Percy about all this!'

'Percy . . .' she said dreamily. 'Percy is stopping being Percy, have you noticed? The man I love is . . . what . . . receding, diminishing like a figure in a painting with deep perspective. I wonder how much longer I'll be able to communicate with him even by shouting in his ear.'

'Ask *me* then, I'm your doctor, right? Have you invited Polidori into your presence yet?'

'No – though he hinted that he'd like that.'

'I daresay. *Don't* do it.' He stepped closer to her and put his hand on her chin to tilt her face up. 'Percy Florence will die, if you do,' he said, staring hard into her eyes. Was she getting any of this? 'Repeat that back to me, please,' he said in his best professional tone.

'Percy Florence will die, if I do,' she said weakly.

'Good.' He released her. 'Now go to bed.'

She tottered back toward the house, and Crawford sat

381

down in the sand; he was aware of someone watching him intently from up the slope, but the sky was lightening toward blue, and he knew that the thing that had been Polidori wouldn't try to approach him.

He remembered Byron derisively quoting some of Polidori's poetry, back in Switzerland in 1816. Crawford had laughed at the inept lines, as Byron had meant him to, but then the lord had frowned and said that it really wasn't funny. 'He's terribly serious about all this, Aickman,' Byron had said reprovingly. 'He's a successful doctor, one of the youngest graduates of Edinburgh University, but his only ambition is to be a poet – like Shelley and I. He approached me for the personal physician job just because he thought that by associating with me and my friends he would be able to . . . learn the secret.' Byron had laughed grimly. 'I only hope, for his sake, that he never does.'

Well, thought Crawford now, he did learn it, Byron. But, though he paid the Muses, they didn't deliver – it was much like the deal Shelley thought he could make with his sister, my ex-wife.

The sun was up now, sparking green highlights on the wooded peaks of Portovenere across the Gulf, and the breeze almost seemed to have some coolness in it. Crawford got to his feet and began plodding back through the sand toward the Casa Magni, trying not to step into the indentations of Mary Shelley's feet.

During the next five days Shelley spent more and more time out on the *Don Juan*, letting Roberts and the Vivian boy handle the rigging while he peered at various mountains through a sextant and filled page after page in his notebook – not with poetry anymore, but with obscure, scribbled mathematics. When they returned at dusk he would sometimes try to get Crawford to check his maths, but it was largely Newtonian calculus, and entirely beyond Crawford's skill; Shelley never asked Mary to check it, even though she was clever with numbers and he had clearly begun to doubt his own thought processes.

Crawford thought the man's doubts were justified. No longer did Shelley dominate the dinner-table conversation with long arguments about the nature of man and the universe; he now seemed to find it difficult, in fact, even to follow Claire's ramblings about her shopping expeditions to Lerici — and, though he did still read his mail, Crawford had several times seen him struggling to puzzle out the meaning of a letter, frowning and moving his lips and circling important words.

At last, seven days after Mary's near strangulation, Shelley threw his notebook and a lot of his recent correspondence into the fire, and then asked Crawford and Josephine to accompany him on a walk down the shore.

The sun still shone in the morning half of the sky, but the sand underfoot was hot even through Crawford's shoes, and he wondered how Shelley could stand plodding through it barefoot. Perhaps he hadn't noticed yet that it hurt. Josephine was tense, but held Crawford's hand and even managed a wan smile a couple of times.

'We leave tomorrow,' Shelley told them quietly. 'You two will have to come back here in a week or so, but I want you with me in the meantime.'

Crawford frowned. 'Why do we have to come back?'

'To do the part that has to be done *here*,' Shelley said peevishly, 'and has to be done by *you*. So don't pack everything, leave here any . . . scientific or medical apparatus you might possess.' He frowned, visibly trying to think. 'Actually, Josephine needn't come back here with you — she could stay with Byron and Trelawny and the rest of the crowd. They're all going to be gathering back in Pisa.'

'I go where Michael goes,' said Josephine quietly.

Crawford squeezed her hand. 'And *neither* of us is going to Pisa,' he said. 'We barely escaped being arrested there two months ago. Why do *you* have to go there, anyway?'

'I – because of – oh, of course, to get poor Leigh Hunt set up with Byron. It was because of my urging that he's sailed down here, with his whole damned family, and since I've got to be – stepping out of the picture, I want to see that he's not left – left – '

'Helpless?' suggested Josephine.

'And broke?' added Crawford.

'In a foreign land, right,' said Shelley, nodding. 'You *can't* go to Pisa . . . ? Well, we're stopping off at Livorno on the way, to meet them all, so you could . . . wait for me there. I'll be stopping back at Livorno again, before I . . .'

Crawford interrupted hastily. 'This part that Josephine and I have to do,' he began, but Shelley waved at him to be silent.

When they had walked another hundred yards along the narrow, rocky shore, Shelley waded out into the shallows. 'Let's talk out here,' he said. 'The, uh . . . the *water*, will help muffle our words. I don't want the . . . *vitro* to . . . the sand, I mean, to hear what we say.'

Crawford and Josephine exchanged a worried look, but crouched to take off their shoes.

'What about glass?' Josephine called as she straightened up.

'Glass?' Shelley frowned. 'Oh, like if you're carrying any. Right, leave it there.'

Josephine reached up to her face and poked her glass eye out and put it in one of her shoes, then took

Crawford's hand again and walked with him out to where Shelley stood.

'Now pay attention,' Shelley told them. 'I may not be able to express all this clearly . . . later. After now. Ever again.'

In the early afternoon of the next day the *Don Juan* sailed out of the Gulf of Spezia for the last time, bound south for Livorno. Mary and Claire and Jane Williams and the children stayed behind, and Shelley was half-heartedly helping Roberts and Charles Vivian work the sails, and Ed Williams stayed below deck, out of the sunlight, so Crawford and Josephine had the bow to themselves.

'Six times six is thirty-six,' Josephine was muttering, 'seven times seven is forty-nine, eight times eight is sixty-four . . .'

She had developed this habit during the last couple of days; it still annoyed Crawford, but after she had explained that it helped keep the Josephine personality in control when she could feel it weakening, he was careful not to let his irritation show. The habit had visibly upset Mary, but Shelley had tended to sit nearer to Josephine while she was doing it, as if the chant was an emblem of something he was losing . . . or, as Crawford had sometimes uncharitably thought, because the distraught poet was hoping to overhear a correct answer to one or two of the mathematical puzzles that were so clearly beyond him.

Crawford now simply stared out at the Italian shore that moved imperceptibly past, a mile beyond the port rail. Since yesterday afternoon he had thought of nothing but the thing he was going to have to do in a week, and so when Josephine let the multiplication table stutter to a halt and asked him a question, he answered it with no jolt of a changed subject.

'Will you be able to do it?' she had asked.

'I don't know,' he said, still staring at the coastline. 'I've resisted her before – with your help. And I – ' He stopped, for he'd been about to say that now that he had Josephine he was immune to the inhuman woman's sexual attraction, but it had instantly occurred to him that it might not be true. 'I don't know,' he finished lamely.

A tired smile made the lines in Josephine's tanned face more evident. 'It'll mean the deaths of us all if you don't – as opposed to the deaths of just a couple of us. She'd never let me or the children out of her net.'

'Perhaps,' he said with exaggerated politeness as he pushed himself away from the rail, 'you imagine that I didn't know that.' He walked away from her, back toward the stern where Shelley was listlessly working the mainsail sheet.

Behind him he heard the chanted multiplication tables start up again.

The boat flew along smoothly in a succession of long tacks against the constant wind, and a few hours after sunset they saw ahead the lights that marked the seawall in front of the entrance to the Livorno harbour. They tacked in to the sheltered expanse of water and, after a brief, shouted conversation with the harbour master's boat, found a mooring next to Byron's *Bolivar*; Byron was ashore, at his house in nearby Montenero, and the *Don Juan* was under temporary quarantine, but the crew of Byron's ship obligingly tossed some pillows down onto the deck of the smaller vessel so that Shelley's party could sleep in the open air of the warm night.

Crawford and Josephine slept up by the bow, while Shelley and Roberts and Charles Vivian sprawled themselves wherever they could find room around the mast and the tiller. Williams paced the deck all night, finally crawling below just before dawn.

* * *

386

The quarantine officers cleared them the next morning, and everybody except young Charles Vivian went ashore – though Williams complained of being sick, and wore a wide-brimmed hat to keep the sun off.

Shelley was almost hysterically cheerful now, and with uncharacteristic lavishness hired a big carriage to take them all the six miles to where Byron and the Hunt family waited for them in Montenero.

The summer seemed to be getting even hotter, and when, after a dusty hour's ride, they arrived at Byron's house, the Villa Dupuy, Crawford was discouraged to see that it was painted a particularly warm shade of brownish-pink.

Josephine hadn't spoken during the ride, but Crawford had noticed her fingers working methodically in her lap and had guessed that she was running through the multiplication tables in her head. It hadn't improved his mood.

Byron greeted them at the door, and though Crawford was startled to see that the man had put on weight again, Shelley seemed pleased by the change. Shelley appeared to be delighted with everything, in fact, remarking on how glad he was to see that Byron was still living with Teresa Guiccioli, and that she still liked to go outside on sunny days; and he eagerly introduced Crawford and Josephine to a tall, distracted-looking man who proved to be Leigh Hunt, the luckless Englishman who with his wife and six children had taken ship to Italy to co-edit the journal Byron and Shelley had dreamed up last year.

Byron was clearly hoping to be able to stay up late talking with Shelley, as they had done so often before they had left Pisa, but Shelley claimed to have been exhausted by the trip, and went to bed early.

Hunt was sulking because of some testy remarks Byron had made about his badly behaved children, and he went to bed early too, and so it was Williams and Crawford and Josephine who sat up with Byron in his high-ceilinged hall and drank his wine and listened to his complaints about his servants and the weather. And Byron seemed glad of the company, though Williams seldom spoke and spent most of the time peering out through a pair of glass doors at a side courtyard, and Josephine several times responded to questions with cheerful statements to the effect that some number multiplied by some other number equalled yet another number; but Byron had heard so many non sequiturs from her in the past that he only grinned and nodded each time she delivered another, and twice demanded that they all drink to the sentiment of the latest one.

He was in the middle of a story about how several of his servants had recently had a knife fight in the road out front, when everyone's attention was suddenly drawn to Williams.

The man had abruptly *tensed*, so tightly that his body seemed to curl and his forehead was nearly touching the glass of the window, and he was standing on tiptoe.

Byron had looked across at him in annoyance at first, but there was alarm in his voice now as he said, 'What the hell is it, Ed?' Byron clanked his wine glass down on the table and half stood up, but Williams jerked an arm toward him so imperatively that Byron fell back into the chair. A moment later Byron had reddened in embarrassment and repeated his question angrily.

'Nothing, nothing,' Williams answered quickly. 'I just – I'm not going with Shelley to Pisa. Tell him I'm staying here in Livorno to – buy supplies for the run back up to Lerici. I – I'll be back.'

Still stiff with tension, he hurried to the front door, and a moment later he had disappeared into the night. He had left the door open, and a warm breeze scented with night-blooming jasmine ruffled Byron's greying hair.

Byron's anger had disappeared. He was staring out through the open doorway with an expression of loss. At last he turned toward the couch where Crawford and Josephine sat, and looked hard at them.

'You two do seem to be all right,' he said after several seconds. He picked up his wine glass, ignoring the puddle he'd sloshed onto the table top, finished what was left in it and then refilled it from the decanter on the floor. 'What kind of friend am I, not to have noticed it in him instantly?' He shook his head as he put the decanter down. 'How long has that been the case?'

'A month or so,' said Crawford. 'His wife, Jane, seems to be . . . untouched, so far. Unbitten.'

'They have to be bidden before you can get bitten,' remarked Byron with a bitter smile. 'Damn Shelley.' With a sigh he stood up and limped across the tile floor to a cabinet in the corner and then fumbled in the loose sleeve of his ornate nankeen jacket. 'You're probably curious . . . as to how I've preserved myself and Teresa.' He had found a key and unlocked the cabinet, and took from it a pistol and a cloth bag. 'There's powdered iron in the paint on this house, and a garlic-flavoured stain deeply bitten into all the wood, and whitethorn and buckthorn around the windows, and of course it's easy here to eat lots of garlic, and I have several guns around the house loaded with this sort of ammunition.' He tossed the cloth bag to Crawford and then resumed his seat, carrying the pistol pointed at the floor.

Crawford spilled some of the heavy balls into his palm. They were of silver, with a bit of wooden dowelling, sanded down flush, through the centre.

'Twice I've shot at unnatural figures out in the courtyard,' Byron remarked. 'No luck.'

Crawford kept his face expressionless, but remembered

Byron's excellent marksmanship, and decided that the contempt Byron had shown for his poetry when they'd last talked must have been largely a pose – it seemed that he was willing to *restrict* his vampiric muse, but not willing really to drive it away.

Crawford held up one of the silver-and-wood balls. 'Would one of these kill . . . one of them?'

'Maybe. If the creature were very overextended, or very new, it might. Even a vigorous, mature one, though, would be – discouraged.'

'What does Teresa think of all this?' Crawford asked.

Byron shrugged. 'These are traditional Carbonari protections. I *bought* that ammunition – I didn't have to have it specially made.'

Crawford was getting angry, but it took him several seconds to realize why, and by then Josephine had already begun articulating his thoughts.

'What,' she asked slowly, 'if Teresa should become pregnant? Would you stay with her, and a *child* of yours, under these circumstances, knowing what sort of perilous sea your . . . your admittedly carefully constructed boat is sailing on?'

Byron seemed startled, and not pleased, by these coherent sentences from her; but before he could answer, there came a catlike wail from the dark courtyard outside, rasping on nerves like a bow on violin strings. The wail continued for several seconds before diminishing away in a couple of syllables that sounded like '*Papa.*'

The pistol was shaking in Byron's hand, but he got to his feet and walked to the glass doors.

'*Papà, Papà, mi permetti entrare, fa freddo qui fuorí, ed è buio!*' came the weirdly childlike voice. Crawford translated it mentally: *Papa, Papa, let me inside, it's cold out here, and dark!*

Once before Crawford had seen the little girl who was

390

now hovering in midair outside the glass, but she was plumper now. Her eyes were bright, and fresh red blood was smeared on the white skin around her mouth, and the palms of her hands were flattened against the glass. She was looking into Byron's face, and all at once smiled hideously.

The skin was tight over Crawford's cheekbones, and he forced himself to stay by Josephine and not run.

Byron had gone white and his hands were trembling, but he was nodding gently. '*Si, tesora, ti piglio dal freddo.*'

Without taking his eyes off the child's body he raised his voice and said 'Aickman – Josephine – go upstairs to your rooms. Please. This is between the two of us.'

Crawford opened his mouth to protest, but Josephine caught his arm. 'It's all right,' she whispered. 'Let's go.'

They crossed the wide room to the dark hall, and before they rounded the corner Crawford looked back. Sobs were visibly shaking Byron, but the pistol was steady.

They heard the shot when they were on the stairs, and several minutes later, from the window in Crawford's room, they saw the limping figure of Byron carrying the small body out across the moonlit grass. Crawford remembered having seen a church in that direction, and he wondered if Byron could be confident of finding a shovel.

'He *said* a new one might be killed with that ammunition,' said Josephine solemnly as she unbuttoned her blouse. 'And she was certainly a new one.' She folded the blouse, shed her skirt and then crawled into bed. 'Remember what Claire always used to say?' By moonlight Crawford could see Josephine's haggard smile. 'Well, she can't say it anymore. At last he's done something for Allegra.'

After several minutes of silence they became aware of a distant, inhuman singing that seemed to resonate up from the earth and down from the sky; the chorus was a tapestry of long-sustained notes, but, though it was majestically tragic, it evoked only awe and humility in Crawford, for it was clearly not composed for human emotions.

A gentle rocking woke Crawford at dawn. For a few sleepy moments he thought he was on shipboard, but when he noticed the flowers bobbing in the vase on the bedside table he remembered that he was in Byron's house, and he realized that what he was feeling must be a mild earthquake. The rocking quickly subsided, and he went back to sleep.

Chapter 16

There were giants in the earth in those days . . .

— *Genesis* 6:4

Crawford and Josephine were awakened later in the morning by Shelley's shrill voice down in the yard — when Crawford got up and pulled the curtains back and looked down, he saw that Shelley was directing the loading of the Hunts' luggage onto the roof of his rented carriage, and seemed impatient to be on the road.

Byron could be seen pacing back and forth through the long, stark shadows of the olive trees that bordered the dusty yard, and the fact that he was awake at this hour, and not even bothering to watch as his servants strapped his own luggage onto the rack at the back of his Napoleonic carriage, led Crawford to believe that the man had not slept at all.

The stripes of darkness across the flat dirt made the yard resemble to Crawford a wide stairway, like the flight of steps he'd seen from Keats's second-floor window in Rome two years ago, and he morbidly wondered which members of this party were heading uphill, and which were headed down. Byron seemed likely to be one of those people Crawford recalled who simply stayed in one place on the stairs, waiting for some tourist to pay them to pose for a portrait — and what sort of character was Byron calculated to suggest? Certainly none of the saints.

Crawford unlatched the window and pushed it open,

and the already warm summer air that sighed into the room was scented with coffee and pastries somewhere nearby – apparently being ignored by all the busy people below.

Crawford and Josephine got dressed and went downstairs, and since they were staying in Livorno and not going on to Pisa, they had the leisure to eat a lot of the informal breakfast Byron's servants had prepared.

At one point Shelley took Crawford aside and gave him a hundred pounds. Crawford took the money, but squinted at Shelley.

'Are you certain you want to give me all this?' he asked.

Shelley blinked, noticed the bank notes in Crawford's hand, and then shook his head and reached for them. 'No, I – I should give it to poor Hunt – or have it sent back to Mary, in Spezia – I – '

Crawford kept two ten-pound notes and handed the rest back. 'Thanks, Percy.'

Shelley stared at the money Crawford had given back to him, nodded and smiled uncertainly, then stuffed it into a pocket and wandered away.

By eight o'clock the last of the Hunts' children had been rounded up and bundled aboard the rented carriage – Byron wouldn't permit any of them in his own – and the adults climbed into one carriage or the other, and latched the doors, and then the vehicles got under way, flanked by servants on horseback.

Not all of Byron's servants were leaving, and he had left instructions that Crawford and Josephine were to be allowed to borrow a spare carriage and a couple of horses for the trip back to Livorno. By the time they had got themselves organized, though, the sun had begun baking the dusty road in earnest, and they decided to wait for the cool of dusk.

Crawford took a couple of Byron's books out into the

shaded courtyard and tried to read, but he kept getting distracted by the thought of the child he had seen out here the night before. He was sure the blood on the child's mouth had been Ed Williams's, and he wondered who Ed would get to consume him now.

Josephine spent most of the day lying down – Crawford assumed at first that she was napping, but at around noon he looked in on her and noticed that her eyes were open, staring patiently at the ceiling. He went back out to the courtyard and tried again to read.

West of Montenero the land sloped down for two or three miles to the coast of the Ligurean Sea, and when the sun had sunk enough to make a black silhouette of Elba, Napoleon's island of exile, Crawford became aware of a rhythmic chanting from the road below the house.

He tucked one of Byron's pistols into his belt before limping down the dirt road to investigate the sound, but found only a dozen villagers and a couple of priests standing around a wagon to which a weary-looking donkey was harnessed.

The priests were intoning prayers and sprinkling the dry road dust with holy water, and at first Crawford thought it was some local ritual that had nothing to do with him; then a very old man with a walking stick came hunching out of the sparse crowd and smiled at him ... and Crawford wondered if a pistol would do any real good here anyway.

'They're *aware*,' said des Loges in his barbaric French, 'of the sort of place you people have lately come from.' He waved at the villagers and the priests. 'Portovenere, I'm told. You'd be amazed to know how long it's had that name, and in how many languages. The fourteenth-century poet Petrarch had some things to say about the place, when he wasn't moaning about his unattainable sweetheart Laura.'

He laughed and looked around at his bucolic

companions, then squinted back at Crawford. 'I think that at the right word these people would attack the house up there – note the knives several of them have, and the pitchfork that gentleman at the rear carries. The English lord who was here, Byron, is a member of the Carbonari, yes? These people approve of that – but Byron is gone now, and they can smell the – *Siliconari* – on you. They can smell it on me too, which isn't helping.' He waved his stick back up the road. 'Do you suppose you and I could talk?'

Crawford thought of Josephine, helpless back at the house. 'All right,' he said, suddenly very tired. 'Tell them I'm . . . tell them I've put a nail in a *mazze*, though, will you? We don't need their . . . help.' *Siliconari*, he thought – probably a pun on *silex*, the French and Latin word for flint. *Silex, silicis, silici*.

Des Loges laughed and rattled off a quick phrase in Italian to the priests, who did seem to relax a little, though they didn't stop sprinkling the holy water.

Des Loges stared at Crawford from time to time as the two of them limped ungracefully up the steep, dusty road to the dirt-paved yard. The shadows of the trees were lying to the east now, but the effect reminded Crawford of the stairway illusion he'd noticed that morning, and he wondered now whether he was headed uphill or down himself.

'You're divorced!' exclaimed des Loges at last as they approached the front door. 'But the Venice attempt was a failure, the one your friends made four years ago – you must have gone all the way up into the Alps, am I right?'

'Right,' answered Crawford. 'With Byron, in 1816. And he's backslid since, and I haven't, so I don't see why your priests admire him and fear me.'

'Actually they're not that fond of Byron either, but

he's rich and powerful, and you're not, and he is doing a lot for the Carbonari.'

Des Loges shook his head, and Crawford thought there was a glint of admiration in the ancient man's eyes. 'I never even seriously considered going to the Alps myself – the trip would have been a fearful ordeal for me, and I assumed it would be certainly fatal anyway; or, worse, that it would leave me crippled and unable to try anything else.' He shrugged. 'So why not just get the right man to drown me at home.'

Crawford knocked on the door and self-consciously diverted the conversation from the subject of his failure to drown the old man six years ago. 'It nearly *was* fatal. The trip to the Alps. There are some . . . astonishing creatures in those mountains.'

Des Loges nodded agreeably, accepting the conversational shift. 'And you went in 1816? Old Werner was passing through in those years – his arrival in Venice was what wrecked the scheme your friends . . . and I . . . had there in 1818. His presence in Switzerland must have had the locals particularly upset – there must have been some Carbonari activity – and it would have had the old creatures particularly agitated, too, having the' – he used a word that Crawford could interpret only as *animating focus* – 'pass so close. Did you see Werner, by any chance? He'd have been avoiding the highest passes, since *he* certainly wouldn't be wanting a divorce, but you might have glimpsed his party.'

Crawford had begun to shake his head when des Loges added, 'He'd have been travelling packed in ice, with an escort of Austrian soldiers.'

And it seemed to Crawford that he did remember something like that – a wagon stuck in the mud at dusk, and Byron whimsically climbing up onto its bed to help oversee the efforts to push the vehicle free.

'Maybe I did,' he said. 'Who is this Werner?'

Des Loges didn't answer, for one of Byron's servants was finally pulling the door open. The servant stared with distaste at des Loges, but stood aside when Crawford told him that the old man was a guest of his – though this revelation earned Crawford himself a coldly reconsidering look.

'I'll tell you about him,' des Loges said. 'Where can we talk?'

The servant's look of disdain had deepened visibly upon hearing des Loges's calamitous French. 'Uh, up in our room,' Crawford said. 'Wait here while I tell my . . . wife, my current one, that we're coming up.'

Josephine was sitting on the floor when Crawford returned to the bedroom with des Loges, and Crawford couldn't tell whether she looked at the horribly old man with fascination or loathing, or both; he did see her hands working in her lap, and he knew she was once more mentally running through the halls of the multiplication tables.

Des Loges sat down in a chair by the window and put his feet up on the bed. 'You asked about Werner,' he said. 'Werner is the . . . high king of the Hapsburgs, you might say – the secret but absolute head of the Austrian empire. And he's been that for a long time – he's even older than I am, by a good four centuries. He was born in about the year AD 1000, in the old Hapsburg castle on the river Aar, in the Swiss canton of Aargau.'

Crawford was standing by the window, looking down the road toward where they'd left the priests and the villagers, but he looked around sharply at the name of the canton, and des Loges raised his eyebrows inquiringly.

'Uh, never mind,' Crawford said. He turned back toward the window, for he thought he had caught a flicker of movement in the dusky road. 'Look, I'm not all that curious about this fellow. What do – '

'You have to be,' des Loges interrupted. 'He's the man responsible for all our troubles. He wanted immortality, and he was in Switzerland, so he was very aware of the stories about the Alps being the stronghold of the old gods, being in fact the old gods themselves, frozen in stone by the changed sunlight but not killed. He climbed the mountains at night, young Faust that he was, and he managed to awaken the mountains enough to talk to them, and he learned about their people, the nephelim, the pre-Adamite vampires, whose petrified bodies could still be found here and there, dormant like seeds in the desert waiting for the right kind of rain.'

Des Loges held up his withered hands, the palms about a foot apart. 'They looked like little statues,' he said. 'Little petrified ribs of some pre-Adamite Adam, waiting for the breath of life once more. And Werner found one, and had it surgically and magically inserted into his body, so that it could wake up on his *account*, in a manner of speaking, using his psychic credit. He became a bridge that way, an unnatural overlap, a sort of representative of both races at once, and he – the fact of him – both diminished humanity and revived the nephelim.'

'A Christ from the old gods,' said Josephine softly in French. 'A sort of artificial redeemer-in-reverse.' Her hands lay limp in her lap, as if even the multiplication tables had failed her.

Crawford was peripherally impressed that she'd understood the old man's speech, but his attention had been caught by something else, and he turned away from the window to face des Loges again. 'Surgically inserted,' he said. 'Where did he have that done? Switzerland, right?'

'Yes,' the old man answered. 'You know something about that?'

Crawford remembered the manuscript he'd described to Boyd six years ago, the description in *The Menotti Miscellany* of a procedure for inserting a statue into a man's abdomen. As he'd told Boyd, the manuscript had only survived because it had been mistakenly catalogued as a procedure for caesarian birth. 'I believe I've read the surgeon's notes.' Des Loges started to say something, but Crawford waved for silence. 'This Werner – from Aargau! – what does he *look* like? Does he look . . . young? Healthy?'

Des Loges stared at him. 'You *have* seen him, haven't you? No, he's not young nor healthy, though his condition is notably *stable* now that he's in Venice, near the Graiae pillars. He can't move around, but he can *project* himself, in images tangible enough to pick up wine glasses or turn the pages of books or cast solid shadows in not too bright light, and these images can be as youthful-looking as he wants them to be. He can't project them very far, though – no more than a few hundred yards from where his horrible old body is. And since 1818 that's been Venice, in the Doge's Palace by the Piazza San Marco. I believe that's the only reason he had the Austrians take Italy, so that he could own the Graiae pillars and live in their preserving aura.'

'I met what must have been him – one of his projections – in a café on the Grand Canal,' said Crawford thoughtfully. 'He wasn't very secretive – he told me his name was Werner von Aargau.'

'I guess he hasn't got a lot of need to be secretive,' put in Josephine. 'The only thing he kept from you was – what, the fact that you were specifically furthering the nephelim cause, rather than just the Austrian one.'

'And the fact that the medicine I was supposed to give you would have killed you,' said Crawford.

400

'Of course it would have,' said des Loges, nodding so vigorously that Crawford thought his driftwoody neck would break. 'The Austrians have derived their power from the alliance Werner forged with the revived nephelim, and so they do whatever they can to keep the nephelim happy – and this young gentleman's ... *ex-wife*,' he said, pointing at Crawford, 'would be very happy to have you dead. These creatures genuinely do love us, but they are powerfully jealous.'

There was torchlight visible down the road now, behind the trees, and Crawford wondered if he should warn Josephine; but he decided that Byron's servants could surely handle any visitors. Byron's pistol was still in his belt, and he touched it nervously.

'Who are *you*?' asked Josephine. 'How do *you* know all this?'

The very old man smiled, and his face had such a look of detestable wisdom that Crawford had to force himself not to look away. 'My real name is François des Loges, though I'm remembered under another. I was born in the year Joan of Arc was burned to death, and I was a student at the University of Paris when I fell in love.'

He chuckled softly. 'Near the University,' he went on, 'in front of the house of a certain Mademoiselle des Bruyeres, there was a large stone – you saw it, sir, when you took advantage of my hospitality. The students must have perceived something of its ... *strangeness*, for among them it was known as *Le Pet-au-Diable*, the Devil's Fart. *I* never called it that – *I* had seen the woman it became by night, and I worshipped her. You have both experienced this.'

He smiled reminiscently. 'When I was thirty-two I left Paris and the attentions of men, and for many, many years I wandered with her, a happy pet of hers. I was in the bosom of my new family, and I met other in-laws like myself – including Werner himself, the man who

401

had reintroduced the two species to each other. The fours and the twos, under the gaze of the eternal threes.'

Crawford frowned and looked away from the window. 'That's the riddle isn't it? The one the sphinx asked us on the peak of the Wengern. What does it mean?'

'You don't know?' Des Loges shook his head in wonder. 'What did you do, just *guess* the right answer? You can't have used the answer that legend claims was given by Oedipus – legend has it close, but not nearly close enough.'

Crawford tried to remember the wording of the riddle. *What was it that walked on four limbs when the sunlight had not yet changed, and now is supported by two, but will, when the sunlight is changed again and the light is gone, be supported by three?* 'I thought the riddle might be a . . . a ritualistic demand for diplomatic recognition. A citing of something the two species had in common. So, instead of "man," I gave an answer broad enough to include the nephelim too – I said, "sentient life on earth."'

The old man nodded sombrely. 'That was a lucky guess. You were lucky, too, to have got by the phantom that guards the threshold, the one Goethe refers to in *Faust* – "She looks to every one like his first love," Mephistopheles tells Faust. Actually, the phantom looks to every intruder like the person the intruder loved and has most grossly betrayed.'

Josephine had reddened, but was smiling slightly too. 'So what does it *refer* to?' she asked. 'The riddle, I mean.'

'Skeletons,' des Loges told her. 'Your friend Shelley knows about it. Read his *Prometheus Unbound*: "A sphere, which is as many thousand spheres . . ."' Des Loges's English was even worse than his French, to which he now mercifully returned. 'Matter, every bit of stuff that comprises the world and ourselves, is made up of what the old Greeks called atoms – they're tiny spheres, animated by the same force that makes lightning jump from the sky to the ground, or makes St Elmo's Fire flicker on the spars of ships.'

Corbie's Aunt, thought Crawford, animating the hulks.

'Each of these spheres is "many thousand spheres,"' des Loges went on, 'for the central bit is surrounded by tiny pieces of electricity that occupy distinctly divided spheres — and it's the number of these pieces of electricity in the atom's outermost sphere that defines which other atoms the atom may combine with. The pieces of electricity are the limbs by which the atom can seize other atoms, and three kinds of atoms are the bases for the three kinds of skeletons. Even the surviving legends of Oedipus describe the four-and-two-and-three as means of *support*.'

Crawford nodded dubiously. 'So what are these kinds of skeletons?'

'Well,' said des Loges, 'the nephelim, the *Siliconari*, so to speak, were the first intelligent race the earth had, Lilith's people, the giants that were in the earth in those days, and their skeletons are made of the same stuff their flesh is made of — the stuff that's the basis of glass and quartz and granite. The atoms of that stuff have four pieces of electricity in their outer sphere. Then the sunlight changed and the nephelim all petrified and sort of receded from the perspective of the picture.

'Humanity was the next form of intelligent life, and our skeletons are made of the same stuff as seashells and chalk and lime. And the basic element of those things has two pieces of electricity in its outer sphere.

'And the answer to the riddle implies that after the sunlight changes again and the sun goes out, the only intelligent things left will be the mountains themselves, the gods, and you've seen the stuff of their skeletons — it's the lightweight metal my pots and pans were made of, remember? Back in my little boat-house in Carnac?

It's the most abundant metal in the earth, found most commonly in clay and alum, and of course its atoms have three of these electrical bits in the outermost sphere.'

Crawford remembered seeing a silvery metal exposed in the side of the Wengern by an avalanche – a mountain guide had called it *argent de l'argile*, silver from clay.

Then his attention was distracted by the lights on the road. There were many torches approaching – more than could be carried by the group he'd seen earlier. Byron's servants would not be able to hold off this crowd.

'We've got to get out of here,' he said hastily to Josephine. 'Back stairs, and no time to grab anything.' He was suddenly very grateful for Shelley's twenty pounds.

Josephine's eyes widened when she looked out the window, and instantly she was moving for the door, with Crawford right behind her.

On the stairs Crawford noticed that des Loges was following them. 'Can you distract this gang?' Crawford hissed back at the old man. 'They're your friends.'

'No friends of mine, I assure you,' des Loges panted. 'They'd kill me, but not in the way I need. I'm coming with you.'

There was no chance of escaping unseen by the front door, so Crawford led them out the back door and across the darkening field that Byron had trod only the night before, with his dead daughter's body in his arms. Crawford was glad Byron's servants hadn't seen them leave, for it seemed to him that their loyalty was dubious.

The trio moved slowly through the dry grass for fear of making any trackable noise, and eventually found themselves blundering through the churchyard that must have been Byron's goal. The sky was dimming through deep purple toward black, but Crawford spotted a small mound of fresh-turned earth under an olive tree by the fence. He led them several yards farther before sitting down.

'May as well get comfortable here,' he said quietly. 'There's no use blundering around in the dark with people after us who know every road, and they probably won't look for us on consecrated soil.'

During the long, furtive walk he had remembered some things – such as Byron's identification of the song Crawford had been singing in the Alps, the song Crawford had learned from des Loges – and he was now sure he knew what des Loges's other name was, the one under which he'd said he was remembered.

'And so, Monsieur Villon,' Crawford whispered when they had all sat down on the still warm, grassy earth, 'is it your intention to travel with us?'

The old man laughed softly in the darkness. 'You're a bright boy. Yes, since you have evidently overcome your reluctance to participate in drownings, I want to enlist in the . . . the terminal cruise of poets.'

Crawford realized what the man was asking for, and realized too that he himself now knew enough about the situation to be unable to refuse. 'Well,' he said slowly, 'there's no way Shelley will permit that English boy Charles Vivian to sail along – *he* certainly has no need of this kind of baptism. So yes – I see no reason why there shouldn't be a berth for you aboard.'

Chapter 17

. . . Round the decay
Of that colossal wreck, boundless and bare,
The lone and level sands stretch far away.

— Percy Shelley, 'Ozymandias'

Processions of priests and religiosi have
been for several days past praying for rain;
but the gods are either angry, or nature is
too powerful.

— Edward Williams's journal, last entry
4 July 1822

As dawn scratched away the darkness of the sky
between the trees and the old Romanesque buildings of
the church, Crawford and Josephine and des Loges stole
to the road and began walking north. The air had already
shed the mild chill of night, and was poised for the day's
heat.

At first light the three of them caught a ride northward
aboard a farmer's wagon, and before the rising sun had
even cleared the bulk of Mount Querciolaia they
alighted in a narrow street in the southwestern waterfront section of Livorno. The docks and channels
extended inland quite a distance, and were connected
with a network of canals, and Crawford could almost
believe he was back in Venice.

He knew that Shelley would expect to meet them at
the Globe Hotel, but he knew too that Edward Williams
would be there now, and he dreaded seeing the man

again; so he found an *albergo* to stay at on the banks of one of the canals. The landlord crossed himself when they checked in, but an English ten-pound note for a week's lodging overcame whatever superstitious misgivings the man may have had.

Crawford and Josephine took rooms on the ground floor, overlooking the canal, but des Loges insisted on a room right up under the roof, in spite of the impediment of the narrow stairway. 'Even if I *am* dying in a week,' he told Crawford, 'I'd just as soon keep as much stone as possible between me and the earth.'

Crawford made a show of liking the place, praising the local restaurants and getting to know the neighbours, but to himself he admitted that he was simply hoping to miss Shelley and not have to follow through on the promise he'd made to him . . . and, years earlier, to des Loges.

So he was dismayed when, early on the morning of Monday the eighth of July, their fourth day in Livorno, des Loges came hobbling to the table in the outdoor trattoria where he and Josephine were having minestrone with beans, and told them, 'I feel a twin, a symbiote, approaching by sea, and it's certainly not old Werner. It's time — let's go.'

The *Don Juan* was in the harbour, and Shelley was at the Globe Hotel, in the sunlit lobby. He was tanned and fit-looking in a double-breasted reefer jacket and white nankeen trousers and black boots, but the face under the disordered grey-blond hair was expressionless. An iron case with a carrying handle stood on the floor by his right foot. Williams and Trelawny were with him — Williams was pale and haggard and Trelawny looked worried.

Crawford limped up to them.

'The Vivian boy and I,' Shelley was saying quietly,

407

'*can* work the *Don Juan* by ourselves. And we *will*.' Very slowly, as if saying it for the hundredth time, he added, 'I simply want to do the trip in as much solitude as possible.'

'I don't like it,' said Trelawny. 'And I'm going to pace you in the *Bolivar* and you can't prevent me. If you get into trouble, at least I'll be able to fish the two of you out of the water.'

Shelley's face regained its animation when he saw Crawford. 'There you are,' Shelley said, picking up the iron case and crossing to him and taking his arm. 'I've got to talk to you.' He led Crawford across the tile floor to a far corner.

Crawford tried to get in the first word, but Shelley overrode him.

'Listen,' Shelley said, shoving the iron case into Crawford's hand, 'you've got to leave *now*. I want to be setting sail this afternoon, but you've got to be in Spezia, and all prepared, when I do. Also, this weather will become very bad – I've waited for it – and I don't want *you* to run into trouble.' His smile was both frightened and bitter. 'This coming storm is all for me.'

'And the Vivian boy too, I gather,' said Crawford angrily, setting the case down. 'Doesn't he count? I won't permit you – '

'Oh, shut up, please, of course he's not going. I've already paid him off and told him to get out of Livorno. No, I'm going alone – I can work the *Don Juan* solo, at least well enough to get myself killed – but if Trelawny knew it, I think he would physically prevent me. As it is he's insisting on escorting me, but I've hidden his port clearance papers, so he'll spend the night here, like it or not.'

Then Shelley reached into his jacket and pulled out a little vial of bright red blood. 'I drew this only an hour ago,' he said, 'and I put a little vinegar in it, as I've seen

408

cooks do, to keep it from clotting. It'll be a powerful proxy for me. Now remember, in addition to being my proxy, it's also to let me know when you're ready — so do remember not to dump all of it out for the lure.'

Trying not to gag, Crawford put the vial into his coat pocket; somehow, of all the things he would have to do today, the use of Shelley's blood was the thing he was dreading most. He picked up the case again.

'I've got you a passenger,' he said, a little wildly. 'Someone who wants to accompany you on your . . . cruise.' He waved to des Loges, who had been standing by the front door and now came hobbling toward them, a repulsive grin curdling his ancient face.

Shelley gaped at the old man and then turned to Crawford furiously. 'Haven't you understood *anything*? I can't be taking passengers! What does this derelict imagine — '

Crawford overrode him: 'Percy Shelley, I'd like you to meet François Villon.'

Shelley's voice trailed off, and for several seconds Crawford could see the effort it cost him to think — then finally Shelley smiled, with something of his old alertness. 'Really? It's really Villon, the poet, he's an in-law? And wants to . . . go . . . with me?'

Crawford nodded. 'It is,' he said flatly, 'and he does.'

Des Loges had by now hobbled up to them, and Shelley slowly reached out and shook his hand. 'It will be,' he said slowly in modern French, 'an honour to have you aboard.'

Des Loges bobbed his head. 'It is an honour,' he said softly in his barbaric accent, 'to sail with Perseus.'

Shelley blinked at the old man, then pointed at him excitedly. 'You . . . you were in Venice, weren't you? When I was there with Byron in '18. You called me Perseus then, too.'

'Because you had come to have dealings with the

409

Graiae,' des Loges said. 'And today, still true to your name, you mean to slay a Medusa!' He looked out the window at the hot sky. 'It looks like a good day for doomed men to go sailing.'

Crawford waved for silence, for Edward Williams had stepped away from Trelawny and was approaching them.

Williams stopped beside Shelley. It was obviously painful for him to be up and around in the daylight, but he forced a smile as he took Shelley's arm.

'I-I'm sailing w-with you, Percy,' he stammered. 'Don't try to talk me out of it. She's d-dead, really dead, Allegra is . . . and I really . . . think . . . I can hold this resolve . . . until nightfall, and not try to find another lover. If I keep thinking about Jane, and our children, I think I can.' His smile was desperate but oddly youthful too, and for a moment he looked the way Keats had looked in London in 1816.

'Ed,' said Shelley, 'I can't take you. Go with Trelawny on the *Bolivar*, and – '

Williams smiled bleakly. 'That wouldn't . . . do me any good, would it?' he said quietly. 'The *Bolivar*'s not going to sink.'

For several moments Shelley stared at his friend's wasted face, and then his answering smile was sad and gentle. 'Well,' he said, 'now that I consider it, I can't think of a pilot I'd rather have on this trip.' He turned to Crawford and extended his hand. 'Go,' he said. 'Now, while you can still do this for all of us.'

As Crawford took Shelley's hand he was thinking about the first time he'd seen him, unconscious in a street in Geneva six years earlier. Aware of the losses Shelley had suffered since then, and of the grey hair and limp and scars he himself had acquired, and of Josephine's lost eye and twisted hand – and of all the deaths and suffering – Crawford was choked, at a loss for an adequate parting statement.

'I wish,' he managed to say as he hefted the iron case, 'we'd got to know each other better.'

Shelley smiled, and when Crawford released his hand he further disarranged his hair. 'There's hardly anyone left here to get to know anymore – so go.' He reached across and tapped the lump in Crawford's coat that was the vial of blood. 'Tell Mary I send my . . . love.'

Crawford used some more of Shelley's money to hire the fastest-looking boat he could find in the harbour, and when he and Josephine were aboard, and the single-masted sloop was coursing northward across the clear blue water, he limped through the spray and wind to the bow and stood staring ahead, toward what, one way or the other, would be the culmination of these last six years of his life.

He was still far from sure that he would be able to do what he had promised: the procedure that would save Josephine – and, incidentally, save Mary Shelley and her young son – but which would also bar him forever from the sort of longevity that des Loges and Werner von Aargau had been enjoying for the last several centuries. He could probably become a mere *victim* again, if he searched long enough for a nephelim predator to destructively love him, but he would certainly never again have the chance to actually *marry into the family*.

It was all very well for everybody to expect this of him. Des Loges had had centuries of the easy life already; Shelley had seen nearly all of his children die, and still had one to save; and Josephine had never had membership in the family even offered to her.

He took the vial of Shelley's blood out of his pocket and thought about how easy it would be to simply drop it over the side, into the ocean.

He glanced back at Josephine, who was sitting against the mast with her eyes closed, mumbling – certainly the good old multiplication tables again. Sweat gleamed on her forehead. He tried to see her as an annoyance, as an odious responsibility he'd somehow accidentally been burdened with, and something in the empty sky seemed to help him think it – all at once Josephine seemed too physically hot and organic, and perishable like some kind of stuff for sale in the open air markets, where one had to wave away the buzzing clouds of flies to see what the merchandise looked like, be it vegetable or meat.

But though some power was helping him to see her as a temporary bit of noxious growth – some kind of mushroom that would appear fat on a lawn in the morning and be burst and spoiled by dusk – something in his mind, something more forceful, was making him see her in different contexts: he saw her helpless at sea, while he looked on without acting; trapped in a burning building while he drank nearby; crushed in a bed in which he slept, and went on sleeping.

And then he remembered her pulling Byron and himself back from the abyss on the peak of the Wengern, and kissing him with a mouth full of glass and garlic in a Roman street, and pulling him out of the sea and massaging his leg with tortured hands, and he remembered the beach on which they had first made love, the day of Mary's miscarriage.

And, unhappily, he put the vial back into his pocket.

At a little after one in the afternoon the boat hove to and lowered its sails, and Crawford and Josephine climbed over the gunwale and waded to shore, a few hundred yards south of the Casa Magni; the trip had only taken about five hours.

* * *

The sun glared bright as static lightning in the burned purple sky.

'She'll be weak,' Crawford told Josephine harshly as he dragged a stick through the hot white sand, drawing a wide pentagram, 'since it's daytime. She'll come, though, because she'll imagine that Shelley and I are in danger, and she – ' His throat narrowed, and he had to stop before going on. ' – she loves us.' He had shed his jacket, but still the sweat ran down his face and soaked his shirt.

Josephine didn't say anything. She was standing at the top of the beach slope, just in front of the trees, and it occurred to Crawford that the spot where they had first made love must be somewhere nearby. He couldn't be bothered now to try to figure out where it had been.

Outside the pentagram he put down the iron case Shelley had given him, and he crouched to open it. For a moment the reek of garlic overpowered the sea smell, and even after the breeze had taken the first redolent puff away, the smell swirled back and forth in the warm air like strands of seaweed in a tide pool.

He opened a little jar and turned to the pentagram and shook a mixture of wood shavings, shredded silver and chopped garlic into four of the five shallow grooves, leaving empty the groove that faced the sea. He set the jar down, still open, in the sand nearby. At last he straightened and stared out westward across the glittering blue gulf toward the peaks of Portovenere.

He knew that he was about to change his world forever, rob it of all its glamour and adventurous expectancy and what Shelley had once in a poem called 'the tempestuous loveliness of terror.'

Goodbye, he thought.

'Come,' he called softly.

He bit his finger savagely and held it over the pentagram so that the quick drops of blood fell on to the sand within it; then he took the vial out of his pocket and uncorked it and poured half of the contents onto the spatters of his own blood. There was still an inch or so of red fluid in the glass container, and he looked hopelessly at it for several seconds while he tried to summon the nerve to do what came next.

'Screw your courage to the sticking point,' he whispered to himself, and then drank the blood and tossed the empty vial into the close sea.

And then he was in two places at once. He was still on the beach and aware of the pentagram and Josephine and the hot sand under his boots, but he was also on the shifting deck of the *Don Juan*, back in the boat-crowded Livorno harbour.

'He's there,' he heard himself say in Shelley's voice to the two other men on the boat with him. 'Cast off.'

A mirage was forming way out over Portovenere, and though there was no wind to deface the pentagram or stir Josephine's skirt, Crawford felt something massive rushing toward them across the miles of ocean.

Josephine gasped, and when he impatiently glanced at her he saw that she had clapped her hand over her glass eye. 'I *saw* her,' she said, her voice husky with fear. 'She's coming here.'

'To die,' Crawford said.

He felt the deck of Shelley's boat shift under his feet and he had to resist the impulse to roll with it. 'So is Shelley,' he said, and he spoke loudly, because des Loge's harsh laughter on the deck of the *Don Juan* was ringing in his ears. Through Shelley's eyes he saw the low, dark clouds moving in toward Livorno from the southwest, and distantly he felt too Shelley's rigidly suppressed horror at what was soon to happen.

Then Crawford's attention was entirely on what his

414

own eyes were seeing, for now *she* was there on the beach, standing naked in the pentagram.

She was blinking in the glare of the sun on the white sand, and before he could look at her closely he quickly crouched to pour the wood-and-sand-and-garlic along the last line, closing the geometrical figure and trapping her inside.

When it was done he stood back and then let himself look at her.

She was pearly white and smooth, and the sight of her mouth and breasts and long legs made the breath stop in his throat; and though he could see that the sunlight was hurting her terribly, her weirdly metallic eyes were looking at him with love and, already, forgiveness.

'Where is my brother?' she asked. Her voice was like a melody played on a silver violin. 'Why have you called me and imprisoned me?'

Crawford made himself look away from her, and he saw the sand shifting in waves away from the pentagram. 'Shelley is sailing this way,' he said tensely. 'There's a storm . . .'

He heard her bare feet shift in the sand as she turned to look south. She whispered a sound that was half sigh and half sob, and he knew she was dreading the tortures of the long flight south to save Shelley. 'You don't want him to die,' she said. 'Release me so that I can save him.'

'No,' Crawford said, trying to sound resolute. 'This is his plan. He wants me to do this.'

The woman turned back toward him, and he found himself helplessly meeting her inhuman gaze. 'Do you want him to die?'

'I won't stop him.'

'Did he tell you,' she asked him, 'that it will kill me too?'

Her eyes seemed prodigiously deep, and were as dark

415

as a cool moonless night on a Mediterranean island. 'Yes,' he whispered.

'Do you want *me* to die?'

He felt Josephine's hot hand take his; he wanted to shake it off irritably, but he forced himself to clasp it, even though he knew that he was clasping death – his own soon enough, and Shelley's and the lamia's today. He tried to think about Percy Florence Shelley, and Mary, and the Williams children, and Josephine.

'Yes,' he answered the woman, hoping it would all be over before his fragile resolve crumbled. He looked away from her and saw, through Shelley's tears, the thick skirt of rainy haze that hung under the dark clouds ahead of the *Don Juan*'s leaping bow.

He sat down, for the rocking of the distant deck was making him weave on the sand – but the sand was moving too. The sand-waves moving away from the pentagram were higher now, though they seemed powerless to change the pentagram itself; and humped shapes, apparently made of sand, were beginning to rise up around the three human forms in a semicircle that was open on the seaward side. Rocks in the wooded slope cracked as if flexing themselves.

'My mother the earth would harm you,' the woman said, 'if I let her.'

The three fingernails of Crawford's free hand had dug bloodily into his palm, and he couldn't tell whether the tears blurring his vision were his own or Shelley's. Everything that had happened since his week of glad bondage to the lamia in Switzerland seemed like a frustrating dream. 'Let her,' he said softly.

'How can I?' she asked. 'I love you.'

He was dimly aware that Josephine's hand was no longer in his.

The *Don Juan* was in the haze under the dark clouds when the wind struck, and she heeled wildly, her sails full of the hot damp breath of the storm; Crawford felt the pain as Shelley fell against the rail and clutched at it.

A little Italian boat, a felucca, was visible off the starboard bow, racing in for Livorno harbour, but she lowered her triangular lateen sails when she was near Shelley's boat, and her captain called across the dark water, offering to take the *Don Juan*'s passengers aboard.

Crawford felt the strain in his own throat as Shelley yelled, '*No!*' The felucca was already receding aft, though Shelley had to look upward as well as back to see it from where he was crouched at the edge of the *Don Juan*'s slanted deck.

'Break the pentagram,' the silvery woman said, cringing against the weight of the sun on her, 'and I will spare all of them — the children, that woman there — all of them. But do it now. Already I am so weakened that the task of saving Shelley will nearly kill me.'

'Let her go, Michael,' said Josephine suddenly. 'You can't kill his *sister*!'

Too, thought Crawford bitterly, you mean I can't kill *his* sister *too*, in addition to *your* sister, is that it?

'Remember her promise to Shelley,' he said. His voice was as harsh as the cracking of the rocks and the rustling of the sand.

'You're a woman too,' the lamia said to Josephine, 'and you love him too. We're alike, we're *identical*, in that. I will let you have him — I'll go away — if you will just let me save my brother. I don't know why your Michael wants him to die.'

'He's jealous of Shelley,' said Josephine, 'because Shelley . . . *had* you here, a month ago.'

Crawford turned to Josephine to deny what she'd said, but the captain of the receding felucca had shouted, 'If you will not come on board, for God's sake reef your sails or you are lost!' — and Williams, his earlier resolve

417

shattered by the real proximity of real death, had leapt for the halliards to lower the sails.

Shelley sprang forward and punched him away from the rail, and the *Don Juan* laboured on through the steamy rain, still under full sail, farther into the storm.

Crawford saw Williams — no, it was Josephine — start toward the pentagram, her hand out to break the lines of it, and Crawford seized her by the arm and threw her away across the sand.

Human-shaped forms made of flinty sand were standing around them now, waving fingerless arms in impotent rage or grief, and trees on the slope behind him were snapping and falling as though the hill itself were waking up and throwing off its organic blanket. The sea bubbled like a boiling pot, and the sky was full of rushing, agitated spirits.

'Michael,' said the woman in the pentagram.

Helplessly he looked at her. Burns were visible now on her pearly skin. Horribly, love still shone in her unnatural eyes. No *human*, he thought, could have continued to love me through this.

'It is too late for me now,' she said. 'I die today. Let me at least die going toward him, even though it is certain that I will die on the way.'

He knew that only someone who hated himself thoroughly could do this, could *continue* to do this, and he wondered if Josephine and Mary and her child would ever know enough to be thankful that one such had been chosen for the job.

'No,' he said.

The *Don Juan* had foundered now under the dark, turbulent sky; water was cascading in over the gunwales, and the tightly bellied sails were pulling her over still farther.

Shelley was clinging to the rail. 'Goodbye, Aickman,'

he said, having to spit out salt water before he could speak.

'Crawford,' said Crawford, suddenly thinking it was important. 'My name is Michael Crawford.'

Crawford could feel the tension of Shelley's smile as he held his head up into the warm rain above the solid water surging in over the gunwales. 'Goodbye, Michael Crawford.'

'I could still release her,' Crawford heard himself say.

'No,' Shelley said, with a sort of desperately held serenity. 'Stand with me.'

'Goodbye, Shelley,' Crawford managed to say.

He felt Shelley free one hand from the rail to wave.

Crawford caught a last thought of Shelley's as the young poet despairingly lifted his feet and let go of the rail and let the savagely eager sea batter him off the deck: bleak gratitude that he had never learned to swim.

The hot sand was in Crawford's mouth then, for he had fallen face down, gasping for air even though it wasn't his lungs that were being choked with cold sea water.

In a minute or two his breathing returned to normal, and he was able to lift his sand-caked face.

The woman in the pentagram was impossibly shrinking, shrivelling in the harsh sunlight. She seemed more reptile than human now, and soon she was unmistakably a serpent, her bright scales glittering purple and gold. And as if to match the foggy tempest in which the *Don Juan* had met its doom, the shaking hill had thrown up a cloud of dust, and a savage wind sprang up in which the sand-figures flung themselves apart in clouds of stinging, gritty spray.

With filming eyes the diminished creature gave him a last glance full of love and torment, and then there was just a little statue lying in the centre of the pentagram. The wind died, and he was alone on the beach with

Josephine, who was sitting in the sand where he had thrown her, rubbing her arm.

Crawford felt unpleasantly drunk, out of touch with the world. Throwing my women around, he thought, as he bent to pick up the little statue; he drew his arm back and flung it as far as he could out over the water of the gulf. It seemed to hang in the sky, turning slowly, for a long time before it finally sped downward and made a brief, small splash and was gone.

All the cubic miles of hot air seemed to stagger, as if a vast but subsonic chord had been struck on some cosmic organ.

Josephine had stood up by the time he turned back from the sea, and she gave him a frail, bewildered smile. 'We did it,' she said, her voice quiet but pitched higher than usual. 'We planned it and we did it. I even thought I had some idea of what it was we were going to do. Now I – ' She shook her head, and though she was smiling he thought she might cry. 'I don't have any idea what it is that we've done.'

Crawford went to her and gently took the arm by which he had flung her away a minute earlier. He knew what to say, and he tried to give the sentence a tone of importance. 'We saved Mary, and her son – and helped to save Jane Williams and her children.'

Josephine's lips were slightly parted, and she was squinting around at the sea and the sand and the rocks. The haze of dust from the hill had blown away out over the sea.

'An enormity,' she said. 'I'll never grasp all of what we did, but it was an enormity.'

They walked north along the beach. Crawford wanted to take her hand, but it seemed too trivial an action to be appropriate right now. The taste of Shelley's blood was metallic acid in his head. He was out of touch with the world, and he was vaguely glad that he was dressed, for he didn't think he would be able to put on clothes correctly – to remember what went on where, and which side out. He had to look down from time to time to make sure he was still walking.

The squat stone structure that was the Casa Magni appeared ahead, and shortly after they reached it he found himself drinking wine and chatting cheerfully with Mary and Jane.

He made an effort to listen to what he was saying, and was dimly reassured to hear himself telling the two women that their husbands had planned to leave Livorno in the afternoon, and would no doubt arrive sometime during the evening. 'Percy sent you his love,' he remembered to tell Mary.

They slept chastely that night in the room that Shelley had let them have, and they were awakened at midnight by a remote inorganic singing, a distant chorus that seemed to be in the sky and the sea and the hill behind the house. Without speaking, they both got up and went into the dining room and opened the glass doors and walked out on to the terrace.

The singing was a little louder, heard from out here, and deeper. The tide had receded out so far that if Shelley and Williams really had been coming home tonight they would have had a hard time finding a mooring at all close to the house – and the exposed shells and black hummocks of sodden, weedy sand seemed to be resonating to the inhuman chorus.

The house was creaking as if in accompaniment, and when he had to take a step sideways to keep his balance Crawford realized that the house was shifting in an earthquake.

'It's what we heard last week in Montenero,' Josephine whispered finally, 'the night Byron killed Allegra. It's the earth, mourning.'

When they returned inside, Josephine insisted on spending the rest of the night in the women's servants' room; wearily, Crawford acquiesced and went back to bed alone.

Chapter 18

No diver brings up love again
Dropped once, my beautiful Felise,
In such cold seas.

    – A. C. Swinburne, *Felise*

How elate
I felt to know that it was nothing human . . .

    – Percy Bysshe Shelley

Mary Shelley and Jane Williams were awake early the next morning, and as they drank their breakfast coffee they anxiously scanned the blue horizon of the gulf; Claire got up later, and volunteered to watch from the terrace while the other two women tried to read and to conceal their uneasiness from the children – but it wasn't until the sun began to sink over Portovenere in the late afternoon, with no boat having appeared, that the three of them began to be alarmed.

Josephine had resumed her job as governess of the children, and Crawford spent the day drinking on the terrace. Claire stood by the rail near him, but they hardly spoke.

That night he and Josephine again slept separately.

Josephine was awakened in the middle of the night by a voice whispering faintly from outside the house. She climbed out of her bunk and got dressed without waking the other servants, and went down the stairs to the ground floor, walked past the boat in which she had rescued Crawford three weeks earlier, and out on to the still warm moonlit sand.

A man was standing on the beach, and when she had stepped out of the arches he turned toward her and held out his hand.

For perhaps a minute neither of them moved; then she sighed deeply and reached out and took the proffered hand with her maimed left hand.

They walked south along the shore, moving up the slope when the waves came up and straying out onto the wet, flat sand when they receded.

After a few minutes she looked into her companion's silvery eyes. 'You're my friend from the Alps,' she said, flexing her bent hand reminiscently in his. 'Why do they think you're this Polidori?'

'I am him too, more or less,' the man replied. 'He came seeking my kind after leaving the poets, and I was . . . available and vital. Thanks to you, thanks to what you had given me. So I took him and, when he took his own life, the – what would be the right word? – the bits of attention . . . the seeds, say; the seeds I had planted in his blood quickened, and I emerged from his grave.'

Josephine frowned. 'Doesn't that mean there are two of you now? The one that bit him and the one that grew out of his dead body?'

'Identity is not as rigidly quantized with us as it is with you. We're like the waves that agitate a body of water or a field of grass; you see us because of the material things we move, but we don't consist of those material things. Even the seeds we plant in people's blood aren't physical things, but a sort of maintained attention, like the beam of a slotted lantern held on a moving object in the dark. My sister had to suffer, and labour, to be focused down to a point where she could actually be killed, and even then she would probably not have died if she hadn't been linked to Shelley by the fact of their twinhood.'

Josephine glanced at him warily, but his expression was still placid. 'This person beside you,' he went on, touching his own chest, 'can exist in any number of forms at once, just as he can be both Polidori and the stranger you called to your room that night in Switzerland.'

A wave came swirling up, faintly luminous in the moonlight, and they stepped up the slope to avoid it.

'It's been a long time,' she said quietly.

'Time is nothing to my kind,' her companion told her. 'It needn't be anything to you either. Come with me and live forever.'

Some muted part of Josephine's mind was profoundly frightened, and she frowned in the darkness. 'Like Polidori?'

'Yes. Exactly like Polidori. Float to the surface of your mind only when you want to be awake.'

'Are you in there, Polidori?' Josephine asked, a little hysterically. 'Say hello.'

'Good evening, Josephine,' said her companion in a different voice, one that still carried some pomposity. 'It is my good fortune that we meet at last.'

'Did you find your life intolerable?'

'Yes.'

'Have you managed to jettison those . . . things, those memories, now?' Her face was relaxed, but her heart was pounding.

'Yes.'

'Do you hate my . . . do you hate Michael?'

'No. I did, before. I hated him and Byron and Shelley and all the people who had what I so wanted – the channel to the Muses. I gave everything I had, I gave *me*, but the Muses still withheld that, though they took me.'

'Are you sorry now that you gave in?' she asked,

425

surprised at the urgency in her own voice. 'Since they didn't keep the bargain you thought you were making?'

'No,' he said. 'Now I live forever. I don't *need* to write poetry any longer – I *live* poetry now. The nights are mine, and the songs of the earth, and the old rhythms of the worlds and the atoms, that never change. I've faced the Medusa, and what looks like stony doom to men is actually birth. Men are born out of the hot wombs of humanity, but that's only . . . like a chick in the egg developing feathers. The real, lasting birth is the next one, the birth out of the cold ground. Everything you wished you could leave behind is left behind.'

The moon was sinking low out over the water, highlighting with silver fire the tips of the waves that had closed over Shelley and his slain and petrified sister.

'Polidori is me, and I am him,' her companion said in a different voice.

'His sister,' Josephine said. 'Your sister. She's dead.'

'Yes,' said her companion calmly. 'It's rare that we die, but she is dead.'

'I killed her, helped kill her.'

'Yes.'

Tears glittered suddenly on Josephine's right cheek. 'I – I'm sorry I abandoned you in the Alps,' she said hoarsely. 'And I'm sorry I refused you in that street in Rome, in front of Keats's house. And I'm sorry I helped kill your . . . sister.' She walked on in silence for a while. 'Sisters shouldn't be killed,' she whispered.

'Nobody should be killed,' said her companion. 'We offer eternal life to everyone.'

Josephine stopped, and faced him, though her eyes were closed. 'Will you still have me?' she asked in a humble, hopeful monotone.

'Of course,' he said, placing his hand gently behind her neck and lowering his head to her throat.

* * *

426

Mary and Claire and Jane Williams were nearly hysterical with worry when the next day dragged on till noon without any sign of the *Don Juan*, and Crawford agreed to go back to Livorno to ask whether or not Shelley had actually set out. Josephine was ill in bed, so, alone, already trying to figure out how he would break the news to the ladies on his return, he walked north along the beach to Lerici, where he hired a boat.

He arrived in Livorno in the evening and found Trelawny and Roberts still at the Globe, and their expressions of worried hope turned to despair even before they could ask him any questions, for Crawford's face let them know that the *Don Juan* had not arrived at the Casa Magni after having disappeared into the storm two days earlier.

Byron was still in Pisa, and after a bleak, muted conversation in the lobby, Trelawny volunteered to ride north to tell him that it seemed sure that Shelley and Williams were drowned.

Trelawny left early the next day and was back in the late afternoon. Hunt and Byron, he said, had both been visibly upset by the news, and Byron sent a servant back with Trelawny to act as a courier, and had insisted that Trelawny take the *Bolivar* out and search for the *Don Juan* until Shelley's fate was absolutely known; and the next day, as the courier took a fast boat north to deliver a tersely unhopeful letter to the Casa Magni, Trelawny and Roberts and Crawford sailed slowly in the same direction, closely skirting the coastline and scanning the shore for any sign of Shelley's boat.

Crawford had gone with them, rather than with the courier, because the task of facing the women seemed vastly beyond him. During the past two days his feeling of disorientation had only grown worse — he was bewildered by, and unable to come up with ready answers to, even such innocuous remarks as 'Good morning,' and it was actually a relief that Josephine had not spoken to him since the day of the lamia's killing.

No sign of the *Don Juan* was found that day.

Back at the Globe that evening they learned that Mary and Claire and Jane Williams had returned with Byron's servant that afternoon, and had gone on to Pisa to stay with Byron at the Palazzo Lanfranchi to await word. Josephine, it appeared, had elected to stay on at the Casa Magni with Shelley's servants. Crawford was obscurely glad of it.

He and Trelawny and Roberts kept up the search for five more blurry days, only quitting when word reached them that two bodies, one of them tentatively identified as that of Edward Williams, had been found washed up on the beach near the mouth of the Serchio River, fifteen miles north of Livorno.

The health authorities buried the bodies before Byron and Hunt could get there to look at them, and presented Byron with a bill for the interments; Trelawny showed the bill to Crawford, angry about the charges for health measures, which included 'certain metals and vegetable bulbs.' Crawford told him there were probably better things to be worrying about.

Another body was found the next day, five miles farther north. The port officials were fairly sure it was Shelley's. Trelawny blustered and threatened and made liberal use of the fact that Byron was an English peer, and eventually got them to agree to postpone the burial until the body could be identified.

On Friday the *Bolivar* sailed north once more, and dropped anchor when they saw half a dozen Tuscan soldiers waving at them from the beach near Viareggio. Crawford, leaning on the *Bolivar*'s rail, wondered idly why so many soldiers were necessary to stand watch over one drowned body.

Roberts lowered the boat, and he and Crawford and Trelawny rowed ashore through the low surf.

As Crawford was splashing in through the shallows he noticed the sprawled form around which the soldiers were standing. Several canvas bags lay on a wooden pallet nearby, and there were four shovels stuck upright in the dirt like sailless masts. A crowd of ragged civilians, presumably fishermen, watched from a sandy rise a hundred yards away. Crawford looked down at the body.

The flesh of the face and hands had been nibbled away, right down to the bones, and the soldiers assured the Englishmen that fish had done it.

Trelawny and Roberts just nodded blankly, but Crawford looked up the beach to the crowd of unsavoury spectators, and he remembered an old man who had dressed up as a clergyman to get into Guy's Hospital and steal blood from a certain sort of corpse, and he wondered what the Italian word for *neffy* was, and he thought he knew why so many soldiers were here. He considered walking up to the silent figures, but was afraid he would lose all contact with the sane world if he saw . . . say, a fork . . . in the hand of one of them.

He turned away and spat in the sand, for the taste of Shelley's blood was hovering in the back of his throat like a bad smell.

He returned his gaze to Shelley's stripped skull. Some of the flaxen hair still adhered to it, and he remembered the way that hair used to blow in disarray around his face after Shelley had excitedly run his hands through it. He tried to derive some sense of sadness from seeing Shelley in this state of ruin, but he found that he couldn't see the corpse at his feet as anything more than a corpse; he had said goodbye to the man eleven days earlier, when the blood he'd drunk had linked him to Shelley as he clung to the rail of the foundering boat.

Trelawny on the other hand was striding up and down

the beach with his hands balled into fists, cursing to cover his very evident grief. Roberts looked more embarrassed than anything else.

Even without a face, the body was clearly Shelley's. It still wore the nankeen trousers and the reefer jacket, from the pocket of which Trelawny had melodramatically pulled Leigh Hunt's copy of Keats's *Poems*. Crawford noticed that it was folded open to the poem *Lamia*.

The officer in charge of the soldiers was yawning and shrugging, as if to indicate how routine and unremarkable the whole proceeding was, and when he spoke it was in English, as if to distance himself even further. 'This body,' he said, 'must be buried now, very now. You should burn him later, and the bodies down the coast also. It is the final law. And with this . . . *wherewithal* . . . placed muchly upon the bodies, first, when they are buried.' He waved at the canvas bags. 'Health necessities, of the law.'

'More of their damned health necessities,' growled Trelawny. 'Like the vegetables and metals they made Byron pay for.' He turned to Crawford. 'What the hell's he trying to say?'

'I think,' said Crawford, 'he means that we have to bury the bodies now, but can dig them up later for cremation. And when we bury them we have to dump those bags on to the corpses.'

'What *is* that?' asked Trelawny, his black beard seeming to bristle with suspicion. 'In the bags?'

Crawford crossed the sand to the bags, touched one, and then smelled his finger. 'Quicklime,' he said before the officer could think of the English word. 'It gets tremendously hot on exposure to water, any dampness.' The other two Englishmen looked ready to object, but Crawford looked again at the spectators and said, 'I think it's a good idea.'

* * *

They buried Shelley under the hot sun, and dumped a bag of the quicklime over him and then hastily shovelled sand down on top of the steaming effigy. The crowd of spectators broke up and drifted away, and Crawford and Trelawny and Roberts waded out to the boat and rowed back to the *Bolivar*.

They sailed back to Livorno as the sun went down over the Ligurean Sea beyond the starboard rail. By early evening they were back at the Globe Hotel, but Trelawny paused only long enough to empty a glass of wine before riding south to break the final news to Byron and the ladies.

Crawford sat up late, drinking alone on a balcony overlooking the harbour. The water was dark, but streaked here and there with yellow light from the portholes of a few boats with people staying aboard, and the waterfront was quiet on this Friday night; the only sounds were the faint wash of the surf and the wind fluting in the roof tiles behind and above him.

As had happened once before, in Byron's coach outside the walls of Geneva, the wine seemed to clear his wits rather than dull them, even though the glass he was now drinking from was plain glass instead of amethyst.

Sometime during the long, morbidly hot day he had decided that tomorrow he would use the last of Shelley's money to hire a boat back to the Casa Magni . . . and then ask Josephine to marry him. His life hadn't been one he'd have chosen, but Josephine was the best and most important part of it, and – now that he had begun to recover from the shock of having killed the lamia – he knew he couldn't bear to lose her.

Only by promising himself that he would marry her and make the rest of her life happy and contented could he bear to think of what her life had consisted of since she'd left England – the injuries, the cold and hunger, the loneliness, the recurrent madness . . . or to remember the innate gallantry and loyalty of her, the moral strength that had several times been much greater than his own . . .

In fact, it occurred to him as he poured a fresh glass of wine, her life in England seemed to have been a nightmare too. Clearly she had always been implicitly blamed for her mother's death, both by her father and by her sister Julia, whom he had so carelessly married so long ago. He remembered Julia cheerfully telling him about Josephine's pathetic attempts to *be* Julia, and about Julia's callous public shattering of those pretences.

The fact that Josephine could still love anyone, that she could still care so much about people – like himself and Keats and Mary Shelley and the children – that she would put her abused life in danger to do it, was evidence of a soul that should all along have been treasured, cherished.

The world had no place for her, and would certainly break her – probably soon – if he didn't do what he could to protect her.

The medical profession was undoubtedly closed to them now, in Italy, at least, but surely there was a quiet life to be had, somewhere, for two tired and damaged people. Surely the world had no further malice toward them.

Cheered by the wine and by his new resolve, he went to bed early, for he wanted to be at Casa Magni by noon.

The boat he had hired had no smaller boat for passengers to debark in, and so after the captain lowered the anchor to wait for him, Crawford had to wade waist-deep through the low surf to the beach in front of the Casa Magni; one of Shelley's woman-servants waved to him from the terrace, and was waiting for him in the dining room when he had crossed the sand-streaked paving stones of the ground-floor room and ascended the stairs.

The servant, whose name, he recalled, was Antonia, hurried across the carpeted floor to him. 'There's only me and Marcella and Josephine still here, sir,' she said quickly in Italian. 'Is there word on Mister Shelley?'

'He's dead, Antonia,' Crawford answered in the same language. 'They found his body on the beach yesterday, twenty miles south of here. Williams is dead too.'

'Ah, God.' Antonia crossed herself. 'Their poor children.'

Crawford just nodded. 'They'll get along,' he said in a neutral tone. 'Where is Josephine?'

'She's in the room that used to be Shelley's.'

And was afterwards hers and mine, for a while, Crawford thought as he crossed to the closed door. He tapped softly on it. 'Josephine? It's me — Michael. Let me in, there's something I've got to talk to you about, and I have a boat waiting — for us.'

There was no reply, and he turned back toward Antonia with a questioning look.

'She has been ill, sir,' Antonia said. 'The sun hurts her eyes . . .'

Crawford turned the knob and pulled the door open. The curtains were drawn against the sunlight, but he could see Josephine lying across the bed in her night-gown, her sweaty hair trailing across her face and throat as if she were a drowned body carried up here to await identification. The window was open, though the curtains scarcely shifted at all in the still, hot summer air.

Very slowly he walked to the bed, and he laid his hand on her forehead. The skin was hot, and his eyes had adjusted enough to the dimness for him to notice how pale she was.

He reached out and, hesitantly, pulled the damp

strands of hair away from her throat. Two red puncture marks showed clearly on her white skin.

'No,' he remarked quietly, almost conversationally, though his heart was thudding rapidly behind his ribs. 'No, this isn't what's happened. Not . . .' He sat down on the floor beside the bed, and he only knew he'd begun crying when Josephine's drawn face blurred and dissolved into the pattern of the curtains, like an imagined face seen in the contours of crumpled bedclothes, that disappears when the viewer moves.

Not *now*, he thought, not now that I'm finally free of the lamia, now that Josephine and I are both too old and broken to climb the Alps again . . .

When he blinked away his tears he saw that her eyes were slightly open, squinting down at him where he sat. 'Darling!' she whispered. 'Come along, tonight. We can all share each other . . .' Her lips curled in a strained smile.

Then he was running down the stairs two at a time until his bad left leg buckled and he rolled down to the sandy pavement of the ground floor, twisting an ankle and cracking his head hard against the stones.

He remembered the despair-inducing field that had hung about the top of the Wengern like a subsonic vibration, and he wished he could bask once more in its oppressive influence, for he was afraid he lacked the necessary strength of character to shoot himself, or take poison, or jump from a height, without that kind of help.

Ah, but don't worry, he told himself bleakly as he limped across the sand and into the surf and then began laboriously wading back out toward where the anchored boat waited for him; there must certainly be other ways – not as *abrupt* as guns or cyanide or high balconies, but in the long run every bit as effective, I'm sure. And I have just enough faith left in myself to be confident that I'll find one.

Chapter 19

My head is heavy, my limbs are weary,
And it is not life that makes me move.

— Percy Bysshe Shelley

Byron was squinting against the sun-glare on the water of the narrow Livorno canal below him to his right, and in spite of the nasty things he'd heard about his destination he was looking forward to getting there, for his informants had all agreed that the place was very dark.

He was wearing a broad-brimmed hat, partly so as not to be recognized in this shabby district, but mostly for protection from the sun — his skin had always tended toward paleness, but lately he seemed to sunburn as easily as some British clerk on his first holiday.

Byron was in an irritable temper. His errand today would probably turn out to have been a waste of his time, and time was something he didn't seem to have much of these days; what with the Hunts and their Cockney brats staying in the Casa Lanfranchi on the floor below his own rooms, and Claire Clairmont and Mary Shelley and Jane Williams mooning around in their grief, and all the conferences with the Italian health authorities, he was lucky to have been able to get any work at all done on *Don Juan*.

And tomorrow he had to go along for the exhumation and cremation of the body of Ed Williams, and the day after that there was the same job to be done with the body of Shelley.

He wasn't looking forward to it. The bodies had been buried in the shallow, sandy graves nearly four weeks ago, and he wasn't sure which would be more upsetting: digging the bodies up again, or finding the graves empty. The latter was a distinct possibility – the seawater, and the garlic and silver the health authorities had buried them with, would have slowed them down, but still they'd been in the ground a lot longer than Allegra had. But perhaps small bodies were converted more quickly.

Byron paused, for ahead of him to his right was the narrow stone canal bridge he'd been told to watch for – three stylized wolves were rendered in bas-relief on the water-facing wall of it, and Byron saw without surprise that vandals had hammered away two legs from the middle figure and one from the far one. What was left was a four-legged wolf, a two-legged one, and one with three legs.

He peered under the foot of the bridge's near side, and his heart sank to see the black wooden stairs leading down toward the water. He had been half hoping that the stairs would be gone, and the place they led to closed and abandoned.

He squinted up at the rusty iron balconies of the surrounding houses, but no one seemed to be staring at him from behind any of the flower pots and clotheslines, so he tucked his hat brim down and reluctantly stepped forward.

The stairs were so close to the bridge that he had to duck to get in under the weathered stone arch of it, and their construction was unsteady enough to make him hold the rails firmly, despite the muck they were smearing on to his suede gloves. He could hear voices now from below, and he was grateful for the weight of the pistol in his coat pocket.

The stairs led down to a shadowed dock that extended a couple of yards out over the slow-moving water, and a doorway had been cut into the stones of the canal wall to his left. The wooden door was open, but only dim spots of light gleamed in the darkness within. A dank breeze, rumbling with hoarse voices and heavy with the reeks of wet clay and liquor and unwashed bodies, sighed out through the stone mouth like an exhalation from the earth's own sick lungs.

Byron whispered a curse and stepped inside. His eyes quickly adapted to the dimness.

Bottles on shelves lined one wall behind a long counter, and tables with little lamps on them had been set up on the uneven flagstones of the floor. The hunched forms in several of the chairs, he now noticed, were people; from time to time one of them would mumble something to a companion or lift a glass and drink from it.

A man in an apron was visible now behind the counter, and by the light of a candle on one of the shelves Byron saw the man raise his eyebrows inquiringly. Byron waved vaguely to him and turned back to the room, trying to see into the farthest corners – and suddenly he realized that the low-ceilinged room was much vaster than he had at first thought. The little dots of light that he had assumed were tiny candles set in a fairly close wall were actually the lamps on distant tables.

Through taverns measureless to man, he thought, mangling a line from Coleridge's 'Xanadu', *down to a sunless sea*.

He started forward, slowing to peer into the lamplit face of every person he passed; the bartender called something after him, but Byron dug a pound note out of his pocket and flicked it away over his shoulder, and the man relapsed into silence. Byron could hear him pad out from behind the bar, and then after a moment return.

The floor sloped down as Byron moved farther away from the canal-wall door, and the smells grew worse. The scattered mutter of dozens of conversations or monologues echoed and re-echoed in waves of amplification and interference until Byron thought that out of the noise there must eventually emerge one disembodied, aggregate voice, pronouncing some sentence that it would be fatal to hear.

There was masonry ahead of him, and he wondered if he had at last reached the far wall of the place – then he saw that it was just a blocky pillar, with more darkness receding away on either side of it; but there was a crowd gathered there.

They seemed to be chanting very quietly, and Byron saw that there was a life-sized crucifix mounted on the pillar. A cup, apparently a gold chalice, was ceremoniously being passed from man to man.

Are they saying *Mass*? Byron wondered incredulously. The Eucharist, down *here*?

He moved closer – and noticed that the crucified figure's feet were in a metal bowl, and that dark blood was running down the ankles; and then the figure rolled its white-bearded head and groaned, and flexed its bound hands.

Byron nearly screamed, and he found that his hand had darted into his jacket to seize the butt of his pistol. He lurched to the nearest table and, ignoring the languid protests of one solitary drinker, took the lamp and hurried back to the scene he had thought was a celebration of the Catholic Mass.

One of the men who had just drunk from the chalice licked bloody lips and smiled at Byron, whose face was now lit from underneath.

'Are you the afternoon shift, lover?' the man asked in Italian as he passed the chalice on to one of the other men. 'You look like a fresher keg than our boy up there.'

438

Byron opened his mouth to answer furiously, and he might even have shot the man – but then the figure on the cross opened its eyes and looked down at him, and Byron recognized him.

Crawford recognized Byron too.

Oh God, he thought, go away, I'm within days of getting it all over with, the long suicide is almost consummated, don't drag me back. I won't be dragged back.

He had been here for a month now, opening his veins for the thirsty neffers on a fairly exhausting schedule, and he had been remotely pleased at the way the process had seemed to be fragmenting his identity. Several times when some customer had drunk some of his blood he had seemed to *become* that customer, able to stand back with the taste of his own blood in his mouth and look up at his own crucified body. *Può vedere attraverso il sangue*, in fact – which was Italian for *You can see through the blood* – seemed to be some sort of motto of the place.

Perhaps Byron would leave. Crawford blurrily hoped so.

But Byron was shouting, and he had driven away the neffies who had the chalice, and now he was climbing up to untie Crawford's wrists from the horizontal beam.

The neffies began shuffling back toward the cross, but Byron, hanging on to the upright beam, drew his pistol with his free hand and pointed it at them, and they moved away again.

Crawford had been in this position for hours, and when Byron got the ropes loose he fell forward into his arms. Byron climbed back down supporting Crawford's weight, and lowered him gently to the stone floor.

'What the hell are you doing,' Crawford mumbled, 'leave me alone, I don't need rescue.'

'Maybe you don't,' panted Byron, 'but there's those

that do. Is that stuff in these glasses likely to be plain drink? Not blood or piss or something?'

'Brandy, mostly,' Crawford said, hoping that Byron might just have blundered his way in here looking for alcohol. 'Grappa, you know.'

Byron got up and snatched a glass off the table he'd taken the lamp from, and drank half of it in one gulp. Then he crouched and started to tilt the glass toward Crawford's lips, but stopped. 'My God,' Byron said, 'you *already* stink of brandy.'

Crawford shrugged weakly. 'Brandy in, blood out. It's a living.'

Byron spat in disgust. 'It's a dying,' he said, looking around to make sure the neffies kept their distance. 'Listen, you can come with me or stay here. Shelley's body is to be burned the day after tomorrow, and I think I know a way to use his ashes to get free of the nephelim net. I – '

'I'm already free of it,' Crawford said. 'You go ahead.'

'What about your girl, Julia or Josephine or whatever her name really is? Shelley's servants have come back to Pisa, and I know you saw her at the Casa Magni, and recognized what was wrong with her.'

'She's buttered her bread and now she can lie in it,' said Crawford. He reached up and took the cup from Byron and drained it. 'She knew what she was doing when she gave in. I stay here.'

Byron nodded. 'Fine. I'm not going to . . . *abduct* you, just escort you out of here if you decide you want to come. I'm only doing even this much because I . . . *do* remember what happened on the peak of the Wengern six years ago. You and your Josephine saved my life. If you don't come with me I'll do what I can to save her myself.'

'Fine.' Crawford struggled to his feet and stood swaying in the fetid breeze, massaging his numb, bleeding wrists. 'I hope you do better with her than I did. Do you suppose you could help me back up there, and retie me?'

Byron was angry. 'I'll be happy to, as soon as you know the stakes.'

'Goddamn it, I *know* the stakes. Josephine's going to die if she doesn't shed her vampire. Well guess what, she *likes* her situation. Everybody who's in it likes it. I liked it, while I had it. The people in this place would eat *poison* if they could experience it for half an hour.'

Byron looked at the men hovering nearby, and sneered. 'I think you overestimate their courage. They just like to sniff.'

'*You* haven't been all that eager to ditch it, have you?' Crawford added. 'Now that you're writing so well?'

A bitter smile hollowed Byron's face. 'Josephine isn't the entirety of the stakes.'

'Your sister and children are your concern. And as for Mary, and Williams' children, I've already — '

'That's not it either,' Byron said. 'Josephine's pregnant.'

For the first time since finding this place, this job, Crawford felt real panic building up in him. 'Not by me, she's not. I'm sterile.'

'Apparently you're not. Antonia, Shelley's old servant, is confident that Josephine missed her period last month and this month, and Josephine certainly wasn't — *cohabiting* — with anyone *else* in July.'

'Stress,' Crawford said quickly, 'can easily make a woman miss her periods, that's probably exactly what's — '

'Maybe,' interrupted Byron. 'But what if it *isn't* stress?'

Crawford's heart was pounding, and he tried to drink out of the glass again, but it was empty. 'This is a lie,' he said, in a voice that he made as steady as he could. 'You're just saying this to get me to leave here.'

Byron shook his head decisively. 'I'd never stop anyone from killing himself, as long as he truly knew what he was doing. And now you know what you'll be doing by staying or leaving. *I'm* leaving here in a moment. I only want to know if I'll have to carry you along too.'

Crawford blinked around at the catacombs. He was suddenly tired, and he let the weariness wash through him, dulling the momentary alertness Byron's appearance had provoked.

So what if she *is* pregnant, he thought blurrily. It was that Navy man that did it. Let *him* pull her out of the damned burning house, her and his unborn baby. I'll stay here at the Galatea where I can trade blood for polenta and rice and pasta – and brandy – lots of brandy.

'You go ahead, John,' he said, but when he looked more closely at his companion he saw that it wasn't Keats. Where had Keats gone? He'd been here a moment ago – they'd been drinking claret and Oloroso sherry.

'I'm Byron,' his companion said patiently. 'If you tell *me* to leave, I will.'

Why was the man being so troublesome? Of course Crawford wanted him to leave. Who was this Byron anyway? Crawford seemed to recall having met the man . . . in the Alps? That hardly seemed possible.

The thought of polenta reminded him that he hadn't eaten today, and he reached into his pocket for a piece of the fried corn mush he remembered having put there – but his pockets were full of other things.

He felt a crude iron nail, and it was wet with what he knew was his own blood, and for a moment he remembered having pushed the palm of his hand down onto the point of it on the terrace of Byron's villa in Geneva; and there was a glass vial in his pocket too, but he couldn't recall whether the liquid in it was the poison von Aargau wanted him to give to Josephine or was the dose of Shelley's blood, mixed with gall — no, with vinegar; then he found the piece of polenta, but when he took it out of his pocket it was an oatcake with a little raised image on it of two sisters who were physically joined at the hip. Josephine was supposed to have broken it at his wedding to her sister, so that he could have children.

He held it up in front of his eyes. It still wasn't broken.

And he knew that drunkenness wouldn't save him, wasn't strong enough to let him stay here and die. Tears of disappointment were coursing down his lean, bearded cheeks.

The disgruntled neffies had finished the chalice of his blood, and one of them brought the empty vessel back and set it down at the foot of the now vacant cross.

Crawford broke the oatcake into a dozen pieces and scattered it across the stone floor. 'You're the wedding guests,' he called gruffly to the slouched figures who were watching him and Byron. 'Pick up these pieces and eat them, you pitiful bastards, and the wedding ceremony will finally be finished.'

Byron was still watching him patiently. 'I'm Byron,' he repeated, 'and if you tell me to leave you here — '

'I know who you are,' Crawford said. 'Let's go. This is a good place to be out of.'

Crawford was hardly able to walk. Byron had to get in under Crawford's right arm and then shuffle forward, carrying most of his companion's weight as Crawford's feet clopped unhelpfully on the stones. As the lurching pair made their slow way up the sloping floor and got closer to the door, several of the patrons stepped in front of them, one of them mumbling something about it

443

being a shame to permit two such excellent wineskins to leave the place.

Byron let his snarl of effort curl up in a wolfish grin, and with his free right hand he drew his pistol again. 'Silver and wood,' he gasped in Italian, 'the ball in this is. You can die the way your idols do.'

The patrons backed away reluctantly, and a few moments later Byron and Crawford were scuffling out through the arched doorway. As Byron led him toward the wooden stairs, Crawford blinked over his shoulder.

'That's not the Thames,' he said wonderingly, 'and this bridge isn't London Bridge.'

'Not much gets past you, Aickman, that's certain,' Byron observed as he began dragging the two of them up the stairs.

Up on the pavement they paused to rest. Crawford squinted around at the torturingly bright street, and wondered where on earth he was. He peered down past his nose and was surprised to see that he had a beard, and that it was, though dirty, white.

'Not far now,' said Byron. 'I've got Tita waiting in a rented carriage around this corner. If I'm not back to him in a few minutes, in fact, he's been instructed to come after me.'

Crawford nodded, trying to hold on to his fragile alertness. 'How did you find me?' he asked.

'I got my servants to ask around about an Englishman, with a Carbonari mark on his hand, who might well be trying to kill himself. They quickly learned that you were in one of these dens, and then they kidnapped one of the local *nefandos* – that's what they call the neffies here, you know, it also means "unspeakable" – and they threatened to kill him if he wouldn't give us the location of this place.'

Byron shook his head contemptuously, 'The man broke down immediately, crying and babbling directions on how to get here. These *nefandos* are cowards. Even in their vice, they just want to skirt the unperilous outer edges, like a would-be rake who can't work up the nerve to do more than just peek in through bedroom windows. If they had any real ambition they'd go north to Porto-venere, where they might just actually *find* a vampire.'

Crawford nodded. 'That's true, I guess. They just want the dreams they get from their quartzes and bits of lightweight metal . . . and from the blood of the people who have been bitten. You can see through the blood.' He started forward, but again had to lean on Byron.

'And *I* wasn't even *infected* anymore. They said my blood was still worth a connoisseur's time, though – they said it was like a mild vinegar in which one could . . . still taste the grandeur of the fine wine it had once been.' He laughed weakly. 'They'd love yours. If you should ever fall into penury . . .'

'A job always open to me, right. Thanks.'

For several moments they limped on in silence, while Crawford kept reminding himself of what was going on. 'I'll *try* to go up into the Alps again,' he wheezed finally, 'for the sake of the child, but I'm afraid I'd die now long before reaching the peaks. I was . . . incalculably younger in 1816.'

'If my plan is sound we won't have to go any farther than Venice,' Byron said. 'I think I know a way to blind the Graiae.'

'Blind the . . . Graiae,' Crawford repeated, sadly abandoning his frail hope of being able to understand what was going on.

They shuffled around a corner, and Byron had taken off his hat and was waving it at the waiting carriage.

'You'll stay at my place in Pisa tonight,' Byron said as the carriage got under way, 'and then tomorrow we'll take this carriage to Viareggio, where we'll meet

445

Trelawny, who's sailing there aboard the *Bolivar*. He's built some kind of damned oven or something to burn the bodies in. We'll be bringing leaden boxes to hold the ashes.'

Crawford nodded. 'I'm glad they're going to be burned.'

'I am too,' Byron said. 'The damned Health Office has been dragging its feet on letting us have the permits – I think someone high up in the Austrian government *wants* vampires hatching out of the sand – but we've got the permits now, and mean to use them before they can be cancelled. I just hope it's not already too late.'

'Wait a moment,' said Crawford, 'Pisa? I can't go there – the *guardia* is looking for me.'

'Oh for Christ's sake, do you really imagine that you're *recognizable*? You must weigh all of ninety pounds right now. Hell, look at this!'

Byron reached out and took hold of a handful of Crawford's greasy white hair, and tugged. The clump of hair came away in his hand with almost no resistance. Byron tossed it out the open window and wiped his hand on a handkerchief and then threw the handkerchief out too. 'You look like a sick, starved, hundred-year-old ape.'

Crawford smiled, though his vision was brightly blurred with tears. 'I've always said that a man should have experienced something of life before embarking on fatherhood.'

Leigh Hunt's children also noticed Crawford's resemblance to an ape, and insisted that the lord's menagerie was extensive enough already without bringing in 'a mangy orang-outang,' but Byron cursed them away and got Crawford upstairs and into a bath, then went to fetch Trelawny.

Crawford scrubbed himself with some rose-scented

446

soap that might have belonged to Byron's mistress Teresa – though he was sure she wouldn't want it after this – and washed his hair with it too. When he lifted his head after dunking it in the water to rinse out the soap, most of his hair stayed in the tub, floating in curls like strands of boiled egg white; and when he got out of the tub and used one of Teresa's hairbrushes, he realized that he had gone bald during this past month.

A full-length mirror hung on one wall, and he stared in horror at his naked body. His knees and elbows were now the widest parts of his limbs, and his ribs stood out like the fingers of a fist under tight cloth, and there were sores on his wrists from the daily chafing of the cross-ropes. And he didn't think he would be fathering any more children.

For a few moments he wept, almost silently, for the man he had once been . . . and then bolstered himself with a sip of Teresa's cologne, pulled a robe around his wasted body, and tried to tell himself that if he could somehow save Josephine and their child he would qualify for manhood in a truer sense than he ever had before.

It was a brave resolve, but he looked at his pale, trembling hands and wondered how much he would be able to do; and he considered the fragmented state of his mind and wondered how long he would even be able to remember the resolve.

Byron returned with John Trelawny to discuss the details of tomorrow's pyre – Trelawny only gaped at Crawford twice, once when he first glimpsed him and once when he was told who Crawford was – but Crawford wasn't able to concentrate on what was being said; Trelawny was so burly and tanned and dark-bearded and clear-eyed and *healthy* that Crawford felt battered and scorched by the man's mere proximity.

Byron noticed his inattention, and led Crawford down

a hall to a guest bedroom. 'I'll send up a servant with some bread and broth,' he said as Crawford carefully sat down on the bed. 'I'm sure a doctor would insist that you stay in bed for a week, but this pyre tomorrow will be a sort of practice run for Shelley's on the following day, so I want you along.'

Byron started to turn away, then added, 'Oh, and I'll have the servant bring in a cup of brandy too – and feel free to ask for more whenever you like. It's no office of mine to restrict anyone's drinking, and I can't have word going around that my hospitality is such that my guests are driven to drinking cologne.'

Crawford felt his face heating up, and he didn't meet Byron's eye; but after Byron had left the room he relaxed gratefully back across the bed to await the food. He heard his bath water being dumped out of a window, and he hoped the plants wouldn't be poisoned.

He fell asleep, and dreamed that he was back up on the cross in the underground bar; someone had mistaken him for a wooden crucifix, and was getting ready to hammer an iron nail into his face, but Crawford's only fear was that the man would notice too soon that Crawford was alive, and not do it.

Chapter 20

The only portions that were not consumed were some fragments of bones, the jaw, and the skull; but what surprised us all was that the heart remained entire. In snatching this relic from the fiery furnace, my hand was severely burnt; and had any one seen me do the act I should have been put into quarantine.

> — Edward John Trelawny,
> *Records of Shelley, Byron, and the Author*, 1878

Lady Macbeth: Here's the smell of the blood still: all the perfumes of Arabia will not sweeten this little hand. Oh, oh, oh!
Doctor of Physic: What a sigh is there! The heart is sorely charged.
Waiting-Gentlewoman: I would not have such a heart in my bosom for the dignity of the whole body.

> — Shakespeare, *Macbeth*

The Serchio river at the end of summer was low and narrow between its banks, and the glittering waves that swept in from the Ligurean Sea and crashed along this uninhabited stretch of the Tuscany coast went foaming quite a distance up the river mouth, apparently unopposed by any current. The onshore breeze hissed faintly in the branches of the aromatic pine trees that furred the slopes of the hills.

The *Bolivar* was moored fifty yards out from shore, near a sloop that flew the Austrian flag, and Byron's carriage stood on the dirt road above the beach.

On the sand slope a hut had been built of pine tree

trunks woven with pine branches and roofed with reeds, and Crawford and Byron and Leigh Hunt were sitting in its shade, drinking cool wine while several uniformed men stood around the little structure. Crawford was sweating profusely, and he wondered which of the officers had had the unpleasant duty of living in the hut for the past month, guarding the graves of Williams and des Loges.

'Trelawny is upset,' Byron said. 'He'd *like* to have done this at *dawn* – with a Viking ship for the pyre, I don't doubt. He's a pagan at heart.' Byron had been nervously irritable all morning.

Trelawny stood a few hundred yards away, his arms crossed, watching the men from the Health Office digging in the soft sand. His custom-made oven, a sort of high-sided, four-legged iron table, sat over a lavish pile of pine logs a few yards past him.

Trelawny had told Byron that he wanted the cremation to take place at ten o'clock – but Byron had slept late, and his carriage had not come rolling up to the road above the shore until noon.

Crawford took one more sip of wine, then shrugged. 'It's a pagan business,' he said. The ride had tired him, and he wished he could sleep. He tugged the brim of his straw hat down farther over his eyes.

Hunt looked at him in puzzlement and seemed about to ask a question, but Byron swore and stood up – the men had evidently found a body, for one of them had climbed up out of the sandy hole and picked up a boathook.

'*Somebody* is still here, at least,' Byron muttered, starting to limp forward.

Crawford and Hunt stood up and plodded after Byron through the thick hot sand to the hole. Crawford made himself keep up with Hunt, but in order not to faint he had to clench his fists and stare at the ground and take

450

deep breaths. The bandages around his ankles were wet – the blood draining incisions the *nefandos* had given him had started bleeding again.

Oddly, there was no noticeable odour of putrefaction on the pine-scented sea breeze.

The health officer had dragged a blackened, limbless body out on to the sand. A woven chain of garlic still adhered to the body, and several purpled silver coins tumbled off onto the sand. The Health Office didn't cheat, Crawford thought dizzily.

Byron was squinting, and his mouth was pinched. 'Is that a human body?' he asked, his voice scratchy. 'It's more like the carcass of a sheep. This is . . . a satire.'

Trelawny reached down and gingerly pulled a black silk handkerchief free of the remains of the jacket; he laid it out on the sand near one of the silver coins and pointed at the letters *E.E.W.* stitched into the fabric.

Byron shook his head in disgusted wonder. 'The excrement of worms holds together better than the potter's clay of which we're made.' He sighed. 'Let me look at his teeth.'

Both Trelawny and Hunt turned puzzled glances on Byron.

'I, uh, can recognize anyone I've talked to by their teeth,' he said. Glancing at Crawford, he added, 'The teeth reveal what the tongue and eyes might try to conceal.'

Trelawny muttered some quick Italian to the officer, who shrugged and, with the handle of the shovel, turned the head.

Crawford looked down at the shapeless, lipless face, and nodded. Williams's canine teeth were perceptibly longer than they had been when he'd been alive. The garlic and silver slowed him down, Crawford thought, but the Health Office really should have thought of some plausible, hygienic-sounding reason to put a wooden stake through the chest.

The officer had leaned into the hole again, and this time hooked up a leg with a boot on the end of it. Trelawny stepped forward – he had brought one of Williams's boots for comparison, and when he held it up to the one on the dead foot, they were obviously the same size.

'Oh, it's him, sure enough,' said Byron. 'Let's get this on to your oven, shall we?'

The officers were careful, but as they lifted the body, the neck gave way and the head fell off and thudded into the sand. One of the officers hurriedly stepped forward with a shovel, and, in a grotesque attempt at reverence that made Crawford think of someone coaxing some hesitant animal into a trap, gingerly worked the blade of the shovel under the head, and picked it up. The head grimaced eyelessly at the ocean, rocking slightly as the officer walked.

Byron was pale. 'Don't repeat this with me,' he said. 'Let my carcass rot where it falls.'

Several of the officers had continued digging in the sand; they had found another body now, and wanted to know whether it should be carried to the oven too.

'No no,' said Byron, 'it's just that poor sailor boy, I doubt that he has any family to – '

Crawford took Byron's arm, both to steady himself and to get the lord's attention. 'Add him to the pyre,' Crawford whispered. 'I think you'll recognize him by his teeth, too.'

'Oh.' Byron swore. '*Si, metti anche lui nella fornache!*' Hunt and Trelawny were staring at him, and he added, 'Shelley thought well enough of – whatever his name was – to hire him, didn't he? I'm taking over Shelley's debts, and I choose to regard this as one of them.'

Hunt and Byron and Trelawny walked onward to

452

stand around the open-topped oven on which their dead and sundered friend lay, but Crawford reeled away through the hot air to where the other body was being dug up.

The officers had got the head and an arm out, and Crawford saw here too the garlic and the silver coins. He stared down at des Loges's fleshless smile, noting the lengthened canine teeth, and he managed to smile back at the grisly thing, and tip his straw hat.

Goodbye at last, François, he thought. Thanks again for helping with my passport six years ago. I wonder if that clerk is still around – Brizeau? Some name like that – and if he'll finally manage to get your wife now.

The health officers laid des Loges's remains in a blanket, and Crawford limped along beside them as they carried the burden to where everyone else waited.

At last both bodies were laid side by side in the bed of the oven, and Trelawny crouched and held a burning glass over a particularly dry cluster of pine needles. The concentrated sunlight glowed blindingly white, and then resinous smoke was billowing up. Quickly the fire was burning so furiously that Hunt and Trelawny and the officers all stepped back, and the beach and the sea seemed to ripple through the nearly transparent flames.

Crawford forced himself to stand firm for one second longer, holding his hat onto his head against the blast of hot air that would have whirled it away, and through streaming eyes he watched the heat taking the ruined bodies; and when he finally had to spin away and stagger into the relative coolness of the sea breeze, he noticed that Byron too had hung back to look.

The two of them glanced at each other for a moment, and then looked away, Crawford toward the sea and Byron toward his carriage; and Crawford knew that Byron too had seen the pieces of the bodies moving, weakly, like embryos in prematurely broken eggs.

Hunt had fetched a wooden box from the carriage, and after the first intense heat had given way to a steadier fire, Trelawny opened the box, and then he and Hunt leaned in toward the fire to throw frankincense and salt onto the now inert bodies, and Trelawny managed to get close enough to pour a bottle of wine and a bottle of oil over them. Everyone retreated back to the hut then, for the very sand around the furnace was becoming too hot to walk on, even in boots.

Earlier in the morning Trelawny had curtly turned down the offer of a drink, but now he seized the wine bottle and drank deeply right from the neck of it. He leaned against one of the poles of the hut, but it started to give, so he sat down beside Hunt. Byron was standing just outside the hut, next to where the exhausted Crawford sat.

'A cooked salad,' Crawford heard Byron mutter. Then, louder, Byron said, 'Let's try the strength of these waters that drowned our friends! How far out do you think they were when their boat sank?'

Trelawny stared up at him in exasperation, the shadows of the woven branches striping his bearded face. 'You'd better not try, unless you want to be put into the oven yourself – you're not in condition.'

Byron ignored him and began unbuttoning his shirt, walking away down the sand slope toward the sea.

'Damn the man,' muttered Trelawny, handing the bottle to Hunt and getting to his feet.

Crawford watched the two of them stride to the surf, throwing off garments as they went, and then dive into the waves. He and Hunt passed the bottle back and forth as the heads and arms of the two swimmers receded out across the sea's glittering face. Crawford absently brushed blood-caked sand off the bandages on his ankles.

After a few minutes one of the swimmers seemed to

be having some difficulty — the other had paddled over to him, and now they had both turned around and were labouring back.

Hunt had stood up. 'I think it was Byron that ran into trouble,' said Hunt nervously.

Crawford just nodded, knowing that most of Hunt's concern for Byron's welfare was based on Byron's promised support of the magazine that was supposed to save Hunt from penury.

At last the two swimmers had reached the shallows, and were able to stand up. It had indeed been Byron who had broken down — Trelawny had practically towed him in, and Byron now angrily threw off his supporting arm.

Byron retrieved his scattered clothing, and put it all back on before walking back up to the hut. 'It was an excess of black bile,' he muttered when he had got back into the shade.

Crawford recalled that in the medieval system of medicine black bile was supposed to be the humour that caused pessimism and melancholy. I imagine, he thought, that we're all suffering an excess of it today.

Trelawny had stumped up to the hut now, and though he watched Byron solicitously, the lord avoided meeting his glance. 'I hope you paid attention here today,' Byron said, perhaps to Crawford. 'Tomorrow we do Shelley.'

Crawford stared toward the still raging pyre, and in spite of the day's heat he had to clench his jaw to keep his teeth from chattering.

Trelawny sailed off in the *Bolivar* and spent the night at an inn in Viareggio, while the others returned to Pisa in Byron's carriage. The next day they all met again at a section of beach fifteen miles farther north; and again Byron had made them late. No hut had been built here, and Byron and Crawford and Hunt waited in Byron's carriage.

The sky was as cloud free as yesterday's had been, and seemed all of a piece with the sea, so that the two islands on the southern horizon seemed to float in space.

Byron caught Crawford's eye and nodded toward the islands. 'Gorgona and Elba,' he said. 'To which do you suppose our Perseus has flown? To the Gorgon, or to the isle of exile?'

Hunt rolled his eyes and exhaled loudly.

Trelawny had arrived early in the morning and set up his oven, and now that Byron's carriage was here he told the officers that they could begin digging.

For more than an hour, though, the men dug in the soft sand with no result – aside from unearthing an old pair of trousers which didn't seem to have belonged to anyone who'd been on the *Don Juan*. The officers impatiently threw the sand-caked garment aside, but Crawford leaned out the carriage window to stare at the trousers, wondering if they might have been the pair he'd shucked off two months earlier, in the Gulf of Spezia, just before swimming to rescue the suicidal Josephine.

For a moment he regretted having gone to save her, but then he remembered that she now seemed to be pregnant by him – had possibly become pregnant that very day.

When he finally relaxed back into his seat Byron glanced nervously at him, and Crawford knew what he feared – that the delay had been too long, and that Shelley's body had undergone the stony resurrection and climbed up out of its grave.

'It begins to look like Gorgona,' Byron said.

Crawford shrugged, then sketchily made the sign of the cross. He was weak and trembling, and at the moment hoped they wouldn't find Shelley's body, for then he wouldn't have to get out of the carriage and walk around.

But a few minutes later one of the probing shovels thudded against something, and after the officers had crouched to brush away sand they called to the Englishmen.

'Elba after all, it seems,' said Crawford stoically, putting on his straw hat.

Byron sighed and unlatched the carriage door. 'Not too late,' he agreed, climbing down to the sand-swept pavement. His greying hair shone as he stepped out of the shadow of the carriage into the hot sun.

'"Not too late"?' echoed Hunt irritably as he followed Byron out. 'Did you suppose that he would have decomposed entirely in this time?'

'On the contrary,' Byron said, and started out across the dry grass of the road shoulder toward the sand.

Hunt turned to Crawford, who had now climbed down beside him. 'What does his *lordship* mean by *that*, do you suppose?' Hunt asked.

'He probably meant "on the contrary,"' Crawford told him.

They followed Byron to where Trelawny stood beside the hole in the sand, and then for several moments they were all silent, staring down at Shelley.

The exposed bones had turned a dark blue, and the once white clothing was now all black. Unlike yesterday's exhumations, the smell of rot here was overpowering, and the health officers tied handkerchiefs over their faces before freeing the thing from the hole. At least it held together, and when it was laid out on the sand Crawford noticed that the incisor teeth showed no signs of having grown during the month in the earth.

Crawford looked up at Byron. 'Not even a glance toward Gorgona,' he said softly. Clearly Shelley had died

457

entirely when his lamia sister had expired on the beach below the Casa Magni.

Byron swore hoarsely and turned away, and angrily wiped his sleeve across his eyes.

Trelawny crouched beside the corpse and gingerly prised from the jacket pocket the copy of Keats's poems, but it now consisted only of the leather binding, and he sadly laid it back on the dark ribcage.

The body was then shifted onto a blanket, and the four Englishmen walked beside it like pallbearers as the Italians carried it to the oven and gently laid it into the blackened bed. The rotted leather binding still lay on the body's chest – like, thought Crawford, a Bible clasped in the hands of a dead pope lying in state.

Again Trelawny set fire to the pile of pine logs under the iron table, and again the flames sprang up in a withering rush – but though Byron and Crawford once more braved the shocking heat for several seconds to watch, Shelley's body sizzled on the iron bed but didn't move at all. The two men stepped back from the heat and stood away from Hunt and the others.

Though still high, the flames were steadying, and an aura of gold and purple shone around them. Byron glanced at Crawford, who nodded.

'The thing that attacked us in the Alps glowed with those colours,' Crawford said quietly, 'just before it petrified.'

'So did the rainbow over the . . . dramatically *petrified* Alps. I wonder if human royalty adopted these colours in a spirit of . . . hanging up the dried head of your slain enemy – though in the cases of these things the dried head can often still bite.'

'Bite's the word,' Crawford agreed.

Byron mopped his sweating face with a handkerchief. 'There'll be something here,' he muttered to Crawford.

458

'These days you understand at least as much as I do about this business – watch for it.'

Crawford looked back to the black figure reclining in the heart of the flames. 'What – what sort of thing?'

Byron shook his head. 'I'm not sure. That's why I needed you to be here, to help me. It'll be . . . whatever so drew the attention of the Graiae to Shelley, in Venice four years ago – and drew the attention of some kind of wild lamia on Lake Leman, two years before that.'

Seeing Crawford's baffled look, he added, 'Whatever made him different from people – different from *everybody*, even people like you and I.'

'Ah.' Crawford nodded. 'Right, he was a member of the family – and by *birth*, by *blood*, rather than just by marriage, as I was.' He remembered Shelley's complaints about bladder stones and the stiffening of his skin and the hardness of his fingernails. 'He was mostly human, but part . . . nephelim, part stone.'

'His bones, then, perhaps,' said Byron hoarsely. He raised his hand uncertainly, almost as if in farewell or apology to Shelley, then looked over to where Trelawny stood, sweat and tears running down the tanned face into the black beard. 'Trelawny!' Byron called. 'I'd like his skull, if it can be salvaged!'

Trelawny hadn't caught his words, and made him repeat them – and then visibly comprehended them, and stared at Byron wrathfully. 'Why?' Trelawny demanded. 'So that you can make another drinking cup?'

Byron's voice was level when he answered. 'No,' he said, limping toward the others, 'I will treat it as . . . as Shelley would have wanted.'

Crawford followed Byron across the sand as Trelawny reluctantly picked up a long-handled boathook and approached the fire. The bearded giant leaned toward the blazing oven and reached in with the hook toward

Shelley's head, but at the first touch of the iron the skull fell to pieces, throwing burning bits of flesh spinning up into the sky. Trelawny reeled back, tossing the hook aside and rubbing singed hair off his forearm.

Crawford caught Byron's eye and shook his head slightly. It's not the skull, he thought.

The flames billowed in a breeze from the sea, and Crawford turned away to cool his sweating face. In the last few minutes he had become intensely aware of the charring figure on the iron bed behind him – not as a human figure, much less as something evocative of the man it had been, but as a kink in the fabric of the world, something that violated natural laws, like a stone impossibly hovering in midair. It was as if the heat had crystallized something, quantified something that had only been implicit before.

He looked back at the body, trying to determine the source of the impression, but the body looked like nothing more than dead flesh and bone in a fire.

Crawford looked toward Byron, curious to see if he showed any signs of feeling a wrongness about Shelley's body, but for the moment Byron seemed to have forgotten that Shelley had not been entirely human – he was just clenching and unclenching his fists as he stared at the pyre of his friend.

Hunt had walked up with the wooden box he'd brought to Williams's pyre the day before, and now he and Trelawny opened it and began throwing frankincense and salt onto the fire, intensifying the yellow-gold glow of the flames. Trelawny again plodded up close to the oven, this time to pour wine and oil over Shelley's body.

'We restore to nature through fire,' intoned Trelawny, 'the elements of which this man was composed: earth, air, and water. Everything is changed, but not annihilated; he is now a portion of that which he worshipped.'

460

For a while no one spoke, and the roaring of the fire was the only sound under the empty sky; at last Byron forced a frail smile. 'I knew you were a pagan,' he said to Trelawny, 'but not that you were a pagan *priest*.' Tears glistened in Byron's eyes, and his voice was unsteady as he added, 'You do it . . . very well.'

Hunt walked back through the hot sand to the carriage, and Trelawny walked around to the other side of the fire. Byron, clearly embarrassed at having shown emotion, was blinking around as if someone had said something he chose to interpret as an insult. Crawford was watching the burning body.

'I think it's the heart,' he said.

'What is?' asked Byron belligerently. 'Oh.' He took a deep breath and expelled it and rubbed his eyes. 'Very well – why?'

Crawford nodded toward the fire. 'It's turned black but it's not burning – though the ribs have collapsed around it.' And only when I stare at *it*, he thought, do I get that feeling of cosmic wrongness.

Byron followed his gaze, and after a few moments he nodded. 'You might be right.' He was breathing hard. 'Damn all this. We need to talk – I need to tell you about this thing he and I tried to do in Venice, unsuccessfully, and how I think it *can* be done *successfully*.' Byron looked up and down the shore, then down at the sand under his boots. 'We can't talk here – let's go out to the *Bolivar*. I'll swim, and you can go in the boat. I'll get Tita to go with you and work the oars.'

Crawford looked at the sand too, and remembered that when Shelley had first talked to him about the lamia, on that summer night six years ago in Switzerland, he had insisted that they talk in a boat out on the lake; and before Shelley had told Josephine and Crawford about his plan to run the *Don Juan* into a storm and drown, he had told them to walk a few yards out into the surf first – and he even told Josephine to leave her glass eye on the sand.

So Crawford just nodded, and followed the limping figure of Byron down across the white sand toward the waves.

Tita wordlessly rowed Crawford out toward the *Bolivar* as Byron and one of his Genoese boatmen swam alongside, a few yards out from the boat's starboard gunwale. Crawford assumed Tita and the Italian sailor were keeping track of their master's progress, but Crawford did too, remembering that Byron had had trouble while swimming yesterday.

But Byron was swimming strongly today, his muscular arms metronomically knifing ahead of him to pull him forward through the glassy water – though Crawford noticed that his shoulders were red with sunburn. He should call for a shirt when he gets to the *Bolivar*, he thought.

The three bare masts of the *Bolivar* grew taller and clearer and farther apart with each powerful pull on the oars, and soon Crawford could recognize the men on her deck. He waved to them, but though they waved back they clearly didn't recognize him as the man who had helped them search the shoreline for signs of the *Don Juan* a month earlier.

He looked back at the shore. The smoke was a tower in the nearly windless sky, and the men standing around on the distant beach looked like the dazed survivors of some disaster.

The *Bolivar* was close enough now to blot out a third of the sky. At a call from Byron, Tita pushed strongly on the oars, and a few moments later the boat had stopped and was rocking in the water under the arch of the *Bolivar*'s hull.

The rope boarding-ladder hung to the water from the

rail above, but Byron stayed a yard or so out away from it, treading water. He looked sceptically up at Crawford. 'Can you handle the oars well enough to keep the boat from bumping the hull? Or drifting away?'

Crawford flexed his bony shoulders. 'I have no idea.'

'Oh hell, in a pinch I can swim over and give the boat a push or a tug. Tita, up on deck with you — and lower us a cold bottle of *sciacchetra* and a couple of glasses.'

The sailor had come paddling and gasping up to the ladder, and after catching his breath he pulled himself up the rungs to the rail, followed closely by Tita, who had paused to manoeuvre the boat in to within a yard of the hull.

The creaking of the timbers and the slap of low waves against the hull were the only sounds now, and in spite of his broad-brimmed hat Crawford felt the hot sun as a weight on his head.

Through the clear water he could see Byron's legs kicking at a relaxed pace, and there was no sign of strain when he raised one hand to carefully push his wet hair back away from his forehead.

Byron looked up at him. 'Trelawny or Hunt might want the heart,' he said quietly. 'Or Mary — she might already have asked for it.'

Crawford nodded. 'People get sentimental about such things. Hunt tells me that Jane Williams already has Ed's ashes in an urn on the mantel of the house in Pisa.'

Byron spat. 'She'll forget and make tea in it one of these days.' He tilted his head back to peer toward shore. 'Well, they can have the bones or something — we've got to make sure we get the heart.'

A basket was being lowered on a rope, and Crawford leaned out and caught it and took from it a bottle and two napkin-wrapped wine glasses. The cork had been pulled out of the bottle and stuck loosely back in, but it took all of Crawford's strength to tug it out again, and his hands were shaking as he poured the wine into one of the glasses and held it out over the gunwale to Byron.

'Thank you,' Byron said, taking a sip and then effortlessly holding the glass steady above the water as his legs continued to pump below the surface. 'You seem to be a moderately educated man, Aickman – have you heard of the Graiae?'

'Graiae as in the Greek myth?' asked Crawford. 'They were the three sisters Perseus consulted, before going to kill the Medusa.' He carefully filled his own glass and tasted the wine. 'They had only one eye among them – didn't they? – and they had to keep handing it back and forth.'

Byron confirmed this, and then went on to describe the attempt he and Shelley had made to awaken the blind Graiae pillars in Venice in 1818. The narration took several minutes, and twice during it Byron paddled closer to the boat and held out his glass for a refill.

Crawford had finished the wine in his own glass, and was debating the wisdom of pouring himself some more. He decided not to – he was already dizzy, and this story would clearly require all of his concentration. 'So – what is it we want the heart *for*?'

'I think *it's* what drew the attention of the Graiae to him. The fresh blood that was splashed all over the pavement acted as a sort of jury-rigged eye for them, and – goddamn me, Aickman – when Shelley was wavering at a point about the same distance from each of the columns, that blood just *raced* across the paving stones from one column to the other, and back! You could *feel* the attention they were paying to him, like . . . like the pressure on your ears when you're under water.'

He held up his glass, and Crawford leaned over the gunwale to refill it again.

'And then when we were fleeing in a gondola,' Byron went on, 'the third sister – the pillar they'd dropped in the canal centuries ago – came rearing up out of the water as we passed. I think if we hadn't very quickly got out of their . . . *field of influence*, the blood would have sprayed horizontally out over the water to that pillar. They wanted to stare at him as closely as they could, and so they were throwing their eye back and forth, to whichever of them was closest to him.'

'What's so . . . astonishing . . . to them, about his heart?'

'I can only guess, Aickman. Since it's half human and half nephelim – '

'Carbonari and siliconari,' commented Crawford.

Byron blinked. 'If you like. In any case, since it's a mix that probably isn't logically possible, I think it's a violation of the determinism that the Graiae project with their eye, and so the eye can't leave it alone. I don't think such a creature as Shelley could have been conceived in the field of the eye . . . though I'll bet such a creature couldn't be easily killed in the field, either. The eye prevents randomness, the vagaries of chance. As I told Shelley then, it not only checks on things, it checks them.'

Crawford opened his mouth to speak, but Byron was already talking again. His upthrust hand was still steady, though the moisture beading his face now was clearly sweat.

'The reason the Austrians brought the eye to the pillars,' Byron was saying, 'was that they were also bringing some enormously old Austrian king or something there too, so that with specific treatment he can live forever in the deterministic focus of the wakeful, sighted Graiae,' Byron raised his sunburned shoulders above the water in a shrug. 'Maybe this king is a half-and-half too, like Shelley.'

Crawford's stomach had gone cold, though the sun on him was as hot as ever. 'Yes,' he said. 'He is. But unlike

Shelley, who was born that way, this king was . . . surgically made into one.'

For the first time that day, Byron really looked squarely at Crawford. 'You know of him?'

'I – ' Crawford laughed uneasily. 'I used to *work* for him. Werner von Aargau, he's called these days. You and I saw him – or his vehicle, at least – when we were going through the Alps. Do you remember a wagon that was bogged down in mud? You jumped up into the bed of it to oversee the job of freeing it, and you said there was a box in it full of ice. I'm pretty sure our Austrian was in that, in the box.'

'Huh. Well, he's no concern of ours. The thing is, when the Graiae are awake but *without* their eye, then everything is *very* randomized, *supremely* uncertain. And this priest I got to know there said that if you were in the focus of them while they were blind, you could shed the attention of a vampire. The vampire can't track you in the . . . the spiritual darkness, the chaos of unresolved probabilities. The creature can't hold its beam of attention on you. Of course you'd have to cross a lot of salt water directly afterwards so that the vampire wouldn't eventually be drawn back to you.'

'America, you once told me.'

'Or Greece. Now I think Greece would be good enough.'

'But even if your vampire *did* find you again, it'd need a fresh invitation, wouldn't it?'

The corners of Byron's mouth turned downward in a bitter smile. 'Yes – but even though you never gave in and asked yours back, as your wife and I both did eventually, I'm sure you'll agree that it's a . . . powerful temptation. I'm sure there were moments of loneliness and fear, in which even you *just about* gave in.'

Crawford lifted his eyes and looked past Byron, up the coast to the point where the shoreline seemed to dissolve in the wavering heat-mirages, and he nodded. 'So,' he said after a moment, 'we go to Lerici, catch Josephine and tie her up, and take her to Venice, and then use Shelley's heart to draw the eye out of whichever of these sisters has got it, and catch it.' He grinned and looked down at his pale, trembling hands. 'And then run like hell.'

'That's it.' Byron's face was shining with sweat, and the hand in which he was holding his glass had at last begun to tremble. 'Here,' he said, thrusting the glass at Crawford, who managed to take it without dropping it and the bottle into the sea.

Byron ducked under the surface, and when his head bobbed back up into the air he even seemed to have swallowed some of the seawater.

'Are you all right?' Crawford asked.

Byron nodded and tossed his head back. He was using his arms too to tread water now, and didn't ask Crawford to return the glass. 'I'm fine,' Byron said shortly. 'I seem to – lately I seem to *think* better if I'm surrounded by salt water; and even better if I'm actually *immersed* in it.'

'I think it insulates you from the nephelim influence,' Crawford told him. 'The only times I really wanted to escape the nephelim net, when I was infected, were moments when I was under water. You recall Noah didn't escape by climbing a mountain.' He stared at Byron, who was panting now. 'You're doing a lot of swimming lately, it seems. Are your Carbonari precautions beginning to falter?'

'Don't – ' Byron began angrily; then he shook his head. 'I guess you do have the right to ask.' He swam to the boat and flung his elbow over the gunwale and let his arms and legs relax. The boat tilted with his weight, and Crawford had to grab the bottle to keep it from falling over.

'Yes,' Byron said, 'the precautions don't seem to be a

permanent solution. Hell, I'm like a drunk who keeps telling himself that there *is some way* to have his gin and have a normal life too. I thought I could hold – whatever you want to call it, Lord Grey de Ruthyn, Margarita Cogni – *it* – at bay; so that I could still write, but at the same time that I would be free to go out in the sun, and that Teresa and my remaining children would be safe. But lately I've been getting weaker during the day, and less able to concentrate. I don't think I've been entirely without a fever for months. I want to do this, this *exorcism*, while I still have the strength – both of mind and body.'

Crawford thought of the strength of his own mind and body. 'Will we be bringing Tita along with us, or Trelawny?'

'No.' Byron brought his other arm to the gunwale and laboriously hoisted himself up into the boat. His shoulders were even redder now than they had been when Crawford noticed them earlier, and had begun to blister. 'No, Tita won't touch that kind of work since that night in Venice when the pillar rose up out of the water, and I know that Trelawny wouldn't believe us if we told him what his revered Shelley really was.'

Byron took hold of the oars and, weakly, manoeuvred the boat back close to the boarding ladder so that Tita could climb down and row them to shore. 'It'll just be you and me – and Josephine.'

'God help us,' said Crawford softly.

'If there is one.' Byron grinned. 'A whole lot of ghastly things have turned out to be possible, remember.'

By four o'clock the fire had burned down enough so that they could approach the oven without being scorched. The rib cage and pelvis had collapsed into broken, charcoal-like chunks, but the heart was still whole, though blackened. The sight of it made Crawford dizzy again, and he sat down in the hot sand.

Byron took a deep breath. 'Tre,' he said, 'could you get the heart for me?'

Trelawny shook his head firmly. 'I tried to get the skull for you. Hunt has asked for the heart.'

Byron glanced worriedly down at Crawford. 'That's absurd,' he told Trelawny, 'I knew Shelley longer than either of you! You're both guests in my home! I demand that – '

He paused and stared at Hunt and Trelawny. Crawford could guess what the lord was thinking: Trelawny wouldn't budge, and Hunt might, out of injured pride, actually move out of the Casa Lanfrachi, taking the heart with him; and if Byron made a scene about wanting the thing, Hunt might very well ship it to his home in London at the first opportunity.

'Sorry,' Byron said. 'It's just been a trying day. Of course you can have it, Leigh – I'll make do with a bit of bone.'

Hunt had brought a little box to carry away relics in, and now he held it open while Trelawny leaned over the blackly littered oven and snatched out the heart. He whistled in pain, but juggled the thing toward Hunt, who managed to catch it in his box and slam down the lid as if the heart might try to escape.

Hunt glanced at Byron nervously, but the lord was smiling – though Crawford noticed that his jaw muscles were tightly flexed, Byron took out a handkerchief and with it picked out a segment of a rib. 'This will do for me,' he said in a neutral voice.

The ashes and remaining bone fragments were scraped into the little lead and oak coffin Byron had bought, and then the health officers helped Trelawny slide poles under the oven and carry it down to the surf. Steam billowed up when they lowered it into the water, and

Crawford thought the sudden hiss sounded like the sea reacting in pain.

An hour later Trelawny and Byron and Hunt and Crawford were having dinner in Viareggio. Byron puzzled Hunt by asking the innkeeper if they could drink their wine from amethyst glasses – plain glass ones turned out to be all that was available, but the four of them got drunk on the house's harsh red wine anyway, and on the drive back south to Pisa in Byron's Napoleonic coach they sang and laughed hysterically.

Crawford recognized their mirth as a reaction to the horror of the day; but in his own laughter, and Byron's, he heard too an edge of fear, and as the shadows of the roadside trees lengthened across their route he couldn't help throwing frequent glances at Hunt's little relic box on the seat beside Trelawny.

Chapter 21

And bats with baby faces in the violet light
Whistled, and beat their wings
And crawled head downward down a blackened wall
And upside down in air were towers
Tolling reminiscent bells, that kept the hours
And voices singing out of empty cisterns and exhausted wells.

— T. S. Eliot, *The Waste Land*

The next day was a Saturday, and Crawford did little besides eat and sleep.

He was awakened early Sunday morning by birds twittering and hopping around in the branches of the tree outside his window, and for at least an hour he just lay in the bed, enjoying the softness of the mattress and the warm weight of the blankets.

Eventually the door swung inward quietly, and Byron's servant Giuseppe peered in at him; seeing that Crawford was awake, the man left and returned shortly with a bowl of bean soup. Crawford ate it happily and had lain back in the bed, vaguely wishing he'd asked the servant to fetch him some books . . . when it occurred to him that Josephine must only recently have gone to sleep. He hoped she was still staying at the Casa Magni, and not sleeping out among the trees somewhere.

He looked at the scraped-clean soup bowl on the bedside table and wondered what she was eating these days. She *should* be eating liver and raisins, he thought, just to restore the blood she's certainly losing every night; and she should be eating for two now. I wonder if she even knows that she's probably pregnant.

'Damn,' he whispered wearily, and swung his narrowed legs out from under the blankets. He was wearing a long nightshirt, and he pulled it down over the depressing spectacle of his white, bony knees. A moment later he took a deep breath and stood up, swaying and dizzy at the sudden altitude, and then shuffled to the door.

Giuseppe came in just as he was reaching for the knob, and the door hit Crawford in the shoulder; he lost his balance and sat down hard on the rug.

The servant shook his head impatiently and bent down and, with humiliating ease, wrapped his hands around Crawford's upper arms and hauled him back up to a standing position.

The man pointed over Crawford's shoulder at the bed.

It took an effort of will for Crawford not to rub his bruised arms. 'Very well,' he said, 'but tell Byron when he wakes up that I have to talk to him.'

'He is awake now,' Giuseppe said, 'but too sick to speak to anyone. He will see you when he wants to. Now get back in bed.'

Crawford wondered why the man seemed to dislike him. Perhaps he'd heard how Crawford had spent the last month, and disapproved of *nefandos*; or perhaps it was just that the Hunt children had got all the servants in a bad mood.

Crawford obediently went back and sat down on the bed, but when the servant had left, he once again struggled to his feet.

There was no one in the hall, and he padded down the cold stone floor to Byron's room and knocked on the heavy door.

'Come in, Seppy,' Byron called, and Crawford opened the door.

472

Like most inner rooms of Italian houses Crawford had seen, Byron's bedchamber was dark and cheerless. The bed in which the lord lay was an immense black canopied structure with, Crawford noticed, the Byron coat of arms painted on the foot of it.

'What the hell are you doing here?' asked Byron irritably, sitting up.

'I hear you're sick.'

'I doubt that you came to ask about my health.' He lay back on the tasselled pillows. 'Yes, I'm sick. I think he resents it when I spend so long in the sea. She's jealous of the time spent out of her control, and so hits me with the fever *redoubled*, as punishment.'

Crawford knew that both pronouns referred to the same creature. 'Let's start soon,' he said, taking the liberty of sitting down in an ornate chair near the bed. 'Hunt may ship the damned heart to England any day, and you're not getting any stronger.'

'Don't be *importuning* me, Aickman – I'm doing this for your damned wife – '

'And yourself and your remaining children.'

' – And don't interrupt me, either! I can't possibly travel in this condition! And you're a ruin yourself, look at you! We daren't risk attempting this until we've . . . done everything we possibly can to make our success likely.'

A writing board and sheets of manuscript lay on the bed by Byron's hand, and Crawford's eyes had adjusted to the dimness of the room enough for him to see that the sheets were scribbled with six-line stanzas. It was probably more of *Don Juan*, the apparently endless poem Byron had started writing in Venice in 1818.

Byron had followed the direction of his gaze, and now opened his mouth angrily – but Crawford waved him to silence.

473

'Did I say anything?' Crawford asked. 'I didn't say a word.'

Byron seemed to relax a little. 'Right. Well, if you want to be so active, why don't you go steal the heart? Hunt's got it on a shelf downstairs.'

'Out of reach of his children, I really do hope.'

Byron blinked. 'Not if they were to fetch a chair, now that you mention it – if there still is an unbroken chair down there. Yes, I think it would be a good idea if you went and did it right now.'

Byron clearly wasn't going to offer to accompany him, so Crawford left the room and tottered to the stairs and started down.

Byron's bulldog sat on the landing, but merely lifted its head to squint at Crawford as he shuffled nervously past. Crawford recalled Byron having told the dog not to 'let any damned Cockneys' up into his apartments. He smiled now as he descended the last of the stairs. On your way back, he told himself, be sure to say *Hello, doggie* in your most cultured accent.

Once in the main hall, he shuffled quickly to the arch that led to the room the Hunts were using as their parlour. The room was empty, though the scribbling on the walls reminded him that the children might appear at any moment.

The box was on the mantel, and he crossed to it and took it down. The top wasn't locked – impulsively he opened it and stared down at the charred lump inside it.

Again he got that feeling of a profound contradiction in terms. It nauseated him, and he closed the box.

He walked back out to the hall, but had taken only two steps toward the stairs when he heard someone fumbling at the heavy front door behind him; he quickly side-stepped through a narrower arch on his right, and found himself in a wide, stone-flagged room dimly lit by sunlight through a couple of small hexagonal windows.

The air was warmer here, and heavy with the smells of garlic and cured ham. The old woman who was Byron's cook glanced up at him disapprovingly from her seat by the fire, but just shook her head and returned her attention to the pot of broth she was stirring.

Crawford could hear the cheery scream and clatter of the Hunt children in the main hall. Were their parents following? Leigh Hunt would certainly notice the absence of the box, and might well begin shouting about it before Crawford could get safely back upstairs.

Several sheets of butcher paper lay on a wooden counter by his right elbow, along with some chickens in various stages of dismemberment, and on a sudden inspiration Crawford spread out one of the sheets of paper, opened the box, and rudely dumped Shelley's heart out onto it; then he snatched up a big, wattled rooster head and dropped it into the box. He closed the lid and hefted the box – noting with anxious satisfaction that its weight was roughly the same as it had been when it had contained the heart – and then wrapped the paper tightly around the heart and picked it up in his other hand.

The sight of Shelley's split and blackened heart had made him think of his own, which was pounding so hard in his rib cage that his head was bobbing in time to it. God knew what the Hunts and the servants would make of his burdens if he were to pitch over dead right now. Even Byron would wonder what had possessed him.

He couldn't hear the children – apparently they had run right through the house and out the back door. Panting, Crawford limped once more across the hall and through the arch into the Hunts' parlour.

He slapped the box back up onto the mantel and forced himself to actually run back toward the arch.

He made it into the hall, but the effort had cost him.

His vision was dimming and he had to sit down on the stone floor with his knees drawn up, clutching the paper-wrapped heart tightly to be sure his numbed, trembling hands wouldn't drop it. His ankles had started bleeding again, and his heels kept slipping.

'What have you got?'

Crawford looked up. One of the Hunt boys, apparently about seven years old, was standing over him. The child slapped Crawford's clasped hands. 'What have you got?' he repeated. 'Something from the kitchen, I can tell.'

'Scraps,' Crawford gasped. 'For the dog.'

'I'll take 'em to him. I want to make friends with him.'

'No. Lord Byron wants *me* to bring them to him.'

'My mom says you're a nasty man. You surely do *look* nasty.' The boy stared speculatively at Crawford. 'You're a weak old thing, aren't you? I'll bet I could *take* the scraps from you.'

'Don't be silly,' said Crawford, in what he hoped was an intimidatingly adult tone. He tried to straighten his legs and stand up, but his heels slipped in his blood again and he wound up just thumping the floor with his withered buttocks. The dizziness and nausea that the heart induced in him were very strong.

The boy giggled. 'I'll bet you were taking scraps for yourself, so you could chew 'em up raw in your room,' he said. 'Lord Byron never said you could have 'em, did he? You're a thief. I'm gonna take that bag away from you.' The boy was excited and breathless – clearly the idea of having a grown-up whom he could torment with impunity was a heady one.

Crawford opened his mouth and started to shout for help, but the boy began singing loudly to cover Crawford's noise, and at the same time he reached out and slapped Crawford hard across his white-bearded cheek.

To his own horror, Crawford could feel tears seeping out at the corners of his eyes. There wasn't time for this.

If the heart were discovered, Hunt would lock it up securely and ship it straight back to London — and what if the boy brought it to the dog and the dog actually *ate* it?

He tried again to stand up, but the boy pushed him roughly back down.

Crawford was close to panic. The lives of Josephine and his unborn child — their lives as humans, at least — depended on his escaping from this little boy, and he wasn't confident that he'd be able to do it.

He started to yell again, and again the boy began singing — '*O say, thou best and brightest, my first love and my last*' — and slapped him backhanded on the other side of his face. The boy was panting now, but with pleasure instead of exertion.

Crawford took a deep breath and let it out, and then he spoke, very quietly. 'Let me take it and go,' he said evenly, 'or I'll hurt you.' Over his sickness he tried to concentrate on what he was saying.

'You couldn't hurt me. I could hurt you, if I wanted to.'

'I'll . . .' Crawford thought of Josephine, whom he was so ludicrously failing to save. 'I'll bite you.'

'You couldn't bite a noodle in half.'

Crawford stared hard at the boy, and slowly smiled, keeping his eyes wide open to magnify the wrinkles over his cheekbones. He held up his left hand and waved the stump of his wedding-ring finger at him. 'See that? I bit that off, once when I was bored. I'll bite *your* finger off.'

The boy looked uneasy, but angrier too, and when he drew his hand back again it was clear that he meant to hit Crawford a good deal harder this time. Crawford thought this blow might, in his weakened state, knock him unconscious.

'Like this,' he said quickly, and thrust his own little finger into his mouth. He tasted bean soup on it, and the thought that he might also be tasting Shelley's heart very nearly made him vomit.

The boy's hand was still drawn back for the blow, but he had paused, staring.

Crawford bit down on his finger. He couldn't really feel any pain, so he bit harder, wanting some blood to scare the boy with. The hard pounding of his heart seemed to make coherent thought impossible.

The Hunt boy didn't seem to be impressed; he brought his hand farther back and squinted at Crawford's face.

A vast bitterness almost made Crawford close his eyes, but he kept them locked on young Hunt's; and even as he wondered if there might have been any other way out of this, he expressed all of his despair by clenching his jaw on the last finger-joint with every particle of strength he had left. Cartilage crunched between his teeth, and the horror of that seemed only to give him more strength.

Crawford's hand flew away from his mouth, spraying blood across the floor.

The last joint of his little finger was still in his mouth, severed. He spat it out hard, bouncing it off the boy's nose.

Then the boy was gone, screaming hysterically as he ran through ever more distant rooms, and Crawford rolled over on to his hands and knees and crawled away toward the stairs, dragging the paper bundle with him and leaving a trail of blood smeared across the stone floor.

Giuseppe found him on the stairs and carried him to his room.

Byron visited him shortly after Giuseppe had tied a bandage around his fresh finger-stump. The lord looked pale and shaken.

'That's . . .' said Crawford weakly, 'the heart, there. On the table.'

'What the hell did you do?' asked Byron in a quiet but shrill voice. 'Hunt's brat is saying that you bit off your finger! Is that what happened?'

'Yes.'

'Did you have a fit? The boy says you – *spat* the finger at him! Everyone's shouting downstairs. Moreto got down there and seems to have *eaten* your finger. God-damn it, why do I get involved with such horrible people? I've got Hunt and his sow and litter underfoot, because of this impossible project of his magazine, but that wasn't enough for me, was it? I had to get into an even more impossible project, with a man who bites his fingers off and his wife, who pulls out her eyes!'

Crawford's shoulders were shaking, and he honestly couldn't have said whether he was laughing or crying. 'Who's,' he choked, 'Moreto?'

Byron stared at him. 'Who the hell do you *think* Moreto is?' He was frowning, but the corners of his mouth were beginning to twitch. 'One of the servants? Moreto's my *dog*.'

'Oh.' Crawford was definitely laughing. 'I thought it might be that old woman in the kitchen.'

Byron was laughing too now, though he still seemed to be angry. 'Just because you're driven to drink cologne doesn't mean I starve my help.' He leaned against the wall. 'So how *did* you come to bite off your own finger? A seizure of some sort, I assume.' He stared at Crawford. 'I mean, it *was* an accident, right?'

Crawford was still shaking. He shook his head.

'Jesus. Then . . . *why*?'

Crawford wiped his eyes with his maimed hand. 'Well, it – it really seemed, at the time, to be the only way to keep him from feeding Shelley's *heart* to the dog.'

Byron shook his head wonderingly. 'That's . . . crazy.

I'm sorry. That you could imagine such a thing is plenty of evidence that you're not ready for this undertaking of ours. Good God, you could have . . . yelled for help, couldn't you? The cook was right there. Or just *walked away* from the boy, surely? Or hit him? I just don't see – '

Now Crawford was crying. 'You *didn't* see. You weren't there.'

Byron nodded, and seemed to be working not to let pity – or it could have been disgust – show in his face. He crossed to the bedside table and picked up the paper-wrapped bundle. 'I'd better hide this. Hunt will probably notice its loss soon.' He hefted the heart. 'Even if he just picks up the box, he'll realize it's light.'

'No,' Crawford choked. 'The box weighs the same.'

'The box,' Byron said carefully, 'weighs the same. What did you put in it?'

'A – oh, God – a rooster head. From the kitchen.'

Byron was nodding gently, and didn't seem to be about to stop. 'A rooster head. A *rooster* head.'

Still nodding, Byron left the room, closing the door softly.

Crawford and Byron both developed high fevers, and during the ensuing week Byron's sun-burned skin peeled off in great patches, and he took delight in making jokes about snakes shedding their skins.

Crawford, tormented by his own helplessness and his impatience to find and save Josephine and his unborn child, didn't find the jokes funny.

For quite a while he could work up no enthusiasm about food or any activity, but forced himself to eat three meals a day, and to exercise – at first simply lifting the iron lamp on his bedside table a few times was enough to set him sweating and trembling, but by the end of the second week of his convalescence he had improved enough to ask Giuseppe to fetch him a couple of bricks, and he soon got to the point where he could lift them from below his waist to above his head fifty times in a row.

Shortly after that he began going downstairs and outside to the narrow kitchen garden to do his exercises, for there was a stout overhead beam there, on which various trellises were anchored, that proved to be sturdy enough for him to do chin-ups on. Byron's cook visibly disapproved of his presence in her garden until one day when he helped her pick and carry several bags-full of basil leaves; after that she stopped frowning at him, and once or twice even smiled and said *Buon-giorno*.

Byron seemed to recover more quickly. Crawford saw him frequently at dinner, but these days Byron was always accompanied by a vapidly gossipy friend called Thomas Medwin, one of the old Pisan English circle, and, on the two occasions when Crawford had tried to hint to the lord that he'd like to discuss their proposed journey, Byron had frowned and changed the subject.

And when Medwin finally left, on the twenty-eighth of August, Crawford found himself unable to talk to Byron at all. The lord spent all his time locked in his room reading, or lounging with Teresa Guiccioli in the main garden, and when Crawford had one day presumed to interrupt the two lovers, Byron had angrily told him that any further intrusions would result in his abandoning their plans altogether.

Byron slept late into the afternoons, apparently spending the entirety of the nights drinking and feverishly scribbling more stanzas of *Don Juan*. He never went out in the *Bolivar* anymore, and had apparently given up riding.

When Crawford felt well enough to go outside, he took to walking up the Lung'Arno and crossing the bridge over the Arno's mud-yellowed water – on which

Shelley had so loved to sail – and knocking at the door of the Tre Palazzi, where Mary Shelley was once again staying. He hoped to get her to intercede for him with Byron, but she was still too distracted by Shelley's drowning, and angered by Leigh Hunt's refusal to let her have Shelley's heart, to pay much attention to him.

Crawford thought he knew why Hunt was so adamant. One recent evening, after a long dinner-table conversation about Percy Shelley, Hunt had retired downstairs to his own rooms – and had then been heard to yell in alarm. Byron had sent a servant down to find out what the matter was, and Hunt had assured the man that he had simply stubbed his toe . . . but a few minutes later the entire household was made helplessly aware that Hunt had, for once, abandoned his often-boasted conviction that children should never be beaten.

Crawford often wondered now, half fearfully and half amused, whether Hunt had believed his children's no doubt passionate denials of any knowledge as to how a rooster head had got into the box that was supposed to contain Shelley's heart.

On the eleventh of September, Mary moved out of the Tre Palazzi, bound for Genoa. It occurred to Crawford later that Mary might in fact have been speaking well of him to Byron while she'd been in Pisa, for on the day after her departure Byron summoned Crawford to the Palazzo Lanfranchi's main garden, in which the lord and his mistress Teresa sat over a leisurely lunch under the spreading orange tree branches, and told Crawford curtly that the house was shortly to be closed down and vacated, and that Crawford would have to leave.

Crawford decided to give Byron a few days to cool off and then to just confront him somewhere, now that there seemed to be nothing to lose – at least there were currently no houseguests.

But four mornings later Crawford awoke to discover that Byron's old friend John Cam Hobhouse had arrived for a week's visit. Crawford remembered Hobhouse from the trip they'd taken through the Alps six years before – Hobhouse had been a fellow student of Byron's at Trinity College, and was now a politician, worldly and sophisticated and witty, and Crawford despaired of ever getting Byron's undivided attention.

After doing his exercises – he could now do twenty chin-ups in a row – Crawford spent the day walking around Pisa, noting places he'd been to with Josephine and savagely wishing that the two of them had got married when they had first arrived in the city, and that they had never renewed contact with the damned poets. Back at Byron's house, he drank brandy in his room for a couple of hours, then went downstairs and ate polenta and minestrone in the kitchen. Feeling sleepy at last, he went back out into the hall.

He paused outside the kitchen arch. In the dim illumination of a couple of lamps in niches in the walls, the Palazzo Lanfranchi's main hall looked like a disorganized warehouse these days — crates of books and statuary and dishes were stacked everywhere, and a dozen ornate swords and rifles stood like umbrellas in a barrel by the door. The usual sour milk and stale food smell of the children was overwhelmed by the musty exhalations of old leather.

Crawford sidled between the crates to the barrel, and he had lifted out an old sabre and drawn it from its scabbard and was sighting along the blade when footsteps sounded on the pavement outside and the door was ponderously opened.

Hobhouse stepped in, glimpsed Crawford and ducked right back out with a smothered yell. A moment later

Byron sprang in with a pistol in his hand, but relaxed, frowning, when he saw Crawford.

'It's just St Michael,' he called out through the open door, 'looking for the serpent.'

Crawford hastily sheathed the sword and poked it back into the barrel as Hobhouse re-entered.

'You might not recognize this old boy,' Byron said to Hobhouse, 'but he was my personal physician during that trip we took through the Alps in '16.'

Hobhouse stared at Crawford. 'Yes, I do remember,' he said quietly. 'You fired him for talking about living stones. St Michael, eh?' To Crawford he said, 'I'm glad you're here.'

Both Byron and Crawford looked at him in surprise.

'You . . . said something about brandy,' Hobhouse remarked to Byron.

The lord nodded. 'Upstairs,' he said, pointing the way with the pistol he still carried. He noticed it and set it down on one of the crates.

'No, bring it along,' said Hobhouse, 'and your physician too.'

Byron was still frowning, but smiling now too. 'He's no longer my — '

Hobhouse was already making his way through the angling corridor between the crates. 'Whatever he is,' he called back over his shoulder, 'bring him along.'

Byron shrugged and waved toward the stairs. 'After you, doctor.'

The paintings had been taken down from the walls of Byron's dining room, and faint white squares on the plaster marked where they had been. Hobhouse closed the windows while Byron poured brandy.

Hobhouse sat down and took a sip. 'I talked to your half sister Augusta recently,' he said to Byron. 'She showed me some stones you sent her, that summer

484

when we toured the Alps. Little crystals, from Mont Blanc. And she showed me some of your letters.'

'I was drunk that whole summer,' Byron protested, 'those letters are probably just – '

'Tell me about your involvement with this Carbonari crowd.'

'I – ' Byron cocked an eyebrow at his old friend. 'I could tell you I'm helping them overthrow their new Austrian masters, couldn't I?'

'Of course you could. But I was there when you met Margarita Cogni, remember?' Hobhouse turned to Crawford. 'It was in Venice in the summer of 1818; we were out riding one evening, and met two peasant girls, and Byron set about impressing one, and I the other.'

He looked back to Byron. 'When I got mine alone,' Hobhouse went on, 'it developed that she wanted to *bite* me. And she led me to believe that the Cogni woman had the same interests. I've always had to save you from . . . inappropriate women, and you recall I tried to talk you into ridding yourself of her too. But at the *time* I thought I was simply trying to rescue you from a mistress with perverted tastes.'

Byron looked shaken. 'Christ, man, I'm glad you didn't let her bite you.' He sighed and took a long sip of the brandy. 'The Carbonari *are* trying to drive out the Austrians, you know – and I *do* think that's a good cause.'

He held up his hand to stop Hobhouse from saying more. '*But*,' Byron went on, 'you're right, there's more to my association with them than just that. In the eyes of the Carbonari, the species of which Margarita was a member is much more specifically the enemy than is the literal category of *Austrians*. The Carbonari have methods of keeping such creatures at bay, and I've been making use of those methods. You'll have noticed that Teresa is

485

entirely human, and unharmed – and so are Augusta and her child, and my ex-wife and her child.'

'"At bay,"' said Hobhouse. 'Is there a way to *free* yourself and your dependants from her – from her species entirely?'

'Yes,' said Crawford.

Hobhouse looked at him, then back at Byron. 'And do you intend to *do* it?'

'Just out of curiosity,' said Byron stiffly, 'do you know what *doing* it will mean? The most . . . *trivial* consequence is that I'll dry up, poetically.' Crawford noted with admiration that Byron did seem to be honestly trying to regard it as trivial. 'I will have written my last line.'

Hobhouse leaned forward, and Crawford was surprised at how stern the man's round, mild face could look. 'And your children won't become vampires.'

'They probably wouldn't anyway,' said Byron irritably. 'But yes, Aickman and I are going to do the trick shortly. And then I'll be going to Greece, where I shall no doubt encounter *another* consequence before very long.'

Hobhouse glanced at Crawford, who shrugged slightly. Don't look at me, Crawford thought, *I* can't tell his sincerity from his posturing.

'You almost sound,' said Hobhouse carefully, 'as if you believe that freeing yourself from this thing, from these things, will cause your death.'

Byron emptied his brandy glass and refilled it. His hand was shaking, and the decanter lip rattled on the edge of his glass. 'I do believe that,' he said defiantly.

Crawford shook his head in puzzlement. 'But people live *longer*, free from these creatures. You've been able to avoid the worst of the emaciation and anaemia and fevers that their victims usually suffer, but it's cost you a lot of effort, and even so hasn't been entirely effective.

Free of your vampire, you'd be *really* healthy, and with no necessity for your Carbonari measures.'

'You certainly haven't lost your doctory tone, Aickman,' Byron said. 'Hell, I'm sure what you say is true in most cases, but . . .'

After a moment's silence Crawford lifted a hand inquiringly.

Byron sighed. 'In my case, the creature has preserved me. I know I wouldn't have lived as long as I have without its . . . its watching over me. Even though I insulted Lord Grey after he had come into my bedroom at Newstead Abbey when I was fifteen, and though I abandoned Margarita Cogni for Teresa, the thing . . .' He smiled. 'It loved me, and loves me still.'

Crawford caught Hobhouse's eye, and shook his head slightly. Their regard for us, he thought, is *why* they're so destructive of us.

'And you,' said Hobhouse softly, 'love *it* still.'

Byron shrugged. 'I could love any creature that appeared to wish it.'

Hobhouse shifted uncomfortably in his chair. 'But you . . . *will* do it, right, this . . . exorcism?'

'Yes, I said I would and I will.'

'Is there any way I can help?'

'No,' said Byron, 'it's – '

'Yes,' interrupted Crawford.

Both men looked at him, Byron a little warily.

To Hobhouse, Crawford said, 'Make him promise you – promise *you*, his oldest friend, schoolmate at Trinity and all that – that he won't publish any more poetry. That would eliminate one of the strongest attractions the nephelim hold for him.' He turned to Byron. 'In spite of your manner of seeming to despise poetry, I think it's a huge part of how you, I don't know, *define* yourself. As long as it's still available out there, I can't imagine you really wanting to abandon your vampire.'

Byron had been sputtering while Crawford spoke, and now burst out, 'That's ludicrous, Aickman, for a dozen reasons! For one thing, would you trust me to keep my promise?'

'A promise you made to Hobhouse – yes. Even more than your poetry, I think your honour is central to your definition of yourself.'

Byron seemed to flinch. 'Well, what would there be to stop me from writing just *for* myself, for no audience but me and the monkeys? Or publishing under a pseudonym?'

'On the one hand it wouldn't be read by the world, and on the other it wouldn't be perceived as being Byron. For you, there'd be no *point* in it.'

Byron was looking hunted. 'So you figure that this will eliminate any hesitancies I may have – that since I would have abdicated the poetry *anyway*, I'd have no reason not to do this.'

'Right.'

Byron looked up at Crawford with hatred. 'I'll . . . do it.' He raised his eyebrows sarcastically. 'I presume it would be acceptable if I publish the stuff I've *already* written? There's quite a bit of it.'

'Sure,' said Crawford. 'Over the next few years you can . . . bleed it out.'

Byron barked one harsh syllable of laughter, then turned to Hobhouse. 'I promise,' he said.

Hobhouse reached across the table and squeezed his old friend's hand. 'Thank you,' he said.

Chapter 22

Quaff while thou canst: another race,
  When thou and thine, like me, are sped,
May rescue thee from Earth's embrace,
  And rhyme and revel with the dead.

> — Lord Byron, 'Lines Inscribed upon a
>   Cup Formed from a Skull'

Hobhouse left six days later.

The Casa Lanfranchi by this time was in chaos. The Hunts were staying at a nearby inn until Byron should have got all his belongings packed for the trip to Genoa, but Byron's dogs and monkeys had been moved into a couple of emptied rooms in the house while their cages and kennels were disassembled and packed, and the animals made up for the racket of the vacated Hunt children. Byron occasionally pretended to have forgotten that the children had left, and interpreted the barking and chattering as idiot demands and complaints in Cockney voices.

Byron was drinking wine all day and gin all night, and he alternated from moment to moment between giddy cheer and resentful gloom. He told Crawford that on the same day that he had rescued Crawford from the *nefando* den he had made arrangements to see a notary and get his will drawn up, but that Teresa had become so upset at the very idea of his ever dying that he had had to cancel the appointment. She had made him promise to forget the idea, and Byron liked to imply that he was sure to die in this upcoming enterprise, and that it would be Crawford's fault that Teresa would get none of his money.

At last, on the twenty-seventh of September, Byron was ready to leave. Most of his servants and possessions were being shipped north aboard a felucca out of Livorno, while he and Teresa and Crawford would travel by land in the Napoleonic coach; the animals had been noisily confined in temporary cages and packed into and on top of two carriages that would accompany their master's.

Shelley's heart was in an under-seat cabinet in Byron's carriage, still wrapped in butcher paper.

Byron was irritable at having had to get up early, and he curtly ordered Crawford to ride up on the bench with the coachman. Teresa was accompanying them only as far as Lerici, and would complete the journey to Genoa with Trelawny, and Byron told Crawford that he wanted as much time alone with her as he might have left.

The three carriages got under way at ten, but it took half an hour for them to move a hundred yards down the Lung'Arno: the horses of other carriages were panicked by the screeching of the monkeys and parrots, and children and dogs crowded up around the wheels, and women in second and third floor windows leaned out to throw flowers and handkerchiefs. Crawford took off his hat and waved it at them all cheerfully.

The festival mood dissipated when they turned north on a broader street – mounted Austrian soldiers rode ahead and behind, emphasizing the government's approval of Byron's departure, and Crawford could see, off to his left, the buildings of the University, where he and Josephine had worked together so peacefully for a year.

The famous Leaning Tower was tilted away from them, making it seem that they were travelling downhill.

* * *

490

Byron insisted on stopping a number of times through-out the day's drive, to eat, and drink, and reassure the animals, and walk around in the roadside grass with Teresa. Crawford hid his impatience, and didn't even look northward if Byron was watching him, for he was sure that the lord would interpret the intensity of his gaze as a protest against the delays, and out of spite insist on even more of them.

It was dusk when the three carriages finally turned west on a seaward road, crossed the bridge over the Vara River and rolled into Lerici. The carriage the Hunts had travelled in was empty behind the inn, and the *Bolivar* rode at anchor in the little harbour, but when Crawford and Byron and Teresa got out and went into the hotel, they learned that Hunt and Trelawny had set out to walk south along the coast to the Casa Magni. Crawford and Byron went back outside.

'They'll be composing sonnets to Shelley,' Byron said as he watched his coachman unstrapping the luggage from the top of his carriage. A chilly wind blew in from off the sea, and he shivered and buttoned up his jacket, though his face shone with sweat in the light from the inn's windows. 'No point in going down there ourselves.'

Crawford looked south longingly. 'Shouldn't we . . . reconnoitre? Josephine is down there somewhere . . .'

Byron coughed. 'Tomorrow, Aickman. If she sees you sooner, she might simply flee, mightn't she? Inland to Carrara, drawn by the marble they make all the statues out of, or across the gulf to Portovenere. If you can't – '
He began coughing again, then swore and pushed open the inn's door.

Crawford followed him back inside. 'Are you . . . well?' he asked nervously.

'No, I'm not *well*, doctor – do I *look* well?' Byron took a flask from his pocket, unscrewed the cap with trembling fingers, and took a long sip. The fumes of Dutch gin roused nausea in Crawford. 'I'm vulnerable here,' Byron went on. 'My Carbonari measures are getting less effective *anyway*, but in this cursed gulf they're tenuous indeed.' He looked toward the stairs. 'I was mad to have brought Teresa here at all.'

'Do you think,' began Crawford; then he considered how he'd been about to finish the question – *that you'll be able to go with Josephine and me?* – and he stopped, not wanting to let Byron think the issue might be in doubt. 'Do you think you should get some sleep then?'

'Brilliant prescription. Yes.' Byron screwed the cap back onto the flask and pocketed it. 'Don't get me up early tomorrow.'

Byron limped away toward the stairs, shivering visibly, and as Crawford watched him recede he wondered if Byron *would* be able to go, or, if so, would be able to survive the trip to Venice and the exertions they'd be in for there.

For that matter, he thought, will *any* of us survive it?

Not wanting to meet Hunt and Trelawny when they returned, Crawford went upstairs to his own room.

His room was narrow and windowless, and the bed's mattress seemed to be blankets wrapped around dried bushes, but he fell asleep as soon as he lay down, and dreamed all night that Josephine had already died, and been buried; and, a cold, silver-eyed vampire now, had clawed her way back up to the air and was giving solitary birth beside the erupted grave. Toward dawn the baby's scalp began to be visible between the inhuman mother's thighs, and Crawford forced himself to awaken rather than see its face.

The skin around his eyes was stiff with dried tears, and he washed his face in the basin before getting dressed and going downstairs. He ignored the cornmeal smell of hot polenta wafting from the kitchen and walked to the inn's front door, trying to suppress his limp.

The air outside seemed even colder than it had last night. Fog hung over the grey slate roofs – for a moment he didn't know in which direction the sea lay, and he was surprised to find himself a little frightened by the uncertainty.

Get used to it, he told himself. Soon enough you'll be crossing the Apennines, and dozens of miles distant from the sea in any direction.

He walked downhill through the narrow streets, shivering whenever a drop of cold dew would fall from one of the iron balconies overhead and strike his bald scalp, and in a few minutes he had left the buildings behind and reached the drab beach; Portovenere was invisible beyond the fog, and the *Bolivar* was a dim, vertical brush-stroke of slightly darker grey far out on the leadenly shifting sea.

He began walking south along the dark, surf-firmed sand, still trying to suppress his limp, and he tried to assess his capabilities, mental and physical.

He had lost the inhuman pallor the *nefando* den had given him, and he really thought he was stronger now than he had been in many years; still, he felt fragile, and he hoped no great exertions would be required of him. His left hand wouldn't be much good for holding a knife or a pistol, with its maimed little finger and absent ring finger, but his right hand was still good. And, since trimming his white beard and remaining hair, he no longer drew wondering stares from strangers.

And he was fairly confident that he would be able to maintain his resolve, for he'd been firmly decided for six weeks now – without any of the passion and drama that accompanied Byron's decisions – that he would do everything he could to free Josephine and his child from

493

the nephelim infection, even if the effort should involve his own death.

The fog was beginning to glow – perceptibly brighter to his left, where the unseen sun was rising over the eastern mountains. He turned and began walking back toward the inn.

The fog had burned off and the sky was a hot, empty blue by the time Byron arose at noon, and Crawford had to find his hat in order to be able to accompany the lord and Trelawny down the hill again to the shore. The sand was hot underfoot.

Byron was sweating and trembling, but after walking up to the surf and letting it swirl around his ankles he suddenly insisted that he would swim out to the *Bolivar* and have lunch alongside, treading water.

Trelawny was unable to talk him out of it, and so once again the two of them stripped and waded into the surf, Byron looking desperate and Trelawny impatient, leaving Crawford to watch their clothing.

Crawford sat down in the hot sand and watched the two heads recede beyond the low waves.

He soon lost sight of them against the distant wedge that was the dark hull of the *Bolivar*, but after a while, squinting against the glitter of the sun on the water, he could see bundles being lowered from the ship's deck, and he knew the swimmers had arrived and were about to start their lunch.

Crawford got to his feet and plodded up the sand toward where the early-morning fishing boats rested upside down against the crumbled edge of the street pavement, faintly shaded by their spread, drying nets. Up on the pavement he turned and looked back at the *Bolivar*. He still couldn't make out the heads of Byron and Trelawny.

The thought of food wasn't at all attractive, but he

knew he should eat something. An old woman was selling tiny fried squids out of a wheeled cart nearby, and he walked over, allowing himself to limp, and bought a plateful. They were redolent with garlic and green olive oil, and at the first bite his hunger awoke; he ate the squids as fast as he could cram them into his mouth, and then bought another plate and ate them at a more leisurely pace, standing by the old woman's cart and glancing occasionally at the piles of clothing and out at the *Bolivar*.

At last he could see white arms flashing in the sea between the shore and the ship, and he handed the empty plate back to the woman, hopped down off the pavement into the soft, hot sand, and began limping back toward where the swimmers' clothes lay on the shore.

And he began to run down toward the surf, though there was nothing he could do, when he saw the figure that was Trelawny begin swimming rapidly toward the other.

The two heads were stopped out there; almost certainly Trelawny was arguing that Byron should let him help him, and Byron was – no doubt angrily – refusing.

'Let him help you, damn it,' Crawford whispered, knuckling sweat from his eyes.

Trelawny didn't get any closer to Byron, but after a few moments Crawford could see that the two men were swimming back to the *Bolivar*.

Fine, he thought. Now come ashore in the ship's boat. This is no time to be airing your damned *pride*, Byron.

He didn't see any figures climbing the ladder, and no boat was being lowered; and, a few minutes later, he once again saw the swimmers working their way shoreward through the low waves.

'You *idiots*,' Crawford said softly.

It took five minutes for Trelawny and Byron to swim

495

in to the point where they could stand, and Crawford met them there, the surf swirling around his waist.

'What the hell do you think you're doing?' Crawford demanded furiously. 'What right have you got to risk your life – unnecessarily! – when so many people are depending on you?'

Byron had waded in a few yards farther and was leaning forward, his hands on his knees under water, apparently devoting all his attention to filling and emptying his lungs.

Trelawny had backed away a couple of steps, so that the incoming swells twitched at the spiky ends of his black beard. 'You might go get our clothes,' he told Crawford.

Crawford hesitated a moment, then nodded and turned and began wading back to the beach. Luckily no one had stolen the clothes.

Trelawny and Byron dressed in the water. Trelawny started forward toward the wavering surf line, then paused and looked back when he realized Byron and Crawford weren't following.

'You go ahead, Tre,' panted Byron. 'We'll meet you at the inn. Have a bottle of something cold waiting for us, there's a good lad.'

Trelawny's bushy eyebrows went up. 'Aren't you at least going to get out of the water?'

'Soon enough,' Byron told him.

Trelawny shrugged and splashed ashore.

Byron turned to Crawford. 'I'm doing this – ' he began. Then, 'God, you reek,' he said. 'What have you been eating?'

'Squids. You should eat something, too – we might need our strength tonight.' He smacked his lips. 'And the garlic can't hurt.'

'I already eat God's own amount of the damned stuff. Garlic, not squid.' A knee-high wave slapped at them,

496

and Byron stumbled but caught himself. 'It's not without defence value, but . . .' He was squinting in the bright sunlight, and his shoulders were already red.

After a pause while another, smaller wave foamed around their knees, Crawford said, 'But . . . ?'

Byron visibly regained his train of thought. 'Damn you, Aickman, do you suppose I *like* wringing my body out on these swims? Do you imagine I'd do it if eating some . . . goddamned garlicky *squids* would insulate me sufficiently to let me save your strayed wife? Do you . . . do you imagine that I'm *showing off*?'

Crawford could feel his face heating up. 'Actually,' he said, 'I guess I did. I'm sorry.'

'I've got nothing to prove when it comes to swimming. I swam the damned *Hellespont*, from Sestos to Abydos.'

Ten or twelve years ago, thought Crawford. But aloud he said, 'I know.'

'*I'll* be ready tonight,' Byron said resentfully, limping away through the shallow water toward the sand. 'Just see to it that *you* are.'

At dusk Byron and Crawford left the inn and walked slowly and without speaking down the Lerici streets, past windows and doorways that were already beginning to glow yellow with lamplight under the purpling sky, to the lowest, farthest-seaward edge of pavement. Byron gave Crawford an ironic look, and made the sign of the cross before stepping carefully down from the masonry into the sand.

Crawford smiled tightly and followed him, and they plodded side by side down the shoreline. Each of them carried in his pockets a jar full of minced garlic and a pistol loaded with a wood and silver ball, and Crawford kept having to hitch up his pants because of the weight of the coil of rope twined to his belt; the slip-knotted loop thumped his thigh, separate from the coil, at each

497

step. Byron was swinging an unlit torch as if it were a walking stick.

The wind was cold from Portovenere across the gulf, and Crawford shivered and tucked his chin into his coat collar, wishing his scarf hadn't been packed up in the luggage he and Byron would be taking with them later tonight.

After a few minutes of walking, they heard the rattle and jingle of a carriage going by on the road over the beach. Byron nodded. 'Tre's right on time,' he said quietly.

With my scarf, thought Crawford. 'I hope he's done what you said, about bringing a spare horse to ride back to Lerici on.'

'So do I,' said Byron. 'He's far too chivalrous about women – and ignorant of the nephelim – to condone a forcible kidnapping.'

They trudged on as the sky darkened, and soon they heard the repeated triple-thudding of a horse riding back, northward toward Lerici.

'He did what I said,' observed Byron. 'Our carriage awaits us above the Casa Magni.' He began coughing, pressing his face into the collar of his jacket to muffle the noise, and Crawford hoped his fever wasn't as bad as it seemed to be. 'Teresa is very upset,' Byron whispered when he had recovered, 'at having to go on to Genoa without me.'

Crawford knew this was an appeal for sympathy, but he was too aware of Josephine, somewhere ahead, to spare concern for Byron or Teresa. 'If *she* ever gets pregnant, she'll be glad of this.'

He thought Byron might get angry at his callousness, but after a long, plodding silence Byron just said, 'You're right.'

Soon Crawford caught Byron's arm, and pointed ahead. Faintly against the nearly black sky, above the silhouettes of the pines, stood the rectangular bulk of the Casa Magni.

There was no faintest light in any of its windows.

'Do you think she's still here?' asked Byron when they had walked around to the sand-gritty pavement between the house and the sea. He had wedged the torch into a crack in the rocks, and had fished a tinder box from his pocket and was striking showers of dazzling sparks from the flint.

'Yes.' Crawford spoke with certainty.

The sparks had ignited a frail flame in the lint in the box, and Byron quickly unwedged the torch and held the splintery, frayed end of it over the light; in a moment the resinous wood was flaring, lighting in its orange glow the startled-looking arches and windows of the house, and he closed the tinder box and tucked it back into his pocket.

'Call her, then,' said Byron, holding the torch up so that the trees were visible on the hill behind the house and shadows crawled and darted among the trunks.

'Josephine,' said Crawford loudly. His voice disappeared in the vast night like wine spilled on sand. '*Josephine!*' he shouted. '*I need you!*'

For several moments the only sounds were the continuing rustle of the wind in the pines and the waves crashing at his back. Crawford looked up at the terrace railing, remembering how Shelley would lean there, staring out at the gulf waters, during the long June evenings.

Then in the pauses between the waves he could hear a soft but echoing shuffling from the darkness behind the ground-floor arches — and a moment later a figure in a tattered dress was visible standing in the central arch, the arch through which Josephine had single-handedly dragged the rowboat on the day she had saved him from drowning.

'Michael,' said Josephine hoarsely. Some dark substance was caked around her mouth, as if she'd been eating, but she looked weak and starved, and her eyes were enormous.

Crawford took a step forward, and she instantly disappeared back into the darkness. 'Don't . . . *approach* me,' she called. 'I'm not supposed to let people approach me.'

'Fine,' said Crawford, backing away with his palms held out. 'Look, I'm way back here – you can come out again.'

For several moments there was silence – he and Byron exchanged tense glances – then Crawford heard sandy scuffling inside, and, very slowly, she re-emerged into the flickering orange light. Crawford tried to see if she looked pregnant, but wasn't able to tell.

'Can you approach *us*?' Crawford asked.

She shook her head.

'Not even so that we can talk? Maybe I want to rejoin the flock. Byron here is . . . one of you, I'm sure you can see it in him.' He felt Byron shift beside him, and he could tell from a wobble in the light that he had moved the torch from one hand to the other. Crawford prayed that he wasn't getting impatient, wasn't going to say anything.

'I can't do anything for you,' Josephine said. 'You know that. You need one of them to look favourably on you.' She smiled, and he could see what her skull would someday look like. 'They will, though, Michael. Find one of them and ask for forgiveness. They'll give it. I'm forgiven for . . . for what you and I did.'

Her bare feet on the flagstones looked like white crabs.

Crawford blinked back tears. 'I want you to come with me, Josephine. I love you. I – '

She was shaking her head. 'I think I loved you,' she said, 'but now I love someone else. We're very happy.'

He squeezed the rope, the useless rope. 'Listen to me,' he said desperately.

'No,' she said. 'The sun is down, and he's waiting for me.' She started to turn.

'You're pregnant,' he said loudly.

She had paused. Crawford thought he had heard a sound on the dark hillside, something different from the hiss of the sea wind in the branches, but he didn't look away from her.

'Think about it,' he went on quickly, 'you were a nurse, you know the symptoms. It's our baby, yours and mine. Maybe this . . . *life* is what you want for yourself, but is it what you want for our child?'

For several long seconds she didn't speak. 'You're right,' she said finally, wonderingly. 'I think I *must* be pregnant.' Her face was expressionless, but tears gleamed now on her hollowed cheek.

Again there was a faint sound from the hillside. Crawford glanced up there for a moment but couldn't see anything among the dimly lit pines.

She turned back toward the sea and took a hesitant step out from the arch, and Crawford broke the twine that held the rope to his belt; the coiled rope was in his hand now.

She had noticed Byron now, and was staring at him as anxiously as a half-tamed cat.

Byron waited until a wave had crashed on the rocks and receded. 'It's all right,' he said, just loudly enough for her to hear. 'Two times two is four, two times three is six, two times four is eight.' His voice was almost harsh with compassion, and Crawford wondered if he was remembering her rescue of them on the peak of the Wengern.

'Come with us,' said Crawford.

'Two times five is ten,' said Byron, softer now, as if reciting a lullaby to a child, 'two times six is twelve . . .'

She opened her mouth to answer, but was interrupted by a loud, musically resonant voice from the darkness on the hill.

'*No,*' it said. '*You're mine, and your child is mine. I'm the father.*'

'Christ,' grated Byron, sliding his free hand into his pocket, 'that sounded like Polidori.'

Josephine had stopped. Her tattered dress was fluttering in the chilly breeze.

She was staring at Crawford intently. He smiled at her – and then flipped the rope out away from his side and tossed the loop over her shoulders.

She turned and lunged for the arch and the darkness beyond it, and Crawford was pulled off balance and fell painfully onto his knees; but he pulled her strongly back, and she fell across him.

She was struggling furiously, and even though Byron knelt on her – awkwardly, for he wouldn't drop the torch or take his hand out of his pocket – Crawford wasn't able to get another loop of the rope around any part of her. He could hear something scrambling down the hillside, and in desperation he hauled back his maimed hand and slapped her very hard across the face.

It rocked her head and she went limp, and as Byron stood up Crawford hurriedly rolled her over and tied her wrists together tightly.

The hand he'd hit her with was gritty with clay. The stuff smeared around her mouth was clay. Had she been *eating* it?

When he looked up, Byron had drawn his pistol and was pointing it past Crawford, toward the trees. His free hand held the torch steadily.

Crawford looked in the direction the muzzle was

pointing. A man stood on the pavement beside the house.

He was dressed in a shirt and trousers as shabby as Josephine's dress; but, unlike Josephine, he looked well fed, with a visible paunch and the beginnings of a double chin.

He was smiling coldly at Crawford. 'I,' he said, 'have not ever hit a woman. I'm proud to have resigned from a race whose members would.'

Josephine was recovering from the blow, and flexing weakly under Crawford, and he ran the rope back from her wrists and looped it around her ankles and drew it tight. He began tying a knot, with trembling fingers.

'Polidori,' called Byron, his voice a little unsteady. 'The ball in this pistol is Carbonari issue — silver and wood.'

Crawford drew the knot tight, and looked up.

With an explosive tearing pop that made Crawford jump, Polidori's clothing flew away in rags in all directions — and to judge by the way the torchlight guttered and flared, Byron had been startled too — but when the light steadied, Crawford saw that a serpent with buzzing wings hung now in midair where Polidori had been standing.

It curled heavily in the air, its metallic-looking scales glittering in the torchlight. Its long snout opened, showing a white brush of teeth, and its glassy eyes swivelled from Byron to Crawford, and then down to where Josephine lay on the stones.

'Don't shoot now,' said Crawford hastily. 'I've seen them in this form before — pistol balls just bounce off them.'

'My darling!' breathed Josephine, staring at the serpent.

The thing rose up into the air, buzzing loudly, and then sailed off into the darkness toward the hillside.

Crawford had wrestled the resisting Josephine half-way to her feet when the musical voice sounded again from among the trees.

'Your ball wouldn't have killed me,' it said, and though its tone was urbane, Crawford could clearly hear anger in the precision of the syllables, 'but it would have hurt me. *You* hurt me before, Mister Crawford, in the Alps. Do you recall?'

Crawford couldn't hold up the struggling Josephine any longer; but he knelt under her as he let her fall, so that it was his already bleeding knees, and not her head, that cracked against the stone. 'Why the hell didn't you shoot when you had the chance?' he asked Byron, his voice an exhausted sob.

Then he took a deep breath and looked up. 'No,' he shouted, answering the voice.

He was glad the thing apparently wanted to talk, for he needed time to think. Could he and Byron drag Josephine into the surf, and use the insulating qualities of seawater to keep the thing away from them until dawn? It would be, he thought hysterically, like children swimming in a pond, ducking under water when a hornet was hovering near.

Josephine was panting, staring up into the dark trees.

'With the mirror,' said the voice. 'When you reflected sunlight onto me.'

Crawford did remember it. 'But that wasn't Polidori,' he panted. 'Polidori only killed himself last year.'

'We're not such divided entities as humans,' came the voice. It laughed, a harsh ringing like bronze bells. '"What you have done to the least of my brethren, you have done to me."'

'How,' demanded Byron, 'do you dare to quote Scripture?'

'How do you dare to publish poetry as your own?' returned the voice, its rage abruptly very evident. 'The

504

great Lord Byron! Secretly sucking away at the Gorgon's teat! Presuming to despise anyone who hasn't found their way to it! My poetry may not have been brilliant' – the voice was shrill – 'but at least it was my own!'

Byron still had the pistol in his hand, and he laughed now and swept its muzzle across the hillside. 'Poetry,' he said good-naturedly, 'was the least of the things in which I excelled you.'

A scream sounded from the hillside, and for a moment Crawford glimpsed a naked man rushing toward them between the trees, and Byron levelled the pistol; but an instant later the buzzing curdled the air again and it was the winged serpent that flew at them.

Byron's pistol went off just before the thing hit him, and the ball ricocheted off the serpent and the house wall as the torch spun through the air and hit the stones, scattering sparks.

The light was gone, and over the ringing in his ears Crawford could hear Byron's panicky gasping and the slither and heavy slap of the serpent's coils; then there was a sharp, tortured wheeze, and he knew that the thing had wrapped itself around Byron and was squeezing the breath out of him.

Crawford had taken one step toward the sea – the only thought in his mind being to swim out as far as he could – when he saw that the torch was not quite extinguished. It lay on the stones a couple of yards to his left, and the head of it was still smouldering.

Still not giving up the idea of fleeing, he snatched it up and whirled it in a circle in the air. It flared back into flame, and the first thing he could see was Josephine's face staring anxiously toward Byron and the serpent.

Her concern, he realized, was not for Byron's safety but for her lover's – and Crawford's panic hardened into a leaden, despairing rage.

He turned away from her.

The thing had Byron down, its long rippling body coiled around him, holding his arms helpless against his constricted ribs, and even as Crawford stepped forward it lowered its head to Byron's neck and delicately lanced its narrow teeth into the man's corded throat.

Byron's eyes clenched shut and his lips pulled back from his teeth in a snarl of pain and rage and humiliation – but of reluctant pleasure, too – and Crawford leaned down and thrust the torch against the serpent's eyes.

Josephine screamed, and the flames licked Byron's cheek and withered the grey hair at his temple, but the reptile's eyes just rolled upward to look at Crawford incuriously as the scaled throat worked, swallowing Byron's blood.

Still holding the torch in one hand, Crawford pulled the jar of minced garlic out of his coat pocket and lashed it down onto the stones, then scooped up a handful of glass and garlic and, shivering with revulsion, leaned down to scour it across the reptile's eyes. Shards of glass lanced into his palm, but the chance that it might hurt Josephine's new lover made him ignore the pain.

The snake-thing convulsed, hissing and spitting out a spray of blood and blinking its huge eyes. Its coils loosened, and Byron shook them off and rolled weakly away, sobbing and whooping.

Crawford backed away from the monster, toward Josephine, as the gold-foil wings began thrashing and buzzing, blowing sand away across the flagstones.

The thing that had been Polidori rose up into the air again, its weight apparent in the ponderous swinging of its body. For a moment the head swung back and forth in the chilly breeze, peering uselessly through the blood and glass and garlic that fouled its eyes.

Then, hanging in the air at shoulder height, the thing shuddered, and its face began squirming, reshaping itself. The snout crumpled inward and widened and, grotesquely, became a fleshy human mouth in the reptilian face. 'Where is the child?' said the mouth. Its voice was hoarse and breathless, as if the creature had not had time to mould more than rudimentary vocal organs. 'Where are you, Josephine?'

Suddenly Crawford guessed that the child was terribly important to it, much more important than Josephine; that children who were *born* into submission, as Keats and Shelley had been, were a particular victory for its species. He crouched over Josephine and clamped his bleeding hand over her mouth, but she squirmed away from under him with surprising strength.

'Here,' she gasped. 'Take me.'

The thing's head snapped around toward her hungrily, and as the long body shot forward through the air Crawford grabbed Josephine around the waist with his free arm and, with an effort that seemed to dislocate his shoulder and spine, heaved her back.

The serpent's head cracked so hard against the pavement where she had been that chips of stone whistled through the air, and its body rebounded up and crashed against the top of one of the building's pillars with an impact that made the Casa Magni resound like a vast stone drum.

The thing hung higher in the air now, about twenty feet above the pavement, and its furiously buzzing wings were blurs of reflecting gold around the downward peering face. The mouth had been shattered against the stones, and blood ran from it in a long, swaying string, but it managed to produce one word.

'Where?'

Crawford's arm was still around Josephine, and he felt her draw in a breath to answer.

In an unreasoning burst of jealous fury he released her and snatched the pistol from his pocket, and only after he had cocked it and aimed it up at the devastated

507

mouth that she preferred to his own did it occur to him that Polidori had compromised his invulnerability by adopting this piece of human anatomy.

Crawford pulled the trigger, and beyond the flare of the explosion he saw the serpent cartwheel away upward through the air, and over the echoes of the bang he heard it scream shrilly like blocks of stone sliding rapidly across each other.

Josephine screamed too, wrenching at her bonds so hard that Crawford thought she would break bones.

He stood up, and limped over to where Byron lay. The lord was staring blankly at the pavement under his face, but he was breathing.

'I hate you,' sobbed Josephine. 'I hope this child *is* his. It *ought* to be – he and I have been living out here as husband and wife for months.'

Crawford smiled savagely at her and blew her a kiss with his bleeding, garlic-reeking palm.

Chapter 23

I am moved by fancies that are curled
Around these images, and cling:
The notion of some infinitely gentle
Infinitely suffering thing.

— T. S. Eliot, *Preludes*

Byron had rolled over, his hand clamped to his bloody throat, and was staring up at the stars. 'Well done,' he said hoarsely. He sat up, groaning and bracing himself on his free hand. 'That won't have killed him, you know. He'll be petrified, and with luck he landed somewhere where the sun will shine tomorrow, but he's not out of the picture.'

'True,' came a grating voice from the darkness, harsh with inorganic pain.

Byron and Josephine and Crawford all jumped, and the torch in Crawford's hand swung wildly.

'Take me!' screamed Josephine, managing to prop herself up on one elbow.

'Soon,' said the voice.

Crawford shook his head unhappily, staring at Josephine and dreading exertions to come. He looked back up at the dark hill. 'And you rebuked me for having *hit* her! *You* tried to *kill* her!'

'Jesus, Aickman,' said Byron as he struggled to his feet. 'Don't be *talking* to the thing. We've — '

'To *kill* her,' came the voice, every syllable sounding as if it cost the thing unimaginable pain, 'is not an *insult*.'

'You,' Josephine called into the night, 'you want me

509

. . . *dead*?' She had managed to get up into a wobbling crouch, with her hands behind her back.

Crawford stared at her. 'Of course he wants you dead. Look at the goddamn *hole* in the pavement where you'd still be lying, smashed like your sis — like a bug, if I hadn't pulled you away!'

He walked back and crouched by her. 'Listen to me,' he said. 'Are you listening? Good. He wants you to die and be buried so that you can hatch like an egg and give birth to the seed he's sown in your blood, the extension of himself that will climb out of your grave. And then after a while you'd give birth to what would once have been *our child*, but would by this time be one of these creatures.'

He laughed grimly. 'Talk about there being no "well-at-any-rates"! Our child would be like Shelley or Keats, condemned to nephelism by the circumstances of birth, except that this child would be deprived of ever having any human life. This may be unprecedented, at least since the good old days before Noah.'

Josephine nodded, seeming to have comprehended what he'd said, and he had begun to relax a little, and even to smile, when she suddenly arched powerfully backwards, striking her head with a sickening crack against the pavement.

'God!' Crawford squeaked in horror. He lunged forward onto his aching knees and for a moment just cradled her head, his mind as blank as if it had been his own head that had hit the stones; then he laid the torch down carefully and began feeling her skull. Hot blood was rapidly clogging her already matted hair, but she was breathing and her skull was at least not broken in.

He was crying, remembering having given her the same desperate, frightened examination after the two of them had been shot in a street in Rome; then too there had been the powerful reek of garlic and blood, but then

510

it had been because she had kissed him to save him from giving in to the lamia.

He tore a strip from his shirt and tied it around her head so that there would be pressure on the cut. Her hair stuck up ludicrously in all directions.

'She should really be in a hospital,' he was mumbling, more or less to Byron, 'she's bleeding and she hasn't been eating, you can see that – God knows what that fit was, it was like the convulsions you get if you eat strychnine, but at least it's worn off for now, apparently – '

'Aickman,' said Byron, swaying unsteadily, 'that wasn't a convulsion.'

'You must not have been looking, man! I'm a physician, but *anybody* could see – '

'It was,' said Byron, his voice weak but very clear, 'a suicide attempt. She learned that the Polidori-thing wants her dead, and so she tried to comply. It's a good thing you had her tied up – otherwise we'd be out in the sea right now trying to catch her.'

Crawford laid her head down gently. '. . . Oh.' He stood up, absently grateful for the cold wind in his sweat-drenched hair. 'I suppose it could . . . I suppose that was it. Yes.'

Byron leaned, then caught himself with a quick forward step and sat down hastily. '*I*, however,' he whispered, 'may shortly be able to show you a genuine convulsion.' Both his hands were palm down on the ground, and Crawford could see the blood coursing steadily down his neck.

Crawford shambled over to him, sat down and, hopelessly, lifted one of Byron's hands and put his fingers on the man's wrist. The pulse was fast and thready, and the skin was hot. The characteristic fever of a newly bit vampire victim was already setting in, building on the fever Byron had already had.

Crawford dropped the hand and sat back, at last recognizing the huge, unalterable fact that had changed the evening, made their efforts and heroics pointless.

'You can't physically *make* it to Venice, can you?' he asked, his voice flat with the effort of concealing the bitter resentment he felt; he would never know if Byron had secretly wanted the evening to end this way, but he vividly remembered the two opportunities Byron had had to shoot the vampire – before its first metamorphosis, and in the instant when it was again a man rushing down the hill at them – before it could bite him. And Crawford knew Byron was a good enough marksman to have made either shot. 'Over the Apennines, and down the Po Valley . . . especially starting tonight – which,' he added with a bleak look up at the hillside, 'I'm afraid we would have to do.'

All for nothing, he thought. My shredded hand, Josephine's cracked head.

Byron put his hand back on his throat and shook his head. 'I'm sorry. I'm nearly certain I'll die if I try it now.' He glanced across at Josephine's sprawled form, and sighed. Then he looked back at Crawford, and all of the usual bluster was gone from his eyes. 'But let's put it to the test.'

Crawford blinked at him, a little ashamed now of his earlier suspicions, but still angry. 'No. Thanks, but no.' He tried to think. 'Maybe I could do it without you,' he said, knowing even as he spoke that it wasn't true.

'No, you couldn't. You don't know . . . nearly enough about the eye, and the Graiae. For one thing, the eye isn't usually free to jump – it was jumping in 1818 because Shelley was right there when they woke up, but ordinarily it stays with one of the columns. There are a number of chants that *will* free it up, but you have to be able to gauge a number of factors to know which chant will work on the night you're there. I studied these things at an Armenian monastery there for months, but I'm not even sure *I* could do it.'

After a moment Crawford nodded reluctantly. He knew Byron was right.

There was a word Crawford was trying to think of, something with the dryness of a legal term, but which had come to have a physically unpleasant meaning for him . . . a taste of iron and vinegar.

Then he had it. 'Proxy,' he said, his voice hollow with hope and nausea.

'Proxy?'

'You can be there – enough to advise me, and to draw the attention of Lord Grey and then lose him – and still be here. How's your neck bleeding?'

'Steadily, thank you.' Some of the old irritability was seeping back into Byron's voice. 'Aren't you supposed to know about bandages and such things?'

'I'll put a bandage on it in a moment. First, give me your jar of garlic.'

Byron dug it out and handed it to him, and Crawford opened it and with his fingers dug out as much of the minced garlic as he could and dropped the stuff onto the pavement. Then he held the jar against the skin of Byron's neck. 'I just need a bit of your blood.'

For a moment Byron looked as if he would resist – then he just nodded weakly and lifted his chin and turned away so that Crawford could hold the jar to the bite.

When the jar was half full, Crawford shut it and set about bandaging Byron's neck.

'When I drink this blood,' he began.

'*Drink* it?' Byron exclaimed. 'You spent too much time in that *nefando* den!'

'Just enough time, actually. I remember thinking that when those men drank my blood I was able to look out of their eyes, see myself on that cross, if only dimly and fitfully, from the other side of the room. And when I drank Shelley's blood – '

Byron gagged. 'You really are a neffer, Aickman.'

'When I drank Shelley's blood,' Crawford went on steadily, 'I was able to see and feel everything he did, and I was even able to talk to him, converse with him.'

Byron was interested in spite of himself. 'Really? I wonder if something similar may be the original basis for the Christian Eucharist.'

Crawford rolled his eyes impatiently. 'Conceivably. So when I drink this, I'm pretty sure I'll be able to be you, to some extent, and you be me. So you'll know when I've got there, and am ready to start. Now listen, I'll spill what I don't drink, so Lord Grey will come rushing to your rescue in Venice as surely as my lamia rushed to where I'd spilled Shelley's and my blood. The thing is, and do pay attention to this, *you must not be visible to him anywhere else when I do it*, or he won't be fooled. Shelley made himself invisible to his half sister by being out in the boat – seawater, right? So you have Fletcher or Trelawny or somebody bring a tub of seawater into your room, and you make sure you're immersed in it when I spill your blood in Venice.'

They set out for the road above the house, where Trelawny had left the carriage. Byron held the torch and Crawford half carried, half dragged the unconscious Josephine, and they managed to work their way to the back of the house in only a few minutes.

The upward sloping path behind the house was more difficult; Byron couldn't climb more than a few feet before needing to sit down and breathe deeply for a while, and Crawford found, to his confused horror, that the only way he could get Josephine up the slope was to tie a fresh length of the rope around her ankles and loop it around a higher trunk and then lean into the free end, so that his own weight dragged her up the hill backwards; though it delayed them still further, he couldn't help pausing frequently to go to her and pull her skirt back up over her knees.

His heart was pounding alarmingly, and not just from the physical effort; he kept imagining that he heard Polidori whispering over the crash of the surf and the rustle of the branches and the scuffing and slithering and panting of his own progress, and during one of the pauses for rest he was sure he heard a soft chuckling from the darkness beyond the torch's frail light.

At last he had got Josephine up to the road, and had rolled, hiked and folded her into the carriage. Byron followed her inside and Crawford climbed slowly up to the driver's bench with the torch, which he wedged into a bracket in the luggage rail. The two horses harnessed to the carriage seemed impatient to be gone.

The clouds had broken up, and the moonlight was bright enough so that he was able to drive at a fairly good speed; within minutes they had reached the streets and overhanging buildings of Lerici, and he reined in the horses in front of a house a few hundred feet from the inn where Byron's party was staying.

Crawford climbed down and opened the door, and Byron got out, as carefully as someone's great-grandfather. Crawford couldn't help remembering the vital young man he'd first met in a Geneva street in 1816.

The paving stones ahead were streaked with light, and faintly on the breeze they could hear music and laughter. 'Trelawny will be carousing,' said Byron hoarsely, 'and the Hunts will probably have already gone to bed, in their sensible way. I should be able to get to my room without anyone asking me about this bandage.' He reached back into the carriage and pulled out a cane, which he handed to Crawford. 'You remember it?'

Crawford nodded, a faint, sad smile touching his bearded face. 'Your sword cane. I remember you waving it around in a lightning storm at the foot of the Wengern.'

'It's yours now. Twist the metal collar of it, that ring there, and you can draw it. It's good French steel.' Byron seemed ill at ease. 'You know where the money and guns are in the carriage. And poor Shelley's heart. And I've got my passport and you've got yours. I don't imagine you'll – '

He stopped, and took Crawford's good hand in both of his. 'I've been a lot of trouble, haven't I? During these, what, six years.'

Crawford was embarrassed, and glad that the flaring torch was above and behind Byron so that he couldn't see if there were tears in the lord's eyes. 'A lot of trouble,' he agreed.

Byron laughed. 'You've been a good friend. It's not terribly likely that we'll see each other again, so I do want you to know that. You've been a good friend.'

'Oh hell.' Crawford freed his hand and hugged the man, and Byron pounded him on the back. 'You've been a good friend too.'

Clearly embarrassed himself, Byron stepped back. 'Do you think it's midnight yet?'

Crawford laughed softly. 'It feels like tomorrow's midnight – but no, it can't be past ten.'

'In two hours it will be Michaelmas. St Michael's day.' Byron waved clumsily. 'Kill our dragon for us, Michael.'

'You'll know,' said Crawford. 'You'll be there, in all but the flesh.'

Byron nodded dubiously. 'That's right. Jesus. Don't go getting us up too early in the morning.' He turned and began limping away, toward the inn.

Crawford leaned into the carriage and made sure Josephine's pulse and breathing were still steady, then

516

closed and latched the door, wearily climbed back up on to the bench and snapped the reins.

He drove northeast until he'd crossed the arching stone bridge over the Vara River, and then he took the old road that paralleled the Marga River, between high mountain shoulders that were a deeper black than the starry sky.

The road was getting steeper as it curled up into the Apennines, but the moon was high and the horses were fresh, and Crawford felt better with every mile he put between the carriage and the stony thing that lay injured but aware somewhere on the hillside behind the Casa Magni.

Finally it was the cold and his own exhaustion that made him stop. The torch had long since burned out.

Seven miles northeast of the Vara a stream flowed into the Marga from up in the mountains, and around the bridge over the stream were clustered the lightless wooden buildings of a little village called Aulla. Crawford found a stable and banged on the broad door until a light appeared in a window overhead, and the door was eventually unlocked and slid open by an old man with a lantern.

Crawford paid him to take the two horses out of harness and groom them, and to fetch a cup of vinegar from somewhere, and to ignore the fact that Crawford and his companion chose to sleep in the carriage.

When everything had been done and the old man had returned upstairs, Crawford checked Josephine – her breathing and pulse were still regular – and then carefully poured about a tablespoonful of the vinegar into the jar of Byron's blood, to prevent its clotting, and closed the jar and tucked it safely into one of the bags on the floor.

Josephine was lying on the rear seat, and he lay down

517

on the front one; in order to fit he had to tuck his legs up and bend his head down over his knees, but he managed it, and was asleep in seconds.

He woke again, hours later, feeling painfully constricted and breathless. He had sat up, and gingerly stretched his legs out and rearranged his clothing and loosened his belt, before it became clear to him, to his dull astonishment, that it was sexual excitement that had forced him awake.

He looked at the dark form of Josephine, only a yard away, and after a moment he realized that the glints of light in her face were reflections of the dimly moonlit stable in her open eyes. He smiled at her, and started to get up.

Then he noticed that she was hunched up on one elbow, and staring out of the carriage window and not at him. Crawford followed the direction of her gaze — and jumped when he saw several erect forms standing on the straw-covered stable floor outside the carriage.

There was a regular squeaking noise — the carriage springs. He looked back at Josephine and noticed that she was rocking her hips against the upholstered seat.

And she was still staring out the carriage window.

Teeth glinted in the hollow faces of the things outside, but Crawford couldn't work up any fear; he could only look at the dim outlines of Josephine's emaciated body under the ragged dress; he thought his own clothes must explode, the way Polidori's had earlier in the evening, if he weren't able to get out of them.

He reached across the carriage and tremblingly cupped her hot right breast; the contact stopped the breath in him, and made his heart beat like a line of cannons being fired by one continuous, insanely quick-burning fuse.

She snarled at him, and her head jerked down and her jaws clicked shut only an inch from his hand.

Even in the dim light and the musty air it was clear that she was excited too – in fact sexual heat had flexed the whole fabric of the air to a tightly strained point, the way imminent lightning causes hair to stand up on scalps, and Crawford imagined that the horses, their very fleas, must be having erotic dreams.

With nothing but hot jealousy Crawford looked through the glass at the creatures Josephine so very evidently found more attractive than himself – and then he remembered something that had been said to him by a young woman he'd encountered six years ago in the streets of Geneva, on the day he'd first met Byron and Shelley: '. . . we could share in their interest in us, Michael, and at least be interested in each other that way . . .'

At least one of the forms swaying outside the glass was female – if he opened the door and gave himself to her, to the crowd, would he thus be able to have a willing Josephine at second hand, at least? Vicariously?

By . . . proxy?

The carriage already smelled of vinegar and blood, but the word brought back with extra clarity the memory of the woman with whom he had killed the lamia on the beach below the Casa Magni – the woman who had made love with him willingly, joyfully.

He didn't want to have her now if her attention was on someone, something, else.

Byron had laid in a good stock of minced garlic, and Crawford opened a fresh jar and smeared the stuff around the cracks of all the windows and both doors.

As soon as the smell began to drift outside the carriage, the figures in the stable diminished into sluglike things and crawled away across the straw-littered floor and up the wall and out through the stable window. Crawford watched until the last of them had heaved its bulk over the sill and thumped away outside into the moonlit night.

Then he checked the knots on Josephine's bonds, being resentfully careful not to touch her at all as he did it; and finally he sat back and opened his flask and drank himself into oblivion.

At Michaelmas dawn the old man burst into the stable with a priest, and as the stable owner harnessed the horses the priest shouted angry, incomprehensibly fast Italian sentences at Crawford, who just nodded miserably.

The carriage was on the road again before the sun had quite cleared the mountains ahead.

'Making friends everywhere you go, hey?' shouted Crawford from the driver's bench to the sleeping Josephine as he snapped the reins over the horses' backs. 'Good policy.'

They drove north under the blue summer sky, through the Cisa Pass between the vertically remote and snow-fouled peaks of the Apennines – the sun was rising ahead of them, and the sunlight was hot in the moments when the mountain wind was not rasping down through the sparsely wooded pass – and by midmorning Crawford knew, from Byron's maps and roadside markers, that they were very near the border between Tuscany and Emilia.

The road had got narrower, and the rocky wall on his right and the abyss to his left had both grown steeper, and when he knew that they must be within a hundred yards of the border crossing, Crawford gave up on finding a place to pull over, and simply halted the carriage in the road. At least there didn't seem to be any traffic right now. He hurriedly climbed down and opened the carriage door – and then gagged and reeled away.

He had left the windows half-open, but the sun had nevertheless made a garlic steam-room of the carriage's interior. Josephine was only semiconscious. He checked her pulse and breathing – they were still regular, and Crawford wondered what he would have done if they had not been.

There was a strongbox under the front seat, and Crawford made sure that all of Byron's pistols and all the knives from the cutlery set were in it, and that it was locked and the key in his pocket. He climbed back outside for a breath of fresh air, then leaned in for one more look around.

He supposed she could break one of the windows and saw open her neck on the jagged edges, or open the door and throw herself off the precipice, but he would hear her beginning either of those, and could conceivably get down in time to stop her – and she looked too weak for any strenuous suicide anyway.

He leaned out for another breath, and then quickly but gently untied the knots he'd pulled tight twelve hours ago in front of the Casa Magni.

He closed the door and climbed back up to the driver's bench and started the carriage rolling again.

At the border crossing Josephine was so clearly ill and incoherent, and Crawford's explanation that she needed to get to the hospital in Parma so desperately convincing, and his bribe so handsome, and the smell of garlic so appalling, that the border guards quickly let them continue on the road east, the road that would lead them down out of the mountains.

A few hundred yards farther on, Crawford halted the carriage and climbed down. He roused Josephine enough to get her to eat some bread and cheese with him, and he made her drink some water, reminding himself to plan a rest stop before too long.

She cursed him weakly as he retied her hands and ankles. After a minute he realized that he was cursing her in return, and he made himself stop.

Hand-sized wooden crucifixes stood on poles every few miles along the roadside, sheltered by tiny shingled roofs, and as the sun climbed by imperceptible degrees to the zenith, and then began to throw Crawford's shadow out under the horses' hooves, Crawford found himself praying to the weather-greyed little figures.

He wasn't precisely praying to Christ, but to all the gods who had represented humanity and had suffered for it; curled around his mental image of the wooden Christ were vague ideas of Prometheus chained to the stone with the vulture tearing at his entrails – and Balder nailed to the tree, around the roots of which flowers grew where the drops of his blood fell – and Osiris torn to pieces beside the Nile.

He had his flask with him on the driver's seat, and the brandy worked with the fatigue and the monotonous noises and motions of driving to lull him into a state that was nearly dreaming.

He wished he had the time, and the hammer and nails, to stop the carriage and go pound an *eisener breche* into the face of one of the little wooden Christs – it would be a gesture of respect and a declaration of solidarity, not vandalism – and, after a couple of hours of wishing it, he began to imagine that he was doing it.

The figure, in his hallucinatorily vivid daydream, lifted wooden eyelids and stared at him with tiny but unmistakably human eyes, as red blood ran down the pain-lines of the crudely chiselled face, and then it opened its wooden mouth and spoke.

'Accipite, et bibite ex eo omnes.'

It was Latin, and he translated it mentally: *All of you take and drink of this.*

He was pretty sure it was a line from the Catholic Mass, said when the priest changed the water into Christ's blood.

Crawford noticed now that a rusty iron cup hung under the crucifix, and that the blood had run down the legs into the cup. He reached for the cup, but a cloud passed over the sun then, and the figure on the eclipsed cross was himself, and while he was watching himself from someone else's eyes he thrust an *eisener breche* into the side of the crucified figure.

Water ran out of the wound, and he didn't have to taste it to know that it was salty — seawater. The water puddled and deepened, and filled the cellar and spilled out into the Arno, which somehow was also the Thames and the Tiber, and flowed out to sea; the little roof over the crucifix became a boat, but it was too far out at sea by now for Crawford to know which boat it was. The *Don Juan*? The ark? One boat to save us by sinking, Crawford thought dizzily, one to save us by surviving.

He realized that his flask was empty, and that the sun had set behind them. They were down among the wooded foothills now, and he blinked back over his shoulder at the red-lit mountain peaks, through whose stony domain this little box of warm organic life had travelled, and he shivered and thanked the hallucinated Christ, or whoever it had been, for the horses, and even for Josephine.

Somewhere ahead lay the ancient walled city of Parma — once a Gallic town, then an important Roman city, and now a possession, with the blessing of the Austrians, of the French; its royal gardens and promenades were supposed to be among the most beautiful in

Italy. Crawford just hoped that whatever stable he would find for them to sleep in would have straw lying around, so that he and Josephine could sleep out of the malodorous carriage.

Chapter 24

Their watchmen stare, and stand aghast,
As on we hurry through the dark;
The watch-light blinks as we go past,
The watch-dog shrinks and fears to bark . . .

— George Crabbe

Perhaps because Parma was occupied by Austrian-sanctioned forces, no priest came to the stable to harry the vampire's woman out of town. The stable owner slid open the heavy wooden door at dawn, and plodded inside to open one of the stalls and lead a horse out, but he didn't even look toward where Crawford and Josephine lay on a luxuriously thick pile of straw, covered by a spare horse-blanket.

Crawford wished Byron had thought to pack blankets.

The man led the horse outside, and Crawford threw the blanket aside and stood up. He went to the carriage, but the jug of water had somehow picked up the ubiquitous garlic smell, and he cursed and took one of Byron's crystal glasses to a horse-trough and dipped up some water. It didn't taste bad, and he refilled the glass and took it over to Josephine.

He crouched by her, and for several seconds just looked at her lean, strained face. She had still been awake when he had gone to sleep, staring at the ceiling and flexing her bound wrists and ankles, and he wondered when she had finally let herself sleep.

He shook her shoulder gently, and her eyes sprang open.

'It's me, Michael,' he said, trying to make it sound reassuring, even though he knew that his was the face she least cared to see. 'Sit up so I can give you some water.'

She hiked herself up and obediently sipped from the glass he tilted to her mouth. After a few sips she shook her head, and he held the glass away.

'You can untie me,' she said hoarsely. 'I won't try to run.'

'Or kill yourself?'

She looked away. 'Or kill myself.'

'I can't,' he said wearily. 'Even if it was just you, I wouldn't. I love you, and I won't cooperate in your death. But anyway, it's *not* just you. There's a child.'

'It's his,' she said. Her voice was listless. 'I really think it's his. They can have children by us, you know.'

Crawford thought of Shelley's half sister, who had grown inside Shelley's body while he was still in his mother's womb, and had by that prolonged contact infected him and made him not entirely human. Josephine's haggard face reminded him of the wooden Christ-face he had imagined yesterday, and he prayed that the human foetus was all that Josephine carried.

'The child is human,' he told her. 'Remember I'm a doctor that specializes in this. You were already pregnant when you first – when you first *screwed* Polidori.' He looked away so that she wouldn't see the rage in his eyes. 'Even if Polidori *has* succeeded in impregnating you too – they can do that, the inhuman foetus grows with, or even in, the human one that was already there – *our* child is still there, and will be at least as human as Shelley was.'

She closed her eyes – he saw with sudden compassion that her eyelids were deeply wrinkled – and tears ran down her cheeks. 'Oh,' she said miserably.

For perhaps a full minute neither of them spoke. A

526

horse poked its head around a stall partition and peered at the two of them, then snorted and stepped back out of sight.

Josephine sighed. 'So it might even be . . . twins.'

'Right.'

Josephine shuddered, and Crawford recalled that she herself had been one of a pair of twins, and that her mother had bled to death within minutes of giving birth to her.

The stable owner walked back into the building and, still not looking over at Crawford and Josephine, opened another stall. Crawford tensed, ready to jump on Josephine and cover her mouth – but when it became clear that she wasn't going to shout for help he was grateful for the interruption; he needed to think.

Would it help, he wondered as the man led another horse out, to remind her of her mother's death? It had, with the help of her sister Julia, effectively wrecked her youth. Would being reminded of it make her more suicidal, or more concerned for the well-being of her child? Would it help to remind her of what Keats went through so that his sister would not become the prey of his vampire?

She had now gone two full nights without giving blood to Polidori, and Crawford remembered, from his long-ago week in Switzerland, how hard it was to do without that erosion of personality, once one had grown used to it.

She's probably only now beginning to be able to think for herself, he thought. And she'll be hating it. Will she acknowledge the responsibilities that she can now clearly see, or will they be so appalling that she'll just want to return to the selfless haze?

'I thought,' she said when the man had left, 'that there'd be no difference if I killed myself. If the baby was his, suicide would just . . . speed up its birth.'

'And your . . . rebirth.'

She nodded. 'I'd finally be able to *stop* being me, Josephine; I really *would* be just a walking . . . thing.'

'But now,' said Crawford carefully, 'you know that our child would be too.'

Josephine's eyes were wide now, and it occurred to Crawford that she looked trapped. 'But we,' she whispered, 'we killed her, the woman that loved you. I can't . . . *know* that, I can't let myself know that.'

Crawford took her shoulders. '*It wasn't Julia*,' he said. 'It wasn't your sister. I know you know that, but you haven't . . . what, digested it. The thing we killed was a goddamn flying lizard, like that thing that tried to kill you – and our child – two nights ago. It was a *vampire*.'

She lowered her head and nodded, and he saw a tear fall onto the knot at her wrists.

Too tired to worry anymore, he released her shoulders and began untying the knot.

When the stable owner came in again, Josephine and Crawford were standing together by the carriage, clinging to each other. The man smiled and muttered something about *amore* before going to the next stall.

They traded Byron's carriage for a less elegant but fresher-smelling one, loaded all their baggage into it, and then paid for a room at a hotel just so that they could bathe and get into clean clothes. Crawford even shaved – and, after agonizing about it for a minute, decided not to hide the razor.

Crawford was careful to wait in the hall while Josephine took her bath and got dressed; he was dimly and incredulously beginning to hope that the two of them might someday marry after all – if they weren't killed in Venice, and if she was carrying only one child – but he could imagine her withdrawing totally if he even *seemed* to be attempting familiarities right now.

When she stepped out of the room Crawford thought she must have left years in the bath water: her hair was clean and combed, and lustrous even in the dimness of the hall, and in one of Teresa's dresses that Byron had packed for her she actually looked slim rather than gaunt.

He offered her his arm; after only the slightest hesitation she took it, and together they walked to the stairs.

They walked down the sunlit Emilian Way to the Piazza Grande, and at an outdoor table under a statue of Correggio they ate hard-boiled egg slices in tomato sauce with grilled bread and olive oil, and drank most of a bottle of Lambrusco.

Beggars were huddled in the sun in front of the Renaissance arches of the Palazzo del Commune, and a barefoot old couple in ragged clothes had ventured out among the tables; the man was wringing a devastated hat in his hands and was talking to the well-dressed people at a table near Crawford. Thankful for his own clean clothes and good food and wine, Crawford pulled a bundle of *lire* from his pocket and waited for the couple to make their way to the table at which he and Josephine sat.

Then he noticed the Austrian soldiers. They must have come into the square several seconds earlier, for they were already spread out and walking purposefully across the square. Two of them seized the old couple and began marching them away, and, looking past them, Crawford saw that the soldiers had rounded up all the beggars and were herding them out of the square.

Suddenly ashamed of his apparent affluence, he crumpled the bills and let them fall to the pavement. In the breeze the wad of paper scooted away across the flagstones like a little boat.

'Parma's new Austrian masters don't seem to approve of beggars,' he said to Josephine as he pushed his chair

529

back and stood up. 'Let's go – I hate seeming to be part of the crowd they're protecting from them.'

Josephine too looked sickened by the spectacle, and stood up. 'I think we've *done* Parma,' she said in a sprightly imitation of the voice of an English tourist. '*Do* let's be moving on toward Venice.'

Crawford was delighted to see even weak, ironic humour in her. 'The Tintoretto *Last Supper*!' he exclaimed fatuously, trying to maintain her mood.

'The Veroccio *Colleoni*!' she chimed in; then, perhaps because she'd seen drawings of that grim mounted statue, her affected smile collapsed. 'Back to the hotel?'

'Just for the carriage. Our old clothes they can keep.'

Austrian guards were checking everyone who was leaving the city through the high stone arch of the north gate, but the soldier who checked their carriage just leaned in the window and looked at Josephine, then peered up at Crawford with a disapproving air; he sniffed officiously and waved them on.

The carriage moved forward out of the shadow into the hot sunlight, and then the horses bounded forward, as if tired of the slow pace of city traffic. The road northward curled away ahead of them across the Po Valley, and for several hours Crawford drove happily between wide fields of yellow earth on which the vines and peach trees made geometrical figures in livid green.

A number of horses and carriages passed them, but he was not anxious to reach the nightmare end of this journey and he wanted the horses to be fresh for the drive through Lombardy and Venetia tomorrow, so he maintained their leisurely pace.

In a couple of hours they had reached a village called Brescello that sat on the marshy banks of the Po. Crawford thought about stopping, but the air was full of some kind of lint that was making him sneeze, and he tilted his hat back and squinted along the western river bank to see where the bridge was.

Suddenly the carriage rocked violently on its springs, and a black-bearded young man was sitting beside him.

Crawford darted a hand toward the pistol under his coat, but the man caught his wrist with a browned hand. Crawford instinctively looked at the hand, thinking of breaking the grip – and then noticed the black mark between the thumb and forefinger. It looked very much like the two-year-old stain on his own palm.

He looked up into a pair of fierce brown eyes. 'Carbonari,' the man said.

Crawford nodded, a little relieved. '*Si?*' he said.

The man spoke rapidly in what Crawford at first thought was French; then he recognized it as the patois of Piedmont, which lay westward up the valley, and he managed to translate it mentally. 'You must go down the river,' the man had said, 'not across into Lombardy. Running water – it throws them off the scent.'

'Uh . . . who,' asked Crawford carefully, unconsciously trying to match the accent, 'do you think we are?'

The man had taken the reins from Crawford and was goading the horses east down a narrower dirt track, away from the bridge.

'I think,' he said, 'that you are the couple who traded in a carriage reeking of garlic, in Parma this morning; the couple who got by the border guards at the Cisa Pass yesterday because of a sick woman, and a big bribe to men who are in some trouble now.'

Suddenly Crawford remembered the guards in the Piazza that morning, who had been arresting everyone who looked as shabby as Crawford and Josephine had the day before; and he remembered the guard who had passed them through the Parma gate after having *sniffed* the carriage. Crawford was profoundly glad that he and Josephine had happened to abandon Byron's vehicle.

The new carriage was among wooden shacks now, and the lint in the air was worse. Crawford sneezed six times in succession.

'They're steeping the harvested flax crop,' Crawford's guide said. 'The air will be full of the stuff for days.' He threw a quick glance sideways at Crawford. 'You have no drink to offer a fellow soldier?'

'Sorry. Here.' Crawford handed him the flask, and the man drank everything that was in it and handed it back. 'Thanks. My name's della Torre.'

'I'm – ' Crawford began, but the man quickly held up his stained hand.

'I don't want to know,' he said. 'There was a description of the two of you, mentioning your Carbonari mark, in a message an Austrian courier was bringing from Lerici yesterday. Our people killed him in the mountains.' He looked over his shoulder, back toward the bridge. 'Clearly the courier they killed was not the only one they sent.'

'Have the Austrians followed us here?' Crawford asked. 'Perhaps we should abandon this carriage too . . .'

'Yes, you should and you will, but not at this moment. They are not here yet – I passed them half an hour ago on the road from Parma, on a faster horse than any of the soldiers had, and I only got here a few minutes ago.'

'Do you know . . . what it is they want us for?' Crawford asked. Shelley's heart? he wondered; the men I killed in Rome? Both?

'No,' said della Torre, 'and I don't want to know. I just assume you're on Carbonari business.'

'I am that.'

A series of decrepit wooden docks segmented the roadside on their left now, and della Torre slanted the carriage into a narrow alley between two warehouselike buildings on one of the docks. Crawford heard a squeal and a splintering snap as some part of the carriage caught against the corner of one of the buildings and apparently broke off.

Della Torre ignored it. 'There will be a boat here,' he said, and hopped down to the resounding boards.

Several big, scarred-looking men emerged from a dark doorway in the building they'd collided with, and della Torre began arguing with them so immediately that Crawford thought they must be old enemies resuming some long-standing conflict.

Alarmed both by the pursuing Austrians and by his new ally, he climbed down and opened the carriage door. Josephine was asleep, and he reluctantly shook her shoulder.

She opened her eyes, but there was no particular alertness in them.

'We're abandoning the carriage,' he said to her clearly, 'and proceeding by boat. You might want to step out.'

'Boat?' she asked doubtfully.

'Boat,' he said. 'What's wrong? Do you *want* him to be able to follow you?'

She closed her eyes. 'You know I don't,' she said. She climbed out of the carriage and stood by him, swaying. He put his arm around her. 'But,' she whispered, 'you know my blood does.'

Della Torre walked around the carriage; he was slapping his forehead. 'The men of Emilia are corrupt,' he said when he had paused before Crawford and lowered his hand. 'These men want a thousand *lire* for the use of one of their boats. It is their best boat, understand, and in it I and one of them can take you to Porto Tolle, on the Adriatic, in two days at the most.'

Crawford's stomach felt hollow. He only had about fifteen hundred *lire*. Still, he couldn't see that he had any choice but to deal with these people, and there didn't seem to be time to try to talk the price down.

'We'll take it,' he said, despising the way his voice sounded like a very old man's.

Della Torre nodded bleakly, then shrugged. 'For nothing, though, they will take responsibility for the carriage and horses that the Austrians are looking so hard for.'

I daresay they will, thought Crawford bitterly. But, 'Very well,' he said. And how much of this are you skimming off? he wondered.

'I,' della Torre went on stoically, 'will help you take your baggage onto the boat.'

'You're *too* kind,' said Josephine in English as they started across the dock.

The boat was about thirty feet long, with apple-shaped bows and a leeboard like a wooden wing on each side; the mast was hinged and lying back across the stern, and Crawford could see that it would carry a gaff-rigged mainsail and a jib. He admitted to himself that it did look serviceable.

Within minutes the mast had been raised and locked in place, and as soon as the baggage and the four passengers were aboard, the lines were cast off and the sails were raised and the land-side leeboard was swivelled down into the water, and the boat began angling out away from the dock.

Josephine had gone straight to one of the narrow bunks below the deck, but Crawford refilled his flask and sat with it by the starboard rail, and he watched the village recede away behind them.

Today was Monday. They had left Lerici on Saturday night, and already he had spent more than half of the two thousand *lire* Byron had given them . . . and lost Byron's carriage and horses.

But the brandy made him optimistic. With luck, he

534

thought, we've also lost our pursuers, both human and inhuman.

All afternoon the boat beat on down the Po, between green fields dotted with white cattle, and at sunset Josephine came tottering up onto the deck.

Della Torre stared at her for a moment, then walked across the deck to where Crawford sat. 'She's bitten,' he said.

Crawford nodded drunkenly. 'We're going to get her unbitten.'

'Why do you go toward the sea, then? The Alps, I'm told, are where one goes to shed the vampires.'

'We're going to do it in Venice.'

'*Venice?*' Della Torre shook his head. 'Venice is their stronghold! That's where their king is supposed to be living.'

Josephine walked up and without a word took Crawford's flask and drank deeply from it. 'God,' she said in English, 'I'm – ' She shook her head, staring at the distant riverbank.

'I know,' said Crawford. 'I've felt it too. Fight it – for the child's sake if not your own.'

She shivered, but nodded and took another sip.

'Talk Italian,' said della Torre. For the first time, Crawford heard real uneasiness in the man's voice.

The sky was darkening ahead, and clouds curled solidly in the sky.

At dusk the man from the docks – whose name, Crawford gathered, was Sputo, the Italian for spit – started to tack in toward the lights of a city, but della Torre told him to keep going, to sail all night. The man shrugged and obeyed, only remarking that if they were to go on they'd have to kindle up running lights. Della Torre walked around the boat with a firepot, carefully lighting the lamps that swung on chains out over the water.

The wind had picked up, and the boat was scudding along under only the half-reefed mainsail.

Crawford was in the bow, fingering the grip of the pistol under his jacket and watching the turbulent sky – but he was nevertheless taken by surprise when the thing struck.

A loud, musical rushing sound slashed the air like a sword across the strings of a harp, and then the deck was heavily struck and resounding hollowly – the boat was jarred sideways with a loud crack and a ripple of popping rigging, and when Crawford scrambled around and looked back toward the stern the hair stood up on the back of his neck.

A translucent human figure, a woman, was rising slowly in the dark sky above the mast, its long hair streaming out behind it like the fine tentacles of a jellyfish. The long glassy arms and legs were flailing, and Crawford realized that the creature had rebounded upward after hitting the deck, and was now about to dive into it again. The face of the thing was contorted with idiot rage.

Della Torre and Sputo had scrambled to the stern and were cowering there, though della Torre had drawn a pistol; Josephine was standing beside the mast, staring up into the face of the woman in the air. It seemed to Crawford that Josephine's head was canted, that she was looking upward through her glass eye.

Crawford drew his pistol and aimed up at the inhumanly beautiful form, wishing the boat would stop rocking and that his hands were steadier, and that he had a few more pistols with him – and then he let out the breath he'd been holding, and squeezed the trigger.

The explosion jolted his wrist and the long yellow-blue muzzle flash blinded him, but over the ringing in his ears he heard the harsh metallic music of the thing's scream.

Crawford rolled away to the other side of the bow as the air shook with the firing of della Torre's gun.

Again the boat was struck. Crawford got to his knees on the slanting deck, blinking furiously to rid his eyes of the red dazzle-spot that stained his vision.

Dimly he could make out the inhuman woman's form; it was contorting in midair only a couple of yards over the deck, its fine hair spread out around its head like a flexing crown. One perfect leg was stretched behind the body and its clawed left hand was slowly stretching out toward Josephine's face.

Josephine was just staring at the approaching hand.

Crawford sobbed a curse and lunged aft at the thing, but even as he took the first of the two steps that would propel him uselessly into the creature he saw Sputo draw a knife from behind his collar and throw it.

The woman exploded in an icy gust that punched Crawford backwards off his feet and filled his nostrils with the smell of cold clay.

Crawford wanted nothing more than to lie on the deck; but he rolled over and got up onto his knees and then, gripping the rail, he stood up.

The woman-shaped thing was gone – a wisp of fog out over the water might have been what was left of her. The boat had lost headway and was heeled around almost perpendicular to the current, and it disoriented him to look aft and dimly see the shoreline beyond the stern.

Josephine had sat down against the mast; Sputo walked up next to her, and he crouched to pick up the knife he had thrown. He grinned at Crawford and held the blade up. '*Ferrobreccia*,' he said.

Iron breach, thought Crawford. *Eisener breche.*

Della Torre barked some harsh order at Sputo, who

shrugged, tucked his knife back behind his collar, and went back to the stern.

For the next ten minutes everyone, even the subdued Josephine, was kept busy lowering the sail and splicing and repairing lines and bailing water out of the hold. At last della Torre took the helm and had Crawford raise the gaff-spar halfway, and the sail filled without snapping the rigging, and the bow began ponderously to come around into the wind.

Crawford was crouched by the broken-off leeboard, where until a moment ago he'd been ready to release the runner line if the sail or the gaff-spar had looked overstrained, and della Torre now left the helm to Sputo and walked over and leaned on the rail near Crawford.

'She,' he said, nodding toward Josephine, who was up at the bow, staring ahead, 'summoned that thing. To kill us.'

Crawford laughed weakly. 'You know that's not true.'

'How do I know?' Della Torre's tone was one of token anger, and when Crawford looked up at him the only expression he could see in the man's eyes was haunted bewilderment. 'The thing came to her, was reaching for her.'

'Not to do her any good. If Sputo's knife-cast had missed, I'm pretty sure my . . . my wife's face would have been torn off.'

Della Torre shook his head. 'It *came* to us – something drew it.' He heaved himself away from the rail and went back to talk to Sputo.

Only Sputo slept that night; Josephine refused to go below, and della Torre worked the tiller with one hand so that he could clutch a pistol in the other, and his eyes were scanning the currents of the sky as much as the dimly visible river ahead of them, and Crawford paced ceaselessly from one side of the boat to the other, peering out at the dark lands moving past.

The creature's screams and the gunshots must have been heard by some villagers, he thought, and fishermen and other boatmen out on the Po. Would the Austrians hear of it? What would they make of it?

Several times he heard distant singing, and once when a breeze brought a few particularly clear notes he looked back at della Torre, who just shook his head.

And once there was a rushing in the sky, high in the empty vaults through which the clouds sailed, but though both men crouched tensely, pistols drawn and cocked and aimed upward, the sound was not repeated, and after several minutes they cautiously relaxed again.

Crawford allowed himself a swig of brandy and leaned against the rail. Sometime during this silent watch he had figured out what it was that must have drawn that air-creature, and he prayed again that Josephine was carrying only a human baby, and not the sort of pair Shelley's mother had carried.

The thing had been drawn by Shelley's heart, which was currently packed, still wrapped in butcher paper, in one of Crawford's bags.

Shelley had been an inadmissible mix of species, like a baby bird who has been handled by humans and now carries their smell; and like a mother bird, most of the pure examples of either species had found him repugnant — though in the case of the human species, the members had not been able to say exactly why he was so intrinsically offensive, and had had to use the excuses of his atheism and his revolutionary poetry and his morals as reasons to disown him and hound him from country to country, so that his only friends had been other outcasts.

His heart still embodied the appalling mix, and was

therefore still a tangible offence against the inherent separateness of the two forms of life.

Shelley had once told him about having been attacked by one of the airy creatures in a boat on Lake Leman, and how he had been strongly tempted – since in that case the boat had very nearly been sunk – to use the incident as an excuse for the watery suicide that he had always known could free his family from the consequences of his existence.

Crawford thought now that the main reason Shelley had considered drowning must have been the awareness of rejection by both forms of life on earth. Crawford didn't want a child of his to have to face the same exile.

At dawn Crawford and Josephine went below, to two separate bunks. Della Torre stayed on deck with the refreshed and chatty Sputo.

Crawford woke up to someone shaking his shoulder.

'Good morning-which-is-evening, *Inglese*,' said della Torre. 'I think you will want to be leaving the boat.'

Crawford struggled up in the bunk, bumping his head on the close underside of the deck. He didn't know where he was. 'Leaving the boat,' he said cautiously, stalling for time.

'We are only a mile short of Punta Maestra, where the Po River empties into the Adriatic Sea. Austrian military boats are blocking the river ahead of us. We're moving slowly, but you will nevertheless have to swim away – you and the woman both – soon, if you hope not to be noticed. Already it is too late for us to slant in to shore without drawing their attention.' He shrugged. 'Sorry.'

Crawford suddenly remembered everything, and he was grateful that he'd been able to get a lot of sleep. 'I understand,' he said quietly, rolling out of the bunk and shaking Josephine's shoulder. 'Josephine,' he said. 'We've got some swimming to do.'

Sputo and della Torre helped them tie their luggage onto a couple of planks. 'These articles are likely to get wet,' della Torre advised Crawford, 'when you are swimming.'

'That's . . . quite a thought, della Torre,' said Crawford, absentmindedly speaking in English.

The riverbanks were shrouded in fog; and the setting sun was just a red glow astern, but Crawford could see the line of boats ahead, toward which they were drifting.

For several long seconds he tried to think of some way to keep from having to swim. At last he shook his head and took Josephine's arm and walked to the stern, and the two of them sat down and took off their shoes and added them to the raft, tying them down securely.

'Thank you,' he said as he swung one leg over the transom, 'but I don't think we quite got our money's worth. If we come back this way, I'll want a ride back up the river.'

Della Torre laughed. 'You're going to Venice, you said? If you manage to come back, we'll sail you to *England*.'

Crawford jumped off the back of the boat.

The water seemed icily cold after the recent warmth of the bunk, and when he had bobbed back up to the surface he could only breathe in great, whispered hoots. The makeshift little raft splashed in next to him, followed by Josephine, who, more stoic than Crawford, was breathing normally when she surfaced. Crawford caught his floating hat and set it back on his bald head.

He waved to della Torre – and softly called, 'We might just take you up on that!' – and then he and Josephine each took an end of the little raft and began paddling toward the north bank.

Chapter 25

They ferry over this Lethean sound
Both to and fro, their sorrow to augment,
And wish and struggle, as they pass, to reach
The tempting stream, with one small drop to lose
In sweet forgetfulness all pain and woe,
All in one moment, and so near the brink;
But Fate withstands, and, to oppose the attempt,
Medusa with Gorgonian terror guards
The ford, and of itself the water flies . . .

— John Milton, *Paradise Lost*

It was only early evening, and the breeze that swept the lagoon from over the low sand-hills of the Lido behind the gondola was warm; but Crawford was shivering as he saw the filigreed white bulk of the Doge's Palace, and the tower of the campanile, rising on the dark horizon beyond the gondola's beak. The lagoon was calm, and the gondola's bow hardly rose and fell as the keel skated through the water.

Crawford was holding the jar of Byron's blood in one hand and Shelley's charred, paper-wrapped heart in the other. The poets return, he thought nervously.

He dreaded what he was going to have to do, and he took a frail comfort in the expanse of water, glittering with reflections of the many-coloured lights of the city, that still lay ahead to be crossed. Several minutes at least you've got, he told himself.

For the first time he noticed that the upswept stem of the gondola was metal, and shaped vaguely like a trident blade. He turned around in his seat and waved at the gondolier, then pointed forward at the stem. 'Why is it shaped like a blade?' he asked.

The gondolier managed to shrug without breaking the rhythm of his sculling. 'Tradition,' he said. 'Gondolas in Venice have always had it. It's called the *ferro*.'

Crawford nodded and looked forward again. From where he sat the *ferro* did make a breach across the many-eyed and toothy-looking face of the Doge's Palace.

He looked worriedly at Josephine, who was slumped on the seat across from him, beside their bag and Byron's sword cane. She was shivering too, but from fever more than fear.

The two of them had had to walk eastward last night for several hours, slogging through marshes as often as walking on roads, to get past the line of Austrian boats blocking the Po, and by the time they had found an early-morning fisherman who would agree to sail them north to the Lido, Josephine had been hot and trembling and unsure about where they were or what year it was. More often than not she had seemed to believe that they were back in Rome, fleeing south from Keats's apartment through the ruins of the Roman Forum.

And several times she'd been doubled up with cramps, though when he'd become alarmed she'd told him that she had them frequently, and that they always passed within a few minutes. He worried that something might be going wrong with her pregnancy – certainly her life recently wasn't the sort of regimen he'd have recommended for an expectant mother.

The white pillars of the Church of San Giorgio were squarely off the portside now, a hundred yards away across the low waves, and the gondola was slanting across the wide mouth of the Canale di San Marco toward the domes of the Church of San Zaccaria, a hundred yards to the east of the Ducal Palace. Crawford could now see the two columns standing on the seaward side of the brightly lighted Piazza.

Within minutes San Giorgio was astern, and away off to port was the broad, boat-spangled corridor of the Grand Canal; the façades of the tall palaces, seen end-on, were a Byzantine glory of lights and arches and ornate balconies.

Crawford stared at the spectacle until he noticed a turbulence in the water out between the gondola and the lights.

'Faster,' he called to the gondolier, who sighed but increased the rhythm of the oar.

Crawford realized that they were on the fringes of the Graiae's focus – the agitation in the water had undoubtedly been the third sister, heaving blindly under the surface at the perception of the heart moving past.

It was time. He laid the heart on his knees, and then, with infinite reluctance, he opened the jar. If only this cup could pass away, he thought with forlorn irony – and he took a deep breath and raised it to his lips.

Somehow his disgust was so great that he didn't even gag at the garlic and vinegar and rust taste. When only a couple of spoonfuls remained in the jar, he surreptitiously poured the stuff out onto the floorboards and placed the sole of one shoe in the puddle; then he dropped the empty jar into the sea, feeling as though he were handing it to a friend. He recalled that, until the Austrians had taken over, the Doges had annually taken part in an ancient ritual that was supposed to marry the city to the sea. Help me tonight, he mentally asked the dark waves.

The canal scene faded, and he was lying on his back in a narrow bed under a low wooden ceiling. His eyes burned and his throat was dry.

'Good evening, my lord,' he said in English. The lips were cracked and chapped.

'You're there,' he felt the body say. 'Am I, yet?' The head rolled to the side, and Crawford could see a tub of water on the floor.

'Not quite yet. When I step ashore you will be. I'll give you plenty of warning so you can be in the tub when I do it.'

'Damn this scheme of yours,' said Byron. He was quiet for a moment, then said softly, 'God, she is the most beautiful city on Earth,' and Crawford knew Byron was looking at Venice through his eyes while he was seeing Byron's room in Lerici.

With a slight effort of will Crawford resumed his own body. The gondolier was staring at him dubiously, and Crawford realized that he must have seemed to be talking to himself. Byron had clenched Crawford's hand on the package that contained Shelley's heart, and Crawford loosened the fingers a little.

The gondola had slanted back westward a little, and the bow now pointed just east of the Ducal Palace. Close ahead were bristling ranks of docked gondolas moored at right angles to the wide stone stairs, and Crawford's gondola had already passed between two of the outer mooring poles.

'Get in the tub,' he said.

Crawford saw the docked gondolas grow nearer and then flank them as the one he was in was deftly edged into a space between two others, and he tensed for the exertions to come – but he nevertheless gave an involuntary shout, for he could suddenly feel cold water up to his waist.

Josephine jumped and stared at him, and he managed to wave reassuringly. 'It's all,' he said through chattering teeth, 'going according to plan, yes, great God. We're . . . in the tub.'

Behind him the gondolier was muttering something about *l'Inglese pazzo*, the insane Englishman.

In his head he heard Byron say, 'Do you like that, Aickman? I'm letting you do the feeling for a while.'

Then Crawford thrashed in the tub, for his body in Venice had stood up without his volition. He was *seeing* what his body was looking at in Venice but *feeling* what Byron's body felt in Lerici.

'The . . . blood,' Crawford made his own body say, 'is on the sole of . . . our left shoe. Don't rub it off or get it in the water before you step ashore.'

The gondolier had stepped on to a little floating dock that projected a few yards out into the water, and he reached a hand down to Josephine and helped her up out of the gondola and then handed her the bag and the cane.

Crawford found himself waving the help away and then hopping on one foot up on to the dock and then down its thumping boards to the lowest of the stone steps. God only knew what the gondolier was making of this.

On the pavement he paused for a moment on one leg. 'So this is what a sound right leg feels like,' said Byron through Crawford's mouth.

'Don't try the left one,' said Crawford through the same mouth. He was growing accustomed to the water in the tub, and was able to talk without chattering the teeth they shared. 'A pistol ball in Rome made a mess of the thigh muscles.'

Byron lowered the left foot and pressed its wet sole against the step.

Like the whisper of a loosed arrow diminishing in one ear and then being audible to the other, Crawford felt a focus of attention leave the body in the tub and arrive at the body standing on the step.

'You're here now,' said Crawford tightly. 'Go.'

Crawford relaxed in the tub and simply rode his body passively, like a man riding a horse that knows the way.

Byron was walking across the canal-side pavement awkwardly, apparently from his lifetime habit of putting his weight on his left leg, and he was tearing the paper off the heart.

'You do understand that I'm Byron?' he asked Josephine, who was reeling along beside him. 'Even though I'm in Aickman's body?'

Josephine frowned in concentration, but finally nodded. 'Right,' she said. 'You're going to free the eye for jumping from one sister to the other, and then you're going to try to catch it in the heart.'

'Very good. Now in a moment I'll want you to walk away from me, stand clear, and watch me and the people around me; I'm going to be busy, and might well miss something. Act like a tourist who's out shopping. Hell, *do* some shopping — Aickman, how much money do you have left? — *Uh, about two hundred* lire — two hundred? Out of two thousand? And I suppose the horses and carriage are gone? — *Well, yes* — Damn me!' Crawford could feel Byron clenching Crawford's fists. 'Well, if we're not killed here we'll talk about that later. Where is it? — *In our right coat pocket.*'

Byron dug out the bills and handed them to Josephine. 'Here. Anyway, buy some touristy junk but keep watching for anyone, especially soldiers, watching me. Got that?'

'Yes,' said Josephine. 'Do you want to carry the . . . cane?'

'No — this doesn't seem to be a night for close work. And if it all goes very wrong, you can use it to defend yourself.'

They had passed the darkly pillared façade of the building that had been the city's prison centuries ago, and reached the foot of the Ponte della Paglia, a stone bridge over the narrow canal that flanked the Doge's Palace.

547

Halfway across the bridge Byron paused, and for Josephine's sake pointed and for Crawford's sake looked up the dark little canal to the archingly roofed Bridge of Sighs, which looked in the dim light like a jawless skull wedged between the walls of the two forbidding buildings.

'That's the bridge across which prisoners were taken from the prison, for execution between the pillars on the Piazza. Thank God we don't cross *it* though we're crossing a bridge that parallels it. *Keep moving*,' he added involuntarily as Crawford took control of the mouth for a moment.

Byron laughed, and resumed his limping pace. 'It's clear you're no longer infected, Aickman,' he said. 'You have no poetry in you.'

He turned to Josephine and went on, 'Now if any soldiers *are* watching me, and coming toward me, I want you to scream, as loud as you can. Pretend you saw a bug or something. And if they're pointing *guns* at me, scream several times, as if you've become hysterical. Have you got that?'

Josephine sighed, and Crawford thought it was a good sign that she evidently dreaded the possible necessity of making a spectacle of herself. 'Yes,' she said.

'Good.' They had reached the lowest, widest-set pillars of the Ducal Palace. It took them a minute to limp and lurch past the building to where the Piazza opened away on their right.

The Graiae columns were only a dozen yards away. Crawford would have flinched a little if he'd been working his body – the marble pedestals of the columns alone were half as high as a man, and the wide stone shafts soared away far upward against the night sky.

At that moment bells began ringing – the bronze figures on top of the Coducci clock tower at the far end of the Piazza had moved forward on their tracks and begun swinging their hammers at the bell. 'Now start slanting away from me,' said Byron.

Since Byron didn't turn his head Crawford couldn't see Josephine go, but from his tub on Italy's west coast he wished her well. Crawford felt a strong sense of being watched — it seemed to partake of the echoing of the bells, and set all the stones of the buildings vibrating like plucked violin strings.

Byron was limping toward the nearest of the two columns, the one with the statue of the winged lion of St Mark at its top. The far one was capped with a statue of St Theodore standing on a crocodile, and Crawford thought of St Michael killing the serpent.

The fourth shivering bell-note rang away across the water.

There was a fist-sized spot moving down the near column. Byron stared at it, and Crawford tried to figure out what it consisted of. It wasn't a patch of darkness or light . . . and then he realized that the stone of the column, the minute pocks and scratches, were particularly clear in the spot, as if a clarifying lens were moving down the shaft.

'I believe that's the eye,' muttered Byron tensely as the sixth note rang from the clock tower.

He walked past the column toward the farther one, and Crawford was grateful that Byron looked back; the spot of clarity was round on this side of the lion's column now. The sense of a vast attention focused on him was now terribly strong, like a pressure in the air. The bell in the clock tower was still ringing, though Crawford had lost count of the notes.

When Byron was nearly halfway to the far pillar he paused and crouched — like, thought Crawford, a mouse between the feet of a giant.

'Sorry, Aickman,' Byron said, then stuck Crawford's

maimed little finger into Crawford's mouth and bit the scarcely healed stump with Crawford's teeth.

It bled freely, and Byron shook Crawford's finger over the rippled pavement, spattering blood onto the stones.

Crawford shivered, but not at the cold of the water in the tub – for the drops hit the pavement in a symmetrical pattern, as if defining the points on a crystal. They seemed to resonate almost visibly in the vibration of the bells.

Byron looked up at the sky, gauging the clouds and the positions of the stars, and then he looked out at the water of the Canale di San Marco, apparently noting the level of the water; and Crawford for a moment sensed Byron's thoughts, and knew that he was choosing from among a number of incantations the one that would work in this particular alignment of the elements.

Then he began chanting under his breath, against the rhythm of the bells, but though Crawford listened closely to his own voice he couldn't decide whether the language he was speaking was Greek or Latin – or, conceivably, some much older tongue.

Still chanting quietly, Byron straightened and resumed walking toward the St Theodore column.

Crawford heard a sustained musical note rush past close over his head, and then the spot of clarity was on the broad surface of the far column.

The eye was freed to be passed back and forth among the sisters.

The bells had ceased, and the last harsh echoes rolled away across the water toward the domes of the church of Santa Maria della Salute.

Byron had stripped all the paper off of the heart now, and he gripped it in Crawford's good hand so that the split open side of the thing faced outward. He held his hand up, with the palm toward the spot of definition, and began walking backwards.

'Hope I can catch it,' he whispered.

Josephine screamed; and then screamed again, and again.

Byron threw Crawford's body to the ground and began rolling across the wavy pavement toward the ranks of gondolas, and Crawford heard two bangs from the far end of the Piazza, and then heard the *twang* of a leaden ball darting past next to his ear.

'That's torn it,' gasped Byron out of Crawford's throat as he rolled to his feet and ran in a low crouch toward the water. 'We can – try it again sometime. *No, get into one of the gondolas.* Are you crazy, Aickman? Swimming's the route now. *Damn it –* '

Crawford exerted his will and forcibly took control of his body. They had reached the steps now, and he ran down them, tossed the heart onto a seat in one of the gondolas and began untying the little boat from its mooring.

When it was free he ran down the short dock it had been moored to, pushing the blade-shaped stem of it ahead of him, and then when the dock ended he jumped into the seat beside Shelley's heart.

The boat was arrowing backwards out away from the stairs, and he scrambled aft and, trying to keep low, grabbed the steering oar.

He kept his jaws clenched, but he could still hear the words Byron was making his throat form: *There's nothing to be done out here – we had to be equidistant between the two pillars, so that the eye would dart back and forth between them!*

Another gunshot sounded behind them, and the ball skipped away past them across the water with a sound like startled birds in tall grass.

Dive overboard! hummed the voice in his throat. *I can swim us to safety! I know a hundred places I can swim to in this city where we'll be safe!*

'Soon,' said Crawford. He had worked the gondola around and was sculling furiously, working up speed. As his arm worked he was peering ahead, trying to judge the relative distances of the Grand Canal and the Church of San Giorgio and the Piazza behind him.

'I guess those bells,' he panted, 'weren't – tolling the hour. They were – an alarm.'

He was just beginning to wonder desperately if he could have miscalculated the place where he'd seen the turbulence in the water earlier, when he saw it again, ahead.

The water was churning at a spot a hundred yards ahead of the prow, and then splashing violently, flinging up a cloud of spray that glittered in the multicoloured lights – and then the third sister raised her head above the white water, into the warm night air.

His mouth formed the word 'Jesus,' and he didn't know whether it had been Byron or himself who had spoken.

Perhaps the thing had lost its shape in its long years underwater; or perhaps she had never been carved into as symmetrical a pillar as her sisters, in which case it had probably not been an accident when the workmen had dropped her into the canal in the twelfth century.

Her head was a barnacled boulder twelve feet across, and under a single gaping socket her mouth – as wide as Crawford's gondola was long – lowered open and then crashed shut with an explosion of iridescent spray and a sound like a stone door dropped closed over the whole city. The head swung slowly, blindly, back and forth over the water.

Crawford stood up – having to grip the gunwale, for the boat was rocking in the suddenly choppy water – and, gripping the heart the way Byron had, turned away from her and faced the other two pillars. He raised the heart over his head.

Again he heard the musical note, distant at first but getting rapidly louder, and in the space of an instant a dozen stars in quick succession became momentarily brighter and steadier. As soon as he had noticed the effect they had resumed their dim twinkling.

'*You missed,*' he heard himself say. '*And here come the Austrians.*'

He had been peripherally aware of another, bigger gondola angling out from the docks, and when he looked closely at it he could see the barrels of long guns against the lights of the distant Piazza.

He looked back toward the third sister. The socket above her mouth was no longer empty – it was darker than it had been before, but it gleamed, and every needle of light it reflected seemed aimed straight into Crawford's own blinking and ephemeral eyes. Shelley's heart flexed in his hand, with a faint crackling sound.

Hastily he tossed the heart onto the seat and sculled his gondola around, and then began heaving at the oar to get closer to the Piazza.

'A little farther,' he panted, his face running with sweat, 'past the equidistant point, and then I'll try it again.'

He spared a glance to port, toward the Austrian boat; they were still moving in the opposite direction, as if intending to pass the third sister on the far side.

They're afraid of her, he realized, afraid to shoot toward her; they want to get to a position from which they can shoot at us with only the lagoon and the distant Lido behind us.

He looked back, toward the third sister. '*You'll have to row farther than you thought,*' said Byron, unnecessarily. '*She's following us.*'

Crawford leaned hard into the oar, sweeping it back and forth through the water so hard that he was afraid it would break, and he was desperately pleased to see the wake his gondola was throwing; and when he thought that he had outdistanced the advancing thing by a few more yards, he dropped the oar and picked up the heart and again held it up.

Again the music swept past him, briefly clarifying a line of stars. 'Missed again,' he gasped, before Byron could say it.

Then the night lit with a yellow flash in the east, and the gondola was jarred by a dozen hammer-blows; stung with flying splinters and off-balance, Crawford rolled over the gunwale as the multiple booming of the Austrian guns shook the air. Instinctively he kicked off his shoes.

He nearly lost his breath when Byron spoke in his throat underwater. *We're invisible to everyone now*, came the muffled sound from his closed throat. *Let me swim back*.

Crawford gratefully relaxed back in the tub of water in the Lerici inn and watched the black Venetian water rush past his eyes.

When Byron had thrashed Crawford's body several yards back underwater toward the third sister, he hunched it and then kicked strongly with the legs, and Crawford was for a moment out of the water to his waist, and his hand, holding the heart, was lashed upward hard enough to nearly sprain his shoulder.

And the music swept up in volume, and then held steady at a tooth-razoring pitch. Time seemed to have stopped – he could see drops of water suspended in the air, and he wasn't falling back into the water.

He had caught the eye.

He forced his head up to look at it. The stars were as clear and bright as luminous diamonds just in front of the ragged bulk that was Shelley's heart. The eye was wedged in the split, barely captured.

He forced his hand forward, closing the cloven heart

around the patch of unnatural clarity, and he squeezed his hand hard to hold the eye in.

Motion crashed back in on him as the music was muffled, and then he had fallen back into the water. His legs and his free arm began pumping, propelling him back toward the Piazza.

Crawford knew his body was very close to total exhaustion, and he was horribly aware that the canal bottom was far below his feet, and that the nearest solid ground was a hundred yards away in either direction; he didn't try to resist when Byron again took over the job of swimming.

And even Byron seemed to be finding it difficult. The current had carried them well east of the glow on the horizon that was the Piazza, and though he swam in at a slant against the current, at a fairly good speed considering that one of his hands had to grip the heart, he had to pause frequently simply to float and work his heaving lungs.

At one point his bad leg began to tighten up painfully, and Crawford thrashed Byron's body in panic in the tub at Lerici, but Byron just gasped a curse and folded double in the water to massage the thigh muscles with his free hand. He had clearly had to do this many times before – his hand worked neither too quickly nor too hard, and within a minute the muscles were unkinked.

Byron breathed deeply when he hauled Crawford's head back up into the cooling night air. 'You did mention your leg,' he said stoically. 'Onward.'

Three times they heard gunshots, followed by the soft whipping sound of lead balls snipping the wave-tops as they flew away toward the Lido, and for several minutes after each shot Byron swam with a sort of dog-paddle stroke that, though slower, was quieter. The hand holding the heart was beginning to cramp now.

Crawford's lungs seemed to be wringing themselves empty and then filling to capacity every second, and his heart was a staccato hammer in the soft tissues of his chest. His left hand, holding the heart, was an aching claw. The lights of the Piazza were closer, but when Byron next paused to rest he gasped, 'Your body's – not going to – make it.'

Before Crawford could use his mouth himself, Byron was speaking again. 'I'll – try something.'

Suddenly Crawford was entirely in the room in the Lerici inn. Trelawny was standing in the doorway and staring at him. 'You had a fit,' Trelawny said worriedly. 'Let me get you out of that tub.'

'No, damn you,' said Crawford in Byron's voice, 'leave me alone.'

Had Byron decided to throw Crawford to safety and ride Crawford's used-up body down to the canal bottom? But that wouldn't work – after a couple of hours, at the most, the blood-induced link would dissolve. Byron's body would simply die, and Crawford would find himself, for a few terrible minutes, in the drowned body.

All at once the body he was in sagged with stunning fatigue, and was panting violently. Sweat sprang out on Byron's forehead as Trelawny swore in alarm and rushed to the tub, but Crawford managed to choke out a strangled laugh as Trelawny lifted the body from the tub, for he realized what Byron had done.

Just as he had, earlier, let Crawford be the one to feel the cold water of the tub, he had now let his own body take the exhaustion Crawford's felt. He had used the blood link to send the fatigue poisons to his own body, and send whatever it was that made blood fresh to Crawford's.

Trelawny had gently laid him down on the narrow

556

bed. 'Where's that damned Aickman when we need him?' he muttered to himself as he flung blankets over Byron's shivering, gasping, nearly unconscious form.

After a few minutes the panting began to subside, and Crawford opened his eyes to see the gondola docks close ahead, and he felt his right hand close around the upright wooden trunk of one of the outer mooring poles.

His body was panting, but evenly. *'Did I kill myself?'* asked Byron bitterly through Crawford's mouth.

'No,' said Crawford, staring gratefully at the nearby hulls rocking in the water. 'Trelawny thought you'd had it, but . . . you're fine now. *I'll bet it did me a world of good,'* Byron added. *'Does Josephine have dry clothes for you in that bag?* Yes. *Then let's get out.'*

He climbed up onto the little dock, noticing with respect that he was still somehow clutching the heart.

With even more respect he saw that Byron had swum to the same dock they'd arrived at earlier in the evening. Helps to have a native guide, he thought. 'Byron,' he said feelingly, 'thank you for . . . for everything.'

The gondolier who had boated them in from the Lido was standing on the shoreward end of the dock; he had been talking to some other gondoliers, but was now staring at, and clearly recognizing, Crawford.

Crawford took back control of his body and smiled at the man, and he was wondering what he could say to make this unconventional reappearance seem mundane, when he saw Josephine hurrying toward them down the *fondamenta*, the sword cane and their one remaining bag still blessedly clutched in her hands.

Crawford set the heart down on the dock and then stood up and began taking off his clothes, and the gondolier shouted to several saints and took a step toward him as if intending to throw him back into the water.

Josephine's call for him to stop was so imperious, though, that he paused; and when she had come panting up and shoved a handful of *lire* into his hand, he actually bowed. Crawford by this time was naked.

'Take us back to the Lido,' Crawford gasped as he opened the bag Josephine handed him and began pulling on a dry pair of trousers. When he had got them on he wrapped Shelley's heart tightly in a shirt.

The gondolier shrugged, and waved toward the boat they'd come in on. Josephine stepped into it, followed by Crawford, who was carrying the balled-up shirt.

The gondola was expertly poled out into the water, and Crawford looked back toward the Piazza. The soldiers' boat was still crisscrossing the water well to the west, and such soldiers as he could see on the pavement of the Piazza were looking out toward it.

The gondolier turned the boat, and now the bow faced the darkness of the lagoon, away from the lights of the city. The breeze was colder now, but Crawford didn't even bother to dig in the bag for a shirt or jacket or shoes.

'We . . . goddamn . . . did it,' he breathed wonderingly. '*Great God, my body's a wreck!*' he said helplessly then. '*I guess I'll live, though – for a while, anyway. Now what about the eighteen hundred* lire *you spent, and what about the horses and carriage?*' Crawford laughed in plain relief. 'Byron,' he said, 'I will curry your horses and mop your floors for twenty years to pay you back. I – '

He paused, staring at Josephine.

She was sitting with her legs crossed. She had got mud on her shoes at the dock, and now she dragged a finger down the sole, and stared at the resulting ball of mud on her fingertip.

Then she put her finger into her mouth and licked it clean and began scraping her sole again.

Expectant mothers, he knew, often ate odd things – it

was as if their bodies knew what the growing babies needed to form themselves.

Abruptly he remembered the clay he'd seen around her mouth when she'd first appeared at the Casa Magni four nights ago – and he remembered too the uncharacteristic pain her three-month pregnancy was giving her.

For several seconds he tried to think of some explanation besides the one he knew must be the true one, and at last he had to abandon them all.

Clearly she carried more than just a human baby. '

He became aware that she was looking at him, and he tried to reassume the satisfied smile he'd been wearing moments before.

She wasn't fooled. 'What is it?' she asked.

Byron repeated aloud the thought Crawford had just had. '*It's twins*,' Crawford heard his own mouth say.

The gondola surged on through the dark water for a full minute while Josephine stared at the bloodstained floorboards. At last she looked up at him from eyes exhausted of tears. 'I guess I knew that.'

Crawford leaned forward and took her hand. In his other hand he clutched the shirt that wrapped Shelley's heart, and he hefted it. 'Shelley had a good life,' he said, forcing each word out as if it were a stone he was pushing in through the doorway of a house, 'all things considered.'

Now she was sobbing, but still without tears. 'What did we accomplish tonight, then?'

'We . . . freed you, the child's mother,' Crawford said. 'And we bought for the child at least as human a life as Shelley had, as opposed – ' He paused. The effort of speaking was almost too much. ' – As opposed to a life of pure . . . stone. We saved Byron, and his children, and Teresa. It was . . . a . . . worthwhile endeavour . . . on the whole.' His own throat was closing, and he turned away so that she wouldn't see the tears in his eyes.

For a while neither of them spoke. 'And all of us,' she said finally in a desolated voice, 'have to flee across oceans now, or else be constantly afraid that they'll find us again, and that we'll eventually one night be weak enough to invite them back. And our child will be *born* into their . . . their slavery. *I* asked them in, for little him or her.'

She leaned back in her seat and stared up at the stars. 'I suppose if you add it all up it's a victory – of sorts – at least – for most of us,' she whispered. 'But God, I wish there was a way to *free* people, to *cut* the string between our species and theirs.'

Crawford trailed the fingers of his maimed hand in the water and watched the dim silhouettes of the church domes filing silently past on the port side, and he thought about the link between the species. He mentally re-heard conversations he'd had with Shelley and Byron and Villon.

And at last he took a deep breath and said, 'I think there may be.' He turned around to face the gondolier. 'Take us back to the Piazza, please.'

'*No!*' he shouted a moment later in Byron's unmistakable tones. '*No, onward to the Lido. Aickman, listen to me – as soon as the Austrians catch on that the eye is gone, they'll just cut somebody's head off in the Piazza, and the blood will work as an eye. If Josephine is there she'll be seen, she'll be back in the net.*'

Crawford took back control of his throat. 'I'm not going to bring Josephine along. She won't step out of the gondola, so she shouldn't be visible to her vampire even if they have already done the blood trick. And *I* wasn't in their net even before we took the eye, so it's no danger to me.' He turned and spoke to the gondolier. 'Take us back to the Piazza, please.'

Josephine leaned out over the gunwale and cupped up some water in her clawed hand. She leaned forward and splashed it across Crawford's forehead.

Crawford blinked at her in irritable puzzlement for a moment, then smiled. 'I said in Rome that I might want that sometime, didn't I? Thank you.'

He dipped his own hand in the water and rubbed his wet hand across her forehead too.

Now baptized, they turned to look anxiously back toward the Piazza San Marco.

Chapter 26

Nothing is sure but that which is uncertain,
What's evident to all is most obscure;
Only when snared in doubts can I be sure.
Only to enigmas, never to Logic's lure,
Knowledge surrenders, and draws back her curtain . . .

— François Villon, 'Ballade for the Contest at Blois'
the W. Ashbless translation

The gondolier sighed theatrically and waved one imploring hand to heaven, but he obediently swung the gondola into a wide curve, back the way they'd come, probably because they were closer to the Piazza than to the Lido, and he'd be rid of these mad people sooner.

Crawford's mouth opened again. *'They might just arrest both of you at the mooring stairs.'* Crawford massaged his throat and wished Byron wouldn't speak so harshly. 'If we see soldiers near the stairs we'll go on by, and let me off somewhere else.'

Josephine had been staring at him with desperate hope. 'What is it you're going to *do*?' she asked now.

'I'm going to undo — *try* to undo the link between the species.'

'How?'

'I don't know, precisely.' He rapped one knuckle against his head. 'Byron — the Graiae are still awake, but right now they're blind. What does that mean? *It means that, unless the Austrians keep a steady flow of blood running in the Piazza, my friend Carlo has lost his livelihood as the premier coin-lagger in Venice. He'll be unable now even to*

562

toss a penny reliably through an open window from three paces – and if he can, there's no way anyone will be able to predict with any certainty where it will land – and it won't even still be the same penny in any sense that makes sense. The field the Graiae are projecting right now is one of indeterminacy and imprecision. I wish Shelley had lived to see it, he did so love disorder.'

It was clear from the tone Byron put into Crawford's voice that Byron did not love disorder.

'Did your Armenian priests tell you how quickly the whole field changes, once the radiating heart of it is altered? *It changes instantaneously, Aickman – or, as the fathers insisted on putting it, at the speed of light. But they told me that it's like St Elmo's fire, or the electricity stored in a roomful of Leyden jars: it's not a current, it's a static field, and so there will probably be patches where the old field is still standing – leaky, but still standing – though such . . . high spots . . . will probably have faded out and conformed with the predominant field within a day or so.'*

Crawford nodded. 'Unless they get the eye back, or keep drenching the pavement with blood. Can you find Carlo? *If he's still alive. He won't have moved – until tonight this was coin-lagger heaven.'*

Crawford watched the lights of the Piazza drawing closer. The Graiae columns seemed slightly flexed, and the Doge's Palace was a motionless but unpredictable beast crouching on a thousand stone legs.

He dug into Josephine's bag and pulled out one of her blouses. 'This looks nothing like the shirt I was wearing earlier,' he observed, pulling it on. He smiled at her tiredly. 'I don't suppose there are any shoes in here?'

She shook her head. 'Your last pair you lost in the canal.'

'Huh.' He pulled out a blue shirt of his own and, with some effort, tore off the sleeves and drew them over his feet. The cuffs flapped loosely a few inches in front of his toes, so he unlaced a couple of ribbons from one of Teresa's dresses and bound up the loose sleeve-ends with them, lacing the ribbons up around his insteps and ankles and then tying them off low on his shins. 'There,' he said. 'They may be looking for someone who has shed his shoes.'

Josephine shook her head doubtfully. The gondolier was making the sign of the cross.

'I think,' Crawford said, 'that there will be one main pocket of the old, determinate field still standing; it'll be near the Piazza and the Ducal Palace, and it'll be where Werner is being kept. He'll have made sure he's living in the equivalent of a Leyden jar.'

A boat was approaching them, and belatedly he noticed the guns in the hands of the men aboard it – these were the Austrian soldiers who had shot to pieces his hijacked gondola only half an hour ago.

He tensed, ready to tell his gondolier to angle away from the boat, then realized that there was no possibility of eluding the Austrians. Instead he gaped at them as they drew near, and nudged Josephine and said, 'Look, dear – those men have *guns!*'

'*Gracious!*' Josephine exclaimed.

The Austrians stared at them, but rowed on past to look at other gondolas.

Crawford relaxed, one muscle at a time. 'I guess they're not looking for a couple, especially two people on their way *in*.' He took several deep breaths. 'Anyway, Byron, if your friend Carlo can't help us find the field, and if we can't manage to . . . undo Werner, Werner will probably have his Austrians put the Graiae back to sleep before his determinacy pocket bleeds away, and then he'll be at least no worse off than he was before he came south from Switzerland. And then he can set his people searching for the eye.'

He had paused for only a moment when Byron took his throat again. *'Who cares about this Werner?'*

The gondolier swung the craft's stern out to port and then leaned on the oar to push the gondola forward into an empty space between the lean hulls of two others.

Crawford stuffed into Josephine's bag the balled-up shirt that contained Shelley's heart and the Graiae's eye. 'Don't lose that,' he told her, handing it to her and standing up.

'Werner,' he said quietly as the gondolier hopped out and began looping lines around the mooring poles, 'constitutes the link between the two species, human and nephelim. Eight hundred years ago he revived the nephelim, who at that time had been dormant for thousands of years, by having one of them – a little, petrified statue – surgically sewn into his abdomen. And the two of them, one being contained inside the other, now constitute the overlap between the two forms of life on earth – the overlap that keeps the nephelim species revived, and able to prey on humans.'

He started to step out of the boat, but Josephine caught his arm. 'I'm coming with you,' she said. 'Look at the square – obviously they haven't spilled a lot of blood there. They have no eye.' Her own glass eye was staring into the sky, though her human eye stared intensely at Crawford.

'Not *yet*,' Crawford told her, 'but they might do it at any moment. If – *He's right*,' Byron interrupted. *'Go back to the Lido and wait for us.'*

'No,' said Josephine calmly. 'You're sure to need help, you're *sure* to fail without help. I'm not going to the Lido to wait for someone who won't be returning.'

She held up her hand. 'Listen to me, and believe me – if you don't let me come, I swear to you I'll . . . fill this dress with stones and jump into the middle of the lagoon. Enough weight and a couple of fathoms of salt water should prevent any of us from ever reappearing: these two foetuses, the heart, the eye, or me.'

Crawford was shaking his head and moaning. 'But what if they do cut off somebody's head or something when you're ashore?'

'If you succeed in this, it won't matter. And if you fail, I'll drown myself anyway.'

Crawford knew she meant it. He shook his head, but took her hand. '"If 'twere done, 'twere well done quickly,"' he said. *'Macbeth again,'* observed Byron as they stepped out onto the dock.

She offered the gondolier more money, but he waved her off, again making the sign of the cross.

'Fine,' she told him. 'Thanks.' She linked her arm through Crawford's, and they walked down the dock to the pavement and began strolling toward the Piazza. 'So,' she said, as casually as if they were tourists deciding where to dine, 'you plan to cut this statue out of him?'

'That's it,' said Crawford. He swung Byron's sword cane with despairing jauntiness.

'What if our human child is already infected with the nephelim stuff? Like Shelley was?' She looked at him brightly. 'Wouldn't he or she constitute another overlap?'

Crawford stopped walking. He hadn't thought of that. 'Jesus.' He ran his maimed hand over his bald scalp. 'How long have you been . . . eating dirt?' he asked.

She shrugged. 'A week? Less.'

'We're probably all right, then. I doubt that the inhuman foetus could get around to interfering with his womb-mate until he was fairly well formed himself and it doesn't sound as if he is yet.'

He tried to put more conviction into his voice than he felt, and he mentally cursed any God that there might be, for having made this coming ordeal not only tremendously difficult and dangerous, but possibly pointless too. 'Take the legs, Byron,' he said hoarsely.

Byron did, without comment; Crawford relaxed in the Lerici bed and watched the pillars of the square-facing side of the Ducal Palace sweep past on the right side of his vision. The Palace's white pillars were so near that he could clearly see the rust stains on the undersides of the Corinthian capitals, and he realized that Byron was skirting the Graiae columns as widely as possible.

Crawford assumed just enough of his body's sensations so that he could feel Josephine's arm in his. A frailer overlap, he thought – but just possibly the one that will prevail tonight.

A hundred yards ahead, torchlight outlined the Byzantine arches and spires of the Basilica of St Mark in luminous orange dry-brush strokes against the starry blackness of the night, and Crawford tried not to see the main entry arch as a gaping stone mouth. Dozens of people were strolling across the broad mosaic pavement, and several of them wore the uniforms of the Austrian military, but at least none of the soldiers was escorting a prisoner and carrying an axe.

The faces of many of the people he passed were blurred slightly, and seemed to shimmer with multiple, contradictory expressions, and it was difficult to be sure in which direction they were looking.

All potential, Crawford thought, and minimal actuality; it would be interesting to live in an indeterminacy field. Imagine cooking, trying to get a three-minute egg just right.

Byron walked Crawford's body quickly past the Palace and then past the high arches of the basilica's west face, hurrying Josephine along whenever she slowed, and under the broad face of the clock tower he turned left, toward the narrower north end of the Piazzetta.

Crawford's face was for a moment lifted toward the

ornamental architecture above the clock face, and he wondered if Byron was as uneasy as he was to see the winged stone lion staring down at them, and above it the two bronze giants poised with hammers beside the great bell.

With scarcely a glance around at the smaller, darker square, Byron hustled the two weary bodies toward a narrow alley-mouth on the north side.

The alley itself, Crawford saw when they were in it, was more brightly lit than the square behind them; lamplight spilled from shops tucked in under the arches on either side, casting onto the worn brick walls the shadows of hanging sausages and cheeses, and lights behind opened windows overhead illuminated flower-pots and balconies and frail curtains flapping in the night breeze.

'Give me a coin,' rasped Byron with Crawford's voice.

Josephine dug one out of her bag and put it in Crawford's hand, which lifted and tossed the coin against the wall, deftly catching it again when it bounced back and tossing it again.

The alley was noisy with conversation and laughter and the strains of a man singing drunkenly somewhere nearby, but the *clink . . . clink . . . clink* of the coin seemed to undercut and dominate all the other sounds. Before his body had taken six more steps Crawford had become sure that the other sounds were now coordinated with, their pace dictated by, the rhythm of the ringing coin.

Then there were two clinks for each impact of the coin against the wall. Crawford's hand caught the coin and his face looked upward.

On a balcony above, a fat man was tossing coins against the far wall. The coins rang against the bricks, but none of them fell down into the alley, or were even visible after hitting the wall.

The man looked down, apparently with recognition. 'They're awake now,' he said in Italian, fear putting a quaver into the careful nonchalance of his voice. 'And blind.'

'We need your help, Carlo,' Byron said. 'I'm Byron, the – '

'I know,' the man interrupted. 'Byron's face is visible behind the face you're wearing, like one patterned veil behind another. This is an evil night.' He threw one more coin into ringing oblivion, then gripped the balcony railing firmly with both hands, as if to stop it from vibrating. 'What help?'

'We believe that somewhere nearby is a pocket of the old way – in this pocket you would still judge that they can see. We need you to help us find it.'

'What will you do there?'

'If we succeed we'll kill the columns, and the vampires – all the unnatural stony life – or at least reduce them to a dormant state they haven't been in for eight hundred years.'

'I've got a wife,' Carlo said thoughtfully. 'And children.'

'You rent, don't you? I'll buy you an estate anywhere in Italy.'

After a long pause – during which Crawford, in the room in Lerici, whimpered with impatience as he imagined soldiers leading a prisoner out onto the square and drawing a knife – Carlo nodded. 'But you don't speak to me or in any way indicate that I am with you.'

'Fine.'

The fat man turned and entered the building.

With some of the *lire* Josephine still had they bought a bag of coins and gave it to Carlo, who took it and walked out of the alley into the Piazzetta; Crawford and Josephine followed him at a distance of a dozen feet.

Carlo walked halfway across the pavement toward the basilica, then flipped a coin into the air. It glittered for a moment in the torchlight and then Crawford lost sight of it; a few seconds later he heard a metallic clink-and-roll far out to the right, toward the tall brick tower of the campanile.

Carlo walked in that direction for a few steps, then flipped his thumb up again. This time Crawford never saw the coin, and heard nothing but the voices and laughter from the alley behind them.

Carlo turned around and walked the other way, toward the rear of the basilica. After twenty steps he tossed another coin. Byron was able to keep Crawford's eyes on it, but it landed well behind Carlo, and for an instant after it hit the pavement it was clearly *three* coins, then two, and then it was simply gone.

Carlo nodded, and kept walking.

Crawford took control of his mouth long enough to whisper; '*We* could have done this.'

'*So* far, sure,' Byron had him saying a moment later. He took a firmer grip of Josephine's arm and walked in the same direction as Carlo without appearing to be following him.

The fat man ambled in an apparently random pattern across the mosaic tiles, each of his tossed coins flying in a different direction and then rolling away at impossible angles.

An alley stretched away in darkness at the northeastern end of the Piazetta, and after several minutes it became apparent that he was walking inexorably toward it.

Eventually he disappeared into it, and after a pause and a yawn and a bored glance around, Crawford found himself escorting Josephine into the shadowed gap between the tall, ornate buildings.

Crawford could hear running water ahead, and he

570

knew it must be the canal on the east side of the palace. The comparative brightness of the open night loomed ahead, and he saw Carlo toss another coin and then disappear around a corner ahead. The coin bounced once behind Crawford, then again *far* behind him, and then rolled to a stop ahead of him.

Carlo had turned right, and Crawford's left leg ached as Byron began walking faster so as not to lose him.

When they had rounded the corner too they found themselves on a catwalk over the narrow canal, with the skull-like Bridge of Sighs silhouetted ahead of them against the glow of the lights along the broad Canale di San Marco.

Byron followed Carlo more closely now, and walked up beside him when he had paused at a closed, iron-banded door at the end of the catwalk.

'Well?' Byron whispered.

'This is the sacristy of the basilica,' said Carlo quietly. 'What you're looking for is somewhere inside.' He shrugged.

Josephine reached forward and took hold of the door latch, and pulled. The door swung open, revealing a dim, high-ceilinged passage beyond.

Muttering prayers, Carlo went in. Crawford followed him, and Josephine pulled the door shut behind them.

Carlo moved forward slowly, pausing every few feet to send another coin spinning into the air. The coins were landing closer to him now, and not rebounding in startling directions.

Crawford could no longer see anything erratic in the courses of the coins. Carlo was catching them easily – but clearly the man was still aware of deviations, for when confronted with a choice of doorways he stepped toward one as he tossed and caught a coin, then toward the other as he did it again, then nodded and walked unhesitatingly through one of the doorways.

After threading a path through a number of ground-floor rooms, Carlo led his two companions up a stone stairway, and halfway down another hall. Pairs of high narrow windows slitted the canal-side wall between broad wooden pillars, and the light was good enough to throw vague shadows onto the panelled wall on the other side.

All at once Crawford seemed to weigh more, and the light was clearer, and the scuff of his ravaged shirt-sleeve socks on the floor was raspier.

Carlo tossed another coin – he caught it, as he had been doing for several minutes now, but he grunted in surprise.

He tossed it higher, almost to the ceiling, and closed his eyes as he held out his hand.

Again he caught it.

He put his finger into his mouth and bit, and then walked a few yards forward, shook a drop of blood onto the flagstones, and walked back.

He took two more coins out of the bag and began juggling all three, humming a random tune. The coins spun around faster and faster, and his humming became louder and seemed to start up a maddening itch in the stump of Crawford's wedding-ring finger.

Then one of the coins bulleted up, pinging rapidly off the ceiling and against one wall and then the other; it hit the floor spinning so fast that it seemed to be a glassy globe, and it moved in a hissing spiral around the spot of blood, getting closer to the spot with every loop.

At last it wobbled to a stop and fell over, exactly covering the spot.

'We're there,' Crawford heard himself say.

'Not quite,' came a familiar voice from a shadowed doorway ahead of them. 'A tourist has had an accident – quite a bloody accident – in the Piazza.' Polidori limped unsteadily out of the shadows into the dim light, and smiled. 'Right between the columns.'

Crawford was walking toward one of the nearest pair of tall, foot-wide windows, and his hands unlatched one of them and swung it open. He turned and said to Carlo, 'Into the canal with you. Swim back, and go home to your family.'

The fat man hurried to the window and managed to squeeze his bulk into the gap and halfway over the sill, and then he wriggled furiously and scraped his way through it and fell away forward into empty air; a second later they heard a splash.

Byron turned Crawford's head toward Josephine and raised his eyebrows.

'No,' said Josephine. 'I'll see this out.'

'You certainly will, darling,' said Polidori, hunching forward, his smile a grimace of pain now. 'You'll see Mister Crawford's *liver* out, torn out by your own hands, and then you'll eat it. Happily.'

Crawford's body shifted its weight on his feet as he mentally pushed Byron out. 'Where is Werner von Aargau?' he asked, concealing his horror and regret behind a determinedly conversational tone.

'Von Aargau? In his chamber in the Ducal Palace, where else? Perhaps you imagined he'd be out boating on the canal?' He stared at Crawford. 'Were *you* looking for *him*?'

Crawford didn't answer, and Polidori turned to Josephine. 'Were you?'

She threw a pleading look to Crawford, who stepped forward and put an arm around her shoulders. 'Yes we were,' he said quietly. He was certain that they had lost everything, including their child, but he couldn't bear to let this . . . rival for Josephine's affections see despair in him.

Crawford looked up at Polidori with raised eyebrows. 'Tell me,' he said politely, 'can one get to his chamber from here?'

Polidori laughed, and Crawford was fiercely glad to hear pain putting anger into the sound.

'Well,' said Polidori, mockingly imitating Crawford's courteous tone, 'I'll tell you a secret, doctor – yes one can. His projections of himself, the substantial, handsome ghosts through which he lives, often use this hallway to enter and leave the palace discreetly. There's a door at the end of the corridor behind me, and a little dock downstairs – he likes to emerge into Venice from under the Bridge of Sighs.'

'Fitting.'

'Why were you looking for him?'

'We mean to kill him.'

Polidori laughed – a strangled, wheezing sound. 'That would be difficult. He's got many, many guards, and none of them will ever take bribes or bring him poison or fight half-heartedly, for they're all his handsome, muscular projections. And even if you *did* succeed in killing him, you'd die yourselves a second later.'

Footsteps echoed on the stairs behind Crawford.

'Austrian soldiers,' Polidori said. 'I'd advise you not to resist.'

Crawford let his shoulders slump, and he clasped his hands on the head of the cane, and part of his evident resentful surrender was genuine, for he hated the necessity of letting Byron do this – and then he forced himself back into the bed in Lerici and let Byron take his body.

Instantly the two good fingers of his left hand spun the collar below the cane's grip, and then he sprang forward in a thigh-straining, long lunge, simultaneously whipping free the length of steel and whirling it into line.

Polidori lurched aside to Crawford's right, but in midair Byron twisted Crawford's wrist outward into a deep *sixte* line and managed to drive two inches of the blade into Polidori's side.

'*Eisener breche*, you bastard!' Byron gasped as Crawford's right foot slapped down at the end of the lunge.

Polidori *shrank* off the end of the blade; he was still human in form, but only a couple of feet tall now. His facial features, handsome a moment ago, had now cramped together in a toadishly broad face. He scuttled away backwards down the hall, burping and retching.

Josephine, biting her lips, watched him go but at least didn't follow.

The footsteps were in the hall now, and running, and Byron spun to face them. Six soldiers with drawn swords skidded to a halt at the sight of his sword, and then advanced cautiously, their blades extended. Oddly, not one of them carried a gun, and their eyes shone with an uneasiness that clearly had nothing to do with Crawford or Josephine.

Reminded of something by Byron's cry, Crawford took advantage of the momentary pause to override Byron and swing the sword at one of the wooden pillars between the windows, leaving a horizontal dent in the wood.

Byron swore as he resumed control, and then he hopped forward impatiently with a feint at one of the soldiers and a corkscrewing bind to the blade of another; Byron's point darted in and gouged the man's forearm, and then Byron had leapt back out of range.

The wounded Austrian fell back with a startled curse, and the two of his fellows who had been flanking him ran forward with their swords held straight out, and Byron feinted high and then flung himself down and sideways so that he was in a low crouch, supported by Crawford's left hand and holding the sword extended in the right, and the window-side soldier unwittingly lunged himself on to the point.

Byron straightened, yanking the blade free as the man tumbled backwards, and Crawford intruded for a moment to make his hand lash the sword at the wooden pillar again, cutting another dent next to the first.

'*Stop that!*' yelled Byron as the four unhurt soldiers all attacked at once. Byron swung his blade in a horizontal figure-eight, parrying all four of the blades for the moment, and then he hopped forward in a short lunge and darted his point into the cheek of the man on his far right — instantly he swept the blade down and across, knocking aside the other three swords, and ducked to quickly but deeply stab the kneecap of the next man.

He was going to advance, but Crawford halted him and swung the blade very hard at a section of the pillar below his two previous cuts.

'*God damn you!*' Byron yelled, and hopped forward with a furious beat to the blade of the nearest Austrian.

The blow jarred the man's blade out of line, and Byron slashed his throat in the instant before two of the others could bring their own blades to bear. Blood sprayed from the opened throat and the Austrian folded to the floor as Byron shuffled back.

'Your clowning will get you killed,' Crawford heard his own mouth say; nevertheless Crawford took possession of his body one more time and, ignoring the advancing men, drove his point into the crude face he'd hacked into the wooden pillar.

The sword's grip was suddenly red-hot, and he had to force himself to hold on to it.

And then one of the advancing sword-points slashed along his right ribs, twisting as it darted in. Josephine gasped, and through the hot flare of the pain Crawford was peripherally glad to know that she was still there.

Byron spasmodically took back control and lashed his

sword forward; it chopped across the Austrian's eyes and physically knocked the man over backwards, and then Byron was rushing at the three Austrians who were still standing.

None of them was unwounded, and they turned and ran from this embodiment of murderous fury. Their footsteps clattered down the stairs, and Crawford could hear them calling for reinforcements.

Tense with the pain of the gash in his side, Crawford swished the sword through the air, and realized that Byron had relinquished control of his body.

He heard Trelawny's voice, raising no echoes in the narrow room of the inn at Lerici: 'How do you feel?'

'Feel!' yelled Byron from his own body on the bed. 'Why, just as that damned obstreperous fellow felt, chained to a rock, the vultures gnawing at my midriff, and vitals too, for I have no liver.'

Crawford took a step back toward Josephine, and the cut in his side sent such agony lancing through him that he sagged and had to take a deep breath to keep from fainting.

Apparently Byron felt it too, for in his bed he shouted, 'I don't care for dying, but I cannot bear this! It's past joking, call Fletcher; give me something that will end it – or me! I can't stand it much longer.'

Faintly through the window Crawford heard the echoes of gunshots, and he prayed that they were Carbonari guns summoned by his stabbing the makeshift *mazze*. He took Josephine's arm and limped away up the hall in the direction the midget Polidori had taken, pressing his sword-gripping fist against his bleeding side and leaving the scabbard lying on the floor behind him.

'Here, my lord,' said Fletcher, seeming to be speaking at Crawford's ear despite the hundred and fifty miles between them.

A moment later Crawford shook his head and exhaled

explosively, for his head was full of the fumes of spirits of ammonia. Then the smell was gone – and so was his link with Byron.

'We're on our own now,' he told Josephine grimly.

He took her arm and hefted the sword, and together they limped on down the hall, through patches of moonlight and darkness.

At last he could see a door in the wall ahead, and he was dizzily hurrying Josephine toward it when he heard heavy steps on the stairs behind him.

He fell forward into a jolting, flapping run, dragging Josephine along beside him. His lungs were heaving and his sleeve-socks had completely come apart, the ribbons loose and whipping at his ankles, but he didn't slow down until he and Josephine had collided with the tall door.

There was a plain iron latch, and he had fumbled at it for several seconds before he realized that it was bolted on the other side.

He turned around and raised his sword.

The stairs were far behind now, and the three Austrian soldiers were uneven piles on the floor in the middle distance. It occurred to him that the hall stretched so far south that he and Josephine must by now be within the walls of the Ducal Palace.

'Stay away from the windows!' came a call in Venetian Italian from the head of the stairs. 'The Austrians have a cannon loaded with shot in a boat in the canal.'

Crawford let himself fall against the wall in relief – it was the Carbonari.

Bearded men were running up the hall toward him, with pistols drawn, and a couple of them crouched briefly over each of the three downed Austrians and worked briefly with knives.

The man in the lead came sprinting up to Crawford in a low crouch, a pistol in each hand. 'What in hell are you doing? This is no place for humans.' He gave Josephine a hostile stare. 'Though it's where I'd expect to find *nefandos.*'

'Help me,' gasped Crawford, 'kill the man we'll find behind that door.' He waved over his shoulder.

'No,' the man said angrily. 'He can't be killed. Two of my men are dead on the Piazzetta – is that what you called us for, to try to kill *him*?'

From beyond the narrow windows Crawford could hear voices, and the splashing of an oar in the water of the canal.

'You've got guns,' Crawford said.

'We couldn't have got in here if we didn't,' the man said impatiently. 'Guns weren't working when the sisters were blind this evening. The Austrians found that out and then tossed theirs aside. We saved ours.'

'Can you at least shoot up the lock on this door?'

'We may not even be able to do that,' said the Carbonari. 'The blood on the pavement is drying and cooling, and if the sisters lose their blood-eye the iron won't spark the flint.'

But a moment later he had beckoned three of his followers forward and given them orders, and each of the four men aimed a pistol at the latch. One after another they fired at it, the four detonations lighting the hall in livid yellow flashes and battering at the windows.

And a second later the pair of windows nearest to Crawford exploded inward in a spray of glass, and as a mattress of hot, compressed air flung him into the far wall, and as he rebounded on to his back on the floor, he dimly heard the echoes of a cannon shot batting away between the buildings along the canal outside.

Two of the Carbonari were lifting him up – they had all been crouching below the window sills, but several were bleeding freely now from glass cuts – and their leader was staring at him angrily. Crawford's ears were ringing loudly, and he could hardly hear the man say, 'Are you hit?'

Crawford weakly brushed splinters of glass off his shoulders. 'Uh . . . apparently not,' he said, speaking loudly to be able to hear himself. 'I was to the side.'

'Do you think you can kill him?' the Carbonari leader demanded.

Blood was running from Crawford's nose, and he wasn't at all sure he would even be able to stand unaided. 'Yes,' he mumbled through chipped teeth.

'And is this woman . . . *helping* you? Sincerely?'

'Yes,' Crawford said.

The man visibly made a decision. 'Very well.' He handed Crawford his unfired pistol and then pulled a long, narrow knife from his belt and slapped the grip into Josephine's hand.

'We will hold them off,' he said, 'for as long as we can.' He tossed his spent gun to one of his men, who caught it and threw a fresh one to him, and then he went to the window and pointed the gun down toward the canal.

He pulled the trigger, and the hammer snapped down, spilling powder, but there was no detonation.

'The blood has cooled,' the Carbonari leader said, tucking the useless gun into his belt. 'That cannon shot was the last shot there will be in this area until they spill more blood. We have knives, and can use them – but do be quick.'

He gathered his men with a gesture, and Crawford sat down hard when the two men released him and went loping away down the hall with their fellows.

Josephine rushed to him and helped him stand, but for a moment he forgot the door ahead, and simply stared at the wall across from the devastated windows.

The wood panelling was peppered with shot pellets in vertical patterns – but not in *two* lines, as he would have expected from the fact that the blast of shot had come in through two windows. Instead there was a series of vertical strips of splintering, and the strips were widest in the centre of the pattern and narrower and fainter toward the edges. It was a wave pattern, similar to the ones he had often seen in the water between a long ship and a long dock.

He knew instinctively that this was a consequence of the indeterminacy field that the Graiae, blind again, were projecting; and he knew too that it meant that von Aargau's pocket of determinacy, his individual Leyden jar, had lost a good deal of its potency, perhaps all of it. If Carlo had been here tossing his coins now, they'd still be disappearing.

Josephine had been cutting her skirt hem into long strips, and now she knotted a couple of them tightly around his ribs, over his sword cut.

'Can't have you bleeding to death,' she muttered when she had cinched the knots.

'Not yet, anyway,' Crawford said.

Leaning on Josephine, he reeled to the door the Carbonari had shot at. The latch had been shattered and the wood around it was splintered away and the bolt broken, and the door swung open at his first tentative push.

Chapter 27

What rites are these? Breeds earth more monsters yet?
Antaeus scarce is cold: what can beget
This store? — and stay! such contraries upon her?
Is earth so fruitful of her own dishonour?

— Ben Jonson, 'Pleasure Reconciled to Virtue'

A narrower hall doglegged away beyond the door, its brick walls dimly illuminated by lamplight from around the corner. Crawford was staring blankly, so Josephine took his hand and pulled him forward; he took a step to keep from falling, and then the two of them were shambling down the little hall.

Crawford's nose was still steadily dripping blood on to the front of the blouse of Josephine's that he was wearing, and he was leaving the red track of one bare foot on the stones of the floor. His arms were too tired to hold the sword and gun extended, but he thought he could raise them if he had to, and he was pleased with his hands for being able to stay clamped on the grips.

Josephine had tucked the knife into the waistband of Teresa's skirt, and was holding the leather bag in front of herself with both hands. Crawford thought it was a good idea, but he wondered what would happen if a sword or a pistol ball should strike the heart

They shuffled around the corner — a lamp burned in a niche in the wall, and Crawford could see that the floor was carpeted ahead, and the walls panelled in dark wood. The hall made another turn a few yards beyond that point, and the light from around that corner was brighter.

Crawford was dully surprised to realize that the only emotion he felt was anticipation of the softness of the carpeting under his bare feet.

They reached it and turned the corner, and then for a moment they both paused, swaying.

An open doorway stood only a few paces ahead, and the room beyond it was wide. Crawford could see a lot of elegantly dressed men standing on the marble floor, though none of them moved or was speaking.

'There's nowhere else to go,' Josephine whispered.

He nodded, and they walked forward.

The room was vast and high-ceilinged, and brightly lit by candles in crystal chandeliers high overhead. The two dozen men in the room were all staring blankly at the walls, as if drugged or listening intently for something.

They're all brothers, he thought — and then he realized that the features they all shared were those of the young Werner von Aargau whose stab-wound he had sewn up in Venice six years earlier, and for whom he had subsequently worked.

'Good evening, Werner,' Crawford said loudly.

The men all turned toward him — and a moment later he swore in panic and stepped back, and Josephine had dropped the bag and convulsively drawn her knife.

The men's bodies were changing.

One man's head was stretching away toward the ceiling like a pulled piece of dough — the tongue emerged, seemed to try to speak for a moment, and then rapidly lengthened for yards like a long, weightless snake and commenced busily curling around the elongating head; another's eyes had by now swelled so grossly that the head was just a toothy bump behind the two gleaming, staring globes; a third had one giant horny plate like a toenail growing out of its shirt collar, concealing the mouth, and then the nose, and finally the eyes of the face.

Most of them had lifted their feet from the floor, and were floating in the air.

Crawford noticed that each right hand, whether that member was a tight bunch of flesh like pink broccoli or was a cluster of long tentacles, now gripped a gun or a sword; and he realized that all the different shapes and sizes of eyes were focused on *him*.

As if a load of bird-shot had been fired at a stretched rubber sheet, the holes of all the mouths opened simultaneously in all the faces. 'Get out of here,' they chorused, speaking Italian with a thick German accent. 'Whoever you are, you are well advised to leave.'

'You don't recognize me?' asked Crawford with fatalistic bravado. 'Look closely,' he added to the man whose two eyes were still growing – at the expense of the body, which had shrivelled up and was now hanging under the suspended globes as its shoes and clothing dropped one by one to the floor. 'I'm Michael Aickman.'

All the varieties of left hands were raised in the air and hideously flexed. 'Aickman!' croaked and whistled all the voices. 'Biting the hand that fed you?'

Crawford tucked the presently useless pistol into his belt, then took Josephine's free hand and walked forward.

A bell rang somewhere to Crawford's right, and a moment later the high double doors at the far end of the room were swung open and several Austrian soldiers burst into the room.

Crawford noticed that even as they entered the soldiers looked frightened and desperate; and when they saw the warping and swelling bodies moving slowly through the air like diseased fish in a vast aquarium, they simply screamed and ran back out of the room. The doors were dragged closed, and the boom of a bolt being shot shook the air and rippled the floating bodies.

'Evidently the blood between the columns has cooled,' calmly observed all the stretched or puckered mouths. 'They'll spill more, Aickman, at any moment, and in the restored determinacy field these bodies will resume their solidity. Go while you can.'

'We can ignore the guns,' Crawford told Josephine quietly, and together they stepped forward.

The floating bodies thrust awkwardly gripped swords at them, but even Josephine with her dagger was able to knock them away. Some of the twisted hands were able to pull the triggers of their pistols, but the hammers snapped down quietly on the inert powder.

The bodies were becoming more distorted with every passing second, like clouds or smoke rings. 'Wait,' said the mouths that were still capable of forming words. 'I'm willing to . . . call it a draw, a stalemate. If you leave now, I'll see to it that you two, and anyone else you designate, will be left alone by the nephelim.'

'For the rest of our lives, no doubt,' said Crawford, still pushing his way forward through the insubstantial crowd, with Josephine audibly parrying blades beside him. He heard the clang of several swords hitting the marble floor, released by hands too stretched to continue holding them.

'For eternity,' replied the mouths.

Crawford didn't answer. He took three more limping strides, and glimpsed through the warping forms a nude figure lying in a glass case against the right-hand wall.

He began angling toward it, making sure not to get separated from Josephine and being careful to clang the weakly obstructing swords out of the way. All around him he heard the clicks of pistol hammers falling into impotent flashpans.

Only a few of the mouths were still capable of

producing human sounds now, but the ones that could laughed heartily. 'I never anticipated someone being able to free, and then *catch*, the eye,' they chorused. 'I should have anticipated it – Perseus did it, after all. And I should have had braver *human* guards, or even blind ones. Still, it doesn't matter.'

'No, it doesn't matter,' came a different voice from overhead, and when Crawford looked up he thought for a moment that the winged stone lion from the clock tower had left its post and was now clinging to the wall, head down.

It wasn't until Josephine weakly said 'Polidori . . .' that he recognized the grey face below the long, winged body.

A stone wing swept out to each side, throwing a gust of wind that Crawford knew must have swirled all the von Aargau duplicates to homogenous ribbons, and then the stony mouth creaked open and the claws retracted from the holes they had punched in the marble wall, and the thing that had been Polidori sprang.

It sprang toward Josephine – and in the instant when it was launched Crawford remembered the way it had tried to smash her against the pavement in front of the Casa Magni four nights ago, and in one flash he remembered too an overturned boat in grey surf and a burning house and a destroyed body in a bed – and he threw himself at her almost joyfully, slamming her out of the thing's way and falling where she had been standing.

A blast of air hit him and bounced his chin off the marble floor, but the impact against which he was cringing didn't come; he rolled over and saw that the creature had stopped its dive and flown out into the high reaches of the room, setting the chandeliers swinging with the wind of its wings. The false von Aargaus were now just slivers whirling in the air, and all their clothing was scattered across the floor.

Josephine had fallen to her knees, but was looking over her shoulder at Crawford, and her eyes were wide with wonder and gratitude.

The winged thing flapped down to the floor, and for several seconds Crawford hoped it was undergoing the same loss of form that the von Aargau duplicates had suffered – its wings broke noisily and folded into the white body, which tilted upright and began to narrow in the middle, and its forepaws stretched, separating into fingers. The face was rapidly narrowing, and he heard the snap as the more slowly shrinking jaw was dislocated.

But it stopped warping itself, and stood up and faced him and Josephine, and his heart sank to see that it had taken the form of Julia, Crawford's long-dead wife.

'Look at me, Josephine,' said Julia's mouth. 'Look at me and relax.'

'Don't listen to it,' Crawford wheezed, hiking himself up on one elbow, 'don't look into its eyes . . .'

But Josephine already had, and was staring into the eyes of the thing that still had power over her.

'Who am I, Josephine?'

'You're . . . Julia.'

The woman figure nodded and walked forward, smiling. 'My poor little sister! Look at your hand, and your eye! What have they done to you?'

Josephine lowered her head jerkily and held up her skeletal arms. She looked as inorganic as the bronze men on the clock tower, and the knife she still clutched in her hand looked as if it had been cast with her arm. 'They've,' she said in a rusty voice, 'taken away nearly all of my flesh.'

'Did you want them to?'

Josephine shook her head, and Crawford bared his teeth in empathic pain to see the tears in her eyes. 'I don't remember,' she said. 'I couldn't have . . . *wanted* it, though, could I?'

'They've used you up,' the shape of her sister said.

'Yes. They've used me up.'

'You've always wanted to be me,' said the Julia-thing. 'You can have it now.' Its tone was infinitely comforting. 'You can be me.' It took another couple of steps, and was now standing in front of Josephine. Its smile was radiant, and even for Crawford it evoked dim memories of the house in Bexhill-on-Sea.

'I *have* always wanted to be you,' Josephine said softly. 'But . . .'

The thing was reaching out white hands toward her. 'But what, dear?'

Josephine took a deep breath.

And the dagger lashed forward so quickly that the thing had no chance to get out of the way, and to Crawford it looked as though the obstruction of the hilt was all that prevented Josephine from driving her fist right through the figure.

'*But I hate you!*' Josephine screamed, falling to her knees with the figure of Julia and dragging the blade upward through the abdomen. 'You *wanted* me to worship you, and live only as a . . . a reflection in one of your mirrors! You *loved* it when I'd dress up as you and pretend to be you, so that you could . . . have everybody make fun of me, expose me as horrible little Josephine, and you could drink up the bit of yourself I'd made!' She pulled the dagger out and drove it into one of the struggling figure's eyes. 'I'm like Keats and Shelley – I was *born* into submission to a vampire!'

The figure had stopped struggling, and was clicking and creaking under her, and moving only as its shrinking limbs were drawn in, and Josephine tugged the dagger free and slowly got to her feet.

Crawford gathered his remaining strength and then

made himself stand up and cross to where she stood. He approached her cautiously until she looked at him and he saw recognition in her eyes.

'It wasn't really Julia,' he said, putting his arm around her shoulder.

'I know,' said Josephine, staring down at the little statue on the floor. 'But everything I said was true. How . . . *could* I not ever have known, until now, that all of that was true?'

Crawford pulled her away, and together they turned and slowly walked over to the glass case against the wall. The figure within it shifted weakly on its ornately embroidered mattress, and seemed to chuckle.

For one moment Crawford thought it must be a terribly old woman, with one hip shoved into a hole in the wall, who had somehow become pregnant – the face was as wrinkled and collapsed as a sun-dried apple, but the belly was tightly distended as if with a huge baby. Then he noticed the wispy beard, and the scar on the abdomen and, finally, tucked away like forgotten schoolboy textbooks in an old man's basement, the withered male genitalia.

The scar was stretched by the swollen belly, but he recognized it – he had noticed it on the flat stomach of the von Aargau duplicate whose wound he had sewn up in a canal-side café, so long ago.

'Good evening, Werner,' Crawford said unsteadily. 'Do you know who this lady is? She's the nurse who you tried to get me to poison in Rome two years ago.'

'Look at the ceiling,' the appallingly old man said.

Crawford looked up.

And his chest went cold. The ceiling was a chequerboard of heavy, square stone blocks, and Crawford's very spine cringed with the sudden awareness that there weren't enough pillars to support it.

'Now look at me.' The old man waved a skeletal hand

589

toward his own left hip, which at first glance had looked as though it had been thrust into a hole in the wall. When Crawford looked more closely, though, peering over the tight expanse of the abdomen, he saw that the pelvis and thigh seemed to have been pared down nearly to the spine, and the body then somehow spliced to the stone.

He and the building are joined at the hip, Crawford thought. It's like the two women on that little cake that Josephine was supposed to break when I married her sister.

And Crawford thought of a line from Shakespeare, from *Macbeth*, that Shelley had frequently quoted: *like two spent swimmers that do cling together and choke their art*; and for a moment it seemed to him that he, and Josephine, and all the poets, had also consisted of two persons intolerably joined. Werner, and the women portrayed on the oatcake, were simply more obvious examples, and thus a concealment of the subtler forms of it.

'I'm a part of the building,' said Werner. 'It's my continuing vitality alone that prevents the ceiling from falling.' From webs of wrinkles in the ancient skin of the face the two gleaming eyes stared up at him. 'Do you understand?'

'Yes,' said Crawford. 'If you die, we die.'

The crumpled, papery mouth worked: 'Those are the facts of the case. So you can forget your ideas about cutting the statue out of me. And my offer nonetheless still stands: leave now and I will instruct the nephelim to forget all of you forever.'

Crawford was trembling, but he forced a laugh. 'I know what their word is worth. Percy Shelley put it to the test recently.'

I could force Josephine to leave, he thought, and then do it, cut it out of him.

Then he remembered her promise to drown herself if she were not allowed to accompany him in this. He knew he would not be able to force her to leave.

For a moment he considered taking Werner's offer – but he knew Josephine would not ever agree to that either.

Perhaps Werner was *bluffing* about the ceiling?

Crawford glanced up, and then shudderingly looked down again. No, he was not bluffing.

He was snapping his fingers, and he avoided looking at either Werner or Josephine.

And you don't have infinite time, he told himself. You've got to do *something*.

He stared down into the glass case at the ancient scar that stretched across von Aargau's distended belly, and then very slowly he turned to Josephine. 'You've been a nurse for how many years?'

'Six,' she whispered.

'How many times do you think you've – ' He had to pause and take a deeper breath. 'How many times do you think you've assisted at a caesarian birth?'

Werner was saying something quickly, but Josephine's voice overrode his. 'Say, six times.'

'Good – because you're about to do it again.'

Crawford climbed into the glass case and, ignoring Werner's bony hands plucking weakly at his trousers, began carefully breaking the glass walls outward with the butt of his pistol – he and Josephine would need room to work.

Werner's frail shouting stopped consisting of words when Crawford, holding the dagger wrapped in cloth so as to be able to grip it near the point, pinched up a tight fold of flesh and made the first incision.

And though Werner's struggling became even more violent then, Josephine had tied him down well, and was able to hold him still with one arm and use the other hand to blot up the flowing blood with a piece of cloth soaked in brandy from Crawford's flask. Every few seconds she held the flask to the old man's lips – after the first cut he had stopped refusing it. Exhaustion was beginning to darken Crawford's vision, and it took a powerful effort of will to keep his hand from trembling or cutting too deeply. He kept forgetting that he was not in a hospital delivering a baby, and more than once he irritably asked Josephine for a bistory or probe-scissors.

He forced himself to remember the series of drawings he had seen in *The Menotti Miscellany*, the drawings that had been miscatalogued as illustrations of a caesarian section but had actually been a record of the operation in which the statue had been inserted into Werner. He remembered where the incisions had originally been made in the *membrana adiposa* and the peritoneum, and he tried to cut in the same places.

His fingers seemed to remember their old skill, and moved with increasing deftness, and in only a few minutes he was able to press aside the split skin and muscle layers and see the statue.

It had grown during its centuries inside Werner, and was now about the size of a two-year-old child, but he recognized it from the drawing in the ancient manu-script. Like a real baby it was curled up head-downward, its feet and hands up around its cheeks, and Crawford had to remind himself that this form was stone, and that he wouldn't be cutting an umbilical cord. He carefully worked his hand in behind the slippery head.

'Carefully now,' he said tightly. 'Here it comes.'

He began lifting.

'Haemorrhage, doctor,' said Josephine urgently.

Crawford had been blinking sweat out of his eyes and staring at the statue's head; now he looked down and saw that purple venous blood was flowing in strong spurts from under his probing hand.

Werner's gasps sounded like weak laughter now.

'Get your hand in under mine,' Crawford told Josephine, 'and push against the area of the bleeding.'

Crawford kept his own hand behind the statue's head as Josephine's blood-slick fingers wormed in under his knuckles. For a moment he was afraid that the stretching of the incision might cause more bleeding from somewhere else, but Josephine was skilled at her job – her hand moved quickly but carefully, probing and testing the tension of the tissues, and in seconds the bleeding had slowed.

'Good,' Crawford said between clenched teeth. 'We'll have to sew that up soon, or tie it off or something, but that's good for now.'

He began lifting the stone head.

The statue flexed, making its stone substance squeal in stress. It was resisting him, trying to tense itself wider and stay in the fleshy nest it had occupied for eight hundred years.

'The tissues are too tight,' said Josephine quickly, 'something'll tear if it keeps that up.' She glanced up at Crawford and gave him a haggard smile. 'The mother's life is definitely endangered.'

Crawford instinctively winced, for in childbirth that sentence generally meant that the baby would have to be sacrificed, killed and brought piecemeal out of the womb.

The statue had had to soften its substance to move, but nevertheless Crawford could see cracks, filled with Werner's blood, where its stony substance had given way.

One stretched across the thing's neck, and he inserted the point of his blade into it, and pushed.

The thing stopped moving. He pushed harder, and felt

593

the knife blade slide a little farther into the stone as it extended the crack.

The statue blinked at him from its upside-down face, and its mouth opened and, in a bird-shrill voice, said something rapidly in German.

Crawford hadn't caught what it had said, and he passionately didn't want to hear what the thing might say; he pushed harder, ignoring Werner's screams and the pain in his own left hand, wedged under the statue's head –

– And the tip of the knife blade broke off. Crawford managed to yank his hand back before the jagged end of the knife could do more than slightly nick the exposed peritoneum.

The statue was frozen now with the *eisener breche* in its throat. Its mouth was still open.

Crawford put down the broken knife and resumed pulling at the stone head. He tried to hold Werner's incised tissues apart with his free hand.

The old man had fainted, but he was still breathing, and Crawford knew that if his pulse had begun to weaken Josephine would have told him.

He could feel his own strength failing, so he cursed and braced himself, and then gave the statue one very strong tug – and a moment later he fell over backwards on to the floor with the horrible thing in his arms.

The room shook ponderously, and the chandeliers were swinging, and he could hear a roaring from outside the building as the city of Venice rocked in the grip of an earthquake.

Josephine had fallen too, and her eyes were clenched shut in pain and she was pressing her bloody forearms across herself. Crawford guessed that the nephelim twin was dying inside her.

He rolled the statue away and, after an anxious glance at the ceiling, he leapt back to his patient.

The broken vein had started spurting again when Josephine had fallen, but he found it and pinched it off. Werner's breathing was fast but regular and deep, and Crawford let himself relax for a moment with his left hand inside the ancient man's abdomen.

Josephine slowly sat up, opening her arms cautiously, as if too fast a move might bring the pain back.

With his free hand Crawford had now begun mopping blood away from the edges of Werner's gaping wound, but he took a moment to glance at Josephine. 'Are you all right?' he asked.

'I . . . think so,' she said, resuming her place beside him.

'Be ready with the sutures,' he said, and Josephine picked up one of the long strings into which they'd torn the ribbons from his ankles.

He took it from her and, after cutting the vein free of the surrounding flesh with the edge of his broken knife blade, he one-handedly tied the ruptured vein off between where it was split and where his left thumb and forefinger were squeezing it shut.

He let his cramping fingers relax — the vein bulged against the knot of ribbon, but nothing broke. If blood was leaking through the constriction of the knot, it was doing it very slowly.

He turned his attention to closing up the incision.

'Josephine,' he said thoughtfully, handing her the truncated knife, 'do you think you could break the heel off one of your shoes? and then use the edge of this knife to pry one of the nails free?'

Josephine looked at her shoe, then at the knife. 'Yes.'

Within a minute she had handed him a nail, and he went to work.

His attention hanging agonizedly on each inhalation and exhalation of the old man, Crawford carefully used the point of the cobbler's nail to poke holes into the edges of the cut tissues – then he took one of the ribbonstrips from Josephine, sucked the end of it to stiffen it, and began lacing up the deepest incision.

After a long minute of the delicate work he drew each successive inch of it tight, so that the incision in the peritoneum had been drawn closed, and nothing gave way.

He breathed a sigh and held out his hand for another piece of ribbon.

When they had stitched up the muscle layer and finally the skin, Werner was still breathing, though he hadn't recovered consciousness. Blood was seeping from the incision, but not at an alarming rate.

Crawford stood up, his scalp itching with awareness of the ceiling stones six yards over their heads. He crouched by the blood-smeared statue, got his hands under it, and then made himself straighten his legs and stand, though the effort darkened his vision and started his nose bleeding again. 'Out,' he gasped. 'Quickly, the way we came.'

Josephine snatched up the leather bag, and they reeled and limped toward the door that led to the wide hall.

The statue just fitted through one of the narrow windows that had had the glass blown out of it by the Austrian cannon. Not trusting his own battered ears, Crawford wouldn't move on until Josephine assured him several times that she had heard it splash into the canal below.

At last he nodded, took her hand, and started toward the stairs.

Figures were running back and forth across the square, and twice Crawford heard the boom of gunfire echo back from the lacy pillared wall of the Doge's Palace, but no one approached them until they had limped and shuffled past the massively tall but inert Graiae columns and had started toward the stairs and the gondolas.

A man stepped out of one of the shadowed arches of the palace and held up his hand. Crawford raised his sword and his still unfired pistol.

'I'm Carbonari,' the man said quickly, and when Crawford made his eyes focus he recognized the bearded face. It was the leader of the group of Carbonari they had met in the hall upstairs.

'There's a boat to take you to the Lido,' the man said, speaking quietly and quickly, 'in the little canal below the Drunkenness of Noah.' He stepped behind Crawford and Josephine and began pushing them along by their elbows.

He marched them down the length of the south face of the palace, with the broad waters of the Canale di San Marco stretching away a quarter of a mile wide on their right, and just at the foot of the Ponte di Paglia he pushed them to the left, away from the stairs and between two of the pillars of the palace. Ahead lay the canal into which Carlo had jumped earlier, and Crawford saw a gondolier waiting for them with one foot up on the pavement and the other on the stern of his narrow craft.

'The Austrians are in confusion,' their guide said tersely, 'and the guards of their secret king have gone mad. We are grateful to you.' He gave them one last forward shove. 'But don't ever come back to Venice,' he added.

Crawford looked up, and belatedly realized what his guide had been referring to, a minute earlier – above the pillars at this southeast corner of the building was a sculpture of Noah reeling below a grapevine, spilling wine from a cup and about to lose the robe that was loosely bunched around his waist.

As he and Josephine climbed into the gondola he kept his eyes on poor Noah, who, it seemed to Crawford, had had every excuse to get drunk and lose his trousers, after having piloted the entirety of organic life to safety.

Crawford uncapped his flask and passed it to Josephine as the gondolier cast off, and when she handed it back he raised it to Noah and then drained off the swallow of brandy that was left. The Bridge of Sighs was behind him, but he looked ahead, toward where the towers and domes of the Church of San Giorgio Maggiore rose against the night.

When they were well out on the water, and the gondolier had begun to lean into the oar to turn them east toward the lagoon, Crawford fumbled Shelley's shirt-wrapped heart out of Josephine's bag. He whispered a prayer to the splintered, weathered head of Christ, and then leaned across the gunwale and held the charred-smelling, flapping thing at arm's length out over the dark water.

Nothing disturbed the calm skin of the water but the faintly reflecting points of jellyfish hanging like pale splashes of milk at the surface, and the ripple of the boat's wake sweeping out to both sides behind them in the starlight.

When the low waves cast by the knife-narrow prow had eclipsed the whole of the ancient city in their skirt, and no slightest swirl gave evidence of the third sister moving below, he sat back and tucked the heart into the bag.

The nephelim were dormant again, for the first time in eight hundred years.

He put his arm around Josephine, and she laid her head on his shoulder and slept.

My illness is quite gone – it was only at Lerici – on the fourth night, I had got a little sleep and was so wearied

that though there were three slight shocks of an Earthquake that frightened the whole town into the Streets —
neither they nor the tumult awakened me. . . . There
seem to have been all kinds of tempests all over the
Globe — and for my part it would not surprise me — if the
earth should get a little tired of the tyrants and slaves
who disturb her surface.

— Lord Byron, to Augusta Leigh, 7 November 1822

EPILOGUE
Warnham, 1851

I have heard the mermaids singing, each to each.
I do not think that they will sing to me.

— T. S. Eliot

'Italians?' echoed Lucy, pausing, her polishing-cloth suspended an inch above the worn surface of the bar. 'I can't do nothing about Italians.'

'They speak English,' the innkeeper told her. 'And their address is in London. All they want is some wine to drink on the back porch before supper. Do you think you could . . .?'

Lucy had resumed her polishing. 'Italian *men*? I hear they're as bad as sailors. They'd better not get fancy with me.'

It was a token objection; though she was still slim, Lucy was in her fifties, and her face was scored by decades of hard work.

'It's a very old couple and their son. They're not wanting to get drunk, Lucy, just – '

'Oh, very well.' She put down her cloth and set a bottle of claret and a corkscrew and three glasses on a tray. 'But the new girl can do the cleaning up tonight.'

'Certainly, certainly,' agreed the innkeeper.

Lucy walked around from behind the bar, picked up the tray, and walked out of the taproom.

Ahead of her was the oak staircase that led up to the rooms; she turned left at the foot of it and walked through the spare dining room to the back door; holding the tray in one hand, she pulled the door open and stepped out on to the porch, where her three customers were sitting at a little table in the shade.

The son was about thirty. He didn't look Italian at all – his hair was brown and straight, combed back off his forehead, and his eyes were pale blue. His smile as she set out the bottle and glasses was only polite.

'Thank you,' he said, and there was a trace of an accent in his voice.

She turned to the old couple.

They really were old. The man was bald except for a short fringe of white hair above his ears, and his face was as dark and seamed as a piece of oiled driftwood. A stout, worn walking stick hung on the arm of his chair, and Lucy imagined that when he gripped it, his brown, gnarled hand must seem to be part of the stick.

His wife's hair was grey. She just kept her eyes on Lucy's hands as the old barmaid twisted the corkscrew into the neck of the bottle, but a smile deepened the lines in her lean face, and seemed to indicate the cause of many of the lines.

When Lucy had poured wine into the three glasses, the old man raised his glass, in a hand that was missing at least one finger.

'Thank you, Lucy,' he said.

Crawford sipped at the wine and looked out over the inn's back yard. The leaves on the trees glowed green and gold with the noon sun over them, and he tried to imagine that he was thirty-five again, and that Boyd and Appleton would shortly be emerging from the door behind him.

He couldn't imagine it.

The far end of the yard was a peach orchard now – God knew when the old carriages had been dragged away. He wondered if the ancient carved pavement he'd tripped on in the rain thirty-five years ago was still out there. He didn't care to go and find out.

John was looking at him uneasily. They'd taken the London-and-Brighton train south as far as Crawley, and then hired a carriage-ride west to Warnham, and John wanted to be back in London tonight to see his own wife and children.

'So,' John said, 'here we are, wherever this is, exactly. You two wanted to tell me . . .?'

'How your father and I met,' said Josephine. 'How you were conceived, and how we got married.'

John blinked. 'I . . . always thought you . . . would never bring it up. I thought you didn't . . . that it wasn't a story you wanted to tell.'

'Mary Shelley died last month,' said Crawford, 'and so our promise to her is finally voided. And Percy Florence Shelley is Sir Percy now, and I don't think he's even aware of the truth about his father.' Crawford laughed, exposing uneven teeth. 'I can't imagine that he believes it, even if he's been told.'

And you probably won't believe it yourself, John, he thought; but I owe it to you – and to your children – to tell you anyway.

'Mary Shelley?' said John. 'The wife of Percy Shelley? You knew her?'

'Yes.'

Crawford sipped his wine and thought about Mary Shelley. He had given her Shelley's heart, which had still contained the eye of the Graiae, in a jar of brandy, and she had kept it all her life; and he had wondered sometimes if the eye was still dimly able to cast its static, determinist field, for Mary had subsequently lost all the spirited spontaneity that had drawn Shelley to her so long ago. Her writing had slowed down and become more formal and stilted, and she'd seen fewer and fewer people as the years went by, and he had heard that before her death she had lain motionless and silent for ten days.

Trelawny had asked her to marry him in about 1830, but by then the authoress of *Frankenstein* had already begun to settle into the inertia that was to characterize the remainder of her life, and she had refused him.

Trelawny had followed Byron to Greece after Shelley's death and, after Byron had died there of swamp-fever while trying to organize an army to drive out the Turkish invaders, Trelawny had stayed on for a while as a sort of mercenary-adventurer. Later he had gone to America, where he swam the Niagara River within hearing distance of the Falls, and Crawford had heard that he had returned to England and got involved with a married woman and was now living in Monmouthshire.

Crawford had often thought of Byron, who had died in 1824. Crawford and Josephine had not seen him again after the Venice adventure — they had meant to look him up and thank him, but then he had died in Missolonghi at the age of thirty-six, and it had been too late.

'I'm sorry,' said Crawford, 'what did you say?'

'I said,' John told him patiently, 'did you know Shelley too?'

'Yes. And Byron, and Keats. You're named after Keats, incidentally, I doubt that we ever told you. And it all started,' he said, waving his glass at the grassy yard, 'here.' He put the glass down and massaged his left hand; perhaps because of the maimed fingers, it had begun aching lately. The whole arm ached, all the way up to the shoulder.

Josephine refilled all three glasses. 'Go ahead,' she said.

The sun was low in the west by the time he had finished the story, and the long grass was streaked with the shadows of the old oaks that bordered the yard.

John was shaking his head. 'And did the . . . did this Werner person . . . what happened to him?'

Crawford grinned. 'We kept track of the news from Venice for a while after that, after we'd left. A week later there was a report of a couple of rooms collapsing in the Doge's Palace. It was blamed on structural weakening caused by the earthquakes.'

'A *week* later?' John asked.

'Your father's a good surgeon,' Josephine said.

'So . . . so he never did find his statue, or any statue, and get to renew the overlap.' John's voice was quiet – he might doubt all this eventually, but clearly he was accepting it now.

'Apparently not,' Josephine said. 'But the . . . potentiality is always out there.'

'That's why you two were always warning me against inviting strangers into the house.'

'Right, John,' said Crawford. 'And I trust you've done what we've said, and passed the advice on to your own children.'

'Well, sure, I just – never quite – knew the whole extent of *why*.'

Crawford finished his wine. 'You do now, son.'

He leaned back in his chair and closed his eyes.

Somehow he could still see the yard, the trees and the grass . . . but it couldn't be the yard of the inn at Warnham, for he could see for miles, across a valley, on the floor of which stood hundreds of tall stones, and he was pulling a wagon in which sat a wickedly grinning old man, older by far than even himself, and the old man was singing a French song with a merry tune but sad lyrics . . .

Keats, young and healthy again, was riding a horse past them. He waved as he passed, and Crawford thought there was gratitude in the look he flashed to him as he galloped away.